LEGENDS OF THE STRAIT

A novel about Benicia, California
during the Prohibition Era

by
Bruce Robinson

authorHOUSE®

AuthorHouse™
1663 Liberty Drive
Bloomington, IN 47403
www.authorhouse.com
Phone: 1-800-839-8640

Because Legends of the Strait *is historical fiction, the narrative closely parallels many events that actually occurred in the distant and more recent past of Benicia. Many geographical locations, commercial enterprises, and street names are (or at one time were) also real. Nevertheless,* Legends of the Strait *is strictly a work of fiction. All character names and events recounted are either creations of the author's imagination or are used fictitiously.*

First published by AuthorHouse 04/02/2011

ISBN: 978-1-4567-5987-2 (e)
ISBN: 978-1-4567-5988-9 (sc)

Printed in the United States of America

Archived photos of Benicia sites © 2004 by Benicia Historical Museum
Archived photo of Vallejo site © 2004 by Vallejo Naval and History Museum

Any people depicted in stock imagery provided by Thinkstock are models, and such images are being used for illustrative purposes only.
Certain stock imagery © Thinkstock.

This book is printed on acid-free paper.

To my father, Lloyd G. Robinson—a man of
common sense and uncommon courage.

Table of Photo Illustrations

Parade Day on First Street 1
(courtesy of the Benicia Historical Museum)

The Commandant's Quarters at the Benicia Arsenal 53
(courtesy of the Benicia Historical Museum)

The Majestic Theater 115
(author's photo)

Singler's Barbershop 131
(author's photo)

The *Contra Costa* train ferry 157
(courtesy of Benicia Historical Museum)

The Lido 187
(author's photo)

Diamond Beach at low tide, showing decayed hull of
Black Diamond Mine coal barge 229
(author's photo)

Carquinez Bridge under construction 265
(courtesy of the Benicia Historical Museum)

Carquinez Bridge opening day 279
(courtesy of the Benicia Historical Museum)

The Capitol Building 323
(courtesy of the Benicia Historical Museum)

The Alamo Rooms 391
    (author's photo)

The Bank of Italy..433
    (author's photo)

The Vallejo General Hospital..465
    (courtesy of the Vallejo Naval and Historical Museum)

The Washington Hotel 499
    (author's photo)

The "Manse" on West G Street.......................................551
    (courtesy of the Benicia Historical Museum)

Preface

Many who live outside of the San Francisco Bay Area may never have heard of Benicia, California. Even those who have visited this North Bay community probably don't know that, for a brief shining moment in its early history (1853 to 1854), Benicia was the State Capitol. Some local cynics may say Benicia's only claim to fame is its past reputation as a "red-light" district—a reputation acquired during World War II because of the town's proximity to two major military installations, the Benicia Arsenal and the Mare Island Shipyard in near-by Vallejo.

Benicia's history encompasses much more than bars and bawdy houses, though. It was the birthplace of Mill's College for women— today considered every bit as prestigious as the "seven sisters" on the East Coast. Benicia was also the childhood hometown of the American poet Stephen Vincent Benet and the world-renowned architect Addison Mizner. As young men, novelists Sinclair Lewis and Jack London vacationed in Benicia. In fact, London wrote several books about his early experiences in Benicia including *John Barleycorn* and *Tales of the Fish Patrol*. From 1872 to 1874, one of the Bay Area's first feminist writers, Gertrude Atherton, attended Saint Mary's of the Pacific school in Benicia. Her 1906 novel *Rezanov* told the true unrequited love story of Sister Maria de la Concepcion Arguelo—who is buried in Benicia's Dominican cemetery.

Visitors to Benicia today will discover that it is rapidly becoming a new Sausalito, complete with upscale restaurants and luxurious new waterfront town homes. A growing community of artists has moved into the old industrial part of town where the Yuba Manufacturing Company once filled the air with smoke from its foundry chimneys. Long gone too are the several tanneries and canneries that besmirched the landscape and fouled the air. Benicia today has its own Yacht Club and marina, municipal pool, and numerous historical buildings that are now being restored and renovated. In short, Benicia at last seems to be fulfilling the "great expectations" of its original founders.

On January 19, 1847, a dentist from Kentucky named Dr. Robert Baylor Semple participated in the Bear Flag revolt against the last Spanish Commandant in California—General Mariano Vallejo. When Vallejo's forces were defeated, Semple and his business partner Thomas O. Larkin induced the captive General to sell them a one-by-five-mile plot of land on the north shore of the Carquinez Strait, where the Sacramento River flows into San Pablo Bay. As partial compensation, Semple and Larkin allowed Vallejo to name their new acquisition *Benicia*, after the General's wife—Francisca Maria Felipa Benicia Carrillo de Vallejo.

Semple and Larkin knew this area provided the only deep-water port in northern California. In the early 1840s, San Francisco (then called Yerba Buena) had too many sandbars and shoals to accommodate ocean-going vessels. These two pioneer venture capitalists assumed Benicia would therefore become the commercial capitol of the entire Bay Area. The gold rush of 1849 brought thousands of immigrant prospectors first to San Francisco, thus making that city rather than Benicia the commercial hub of the Bay Area.

Still, Benicia played a major role in California's industrial growth. In 1879, the Central Pacific Railroad (soon after purchased by the Southern Pacific Railroad) routed its main southbound line from Sacramento through Benicia. The company erected a ferry terminal on Benicia's waterfront and built what was then the world's largest train ferry, the *Solano*, to transport rolling stock across the Carquinez Strait.

In 1914, a second and even larger train ferry was added—the *Contra Costa*. Until 1930, when the Southern Pacific Railroad built a bridge across the Carquinez Strait, these ferries were the only means of rail transport across the Sacramento River. For that reason, many at the time referred to Benicia as the "great bottleneck" of the Transcontinental Railroad. It was precisely this "bottleneck" feature, though, that made Benicia a key funnel of commerce in the region for more than half a century.

From the end of World War I until the first vehicular bridge was built in 1927, most auto and truck traffic between northern and southern California also flowed through downtown Benicia. From there, it too had to be ferried across the Carquinez Strait to Martinez. During approximately the same time period, bootlegging became the moneymaking industry of choice for millions of Americans. In California, Benicia was a major transit point for that industry as well.

All of these factors have prompted me to choose the Prohibition Era (1919 to 1933) as the timeframe for *Legends of the Strait*. This was a fascinating period in American history when, soon after passage of the 18th Amendment in 1919, numerous California citizens became involved with the production, distribution, and consumption of bootlegged "booze." Understandably, this fact is rarely noted among California chroniclers. Another seldom-noted historical fact is that, more than passage of the 19th Amendment in 1920 giving women the right to vote, passage of the 18th Amendment enabled them to take their first giant steps toward equality with men. During the 1920s, many more women patronized speakeasies than registered to vote.

At the vortex of these economic and social revolutions are the two central characters in *Legends of the Strait*—Adelaide, the headstrong daughter of a prominent local judge named Clyde Lanham; and Jack, the rebellious son of an independent-minded but poor World War I widow named Gail Westlake. The narrative traces the maturing relationship between Jack and Del as they pursue diverging career paths to success, Jack's in the viticulture industry and Del's in law and politics.

Legends of the Strait is about much more than its fictional protagonists, however. It's also about a time when new technologies like the electric light, the telephone, and the combustion engine were transforming society worldwide; when broadcast radio and motion pictures began homogenizing America's cultural values; when the Scopes "monkey trial" challenged the most basic precepts of religious tradition; and when Margaret Sanger's crusade for birth control and eugenics forecast some of the most compelling political issues of the 21st Century.

The Author

Acknowledgments

One of the hardest parts about writing historical fiction is crafting an interesting story out of historical facts that often seem boring and disconnected. For *Legends of the Strait*, many good people have helped me with this task by reading and critiquing early drafts of my manuscript. The most important of these is my wife Barbara who has been my first and most honest editor. Others who have also generously given of their time as test readers include Benicia's first Poet Laureate Joel Fallon and Benicia-based criminal defense attorney Steve Naratil.

Of the many secondary sources I have used in researching the history of Benicia and the Carquinez Strait, undoubtedly the most useful have been Richard Dillon's *Great Expectations: The Story of Benicia, California* (1980) and Earl Bobbitt's *Looking Back Benicia, 1900 to 1978 (1988)*. I am also grateful to *Solano Historian* editor Jerry Bowen for helping me gain access to the resources of the Solano Historical Society.

For permitting me to illustrate *Legends of the Strait* with archived photos from the collections of the Benicia Historical Museum and the Vallejo Naval and Historical Museum, I want to thank museum curators Beverly Phelan and James E. Kern. In addition, I wish to thank Jim Turner and Thomas and William Rubarth for researching, building and bringing their remarkable scale model of the *Solano* train ferry to Benicia in October of 2004. Their dedication to this project has been a critical source of information about the history of technological innovation in the North Bay Area.

It is my in-person interviews with life-long Benicia residents, though, that have been the most interesting and revealing. These oral history informants include people who were born as early as 1912 and as late as 1928. They have revealed facts and events that are probably not recorded in any memoire or history book but that are the essence of what life was really like in Benicia during the Prohibition Era.

As a first-time novelist, I owe special thanks to *New York Times* best-selling author and fellow North Bay resident John Lescroart. During the Jack London Writers Conference I attended in 2004, John gave a nuts and bolts seminar on the craft of fiction. Among the many excellent tips he offered, probably the most valuable to me has been this: "Write scenes. Every scene has to be a little gem. If you have to explain, you've failed." What matters most where regional fiction is concerned, of course, is what local readers think. That's why I'm especially grateful to *Benicia Herald* editor Marc Ethier for promoting *Legends of the Strait* to local readers long before it became available on Amazon.com.

The Author

1919

Parade Day on First Street

CHAPTER ONE

"Roses of Picardy"

FOR ALMOST A YEAR NOW, every other Saturday afternoon Gail Westlake had been sending her son Jack to fetch a bucket of beer for her "gentleman caller," Mister James Soames of San Francisco. Though there were rumors in town Soames was a married man and that his visits with a young war widow like Gail were shameful, Jack knew there was little he could do about it. "Best to leave sleepin' dogs lie," his friend Adam Tucker told him.

"Here's the money," Gail said, giving Jack a tin pail and a handful of coins, mostly pennies. "Hurry! Mister Soames will be here any minute."

"Luigi won't like this," Jack protested. "He hates pennies."

Gail looked sternly at her son. He had his father's square jaw and wide-set blue eyes. It was a handsome face, but at moments like this she saw weakness. There was something furtive and desperate in Jack's eyes. Like his father, he was too eager to win the approval of others. "Never mind what Luigi likes!" she retorted. "Get going!"

Jack walked slowly along the wooden boardwalk on First Street until he came to the entrance of Campy's Tavern. Because it was a hot August day, the bartender Luigi Berico had wedged the door open to keep a cross draft from the open windows at the rear of the barroom. The only patrons in Campy's at this early afternoon hour were half a dozen farmers from out of town. Berico was engaged in animated conversation with one of them when Jack entered.

Placing his bucket on the bar top, Jack gazed around the dark and sparsely furnished interior. Apart from the long bar itself, there were only a few battered wooden tables and chairs. The only décor consisted of four trophy elk antlers hung haphazardly against the long wall opposite the bar.

There was one feature of Campy's Tavern that fascinated Jack, though. To discourage patrons from spitting on the floor, Campy's brother-in-law, a plumber by trade, had installed a long metal trough on the floor directly in front of the bar. A steady stream of water flowed through this trough and emptied into a drain near the front entrance.

As he stood waiting for Luigi to serve him, Jack suddenly noticed a five-dollar bill floating toward him in the trough. First checking to make sure no one was watching, Jack quickly reached down, picked up the bill, and stuffed it in the back pocket of his overalls.

Jack's swift movement attracted Berico's attention. "What d' y' want, kid?" he shouted.

Jack pointed to the empty bucket on the bar top. "Mom wants a bucket of beer."

"Oh yeah?" Berico asked sarcastically as he ambled toward Jack. "And did your Momma give you the money to pay for that bucket of beer? Thirty-five cents, y' know."

Grimacing, Jack dumped his handful of coins on the bar top.

Angrily, Berico grabbed the bucket and quickly filled it from a barrel tap. Before giving the foaming bucket to Jack, though, he slowly and methodically counted each coin and dropped it into the till behind the bar. Jack had watched Berico go through this insulting ritual many times before. This time, Jack didn't care. All he wanted now was to escape from Campy's Tavern before one of the farmers realized he had lost his five-dollar bill.

Out on the street again, Jack carried the heavy bucket as fast as he could back to his mother's second floor apartment. As he climbed the outside stairway, Jack heard the tinkling sounds of Gail's upright piano. She was playing one of her favorite ragtime tunes, her long fingers flying over the keys with joyful abandon. His mother was happy. Obviously, James Soames of San Francisco had arrived.

A tall, lean man with slicked-down black hair, a tiny moustache and shifty green eyes, Soames was lounging in his mother's favorite mohair armchair when Jack entered the apartment. The man had removed his coat, collar, and tie and was cooling himself with a hand-fan Gail had given him. He nodded a perfunctory greeting at Jack but concentrated on fanning himself.

"Did you bring Mister Soames his beer, Jack?" Gail asked as she continued playing.

Jack lifted the bucket onto the kitchen counter, slopping some of its contents on the floor.

"Be careful, Jack!" Gail scolded. Abruptly, she stood up from her piano stool and ladled beer into a ceramic mug for her guest. As she handed the mug to Soames, Gail said softly, "You may go out and play now, dear. Just stay close by so I can call you from the window."

Jack did not reply. It was all part of the routine. His mother always sent him out to play whenever Soames came to visit. He knew she didn't really care how far he roamed in the streets of Benicia as long as he returned by suppertime.

Besides, Jack was eager to tell his friends about the treasure he had found. Five dollars was more than some grown men earn in a week. He could buy just about anything he wanted. The only problem was what —a Daisy air rifle, a shiny new Montgomery Ward bicycle? These were things Jack had always wanted but his mother could never afford. Even if he bought both of them, he might still have money to spare.

* * *

Because it was Saturday, First Street was busy with traffic. Scores of vehicles—from buckboard wagons drawn by old nags to new Model Ts—were trundling up and down between Military Road and City Dock at the waterfront end of First Street, where several vehicles were now lined up to take the car ferry across the river to Martinez.

In 1919, Benicia was a hub of commerce for farmers that brought their grain, nuts and fruit there for shipment by train to Oakland and beyond, shopped for tools and clothing at Wilson's Dry Goods, and purchased their harnesses, boots and saddles at McClaren's Tannery. While the farm wives shopped, many of their husbands would visit local saloons like Campy's Tavern, The Pastime Card Room, or Wink's Bar. There were more than eighteen of these establishments on First Street, especially close to the waterfront.

The air was filled with dust from the sun-baked dirt surface of First

Street—dust that, on a hot summer day could be as thick as the fog that rolled in through the Carquinez Strait from San Pablo Bay during the winter months. Everywhere you looked, there was dust—especially on people's boots and shoes, Jack noted, as he stepped down into the street from the wooden sidewalk.

"Watch where you're goin', boy!" an angry driver shouted at him as Jack barely missed being struck by the fender of a passing flatbed truck.

His friend Del Lanham was waving at him from the stoop in front of Wilson's Dry Goods. "Hurry up, Jack. I want to show you something." She ran into the store ahead of him.

Del was different from most other girls Jack knew. Even though she usually wore a pinafore, Del preferred overalls so she could do daring things like climbing to the top of the big water tower near the railroad tracks and throwing rocks at the turkey buzzards when they flew low over the tule flats.

It was dark and cool inside Wilson's store, which was full of interesting smells and sights—everything from sweet-smelling spices and local-grown apples to shiny new shovels and headless wire dummies displaying women's outer garments.

Del stopped in front of the big glassed-in display case where Wilson had filled several wooden trays with penny candy. "Look, I have some money!" Del declared, holding up two shiny quarters. "We can buy us a whole bunch of candy with this!"

Jack wanted to say he had some money too—a lot more than Del! But he decided to say nothing. After all, Del's father was a courtroom judge and owned two cars and a big house on West G Street. He and his daughter could well afford to be generous.

Then he saw it on a shelf high above the candy counter—a sleekly varnished wooden box with an iron footrest on its top. Instantly, he knew how he would use his five-dollar bill. He would buy that shoeshine kit and start his own business. What better place to do it than here in Benicia? There were bound to be hundreds of shoeshine customers in a town where one of the biggest industries was McClaren's Tannery.

"So what kind do you want?" Del asked, startling Jack out of his train of thought.

"Ahm ... let's see," he answered, studying the trays full of multicolored gumballs, black licorice sticks, chunks of chocolate fudge, and cherry-colored jawbreakers. "I'll take five licorices and ten of them jawbreakers."

"You mean *those* jawbreakers," Del corrected.

Del was always doing that—correcting his grammar or telling him how to pronounce some new word he tried to use. Jack supposed that was because Del was a teacher's pet at Saint Catherine's Seminary. He put up with it, though, because Del was a good friend. She was always generous about sharing things.

"Hello there, Missy," Vernon Wilkie chirped as he leaned over the counter and grinned at Del. "What do ya wanna buy today?" Wilkie was one of the clerks who worked in Wilson's store. He was a scrawny little man with buckteeth and one eye that constantly twitched.

"Five licorice, ten jawbreakers, and fifteen gumballs, please." Del loved gumballs because she could blow bubbles with them. In fact, Jack thought, she could blow bigger bubbles than anyone else he knew.

Wilkie dropped the candy into a brown paper bag and handed it to Del. "That'll be thirty cents, Missy."

Del gave Wilkie the two quarters. "Kaching!" sounded the cash register behind the counter. Wilkie dropped the quarters into the till and handed Del two dimes in change. These she put into the snap-purse she always carried in a side pocket of her pinafore. Then, turning to Jack, she said, "Come on. Let's go down by the docks to eat our candy."

Jack stood his ground. "No. I wanna buy something else first."

Del looked at him in astonishment. "What do you mean?" she demanded. "You can't buy anything. You don't have any money."

"That's what you think," Jack said as he reached into his pocket and pulled out the still moist five-dollar bill.

"Where'd you get that?" Wilkie demanded. "You didn't steal it from your Momma, I hope!"

"I didn't steal it," Jack said, keeping calm, even though he was very angry with Wilkie for accusing him. "I found it, and I want to buy that shoeshine kit up there."

Wilkie shook his head, still convinced that Jack had done something dishonest. "Lemme see that bill."

"Not 'til you let me see that shoeshine box first," Jack insisted.

Again Wilkie shook his head suspiciously. "I s'pose I could let you *see* it," he admitted. Pulling a step stool from under the candy counter, he climbed up to take the shoeshine box down from its shelf. Then, keeping a firm grip on the box, he slid it across the counter toward Jack.

Jack reached inside and pulled out some of its contents, which included three small glass jars of different colored shoe polish, two flannel rags, and two stiff-bristled shoe brushes. After carefully examining each of these items, Jack placed his five-dollar bill on the counter.

Wilkie quickly reached for it. But, as soon as he felt its moist surface, he drew back his hand. "Where'd you get that slimy thing—out o' somebody's privy?"

Del promptly leaned over the bill and sniffed it. "Nope. Doesn't smell like it to me," she announced with a defiant grin.

"I ain't pickin' that thing up with my bare hands!" Wilkie declared. "You'll jus' have to wait 'til I get a rag or somethin' t' clean it off." Taking the shoeshine box with him, he disappeared into a room at the back of the store.

"Don't know why he's so fussy," Jack said to Del as he retrieved his bill and stuffed it back in his pocket. "Money's money, ain't it?"

"*Isn't* it," Del corrected. But she did so with a smile that told Jack she agreed with him. "So where'd you find it?" she asked.

"In the spittoon trough at Campy's."

"Eeww! You mean you just picked it up out of a filthy trough?"

Jack nodded. Then, noticing that Wilkie was returning, he put his index finger to his lips. "Shhh!"

Wilkie came back to the front of the store, still clutching the shoeshine kit in both hands along with a clean dust rag. "Now," he said, "Lemme see that bill."

Jack again put his five-dollar bill on the counter. Gingerly, Wilkie placed his dust rag on top of it and tried to wipe it dry. Then, with one finger, he flipped it over and tried to dry the other side. Next, he picked the bill up with both hands and carried it over to the big store window where he carefully examined it in the light from the street. "Guess it's alright," he said at last and returned to open the cash register drawer and drop in Jack's five-dollar bill.

"Wait a minute!" Jack declared. "You ain't told me how much it costs yet."

Wilkie looked surprised at first, but his expression quickly turned to anger. "Two dollars and fifty cents!" he snapped.

"That's too much!" Jack retorted. "It's nothin' but an old wood box with some little jars, rags and brushes in it. I could buy them things separate for a lot less."

"So go ahead!" Wilkie growled and slammed the cash register drawer closed. "I ain't sellin' this kit for one penny less!"

"Then gimme my five dollars back," Jack said.

"What's goin' on here?" another voice asked. It was Cliff Wilson, the storeowner. Wilson was a big man who moved and talked very slowly as if he were never in a hurry to do anything.

"This kid comes in here with a filthy old fiver and tells me he won't pay for this shoeshine kit he wants," Wilkie whined.

"Why not?" Wilson asked.

"He says it costs too much."

Wilson took the shoeshine box from Wilkie and held it up to look for the price tag he himself had pasted to the bottom. "Dollar forty, it says here."

"That isn't what Mister Wilkie told Jack!" Del angrily protested. "He said it was two dollars and fifty cents."

Wilkie's face turned white with fear.

"Well," Wilson said without so much as glancing at his store clerk, "the price tag says a dollar forty. You want it for that price, young man?"

"Yes sir," Jack said.

"Give the boy his change and wrap that shoebox up for him," Wilson said to Wilkie and then calmly walked back to the rear of the store.

"Sorry, kid. Guess I shoulda checked the price tag," Wilkie admitted grudgingly when he handed the wrapped package and three dollars and sixty cents change to Jack.

"You better be careful, Mister Wilkie," Del warned as she and Jack walked out of the store with their purchases. "Guess you showed him!" she whispered triumphantly to Jack.

"Aw, forget it," Jack said. "Let's go see what Adam's doing."

* * *

Adam Tucker was an African American who had been a munitions and motor pool officer stationed at the Benicia Arsenal during The Great War. He had been discharged from the Army in 1917 because of an accidental explosion that blew off his right hand. An Army surgeon had replaced it with a steel hook.

In spite of his handicap, Tucker was a skilled auto mechanic. He knew more about car repairs and could do more with his left hand and his steel hook than almost any other skilled artisan in the North Bay. People from miles around went to Tucker whenever they needed work done on their wagons, cars and trucks.

Many children and teen-aged boys in town liked to watch Tucker while he worked on the vehicles in his garage, which was in an old blacksmith's shop on West H Street. The young people were fascinated by the mysteries of the combustion engine and the skill with which Tucker could manipulate tools with his hook. A patient and gentle man, Tucker didn't mind these spectators as long as they didn't get in his way or stand too close to the mechanical equipment he used.

"Whose car are you working on, Mister Tucker?" Del asked as she and Jack stood in the open doorway of his garage.

Tucker, who was leaning over the engine compartment of a 1917 Model T Touring Car, did not look up from his task. "This be Miss Ebert's car. Gotta fix her carb'retor," he explained.

Not knowing what a carburetor was, Del simply said, "I see." She didn't want Tucker or either of the two teen-aged boys who were standing near her know how ignorant she was. So she whispered in Jack's ear, "What's a *car brator?*"

"How should I know?" Jack said out loud.

One of the teen-agers named Calvin Watrous laughed derisively. "Carburetor's what feeds gas to the engine," he explained superciliously.

Del felt her face turn red with embarrassment.

"Well no, Cal. Actu'ly it don't just do that," Tucker corrected, straightening up and looking around at his young admirers. "Carb'retor mixes gas with air. You got to have air to ignite the fuel. I had to put a new float in this one."

Del stuck her tongue out at Calvin Watrous.

"Let's see if she works now," Tucker said as he shoved a hand crank into the slot under the radiator at the front of Miss Ebert's car and gave it a quick turn with his left hand. The engine sputtered several times but did not start. Tucker cranked it again. This time, the motor rattled into action. Again, Tucker leaned over the engine block and adjusted something that made the engine run more smoothly. "Guess she's all fixed," Tucker announced and closed the metal hood. Then, turning to Del and Jack, he asked, "You two wanna take her for a tes' ride?"

"Sure!" Del and Jack said simultaneously.

"How 'bout me?" Calvin protested.

Tucker gave him a stern look. "You boys stay here with Billy and guard the garage."

Billy Sparks was the seventeen-year-old mulatto who worked as Tucker's apprentice. The rumor around town was that Billy was Tucker's son, though nobody had any proof of that and Tucker himself claimed the boy was an orphan.

Tucker opened one of the back seat doors of the Model T. "Hop in, you two. We's off an' runnin'!"

As soon as Jack and Del climbed in, Tucker closed the door. "Don't you be touchin' them door handles, now," he warned. "You can fall out an' get hurt."

"We won't. We promise, Mister Tucker," Del assured him.

Nodding his approval, Tucker climbed into the driver's seat, released the hand break, and slowly eased Miss Ebert's Touring Car out toward the heavy traffic on First Street. Turning right, he drove the vehicle toward the waterfront.

Jack and Del were very excited. They waved proudly at all the pedestrians they passed on the street. Several people gave them dirty looks, appalled that two white children would be riding in a car driven by a Negro.

"She sounds pretty good," Tucker announced proudly. But then, suddenly, the car's engine began to sputter again. "Uh-oh!" Tucker exclaimed. "Somethin' wrong." As the engine stalled out, he guided the vehicle toward the side of the street where he locked the hand brake and stepped out of the car. "You stay put while I check to see what's wrong," he said.

Tucker opened the hood and examined the fuel line. "Well, I'll be!" he declared. "I do believe she's out o' gas. You two stay here while I goes back 'n' gets us a can. Don't you be touchin' nothin' now!" he warned again as he headed back up the street toward his garage.

"Want a gumball?" Del asked, reaching into her paper bag to add to the two she was already chewing.

"Nah," Jack said. "I don't like them things. They're too sweet. Gimme a licorice."

"*Those* things," Del corrected as she drew a black licorice stick out of her paper bag. "And you should always say *please*," she added.

"Please, Miss Lanham—can I have a licorice stick?" Jack mocked.

"You *may*, Mister Westlake," she replied with equal sarcasm. They both giggled.

For the next several minutes they sat contentedly chewing and watching the busy activity on First Street. "Have you heard about the big parade next Sunday?" Del suddenly asked.

Jack nodded. "Mom told me about it. She said it's to celebrate the new law against drinking."

"That's not all it's about," Del said. "It's also about women's suffrage."

"What's that?" Jack asked. He had heard the term before, but he had no idea what it meant.

Del gave him a withering look. "Women's right to vote. It's another new law they're passing. It'll mean every woman over 21 can vote. Papa says he thinks it's a silly law, but I think it's wonderful."

"Why?" Jack asked

Before Del could answer, their conversation was interrupted.

"Where's the driver of this car?" a deep male voice asked. Startled, Jack and Del looked up to see a tall man in a dark blue uniform leaning in over the steering wheel. It was Constable Frank Cody, a man whom Jack immediately recognized because he had often seen him patrolling the street in front of Campy's Tavern.

"He went to get some gas," Del promptly answered. "He'll be back soon."

"Who is *he*?" Cody asked, pulling a booklet out of his back pocket and starting to fill in a summons form.

"Oh, please don't give him a ticket, sir," Del begged. "It's Mister Tucker. He just fixed Miss Ebert's car and was taking it for a road test."

"He didn't know it was out of gas 'cause Model T's don't have gas gauges," Jack explained, hoping to impress both Del and Cody with his knowledge of automobiles.

The constable acted as if he did not hear them. He finished filling out the summons, tore out a copy and dropped it on the driver's seat. "You tell Tucker t' test his cars someplace else. First Street ain't no place for test drives."

"But he isn't driving it now," Del corrected. "He just parked it here for a few minutes to go back and get some gasoline."

"Ain't no parkin' on First Street neither," Cody said with a sly smile.

"What do you mean?" Del demanded angrily. "Look at all these other cars parked along here? People can park their cars anywhere they want."

"Regular people maybe," Cody snarled, "but not Niggers like Tucker." Having made this point, the constable walked on down the street.

"He's terribly mean!" Del declared. "I'm gonna tell Papa."

"Won't do any good," Jack said. "That's Frank Cody. He's the Mayor's son."

"We'll just see about that!" Del retorted.

When Tucker returned with his can of gas and saw the summons, he quickly stuffed it into his over-alls pocket. Then, he poured gasoline into the tank of the car and cranked the engine again.

Del tried to tell him how mean Constable Cody had been, but Tucker waved his hand indifferently. "Don't pay it no mind, Miss Del."

"I'm still telling Papa," Del insisted. "It's not fair!"

Behind the steering wheel again, Adam released the handbrake and carefully eased the Touring Car into the traffic. At the next intersection, he turned right and drove around the block. As they pulled into the garage, Jack suddenly realized he did not have his shoeshine box.

"Where'd you leave it?" Del asked anxiously. "Hope nobody stole it."

"I think I left it on the ground when we got into the car, right near where we were standing," he told Del.

"Don't you be worryin', boy," Tucker said. "We fin' it." He called out to Billy who was working on the metal lathe. "Billy, you seen a package layin' aroun' here?"

Billy did not look up from his work. He simply gestured toward some large open shelves along the back wall of the garage.

"Tha' she is," Tucker said as he retrieved Jack's package from a collection of cans and small engine parts on one of the shelves and handed it to Jack.

"Thanks, Mister Tucker," Jack said. Then, turning to Del, he asked, "You think your Papa'd mind if you took it home with you and kept it at your house?"

"Why? Don't you want to take it with you?"

"I don't want Mom to see it," he explained. "She'll ask too many questions about how I got it, and I don't want her to know."

"Why not?" Del demanded. "You didn't steal it, so why worry?"

"Well, no. I didn't steal it. But she'll want to know where I got the money to buy it. And then she's liable to say I should take it back to Wilson's and get my money back and then give the whole five dollars to old man Campy."

"That's silly!" Del declared. "You didn't steal that money. You just got lucky and found it. Finders keepers."

"You don't know Mom. She's very particular about things like that. 'Honesty's the best policy,' she always says."

Del still thought Jack was being foolish, but she decided not to argue. Instead, she asked, "So what do I tell Papa? You know he's going to want to know why I'm keeping that package for you."

Jack thought for a moment, then said, "Why don't you just tell him it's a surprise birthday present for your teacher at school or something?"

"That's an even sillier idea!" Del declared. "You know he's going to ask me what's in the package."

"Never mind," Jack said and started to leave with his package.

Tucker, who had been standing and listening to this dialogue, intervened. "You can keep it here if you wants, Jack," he suggested.

Jack's face lit up. "I can? Gee, Mister Tucker! Thanks!"

Tucker smiled and put the package back on the shelf. "You can come get it any time you wants," he said. "It'll be safe, an' I won't tell nobody."

"He's such a nice man," Del said as she and Jack left the garage and walked back toward First Street.

"That's because he knows what it's like to be poor," Jack observed.

"What do you mean?"

"When you're poor, you got to keep secrets," Jack answered. "'Cause people are always trying to steal from you."

"Why would they want to steal from you if you're poor?" Del giggled.

Jack did not respond. He decided Del would probably never understand. Just then, they heard the sound of a train whistle. "Oh, that's the 5:15!" Del exclaimed. "I've got to go now, or Papa will be very angry." Immediately, she ran to the corner and down First Street toward home.

*   *   *

The traffic was even heavier now as Jack walked slowly south on First Street. Most of the pedestrian and vehicular traffic was moving toward the Benicia depot as people rushed to meet the passenger train from Sacramento.

Unlike Del, Jack was in no hurry to get home. He knew his mother would be in a bad mood when he returned, as she always was after a visit from Soames. Often on such occasions, he had found her sitting in her mohair armchair weeping.

Jack didn't understand exactly why his mother acted the way she did, but he did not like to be around her when she was unhappy. He decided to walk down to the depot and watch the switch engine push the passenger cars onto the train ferry that would carry them across the river to Port Costa.

Walking past the entrance of Campy's Tavern again, Jack noticed the place was now filled to capacity with boisterous male patrons. By sundown, many of these patrons would start reeling across First Street toward the Lido—the largest of several bordellos located near the railroad depot. On either side and to the rear of this two-story building, rows of small private rooms or "cribs" had been erected where the women who worked at the Lido would entertain their customers.

The Lido was a source of considerable embarrassment to many upright citizens. It had long been one of the most successful business

15

enterprises in Benicia, though. The town fathers had little alternative. All they could do was confine the nefarious activities at the Lido through strictly enforced zoning laws.

To protect the health of Benicia's citizens, the town fathers also passed an ordinance requiring that the Lido's proprietor, Mrs. "K. T." Parker, send all of her female employees to a local physician for weekly checkups—a requirement with which Parker was perfectly willing to comply, since it enhanced the quality of her services.

Jack and his friends always stayed on the opposite side of First Street when they passed the Lido. For parents, teachers, preachers and policemen constantly warned that severe punishment would be meted out to any minor who so much as exchanged a civil word with Mrs. Parker or one of her "girls." Even so, nine-year-old boys like Jack couldn't resist sidelong glances at the attractive young women who often waved at them from the second floor bay windows of the Lido.

The depot was crowded when Jack got there. Hundreds of people were greeting newly arrived passengers from Sacramento or bidding others farewell as they climbed aboard the Pullman cars. Porters scurried here and there with luggage, and train yard workers shouted to each other as the locomotive was decoupled from the front of the passenger train and moved slowly onto a sidetrack.

Jack loved the sound of hissing steam the huge engine made as it moved, its enormous steel wheels revolving slowly but potently, its connecting rods sliding back and forth like the limbs of some giant preparing to charge.

Even as he lay in bed at night, Jack took comfort in the hooting, clanging and chugging racket the steam locomotives made only a few hundred yards away from Mrs. Brown's boarding house where he and his mother lived. They evoked an almost supernatural power that he felt driving relentlessly forward within himself. They were both the monsters and the angels of his boyhood dreams.

Jack joined the crowd of spectators at the waterfront end of First Street to watch as the passenger cars were slowly pushed aboard the *Solano*—one of the two large ferries that carried rolling stock across the Strait.

Loading the *Solano* was an arduous and time-consuming task. The passenger cars in the original train had to be pushed aboard in coupled sets, each on one of four parallel tracks built onto the ferry deck, as long and wide as a football field. After each set of cars had been pushed into place, it had to be uncoupled. Then a switch engine pulled back the rest of the train so the next set of cars could be pushed aboard on a parallel track.

Jack yearned to watch all of these mechanical operations, but there were so many others already crowding for a view that it was impossible for him to get close enough. He decided to walk toward the other side of the depot so he could at least watch the switch engine as it moved backward and forward on the tracks approaching the ferry.

As he passed the waiting platform, Jack overheard the conversation between a young couple who had apparently just gotten off the train from Sacramento. The man was wearing a two-piece white linen suit and a Panama hat. The woman wore a Canary yellow dress and carried a matching purse and parasol.

"Good heavens!" the woman complained. "What a dreadful smell! What is it?"

"I have no idea," her companion replied. "Perhaps we should get back on the train instead of waiting here."

"Yes. Let's do!" the woman said as she led the way back down the steps.

Jack couldn't help smiling at this conversation. It was obvious these travelers had never stopped in Benicia before. Like most newcomers, they were reacting to the rancid odors coming from McClaren's Tannery.

They did not realize that, inside the five-story brick building just a few blocks away, teams of men were busily scraping hair and flesh from the hides of recently slaughtered cows, horses, pigs and goats—the first step in a manufacturing process that created a horrid stench in Benicia, both day and night.

But then Jack noticed something much more offensive. His mother's friend Soames was standing near the entrance to the Express Office, flirting with one of the pretty young women who worked at the Lido.

Now he understood why his mother was unhappy when Soames came to visit.

CHAPTER TWO

"Pack Up Your Troubles in Your Old Kit Bag"

EVEN THOUGH IT WAS SUNDAY, Del woke up an hour before sunrise. As she knelt beside her bed to say morning prayers, she heard the seals barking out on the water. Quickly she ran to the window, hoping to glimpse some of these creatures frolicking close into shore.

But the faint light of pre-dawn was only beginning to define the eastern horizon. The shoreline at the foot of the bluffs in front of Del's house was still completely shrouded in darkness. All she could see were the lights at the train ferry terminal a quarter of a mile away and, more than a mile away on the opposite shore of the river, the flickering lights of Martinez.

Del knew the seals were not far out there in the darkness, though. For it was August—the time of year when millions of salmon crowd through the Carquinez Strait and rush up the Sacramento River to their spawning pools. Always the predatory seals were in hot pursuit of this sumptuous fare. Feeling compassion for the desperate salmon, Del murmured a special prayer to their patron Saint Francis. Then, putting on her bathrobe and slippers, she tiptoed down the staircase, careful not to wake her father.

Because it was Sunday, their live-in housekeeper Ruby Hicks had the day off so she could perform her duties as Head Deaconess at the Evangelical Baptist Church in Vallejo. Del would have the whole house to herself for at least an hour. Very quietly, she crept into the kitchen pantry where she knew she would find the bowl of cherries Ruby had

19

picked the day before. Taking a large handful, she went into her father's study to find something interesting to read.

Next to her own bedroom, her father's study was Del's favorite room in the house—even though it often reeked from the stench of his cigars. With its high ceiling, dark mahogany paneling, and comfortable Mission-style armchairs as well as its three tall windows looking out onto the street and back yard, her father's study made a wonderful retreat.

Two full walls in this room were covered floor-to-ceiling with bookshelves crammed full of thick leather-bound volumes. Most of these were books about California law and history. But there was a special low-level shelf the Judge had reserved for Del containing books he considered appropriate for a nine-year-old girl to read. Among the titles he had chosen were Bronte's *Jane Eyre*, Defoe's *Robinson Cruso*, London's *Call of the Wild*, and Stevenson's *Treasure Island*.

Del had already read many of these books, even though her Aunt Lucy thought most of them more suitable for older readers. Del had not yet tried one of the newest additions to her special library—Burnett's *The Secret Garden*. She decided the title looked interesting. Pulling this volume from its shelf, she sat down in her father's large, leather-cushioned armchair and, within minutes, was completely absorbed.

Two hours later, her father suddenly appeared in the doorway to his study. "Adelaide, hurry and get dressed! It's time to go to Mass! Didn't you hear me calling you?"

Surprised that she had not even heard the hourly chiming of the big grandfather clock in the front hallway, Del immediately jumped up. "Oh! Yes, Papa," she said. "But this is such a wonderful book. Why didn't you tell me about it?"

Her father walked over and took Burnett's novel from her hands. Looking at its title, he said, "Hmm—*The Secret Garden*. I'm afraid I've never read this book. Your Aunt Lucy recommended it to me. I'm glad you're enjoying it, my dear. But we really must be going now. I'll wait for you in the car." As Del rushed upstairs to her bedroom, the Judge called after her, "Don't dilly-dally," he ordered sternly.

Unlike most Benicians, Judge Lanham owned two cars—a 1916 Model T Roadster and a 1915 Twin Six Packard Phaeton. The latter was a huge and very powerful black four-door sedan and was the envy of everyone in town. Both vehicles Judge Lanham kept in a large car barn in his back yard.

This morning, he chose to use the two-seat Roadster because it was only a short drive from his home on West G Street to St. Dominic's Church on East I Street. Parking the much larger Phaeton would be a great nuisance. Besides, though proud of his possessions, the Judge was averse to ostentatious display of any kind. He considered it unbecoming to a seated member of the Solano District Court Bench.

Del thought differently. She liked nothing better than to be seen driving through town in her father's big Phaeton. She was very disappointed when she learned they were driving to Mass in the much humbler Roadster. "Oh Papa!" she declared. "I do wish we could ride in the Phaeton."

"The Phaeton, young lady, is only for long trips," her father said emphatically.

It didn't take long for Del to spot her friend Maggie in the crowd of people leaving St. Dominic's Church after Mass that morning because Maggie's father, George Woolsey, was one of the tallest men in the parish. As President of the Bank of Italy on First Street, he was always stopped after Mass and engaged in lengthy conversation by the pastor and one or more of the parishioners who did business with George's bank.

As soon as she saw Del, Maggie boasted, "Guess what! My sister Colleen's going to be The Temperance Queen in the parade next Saturday. She's the prettiest girl in town. Everybody says so."

"Oh, that's wonderful!" Del declared, trying to sound enthusiastic even though she did not at all agree Colleen Woolsey was the prettiest girl in Benicia. There were many others who were prettier—even some of the young women who worked at the Lido! Del would never say that to her friend Maggie, however. "Is there going to be a marching band in the parade?" Del asked, hoping to change the subject.

"Of course. Momma says there's going to be lots of marching bands. There's the drum and bugle band from the Arsenal, of course. And then there's the Benicia High School band, the Navy band, and even Doc Blackburn's Montezuma Minstrel Band from Vallejo."

"A minstrel band?" Del asked, astonished that such a group would be allowed to participate, for many of its members were Negroes.

"Yes. They're going to march in front of the John Barleycorn float. Momma says the float's going to be fixed up to look like a hearse with a coffin inside and inside the coffin they're going to put a dummy dressed up like John Barleycorn and the minstrel band's going to play a funeral march—just to make fun of people who drink liquor."

"That's silly!" said Del, recalling her father's disparaging remarks about the 18th Amendment. "John Barleycorn's just an imaginary character in one of Jack London's books."

"No it's not!" Maggie retorted. "Momma says it's very serious and thank goodness they passed the new law so now there'll be no more drunks."

Del had to admit that it would certainly be better if they got rid of all the drunks in Benicia. Even her father would agree with that. "Well, I hope your Momma's right," she said.

"Momma's *always* right!" Maggie declared, astonished that her friend could think otherwise.

At this point, Maggie's older sister Colleen interrupted their conversation. Grabbing Maggie's wrist, she commanded, "Come on, Maggie. We've got to go now."

Del was furious. Colleen had been terribly rude. She had not even said hello to Del. *Prettiest girl in town indeed!* she fumed.

* * *

As was customary for several of Benicia's more prosperous families, after church on Sundays Del and her father brunched in the formal dining room of the Palace Hotel on the corner of First and H Streets. Locally, the Palace was billed as "Benicia's only first-class hotel." Its two upper floors of side-by-side Bay windows rose above its covered ground-floor esplanade like the tiers of a giant wedding cake.

The walls of the Palace Hotel dining room were decorated with murals depicting scenes of the Carquinez Strait when the indigenous Patwin Indian tribes had fished for salmon and shad in its swift-moving waters and hunted the beaver, elk, and grizzly bear that roamed and foraged freely in the surrounding marshes and hills. Del particularly liked the mural closest to the table where she and her father were now sitting. It depicted a Carquines hunter crouched in his balsa canoe, poised to launch his spear at a beaver swimming in the tules.

Del's imaginings were suddenly interrupted by the loud contralto voice of Florence Henshak. "Hello there, Clyde!" she trilled flirtatiously from two tables away where she was sitting with her husband Oscar and their two children—fifteen-year-old Rowena and nine-year-old Greg. "Why don't you come join us?"

Greg was one of Del's best friends, but she did not like Florence Henshak. Though superficially cheerful and solicitous, Florence would explode in a rage at the slightest provocation. She bossed her husband and children around mercilessly and constantly bragged about the famous people she knew.

Judge Lanham waved cautiously at this woman and focused on the menu the waiter had just given him. Florence Henshak was not to be ignored, however. Standing up, she called across the dining room, "Don't be standoffish, Clyde! Come over here and sit with us." To this loud command several other patrons in the dining room reacted with scornful stares. Del felt terribly embarrassed.

"I suppose we really should accept her invitation, Adelaide," the Judge murmured sheepishly. Rising from his chair, he motioned Del to follow him to the Henshaks' table. "Are you quite sure we're not imposing?" he asked as they approached.

"'Course not!" Oscar said offhandedly. Although Oscar Henshak was in his late forties, with his plump, clean-shaven face and full head of flaxen hair, he looked not a day over thirty. Without standing up to greet his guests, Oscar signaled the waiter to bring two additional chairs for their table. Then, nodding indifferently at Del, he resumed eating his plate of oysters. "Plenty o' room," he somehow managed to say with his mouth full.

"How are you, my dear?" Florence asked, embracing Del as if she were a long-lost relative. "We haven't seen you in ages. Where have you been hiding all this time?"

Caught short by this question, Del looked desperately at her father. She had no idea how to answer.

"Del hasn't been hiding, Florence," the Judge said firmly. "She has been very busy this summer helping Ruby around the house. She's old enough now to take on some of the household chores."

Del couldn't help smiling. Her father rarely if ever asked her to perform household chores. Raised in a Victorian household himself,

Clyde Lanham believed female children should be treated as hothouse flowers.

There were several reasons why Del and her friends rarely visited Greg Henshak at his parents' house. For one, it was almost a mile north of town, high in the hills overlooking Benicia. A sprawling two-story ranch house, it had scores of rooms and hired help, including two maids, four groundskeepers, a cook and a butler. That was another reason—all those servants monitoring everything.

What made Del and her friends most uncomfortable, though, was Florence's constant bullying and cajoling. "Stay away from the horse and car barns, children!" she warned. "And don't you dare go near my perennial gardens! No tree climbing and no running around in the yard or the house either!"

Now in the genteel dining room of the Palace Hotel, however, Florence Henshak was all sweetness and light. "Come sit here next to me, dear," she urged as the waiter brought an extra chair for Del. "My! What pretty yellow flowers!" Florence gushed, touching Del's coronet of daisies.

"They're to show my support for Women's Suffrage," Del said, knowing full well this remark would not sit well with Florence, who believed very strongly that a woman's proper place is in the home.

"I can't imagine why a nice young girl like you would want to do that," Florence snapped irritably. "Those suffragettes are just a bunch of hussies!"

"So who you puttin' behind bars this month, Judge?" Oscar quipped as Del's father sat down beside him.

"Actually, I have an estate settlement hearing tomorrow. There are no criminal charges involved—just some greedy relatives squabbling over their share of the spoils."

Oscar snickered. "Oh, I know all about that! You shoulda seen what a mess we had when my old man died. Why, they was relatives comin' out o' the woodwork! Even one of our own servants tried to stake a claim. Didn't do 'em no good, though, 'cause I had me one o' the meanest lawyers in San Francisco. He chewed up all them phony claims in no time."

Oscar Henshak III was the grandson of an entrepreneur who had hit the "mother load" when gold was first discovered in California.

The grandsire had made his fortune not from mining or panning gold but from selling camping supplies and equipment to the thousands of prospectors who poured into the state in 1849. In the years that followed the Gold Rush, Oscar's grandsire had invested his profits in the railroad industry—adding even more to his wealth. Oscar and his family were now living off this accumulated horde.

Del was desperate to correct this man's grammar. How, she wondered, could such a wealthy man be so ignorant! But at least Oscar's outburst had distracted Florence. For the woman immediately jumped into the men's conversation with more details about the people who had tried to break her father-in-law's will. This gave Del a chance to tell Greg about Jack's good fortune. Leaning close to him, she whispered the story in his ear.

"What are you two conniving about?" Florence suddenly demanded.

"Oh nothing, Momma," Greg said softly, his face white with fear.

"Then, why are you whispering?"

"We didn't want to interrupt you and Mister Henshak and Papa," Del quickly explained.

"Hmff!" Florence expostulated. But a waiter had just placed in front of her a sumptuous plate of roast duck with orange sauce, *au gratin* potatoes, and fresh green string beans to which, along with a second glass of champagne, she now eagerly gave her full attention.

By the time dessert was served, Oscar and Florence Henshak had polished off a full bottle between them. Both were in a holiday mood when the Judge politely explained he had to return home to work on the next day's court hearing, so Del and her father made their escape with little fanfare.

*   *   *

Cave Beach was located only one block west of Del's house, at the end of the boardwalk that ran from City Beach on West E to Rosario's boat dock on West G. Unlike City Beach, which was a bona fide public facility, complete with clean white sand and a row of wooden beach houses where bathers could change their clothes, Cave Beach was a shallow inlet which, at low tide, became a mud flat the size of two adjacent football fields.

Local residents referred to this area as Cave Beach because of a seven-foot deep hole the waters of the Strait had carved out in the sandstone bluff adjacent to Rosario's dock. It was rumored that lovers would meet in this "cave" for late night trysts.

What attracted Del and her friends to Cave Beach on hot summer days was not the cave but the mudflat. Here boys from all over town would gather at low tide to launch their homemade wooden sleds and race with each other by paddling across the broad swath of slippery brown muck. It was a messy sport of which few respectable parents in Benicia (if they knew about it) would approve, for at the north end of Cave Beach a large rusty pipe dumped raw sewage into this makeshift playground.

Wearing old overalls and sandals, Del had sneaked out of the front door that Monday afternoon while Ruby was beating rugs on the back porch. Knowing she would need a change of clothes, Del had stuffed her pinafore and a towel in a canvas bag. She would change later in one of the public beach houses.

As she walked down the boardwalk toward Cave Beach, she saw her friends Jack, Greg, Sam Geddis and dozens of other boys propelling their boards across the flat, shouting at each other to get out of the way and often colliding. Del ran to the edge of the mud flat and called out, "Jack! Let me borrow your sled!"

But Jack was too preoccupied with racing Sam across the flat. Then she saw Greg, who was just about to launch his own board. "Greg, wait!" she commanded. "Ladies first!" she added, assuming Greg would respond to this reminder of his gentlemanly duties.

She was wrong. Even though he had looked directly at Del, Greg simply waved and flopped down on his board. Then, paddling furiously, he quickly propelled himself beyond the reach of her voice.

Crestfallen, Del decided she would have to wait until one of her friends was ready to share. She walked back along the beach toward Rosario's wharf, climbed onto it, and sat gazing out across the Carquinez Strait. The broad expanse of water in front of her was as smooth as a glass mirror reflecting the bright blue sky of a cloudless summer day.

It was not always so. In early spring and late fall, the waters of Strait were often roiled with white caps as the strong wind swept in from the northwest. Every morning during the winter months, heavy fog rolled in from San Pablo Bay, completely obscuring the high green hills on the opposite shore.

No matter what the season of the year, Del delighted in the changing moods of the Carquinez Strait. Often she felt they complemented her own. Right now, she reveled in the stillness of the water and landscape before her. Indifferent to the frantic shouts of the mud-sledders behind her, Del identified with the tiny bodies of two seagulls drifting soundlessly out on the water and with the solitary turkey buzzard that was making slow circles in the sky directly overhead.

The staccato sputtering of a gasoline engine interrupted her reverie. Glancing in the direction of the sound, she saw the long white hull of Rosario's twelve-passenger ferry approaching. Only one person was aboard on this vessel's return trip from Port Costa. Miguel Rosario himself stood at the wheel in the stern of his converted whaleboat with its canvas roof and single-cylinder engine. "'Oy, Francisco!" Rosario shouted as his vessel approached.

A door in the storage shed at the end of the long narrow wharf popped open and a thin, shirtless boy with thick black hair ran out to catch the bowline Rosario threw at him. Bracing one of his feet against a piling, the boy strained to keep the boat from drifting farther.

Del had known this Irish orphan ever since he first started living with the Rosarios three years before. Miguel and his wife Inez had taken Francis in, primarily for his usefulness as a dockworker and farmhand. Like many residents of Benicia, Miguel was involved with multiple enterprises. He operated the small passenger ferry that daily transported railroad workers between Benicia and Port Costa and he raised pigs on a hillside farm west of Benicia.

Despite being abandoned by both of his parents when he was only five years old, Francis Flanagan was fiercely proud of his Irish ancestry. Rosario, being his boss and being equally proud of his own Portuguese heritage, insisted on calling him Francisco.

Del moved down the dock toward Rosario's boat. "Hello, Mister Rosario. Hello, Francis."

Rosario only grunted, his thick eyebrows knitted in a scowl.

"'Lo," Francis answered without looking at Del. Francis knew he had to keep his full attention on the cranky old man in the boat who, at any moment, might bark some new monosyllabic command.

Rosario climbed awkwardly onto the dock, handed its stern line to Francis, and headed toward the storage shed. As soon as she saw Rosario enter the shed and close its door, Del asked, "What's he do in there?"

"Drinks his rotten brandy an' sleeps," Francis snorted contemptuously as he secured the stern line to a piling

"What were *you* doing in there?" Del taunted.

"Readin' a book."

"What kind of book?" Del asked, surprised. It had never occurred to her that an orphan boy like Francis would be interested in books.

"A book about engines. I wanna learn all 'bout 'em, so I can get better job an' make some damn money!"

"You want to be a mechanic like Mister Tucker?"

Francis glared at her. "Not *like* him. *Better* 'n him—*way* better! I wanna be like Henry Ford an' make millions o' dollars."

"You'll have to go to college for that," Del cautioned.

Francis' thin lips twitched a fleetingly sarcastic smile. "College—hell no! That's a waste o' time. Ford didn't go to no college, did he? All y' gotta do is work on all kinds o' diff'rent engines. There's new engines bein' invented ever day for all kinds o' things. You take this little one-banger, for instance," Francis said as he stepped aboard Rosario's boat and pointed at the small gasoline engine mounted in the center of the hull. "You know where this come from?"

Del shook her head.

"Out of a 1912 REO run-about Tucker found in a junk yard someplace. All he did was clean that old engine up an' add a few new parts. Then, he put a chain pulley on the flywheel and run it over a homemade drive shaft to turn the prop. Runs like a charm! Hell I could do that easy!"

"Do you really think so?" Del asked.

Before Francis could answer, Del heard Jack calling to her from the edge of the mud flat. "Hey, Del! You wanna use my board now?"

Del turned and jumped off the dock. "Bye, Francis. See you later," she said and ran toward Jack.

Francis shook his head in disgust. "Stupid girl!"

CHAPTER THREE

"Mademoiselle from Armentieres"

THE SUN WAS SINKING FAST over the western horizon, as Sam Geddis and his younger brother Tully returned home from Cave Beach through the hills north of Benicia. Sam was leading the way with long strides that made Tully cry out, "Wait for me!"

Sam turned and looked back down the slope. At nine, Sam was tall for his age, with long legs and an unusually large head. Sam smiled, pleased to see he was at least thirty yards ahead of his brother. Tully was thin and frail—a pesky five-year-old who constantly whined and complained. Sam scowled, but stopped and waited anyway. "We're late, Tully," he warned. "If we don't hurry up, Momma will burn our supper again."

Sam knew all too well how easily this could happen. Ever since their father Talcott Geddis had killed himself with a shotgun a year before, their mother Florin had turned to drink. Often, when they came home from playing with their friends after school, the boys had found her so intoxicated with wine that she had fallen asleep and overcooked their evening meal.

When both boys reached the top of the hill, they saw Florin's 1919 Maxwell Touring Car moving slowly up the winding dirt road from downtown Benicia. Sam waved at her to stop and pick them up. As they climbed into the back seat, Sam noticed several brown paper bags in the front passenger's seat. "What's in the bags?" he asked.

"Ah!" Florin said distractedly. "I went to the Farmer's Market. I found *haricots verts* for us. Also *des baguette fraiche,"* she explained, lapsing into the vocabulary of her preferred ancestral French.

Sam leaned forward and peered inside the largest of the paper bags. It was filled with bottles of red wine. Extracting one of these, he held it up and asked sarcastically, *"Baguette,* Momma?"

"Ah—that too," she replied with a vague smile. "Some very fine *vin du pays."*

Sam flopped back into his seat, giving his brother a disgusted look. Tully only looked puzzled.

As they rounded the last bend in the road, the Geddis' house came into view—a large two-story stucco and wood frame structure with a mansard roof and six bay windows. Though impressive in size, the house was a grotesque mix of French Provencal and Queen Anne architectural styles. It had been built three years before when Talcott Geddis had moved his family to Benicia from southern California where he had been an engineering consultant for several independent oil-drilling firms.

After visiting Benicia on business several times in the past, he had decided Suisun Bay would be the perfect location for an oil refinery. The deep-water channel of the Carquinez Strait offered ready access for sea-going tanker ships coming from the Golden Gate through San Pablo Bay. Such a refinery's close proximity to the Benicia Arsenal and the Mare Island Naval Shipyard in nearby Vallejo ensured a reliable and growing market for its products.

Talcott also knew the increasing slaughter of British and French troops on the Western Front made it likely the United States would soon enter the war against Germany. Accordingly, in early March of 1917, he purchased seventy-five acres of land on the western shore of Suisun Bay as the site for his new refinery. This venture proved tremendously successful because of the enormous demand for oil and gasoline that followed America's declaration of war against Germany.

As many local residents said, Talcott Geddis had "the Midas touch." When he shot himself just as his new venture began generating millions of dollars, therefore, it was a great mystery to everyone—everyone, that is, except Sam who knew his mother was contemptuous of her husband.

Sam did not understand exactly why. After all, his father had always seemed reticent and passive—always eager to satisfy Florin's extravagant demands and tolerant of her frequently dark moods. During the years following the Geddises' move to Benicia, Florin had berated her husband mercilessly whenever he was home—especially late in the evening after the boys had gone to bed. All the way from his third floor bedroom, Sam could hear her shouting and slamming around in the kitchen.

Early one morning, just a few days before Talcott shot himself, Sam had come downstairs to find the man on his knees in the kitchen, whimpering softly as he picked up pieces of broken china and glass scattered on the kitchen floor. When Sam asked what had happened, the oil tycoon could only shake his head in speechless despair.

Talcott had met Florin on his first business trip to Benicia in the spring of 1910. She was working as a housekeeper at the Palace Hotel then. Her long brown hair, smooth olive complexion, sensuous lips and flashing eyes had captivated Talcott immediately. Having been raised in the cloistered and all-white world of a wealthy San Luis Obispo family and educated at the Massachusetts Institute of Technology, Talcott knew little about women—least of all, exotic working-class women like Florin.

Florin was the granddaughter of a French Canadian fur trader named Jacques Delong who had come to Carquinez Strait in the early 1840s to hunt beaver, which at that time were plentiful in the tule marshes of Suisun Bay. Her maternal grandmother had been a member of the warlike Suisunes tribe and her mother, the "half-breed" wife of a Portuguese sailor.

Abandoned by her mother as an infant, Florin was taken in by the Dominican Sisters of Saint Catherine's Seminary in Benicia. The nuns did their best to indoctrinate Florin in the ways of Holy Mother Church. From her ancestors, though, Florin had inherited a fierce independence. When she turned sixteen, therefore, the nuns released her from their care and helped her find employment at the Palace Hotel.

Fascinated by this handsome and defiant young woman, Talcott had lured her to his hotel room bed. When he returned to Benicia a few months later and Florin told him she was pregnant, Talcott's carefully cultivated sense of *noblesse oblige* induced him to marry her.

As Florin and her sons turned into the long driveway now, the many tall windows in the front of the Geddis' house blazed with the blood

31

red light of the sunset. "Look!" Florin suddenly declared, pointing at the house. "Papa is home!"

Sam shuddered. "Momma!" he shouted. "Papa's dead!"

"No-no!" she retorted excitedly. "Don't you see? He has left the lights on for us."

Terrified, Sam waited in silence while his mother stopped the car in the driveway, got out and headed for the front entrance carrying only her large bag of wine bottles. "*Apport les provisions!*" she commanded.

Before the boys entered the kitchen, Florin had already lighted a Turkish cigarette, uncorked one of her new bottles, and poured herself a large glass of Cabernet. While Sam emptied the grocery bags, Florin carried her glass into the front parlor and cranked up her Victrola. Placing a record on its turntable, she sat down to smoke, sip her wine, and with her eyes closed serenely slip into the meandering piano rhapsody of Debussy's *Claire de Lune*.

Sam watched Florin warily as he stored the various packages of vegetables, meat, and cheese in the icebox. He felt somewhat less fearful now because his mother was behaving just as she usually did—attending to her own wants first and indifferent to what was happening around her. Sam decided, if he and his brother were going to get any supper that night, he would have to prepare it himself.

Rummaging through the icebox, he found a quart glass jar filled with onion soup his mother had prepared two nights before. Removing this and a block of goat cheese wrapped in brown paper, he placed these items on the kitchen table. Then, loading several pieces of pine kindling into the kitchen stove, he ignited a fire.

By this time, the Debussy piece Florin had been listening to concluded. Roused from her reverie by the noises in her kitchen, Florin came out to investigate. "*Quest-ce que tu fais?*" she inquired sweetly.

"Preparing supper," Sam replied. "It's time, Momma. Tully and I are hungry."

"*Mai sure! Pardon moi, mes chers!*" Florin gushed. Then, noticing the cheese and soup jar on the kitchen table, she said, "*Ah non! Pas le potage!* I make *crepes suzette, nest-ce-pas?*" Opening the icebox, she extracted one of her newest purchases. "And look—I buy *saucisse* for you!"

Annoyed that his mother poured herself yet another glass of wine before she placed the iron skillet on the stove, Sam was satisfied he had sufficiently reminded Florin of her maternal duties. He therefore challenged Tully to a game of jacks on the kitchen floor, directly in front of the stove.

"*Pas ici!*" Florin said sharply as she dropped the sausages into her skillet.

Shrugging defiance, Sam picked up his jacks and moved them to another part of the room where his superior skill quickly reduced his brother to tears.

"Sammy," Florin urged. "Be gentle, *mon cher.*"

"But he's such a cry baby!" Sam protested.

"Perhaps you should both wash your hands now," Florin suggested softly. "Supper will be ready soon."

"I hope so!" Sam groused as he marched to the kitchen sink, splashed cold water over his soiled hands, and wiped them on a dishtowel.

Florin's eyes flickered with anger. Grabbing the towel from Sam, she snarled, "Your trousers and shoes are covered with mud! Go upstairs and change! *Vite! Vite!*"

Sam ignored this directive and continued playing his game of jacks.

Frustrated by Sam's defiance, Florin retaliated as she always did—by showering affection on her youngest. "Tee-Tee," she murmured solicitously, using the nickname she had assigned to Tully when he was born. "Come wash your hands, *mon petit.*"

Tully promptly obeyed, smiling blissfully up at his mother as she took a bar of soap and carefully washed his and her own hands together in a pan of warm water. Then, taking a clean hand-towel from a cabinet drawer, she dried first her son's and then her own hands. Kissing him lightly on the forehead, she warbled, "*T'asseoit, mon petit.*"

Sam had already taken his place at the head of the kitchen table where his father had customarily sat and was now tapping on the tabletop with a fork, impatient for his mother to serve him.

Carefully rolling the crepe on their plates and sprinkling them with powdered sugar, Florin added the crisply sautéed sausages and, spreading wide her arms in a dramatic gesture, declared, "*Voila!*"

Tully applauded vigorously, but Sam continued rapping his fork on the tabletop. Florin signaled her displeasure with this by serving Tully first. Then, as they began eating, she poured each of them a glass of milk and herself a third glass of wine.

She did not sit down with them at the table, preferring to stand at the sink and watch them while she sipped her wine. It was just as she had done when his father was alive, Sam remembered now. Since Talcott often returned home late from work, Florin would wait to dine with and, usually, rebuke him for his tardiness.

The boys devoured their food in silence for several minutes. Satisfied that she had done her duty, Florin returned to the front parlor and put another record on her Victrola—this time a series of lively ballads sung in French by a man accompanying himself on a guitar.

As the music drifted into the kitchen, Florin returned carrying a newspaper and her glass of wine. This time, she sat down at the table and began reading her newspaper. "*Ecoutez!*" she suddenly declared and began quoting a headline on the front page. "'First Daytime Mail Flight from San Francisco to New York in 33 hours.'"

Florin spread the opened newspaper out on the table and pointed to the photograph of a smiling aviator standing in front of a single-engine bi-plane. The caption underneath read: "Veteran aviator James H. 'Jack' Knight stands beside his Havilland DH-4."

Sam moved to get a closer look. His mother leaned over his shoulder and began reading aloud the first paragraph of the news story.

"Let me read it," Sam insisted as he snatched up the paper and started perusing the news report with both of his index fingers.

"Can I see?" Tully asked, running around the table.

Sam pushed him away. "Get out of here! You can't read."

"Come, Tee-Tee," Florin said, taking Tully's hand and coaxing him to follow her back into the front parlor.

Much later that evening, long after Sam had gone up to his room to work on a model plane he was building, Florin awoke from her wine-induced doze. Rising from her chair slowly, she stood unsteadily for several seconds looking around the room until she noticed Tully sound asleep on the sofa. Stepping softly toward him, she touched his shoulder and whispered, "Come, Tee-Tee. It is time for bed."

The boy flinched slightly at her touch. Then, without opening his eyes, he sat up and put out his arms to be carried. Though Tully was small for his age, Florin was not at all sure that in her inebriated condition she was ready to carry him. "No, Tee-Tee. If you want to sleep with Momma, you must walk upstairs yourself."

Reluctantly, the boy stood up and allowed his mother to take him by the hand into the front foyer and up the staircase to her room. After removing Tully's clothes, Florin gently helped him climb into her bed. Then, she removed her own clothes and climbed in beside him.

CHAPTER FOUR

"There'll Be a Hot Time in the Old Town Tonight"

JACK HAD BEEN LATE FOR supper, his clothing covered with mud. "Where have you been to get so dirty?" Gail demanded.

"Just out playin'," he said as he flounced into her mohair armchair and noisily bit into an apple he had taken from the fruit bowl on the kitchen counter.

Gail snatched the apple from his hand. "Don't eat that now!" she scolded. "It's supper time. Go clean yourself up and get out of those filthy clothes!

Furious, Jack bounced up out of the armchair and marched into the bathroom, slamming the door behind him. He emerged minutes later, wearing nothing but his undershirt and boxer shorts. Again, he flounced into the armchair.

"What's wrong with you, Jack? I told you to *change* your clothes, not strip down to your skivvies!"

"What do you care?" he asked sullenly.

Gail began to worry. This defiant behavior was not at all typical of her son who was usually a good boy, obedient and kind to his mother. Her voice softening, she walked over to him and touched his forehead. "Are you sick, dear?"

"No. I ain't sick!" he retorted, pulling away from her.

"I *am* not sick," she corrected.

"Dammit!" Jack shouted and leaped to his feet. "You're always correcting me! You're worse than Del!"

"How dare you swear like that!" Gail shouted back. "I'll wash your

37

mouth out with soap, you fresh thing!" Swiftly, she moved toward the sink to carry out her threat.

This was enough to give Jack pause. Hanging his head, he said, "Sorry!" he mumbled, still resentful. "I'm sick of people always picking on me for my grammar."

"We're not talking about grammar, mister!" Gail warned. "I'm raising you to be a gentleman, and gentlemen don't talk that way to ladies—least of all their own mothers!"

Jack glared angrily at her.

Gail stood with her hands on her hips, studying her son in silence for several seconds. At last, she said, "Go put on a clean shirt and trousers. Gentlemen don't go strutting around half naked in front of ladies either."

Jack eyed his mother suspiciously. "Oh no? Then, why does Soames take off his collar and tie when he's here?"

This retort rocked Gail back on her heels. "That's not fair, Jack! It was very hot when he was here Saturday. Mister Soames was our guest. I suggested he remove his collar and tie so he'd be more comfortable."

"Seems like he's getting a little too comfortable, if you ask me," Jack groused.

Instinctively, Gail cocked her right arm, barely managing to refrain from slapping her son in the face. "Nobody asked you," she said coldly. "Now, go get dressed!"

Jack did what his mother had asked and changed into clean clothes. But the two of them ate supper in silence. As soon as he finished eating, Jack got up from the table and started toward his bedroom.

"You didn't excuse yourself, Jack," his mother said.

Jack ignored this reproof and entered his bedroom, closing the door behind him.

Gail remained seated at the table in silence for several seconds, not sure what she should do. At length, she stood up and cleared the table. Stacking the dirty dishes in the kitchen sink, sat down in her armchair to read the newspaper, determined to distract herself from the turmoil she was feeling.

After the sun went down, she opened the cupboard over her kitchen sink, reached up on the top shelf, and took out the bottle of sherry Soames had brought her as a gift from San Francisco. She filled a teacup with the sweet-smelling wine and sipped it slowly, hoping it would help her sleep. But one teacup full was not enough, so she had another. And then another.

Even this did not help. For, after she went to bed at ten o'clock, she lay wide-eyed with worry, keenly aware of the nocturnal clanking and hooting railroad noises she had long since grown accustomed to.

Was her son also unable to sleep? She wanted to get up and go to him, take him in her arms and hold him as she had when he was a little boy—assure him that everything was alright.

But she knew it was not. "Nothing will ever be *all right* again," she whispered to herself in the dark, tasting the bitter salt of her own tears.

* * *

"Good morning, Gail!" Ira Jacobs chirruped as she entered Ahern's Import/Export building the next morning. "Ready for another exciting day at the office?" he added with a wink.

"Awfully sorry I'm late, Ira," Gail replied. "I had kind of a bad night last night. Couldn't get to sleep for some reason." She had entered just as the big Monitor clock on the office wall was chiming 8:00 A.M.

Ira, Ahern's local branch manager, was a short, chubby man in his late forties. His receding hairline, bulging brown eyes, and wide mouth down-turned at the corners reminded Gail of a perpetually sad frog. "Don't worry, Gail," Ira smiled as best as he could. "You're not late. Look at the clock. It wouldn't matter anyway, my dear. You're so fast and efficient, you could come in at noon and still do all the work you need to do."

Ira had a heart-aching crush on this handsome woman. At five feet and eight inches tall with a long, graceful neck and torso as well as an ample bosom, Gail was what women of her mother's generation called a "statuesque beauty." Though seemingly reserved and even-tempered, Gail simmered with latent sensuality. She was very much like her mother in this respect. But, in her ability to concentrate for long hours on performing repetitive arithmetic tasks, she was like her father.

Ira had been infatuated with this woman ever since she first walked into the office two years before seeking work as a totally inexperienced clerk. His instantaneous assessment of her bookkeeping skills had been unemotional—keen and accurate. In less than two weeks, Gail Westlake mastered all the subtleties of posting and balancing the scores of customer accounts the office handled every day.

"You're too kind, Ira," Gail said as she sat down at her desk and promptly began sorting through the stack of order forms piled on her desk. Shuffling through these in a preliminary inspection, she asked, "Did Mister Grimes drop off those new shipping schedules you wanted yet?"

Ira threw both of his arms up over his head and rolled his eyes in exasperation. "Who's to know with that guy! They were supposed to be ready last week. Tell you what—I'm gonna call him right now. This is making me crazy!"

Ira picked up the candle phone on his desk. "Alice, get me 6324-R2," he barked into the receiver. "And please do *not* eavesdrop!" he added irritably. "This call is none of your business!" Thrumming his fingers on his desk blotter, Ira waited impatiently for the right party to answer.

"Grimes—is that you? Where's my shipping schedules? ... What d' y' mean they ain't ready yet? It's been two weeks since we ordered 'em, already!" There was a long pause during which Grimes was apparently trying to explain the delay, "Don't gimme that!" Ira made a face at Gail, who was now totally engrossed in her work. "You got a problem with your printing press? So what am I supposed to do about it? I got customers to take care of here. They won't wait." Another pause, longer this time. "Tomorrow's not good enough!" Ira snarled. "I got t' have 'em today!" Hanging up the phone, Ira again threw up his arms in exasperation and scowled at Gail "He says he'll drop 'em off this afternoon. He better!"

Accustomed to Ira's irritability, Gail had long since learned to ignore it. She knew it would never be directed against her. She also knew Ira Jacob's bark was bigger than his bite. The man was a showman. He would have been much happier and more effective, she thought, in vaudeville.

Suddenly, the street door opened, admitting a frail, wispy-haired woman with a face like a hatchet and the quick furtive movements of a ferret. It was Gail's friend, Snooky Wells. Though only thirty-eight, Snooky already looked like an old woman—stoop-shouldered, her face heavily creased with wrinkles and her hands mottled with brown spots.

"Hey, lady," Snooky rasped at Gail in her hoarse barfly voice. Snooky was both a heavy drinker and an inveterate smoker. She puffed whenever she could. It didn't matter whether it was one of her many boyfriends' cheap cigars or her own corncob pipe. Snooky thrived in a constant cloud of smoke. "How y' doin', Ira?" she said to Gail's boss.

"I'm good," Ira replied amicably but warily. He was amused by this eccentric creature and, because she was Gail's friend, he tolerated her always-bizarre behavior and questionable morals. "How's Alfie these days?" he asked, peering through the big street-front window at the small figure huddled in a wooden wheelchair outside. Alfie was Snooky's quadriplegic seven-year-old son.

"Alfie's great! Would you believe it? That kid never gets sick!" Snooky eyeballed Gail mischievously.

Gail knew her friend regarded her hopelessly crippled and dependent son as God's punishment for her own sins. Snooky had been raised as a Roman Catholic. Despite her always irreverent views of Church traditions and her defiant persistence in violating its most fundamental moral precepts, Snooky was ruthlessly honest with herself. "I'm a scarlet woman," Snooky had often confessed to Gail. "Ain't no doubt about it, an' I'll prob'ly fry in Hell for it. But—you know what? That little sucker out there could be my ticket to Heavn, so I'm gonna do whatever I gotta do to keep him happy an' healthy!"

Snooky had been faithful to that vow. Though few Benicia residents approved of Snooky's ways, practically everyone commiserated with her plight. Soon after Alfie had been born, Snooky's husband, Zeke Wells—a notorious town drunk and one-time crony of Jack London— had quit his job at McClaren's Tannery and jumped a freight car to travel nobody knew where. Furious and destitute, Snooky used the only talents she had to support herself and her son.

Ever since she was six-years old, Snooky had played the five-string banjo—the only family heirloom passed down to her from her paternal grandmother, who in 1846 had migrated with her family from Minnesota to California in a Conestoga wagon. By the time she was sixteen, Snooky could frail like Earl Scruggs and wail like Libby Holman. With the tough survival instincts she had inherited from her pioneering ancestors, it was only natural for Snooky to seek employment as an entertainer in Benicia's many waterfront saloons.

The patrons of these establishments loved her, and the proprietors rewarded her with nightly engagements where customer tips helped pay her rent and put food on her table. Alfie was always a part of these entertainments, posted front and center in his wheelchair wherever Snooky performed. While she would belt out her raucous "torch" songs or lead her audience in sing-alongs, Alfie collected the coins customers would drop in the tin can he held on his lap. "We got no shame!" Snooky often proudly declared.

Gail stood up and rushed to embrace her friend. Signaling with a quick glance at Ira her wish to share confidences with Snooky. Ira nodded his approval and the two women went outside, where Gail gave Alfie a greeting hug. He responded with a drooling smile and his own garbled greeting, "Hewo, Pail. I wove you."

Gail's eyes instantly filled with tears. "I love you too, dearest boy!"

Extracting a corncob pipe and a box of matches from the gunnysack she always carried with her as a purse, Snooky promptly lit up. Speaking through clenched teeth, she asked, "So how's old Soames these days?"

"Don't ask," Gail said grimly. "I think Jack knows about us. It's not good."

Snooky leered at her friend through a thick cloud of pipe smoke. "Don't worry about it. He was bound to find out sometime. You think boys his age don't already know 'bout that stuff?" Then, laughing harshly, she added, "In *this* town?"

Gail shook her head. "You may be right. Still—it's not good."

"It's all part o' growin' up, honey. Better he learns 'bout it from you than one o' them damn whores down there." Snooky nodded in the direction of the waterfront where they now heard the loud hooting of a train whistle. "You goin' to the parade Sunday?" Snooky asked, realizing it was time to change the subject.

Gail was still looking toward the waterfront, still preoccupied with her own anxious thoughts. Finally, she said, "I suppose so. I understand it's going to be a big event."

"You better believe!" Snooky affirmed. "Just about the biggest thing's happened in town since the Arsenal fire. An' you know who's gonna be one o' the stars in that there parade, don't y'?" Snooky tilted her head coquettishly at her friend.

"You, of course," Gail smiled.

"You bet y'! I got me a place right up front on the John Barleycorn float, and I'll be leadin' Doc Blackburn's Minstrel Band ever step o' the way." Snooky proudly announced.

"I wouldn't miss that for the world!"

"You better not! You bring your lunch today?" she asked, again switching topics.

"I always bring my lunch," Gail replied bitterly. "You know that. I can't afford *not* to."

"Tell you what," Snooky suggested. "How about me and Alfie treat you to a beer and a san'wich over at Wink's Bar. It's only a nickel apiece. We did pretty good with tips Saturday night, so I'm feelin' flush."

Gail smiled gratefully at her friend. "Alright," she said. "But only if it's a Dutch treat."

"Don't be such an ingrate! It's my treat or nothin'!"

"Fair enough," Gail acquiesced. "I'll meet you there at 12:30. But I've got to get back to work now." So saying, Gail squeezed her friend's hand and re-entered her office, but not without first giving Alfie another hug.

*　*　*

By seven o'clock the following Saturday morning, the people of Benicia had already put out chairs, blankets, and pillows along both sides of First Street in preparation for the big Temperance Victory Parade. A makeshift-viewing stand had also been erected at the intersection of First Street and West Military Road where the two contingents of the parade—one originating in Vallejo and the other at the Benicia Arsenal—would join and march down First Street to the waterfront.

Several early-bird youngsters had already commandeered the highest tiers of the viewing stand, from which they were repeatedly jumping or pushing each other off. Constables Frank Cady and David Warwick had stationed themselves strategically at the southwest corner of First and Military and stood watching warily the roughhouse antics of these youthful citizens.

Strands of red-white-and-blue bunting had been hung on buildings and from telephone poles along First Street—all the way to the railroad depot. There a three-foot high wooden platform had been erected for the dignitaries and officials who were scheduled to speak during the culminating ceremony at high noon. To protect the speakers from the hot noonday sun, a white canvas cover had been suspended on wooden poles over the stage.

Here, Women's Christian Temperance Union leader Vicki Callahan and her team of dedicated supporters were now putting the finishing touches on the speakers' platform decorations, which included more red-white-and-blue bunting as well as garlands of yellow roses.

"This will be lovely!" Charlotte Fisk, Secretary of the Board of Trustees at St. Paul's Episcopal Church, declared to Vicki. Looking up at the bright morning sun that had already raised the temperature into the high seventies, Charlotte anguished, "I just hope it doesn't get too hot today."

"Oh, it'll get hot, alright!" Vicki chuckled. "Especially when people hear the speech I've prepared. I wouldn't be surprised if mobs start smashing windows at the Lido this very afternoon," she added, pointing toward the two-story building only a few yards away.

"I'll be happy to throw the first stone!" Gladys Holcomb affirmed, somewhat modifying the original biblical text. "The sooner we get rid of that filthy place, the better is what I say." Gladys, a pillar of the First Methodist Church in Benicia, had long held Mrs. "K. T." Parker's establishment in special contempt—ever since her son Luke, at sixteen, had come home from the Lido late one Saturday night with a bad case of the crabs.

"Well, you know, it's the liquor that did the mischief," Charlotte insisted.

"Obviously," Vicki concurred. "And, once we women get the vote, we'll put a stop to prostitution as well. You can be sure of that!"

* * *

Del heard it long before she saw it—the repeated ra-ta-tat boom sound the Drum and Bugle Corpsmen made as they marched westward along Military toward the intersection with First Street. Del leaned as far forward into the street as she could to catch a glimpse of the lead contingent—Arsenal Commandant Colonel Orrin Wright Morris and his officers in full-dress regalia, riding high and proud on their gallant mounts.

She and her father had been waiting for more than an hour in the throng of spectators who lined both sides of First Street in anticipation of this moment—the beginning of the great Temperance Victory Parade. Then, just as the horsemen rounded the corner, heading south toward the waterfront, the bugles rang out their brisk clarion call and a wave of cheers and applause rolled swiftly down the full length of First Street.

Within minutes, another glorious sound filled the air—that of the Navy Band from Vallejo breaking into a rousting rendition of John Phillip Sousa's *Stars and Stripes Forever*. The spectators roared with delight and everyone began clapping in time and marching in place to this greatest of all patriotic American marches.

Del jumped and squealed with excitement when the big, handsome steeds leading the parade passed in front of her where she stood with her father at the northwest corner of First and G Streets. Then, as the approaching forty-man Navy Band struck up its second inspiring Sousa tune—*The Washington Post March*—she almost ran out into the street to join the parade herself. It was only her father's strong grip on her shoulders that kept her from doing so.

Immediately on the heels of the Navy Band was the first float in the parade. In the middle of this daisy bedecked wagon was Colleen Woolsey, attired in her white Queen of Temperance gown and surrounded by her retinue of, Del thought, much prettier attendants. Much to Del's chagrin, everyone cheered wildly as the big float passed and the snooty Colleen waved gloatingly at the adoring crowd.

The cheering quickly died down, however, when the long, ten-deep troop of W. T. C. U. marchers passed in their black broad-brimmed hats and mourning dresses, many carrying street-wide yellow banners that proclaimed such ominous slogans of their cause as "Lips that touch alcohol shall never touch mine."

Leading this bleak band of determined damsels was the towering figure of Vicki Callahan, carrying her own three-by-four foot sign depicting a large whiskey bottle with a thick black "X" painted over it. Vicki had learned well from her East Coast mentors in the tabloid newspaper industry that "a picture is worth a thousand words."

Meanwhile, three blocks up on the opposite side of First Street, Gail and Jack craned their necks to see the approach of the John Barleycorn float. But their efforts were in vain, for many other marching groups and rolling displays were yet to come before the John Barleycorn float brought up the rear.

First was the Benicia High School band, its meandering lines of mostly inept teen musicians tooting and bleating their off-key cornets, trombones, and clarinets while members of the percussion section vied to see who could pound loudest and fastest with no regard for a single consistent tempo. Del instantly recognized Calvin Watrous as one of these reckless drummers.

Following the high school band was a contingent of men in three-piece suits and straw hats with red sashes across their chests identifying them as members of the Benicia Redmen's Lodge. Following the Redmen were the officers and members of Benicia's newly chartered American Legion Post No. 101, marching in stiff formation and proudly displaying their nation's colors.

Next came a large flatbed truck bearing the Mayors and Town Council members of both Benicia and Vallejo who bowed and waved at the passing throng with as much vote-getting dignity as they could muster. The politicians' flatbed led a motorcade of open touring cars and horse-drawn wagons—each decked with banners and signs advertising various merchants in the two cities.

Finally, Gail heard the sprightly twanging of Snooky's five-string banjo, accompanied by the syncopated jingle of tambourines. In front of the John Barleycorn float—which was really a bulky and ancient horse-drawn hearse with its canvas top removed—were several dozen men in straw hats, prison-stripe suits, and black face (a few were actually Negroes) who twisted and turned as they danced like dervishes to the tempo set by Snooky's banjo.

As the John Barleycorn float approached the point where Gail and Jack were standing, Snooky hooted and waved frantically at them. Then, shouting to her fellow revelers, she commanded, "Come on, boys, let 'r rip!" With stunning promptness and precision, the dervishes lifted their brass and woodwind instruments to their lips and broke into a classic Dixieland version of *Didn't He Ramble*.

Instantly, spectators on both sides of the street went wild with cries of joyful release, and young couples rushed out to join the minstrels, wiggling and kicking their improvised versions of the two-step. As the John Barleycorn float moved noisily forward, the crowds on the wooden sidewalks spilled out into the street and followed Old John Barleycorn on his last journey to the waterfront saloons.

*   *   *

It was almost 1:00 P.M. before the Temperance Victory Parade leaders, with the help of police officers from both Vallejo and Benicia, could subdue the hundreds of people gathered in front of the reviewing stand so that Reverend Herald Twitty of Saint Paul's Church could intone his solemn invocation. "Oh Heavenly Father," he began, "we thank Thee for this glorious day of emancipation for all our brothers so long enslaved by that worst of demons—John Barleycorn."

"Hurrah!" interrupted several in the crowd, not a few of whom were simultaneously sipping inspiration from their own pocket flasks.

"And we pray," the Reverend continued, "that, in Your infinite mercy, You will bring them at last to Your Holy Tabernacle with contrite hearts and humble pledges of everlasting abstinence."

"Hooray!" the rowdiest in the crowd interrupted again.

Finally, raising his hands in a patient but much-abbreviated blessing, the Reverend concluded, "May the Lord bless us and keep us. May He make His Light to shine upon us and give us peace. Amen."

"Amen," echoed scores of voices.

Immediately, a tall man in a white suit and ten-gallon hat—Mayor Tom Cody—stepped up to the podium and, after shaking hands with Reverend Twitty, solemnly addressed the assembly. "Fellow citizens," he began, "we have come here today to celebrate a great victory." Pointing to the open casket on the John Barleycorn float where it was parked directly in front of the speaker's platform, he said, "Here before you lies the visible symbol of that victory." Then, pausing briefly to punctuate his meaning, Mayor Cody proudly announced, "And at sunrise tomorrow, we shall bury this ugly reminder of our past once and for all in the Benicia City Cemetery!"

With a broad but dignified smile, Cody waited until the cheering and clapping subsided. At this point, he gestured toward the stern-faced woman sitting directly behind him. "It is with great honor, my fellow citizens, that I now present to you our featured speaker for this historic day—Victoria Hogue Callahan. Miss Callahan is an officer in the national chapter of the Women's Christian Temperance Union, and she comes to us today all the way from that noble organization's headquarters in New York City. Please join me in welcoming Miss Callahan to our own fair city."

As Vicki rose to full height, her retinue of black-garbed followers, who had scattered themselves strategically throughout the audience, clapped as loud as they could. But the response of this audience was lukewarm at best. Still a small town in 1919, most of its residents were wary of outsiders. Especially those from the crowded ghettos of New York City were viewed with suspicion.

Vicki Callahan was not in the least bit put off by such xenophobia. Indeed, she had come fully prepared to wow these rubes with the full force of her well-honed oratorical skills. She had even prepared a special visual aid for the occasion—an oblong package wrapped in plain brown paper, which she now carried to the rostrum like some mysterious birthday surprise.

Nodding haughtily to the Mayor, who bowed diffidently and returned to his seat, Vicki looked out over the restless crowd for several seconds. Suddenly, she fixed her steely gaze on the bearded face of one of its most intoxicated members. Pointing a long index finger at this individual, she roared, "You, sir, are a disgrace!"

Immediately, hundreds of eyes focused on the object of Vicki's scorn. "This is not a man!" Vicki declared. "This is a mutant—the vile offspring of John Barleycorn!"

Everyone in the audience stood stunned in silence. Even Vicki's most loyal supporters had not expected such an aggressive assault. Vicki smiled, satisfied she now had everyone's full attention. "But I am not here to condemn such pathetic beings," Vicki said, her tone less severe now but still deadly earnest. "Rather, I come here to offer a cure for this plague that has so long enslaved our nation."

There were smatterings of applause from the women in black, and the shocked expression in many faces softened to bewilderment.

"Look around you—at the person to your right and the person to your left," Vicki commanded, noting with satisfaction that almost everyone complied. "Are these people worthless drunkards and reprobates? Certainly not! They are your brothers and sisters, your neighbors and friends. All share utter repugnance for the dissolute and deformed in our society. How, then, you must ask yourselves, have we come to this pass? What barbaric customs and feckless laws have made this possible?"

Snooky, who was standing beside the John Barleycorn float directly in front of Vicki, clutched fearfully at Alfie's shoulders. "You rotten bitch!" she muttered and looked around defensively to see whether others were staring at her "deformed" son. She was relieved to discover that all eyes were on Vicki.

"My friends," Vicki continued, sounding almost amiable now. "I'm sure you know the answer to these questions. First and foremost are the barbaric customs of those primitive tribes in Africa and Asia that have kept women in slavery since the dawn of time—customs that force women to bear thousands of unwanted children every year. Second is the Roman Papacy that has for centuries condemned women to lifetimes of unbridled procreation. Third are the archaic *man*-made laws in our own nation that block the spread of scientific facts about population control."

"Clearly, my friends, it is not we whose foremothers and fathers founded this great nation. No. It is the hordes of ignorant and superstitious immigrants who have been pouring across our borders for decades. And how do we stop those hordes? The answer, my friends, is simple and clear. We must enact strict laws to stop this deluge of unwanted races."

"Isn't she wonderful" Gladys Holcomb exclaimed to her friend Charlotte Fisk.

"Smart as a whip!" Charlotte affirmed.

"What the hell's she talkin' about?" Tom Cody grumbled to the elderly man sitting beside him, tannery owner Ralph McClaren.

"Damned if I know! Who invited this witch, anyway?"

The Mayor shrugged his shoulders, reluctant to risk exposing and thereby alienating the members of the Parade steering committee who had recommended Vicki.

"As many of you know," Vicki resumed, "one of our most respected national leaders, Missus Margaret Sanger, has written and spoken volumes on this issue. Her monthly magazine has edified and liberated women both here and abroad. Among the liberating policies Missus

Sanger advocates is the right of every woman to control her own destiny. And what is that destiny?"

Here, as Vicki had been taught to do in her oratory classes at Vassar, she focused on the enraptured faces of her most ardent supporters. "Is it simply to stay home and have babies as our mothers and grandmothers and their mothers and grandmothers have done for so many centuries? Or is there something more we women can do? Do we not have brains as smart and hearts as stout as men? Were not we too created in the image of God? Why, then, should we not be treated as equal to men in every respect? That is the question Margaret Sanger repeatedly asks."

By now, Vicki sensed she had lost the attention of almost everyone in her audience. Still, she plied on. Like a clipper ship under full sail, she felt nothing but the force of her own gale. "What we most need now, Misses Sanger believes, is a new scientific morality. For only that will solve the most compelling social and economic problems of our time."

When these high-sounding words were greeted only with silence, Vicki decided to move directly to her dramatic conclusion. "We have come here today, ladies and gentlemen, to celebrate two great victories in the annals of human history—the nationwide prohibition of alcoholic beverages and, soon, the enactment of universal women's suffrage. With such triumphs behind us, how can we fail to progress in this new Twentieth Century?"

Yet again Vicki paused, patiently waiting as what she considered her own inane platitudes gradually prompted polite applause. Now she would hit them where they lived! Slowly and tauntingly, Vicki began to unwrap the package she had placed on the speaker's podium. She knew all eyes were riveted on this act.

"And so, my good friends," she declared triumphantly as she raised high the long-handled axe she had unwrapped, "with the firm conviction of my courageous sister Carry Nation, I raise high the implement she used to culminate her crusade against Demon Drink. Down with John Barleycorn!" Vicki bellowed.

Instantly, the crowd roared its approval with repeated shouts of "Down with John Barleycorn!"

Then, suddenly pointing with her axe toward the Lido, Vicki declared even more fervently, "And, with the firm conviction of my courageous *other* sister Margaret Sanger, I say—Down with those Demon Women!"

Immediately, the face of every dignitary and official behind her became either white with fear or red with rage, and from the open bay windows on the Lido's second floor, eight angry women leaned out and simultaneously made the same obscene gesture at Vicki.

Seizing this rebellious moment, Snooky jumped up on the John Barleycorn float and began strumming and singing the opening bars of *You Are My Sunshine*. As soon as they heard the familiar lyrics, hundreds of onlookers joined in singing the refrain. Even the dignitaries on the reviewing stand rose to their feet and began clapping and singing along—all, that is, except Vicki Callahan.

Her face flush with fury, Vicki marched off the platform. Waving her axe and bullying her way through the jeering throng, she fled up First Street to the safety of her room at the Union Hotel. By six o'clock that evening, she would be on a passenger train to Chicago.

The soiled doves of the Lido had saved the day.

1920

The Commandant's Quarters at the Benicia Arsenal

CHAPTER FIVE:

"A Good Man Is Hard to Find"

"OYE! OYE!" CALLED OUT THE bailiff. "All rise and give your attention. The honorable Justice of the Circuit Court of Solano County, Clyde Lanham presiding. This Court is now in session."

After first sternly surveying the courtroom to make sure everyone was respectfully standing, Judge Lanham nodded to the bailiff. "You may call in the jury."

Del, who was sitting in the gallery with Ruby, watched with keen interest as the twelve men filed into the jury box. The first was a handsome young man with blonde hair and bright blue eyes. He looked around nervously and immediately headed for the back row. The other jurors were in their thirties and forties, many of them with the rough and callused hands of tradesmen. The last juror to enter was the oldest, with graying hair and thick sideburns. He confidently took a seat in the front row. All of these men were wearing dark suits, white shirts and ties. Most of them looked very uncomfortable in such formal attire.

Once the members of the jury had taken their seats, Lanham greeted them solemnly and then focused his gaze on District Attorney Joshua Wyman. "We are ready to proceed. Mister Wyman. You may make your opening statement."

Wyman stood up. It was hard to tell, though, because he was just over five feet tall. Still, he had a deep and commanding voice. "Gentlemen of the Jury," he began as he moved confidently to stand directly in front of the jury box. "You have been called here today to pass judgment on a woman who has defiled the most sacred honor God can bestow on any human being—the crown of motherhood."

Wyman paused for several seconds, his eyes ablaze with righteous wrath. "As the evidence in this case will show, on the night of March 3rd, 1920, the defendant Missus Florin Geddis did willfully attempt to murder her own innocent children—Samuel Geddis, age nine; and Tully Geddis, age five." At this point, Wyman turned to glower at Florin who seemed completely oblivious.

Shaking his head in disgust, Wyman turned again to the jury. "As you can see with your own eyes, gentlemen, the defendant is coldly indifferent. Clearly, she considers herself above the laws of both God and man. But God is not mocked! Once you have heard the overwhelming evidence against this heartless and soulless creature, you yourselves will be the instruments of His Almighty Justice and return a verdict of Guilty."

Florin's defense attorney Calvin Patterson immediately stood in protest. "Your Honor, I object! The Prosecution's opening statement is argumentative and completely out of order! Clearly, this is nothing but a hostile attempt to influence the jury with condemnatory epithets."

Struggling to conceal his own anger, Lanham sustained Patterson's objection. Then, to Wyman, he said, "I would remind you, sir, that it is the Court's role, not the prosecution's, to inform the jury what the defendant is charged with."

Without acknowledging this rebuke, Wyman sat down.

Lanham nodded to Patterson. "You may make your opening statement, Counselor."

Though still a young man, Patterson already had a successful private practice in Fairfield, the County Seat. Before he died, Talcott Geddis had named Patterson as back-up trustee of the Geddis Family Estate. Though a trust attorney by specialty, Patterson also occasionally handled criminal defense cases.

Smoothly confident, he now took a position several feet away from the jury box, determined to address not only the members of the jury but also the judge and the hundreds of spectators in the gallery.

"Your Honor, gentlemen of the jury," Patterson began. "Motherhood is indeed a gift from God. We are not here to dispute that. This is not a church or a temple, however. It is a court of law. Our first duty in this case is to determine whether or not a crime has even been committed. Even should the Prosecution somehow manage to demonstrate that a crime has been committed, the discovery documents already offered simply do not support any evidence of guilt. Moreover, as the testimonies of the witnesses will show, the Prosecution's arguments are based entirely on circumstantial evidence. I am confident, therefore, that once you have had an opportunity to consider all of the facts, you will return a verdict of Not Guilty." Turning to Lanham, Patterson said, "Your Honor, the Defense is ready."

Lanham looked toward Wyman. "You may call your first witness, Counselor."

Rising from his chair with calculated calm, Wyman slowly moved toward the witness box. "Thank you, your Honor. The People call Benicia Police Chief Frank Colpepper to the stand."

Plump but pleasant-faced, Colpepper was in his late thirties with prematurely graying hair. Neatly attired in full-dress uniform, he briskly marched into the witness box and was sworn in by the bailiff.

"Chief Colpepper," Wyman began with the cloying formality of a mortician, "it is my understanding that you were the primary investigating officer in this case. Is that correct?"

"Yes, sir." Colpepper's voice was musical and warm, almost caressing in its softness.

"Would you please tell the Court what you observed when you first arrived at the Geddis residence on the night of March 3rd, 1920?"

Colpepper swallowed hard, for the first time indicating that he felt uncomfortable. "Actually, I didn't get there until after the Benicia fire brigade arrived. You see, Officer David Warwick, who was on duty that night, did not receive a phone call about the incident until almost midnight, and he had trouble starting his car and coming to pick me up at my house."

Wyman grimaced with impatience at this answer. "Approximately what time was it when you *did* arrive, Chief Colpepper?"

"I'd guess it was around 12:30 AM and, of course, the first thing we did was talk with Fire Chief Hodges and his men to find out what caused the fire. By then, the Geddis home was almost completely burned to the ground. Bill ... I mean, Chief Hodges told me he didn't know for sure and that we'd have to wait 'til dawn when there was enough light for us to search through the ashes."

"And, when you were finally able to conduct that search, what did you find?"

"Actually, it was one of Chief Hodges' men who found it. It was a knife."

Wyman quickly walked to the evidence table and picked up a wooden tray containing the badly charred remains of a ten-inch carving knife. He carried it over to show Colpepper. "Is this the implement to which you are referring?"

"Yes, sir. I believe it is."

"You must answer simply 'yes' or 'no' to the counselor's question, Chief Colpepper," Lanham warned.

After first looking up fearfully at the judge, Colpepper nodded, "Yes, Mister District Attorney, that is the knife."

After asking that the knife be labeled as Exhibit A, Wyman resumed his interrogation of the witness. "Now then, Chief Colpepper, are you aware of any other tangible evidence found at the site of the fire that morning?"

Again glancing up at the judge, Colpepper answered softly, "No, sir."

"Speak up so the members of the jury can hear you, sir!" Lanham barked irritably.

"No," Colpepper responded, much louder this time.

"No *tangible* evidence," Wyman repeated. "However, you did interview several witnesses at the scene, did you not?"

"Yes, sir. Officer Warwick and I interviewed the Geddis's neighbors, Mister Eli Strohmann and his wife Esther. We also interviewed Missus Geddis' oldest son, Sam."

"And you have filed affidavits to that effect with the Court, have you not?"

"Yes, sir."

To the judge, Wyman said, "As you know, your Honor, the prosecution will be calling these witnesses to present their testimonies to the Court."

Lanham nodded.

"Thank you, Chief Colpepper," Wyman said dismissively. Then, glancing at Patterson with a taunting smile, he added, "Your witness, Counselor."

Addressing Judge Lanham, Patterson replied, "The Defense has no questions of the witness at this time, Your Honor. We reserve the right to re-call on cross-examination, however."

"So approved," Lanham acknowledged. "You are excused for now, Chief Colpepper." With conspicuous relief, Colpepper stepped out of the jury box and exited the courtroom.

"You may call your next witness, Counselor Wyman," Lanham said.

"The People call Benicia Fire Chief, Captain William Hodges."

"Bailiff, you may summon this witness," Lanham directed.

Minutes later, the bailiff re-entered the courtroom accompanied by a long, lean man with the comical features of a scarecrow—coarse canvas-like complexion, small black button eyes, and unruly straw-colored hair that stood out in every direction. Except for a wrinkled blue blazer with brass captain's bars on either shoulder, he was dressed in civilian clothes. After the Bailiff had sworn him in, he sat down in the witness' box and gazed around in wonder at the full assembly.

Wyman stepped forward and, standing a few feet to the left of the witness, began his examination. "Captain Hodges, I understand you and your men were the first to arrive at the scene on the night of March 3rd, 1920 when the Geddis' house was reported to be on fire. Is that correct?"

"Yes, sir."

"Would you recount for the Court, please, the details of that event?"

Hodges crossed one of his long legs over the other in an attempt to appear relaxed and confident. "Well, it must 've been around 11:30 when I got a telephone call from Eli Strohmann. He's a poultry farmer lives out near the Geddis place." Hodges paused thoughtfully for a moment. "Actu'lly, it was Missus Strohmann called. She was pretty worked up. She said the Geddis' place was burnin' like crazy an' I'd better get out there fast."

"What did you do then?"

"Well, right away, o' course, I rousted my boys. Told 'em t' grab their boots and buckets an' meet me up at the Geddis place soon as they could. Then, I went over to the firehouse and got the tank truck. By the time we all got there, though, it was too late to do much of anythin'. That house was already just about burned to the ground. 'Sides, there wasn't no outside well or fire pond, so alls we could do was wait 'til she burned herself out enough to go in an' douse the flames with what water we had in our tank truck. And I'll tell you that's pretty slow goin' 'cause we only got one spigot on that thing."

"I see," Wyman remarked impatiently and began pacing back and forth in front of the witness. "Once the fire was completely out, what did you do?"

"Well, by then there was a whole bunch of us up there, includin' Chief Colpepper and his men and some o' the Army boys from the Ars'nal. So we all started siftin' through the ashes to see what we could find out about what caused it all."

"I see," Wyman said again, still pacing back and forth. He was visibly annoyed with Hodges' rambling responses. Suddenly, he stood still and faced Hodges. "And what *precisely* did you find, sir?" he demanded.

Hodges straightened up, putting both feet on the floor to let everyone in the courtroom know he knew this was serious business. "We didn't find much o' nothin' 'til sun-up. It was way too dark up there, even with all the lanterns we had. Soon as the sun come up, though, Clem Shotwell found a kitchen knife."

Wyman quickly moved to the evidence table and again held up the carving knife to which the Bailiff had now attached an Exhibit A tag. He carried the knife over to the witness and asked, "Is this the knife to which you're referring, Captain Hodges?"

"Yes, sir. That's it."

"Your witness," Wyman said to Patterson and, after returning the knife to the bailiff, sat down again at the prosecution's desk.

"Your Honor," Patterson said, rising from his chair but not coming forward. "The defense wishes to challenge Counselor Wyman's allegation that the knife identified as Exhibit A has some bearing on this case. No clear connection has yet been established between this knife and the accused. The only reasonable conclusion that can be made is that it was a kitchen utensil recovered from the ashes of the fire. Doubtless there were many such implements in the debris left by the fire."

Wyman immediately jumped to his feet. "Objection! According to the police report already submitted to the Court, the knife marked as Exhibit A was found in a part of the house far away from the kitchen area and, by inference, fell from an upstairs bedroom when the floor of that room collapsed in the fire."

Lanham scribbled a note to himself. Then, looking up, he said, "Your objection has been sustained, Mister Wyman—even though it is inferential. Please sit down." Then, to Patterson, he said, "Do you wish to cross-examine this witness, Counselor?"

"Yes, your Honor. I have just one question."

"You may proceed, then."

Still remaining behind the defense's table, Patterson asked, "Captain Hodges, have you made any determination as to what caused the fire at the Geddis residence?"

"Nope. Not for sure, anyways. There wasn't much to go on—just a bunch of ashes an' charred timbers. Could 've started just about anywheres. Coulda been the wood stove in the kitchen or one of the fireplaces. They had one in just about ever room o' that house, and it was a mighty big house!"

"To the best of your knowledge, however, there was no evidence of the true cause of the fire," Patterson said.

"No, sir."

"Thank you, Captain Hodges. I have no further questions of this witness, your Honor," Patterson said and sat down.

"You may step down, Captain," the Judge told Hodges.

Nodding and smiling obsequiously, Hodges exited the courtroom.

"Call your next witness, Counselor Wyman," Lanham ordered, eager to move the case along.

"Thank you, your Honor. The People call Master Samuel Geddis to the stand."

Again, Calvin Patterson stood up to address the bench. "Your Honor, before you call this witness—a point of clarification, if I may."

"You may, Counselor."

"Sam Geddis is a minor—only ten years old as of last month. It is our view, therefore, that his youth may be an impediment to his judgment in this matter."

Lanham fixed Patterson with a withering stare. "As you know,

Counselor, we have already resolved this issue in chambers. I will allow the witness."

"Yes. Thank you, your Honor." Patterson sat down again.

After Sam was sworn in and seated in the witness box, Wyman approached him with a disarming smile. "You needn't be nervous, son," Wyman said reassuringly. "I just want to ask you a few simple questions. All you need to do is tell the truth. Alright?"

"Yes, sir," Sam almost whispered, for he was in fact both nervous and frightened.

"Very well then," Wyman resumed soothingly. "Would you please repeat for the Court what you told Chief Colpepper the morning after the fire?"

Sam couldn't resist the impulse to look at his mother who was sitting absolutely still now, staring into space as if she had no idea where she was. There was absolute silence in the courtroom as everyone waited for Sam to speak.

"Well," he said at last, "Tully and I were asleep in our rooms and all of a sudden I woke up and smelled smoke. And then, when I looked around, I saw my bed was on fire. And then ..." Sam paused, his throat suddenly tightening so much that he thought he would choke.

"Take your time, son," Wyman murmured.

"And then I looked up and saw Momma standing over me with this big knife in her hand. She was leaning over me with this awful look on her face." Sam paused, his lips trembling as if he were about to break into tears.

"What did you do then?" Wyman coached.

"I got out o' there!"

The courtroom erupted in laughter. Sam's response had been so simple and logical that everyone found it comic relief.

Judge Lanham, however, was not amused and firmly rapped his gavel, quickly restoring silence to the courtroom.

"What did you do next?" Wyman asked, still keeping his voice low and gentle.

"I went to get Tully and sneaked him downstairs and out to the woodshed. I told him to stay there 'til I got back. Then I ran across the field to the Strohmanns for help."

Now the spectators broke into uncontrollable applause, punctuated with several loud cheers. Furious with this outburst, Lanham pounded with his gavel. "Order! Order in this Court!" he shouted. Then, as the applause quickly died down, he glared around the room and declared, "If there are any more of these outbursts, I shall order the Bailiff to clear the room!"

Absolute silence greeted his warning. "You may proceed, Counselor."

Wyman stepped back from the witness box a few paces, still keeping his eyes on Sam and his voice low. "Now Sam, what was your mother doing while you were rescuing your little brother?"

Again, Sam looked at his mother. Still, she was staring blankly into space. "She was running all around upstairs in the house, screaming at us. I think she was trying to find us. I don't know for sure. I just wanted to get out of there as fast as we could."

Wyman nodded his approval. "And what happened when you got to the Strohmanns' residence?"

"Well, they were all asleep, I guess. So I just banged on the front door 'til somebody woke up. Mister Strohmann opened the door, and he was really mad. But when he looked across the field and saw our house burning, he told me to come inside. That's when I told him about my Momma chasing us with a knife and about how Tully was hiding in the woodshed. Right away, Mister Strohmann got his shotgun. 'You stay here,' he told me. 'I'll go get your brother.' Then, Missus Strohmann got up and tried to keep Mister Strohmann from going out with his gun. But he told her to shut up and call the firehouse. So that's what she did, I guess."

"And did Mister Strohmann rescue your brother?" Wyman asked.

"Yes, sir," Sam replied. "I followed him and saw him do it."

Again, applause and cheers broke out in the courtroom.

Lanham promptly ordered the Bailiff to clear the courtroom and declared a fifteen-minute recess.

When the court reconvened at 2:30 that afternoon, Wyman resumed his dialogue with Sam. "You have told the Court, Sam, that Mister Strohmann rescued your brother. Where was your mother when this happened?"

"He rescued her too," Sam said. "We heard her screaming from inside the house and he ran in and dragged her out just before the roof caved in. She fought with him, but he threw her on the ground and tied her wrists behind her with some rope we found in the car barn."

"Did your mother still have the knife in her hand when Mister Strohmann rescued her?" Wyman asked.

"No, sir."

Again Judge Lanham scribbled a note to himself.

"What happened next, son?" Wyman inquired.

"Well, we all went back to the Strohmanns' house and Mister Strohmann called the police."

Wyman stepped close to the witness box now and, placing his hand on the boy's shoulder, said, "Thank you, Sam. You have done very well in your testimony. I have just one more question for you. Do you have any idea about how the fire started that night?"

Patterson was caught by surprise with this question. By raising this question to Sam now, Wyman had played a card that could strengthen the case against Florin Geddis. Patterson did the only thing he could to foil Wyman's ruse. Standing at his desk, he said, "Objection. Your Honor, the Prosecution is calling for speculation."

The Judge nodded. "Objection sustained." Then, to Wyman he said, "Either withdraw your question, Counselor, or ask a different one."

Leering devilishly at Patterson, Wyman replied, "Of course, Your Honor, I'll withdraw the question and ask another." Then, to Sam he said, "Let me ask you this, Sam. Does your mother have any habits that might be a fire hazard?"

Somewhat puzzled by the wording of Wyman's question, Sam took his time answering. Once more he looked at his mother and again saw that she seemed completely indifferent to what was happening. "Momma smokes cigarettes," he said. "Sometimes she even smokes in bed. I don't know. Maybe her cigarette started the fire."

Simultaneously, the two lawyers exchanged glances. Smiling smugly, Wyman said, "Your witness, Counselor."

Though stunned by Wyman's skillful recovery, Patterson too recovered quickly. Ordinarily, he would have challenged Sam's speculation about his mother's starting the fire with a lighted cigarette. He decided this approach might backfire with the jury. "I agree with Counselor Wyman, Sam. You are an excellent witness. I too have just one more question, if you please."

"Yes, sir?" Sam sat erect in his chair now, feeling very proud of himself, no longer at all nervous or frightened.

"You have said that, when Mister Strohmann rescued your mother from the fire, she no longer had the knife with her. Is that correct?"

"Yes, sir."

"Are you quite sure that she actually had a knife in her hand when she woke you up earlier that night? Is it possible you just *imagined* she had a knife because you were startled from a deep sleep?"

Wyman jumped to his feet. "Objection! Your Honor, Counsel's question is argumentative and calls for speculation. What's more, Counsel's question is compound and must certainly be confusing to this innocent child!"

"Objection sustained. Counselor, if you have nothing of more substance to add, I suggest you release this witness."

"Your Honor, the Defense is simply trying to establish that the accused actually had a knife in her possession when, in fact, she may simply have been trying to warn her son that a fire had started. We also believe it's important to accurately establish this witness's state of mind at the time."

Lanham smiled indulgently. "The boy has already testified under oath that he saw his mother with a knife. That is sufficient for this Court. As for his state of mind, only God and the witness himself know that. I urge you to release this witness, Counselor."

"Very well, your Honor," Patterson replied. Then, to Sam, he again said, "Thank you, Sam. You've done very well."

"Thank you, son," Lanham echoed. "You may step down."

Not familiar with such courtroom jargon and visibly rattled by Patterson's question, Sam remained in the witness box for several seconds until the bailiff walked over to him and gently ushered him out of the courtroom.

"That lawyer's very mean!" Del whispered to Ruby where they watched from the second floor gallery. Ruby nodded in hushed agreement. Del then leaned over the railing to see what effect Patterson's question might have had on the members of the jury. As she scanned their faces, she saw nothing but intense and stony attentiveness.

The next witness Wyman called was Salvatore Maroni, proprietor of Maroni's Butcher Shop where Florin had purchased meat on the day of the fire. A taciturn man who spoke only broken English, Maroni had very little to contribute as a witness except to confirm that Florin was one of his regular customers and that she had in fact purchased some sausage from him that day. Having elicited similar testimonies from several other vendors, Wyman rested his case.

Lanham nodded toward Patterson. "You may call your first witness for the defense, Counselor."

Patterson rose and moved again to a neutral position in the front of the courtroom. "The Defense calls Missus Helen Moran to the stand."

Helen Moran was a plump matronly woman in her early forties, Attired in a gingham dress that looked as if it had been picked from a mail-order catalog, she had the smooth complexion and perkiness of a much younger woman. She seemed perfectly at ease as she took her oath and sat down in the witness box.

"Good afternoon, Missus Moran," Patterson greeted her affably. "I understand that you are acquainted with the defendant, Florin Geddis. Is that correct?"

"Oh yes, I know her quite well because she brings her boys to our Sunday Bible School every week. She's always seemed to me a very gentle and loving mother."

Lanham leaned toward the witness box. "Please simply answer yes or no to the Counselor's questions, Missus Moran," he courteously advised.

Helen smiled sweetly up at the Judge. "Yes, your Honor."

"Have you ever seen Missus Geddis mistreat either of her boys?" Patterson asked, coming right to the point.

"Oh dear no!" Helen answered vigorously. "In fact, I should say quite the opposite. She is always solicitous toward them. If anything, I have to say Sam has sometimes seemed to me quite rude to his mother. On one occasion, I'm told, he even slapped her in the face while they were shopping at the City of Paris."

Startled by this response, Patterson appealed to the Judge. "Your Honor, this witness's last statement was based on hearsay. Her remark should be stricken from the record."

"I agree, Counselor. The Jury will disregard the witness's last statement." Once more, Judge Lanham leaned toward Helen, this time with a very stern expression on his face. "Missus Moran, I implore you to restrict yourself to simple yes or no answers. I must warn you further not to repeat whatever rumors you may have heard about any of the litigants or witnesses in this case"

"Oh but, your Honor, it's not a rumor!" Helen protested. "I heard it from several of the most respectable members in our congregation."

Furious at this woman's audacity, the Judge growled, "You are under oath, Madam! Any testimony you give in this Court must be restricted to your own first-hand knowledge. Is that understood?"

"Yes, your Honor," Helen said meekly, now no longer smiling.

Realizing he would have to proceed very cautiously with this witness, Patterson asked, "Would it be accurate to say then, Missus Moran, that—based on your own first-hand experience—you consider Missus Geddis to be a responsible and dutiful parent to her children?"

"Most definitely!" she affirmed.

"Thank you, Missus Moran," Patterson said, eager to get this woman off the stand as soon as possible. "Your witness, Mister Wyman."

Wyman eagerly stepped forward. "Madam, we have heard testimony that Missus Geddis smokes cigarettes. Do you yourself have any reason to believe that she engages in such unladylike behavior?"

Looking up apprehensively at the Judge, Helen replied with nervous hesitation. "Well, I've sometimes smelled tobacco on her clothing."

"So you agree with the earlier testimony that Missus Geddis may be a smoker. Is that correct?" Wyman asked.

"Well, yes. I suppose it's possible. But I've never seen her smoking myself," Helen insisted. "She has always seemed to me a perfect lady."

"Have you ever smelled alcohol on Missus Geddis' breath?".

"Certainly not!" Helen declared.

Satisfied that he had sufficiently undermined this woman's credibility as well as underscored Florin's smoking and drinking habits as a possible cause of the fire, Wyman headed toward the Prosecution desk. "No further questions, your Honor."

It was now almost 4:30, so the Judge called for adjournment. Rapping his gavel, he announced that the Court would reconvene at 1:30 PM the following day.

CHAPTER SIX

―――――

"Look for the Silver Lining"

IMMEDIATELY AFTER LEAVING THE COURTROOM, Wyman entered the County Clerk's office to phone his junior partner, Fred Koontz, and tell him what had happened during the first day of the trial.

"Sounds good, Josh!" Koontz declared. "Asking the kid about the cause of the fire was perfect. That guy Patterson must be a real amateur! Oh and listen to this! I got some more good news for y'. I got us an interview with that old nun over at St. Catherine's you wanted to talk to. You know, the one that used to teach Florin Geddis when she was a kid?"

"When?" Wyman asked. "We don't have much time."

"Right now soon enough for y'?"

"Where? At the Convent in Benicia?"

"Right. I'll come over an' pick y' up. It'll only take us a few minutes to get to Benicia."

"Good. I'll be waiting at the front entrance." Wyman hung up the phone and, after making a quick stop in the men's room, rushed out of the building.

A new Model T sedan was already waiting in front of the Courthouse with Koontz at the wheel. Koontz's most distinguishing physical traits were his big feet, long neck, and a face covered with marks left by a childhood bout with Chicken-pox.

Wyman had taken Koontz on as a partner four years before. He knew the man was far too ugly to be a courtroom lawyer. But Koontz was a relentless and skillful researcher. He liked nothing better than to

69

spend hours pouring over the archived documents in the County Clerk's office. He also had an uncanny ability to spot the most abstruse but critical precedents in case law.

As soon as Wyman climbed into the front passenger seat, Koontz gunned his engine and the car leaped into the steady stream of traffic heading westward on Texas Street. Within minutes, they were speeding at nearly fifty miles an hour along the macadam-paved roadway toward Benicia.

"Nice car!" Wyman observed. It was the first time he had even seen Koontz's new vehicle.

"This is old Henry's latest model!" Koontz announced proudly.

Dreading the likelihood that his junior partner—an automobile fanatic—would launch into a long recitation about all of his new car's engine and body specifications, Wyman changed the subject. "How did you manage to get an interview with the nun?"

"Easy!" Koontz chuckled. "I'm a Saint Cat's alum. Donate to the school every year. No way they're gonna turn me down!"

* * *

It was precisely five o'clock when they pulled in at the main gate of St. Catherine's Dominican Convent School on Military Way. They could hear the chapel bell ringing as they drove into the parking area next to the main building, parked the car, and approached the concrete steps at the entrance. Ahead of them, a long line of nuns in white habits was filing into the refectory.

"Good evening, gentleman," said a tall stentorian woman who immediately stepped in their path as Wyman and Koontz entered the front foyer. "How may I assist you?"

"My name's Fred Koontz and this is District Attorney Joshua Wyman, Sister," Koontz explained with the diffidence of an altar boy. "We're here to see Sister Mary Clare."

A smile of recognition softened the nun's rigid features. "Ah yes, Mister Koontz," she said. "Sister Clare is expecting you. But, as you can see, this is our supper hour. I'm afraid you will have to wait here in the foyer for a moment." The nun gestured toward a wooden bench close to the entrance door.

"That will be quite alright," Wyman replied with a courtly bow, though there was a distinct timber of impatience in his tone.

The gatekeeper nodded and disappeared through the open double doors of the refectory where Wyman and Koontz glimpsed several dozen nuns lining up like soldiers at long wooden tables. The double doors were quickly closed, leaving the two men to sit in sacrosanct silence.

"Right now, eh?" Wyman taunted his partner as the two men sat down on the bench.

Koontz swallowed hard in embarrassment, so much so that his Adam's Apple bobbled conspicuously above his stiff white shirt collar. "Sorry, Josh. Afraid you'll have t' be a little patient. These nuns live in a different world—different routines, different time schedules."

"That may be. But time is of the essence, my friend," Wyman reminded his colleague. "Besides, it's Friday night and I promised Carolyn I'd be home by six. We're having some important guests for dinner this evening."

Koontz did not answer. Instead, he sat nervously folding and unfolding his large hands for several minutes.

Suddenly one of the double doors to the refectory opened and a pretty young novice stepped into the foyer. Moving swiftly toward the two men, she asked in a cautious whisper, "Are you the two gentleman who wish to see Reverend Mother Clare?"

"Yes, Miss!" Koontz jumped to his feet, again introducing himself and his partner. Wyman, however, remained seated. This young slip of a girl couldn't have been more than fourteen or fifteen, he conjectured—hardly a figure of authority.

"Please wait in the reception hall, gentlemen," the novice murmured softly and pointed to a wood-framed glass door opposite the entrance to the refectory. "I'll bring Reverend Mother Clare to meet with you there."

"Sister Clare doesn't eat with the others?" the always-inquisitive Koontz asked.

The girl shook her head and placed a cautioning finger to her lips, reminding the two visitors that all in this part of the Convent were constrained by a rule of silence. She then quickly disappeared into a dimly lighted corridor leading toward the rear of the rear of the building.

What first captured Wyman's attention when they entered the reception hall was its Victorian simplicity. Though it was a large room with tall mahogany-framed windows, these were covered with white sheer curtains framed by sage green cotton drapes. The walls above the dark mahogany wainscoting had been painted white and were bare except for two large portrait paintings depicting saintly personages unfamiliar to both Wyman and Koontz. The highly polished hardwood floor was also bare.

In the center of the room was an enormous oak table with elaborately carved legs, its surface obviously dusted and polished daily to preserve a high sheen. A dozen matching straight-backed chairs lined each long side of this table. Apart from this, the room was sparsely furnished. An eight-foot high mahogany armoire stood against one of the interior walls and, facing the marble-framed hearth in the other, was a semi-circle of six wingback armchairs.

"Thank God they have a fire going!" Wyman declared as he claimed the wingback closest to the fireplace. Although it was early April, the dampness and cold of the Carquinez Strait was still penetrating, especially late in the day.

It wasn't long before the novice returned, pushing a wooden wheelchair bearing the withered frame of an aged nun. The woman's face was so creased with wrinkles that any form of expression seemed impossible. Somehow, though, Sister Clare managed a welcoming smile.

"Good evening, gentlemen," she said in a surprisingly strong voice conspicuously tinged with a French accent. "Please forgive me for not greeting you in the front foyer. I am old, and the drafts in that part of our building are most uncomfortable." Addressing the novice, she said, "Thank you, Maureen my dear. I shall summon you with this when our guests are ready to leave." As she spoke, the nun touched a small brass bell attached to the side of her wheelchair.

The girl nodded and promptly left the room.

"Now, then," Sister Clare asked, "how may I help you gentlemen?"

Wyman was impressed. Immediately, he stood and introduced himself with his best courtroom demeanor. "Sister Clare," he began solicitously, "it's very gracious of you to meet with us on such short notice. Please accept our apologies if we have inconvenienced you at the dinner hour. I assure you, we will keep our meeting as brief as possible. We'd just like to ask a few questions about a woman who, as I understand it, was once a student of yours—Missus Florin Geddis? I believe her maiden name was Carvalho."

"Ah yes. Chief Colpepper has told me about her. It distresses me to learn she is in trouble with the law."

"Only as a suspect, Sister," Koontz was quick to explain.

"Actually," Wyman corrected, "she has been indicted as the defendant in a murder trial. I am the prosecuting attorney representing the Court in this case. Mister Koontz here is my associate."

The old nun revealed no emotion in her response. "What is it you would like to know, gentlemen?" she asked.

"It's my understanding, Sister," Wyman said, "that you have known Missus Geddis since she was an infant. Is that correct?"

"Oh yes," the nun replied, her eyes brightening now with keen recollection. "Florin was scarcely more than a few months old when one of our priests found her in a basket left on the front steps of Saint Dominic's rectory." She paused, reflecting for a moment. "I believe it was sometime during the winter of 1894 when Father Lawrence brought her to us. At first, we did not know whose baby she was. But Benicia was a very small town then. It did not take us long to discover that her mother was Anne Carvalho. Anne was the wife of a Portuguese sailor named Jose Carvalho. Alas! Jose was not a good husband. As a merchant seaman, he was often away from home for months at a time. When he *was* at home, he often drank too much and beat his wife."

"And that, I presume, is what prompted you to take this infant in as an orphan?" Wyman was genuinely excited now. Koontz had been right. Sister Clare was a veritable treasure trove of information!

"Our order does not usually take in foundlings. In this instance, however, the Prioress said it was our Christian duty to care for this helpless innocent. As she grew older, Florin proved to be a very bright child, though *intraitable*." Sister Clare hesitated for an instant, aware that the French word she had used might not be familiar to her guests. "I think perhaps you would say headstrong?" she suggested.

Wyman nodded, eager for her to continue.

"I came to know Florin well because I taught her throughout

grammar school, and she was one of the best pupils in my secondary school French classes. Perhaps this was so because Florin's grandfather was French Canadian, a heritage that set her apart from her classmates. Florin was always a very proud and aloof child." At this point, the old nun stopped speaking, suddenly aware she might have revealed too much.

"You said she was headstrong. Could you tell us more about that?" Wyman urged.

"Florin did not respond well to discipline," Sister Clare replied cautiously. "She often quarreled with the other children. Also, she held grudges and could be very ... how do you say—*vindictif*?"

"Vindictive. Yes, I understand, Sister. Please continue. Could you share with us an example of what you mean?"

"On one occasion, when Florin became very angry at Father Lawrence for giving her a severe penance, she tried to poison the parish cat. And several times, when we disciplined her, she attempted to run away."

Wyman studied the nun several seconds before he asked his next question. He wasn't at all sure how she might react. He was not Roman Catholic and was inclined to think all Catholics were ignorant and superstitious. "Do you believe Florin was possessed of the Devil?"

Much to his surprise, Sister Clare merely smiled at this question. "Not in the sense you may construe, Monsieur Wyman. No doubt you have heard the old saying 'The Lord works in mysterious ways.' I assure you, so too does Satan. He rarely takes possession of anyone in a manner that would require an exorcist. It is much easier for him to work through mere mortals like us." The old woman paused momentarily, studying her inquisitor as she might an insect under a microscope.

Wyman was beginning to feel uncomfortable in this woman's presence. She was obviously much more intelligent and canny than he had anticipated. "I'm sorry, Sister Clare," he said. "I don't think I quite understand what you mean. Perhaps you would be kind enough to explain."

"Naughty children are not naturally so, Monsieur. More often than not, their bad behavior can be traced to the emotional atmosphere of their early childhood. In Florin's case, I suspect that atmosphere was very disagreeable. Very early, she learned not to trust the grown-ups in her world. After that, almost any adult who reminded her of that atmosphere prompted her instinct to rebel. Satan, you see, had worked his will through Florin's parents."

Wyman exchanged glances with Koontz. Then, to the nun he said, "I see. That's a very perceptive observation, Sister. Were there perhaps any other adults who may have contributed to this 'atmosphere,' as you call it? You mentioned, for instance, that Florin was hostile toward one of your priests. Is it possible she was physically abused by this individual at some point during her stay here?"

Sister Clare stiffened in her chair. She paused several seconds before answering. It was clear to Wyman the woman was struggling to calm her emotions. Her voice still tense, she said, "As I'm sure you realize, Mister Wyman, even priests are human."

Wyman smiled disarmingly. "I take it, then, that your answer is yes. Florin *was* physically abused by this priest."

"I did *not* say that, Monsieur!" the nun declared. "There has *never* been any incident of abuse at Saint Catherine's Seminary. We are, after all, a teaching order of Holy Mother Church!"

Satisfied that he had gone as far as he could with this line of questioning and convinced that Sister Clare would fiercely defend her faith no matter how it might conflict with secular law or common sense, Wyman stood up. "Thank you for sharing your insights with us, Sister. I think we have all we need for now."

Immediately, the ancient nun's features softened in an expression of relief. "I hope I have been of some assistance to you, gentlemen," she said softly. "I am very old, and I fear my memory is not what it used to be."

Though he couldn't repress an amused smirk at the unintentional contradiction in what the old nun had just said, Wyman made his best effort at departing gallantry. "I just hope mine is half as good as yours when I retire, Sister."

* * *

"Jesus, Mary, and Joseph!" Koontz exclaimed as he and Wyman headed north again toward Fairfield. "Are you out of your mind, Josh, asking a question like that of a nun?"

"No one is above the law, my friend," Wyman said grimly. "Not even a member of the clergy. We've done what we came to do. We've established a motive. Unfortunately, though, if we ever put this woman on the stand, she would blow our case to bits!"

Koontz's Adams Apple bobbled above his collar. "Yeah. You're right about that," he admitted. "Sorry, Josh!"

* * *

Gail Westlake was the first witness Patterson called when the Court reconvened the following Monday afternoon. Dressed simply but tastefully in a gray frock with primly high-cut lace bodice, long sleeves, and a hemline just a few inches above her ankles, Gail looked the paragon of ladylike propriety. Her steady gaze and glowing natural beauty drew admiring glances from everyone in the courtroom. Calvin Patterson especially was captivated by this woman's quiet composure as she took her seat in the witness box.

"I understand, Missus Westlake, that you are well acquainted with Missus Geddis. Is that so?" Patterson began.

"Yes. I would say so. We've known each other ever since the Geddises first moved here four years ago. My boy and hers go to school together and play together often."

"Do you and Missus Geddis socialize with each other—as adult friends, I mean?"

"Oh yes. I frequently go to her house for afternoon tea and, whenever we can, we shop together in Vallejo and Martinez."

Wary now about asking this woman any leading questions like the one he had posed to Helen Moran, Patterson was apprehensive about asking his next question. "Based on your friendship, I infer you have had many opportunities to observe Missus Geddis' relationships with her children. Would you describe her as a good mother?"

"She's a wonderful mother!"

Gail's response was so warm and sincere that it made Patterson's heart flutter. He felt sure it had the same effect on every member of the jury. "Thank you, Missus Westlake." Turning to the Judge, he said, "I have no further questions of this witness, your Honor."

In cross-examination, Wyman approached Gail as if he were a suitor for her hand in marriage. "I hope you'll not think it bold of me, Missus

Westlake," he began. "But I'm sure I speak for everyone here when I say that's a very becoming dress you're wearing."

"Thank you, sir," Gail replied with a modest but wary smile.

Seething with envy, Patterson immediately objected. "Your Honor, the Prosecution is openly flattering this witness!"

"I concur," the Judge snapped irritably. Then, to Wyman he said, "Counselor, please restrict yourself to matters of relevance in this case."

Wyman was not one to be easily dissuaded from his own courtroom strategies, however. Bowing slightly to the Judge, he replied, "Thank you, your Honor. I shall do so." Then, turning to Gail with a sardonic smile, he said, "Since you and Missus Geddis are such close friends, I presume you're aware that Missus Geddis is a smoker."

"Yes," Gail said, unperturbed. "But I see nothing wrong with that. An increasing number of women smoke nowadays. It's becoming quite fashionable in some circles."

"In large cities like Chicago and New York perhaps, but not in Benicia or here in Fairfield, I'm sure you'll agree." Wyman had directed this last comment at the members of the jury, several of whom now registered facial expressions of righteous disapproval.

"I'm not so sure about that," Gail replied coolly. "Since the Great War, manners have greatly changed in our society. I expect they will continue to do so. After all, we women now have the right to vote." Then, parrying cleverly but not at all coquettishly with Wyman, she added. "I'm sure you'll agree, sir, that *that* is a good thing."

Wyman nodded but only to indicate he had heard what she said. He was keenly aware of what most of the men on the jury panel thought of universal women's suffrage. Quickly, he moved to his next pointed question. "And are you aware, Missus Westlake, that Missus Geddis consumes alcohol?" Once more, Wyman directed a meaningful glance at the jury.

Still Gail was unruffled. "I'm aware she enjoys an occasional glass of wine in the privacy of her own home. But, again Mister Wyman, I see nothing particularly wrong about that. Florin is a sophisticated woman. She has often traveled abroad with her husband and has very cultivated tastes."

"Indeed!" Wyman remarked with conspicuous sarcasm. "Am I to

understand, therefore, that you yourself approve of alcohol consumption even though it is now prohibited by both federal and state law?"

Realizing she had been cornered, Gail paused briefly before responding. "I do not approve of anyone's breaking the law, if that's what you mean. But I understand many people do bend that particular law in their own homes nowadays. I'm sure Florin does not do so in public."

Wyman looked up at the Judge, expecting him to intervene as he had with Helen Moran. Lanham, however, remained silent. He admired Gail's pluck and, though he would never publicly admit it, he agreed with her implied argument that the Volstead Act was bad law.

"How can you be so sure, Madame?" Wyman asked, now becoming openly hostile. "Do you yourself *bend* that particular law, as you put it?"

Patterson was on his feet. "I strongly object to this line of questioning, your Honor!" he declared. "Missus Westlake is not on trial here. Counselor Wyman is simply sparring with this witness."

Lanham promptly agreed. "Counselor, I must ask you to get to the point. What is it you want from this witness?"

Raising his hands in feigned surprise, Wyman explained. "I'm simply trying to show, your Honor, that Missus Westlake here is fully aware of her friend's eccentricities and that these eccentricities are clear indications of Missus Geddis' thorough contempt for the norms of decent behavior in our society." Glancing toward the jury, he added: "It is therefore evident, to me at least, that Missus Geddis is quite capable of perpetrating a despicable act such as the murder of her own children."

Everyone in the courtroom was stunned by this open assault. Wyman paused for several seconds after he had made his statement. Then, stepping back from the witness box, he said, "I am finished with this witness, Your Honor."

Aware that there was little he could do to counter Wyman's attack and that any additional good things Gail might say about her friend would fall on deaf ears, Patterson moved on to his next witness—the Geddises' next-door neighbor, Eli Strohmann.

A short, stocky man in his late forties, Strohmann had first come to Benicia with his family from Buffalo, New York in 1912. He had moved to California chiefly because his wife's poor health had been aggravated by the cold winters of upper New York State and because farmland in Benicia, at the time, was relatively cheap.

Though formerly a dairy farmer, he had decided to raise chickens because the care and maintenance of such livestock was far less costly than raising cows. In addition, as a food commodity in California, poultry offered a much better margin of profit than dairy products, which had to be processed and distributed through commercial vendors.

Eli Strohmann was, first and foremost, a practical businessman. Aloof and taciturn, he believed in hard work and had no interest in the community life of Benicia. Nor did he encourage his wife Esther or his eight-year-old daughter Rachel to mix and mingle. Their only outings were occasional shopping trips to Vallejo and their weekly attendance at the Jewish Orthodox Temple in that city.

Strohmann's testimony added little to the arguments of either side in the case. Though he corroborated Sam's account of the fire and rescue, his answers to both counselors' questions were curt and specific. The only new information he provided to the jurors was that, prior to the fire, the Strohmanns had had no social contact with anyone in the Geddis household.

Patterson's final witness was Dr. Scott Merriweather, a physician at the Solano County Hospital where Florin Geddis had been sequestered in the Court's custody since the night of the fire. Still in his late twenties, Merriweather was a recent graduate of Stanford University medical school where he had specialized in the relatively new science of psychiatry. It was because of this background that he had been asked to examine Florin Geddis in order to determine whether she would be able to appear as a witness in her own defense. Merriweather had recommended against it.

"Doctor Merriweather," Patterson began, "would you please tell the Court why you have recommended that the defendant, Florin Geddis, not be allowed to testify?"

"As I stated in my deposition," Merriweather explained confidently, "during the past six weeks, I have conducted numerous physical examinations and administered a number of psychological tests of the defendant. I have also closely monitored her behavior and met with her in private counseling sessions. My physical examinations indicate that Missus Geddis is in good health. The results of the psychological tests, however, indicate a neurosis that may have its roots in hysteria. Moreover, in private counseling sessions, she has been consistently unresponsive. It is for these reasons that I have concluded Missus Geddis may not be prepared to testify in her own behalf."

"Thank you, Doctor Merriweather," Patterson said. "Your witness, Counselor."

Wyman now took a position midway between the witness stand and the jury box. He was determined to choreograph his final assault so that it had maximum effect on the jury.

"Doctor Merriweather," he began, "you have stated that you have found Missus Geddis unresponsive in her private counseling sessions with you. Would you please explain to the jury, sir, precisely what that means?"

"As I trust you are aware, Counselor, the content of a physician's private consultation with a patient is strictly confidential. I am not at liberty, therefore, to divulge any of Missus Geddis' specific responses."

Wyman pursed his lips in mocking skepticism. "Is that so? Well then, perhaps you will allow me to pose to you a few clinical questions about Missus Geddis' condition. You may, of course, answer them or not—however you see fit."

"Fire away!" Merriweather said with a degree of youthful informality and impudence that startled all of his listeners.

Wyman stepped back, closer to the jury box, still keeping his eyes fixed on the young doctor. "In your professional opinion, sir, would you say that Missus Geddis is a psychopath?"

"That's an interesting but relatively new term, sir," Merriweather replied with a sardonic smile. "Very little clinical research has been done on psychopathic behavior, and the results of the few studies that have been done are inconclusive."

"What about this, then?" Wyman asked, moving closer now to the witness box. "Would you say that Missus Geddis exhibits homicidal tendencies?"

"There is nothing in her behavior to support such a diagnosis, sir." Merriweather was clearly beginning to lose patience, which was precisely what Wyman wanted. Pausing momentarily to recover his composure, Merriweather explained, "To make an accurate diagnosis, I would have to observe Missus Geddis over a much longer period of time than I have been able to so far. I would also need to consult with other experts before reaching any firm conclusion."

Wyman raised the index finger of his right hand. "Aha! I detect a slight hint of uncertainty in your response, Doctor. Is it possible then that you believe Missus Geddis could be homicidal?"

"Anything is possible, Counselor. In this case, however, it is highly improbable."

These were precisely the words Patterson had been waiting to hear. Rising from his chair, he addressed the bench. "Your Honor, I would remind the Counselor that it is only guilt beyond a reasonable doubt, not mere possibility, with which we are concerned in this case. Doctor Merriweather's response should put an end to this fishing expedition."

"I agree," Lanham said. "Counselor Wyman, unless you have more substantive questions to ask of this witness, I suggest you release him."

Smiling benignly at the Judge, Wyman said, "I have no further questions, your Honor."

By the time Merriweather was dismissed, it was 3:30 in the afternoon. Lanham therefore called a recess until the following morning when the prosecution and defense counselors would be asked to give their summations and the jury to begin its deliberations as to a final judgment.

CHAPTER SEVEN

————

"When My Baby Smiles at Me"

"HEY, BOY—YOU DO A PRETTY good job!" Bob Jenson said as he looked down for the first time at his newly polished shoes. Jenson had been lounging back in one of the two leather-cushioned chairs in Hewitt's Barber Shop while Huey, the owner, lathered him up for a shave. Jack, having completed his shoeshine duty, was now deeply engrossed in an article about circus clowns in *The Saturday Evening Post*.

"Yeah," Huey said. "He's gettin' pretty good at it. Been with me now almost a year. Ever since Tucker brought him over to work for me las' August. Makin' good money too, ain't y', boy?" Huey added, directing his question at Jack.

Jack looked up briefly from his magazine to give Huey an ambiguous smile. He was not entirely happy with the payroll arrangements Tucker had made for him with Huey, who took five cents from every dime charged for Jack's shoeshine service. Having inherited from his mother and his grandfather a natural affinity for numbers, Jack knew he was being cheated.

Even so, by coming to work at Hewitt's Barber Shop every Friday afternoon and all day most Saturdays, Jack had accumulated a sizeable cash nest egg for himself, which his mother had encouraged him to put in a savings account at the Bank of Italy. From his earnings, she allowed him to keep a weekly allowance of fifty cents. In 1920, this was a princely sum for any ten-year-old boy.

Jenson suddenly interrupted Huey's ministrations to say he needed to use the bathroom. He was gone several minutes. By the time Jenson climbed back into the barber's chair, Huey was visibly annoyed. "I gotta lather y' up again," he declared.

"Yeah, sure you do," Jensen sneered. As the head dyer at McClaren's Tannery, Jenson was notorious for his bravado. "Say, Huey," he asked to recover control of the barbershop dialogue, "wha'd y' think o' the verdict in the Geddis trial las' week?"

"Wasn't no verdict," Huey replied, sharpening his straightedge razor on the leather strap at the back of his barber's chair. "It was a hung jury. Don't seem right t' me. From what I read in the *Times-Herald*, it shoulda been an open an' shut case against that Geddis woman."

"So what 're they gonna do to her?" Jenson asked.

"Judge sent her to some looney house up in Napa. Who knows what they do in them places?" Huey was now scraping the three-day-old growth off of Jenson's face. "Far as I'm concerned," Huey added, "they oughta lock her up an' throw away the key."

"Mmm," Jenson grunted, careful not to move the muscles in his face and risk being nicked by Huey's fast-moving razor.

The shop was silent for several minutes while Huey worked. Outside on First Street, though, there was plenty of noise from the heavy Saturday afternoon traffic. Occasionally, the face of a male passerby would peer through the front window of Huey's shop to see how busy he was.

When at last Huey was finished and began slapping his customer's face with witch hazel, Jenson said, "Wonder what's gonna happen t' them two boys o' hers."

"You mean the Geddis kids?" Huey asked. "I hear they're gonna live with relatives down in Oakland. Can't say as I'd want t' take 'em in. That kid Sam's pretty wild, from what I hear."

At this, Jack looked up from his magazine. He knew his boss was a relentless gossip and liked nothing better than to share any bad news he could garner with every one of his customers. This rumor about his friend Sam, however, he had not yet heard.

"What d' y' mean?" Jenson asked.

"Well, y' remember on Mischief Night las' year when them kids dumped the whorehouse privies into the river an' old man Cooney got caught in one of 'em an' almos' drowned?"

Jenson sat upright in the chair. "No kiddin'! He did?"

"Sure 'nough!" Huey affirmed. "If Terry Duckworth hadn' o' heard him holerin' and swum out an' rescued 'im, sure as shootin' he'd be up in the city graveyard right now."

"Well, I'll be! How come I never heard 'bout that?"

"Don' know, Bob. But one thing I do know—Sam Geddis was one o' the kids they caught dumpin' them privies. Him an' the Holcomb boy an' a couple of others." As he said this, Huey cast a jaundiced eye in Jack's direction. Jack quickly refocused on his magazine.

The bell attached to the entrance door jangled, announcing the arrival of a new customer. "How y' doin', Huey?" asked the redheaded man who entered.

"Not bad, Wally. How's yourself?"

"Got a hot date t'night," announced the newcomer with a self-congratulatory grin as he sat down to wait in the chair next to Jack's.

Looking up from his magazine, Jack instantly recognized the Henshak's red-headed groundskeeper, "'Lo, Mister Sykes."

Sykes threw an arm around Jack's shoulder. "Hey, little buddy! How are y'?"

Put off by Sykes' familiarity, Jack cringed.

"Who's y'r date?" Huey asked, eager for new gossip. "Got one o' them *putahs* from the Lido?" he taunted.

Always resilient, Sykes grinned. "No siree! Got me a date with a real lady. Sara Wilkes at the Express Office. Gonnah take 'er to the big barn dance over at Bert Holcomb's place tonight. Sara says she's crazy 'bout square dancin', so that's how I roped her in."

"Won't be much fun, now Pro'bition's started," Huey observed, determined to needle Sykes. "Y'r gonna have t' be satisfied with lemonade."

"Yeah. Lemonade spiked with some o' Holcomb's home-made schnapps!" Sykes fired back. "Pshaw! That new law don't mean nothin' in this town. You seen any slow-down in business at Campy's 'r The Pastime yet?"

"Mayor says he's gonnah shut them joints down," Jenson commented.

Sykes chuckled. "I'll bet ten-to-one the Mayor's gonna be over at Holcomb's suckin' up that spiked lemonade hisself t'night!"

"Not if them Temp'rance women's there," Huey rejoined.

"You mean like that Callahan woman?" Sykes asked, still chuckling over his own worldly sagacity. "Hell! They run that witch out o' town months ago. Wasn't you there when Parker's girls give her the finger at the big parade las' August?"

"I ain't talkin' about that," Huey persisted. "I'm talkin' about our own lady folk here in town. 'Specially the ones over at Saint Paul's."

Sykes waved his hand contemptuously at Huey and gently poked Jack in the shoulder. "Come on, boy. How about shinin' up these dancin' shoes?"

Reluctantly, Jack obliged by putting down his magazine and sliding his shoeshine kit in front of Sykes. As he did so, the entrance doorbell rang again, and two railroad workers came into the shop—switch-engine operator Kevin Lockyer and oiler Joe Patmos. Both men were still dressed in their work clothes and Patmos' hands were black from the grease and suit he'd picked up from his morning labors. Holding his palms up now, he asked, "I gotta wash up. Can I use y'r bathroom?"

"Sure. But don't f'rget t' clean up the sink when y'r done," Huey cautioned.

"We had a near disaster this mornin'," Lockyer reported as he sat down with an exhausted sigh in the chair next to Sykes.

"That so?" Huey asked, all ears. "What happened?"

"Harry Bettencourt and me pulled a bunch o' box cars on the *Solano* and was waitin' in our goat when all of a sudden we felt ourselves gettin' pushed from behin'. We tried to throw the brakes on, but it didn't do no good 'cause the yard boss ordered the other goat t' help us out. Well, he helped us out alright—our goat an' six box cars right off the deck an' into the river."

"Holy smokes!" Sykes declared.

"Anybody hurt?" Huey asked.

"No. Lucky for us, me an' Harry jumped out before our goat went over the side. But I don't min' tellin' y' we was pretty scared."

"So what happened to y'r engine and the cars?" Jenson asked.

"That goat sank right to the bottom with the cars hangin' off the deck. They had to bring the barge crane over from the shipyard. They're tryin' t' pull the engine an' cars back up right now."

"I seen the whole thing," Joe Patmos announced proudly as he returned from Huey's bathroom. "I was standin' right next to Boss

Chilton when he called up the other goat. He was over t' Campy's for his usual mornin' pick-me-up so he didn' even know they was another goat pullin' from up front. Damn fool!"

"Guess Chilton ain't gonna be Yard Boss no more," Jenson chuckled. "They'll fire his ass for sure."

"They better!" Lockyer said ominously.

"Okay, Bob—you're all done," Huey announced as he removed the cover sheet from Jenson and shook it out for his next customer.

Jenson promptly stood up and paid Huey.

"Don't drink too much lemonade tonight, Wally," Jensen quipped as he headed out the door.

Huey looked disparagingly at the two quarters in his hand. "What a cheapskate! Didn't even pay for his shoeshine!" He promptly dropped the two coins into his cash register and started to work on Sykes.

Seeing this, Jack decided it was time to start asking his own customers to pay him in advance.

*   *   *

Monday in Mrs. Thorndike's class was always recitation day. Every one of the three grade levels she taught had to memorize and recite some passage from their classroom reading text. Children in grade three were usually assigned a nursery rhyme or the abbreviated version of one of Grimm's Fairy Tales, while children in the fourth grade (Jack's class) were assigned more challenging passages such as a few quatrains from Kipling's "Gunga Din." Only the fifth graders were allowed to choose their own passages. Mrs. Thorndike made sure these choices would be even more challenging by prescribing a list of longer poetry and prose passages, such as all of Lincoln's "Gettysburg Address."

Jack hated Mondays. It was not so much having to stand up in the front of the class and recite that bothered him as it was the time it took over the weekend to memorize his assigned passage. He did everything he could to put this off until the last minute—usually after supper on Sunday when he knew his mother preferred to sit quietly and read the *Examiner* rather than goad him to practice his recitation.

As Jack walked down East J Street toward school on this sunny April morning, he noticed the peach trees along his route were filled with bright pink blossoms and chirruping sparrows—signs of spring that sharply contrasted with the lines he had been assigned from Poe's morbid poem *The Raven*. When he reached the bottom of the hill, Jack heard running footsteps behind him.

"Wait up, Jack!" It was his friend Greg Henshak. "You ready for recitation?" Greg asked breathlessly when he caught up with Jack.

"I don't know. I hope so. That Poe poem is really hard. You ready?"

"Oh yeah!" Greg boasted. "I really like the poem I got." Immediately, Greg started reciting his poem:

> *Tiger, tiger, burning bright*
> *In the forests of the night.*
> *What immortal hand or eye*
> *Could frame thy fearful symmetry?*

"What's it mean?" Jack asked, baffled by the strange imagery.

Greg shrugged. "I don't know. Something about a tiger in a forest fire, I guess."

"Is that all you had to memorize—just those few lines?"

"No. There's five more verses. But they're all short like the first one and the last verse is the same as the first. You wanna hear the rest of it?"

"No," Jack said. "It's hard enough trying to remember my own poem without mixing it up with yours."

"Is your poem longer?" Greg asked, feeling sorry for his friend.

"A lot longer and a lot harder!"

Greg threw his arm around Jack's shoulders. "Don't worry, Jack. You can do it. You're really smart!"

"It doesn't have anything to do with being smart," Jack grumbled. "It's just stupid memory work."

"But Missus Thorndike says memorization is very important because it helps you think."

"That's baloney!"

They were approaching the school entrance now where scores of children were crowding into the front hallway and depositing their lunch pails in the wooden cloakroom lockers. Jack did not have a lunch pail but carried the jelly sandwich and apple his mother had prepared for him in a paper bag. He would stuff his bag into his classroom desk..

Emma Thorndike, a stout matronly woman in her early fifties, stood in the classroom doorway marking her attendance book as her pupils filed inside and drifted toward their desks. Emma had taught at the Benicia Primary School ever since she graduated from St. Catherine's Seminary in 1888. Even-tempered and soft-spoken, she was well liked by most of her pupils, though some of them made fun of her behind her back.

Fourth-grader Priscilla McClaren was the classroom monitor this week. At precisely 9:00 A.M., she walked to the front of the classroom and rang the brass bell Mrs. Thorndike kept on her desk. Instantly, all of her pupils stood up at their assigned desks. Even the most rambunctious knew the ringing of Mrs. Thorndike's brass bell was a serious summons to order. Anyone who failed to heed it would face an hour of after-school detention.

Silence prevailed as Mrs. Thorndike mounted the dias at the front of the classroom and solemnly nodded to Priscilla, who promptly covered her heart with her right hand and led the class in reciting The Pledge of Allegiance.

Next, Mrs. Thorndike gestured for the children to sit down and listen while one of her fifth grade pupils read a passage from the Bible. This morning's reader was Rosemary Clinger, a pig-tailed and freckle-faced ten-year-old whom Jack considered an insufferable teacher's pet. Like many of the other boys in the classroom, Jack paid little attention to the Bible reading, for he was focusing on a last-minute review of the verses he was supposed to recite.

The morning rituals concluded, Mrs. Thorndike immediately began calling on individual third-graders to recite their memory passages while standing at their desks. After each pupil recited, Mrs. Thorndike made a mark in her grade book and, without comment, called on the next pupil. These recitations went quickly because the third graders rarely had difficulty with their short and simple memory passages.

Mrs. Thorndike always called on her students in alphabetical order, so Jack was the last in his class to be summoned to the dias. As he stood beside Mrs. Thorndike's desk and looked around the room, he noted that several other boys were making faces at him. Jack tried to ignore them and concentrate on the first words of his assigned stanzas: "Prophet!" Jack sputtered. "Thing of evil …"

Jack's mind went blank. He couldn't remember the next line. Frantic, he looked toward Mrs. Thorndike. But her face was expressionless. The silence in the classroom was deafening. At last more words came back to him. "Tell this soul with sorrow laden, if, within the distant …" Again, Jack drew a blank and again he looked at his teacher.

"Aidenn," she murmured with a slight but compassionate smile.

This was all Jack needed. Suddenly his memory cleared and he began to recite—without much expression but, for the most part, fluently and easily. As he spoke the last lines, he felt a tremendous sense of relief: "And my soul that lies floating on the floor shall be lifted nevermore."

Swallowing hard, Jack stood in exhausted silence. Mrs. Thorndike gave him a little nod and made a mark in her grade book. As he returned to his desk, though, Jack heard someone at the back of the room call out, "Hooray, shoeshine boy!"

Mrs. Thorndike was quick to reprove this miscreant. "Antonio Marino," she scolded, "I will see you during recess!"

Jack stuck his tongue out at the scrawny third-grader who had mocked him. Tony responded by biting the tip of his thumb at Jack. Jack wasn't sure what biting your thumb meant, but he suspected it was much worse than sticking out your tongue. He decided to ignore it.

This was not the first time Jack had had a falling out with the Marino brothers. A year before, Tony had suddenly walked up to Jack in the school playground and punched him in the jaw. The blow had taken Jack completely by surprise. He had no idea why Tony had punched him. Because Tony was much smaller than he, Jack simply warned him not to do it again. But as Jack walked through the cloakroom at the end of recess, he was suddenly grabbed from behind, lifted off his feet and stuffed into a trashcan. "That'll teach you to pick on my little brother!" eighth grader Mario Marino snarled and then stood back to laugh at Jack's humiliation.

When after school Jack told his mother about his latest confrontation with Tony, she did not sympathize. "You're not the only one who has to put up with bullies in this world, Jack. You just have to ignore it."

"What about bullies like Soames?" Jack retorted, determined to punish her for being so indifferent to his plight.

Once again, Gail had to resist the impulse to strike Jack in the face. "Just what do you mean by that remark, young man!" she demanded.

"Well, how come you let Soames bully you when you know he fools around with those women at the Lido?"

For almost a year, Jack had kept what he knew about Soames' flirtation with the girl at the Lido to himself. The expression of pain and distress in his mother's face now made him regret what he had said.

Gail turned her back to him. "That's not true. You have no business saying such nasty things." But she spoke without conviction and her shoulders started to shake.

Jack reached out and touched his mother's arm. "Momma! I'm sorry! You're right. I shouldn't have said that. But it's true. Soames is a bad man."

Gail spun around, her tear-streaked face flush with fury. This time, she did not resist the impulse to strike her son. With the full force of her rage, she slapped him in the face. Jack stumbled under the blow, falling against the kitchen counter. "Get out of here!" his mother screamed. "Get out of here right now!"

Terrified, Jack ran out of their apartment and down the stairs into the street. Stopping at the foot of the stairs, he looked back to see if his mother had followed him. She had not. Suddenly, Jack realized he had crossed a forbidden boundary in his relationship with his mother. There was no going back. Who would take him in after the terrible thing he had done? He burst into tears.

*   *   *

"What'sa matter, honey?" said an unfamiliar female voice. "You lost or somethin'?"

Terribly embarrassed, Jack quickly tried to dry his eyes with clenched fists. Through his tears, he saw the pale face of a young woman with brilliant red hair close to his own. Her hand rested lightly on his shoulder.

"N ... nothing," Jack blubbered forlornly. "I ... I'm OK."

"Don't look it to me, honey," the girl said softly. "Whyn't you come with me an' I'll buy you a hot choc'late or somethin', OK?"

His vision clearer now, Jack recognized the face of this sympathetic stranger. It was one of the young women who had so often waved to him from the second-story bay windows of the Lido. He was speechless with shame. Of all the people in Benicia, this was the last person he would have expected—or wanted—to offer him sympathy. Yet, at the same time, he felt a sudden flood of relief, even joy. The words erupted from his lips: "Gee! You're awful pretty!"

"So are you, honey," the girl murmured affectionately as she pressed her brightly rouged lips against his cheek and then, stepping back, said, "Who could resist those long eyelashes of yours!"

It was the first time anyone had said anything like that to Jack. What did it mean? Was it some attribute women found attractive? He did not know. He did not care. What mattered most just then was that someone else cared.

"Come on," she insisted, grasping his arm firmly and propelling him up First Street. "Let's go get us some hot choc'late."

Overwhelmed with a tumultuous sense of gratitude toward this beautiful stranger, Jack allowed himself to be guided along the boardwalk. "Thank you," he muttered.

Jack was glad that the young woman seemed content simply to walk beside him in silence, though she continued to hold onto his arm. Looking at her more closely now, he realized she wasn't much taller than he. Despite the rouge on her lips, she had the slender figure and wholesome freshness of a girl his own age. "What's your name?" he asked.

"Becky Parsons," she smiled. "What's yours?"

"Jack Westlake. I've seen you before." He was reluctant to say where. He did not want to offend Becky, no matter what her reputation might be.

"I know. I've seen you too, honey." She winked at him. "Don't worry. I won't bite you. I just want to be friends, OK?"

"OK," Jack echoed. He was feeling calmer now. Becky seemed to him much more like a big sister than a 'scarlet' woman. "How old are you?" he asked.

"Fifteen," she said. "I've only been doing this for a year. And it's not as if I want to or anything," she explained. "When you're poor and homeless like me, you don't have too many choices."

"I know what you mean," Jack said sadly, thinking that he too was now poor and homeless.

"So, do you want to tell me what's makin' you so sad?" Becky asked as they crossed First Street toward the entrance to Huey's barbershop and soda fountain.

"I had a big fight with my Mom." Jack surprised himself with his own candor. "She slapped me and told me to get out."

Becky chuckled at this. "Oh, that's all? Don't be silly, honey! Your Mom will get over it."

"I don't think so. She's really mad."

"How old are you, Jack?" Becky asked.

"I'm ten."

"And you've been living with your Mom all that time?" When Jack nodded, Becky laughed again. "Come on, honey! You think your Mom's gonna throw you out on the street after ten whole years of taking care of you? I just wish I had a mother like that," she remarked as she pushed open the door of Huey's shop.

"Hi, kids! How y' doin'?" Mary Lou Hewitt called out cheerfully as Becky and Jack sat down at the soda fountain counter. Mary Lou, Huey's wife, ran the soda fountain and pool hall that occupied most of the ground-floor space in their building. Huey's barbershop took up only a small partitioned-off area in the front of the store.

A grotesquely overweight woman, Mary Lou moved very slowly behind the counter. She was always happy and friendly, though, and especially catered to the many children and teen-agers who frequented her shop. "Well, well!" she said with a chuckle, "I see you found yourself a new girlfriend, eh Jack?"

"This is Becky Parsons," Jack announced sternly, determined not to let Mary Lou's often-tasteless sense of humor get out of hand.

"Oh, don't you fuss now! I know Becky. She's a good girl, ain't y' Becky?" Mary Lou said with a knowing wink.

"We want two hot choc'lates," Becky announced matter-of-factly.

"Alrighty, two hot choc'lates comin' right up!" Mary Lou turned to fill two cups from a steel pot she kept on a gas-fueled hot plate behind the counter. "You want marshmallows in 'em?" she asked.

"Sure," Becky said.

Out of the corner of his eye, Jack noticed two older boys playing pool at the rear of the shop—"Joey Junior" Vitalie and Calvin Watrous. He was glad to see they were too engrossed in their game to notice Becky and him. At the far end of the soda fountain counter, though, Mary

Lou's twelve-year-old daughter "Isty" Hewitt and Priscilla McClaren were giggling and whispering together, obviously gossiping about Jack and his new friend.

Becky poked Jack in the ribs with her elbow. "Forget about them!" she whispered harshly. "Drink your hot choc'late!"

Jack did as he was told, noticing that Becky had extracted a dime from her purse and placed it on the counter to pay for their beverages. Mary Lou put one fat finger on this coin and pushed it back toward Becky. "First roun's on the house, honey," Mary Lou chirped to Becky with another knowing wink. "After all, Jack works here."

"Do you really?" Becky turned to gaze at Jack, her eyes wide with admiration.

"Yeah. I work Fridays and Saturdays shining shoes." Jack noticed with relief that Mary Lou had moved farther down the counter now and was talking to her daughter and Priscilla. It looked as if Mary Lou might even be scolding them.

"Good for you! How long you been doin' that?" Becky asked.

"Almost a year now."

"Your Mom must be real proud of you."

"Not now, she ain't." Jack's lips trembled as he spoke.

Becky patted his shoulder. "Come on, honey. Cheer up. Everything's gonna be alright."

As if on cue, the bell on the entrance door suddenly jangled loudly and Constable Frank Cody entered the shop, his face red with anger. "So here you are!" he declared. Marching swiftly up to the counter, he grabbed Jack's arm and glared disdainfully at Becky. "Come along now, boy! Time for you to go home. Your Momma's been lookin' all over town for y'!"

"See?" Becky said with a big smile at Jack. "What'd I tell y'? Bye, honey."

*   *   *

Gail Westlake was waiting on the landing at the top of the stairs when Constable Cody brought Jack back to Mrs. Brown's boarding house. "Jack, where have you been?" she demanded. "I've been worried sick over you!"

"You best keep a close eye on your boy, Missus!" Cody warned sternly as he pushed Jack up the steps. "I found him up the street at Huey's with one o' them girls from the Lido."

"Oh Jack, no!" Gail exclaimed. "Why would you do such a thing?"

"We weren't doing anything wrong, Mom. Becky just bought me some hot choc'late and told me not to worry. She was very nice to me."

"I bet," Gail said, her face hardening with suspicion.

"Like I say, Missus—you best keep a close eye on your boy," Cody said again. "Next time I find him keeping such bad company, I'll have to take him down to the station."

"That won't be necessary, I assure you," Gail replied archly. Then, realizing her response was unwarranted, she added, "Thank you, Constable." Giving Jack a warm hug, she said, "Come inside, dear. I've made your favorite supper—some nice beef stew."

Perplexed by the sudden change in his mother's demeanor, even suspicious of it, Jack nonetheless followed her inside. The sweet aroma of his mother's cooking immediately softened his feelings toward her. Much to his surprise, she did not even insist he wash his hands before he sat down at the kitchen table to eat.

But, as Gail solicitously served him his bowl full of hot stew and sat down at the table with him, Jack noticed she had poured herself a full glass of sherry. Though he had long known his mother drank an occasional glass of wine when she visited with her friends, he had never seen her do so when she was alone with her son.

Jack immediately thought of what his friend Sam had told him about his mother's drinking habits as well as about the fire and trial that had resulted in her being committed to an insane asylum. Jack felt his mother's eyes on him now as he slowly ate his stew, savoring the delicious flavors of meat, vegetables and gravy but reluctant to return her gaze.

"Jack, dear," Gail said softly. "I'm so sorry! I should never have struck you the way I did. It was awful of me!"

Jack looked up at her. Gail's eyes glistened with tears. "It's OK, Mom. I shouldn't have said that bad stuff about Mister Soames. It's none of my business."

Gail bit her lip. What could she say to a ten-year-old boy? She wished her friend Snooky were there with her now. She would know what to say. Reasoning that whatever she might say would only make things worse, Gail decided to say nothing.

The two sat in silence for several minutes, the only sound that of Jack's spoon scraping the bottom of his bowl. At length, he said, "Can I have some more, Mom? The stew's really good."

"Of course, dear." Gail immediately jumped up and refilled his bowl. "Would you like some bread with it?"

"No thanks." Jack continued to focus on his food. For him, it was sufficient proof that Becky had been right. His mother still loved him.

CHAPTER EIGHT

"Ain't We Got Fun?"

BEFORE DAWN ON A CHILLY April morning, twenty-five men in full hunting regalia gathered in the large front parlor of the Commandant's house at the Benicia Arsenal. Colonel Orrin Wright Morris, the host of this gathering, had provided crystal carafes of fine brandy for all to warm themselves before heading out to Grizzly Island, several miles east of the Southern Pacific Railroad line. He had also provided three Army lorries to transport everyone to the site.

In addition to such charter club members as Colonel Morris, Judge Lanham, James Fisk, and Oscar Henshak, several guests from Concord and Martinez were also present. Among these was Chairman of the Contra Costa County Republican Party, Howard "Gunslinger" Roach. Roach had acquired his nickname by firing a six-shooter to get everyone's attention during a particularly contentious party caucus.

Though not a sportsman, Roach had eagerly solicited an invitation to this outing. For 1920 was an election year when important political issues were at stake. Roach wanted to be sure his party was well represented at any event that might attract the rich and powerful.

"Good idea, this," Roach said as he held up his glass of brandy in a toast to the Colonel. "Bitter cold out there."

"Normal for this time of year, sir," Morris replied briskly, his stern leathery features barely concealing the contempt he felt for this plump and pompous little man. "I hope you brought your long johns, Mister Roach" he added caustically.

Henshak, who was standing directly behind the Colonel and who

97

had been instrumental in securing Roach's invitation, immediately stepped forward to join the conversation. "Oh don't worry, Colonel. I gave Howie plenty of advanced warning. Only thing he needs now is a gun. I don't s'pose you'd have a spare one he could use, now would you?"

Morris, who stood head and shoulders above both of these men, smiled tolerantly. "He may have his choice of several hundred." Then, tilting his head toward the uniformed officer at his side, he said, "Captain Siefert here will see to it you have whatever you need."

Certainly," the alert young officer affirmed. Then to Roach he said, "If you'll follow me, sir, I'll take you to our armaments building."

"Thanks," Roach replied with a wince at the thought of leaving his place beside the giant hearth where a roaring fire filled the room with warmth. "I'll finish my brandy first, if ya don't mind."

"Certainly, sir. Just let me know whenever you're ready."

"That should probably be right now," the Colonel suggested. "We all need to be at our stations as soon as the decoys have been released." Setting his own unfinished brandy glass on the mantel, he added, "Excuse me, gentlemen. I have some important matters to attend to."

"Pretty cocky, ain't he?" Roach said to Henshak as soon as the Colonel was out of earshot.

"Well, he *is* a Colonel, after all," Henshak said. "What d' y' expect, Howie?"

Half an hour later, as the first faint signs of dawn were showing on the eastern horizon, most members of the hunting party had found their places behind one of the fifteen wood-frame blinds that had been erected across an open strip of solid ground at the edge of the tules. Ten more blinds stood several yards farther forward, their supporting wooden stakes stuck deep in the muddy shoal so they were completely hidden by the marsh grass.

The seasoned hunters behind these forward blinds, including Judge Lanham and Colonel Morris, waited in patient silence for almost a full hour. Before long, though, those on solid ground began mumbling discontentedly.

"How long we gotta sit here before the damn birds come?" Roach complained. "I'm freezin' my balls off!"

"Guess you didn' wear them long-johns the Colonel was talkin' about," Henshak observed unsympathetically. Reaching into a side-pocket of his jacket, Henshak extracted an ornate silver flask. Unscrewing its cap, he handed it to Roach. "Here. Take a couple o' swigs o' this. It'll warm y' up."

Eagerly, Roach grabbed the flask and put it to his lips. "Oh my Gawd!" he squawked, drawing fierce looks of disapproval from every hunter who heard him. "What the hell is this stuff?"

"Shhh!" Henshak warned, but added with a grin, "They call it Injun Juice. Special brew cooked up by some o' my friends over in Port Costa. Pure wood alcohol. Prob'ly scraped off the hold of an old coal barge."

Roach gave him a murderous look. "You son of a bitch!" he rasped. "You tryin' t' cause me an early death?"

Ignoring Roach's protest, Henshak pointed up at a wide V of mallards moving in perfect formation directly overhead, "Here they come!"

Instantly, Roach raised his borrowed shotgun to fire. Henshak grabbed its barrel, though, and firmly pushed it to the ground. "You gotta wait 'til they're on the water!" he rasped.

Slowly, the graceful V circled lower toward the open water until at last the birds slid smoothly to rest on its surface a few yards beyond the tules. Even then, Roach noted impatiently, there was silence from the hunters in the forward blinds. When would they begin firing? He decided his best strategy was to imitate whatever Henshak did. As soon as his partner raised and cited his gun, he would do the same.

"Boom! Boom! Boom!" suddenly sounded from three of the forward blinds. Immediately, these initial explosions were followed by the roar of more guns as hunters everywhere fired at will and the squawking creatures on the water either rose in frantic flight or flailed in helpless agony.

By the time Roach and Henshak managed to raise and cite their guns, the fleeing birds were out of range. Nevertheless, Roach emptied both barrels and vehemently rebuked Henshak for his poor timing. Both of them watched bitterly as other hunters released their dogs to retrieve the dead and wounded fowl.

The same scenario recurred several times that morning. Each time, the entire hunting party moved to a new set of blinds in a different location along the shoreline. Every time, Roach thought, it was the same small cadre of seasoned hunters who bagged the birds. This was a tedious and stupid sport, he concluded when the party broke up at 11:00 A.M.

Late that afternoon, Fisk, Lanham, Henshak, Roach and four other men who had been invited guests at the hunt club outing sat comfortably before an open fire in Oscar's study, sipping his Benedictine brandy and puffing on his Cuban cigars. Their conversation was not about duck hunting, though. Instead, it focused on Republican Party plans to disrupt the upcoming Democratic National Convention in San Francisco.

Because of the political turmoil in 1920, there were four separate national conventions and parties vying for control of the federal government that year. Both the Socialist Labor Party and the Socialist Party scheduled separate conventions in New York City, while the Republicans met in Chicago and the Democrats, in San Francisco. For the first time in history, a national convention was taking place on the West Coast.

Businessmen, lawyers and politicians all over California were excited by this milestone event. Especially in the greater Bay Area, political leaders saw the San Francisco Democratic Convention as a perfect test case for putting California on a par with the long dominant states of the East and Midwest. For Republican political machine bosses like Howard Roach, it was the opportunity of a lifetime.

"Any you fellahs ever read Jack London's *John Barleycorn*?" Roach suddenly asked in the middle of a heated discussion about how the California Republican Party should best combat the press coverage of the San Francisco Convention.

"Never read it and never will!" snarled Bert McCutcheon, a Scottish land speculator who owned several hundred acres of prime real estate in northern Contra Costa County. "The man was a communist!"

"My wife read it," James Fisk snarled disparagingly. "She says he was just a damn drunk! Who cares what a bum like that wrote in his books?"

Roach smiled slyly at this last remark. "You might be surprised, Jimmy. Don't get me wrong. I ain't sayin' I agree with 'im. I'm sayin' we can make good use of what he says in that book."

"What d' y' mean, Howie?" asked Tom Horvath, President of

the Contra Costa Growers Association—an advocacy organization representing the large agribusinesses operating in the East Bay and Central Valley.

"There's a part of his book where London tells about this time when a bunch of politicians rounded up the drunks in Benicia and got 'em t' brake up a political rally. London said they put 'em all on a train, shipped 'em down to Hayward, got 'em all crazy on hooch, an' turned 'em loose on the town. Now I'd say that's a pretty smart idea."

"Smart for who about what?" Henshak asked, fully aware of what his friend had in mind.

Roach leaned back in his wingback chair and took several long puffs on his cigar. Then, squinting at the others through a thick cloud of smoke, he said slowly. "I look at it this way, gents. We gotta do whatever we can t' make them Democrats look like a bunch o' damn radicals. You know all the papers is goin' t' be converin' the Frisco ballyhoo. 'Specially that feller Hearst. I say we ship a couple o' ferry loads o' drunks from Benicia over there t' parade aroun' town with commie signs, bust into stores an' get int' fights. It'll turn that Convention into an all-out riot."

Fisk nodded. "Sounds like a pretty interestin' idea, Howie."

"Nonsense!" Judge Lanham declared with uncharacteristic candor. "I could never be a party to such an unconscionable scheme!"

The other men stared at the Judge in disbelief. There was a long pause in which everyone was silent until, at last, Oscar Henshak said, "Now Clyde, don't jump to conclusions. Nobody's said we're really gonnah do anythin' like that. It's just sort of an idea Howie's tossed out for us t' think about."

"It's a preposterous idea!" the judge insisted even more adamantly.

Roach again sucked hungrily on his cigar, exhaling a stream of smoke toward Lanham. "You need to remember, Judge. You're an elected official too—indirectly, anyhow. Maybe you've had your nose in your law books too long."

"I will not be intimidated, sir!" Lanham retorted, his eyes flashing defiance.

"We'll see," Roach said. "There's more than one way t' skin a cat, mister."

"And, like my dear old Momma used to say," Horvath added with a sneer, "all cats are gray in the dark."

Everyone laughed except Clyde Lanham. His glum silence was an ominous portent that no one seemed to notice.

* * *

"Pew! This town stinks!" Bernadette Roach declared as her traveling companion helped her down the steps of the Pullman car.

"It's the tanneries," Guido Pirelli explained, pointing up First Street toward a matching pair of five-story brick buildings with their top floors connected by an enclosed wooden walkway over the street. Thick yellow smoke was pouring out of several chimneys on the roof of each building. "They got a saying here," he added with a chuckle. "'When the West wind blows, hold y'r nose.'"

"I'll say! Noisy and dusty too! How's anybody survive in this burg?"

"Couldn't tell y', Bernie. Guess the locals just get used to it." Guido reached up to take Bernie's two suitcases as the porter handed them down from the Pullman car. Over six feet tall, Guido had the bulk and muscle of a barroom bouncer.

Despite her own much smaller stature, Bernie was very much an independent woman. As the daughter of Howard Roach, she had no illusions about the sinister underside of so-called gentlemanly behavior. "Never mind, Guido," she snarled. "I'll carry this. Just get us out o' this stink!"

"Have it y'r way," Guido shrugged as he hefted his own suitcase. "It's a three block walk to the hotel, though."

"Lead on!" Bernie growled.

As they walked up First Street toward the Union Hotel, Bernie took note of the several old scows tied up to the piers between West A and B streets. On the deck of one of these vessels, a shabbily dressed woman was hanging her wash on a clothesline rigged between the roof of the scow's cabin and one of the pilings. "You mean people actually live on them filthy old barges?" she asked.

"Sure. Greeks, mostly," Guido replied without slowing his pace. "They fish the Strait at night an' sleep all day. Most of 'em's drunks like ol' Jack London. He kep' a barge here once, y' know."

"Yeah, sure. Ever'body knows that!" Bernie puffed breathlessly. She was having difficulty keeping up with Guido's long and rapid strides. She was not about to let an ignoramus like Guido think he knew more about Benicia's history and culture than she did.

"Wait 'til you see some o' the houses." Guido continued with his tour guide lecture, alluding to the several wood frame cottages they were approaching on their left. By *houses* he meant bordellos; for they were now in the heart of Benicia's infamous "red-light" district.

Bernie grimaced. "Yeah. I know all about 'em. 'Heaven or Hell,' they call this part o' town—right?"

"All depends on how y' look at it," Guido chuckled again. "The sailors and soldiers think it's Heaven. The townsfolk think it's Hell."

"Men got no brains!"

Once inside the Union Hotel, the two travelers breathed a sigh of relief. Gone were the rancid smells of the tanneries, the clanging racket of locomotives at the depot, and the incessant rattle of horse-drawn carts and automobiles on First Street.

Edward Fuller, proprietor of the Union Hotel, had taken every precaution to ensure the comfort of his guests by installing double doors in both street entrances, keeping all ground-floor windows firmly shut, and strategically placing sachet-filled urns throughout the hotel lobby. For this last and most important touch of hospitality, Edward was indebted to his wife of twenty years—Rebecca Lynch Fuller, daughter of Rear Admiral Robert Perry Lynch, one-time Commodore of the Mare Island Naval Shipyard in Vallejo.

"Welcome, folks. How c'n I help y'?" Fuller asked as Bernie leaned with both elbows on the registration desk and glared at this meek and soft-spoken old gentleman.

"Name's Roach," Bernie said abruptly. "We booked two rooms tonight—me an' Pirelli here."

"Oh yes, Missus Roach," Fuller replied cheerfully. "Your rooms are ready for you. All you need to do is sign the register here." With utmost deference, Fuller pushed a large open ledger toward Bernie and, extracting a freshly cut goose quill from a marble inkwell, proffered it to this woman he mistakenly perceived to be a lady.

"It's Miss, not Missus!" Bernie barked as she seized the quill and quickly scribbled her own name and Pirelli's several spaces below the last guest name that had been entered. Then, pushing the ledger away, she asked, "Where's the bar?"

At this, Fuller's bland features hardened into righteous disdain. "I'm afraid we don't serve alcoholic beverages, Miss. Prohibition, you know."

"Don't gimme that line!" Bernie snarled. Then, suddenly realizing her belligerence might be counter-productive, she reached into her purse and extracted a five dollar gold piece. Carefully placing this coin on the registration desk, she winked at Fuller. "That's awright. Mayor Cody's a good friend o' mine. He won't give you no trouble."

Feigning offense at Bernie's conspicuous bribe, Fuller scowled. "You're friends with His Honor?" Then, blinking several times but unable to prompt any reply to his question, Fuller rang a bell on the registration desk. "I'll have the boy show you to your rooms."

"Sure," Bernie said. "You do that. Then, we'll come down and have us a couple o' Mickey Finns." Again, she winked at Fuller.

Ignoring this, Fuller summoned the bellhop, a pimply-faced boy in a white dust jacket. Handing the boy two sets of keys, Fuller said, "Charlie, show our guests to rooms three and four."

When Charlie dutifully attempted to pick up Bernie and Guido's suitcases, Bernie intervened. "That's OK, kid. We'll handle the bags." This time, she allowed Guido to carry all of their suitcases.

Minutes later, Guido and Bernie were seated at the bar in the Union Hotel saloon, both contentedly smoking cheroot cigars and sipping shot glasses of Canadian whisky. Apart from Bernie, Guido and the bartender—the Fullers' eighteen-year-old son Martin—the saloon was empty. Since it was only 4:15 on a Tuesday afternoon, most of the usual drinking clientele were still elsewhere engaged.

"So what time he s'posed t' get here?" Guido asked.

"He told me 5:30. I wouldn't count on it, though. That guy's always late to meetings," Bernie was talking to herself more than to Guido. She didn't really care what Guido thought. He was nothing but a hired henchman her father assigned as her bodyguard whenever she was on potentially hazardous missions like this—her first meeting with the notorious bootlegger, James Soames.

Angrily, she glared at her own image reflected in the big mirror behind the bar. She did not like that image—the flat full moon face with close-set eyes and pug nose, all of which she had inherited from her father.

It was no surprise to Bernie that enemies often referred to her as 'the pig woman.' She didn't care what such fools thought, she told herself. She was smarter and tougher than they were. In this world, that's what counts most.

In spite her bitter bravado, Bernie couldn't help entertained romantic fantasies about the handsome young bartender who was now self-consciously busying himself with washing already clean glasses.

Guido, impatient with the prospect of having to wait in an empty saloon for an hour, gulped down the last of his whisky and stood up. "I'm goin' up the street t' see if I c'n fin' me a card game 'r somethin'."

"Go ahead," Bernie said without expression. She didn't really care what the big oaf did. She only tolerated his company because her father insisted on it. Besides, now she would have the bartender all to herself. As Guido exited the saloon, she called out sarcastically, "Hey, kid—how 'bout some more o' that sars'parilla?"

"Yes, Ma'm." Martin promptly tipped the bottle he had left standing on the bar top to refill her whisky glass. "You in town on business, Ma'm?" Martin asked, remembering his mother's instruction to "always be real nice to hotel guests."

Bernie made her best effort at an amiable smile. "Yeah. We're here on business—real important business." At the very least, she wanted to impress this young Sheik with her own importance, even if he too thought she looked like a pig. "What's your name, kiddo?"

When Martin gave her his full name, she said, "So you're workin' for your pa, huh? That's nice. I work for my pa too. Family business. It's the best kind."

"Yes, Ma'm," Martin allowed bleakly.

Like many young men in Benicia, Martin yearned to get away from his hometown—to escape its industrial squalor and the ridiculous hypocrisy of its most 'respectable' citizens. When he had graduated from Benicia High School five months before, one of his favorite teachers had given him a copy of a new novel titled *Main Street*. Instantly, Martin had identified with the social satire of its author, Sinclair Lewis.

"So what d' y' do f'r kicks in this town, Marty?" Bernie asked.

Martin picked up a rag from behind the bar and began polishing its already impeccably high-sheen surface. He wanted to give himself time to think of an answer that would discourage further conversation with this obnoxious woman. "Not much. Friday nights, they have dances over at the Veteran's Hall and every Saturday there's a film at the Majestic."

Bernie shook her head. "Well, whoop-de-do! Don't sound like much fun t' me. How 'bout billiards? Ain't they even got a pool hall in this jerk-water town?"

"Yes. There's one over at Huey's Barber Shop and I think they got one at the Pastime." Martin thought of adding that he considered billiards a bore. He did not, though, because he supposed the ugly woman would only use this as excuse to prolong their conversation. He continued vigorously polishing the bar top.

Several minutes passed during which Bernie sat in silence, puffing on her cheroot and sipping her whisky. She continued to monitor every move Martin made, certain that her intense scrutiny would make him uncomfortable. At last, losing interest in this cat-and-mouse game, she broke the silence. "Where's the John?"

Martin stopped his polishing and pointed toward the entrance into the front lobby. "Down the hall. First door on the right," he said.

Bernie stubbed out her cigar in the big glass ashtray Martin had provided. Then, stepping down from her bar stool, she headed for the lobby. "Refill my glass, kid," she commanded.

When Bernie returned minutes later, she was carrying a copy of the local weekly newspaper, *The Benicia Herald New Era*. Without so much as a nod at Martin, she climbed back onto her stool, lit another cheroot, and began reading the paper.

Taking this as a signal that he was now off the hook and having refilled Bernie's glass as she had requested, Martin picked up a half-filled trash barrel behind the bar and carried it out into the lobby.

"Where y' goin'?" asked his father, who was dutifully manning his station behind the registration desk.

"Just takin' out this trash," Martin replied. "I'll be right back."

"You better be," Fuller senior warned.

"Yes, sir." Martin knew his father, a retired Army officer, never tolerated anyone's neglect of duty. Although he had hoped to role and smoke a cigarette while he was emptying the trash, he changed his mind and immediately returned to the saloon.

This turned out to be a smart decision for, as Martin returned to his post, two new customers entered the bar—a tall, dapperly dressed man with a moustache and a short stocky man wearing a garish black and yellow plaid suit and matching saddle shoes.

"How's tricks, Bernie?" the taller man said as he approached the bar.

Startled, Bernie looked up from her newspaper. But she quickly recovered her caustic mien. "Well, well! You must be Jimmy Soames! Miracles never cease! From what I hear, you're never early to a meeting."

"My mother taught me well," Soames said with an ingratiating smile. "It's not nice to keep a lady waiting."

"Yeah, sure!" Bernie retorted. "So who's the clown in the funny suit?"

"Now, now, Miss Roach!" Soames gently scolded. "Do be nice. This is Ted Peters—one of my most distinguished associates."

Bernie eyed Peters skeptically. Then, deciding she needed to be a little more politic, she reached out and manfully shook Peters' hand. "Pleased t' meet y', Ted."

"Pleasure's all mine, ma'm." Although Peters was forty-two years old, his voice was high-pitched and nasal, almost like a young girl's. In shaking hands with Bernie, though, Peters did his best to seem vigorous and virile. Soames had warned him in advance what to expect of the pig woman.

Throughout this brief exchange, Martin had been standing at attention behind the bar until Peters turned to him and said, "Gimme what she's got, kid."

"I'll take the same," echoed Soames. He winked at Bernie, confident that she demanded only the best booze for her own consumption. As soon as Martin served their drinks, Soames held up his glass to make a toast. "To Gunslinger Roach!" he proclaimed. "May he live long and prosperously."

"To Papa!" Bernie chuckled.

"To y'r ol' man!" squawked Peters, taking his vengeance.

As the three clinked their glasses and tossed off the contents in one swig, Guido entered the saloon.

"Well, well—what d' y' know? Here's Johnny Come Lately!" Bernie snarled.

Guido pulled out his pocket watch and checked it against the time shown on the big Monitor clock on the wall behind the bar. "I ain't late," he said to Bernie. Then, to Soames, he said, "Y're early."

Soames slapped Guido on the back. "Yeah. Too bad, Guido. You missed a free round." Then, tossing two silver dollars on the bar, he said to Martin, "Keep the change, kid. We got t' get goin'."

"Go get my tan suitcase and bring it out to the car," Bernie told Guido as she followed Soames and Peters into the hotel lobby.

Somewhat startled that Bernie was delegating responsibility for fetching this important piece of luggage, Guido nonetheless promptly carried out her order. He had long since learned never to second-guess Bernie's whims.

*   *   *

Peters had parked his brand new 1920 Roamer sedan directly in front of the Union Hotel. The exterior of this luxurious new five-passenger car had been custom-painted black and yellow—no doubt, Bernie surmised, to match Peters' wardrobe. As Soames climbed into the front passenger seat and Bernie and Guido into the back, Peters started his engine with such a loud roar that it forced his three passengers to cover their ears.

"Jeez, Ted!" Bernie protested. "D' y' have t' do that?"

Peters laughed haughtily as he moved his car out into the traffic on First Street, which—both ways—had been brought to a complete stand-still by the loud roar of the Roamer's engine. "It's my new G-Piel Cut-Out. Gives me extra power," Peters proudly explained. "Which way, Soames?" he asked.

"Go around the block and up First to Military. Then, make a right."

Just after Peters made the right-hand turn at Military, Soames directed him to turn left onto the State Highway toward Cordelia—one of the two paved roads out of Benicia. Within minutes, they were traveling through open countryside in the rolling hills north of town. Off to the right, they could see the blue water of Suisun Bay.

"So where y' takin' us, Jimmy?" Bernie demanded to know. "Timbuktu?"

"Not far." Soames said reassuringly, without looking around at the always impatient and querulous Bernie. "Just up the road here a bit."

Actually, they traveled almost twelve miles before Soames told Peters to make another left turn onto a narrow dirt road that wound up the side of a mountain heavily forested with Oak, Spruce and Candle Pine. When they were almost at the top of this mountain, the dirt road abruptly dead-ended in front of an old abandoned farmhouse, behind which was a large hay barn that appeared to be in much better condition than the house.

"This is it," Soames announced. Stepping out of the Roamer, Soames led the way up the front steps onto the porch of the farmhouse. Opening the front door with a key he had extracted from a hiding place under the porch steps, he went inside.

The interior of the house was dank with the smell of mold. The first room they entered had once served as a kitchen. Along one wall was a row of counters and cabinets and an old iron sink, upon which was mounted a rusted hand-pump. Several floorboards in the center of this room were splintered and broken around an opening that revealed the dark crawlspace beneath the house.

"What the hell is this?" Bernie protested as she stood on the threshold of the front door, refusing to enter.

"The perfect hide-out," Soames explained reassuringly. "Follow me."

As he spoke, Soames carefully circumvented the broken floorboards and unlocked an interior door that led to another room. This room was completely dark because its windows had been boarded up on the outside. Soames disappeared inside and, striking a match, lighted a kerosene lantern.

Cautiously, the others made their way across the kitchen floor. As they stepped into the boarded-up room, Soames lighted another kerosene lantern. The two lanterns revealed a well-furnished office space, complete with wall-to-all carpeting, several oak filing cabinets and chairs, and a large roll-top desk. Opening one of the filing cabinet drawers with another key, Soames brought out a bottle of Jack Daniels and four glasses.

"Have a seat," he said, gesturing the others into chairs. Then, filling four large glasses, he handed one to each of his guests and sat down himself. "Now let's talk business."

"Not bad!" Peters remarked, though it wasn't clear to anyone whether his remark was prompted by the elegant appointments of Soames' clandestine office or the crisp bouquet of his bourbon.

"What's in the barn?" Bernie asked, determined to dispel every mystery as soon as she could.

"Let's talk business first," Soames answered.

Soames did not like pushy, ugly women like Bernie Roach. He knew they were not the least bit vulnerable to the whiles he so successfully used with prettier women. The muscles in his handsome face tightened now and his usually soft-spoken tone grew harsh. "First, I need to know what kind of a deal we're making here."

"OK," Bernie said. "We got some friends over in Yolo County that wants t' grow their operation. They already got plenty o' stills and pretty good distribution. But they need sugar. From what I hear, that's y'r specialty, Jimmy. That so?"

Soames nodded. "One of 'em. I'm into a lot o' things," he added with an enigmatic smile. "What quantities are we talking about here and how often do you need delivery and where?"

"Woe, boy!" Bernie held up her hands in caution. "First, we need to know how many labels per hunnert." She was referring to the hundred-pound bags of refined sugar bootleggers use in the fermentation process. The labels she spoke of were the cash-equivalent medium of exchange she was bringing to the table in this transaction.

A month before, Bernie's father had negotiated a deal with none other than Al Capone himself, who had flown to San Francisco with the intention of taking over bootleg booze distribution throughout all of California. Bernie's father had managed to ward off Capone's aggressive move by negotiating an alternative agreement. In exchange for retaining control of local distribution, Roach and his business associates would purchase from Capone all the labels used on bottled spirits in California at five cents per label.

Always a practical businessman, Capone had seen the advantages of such an agreement. Instead of having to send and maintain armies of his own henchmen to enforce collections in California—an enterprise that would be both costly and difficult to manage halfway across the continent—he would simply collect a labeling fee on each bottle distributed in the state.

Soames smiled slyly. "Well now, Miss Roach, surely you realize that the price of everything in this business is determined by the size of the order. Give me a big enough order and I'll give you an attractive offer."

"There's lots of other things, Jimmy," Bernie observed matter-of-factly. "Things like shipping, delivery schedules, and security. All that figures into price."

"Agreed." Soames took a thoughtful sip of his bourbon and waited for Bernie to elaborate.

"I got the shipping part o' this deal," Peters announced. "You need to talk to me about that separate."

"That so?" Bernie reached into her purse for a cigarette to give herself time to think about this unexpected complication. Lighting up, she waved the smoke away from her face. "We're talking at least three tons a week here. Maybe more down the road."

Soames stood up and walked over to the roll-top desk. Unlocking it with yet another key he carried in his vest, he took out a leather-bound ledger, a pad of blank writing paper, and a fountain pen. Then, using the ledger as a support under his pad, he sat down again and began writing calculations.

In the meantime, as was his custom in such situations, Guido stood up and walked back out onto the front porch to smoke and keep watch for any possible intruders.

After several quick calculations on his pad, Soames tore off the top sheet and handed it to Bernie.

Bernie's eyes quickly went to the bottom line. Shaking her head, she said, "Way too much! That's five dollars worth o' labels per bag? You gotta be kiddin' me!"

In point of fact, the four-dollar cash-equivalent price she had planned to cite as her cost was twice the amount her father had negotiated with Capone.

Sipping at his glass of bourbon, Soames paused for several seconds before he spoke. "That's my offer," he said at last. "Take it or leave it."

Bernie puffed furiously on her cigarette. "Guess I'll leave it, then. You c'n take us back to the hotel now."

"Now just hold on, there, you two!" Peters protested. He figured he knew much better than Soames what was at stake. Soames was from San Francisco. It wasn't likely he knew how powerful Bernie's father was—not only in Contra Costa County politics, but statewide. "We gotta give each other the benefit of the doubt here. Lemme see them numbers," he said, reaching over and grabbing the sheet of paper from Bernie.

"Hey!" Bernie shouted angrily. "What d' y' think y'r doin'?" But she resisted the impulse to sick Guido on this small-time crook.

Peters studied Soames' calculations for a moment, while Soames watched cat-like and Bernie fumed. Looking up at last, Peters said, "How 'bout this? I charge fifty cents a bag for shipping an' you, Jimmy, charge three dollars. That saves Bernie here a dollar a bag."

Soames did not respond, his watchful gaze focused on Bernie.

Realizing her father would be very angry if she reported back to him empty-handed, Bernie decided to hedge. "I'll have to talk about it with Papa. See what he thinks. We'll let y' know sometime next week."

Apparently satisfied with this arrangement, Soames stood up and refilled each of their glasses. "I'll look forward to hearing from you," he said with unctuous courtesy. "But you better send a trusted personal courier directly to my office in Benicia. No phone calls. Too many snoopy phone operators in Benicia."

Bernie downed the contents of her glass. "Good enough," she said. "So now how about showin' us what you got in that barn out there."

Soames smiled slyly at Bernie. "Tell y' what—I'll show you if you show me first. You bring some of those labels with y'? How 'bout lettin' Peters an' me see a couple o' samples?"

"Sure. Why not?" Bernie stood up and walked to the door. "Hey, Guido!" she called to her henchman. "Bring that suitcase in here."

With Guido standing at her side, his right hand gripping the handle of the revolver in his shoulder holster, Bernie lifted the suitcase onto her lap and opened it just enough to extract a single package of labels wrapped in brown paper. Tearing open this package, she held it out so that Soames and Peters could see the official-looking seal on the top label.

"How many o' them labels you got?" Peters asked.

"Don't worry," Bernie sneered. "I got enough, an' I can get more any time I want." Quickly she placed the opened package back in her suitcase and closed it. "Now it's y'r turn, Jimmy. Show us what's in the barn out there."

Soames promptly lead the way out of the farmhouse to a large sliding door at the front of the barn. Two heavy padlocks secured iron latches on both sides of this door. Unlocking these with separate keys, Soames slid the door open.

Bernie couldn't help gasping at what she saw inside. Stacked to the ceiling on three sides of the interior were hundreds of bags of refined sugar, and parked in the large open space between these stacks were three two-ton trucks and an armored vehicle, bristling with gun ports and equipped with a machine-gun mounted turret.

"Where'd y' get the tank?" Guido asked.

"Army surplus," Soames explained coolly. "The Benicia Arsenal's full of 'em."

"You plannin' on goin' to war?" Bernie asked, doing her best to sound unruffled.

"You never know what to expect in this business," Soames remarked grimly. Then, suddenly switching to an affable tone, he said, "Now, if your curiosity's satisfied, let's go back to Benicia and have dinner. My treat."

"Sounds good to me," Bernie allowed.

1921

The Majestic Theater

CHAPTER NINE

"Bye Bye Blackbird"

STRIKER'S LANDING WAS LOCATED ON the shoreline of Benicia, midway between West Eighth and West Ninth streets. It was there on a sunny but cool Saturday morning in late March of 1921 that Del's father had directed her to report for her first sailing lesson with Bart Daugherty.

Bart was the thirty-year-old son of Lawrence and Lydia Daugherty, owners of Daugherty's Cannery in Benicia. Bart had worked in his father's plant as a boy. His daily contact with the fisherman who brought their catch for processing had early aroused Bart's interest in boats and ships. Soon after he graduated from Benicia High School in 1899, Bart quit his job at the cannery and signed on as a deckhand aboard a Vallejo-based tugboat.

This proved to be a smart career choice. During the first decade of the 20th Century, shipping traffic in the Carquinez Strait increased significantly. In a very short time, Bart managed to save enough money to buy his own steam-powered tugboat, the *Miss Trudy*, which he used to haul coal and grain barges up and down the Sacramento River. Whenever barge traffic slowed, as it had in recent weeks because of a miners' strike at the Black Diamond Coal Company near Concord, Bart used his knowledge of the winds and currents in the Carquinez Strait to give sailing lessons.

Del felt very uneasy as she walked toward the pier to meet her sailing instructor for the first time. Though her father had assured her Bart was an expert sailor and a perfect gentleman, Del was intimidated by the very idea of sailing. She had often watched the regattas that were a weekly event on the Carquinez Strait during the summer months, but she had never even set foot on the deck of a sailboat. When she saw the flimsy looking little boat Bart Dougherty was now preparing for her to use, she stopped dead in her tracks.

"That you, Miss Del?" Bart called out cheerfully. "Come on down. It's a perfect day for sailing. I'll get you up and running in no time."

"Maybe we should wait for a calmer day. It's awfully windy!" Del shouted back.

Del was still too far away from the end of the dock to see the expression on Bart's face. Clearly, though, he had heard the anxiety in her voice, for he immediately climbed out of the small sailboat and started walking toward her. "Come on, Miss Del! Wind's not bad—only eight or ten knots. You don't want your friends to think you're scared, do you?"

This was all Del needed. The thought that Jack or Greg might call her a scared-y-cat for any reason was enough to strengthen her resolve. "Well, alright," she said and trotted toward the dock.

"At-a-girl!" Bart declared as she stood beside him staring down at the small wooden craft bobbing and bumping against the pilings. "OK now. First thing we gotta do is rig *you* up for sailing." Bart reached into an open storage box on the dock and pulled out a life vest. "Here—try this on for size," he said as he helped her put her arms through the bulky canvas garment. Quickly, he realized his first choice was too large. So he helped her don a smaller life vest. Lacing her into it, he tugged at the drawstrings to make sure it fit snugly. "That OK?" he asked.

Del nodded, thankful for Bart's concern for her safety but also somewhat annoyed by his matronly attentiveness. "I *can* swim, you know," she assured him.

"Well, sure you can!" he laughed. "But that ain't the point. Even the best sailors always wears a life-jacket. Look. See? I got one on myself."

Del smiled, pleased that Bart had had the good sense to let her save face.

"OK—now you need to learn a little somethin' 'bout the parts o' this here sailboat." He looked at her hesitantly for a moment, as if he were unsure whether he had been presumptuous in assuming Del's ignorance. "You ever been on a sailboat before, Miss Del?" he asked.

Not wishing to emphasize the appalling scope of her inexperience, Del simply shook her head.

"OK. Well … there's really not much to it—just a few basic things you need to know." Sweeping his hand the full length of the twelve-foot Beetle Cat he had selected for Del's sailing lessons, Bart explained, "This is what they call the *hull*. Up there's the *bow* and back there's the *stern*. The left side of the boat's called *port*, and the right side *starboard*." Repeating himself, Bart again pointed to each part of the boat. "*Hull, bow, stern, port* and *starboard*—you got that?"

Del nodded and mouthed the new words silently to fix them in memory. She had actually heard of these words before and read about them in books. But she had never really thought of them as specific parts of a boat.

"Good. Now, let's get aboard here so I can show you some other things." Without waiting for Del to respond, Bart firmly grasped her hand and stepped down into the open deck of the catboat, which instantly began rocking with the extra weight of his body. "Woe, girl!" he jokingly chided the little boat. Then, looking up with a big smile at Del, he said, "Don't worry. Everything's gonna be OK, Miss Del. I'll keep her steady for y'. Just hang onto my arm here an' step down."

Hesitantly, Dell moved toward the edge of the dock. Then, suddenly she felt herself being lifted through the air and gently seated on a wooden cross-plank in the center of the boat. "Thank you, Mister Dougherty," Del somehow managed to say as she clutched both hands to the sides of the boat.

Bart sat down in the stern and leaning toward her, fixed her with an earnest gaze. "Tell y' what. S'pose you call me Bart an' I call you Del from now on. That alright?" he asked with a big grin.

"Sure." Del was beginning to feel comfortable with this man. He was like the big brother she had always thought it might be nice to have.

"Good! Now—time for a little test. In what part o' this boat am I sitting?"

"The stern," Del promptly replied.

Pointing to his left, Bart asked, "What do you call this side?"

"Port."

"And what about up there in the front?"

119

"The bow."

"Good!" Bart declared. "You're payin' attention an' that's really important 'cause things can change fast when you're out there on the water. You gotta be awake every second," he winked. "A couple more things for you. You see this piece o' wood in my hand? It's called the *tiller*. Some boats have regular steering wheels, like you see on a car. But that's mostly bigger boats and ships."

"The *tiller*," Del repeated out loud, prompting another approving nod from her instructor.

"You see this rope I have in my other hand?" Bart continued. "It's called a *sheet*. It's got that special name 'cause you use it to control the sail. You'll see how it works once we're under way."

"You mean we're actually going to sail out there today?" Del suddenly felt anxious again, for she noticed several white caps far out in the main channel of the Strait.

"'Course. Why not? That's what we're here for, ain't it?" Bart smiled reassuringly. "Don't worry. I won't ask you to work the sheet an' tiller today. You just sit tight an' watch what I do. Then maybe next time, if it's really calm, I'll let you take the helm." He paused and then laughed and winked at her again. "Oops! Sorry, Del. There's another new term for y'—*take the helm*. That's what y' do when y' sit where I am and use these things." Bart patted the handle of the tiller with his right hand and shook the sheet line in his left.

"Take the helm," Del echoed.

"Right. So let's get started." As he spoke, Bart stood up and untied another line that ran from the top of the mast to a pulley at its base, directly behind Del, and from there to a cleat on the starboard side gunwale. When he pulled on this line, the sail slowly rose up from where it had been folded on the boom. As the sail rose, it began to flap back and forth in the wind and the catboat began to rock. Del shuddered but clenched her teeth, determined not to show her fear.

Securing the downhaul line to the starboard side cleat again, Bart next stepped around Del and released the two lines that had held the boat close to the dock. Immediately, the stern of the catboat began to drift away from the dock and the sail to fill with wind. Del's whole body stiffened. Her anxiety quickly subsided, though, as Bart leaped to the stern and, seizing the tiller, guided the vessel steadily out into the open water. At the same time, he pulled firmly on the sheet to maximize the momentum of the boat. "Away we go!" he shouted jubilantly.

Feeling now as if she were flying rather than sailing, Del relaxed completely.

*   *   *

Three weeks later, Judge Lanham stood with Bart Daugherty and Ruby Hicks at the end of the dock at Striker's Landing, watching in amazement as Del flawlessly guided the Beetle Cat back and forth across the broad sweep of water between Benicia and Port Costa.

"I can't tell whether the girl's part of the boat or the boat's part of the girl," Judge Lanham said.

Bart gave him a puzzled look. He quickly grasped the Judge's meaning, however. "You're right," he said. "She's a natural. That's a twenty-knot wind out there!"

"Just like Jesus," Ruby declared jubilantly, "she got s-w-e-e-e-t harmony!"

Instantly and with uncharacteristic enthusiasm, the Judge threw his arm around Ruby's shoulders and hugged her. "That's it!" he declared.

"That's what?" Bart said, again puzzled by the Judge's locution.

Smiling proudly, he explained. "The name of her boat—*Sweet Harmony*. And you *will* sell me that catboat, won't you, Bart? It's just *got* to be hers!"

Startled by this request, Bart nonetheless nodded agreement. "Sure, Judge. Couldn't be any other way."

"Name your price, my man!" the Judge commanded.

Bart thought about this for a moment. He himself had just recently purchased the Beetle Cat. He had ordered it from a catalog and had it shipped all the way from Massachusetts. He was so pleased with the ease of its handling and the beauty of its all-wood design that he had planned to keep it for many years. "Well," he said at last, "I guess I could sell it to you at cost and get me another one."

Still hugging Ruby with one arm, the Judge now hugged Bart with the other. "I meant what I said, Bart. Name your price!"

Thus the transaction was completed on the spot, the Judge voluntarily adding fifteen percent to Bart's original purchase price.

When Del returned to the dock and learned that the Beetle Cat was now hers, she squealed with delight and gave all three of these people big hugs. She clung especially long to Ruby for coming up with the name for her new possession. "*Sweet Harmony*! Oh, Ruby—it's perfect!

"I think Del's ready for her first regatta," Bart said. "There's one three weeks from tomorrow. I'll sign her up for it, if you want. But I'll have to give her a few racing lessons first."

"Excellent idea!" the judge said. "How about it, Del? You think you're ready to race?"

"Oh yes, Papa. I'd love to!"

* * *

During Mass on the Sunday of the race, Del could barely contain her excitement about the upcoming challenge. Even during the consecration, her brain was filled with visions of *Sweet Harmony* winning the First Place cup.

"You *are* coming to see the regatta this afternoon, aren't you?" Del asked her friend Maggie as soon as she saw her after Mass.

Maggie looked startled. "What regatta?" Neither Maggie nor anyone else in her family had ever taken an interest in sailing. Her father, after all, was a banker; her mother, head of the Rosary Society; her older sister, past Queen of the Temperance Parade; and Maggie herself, a recent winner of St. Catherine School's annual fifth grade spelling bee.

Del was crushed, and then furious at her friend. "Well, just so you know—I'm going to be in it today, racing my new Beetle Cat. And you better come because I'm going to win and you'll be sorry if you don't see it."

"'Pride goeth before a fall!'" Maggie warned, echoing one of her mother's favorite phrases. Confident in her own triumphal retort, Maggie walked quickly away to rejoin her family as they crossed the street and climbed into their big Cadillac sedan.

Right then and there, Del decided she would never speak to Maggie again. Del's resolve was reinforced when she felt her father's hand on her shoulder. "Come along, Del. We must get you ready for the regatta."

* * *

There were scores of sailboats tied up at the City Dock when Del and her father arrived there an hour later—boats ranging in size and design from catboats like her own to forty-foot ketches. Although the Vallejo Yacht Club sponsored these Sunday races, there were sailboats from all over the greater Bay Area, including Oakland, San Raphael and San Francisco.

Suddenly Del felt much less sure of herself. Although Bart had entered her in a trial race with four other local catboat sailors a week before, the realization she would now be out there on the water surrounded by so many larger boats filled her with dread.

She tried to remember what Bart had told her about how the Race Committee always handicaps the bigger sailboats in such regattas, but she couldn't help also remembering how the skippers of these boats would shout at and try to intimidate the smaller boat skippers as everyone maneuvered for position at the starting line. She remembered one starting-line incident in particular when a single-design boat like her Beetle Cat was rammed amidships by a twenty-three foot sloop, shattering the hull of the smaller vessel and toppling its youthful helmsmen into the water.

"That was the kid's mistake," Bart had told her when she mentioned this incident to him several days before. "He shoulda known better than get in line with the wrong design class. That's what happens when you try to be a show-off."

Once she had launched *Sweet Harmony* and was tacking and running confidently among the other one-design boats an hour later, though, Del recovered her confidence. She waved at Greg Henshak and Calvin Watrous as they passed her in this melee of youthful skippers and took particular pride in the fact that she was the only girl skipper in her class.

The entire fleet of larger boats was at least fifty yards ahead of them now, though repeated shouts of "Starboard!" and four-letter epithets were clearly audible among the skippers and crews as each boat frantically jockeyed for position at the starting line.

Then, suddenly, Del heard the sharp crack of the starting gun on the Committee Boat, and the giant wall of crisscrossing sails ahead broke up as the big boats turned to beat their way toward the first marker. Their progress was slow, however, since it was a warm May afternoon with only a light eight-knot breeze. Del felt thankful for that.

With the others in the catboat and dinghy fleet, she trimmed her sail and guided *Sweet Harmony* toward the starting line. Repeatedly, she glanced toward the Committee Boat to see whether the flag signaling the next race had been raised. Once this had happened, she knew it would be only a matter of minutes before the starting gun was fired.

As her fleet got closer to the starting line, several of her competitors began to imitate the aggressive maneuvers of the larger boats, but with much less skill. In the process, two catboats and three dinghies bunched together and quickly became caught "in irons." Their youthful skippers howled angrily at each other and struggled to untangle themselves.

Heeding Bart's warnings about this, Del had kept a safe distance of several yards between *Sweet Harmony* and the other boats in her fleet, even though this meant she was now seventh in the queue of eleven boats approaching the starting line. Glancing again at the Committee Boat, she saw that the warning flag had been raised.

Immediately, Del leaned back over the port gunnel, tightened her grip on the sheet, and pushed the tiller so that *Sweet Harmony* pointed toward the first marker, several hundred yards ahead and just short of the Martinez ferry terminal. Instantly, she felt her Beetle Cat respond— very much indeed like a cat pouncing on a mouse.

"Crack!" sounded the pistol on the Committee Boat, and they were off.

Having kept considerable distance between *Sweet Harmony* and the other boats now proved to Del's advantage. Even though she had crossed the starting line late, her sail picked up the full force of the available air and, slowly but surely, she gained on the on the lead boats.

By the time she was halfway to the first marker, *Sweet Harmony* was third in line. Greg was leading the fleet, with Calvin close on his stern. Remembering Bart's instructions, Del synchronized every move she made with those of Greg and Calvin, coming about on each tack exactly when they did. She was now only a few boat lengths behind Calvin, her whole body tingling with excitement.

As he rounded the first marker, Calvin looked back at her and sneered for he saw that disaster for Del was imminent. In rounding too close, *Sweet Harmony*'s hull brushed against the marker! Del's heart sank. She would have to circle the marker before she could proceed on the next leg. That meant not only that she would fall far behind Greg and Calvin but also that she would probably be overtaken by several of the boats behind her. She might even have to jibe several times to avoid hitting one of the other approaching boats. "Damn!" she hissed.

Before she began the second leg, though, Del managed to go high enough above the marker and the other boats to catch stronger currents of both air and water—just as Bart had told her she would. "Starboard!" she called out as *Sweet Harmony* charged down on them in a reach and blocked their wind in passing.

"Stupid girl!" shouted a boy from one of the boats she passed.

"Bitch!" yelled another.

"Why ain't you playin' with dollies?" mocked a third.

Del ignored their futile sarcasm, concentrating now on catching up with Calvin and Greg who were already rounding the second marker. Again, her heart sank. Since this was only a single-lap race, Greg and Calvin would surely beat her on the final downwind run to the finish line.

Catching a gust on the reach leg, however, *Sweet Harmony* sped toward the second marker and swept smoothly around it. Now on the downwind run—again, as Bart had instructed—Del maximized the Beetle Cat's momentum by raising its centerboard and lifting its tiller completely out of the water. Swiftly, the gap between *Sweet Harmony* and Calvin's boat was closed, so that both of them crossed the finish line bow-to-bow.

Loud cheers exploded from the Committee Boat as Del eased up on the sheet and glided toward the City Dock. When she glanced at Calvin sailing beside her, she was pleased to see that he too gave her a congratulatory salute.

"Good job, Del!" Bart exclaimed as she luffed her sail and gently nudged *Sweet Harmony* alongside the dock. Many others—including her father, Ruby, Jack and his mother, the Henshaks, and even the Woolsies—were there to greet her. Everyone clapped as Del stepped up on the dock and secured her stern line. Her father and Ruby both rushed forward to embrace her, and Jack's face glowed with pride for his friend.

* * *

When the Majestic motion picture theater first opened in October of 1920, owners Earl and Mona Quick advertised in the *Benicia Herald New Era* for a piano accompanist. Knowing that her friend Gail could use the extra money, Snooky told her to apply for the job. Gail was reluctant to do so. "I don't like leaving Jack home alone after dark," she said.

"You only have to work an hour every Friday and Saturday. Jack's old enough to look after himself for a couple hours," Snooky assured her. "It'll be easy for you, and the pay's good—two dollars a night. You're not gonna tell me you can't use an extra four bucks a week now, are y'?"

Gail bit her lip, reluctant to tell her friend she needed to keep Saturday nights open for Soames. "I don't know. Somebody might knock on our door while I'm away. You know how crazy this town gets on Saturday nights."

"So tell Jack to bolt the door and not open it 'til you get home. You can do that, can't y'?" Snooky eyed her friend suspiciously.

"I'll have to think about it. Maybe I could do it on Fridays."

"That ain't gonna work. You gotta work both nights or the Quicks 'll hire somebody else. You know what cheapskates them junk-dealers is!"

To Gail's surprise, Soames told her to take the accompanist job. "Things are getting pretty hectic for me on the weekends these days. Myrtle's doing a lot of entertaining of some important people at our house in the city lately. Big bankers and railroad executives, you know," he winked. "So I gotta be in the city on the weekends more." Seeing the look of panic in Gail's eyes, he added, "Don't worry, baby. We can get together during the week."

Gail knew Soames was lying. She also knew there was nothing she could do about it. After all, she was 'the other woman' in his life. She had to accept the leftovers of whatever he had to offer.

As it turned out, her friend Snooky had been right. The job at the theater was easy. The Quicks knew nothing about music. Neither did most of their customers. All Gail needed to do was weave together fragments of the classical and popular melodies she knew by heart, synchronizing the *largo* and *allegro* of almost any musical composition to the action she saw on the silent screen. The plots of such films were always simple and formulaic. By January of 1921, Gail had become expert at anticipating the rhythms and chords she needed to play for each scene.

*   *   *

It was now April 27—Gail's thirty-third birthday. She had just returned home from the Majestic with Snooky where they had seen Norma Talmadge in *Branded Woman*. To celebrate the occasion, Snooky had taken the night off from her usual job as an entertainer at The Brewery and arranged for a neighbor to take care of Alfie. Since it was 10:30 P.M. when they arrived at Gail's apartment, both women supposed Jack was sound asleep.

"So wha'd y' think o' that one?" Snooky asked as she tossed her woolen shawl and satchel on the tattered green sofa in Gail's front parlor and opened Gail's icebox to look for something to eat.

Gail, who had immediately sat down in her mohair, rubbed her brow and frowned. "I don't know exactly. I liked the part where she tells the old man off for hiding the truth about her mother. But I don't mind telling you that mother really bothered me."

"Why's that?" Snooky asked, still ferreting through Gail's leftovers. "Ain't you got anythin' good to eat in here? I'm starved!"

"There's some cracker jacks in the cupboard over the sink," Gail said wearily.

Snooky promptly opened this cabinet and pulled out the colorful box, which had already been opened and partially eaten. Peering inside, Snooky said, "Hmm. Looks like you got mice."

"It's Jack, of course. He eats me out of house and home."

Snooky jammed a fistful of the stale syrup-coated popcorn into her mouth. "That's one good thing 'bout Alfie," she muttered between crunches. "He can't get to the stuff I put away."

"That's a terrible thing to say!" Gail scolded.

Snooky sat down on the sofa and continued greedily fingering cracker jacks into her mouth. "Maybe," she admitted. "But it's a fact." After chewing thoughtfully for a moment, Snooky asked, "So what bothered you about the mother?"

"In *Branded Woman*?" The exchange about Alfie had almost completely sidetracked Gail's thoughts. Again, putting her hand to her forehead, she sighed, "Oh—you know, Snooky. It's this whole thing about being a bad mother. I'm not talking about the mother in the flicker. She was really sort of a heroine. But what chance do we single mothers have in this world? No matter what you do, you're a branded woman!"

After chewing and blinking at her friend for several seconds like a rodent watching a predator, Snooky shrugged. "Sure. You're right. But who gives a damn?"

"Jack does," Gail said gloomily.

"Oh, don't tell me you're gonnah ride that old horse again! Come on, Gail. You know you're a good mother to Jack. The best!"

Asleep in his bedroom, Jack was suddenly awakened by the sound of the two women's voices. When he heard them mention his name, he sat up and listened attentively. What had he done now, he wondered.

"I think I'm losing him, Snooky. Ever since he ran away with that Lido girl last year? He hasn't been the same. He comes home from school every day and heads right for his room without so much as a hello. And at meal times, he just wolfs down his food and sits staring down at his empty plate. When I try to talk to him about something, it's as if he's deaf. Even when I yell at him for being rude, he just sits there and stares at me."

Dropping the now empty crackerjack box on the sofa cushion beside her, Snooky leaned forward, with her elbows on her knees and her fingertips peaked together in a steeple under her chin. "Look! He's only eleven years old. What d' y' expect? The kid's confused. He sees you foolin' aroun' with Soames while, at the same time, you're scoldin' him for bein' friends with that stupid little whore. No wonder he's messed up! So why don't y' just dump Soames an' get on with y'r life?"

As quietly as he could, Jack got out of bed and tiptoed over to the door, pressing his ear against it so he could hear every word of the women's conversation.

There was a long pause as Gail sat thinking about what her friend had just said. She knew Snooky was right, but her feelings for Soames were so overpowering that she couldn't think of any reply. At last, she stood up and walked over to the kitchen cabinet where she kept her bottle of sherry. Taking the bottle out and uncorking it, she poured herself a glass. "Would you like some?" she asked.

"Nah!" Snooky made a face. "That stuff's too sweet for me. Only hooch I drink is beer an' whisky. The real McCoy, that is," she added with a chuckle. "You ain't got none o' that, I s'pose."

"Sorry," Gail said as she sat back down in her mohair chair.

Again, there was a long silence. Gail sipped nervously at her glass and Snooky continued to stare at her friend—determined not to let her off the hook. "Well?" Snooky finally said. "You gonnah answer my question?"

Exasperated, Gail threw up arms. "Dammit, Snooky! I can't do it! Do you have any idea what life was like for me after John was killed? Even before he left for the War? God! There were months of worry and frustration! We had no money. I had no job. And it's not as if John and I ever had any kind of a real love life. He was much too young and immature. I should never have married him! When Jimmy came along, I was so starved for it! God! He's good!" she exclaimed. "He keeps me going all night long!"

Snooky leaned back into the sofa now, an expression of astonishment on her face that quickly turned into scorn. "All night long? You gotta be kiddin' me!" she declared. "They ain't no men like that! An'—believe me, honey—I know men!"

"Well, Jimmy is," Gail declared emphatically. "And I'm not giving him up!"

"So I guess you're OK with sharing him, right?" Snooky was angry now. "I mean—hell! The guy's married, and Lord knows how many other women he's got on the string. You think you're the only one likes his cherries?"

Gail glared at her friend. "I don't care!"

Suddenly, both of them froze in silence. They had heard a sound coming from behind the closed door to Jack's bedroom.

Snooky stood up and, grabbing her shawl and satchel, said, "I gotta go. Thanks for the stale cracker jacks," she added sarcastically. Then, as she opened the door to the outside landing, Snooky made her parting shot: "Believe me, hon, you'll live to rue the day!"

*   *   *

Though it was December 12, daytime temperatures in Benicia were unseasonably warm. Tucker and Billy Sparks were sweating profusely as they hurried to replace a broken axel on Jeb Hilliard's ice delivery wagon. They did not notice Jack when he stumbled into Tucker's shop, his face badly battered and cut and his arms covered with bruises.

"Look!" Billy declared when he looked up and saw Jack hunched over in the open doorway.

"Land sakes, boy! What you been doin'?" Tucker declared.

"I had a fight with Soames," Jack blubbered. "He beat me up."

Quickly, Tucker moved to help Jack sit down on the only piece of furniture in his shop—an old captain's chair. "There now," Tucker said gently. "You jes' set right there for a spell while gets somethin' t' fix you up."

Tucker ran into the back room of his shop and quickly returned with a bucket of warm soapy water and a clean rag. Squatting beside Jack, he began dabbing Jack's battered and tear-streaked face with the soapy rag. Though he flinched at Tucker's ministrations, Jack stopped sobbing. "Go get the styptic," Tucker said to Billy, who still stood next to Hilliard's wagon, watching in silence.

When Billy returned with the styptic, Tucker used it to staunch the several still bleeding cuts on Jack's face. Through all of this, none of them said a word. Once he was satisfied he had done what he could to clean Jack's face, Tucker inspected the boy's badly bruised arms and legs. Then, shaking his head woefully, he declared, "Boy, you sho' done took a lickin'! You wanna tell me how this happen?"

Jack nodded stoically. "When I got home from school today, I found momma and Soames buck naked in the front parlor. So I got real mad and took a punch at him. I told him to get out of our house. And right away he starts slapping me and throwing me around."

"What'd y'r Momma do?" Tucker asked, standing up and wiping his own face now as it streamed with perspiration and tears. He had seen this before—too many times.

"Nothing," Jack sobbed. "She didn't do nothing!" he repeated, angrily this time. "I ain't never going back there!"

Tucker rested his left hand on Jack's shoulder. "No, boy, you ain't. That fo' sho'! You gonna come live with me an' Billy."

Jack looked up at Tucker's coal black face, its heavily lined features now set in grim determination. "Can I?" he whispered, not really believing what Tucker had said.

"'Course you can! Woman let somethin' like this happen to her boy don' deserve bein' a Momma! Don't you worry, boy. You be alrigh' with us, won't he Billy?"

Billy nodded.

1922

Singler's Barbershop

CHAPTER TEN

"Toot-toot, Tootsie, Goodbye"

B ECAUSE OF ITS LOCATION DIRECTLY across the Napa River from the Mare Island Naval Shipyard, Vallejo was a much larger community than Benicia. During World War I, hundreds of fighting ships had been built and repaired at this federal government facility. The war effort had created steady good-paying jobs that attracted thousands of both skilled and unskilled laborers from all up and down the West Coast.

Soon after the armistice in November of 1918, Vallejo was also suddenly inundated with hundreds of decommissioned cooks and stokers who had served aboard the steam-powered warships. Virtually all of these men were African Americans who, because of their race and poverty, had no choice but to seek some form of unskilled labor and low-cost housing close to the Mare Island shipyard.

As a result, like many port cities on both the East and West Coasts, Vallejo developed a racially segregated ghetto. It was in this run-down neighborhood that Adam Tucker, Billy Stokes, and now Jack Westlake were living.

When Jack went home with Tucker and Billy for the first time on December 13, he felt as if he were being transported into a nightmare world. Abandoned brick warehouses and weather beaten clapboard tenements lined both sides of the narrow, unpaved street where Tucker and Billy lived. From several open doorways, half-naked children stared sullenly out at them as Tucker's 1910 Model T pick-up slowly bounced over deeply cut ruts and constantly weaved to avoid hitting roving children, cats and dogs. Since it was suppertime, the air was filled with the thick, greasy stench of frying food and the shrill shouts of women railing against their drunken mates and wayward offspring.

At the end of this nameless back street, Tucker pulled his truck into a weed-choked vacant lot. In the center of this lot was a one-story windowless shack. Shutting off the truck's engine, Tucker stepped out and walked toward a pad-locked door that was the only entrance to this ramshackle structure. Immediately, the shack exploded with the sound of frantic growling and barking.

Carefully unlocking the door, Tucker opened it just wide enough to reach inside with his left hand. "Shush now!" Tucker commanded. The barking stopped, but the sight of the huge black dog Tucker pulled outside instantly terrified Jack. With its enormous head, glaring eyes, and rapidly snapping jaws full of sharp yellow teeth—the creature looked more like a giant wolf than a mongrel guard dog. Even when Billy got out of the truck and moved calmly toward the animal, it continued to lunge and growl as if it would tear Billy's throat out.

Trembling, Jack huddled in the truck bed and desperately looked around for a shovel or stick with which he could defend himself. Finding nothing but an old canvas tarp, he crawled under it, hoping to make himself invisible to Tucker's monster. This seemed to have the wanted effect, for the dog stopped growling.

Leaning over the side of the truck bed, Billy said to Jack, "Gimme y'r shirt."

"What for?" Jack asked, still keeping himself completely covered by the tarp.

"Jus' gimme it," Billy repeated impatiently.

Jack quickly unbuttoned the front of his shirt and, removing it, gave it to Billy. Then, raising his head just high enough to glimpse over the wooden side-panel of the truck bed, Jack watched as Billy walked over to the dog and held Jack's shirt out for the animal to sniff.

"Tha's Jack. Jack be a good boy," Billy explained to the dog while at the same time he massaged its neck. After sniffing the shirt for several seconds, the dog seemed satisfied and trotted inside the house. Billy beckoned to Jack. "You c'n come on in now."

"You sure?" Jack asked tremulously.

Billy simply nodded. "That be *Peewee*. You calls him that, you be safe."

Jack almost laughed out loud at such an inappropriate name. Still terrified, though, he slowly climbed out of the truck and very cautiously approached the open door. Handing Jack's shirt back to him, Billy led the way inside.

Much to Jack's surprise, the huge beast now lay stretched on the floor several feet from the entrance, its head nestled comfortably on its front paws. Still, its fierce black eyes were wide open and it watched Jack as if it were poised to attack at the slightest provocation.

As he entered, the first thing Jack noticed—besides the supine Peewee—was the stark barrenness of Tucker's residence. The only furniture in this one-room dwelling was a rickety wooden table, two crudely constructed benches, and a pair of folding canvas camp beds.

Along the back wall of the place, Tucker had constructed some open wooden shelves filled with stacks of blankets and clothing as well as several large glass jars and tins of canned fish, fruits and vegetables. Against an adjacent wall was a black pot-bellied stove, its exhaust pipe rising a few feet and then angling outside through a hole in the wall.

The floor of Adam's house was hard-packed dirt; the walls, nothing but the warped and twisted wooden planks on the building's exterior. The only interior lighting came either from cracks between these planks or, after dark, from a single kerosene lantern suspended from a ceiling rafter. Looking up at this, Jack noted that the roof was made of overlapping tin sheets, which probably leaked rain during the winter and turned the interior into an oven during the long hot summer months.

Clearly, Jack's new home offered none of the amenities Jack had been accustomed to in his mother's apartment. There was no running water or flush toilet, no telephone or electric lights. If he wanted to bathe, Jack would have to use the cast-iron tub and hand-pump in a lean-to Tucker had erected against the side of his shack.

As for the privacy afforded by separate rooms in his mother's apartment, a two-hole privy in Tucker's back yard was the only place where Jack might be able to catch a few minutes of separation from his new housemates. As he soon discovered, the stench of that refuge discouraged lengthy sojourns.

Still, Jack was content in his new surroundings. Most important of all, he felt safe—despite the intimidating Peewee and Tucker's warning that Jack should never venture outside by himself, especially after dark.

"Long as you sticks with Billy an' me an' Peewee here," he assured Jack, "you be awright. But don't you be talkin' to none o' the damn drunks an' whores hangs aroun' here. Even the ning-nings is dang'rous. They'll cut you soon as say how-de-do."

Jack had never heard the expression *ning-nings* before, but he quickly surmised that it referred to the numerous small but angry-faced children he had seen wandering around in the street leading to Tucker's shack.

In addition to Tucker's giant guard dog, Jack noticed that there was a double-barreled shotgun hanging on the wall over one of the camp beds and that, over the other, hung a Bowie knife in a leather sheath. Jack felt sure he would be protected as long as he heeded Tucker's warnings.

"Where do you want me to sleep?" Jack asked, noting that there were only two camp beds.

Tucker chuckled. "Well, I guess you have t' sleep on d' flo' t'night, boy. I'll put down some blankets so's you don' catch col'. T'morra I'll scrounge up a cot for y'. They got lots of 'em over to the Ars'nal."

That night, Jack had his first taste of standard Negro fare—an Army-issue tin plate heaped full of fried beans and boiled collard greens along with two thick slices of sourdough bread. The only beverage offered was cold water from the outdoor hand pump.

When he saw that Jack was picking very discretely at his food, Tucker smiled and observed, "You bes' get used to it, boy, 'cause tha's all you gettin' here." Both he and Billy chuckled derisively.

"I'll be OK," Jack said, though he had a very queasy feeling in his stomach.

"Sho you will!" Billy sneered.

Though at first annoyed by his hosts' ridicule, Jack quickly learned to appreciate their "earthy" sense of humor. As they sat eating together at the rickety table that evening, the two men exchanged several reminiscences about the foolish behavior of "uppity white folks" in Benicia.

"'Member the time ol' lady Calvo put sugar in Sergio's tank?" Billy asked Tucker.

"Sho' do. Stupid woman thought she could sweeten up his stinky exhaust," he explained to Jack. "'Course, all it did was gum up the engine so's we had to replace the whole block. We made some good money off o' that one, didn' we Billy?"

Both men broke into raucous laughter. Jack couldn't help himself. He too had to laugh, even though he wasn't quite sure how sugar could ruin an automobile engine. He knew better than to reveal his own ignorance by asking.

Later, as he lay on the thick pile of blankets Tucker had put down for him, Jack realized that Tucker and Billy had probably recounted their humorous anecdotes for his benefit. They had wanted to distract Jack from his feelings of fear and desertion. In the silent darkness now, though, he could no longer hold back his tears.

Then something happened that at first struck terror into Jack's heart, for Peewee had stretched out beside him and was gently licking Jack's face. As slowly and carefully as he could, Jack pulled the Army blanket up until it completely covered his head.

He heard Peewee rise to his feet and sniff at the blanket several times. Finally, with a disappointed grunt, the animal lay down again, its warm body leaning heavily against Jack. Gradually, his fear of this animal subsided and Jack sank into a deep and dreamless sleep.

* * *

Gail Westlake had asked Ira to let her leave work at 4:00 the following Friday afternoon to visit Tucker's garage. She chose that hour precisely because she knew that, by then, Jack would be working at Huey's Barber Shop.

Gail was too ashamed to speak with her son directly. She believed there was nothing she could do to induce him to return home. In fact, she knew it was probably best he not do so. For, in spite of what had happened, she was determined to continue her relationship with Soames.

As usual, Adam and Billy were hard at work on a vehicle repair job when Gail appeared in the open garage doorway. Though he saw her out of the corner of his eye, Tucker did not acknowledge Gail's presence. He was furious that this woman had the audacity even to enter his shop.

"Mister Tucker," Gail finally said after several seconds passed. "I need to speak with you if I may."

Slowly, Tucker stood up straight and turned away from his task. Staring in silent rage at Gail, he growled, "I got nothin' to say to you, woman!"

"I think you do," Gail insisted, biting her lip but standing her ground. "I've brought some of Jack's clothes. He is still my son, after all, and I do not intend to simply abandon him—no matter what you may think of me."

"You already done that, ain't you?" Tucker snarled.

Gail trembled with her own fury now but kept her voice low and steady. "I understand why you may think that, Mister Tucker. What happened last Monday was unforgivable. But I'm not asking for your forgiveness, sir. I'm asking you to let me continue to support my son in the only way I can—by giving you a share of my weekly pay. It's the least I can do in return for your kindness to Jack. Will you please allow me that?"

Tucker shook his head in disgust. "I don' need yo' money, woman. You wants t' pay me t' wet-nurse your boy so's you can keep on doin' what you's doin'? You think I'm some kind o' fool?"

Frustrated with the man's stubbornness, Gail stepped farther inside the garage and placed her suitcase on the ground directly in front of him. "No, Mister Tucker. I do not think you're a fool. I think you are a remarkably kind and compassionate man—a true Christian gentleman. I shall be forever grateful to you for what you have done. That's why I'm pleading with you to let me take at least some responsibility in this situation."

Tucker glared furiously at her. "They's only one way to do that, Missus. An' you knows it."

Gail's expression hardened. "Very well, Mister Tucker. Nevertheless, I shall ask my employer to send you a portion of my wage every week. You may do with it what you wish." Having said this, Gail abruptly turned away and left.

Shaking his head, Tucker carried the suitcase out to his truck, tossed it into the truck bed, and returned to his work.

* * *

In a town of just under 2,000 permanent residents, it didn't take long for the news of Jack's disappearance to spread. As *Benicia Herald New*

Era editor Brad Pincus put it, "All of Benicia's children and livestock are community property." Whether it was stray cow or a lost child, everyone took responsibility for reporting and commenting on the event. Church suppers and committee meetings at the seven different houses of worship in town were the most fertile forums for embellishment. It was the party-line telephone, though, that disseminated local gossip most efficiently.

When Istey Hewett told her mother that Jack had been absent from school on Tuesday and Wednesday, Mary Lou promptly got on the phone to confirm this report with his teacher, Emma Thorndike. "Was Jack Westlake absent from school last week?" Mary Lou asked, getting right to the point.

Emma hesitated before she answered, for she was well aware that Mary Lou was a notorious gossip. "Well, yes," she admitted.

"Do you know why?"

"No. I do not, Missus Hewitt. What's more, I fail to see what business it is of yours."

"Have you talked to Jack's mother?" Mary Lou persisted, ignoring the contempt in Emma's voice.

"No, I have not."

"Did you report it to the truant officer?

A click at the other end of the line told Mary Lou that Emma had hung up. But another voice quickly commented, "That Emma Thorndike certainly is snooty, isn't she?" It was the voice of Sarah Pickett, Mary Lou's next-door neighbor who shared the party line with her and four others in town.

"Sure is," Mary Lou agreed indignantly. "Typical schoolmarm! She's trying to cover up somethin'. I bet it's all about that Soames fella. Everybody knows he's been foolin' aroun' with Gail Westlake for months. That poor dear boy Jack! I feel so sorry for him!"

"Yes, it's terrible! Somebody should tell Reverend Twitty," Sarah suggested. "He's on the Child Welfare Committee, you know."

"That's right. I almost forgot. Good idea, Sarah! You go right ahead and do that!"

In response, at least one other silent party to this conversation, Gladys Holcomb, nodded her approval.

* * *

The parishioners of Saint Paul's Episcopal Church took particular pride in its Anglican heritage, celebrating Sunday worship services with all the pomp and circumstance of High Anglican ceremony. Though the elders of St. Paul's parish tolerated the attendance of such lesser lights as Fire Chief Hodges and his family, the Hodges were definitely not considered members of Saint Paul's elite.

Much more prestigious was the family of Ronald Fisk, Vice President of Operations at the Ford assembly plant in Richmond, California. In fact, Ronald's wife Charlotte was a member of the Boards of Trustees at both St. Paul's Episcopal Church and St. Paul's Episcopal School for Girls. It was Charlotte Fisk who now presided over the emergency meeting of Benicia's Child Welfare Committee.

A plump woman in her late fifties with a white helmet of hair and the pale, swollen features of someone who rarely ventured out of doors, Charlotte devoted her every waking moment to the welfare of others in her community. Her two children had long since left the nest. Eleanor, at twenty-four, was married to a physician and living in San Jose. Twenty-two-year-old Elmer Fisk worked for his father at the plant in Richmond. He was also married and lived with his wife in Oakland.

The members of the Child Welfare Committee had gathered in the front parlor of the rectory immediately following Sunday services that cold January afternoon and were primly seated in strait-back chairs sipping cups of tea prepared for them by Bernice, the demure and pretty young wife of St. Paul's pastor, Herald Twitty.

In addition to Charlotte Fisk and Reverend and Mrs. Twitty, the members of the Child Welfare Committee included the Union Hotel owner's wife Rebecca Fuller, Saint Paul School Headmistress Florence Ebert, *Benicia Herald New Era* editor Brad Pincus and his wife Laura, Dr. William Trent, and Benicia Chief of Police Frank Colpepper. All were generally regarded as Benicia's most upright and respected citizens.

"As I'm sure you all realize," Charlotte began, "we are faced with a very serious situation. One of our children, Jack Westlake, ran away from home last month. It's my understanding that this happened because he was brutally beaten by a man named James Soames."

Because nearly a month had passed since this incident and the latest issue of *The Benicia Herald New Era* had already published a story about it, Charlotte's announcement surprised no one.

"We know very little about Mister Soames," Charlotte continued, "except that he conducts some sort of warehousing business out of a rented office in the Bank of Italy building. I have it on good authority, however, that for some time now Soames has been conducting an illicit affair with Jack's widowed mother, Gail Westlake. Missus Westlake, as you may remember, was one of the witnesses for the defense in the Geddis trial two years ago." Charlotte paused deliberately at this point, fixing every one of her listeners with a glance that was full of righteous rebuke.

All but one of the other committee members nodded in silent acknowledgment. Frank Copepper looked visibly shaken by Charlotte's reference to the Geddis case. As a law-enforcement officer, he knew such allusions might tempt people to draw the wrong conclusions.

Though aware of Frank's discomfort, Charlotte pressed on with her exposition. "It now appears Jack is living with a bunch of niggers in Vallejo. That garage mechanic, Adam Tucker, has evidently taken it upon himself to be Jack's protector."

"How dreadful!" Florence declared haughtily. "We certainly can't allow that to continue!"

"Of course not!" Rebecca agreed.

"The question is what shall we do about it?" Charlotte looked around the room, searching everyone's face for a suitable answer. As she had expected, none was forthcoming.

After several seconds of silence passed, Dr. Trent set his teacup and saucer on a side table and leaned forward thoughtfully in his chair. A recluse bachelor in his early sixties, Trent had a reputation for stoic silence in even the most catastrophic situations. Everyone was surprised, therefore, when he said, "I doubt there's much anyone can do. If the boy's mother won't do anything about it herself, we must leave the matter alone. As for Adam Tucker, I've had frequent dealings with him and he seems to me a very decent man." Glaring at Florence, he added, "regardless of his race."

"I can't believe you said that!" Florence snapped. "I too have had my car serviced by Tucker, and I agree he seems honest and hardworking.

But the fact remains—he *is* a Negro and his influence on an eleven-year-old white boy can do nothing but harm."

"I've even heard Tucker trades in contraband liquor!" Rebecca put in. "He's a common criminal, for Heaven's sake!"

"We have no record of criminal charges against Adam," Frank said firmly. "He's had a few tickets for sometimes parking his cars where they're not supposed to be, but it seems to me we've issued quite a few summons to your hotel guests, Rebecca."

"My husband paid the fines for those—promptly!" Rebecca retorted.

"This is ridiculous!" Charlotte declared. "We're not discussing traffic violations here. We're talking about the moral corruption of an innocent little boy. Didn't Our Lord warn us what would happen to those who harm little children?" Charlotte directed this question specifically at the Pastor Twitty, who promptly blushed but said nothing. He knew all too well that whatever he said would be roundly rebuffed.

"Perhaps we should send a delegation of our members to counsel Missus Westlake," Laura suggested. "I've met her several times in Rankin's and she's always seemed to me a bright and sensible woman. I'm sure she herself is very upset by this turn of events."

Several members of the committee exchanged glances of approval. "I would be amenable to leading such a delegation," Pastor Twitty offered.

"With all due respect, Reverend," Charlotte said, "I don't think a delegation headed by a man would be appropriate. I suggest we form a sub-committee of women. That will be much less intimidating to a young widow like Missus Westlake."

"An excellent suggestion!" declared Florence. "We should draw lots to determine which of us will serve on this sub-committee."

Trent shook his head in disgust. "Meddlesome nonsense!"

Charlotte shot him a disapproving look. "You are outnumbered, Doctor," she snapped. Then, looking around at the others, she concluded with stony confidence: "We are all agreed, then."

Trent stood up. "I want nothing to do with this!" Nodding toward Bernice, he said, "Thank you for the tea, Missus Twitty. Good day, everyone."

Ignoring Trent's protest and quick departure, Charlotte asked

Bernice to bring her some writing paper and a pen so she could draw up lots for the selection of the sub-committee members.

Bernice promptly obliged and, within a few minutes, three women were selected—Charlotte Fisk, Florence Ebert, and Laura Pincus. A date was then set one week hence for the sub-committee's meeting with Gail Westlake.

"Now we need to decide how we will approach Missus Westlake," Charlotte announced. "My own view is that we should tell her to immediately terminate her relationship with this rascal Soames."

"I agree," Florence promptly replied.

"No point in beating around the bush," Charlotte nodded.

"But what if she's offended by such a rude intrusion into her personal affairs? Perhaps we should first try to appeal to her better nature."

"What better nature?" Rebecca barked.

"Missus Westlake has already had ample time to ponder the consequences of her sins," Charlotte affirmed. "We must make her see it is time to make the right decision now."

The determination in Charlotte's voice left no doubt in anyone's mind that open confrontation was the best course for the Child Welfare sub-committee would follow.

* * *

At precisely 1:00 PM the following Sunday, the three members of the Child Welfare sub-committee climbed the outside stairs of Mrs. Brown's boarding house and knocked on Gail's apartment door. Having just left church services, they were all elegantly attired in their best Sunday outfits, complete with hats and gloves.

When the door opened, they saw that Gail Westlake too was elegantly, if much less expensively, attired in her Sunday best. She too had just returned from services at the Stony Ridge Baptist Church. "Good afternoon, ladies," Gail said amicably, almost as if she had expected their visit. "Won't you come in?"

Somewhat surprised by Gail's hospitable welcome, Charlotte gave her visiting companions a doubtful look. She recovered quickly, however. "Thank you, Missus Westlake. We'd like that very much. I'm Charlotte Fisk and these are my friends—Miss Florence Ebert, Headmistress of Saint Paul's School for Young Ladies, and Missus Laura Pincus, Assistant Editor of the *Benicia Herald New Era*."

"Please sit down, ladies," Gail said, gesturing toward her sofa. "Shall I put the kettle on for some tea?"

"Er … no, thank you, Missus Westlake," Charlotte said. "This is not really a social call. We're here to discuss a very serious matter with you."

Gail raised an eyebrow at this. "Oh? And just what might that be, ladies?" On the defensive now, Gail did not herself sit down. Instead, crossing her arms in front of her, she leaned against her kitchen counter and fixed the three women with a wary gaze.

"We are all members of the Child Welfare Committee at Saint Paul's Episcopal Church. We have come to investigate the recent regrettable incident involving you're your son Jack. You see, Missus Westlake, the Committee feels that some measure must be taken to protect your boy."

"Is that so?" Gail stiffened. "And how do you propose to do that, Madam?"

Having rehearsed this part of her presentation many times over in the past several days, Charlotte was well prepared with her response. "We propose that you end your scandalous relationship with Mister James Soames immediately."

Gail stood firmly on both feet now and was about to order all of these women to leave when Laura suddenly leaped up from the sofa and declared, "I smell smoke!"

As if cued by Laura's outburst, the alarm bell on the roof of the Benicia Fire House began clanging. All four women now ran to the door and out onto the landing. Looking up, they saw thick clouds of black smoke rolling over the rooftop of the five-story brick building to the south.

"It's the tannery!" Laura exclaimed. "My Lord! Look at all the smoke! It must be a huge fire!"

"And it's only a few blocks away! We've got to get out of here!" As she spoke, Charlotte was already running down the outside stairway as fast as she could. Florence and Laura were right behind her.

"Go on—run, you pompous busybodies!" Gail wanted to shout. Instead, she stood triumphantly silent on the platform at the top of the stairs and watched with great satisfaction as the three members of the Child Welfare Committee delegation fled frantically north up First Street to safety.

CHAPTER ELEVEN

"I'll Build a Stairway to Paradise"

SINCE IT WAS A SUNDAY, there had been only six men on duty at the Benicia Fire House that afternoon. Four of them were playing Five Card Stud and the other two were asleep when the teletype machine in the second floor barracks suddenly began punching out a warning message from the McClaren Tannery.

Bill Blodget, the fire team supervisor, immediately jumped up from the card game and telephoned Captain Hodges who ordered Bill to ring the firehouse alarm bell and promised to round up as many additional volunteer firemen as he could. The other card-players—Jimmy Espadarte, Rick Agulha, and George Iglesias—woke their sleeping partners Tom Cardoso and Luke Lara. Then, all of them grabbed their helmets and slid down the brass pole to the ground floor garage where the big horse-drawn Phoenix pumper and several smaller hose and tank carriers were stored. Iglesias and Espadarte headed toward the adjoining stable to harness up the dray horses.

"Forget the horses!" Blodget shouted as he threw open the big double doors of the Firehouse garage. "We ain't got time for that. Just grab the carts. We'll let Hodges' men handle the Phoenix."

As soon as the men pulled their carts out onto First Street, they realized this tannery fire was far worse than the run-of-the-mill spot fires they were so often called on to extinguish. Flames were leaping high from the roof of the west-side tannery building and had already engulfed the enclosed wooden crosswalk over First Street. The skeleton crew of tannery workers on the job that Sunday had fled both buildings

145

and were now frantically running north and south along First Street to escape the thick black smoke and falling debris.

"Jesus, Mary and Joseph!" Agulha exclaimed as he and Iglesias pulled their pumper cart down the street. "This is the worst I ever seen!"

"Take the pumper down to the water on C Street," Blodget commanded. "We gotta wet down the buildings this side o' the tannery." While Iglesias and Agulha carried out this order, Blodget and the other three men rushed forward with the two hose carts and the small tank cart.

Within minutes, they reached the intersection of C and First streets and began unwinding the fire hoses. Cardosa and Espadarte unraveled the hoses, and Blodget and Lara dragged them toward the waterfront where the pumper-cart's intake hose had already been immersed in the river.

By the time the firemen had the hoses connected and fully deployed, the fire had already spread to the outer walls of two clapboard residential buildings adjacent to the tannery. Fanned by a brisk west wind coming off of Carquinez Strait, the flames leaped high and wide in every direction.

Farther north, First Street was already filling up with spectators. Police Chief Colpepper and his skeleton crew of duty officers were having great difficulty trying to control this milling crowd of onlookers. "Everybody stay on the boardwalks!" Colpepper shouted through his megaphone. "Keep the way clear for the Phoenix!"

As he gave this order, the big horse-drawn pumper emerged from the firehouse along with Captain Hodges' phalanx of forty-three volunteer firefighters. But, by the time these men managed to connect the hoses to the Phoenix, the ground floor interior of the two residential houses next to the tannery were already in flames.

From a second floor window of one of these buildings, an enormously fat woman was leaning out and screaming for help. Quickly commandeering two other volunteer firemen, Blodget led them through the ground-floor entrance of this building in an effort to rescue the trapped woman. But smoke and flames quickly drove them back outside. In the meantime, Hodges ordered four of his men to place a ladder against the building so one of them could climb up to help the trapped woman.

This effort too proved futile. Espadarte, the fireman on the ladder, wasn't strong enough to extract the hysterical woman by himself. "We need another ladder!" he shouted to his colleagues below.

Immediately, Cardoso and Lara, who had been manning fire hoses, handed them to other newly arrived volunteers and ran to get a second ladder. Lara, the strongest member of the Benicia Fire Department, quickly climbed this ladder and dragged the kicking and screaming woman through the window. Unfazed by her protests, he threw her over his shoulder like a sack of grain and carried her down the ladder to safety.

A loud cheer went up from the watching crowd. None of the firemen noticed this accolade, however, for all were now concentrating on watering down the next pair of buildings north of the tannery. As for the tannery itself, Hodges and Blodget had already made their decision. They would simply let it burn.

*   *   *

Huey's Barber Shop had more than the usual number of customers the following Friday afternoon. Most of them were men who had worked at McClaren's Tannery and were now preening themselves for a week of job hunting. More than three hundred men had worked at the tannery. All were now unemployed.

Although there were two other tanneries in Benicia, they were both much smaller operations. It would be months before either of these plants was likely to increase its labor force. Besides, the astonishing increase in the nationwide sale of automobiles during the past two years had already begun to shrink the market for leather used in the production of saddles and harnesses.

"So where y' lookin' fer work?" Huey asked as Bob Jenson settled into the barber's chair.

Never one to let others think he was unprepared for any extremity, Jenson was quick with a response. "I hear they're hirin' over at the new refinery in Martinez. They're doin' a lot o' new construction so they're bound to need workers."

"Yeah, but what d' you know about construction?" Huey asked

skeptically as he swept his razor back and forth on his sharpening strop.

"Don't matter. I'm a fast learner an' strong as an ox," Jenson retorted, rolling up his sleeves to show his bulging biceps.

"There's lots of us got big muscles," snarled Mark Verde from behind his newspaper. A burly man in his early thirties, Verde had been a scraper at McClaren's Tannery—a job requiring both a strong back and strong arms since scrapers had to wield long steel knives and wire brushes to remove the flesh and hair from newly-arrived hides.

"Couple hundred of us, in fact!" Ted Sena declared, warming to an imminent altercation. At McClaren's Tannery, Sena had been one of the young toughs who loaded long strips of oak bark into the grinding machines so it could be used in the tanning vats.

On the defensive now, Jenson became stoic. "You gotta do what you gotta do."

"Now there's a philosophy!" smirked another former tannery employee, Steve Venizelos, who had been a bookkeeper in McClaren's business office.

"So what are we s'pose t' do?" Jenson retorted angrily. "Jus' roll over an' die?"

The other men chuckled because Jenson had been a "dyer" by trade. Realizing the irony of his own remark, Jenson blushed. But he also smiled and nodded. "Well, you know what I mean. Things is tough f'r all of us."

"You got that right," Verde agreed, putting his newspaper aside. "Only jobs I see in the paper are f'r delivery boys and washer women." Then, looking down at Jack who was shining Verde's boots, he added, "An' shoeshine boys, right?"

Jack smiled slyly up at the big man. However humble his own job might be, Jack was nonetheless proud to be employed.

"How much you make doin' that, anyway, boy?" Sena asked.

"All depends on you," Jack answered. He had long since learned not to disclose to strangers anything about his personal finances. It was one of the first lessons Tucker had taught him.

"Smart boy!" Huey quipped with a wink at Jack.

"Yeah sure! But he's just a kid," Venizelos barked. "He ain't got responsibilities like some us." Venizelos looked angrily around at the other younger men in Huey's shop. All of them were bachelors.

"Everybody's gotta eat!" Verde retorted.

"I hear the Alta plant's hirin'," Huey suggested in an effort to bring more optimism—or, at least, some measure of congeniality—to the discussion.

"I already tried over there. They ain't hirin' Portagees and Greeks," Verde snarled. "They only want Anglos."

"Well now, I wouldn't say that," Huey put in, even though he knew Verde was probably correct. Edward Johnson, the Alta plant manager, was one of Huey's regular customers and Johnson had often expressed his distrust of what he referred to as "Mediterranean niggers."

"I'm thinkin' o' startin' my own bus'ness," Sena announced.

"Oh yeah? What kind o' bus'ness is that?" Jenson asked.

Sena smiled knowingly. "Makin' hooch, o' course. There's big money in it, an' it's pretty easy t' get started from what I hear. All y' need is a still an' some good grapes."

"You better be careful who you tell 'bout y'r plans," warned Pete Coelho, entering the conversation for the first time. Coelho had been a vat tender at McClaren's and knew quite a bit about a variety of brewing processes, including the production of bootleg liquor—since he himself often moonlighted at a small distillery in the hills above Port Costa.

"I ain't worried," Sena affirmed. "Hell! Just about every farmer in the county's already in the business an' you can't tell me Campy or any o' them other so-called '*ex* saloon keepers' in this town is worried. Ever time the Revenues threaten a raid, old Chief Colpepper's on the phone before they even leave Fairfield."

There was now a deathly silence in Huey's shop. Although everyone, including Jack, knew that Sena was correct—that Benicia's constabulary was 'in cahoots' with the local brothel and saloon proprietors—it was not something anyone felt comfortable advertising. 'Live and let live' had long been the unwritten law of the land in Benicia.

Having finished with Jenson, Huey released him from the barber's chair and waved for Verde to take his place. "So who y' bettin' on for the World Series this year, Bob?" Huey asked as Jenson paid for his haircut.

"Well, you can be sure it ain't the Black Socks."

This comment elicited snickers from everyone present because, only two years before, the so-called "Black Sox" scandal had brought nationwide shame to America's favorite sport.

"I'm bettin' on the fights, myself. Dempsey's the hunnert-t'-one fav'rite from what I hear," Sena announced.

"Yeah. Y' think they're gonnah broadcast his next fight out o' the new station they got up in Sacramento?" Venizelos asked.

"Humph!" Verde grunted disgustedly. "Won't make no diff'rence. We won't be able t' get it here anyways. Ain't nobody got a wireless in *this* jerk-water town."

"Y're wrong about that, Mark," Huey said. "Joe Paterno tol' me he's puttin' one in over at The Pastime."

"No kiddin'!" Sena exclaimed. "When's he gonnah do that?"

"He ain't said yet. But you c'n be sure it'll be in time for the Dempsey fight so Joe can pack in lots o' customers."

"Yeah, that greedy som'bitch jus' raised the price on his billiard games," Verde groused as he sat down in the barber chair. "I ain't goin' in there no more."

"Now you're outta work, you won't be able to afford it anyway," Venizelos sneered. "You better stick with baseball. It's healthier an' a lot cheaper." Venizelos was captain of the McClaren Tannery's scrub team that played every Saturday afternoon in Basilio Park on East K Street.

Verde responded to this observation with a dark scowl. Although he was an excellent first-baseman and often joined his co-workers in pick-up games against teams from the other tanneries and the Arsenal, Verede was generally viewed as a hot head and a sore loser.

"See y' later, fellahs," Jenson said as he headed for the door.

Huey was unable to resist a parting shot. "Good luck building latrines at the refinery, Bob!" This had the wanted effect on his other customers, for all immediately burst into laughter.

* * *

Del was waiting for Jack in front of Huey's barbershop when he left work that afternoon. "Where have you been, Jack?" she declared. "I haven't seen you in weeks, and I heard you ran away from home. What happened?"

Jack had been dreading this moment. But he knew that, sooner or later, his friend would track him down. "Soames beat me up," he explained. He hoped Del wouldn't force him to elaborate.

Del inspected Jack's face closely, looking for scars and bruises—all of which, by now, had healed and were no longer visible. "He beat you up! That's awful! Why, for goodness sakes?"

As he had expected, Del was determined to get all the gory details. But Del was such a sheltered flower, Jack wasn't sure how to answer. "I caught Mom and him together," he said.

"What do you mean 'caught them together'?"

"Oh, you know—doing what they do down at the Lido."

Del's face went pale. She was not a complete innocent. She had certainly heard tales from her schoolmates about what happened in places like the Lido, though neither she nor any of her girlfriends had a very clear idea of what it involved. The nuns had sternly instructed them that such activities were nasty and sinful. In this case, though, Del was determined to learn the whole truth—no matter how nasty or sinful it might be. "Well … what do you mean *exactly*?"

Jack studied her for several seconds, feeling suddenly very sad. "You've seen what dogs do to each other, haven't you? I mean, boy dogs and girl dogs?"

"You mean your Momma and Soames were doing that!"

"Well, not exactly, I guess," Jack admitted. "But pretty close."

"That's disgusting!" Del wasn't as shocked now as she was angry. "What did *you* do?"

"I punched Soames in the gut and told him to get out of our house."

"Uh-oh! So that's why he beat you up?"

"Yeah."

"What did your Momma do?"

"Never mind, Del. I don't want t' talk about it." Jack started to walk away from her.

"But you've *got* to tell me about it, Jack," Del insisted, following after him. "I'm your friend!"

Jack stood still then, staring straight ahead up the street. What could he say? When he felt her standing next to him with her hand on his shoulder, he said, "Look—it's all over now. I'm living with Adam and Billy, and …"

"With Adam and Billy!" Del exclaimed in astonishment. "Why them? Why didn't you come to *our* house?"

Jack became angry. "Are you kidding? You think your Papa'd take in an orphan like me?"

"Of course, he would! My Papa's the kindest man in the world!"

"Maybe to you," Jack said bitterly. "But I'm not his son. Why should he take me in?"

Del was silent. She wanted to remonstrate with Jack, but suddenly she realized that he might be right. Her father, after all, was very judgmental and probably very sensitive to what other people in town might say if he were to give refuge to a run-away. "Well ..." she hesitated, tears coming to her eyes. "Isn't there anything *I* can do?"

Jack looked mournfully at her. "I don't think so, Del—except, just keep being my friend."

Impulsively, Del threw her arms around Jack and hugged him. "Oh Jack!" she cried. "You know I'll *always* be your friend!"

Embarrassed by this spontaneous show of affection, Jack quickly disentangled himself. When he saw the hurt expression in Del's eyes, though, he felt ashamed. Suddenly he realized that Del was a very pretty girl. With her high cheekbones and wide-set hazel eyes, glistening now with tears, she looked even prettier than Becky Partridge. "Thank you, Del," he said. "I'll always be your friend too."

"Good!" Del smiled. "Let's go watch baseball practice. Race you!" she declared, sprinting ahead of him around the corner and down East Second Street toward Basilio Park.

* * *

In spite of the devastating impact the 1919 Black Sox scandal had had on fans all across America, in 1922 baseball was still the favorite sport of most Benicia residents. In fact, that year the Benicia Buccaneers had had one of its best seasons on record, winning 18 out of 24 games with a team batting average of .279. So it was not surprising that Jack and Del had difficulty finding a seat in the stands behind the backstop at Basilio Park, even though it was a weekday afternoon and this was only a practice game.

The number of both spectators and players at this event had been significantly increased by the recent lay-off at McClaren's Tannery.

152

Some 300 workers, mostly single young men, now roved the streets of the town in idleness, desperate for something to do that didn't cost money. What better place to work off their boredom and frustration than at a pick-up baseball game?

There were only fourteen regular members of the Benicia Buccaneers' team, but their unofficial volunteer membership had now swelled to thirty-seven. Coach Mario Vitalie had taken advantage of these extra players to mount a full-fledged nine-inning game that would give his boys an excellent opportunity to test their mettle. He hoped he might even discover a few new talented rookies he could persuade to join his team.

During pre-game practice now, Vitalie was particularly interested in one of the laid-off tannery workers from Martinez. Sixteen-year-old Matt Frabizio darted back and forth in left field, effortlessly scooping up hot grounders and gracefully catching long fly balls. Jack knew about this young prodigy because Benicia Primary principal Teresa Frabizio had often sung his praises as her favorite nephew. Even though Frabizio had played in a few pick-up games with workers at the tannery, Vitalie had not noticed his agility as a fielder until now.

"Hey you!" Vitalie called out, pointing at Frabizio. "Come on in an' hit a few." Because Frabizio was tall and skinny, Vitalie doubted the boy's batting would match his fielding skills.

Flashing a broad smile, Frabizio quickly trotted into home plate. Then, crouching into what Vitalie thought was a very awkward stance at the plate, the boy pounded the first pitch deep into center field. He did the same with the next three pitches. Each time the ball went farther, the last one bouncing off the scoreboard marking the center-field boundary of the park.

"You wanna play ball for the Buccaneers, boy?" Vitalie asked.

"Sure!" Frabizio said, flashing another smile.

Immediately, Vitalie ordered all the players off the field. "Everybody in," he shouted, "so's we c'n make teams an' play some *real* baseball."

Eager to watch, Jack and Del headed toward the left-field sideline.

"Jack!" someone called out from a group of people sitting on the grass just beyond the home-team dugout. When Jack looked, he saw his mother's friend Snooky Wells standing in their midst and waving at him. "Come on over here by us," she commanded.

153

As Del and Jack approached, Snooky came forward to greet them. "Jack!" she declared excitedly. "Good t' see y', honey!" Again, Jack found himself clasped in a female embrace. This one was not only embarrassing but also repugnant. Snooky's breath and clothing reeked with the acrid smell of cheap pipe tobacco.

Fortunately, her greeting hug was short-lived. She stepped back quickly and, holding Jack by the shoulders at arms' length, scrutinized him from head to foot. "I hear you got pretty beat up the other day. Don't look so bad to me." Then, glancing suspiciously at Del, she asked, "Who's this?"

"This is my friend, Del Lanham."

"Oh yeah! The Judge's daughter!" Then, with a shrug, she said, "Who cares? I ain't scared o' no judges. Both o' y's, come on over an' meet my friends." At this, she grabbed Del and Jack's hands and guided them to a chattering cluster of men, women and children who looked as if they had just arrived on a packet-boat from Eastern Europe.

Most of the women were wearing babushkas and ankle-length dresses made of faded calico or gingham. Their shoes were wooden togs lashed to their naked ankles with criss-cross leather bindings. Several of the men and children were bare-foot. Their attire consisted of twilled cotton trousers and tattered sleeveless shirts.

"Hey, Sabina!" Snooky called out to an enormously fat woman sitting on a stool in the middle of this noisy group. "Lookey here what I found! Couple o' lost waifs from the West Side," Snooky chuckled. Putting her arms around Jack and Del's shoulders, she urged them forward. "Del an' Jack," she announced with mock formality, "meet Sabina Keet, Queen o' the Gypsies!"

The chattering among the gypsies stopped instantly. All eyes focused on Jack and Del, and the Queen glared at the newcomers as if they had just interrupted a very confidential conversation. At the same time, a pixie-faced man who had been crouching beside the Queen slowly rose to his full six-and-a-half foot height. "Howdy," he drawled. Though he seemed to be addressing Jack and Del, the man's colorless eyes were unfocused—almost as if he were in some kind of trance.

Instantly, Del felt the impulse to run away. But then she noticed Snooky's crippled son Alfie in their midst, smiling and nodding at her in welcome reassurance. "Hi," she said to him softly.

As if prompted by Del's friendly greeting, the Gypsy Queen handed a large paper bag to her tall attendant. "Belcher, give the children some kettle corn," she commanded.

When the stoop-shouldered Belcher advanced toward them with the bag, his loose-fitting jacket opened to reveal a wicked-looking dagger hanging in a sheath from his belt.

Terrified, Del stepped back. "N ... no thank you, sir."

Belcher shrugged indifferently and returned to his crouching position beside the Queen, who now looked even angrier than before. Queen Sabina was obviously not accustomed to anyone's rebuffing her generosity.

Sensing both Jack and Del's anxiety, Snooky sat down on the grass next to Alfie's wheelchair and, patting the ground in front of her, urged them to join her. "Come on, you two. Make y'rself comfy. We got a game t' watch."

1923

The *Contra Costa* train ferry

CHAPTER TWELVE

"Yes, We Have No Bananas"

"**G**ET UP!" ADAM ORDERED, SHAKING Jack out of a deep sleep. When he opened his eyes, all Jack could see was the flickering light of the coal fire in Adam's pot-bellied stove. All he could hear was the steady patter of rainfall on the tin roof overhead.

"What's wrong?" Jack asked, remembering now that it was Sunday morning and that Adam usually allowed both Jack and Billy to sleep late on Sundays.

"Ain't nothin' wrong," Adam said. "We's goin' fishin'."

"Going fishing? In the rain?" Jack groaned and rolled over on his cot. "I don't want to."

"It don't make no diff'rence what you wants, boy. We's goin' fishin'. Get on up now." Then, calling out in the darkness, Adam barked, "You too, Billy!"

A few minutes later, the three of them were jammed together in the front seat of Adam's truck, headed toward the quays along the Napa River. It was 4:30 AM and still pitch dark outside. The only light came from the truck's headlamps.

Glancing sidelong, Jack saw the outlines of Adam's face. The man's features were set in an expression of grim determination. Wherever they were going, it was clear Adam would tolerate no resistance from him or Billy.

Suddenly, the truck stopped in front of a three-foot high concrete wall. Shutting off the truck's headlights and engine, Adam got out and began unloading the back of his truck.

"Billy, you rig up," Adam ordered as he gave Billy a large spool of heavy fishing line and a small knapsack. Then, handing a tin box to Jack, he said, "You bring the bait." Quickly lighting a kerosene lantern, Adam shouldered two large knapsacks and moved toward a wooden gate in the concrete wall. Opening it, he passed through and led the way down a steep flight of concrete steps to a rickety wooden dock.

Tied to the pilings on this dock was a white-hulled longboat, similar to the one Rosario used to transport railroad workers between Benicia and Port Costa. This one, Jack noted, had no canopy or gasoline motor. Adam set his lantern down on the dock and threw his knapsacks into the boat. Then, stepping down into the boat, he lashed the kerosene lantern to a stanchion in its stern. "Gimme that bait box, Jack," he commanded. "You boys row."

Still groggy, Billy and Jack sat down on opposite sides of the longboat and grabbed their oars while Adam released the boat from its moorings. As they drifted away from the dock, Jack had difficulty with his starboard-side oar because it was much longer and heavier than the ones he had used in smaller boats. By watching Billy's sure and easy movements beside him, though, he quickly caught the rhythm. Soon they were moving swiftly and easily with the current in the center of the Napa River.

For a long time, the only sound was that of their oars splashing in the water. Jack felt grateful the rain had stopped, even though a cold morning breeze was now blowing directly in his face. He was also grateful that Adam had insisted he wear long johns and two heavy sweaters under his Army poncho as well as a pair of rubber boots and woolen gloves.

Suddenly they heard voices several yards ahead.

"Oars in!" Adam ordered. As Billy and Jack swung the blades of their oars forward and into the boat, a loud splash told them Adam had dropped the anchor.

Off to his right, Jack saw two other longboats riding at anchor. Each of these had its own lantern, its occupants already drifting their fishing lines. "Good morning, Adam!" one of the men from the other boats called out.

"Mo'nin', Harry," Adam replied. "Catchin' any?"

"Catch one bass. No sturgeon. We wait long time. They come," the man in the other boat announced, his clipped syntax signaling to Jack that the speaker was probably Asian.

Billy handed one of the long bamboo poles to Jack, keeping hold of the end-tackle while Jack moved the tip of his pole out over the water. "Ready?" Billy asked.

"I think so," Jack answered. He heard the heavy weight and long-shanked hook laden with mud-shrimp drop into the water.

"Jus' strip her out slow," Billy said. "Let her drift 'til she hits bottom. Then, set yer drag. But not too tight," Billy warned.

Jack had fished these waters before, but never for sturgeon and never with mud-shrimp. They were nasty, sticky things that easily broke apart when you tried to bait your hook. He was grateful that Billy had rigged his line for him.

A full hour passed with no sign of fish. The gray light of dawn was now beginning to define the outline of the high hills on either side of the entrance to Carquinez Strait, and the cold morning air was beginning to make Jack's fingers ache. "How long are we gonna sit here like this?" Jack asked.

"Long as she takes," was Adam's cryptic reply. "You hungry, boy?"

"A little," Jack said. "But mostly I'm cold."

Adam reached deep into one of his knapsacks and pulled out a ceramic jug. Uncorking it, he handed it to Jack. Steam poured from the open mouth of the jug as Jack brought it to his lips and his nostrils filled with the acrid smell of hot brandy. "You want me to drink this?" Jack asked, amazed that Adam was offering him hard liquor.

"You wanna get warm, drink it. Jus' a li'le bit, though. That stuff 'll knock y' flat!"

Carefully, Jack tilted the jug and sipped the hot liquor. Just at that moment, Billy yelped. "Got one!"

Jack almost dropped the jug as he turned to look at Billy standing up in the bow of their boat. Billy's rod was bent in a tight arc, its tip almost touching the surface of the water. Billy dropped to one knee, bracing the other against the gunnel to keep himself from being pulled overboard.

"Reel in! Reel in, Jack!" Adam shouted as he himself quickly retrieved his own line to avoid entangling it with Billy's.

At the same time the men in the closest boat shouted excitedly to each other in Chinese and also began reeling in their lines. They knew the movements of a big sturgeon were unpredictable. They also knew that, if Billy made his catch, he would share it with all of the boats in the fleet. Among the Chinese, sharing the catch was unwritten law.

There was now enough light in the sky so that Jack could see all this activity clearly. He watched, fascinated, as Billy's rod continued to follow the zigzag movement of his line in the water.

Suddenly, the zigzagging stopped, though Billy's line was still taught. "Let it out! Let it out!" Adam shouted. "He gonna run!"

Billy immediately released the drag on his reel and dropped his rod tip parallel to the surface of the water. Almost as if the fish itself had heard Adam's warning, Billy's line moved like a bullet away from their boat, his reel screaming with the speed and force of the sturgeon's attempt to escape. Jack felt sure the fleeing fish would quickly run Billy's line to its limit.

But no. As suddenly as it had rushed away, the fish reversed direction and came charging back toward Adam's boat. Billy cranked furiously on his reel to keep tension on the line.

"Get the gaff!" Adam shouted at Jack.

Quickly, Jack retrieved the metal pole with its curved and sharply pointed tip from where it had been stowed under the port gunwale. Handing it to Adam, he sat down to watch as Billy continued to struggle for control of his line. Whatever monster was at the other end of that line was still determined to escape. For again the line shot away from the boat, and again Billy had to release his drag.

This back-and-forth battle between man and fish continued for another thirty minutes. Suddenly, in a last desperate attempt to break away, an enormous snake-like form exploded out of the water several feet into the air and fell back with a loud splash. Slowly—almost reverently—Billy reeled in his catch and brought the still flailing sturgeon close to the boat.

Moving swiftly, Adam raised the gaff high over his head and brought it down with all his force on the broad flank of Billy's fish. The huge creature writhed franticly for several seconds but at last seemed to give up.

"Careful now!" Adam warned. "He ain' done with us yet. Jack, you take Billy's pole. Billy, get the lasso."

Jack had never heard of anyone lassoing a fish before. But, as he gazed in awe at the huge creature beside their longboat—it was at least six feet long—he realized several lassoes and several strong men might be needed to bring this monster into their boat. It was at this point that he heard the sound of oars creaking and splashing. The other two longboats were moving in to assist them.

* * *

The red disk of the sun had already dropped below the jagged skyline of the Mare Island Shipyard. Its many warehouses and machine shops loomed black against the glowing horizon, the long necks of its heavy cranes rising like prehistoric monsters to protest the approach of darkness.

Jack sat exhausted on the top step of the concrete steps while Adam, Billy and eight other fishermen cleaned the day's catch, which included thirty-seven striped bass and six large sturgeon. The men were very excited, their constant chatter in English and Chinese often punctuated with laughter.

After measuring and weighing each fish, they divided up the catch into three equal parts—one for each boat. Then, washing their hands and arms in buckets of river water, they sat down on the steps and passed around several earthenware jugs of brandy. Some of the fisherman lighted up cigarettes and corncob pipes.

Jack hoped this victory celebration would be short-lived. He yearned to get back to his Army cot and the warmth of Adam's coal-burning stove. Oblivious to Jack's wants, Adam and Billy were totally absorbed in their conversation with the Chinese fishermen.

"Hey, boy!" one of the Chinaman sitting next to Adam suddenly called up to Jack. "You want learn sail big boat?"

Startled that he was suddenly the focus of everyone's attention, Jack didn't know what to say. He had no idea why he was being asked this question.

"Sho he do," Adam declared with a broad grin. "Come on down here, boy."

Wearily, Jack rose to his feet and descended the concrete stairs. Adam patted an open space on the step to his right. "Sit down, boy.

This here's Harry Lee," Adam announced, nodding to the smooth-faced young man on his left.

Harry eagerly stood up and pumped Jack's hand. "Velly happy to meet you!" he declared.

Jack tried to smile, but he felt so tired the effort seemed futile.

Adam grabbed Jack's wrist and pulled him down on the step. "Guess you plumb wore out, ain't you, boy?" Then, putting his arm around Jack's shoulders, Adam gave him a manly hug. "Da's awright. You a good boy!"

"Velly good boy!" Harry echoed, squatting in front of Jack and studying his face with an intense but friendly gaze. "You come with me. I show you how sail, yes?"

Still puzzled, Jack looked at Adam. "You want me to learn to sail?" he asked.

Adam nodded. "Sho' do. I gots a new job f' you. Only you gots t' learn t' sail a junk t' do it."

"What kind of job?" Jack could barely keep his eyes open, but he was determined to seem alert.

Adam exchanged a knowing glance with Harry, but neither of them spoke for several seconds. At last, Adam said, "Le's see how fas' you learns, fus'. If you catches on fas', then I'll tell y'."

Ordinarily, Jack would have challenged such an ambiguous reply—even from Adam. Right now, though, he was too tired. "Alright," he said.

Fifteen minutes later, Jack was sound asleep, his head resting on Billy's shoulder as Adam drove them back to the shack.

* * *

The offices of Feldman, Jacoby and Stern Associates were located on the top floor of the ten-story Diablo Towers. In 1923, the Diablo Towers was one of the tallest buildings in Concord, California. Despite the prestige of this address, the space occupied by this highly successful accounting firm was modest, almost austere, in its décor. As might be expected, the partners were more concerned with minimizing their overhead costs than with impressing their clients.

Arthur Jacoby looked up startled when he heard Bernie Roach's shrill voice in the hallway outside his office. He had seen but not formally met this woman before on only one occasion—during the Presidential election of 1920 when her father had first engaged Jacoby's firm to handle the accounts of the Contra Costa County Republican Party. "She's trouble for us," his senior partner Larry Feldman had warned, "a shiksa with a big mouth!"

"Hey Art, how y' doin'?" Soames cheerfully declared as he marched into Jacoby's office and promptly sat down on the only other chair in the room.

Lifting his green eyeshade, Jacoby looked up at his client and smiled nervously. "I'm here. I'm working. So who's to complain?"

"Got a new customer for y'," Soames announced. Then, calling out toward the open doorway, he added, "Hey, Bernie! Come on in here an' meet my boy Art Jacoby."

Now almost seventy years old, Arthur did not appreciate being called a boy. Still, Soames was one of his best clients, so he tolerated the man's insolence with professional stoicism.

Dressed in a full-length mink coat and incongruous moleskin cap, Bernie bounded into the room followed by her bodyguard Guido Perelli. "Yeah, so?" she asked, eyeing Jacoby suspiciously.

Slowly and painfully, Arthur rose to his feet as the dreaded woman approached his desk and stuck out her hand toward him in a contemptuously manly gesture. "Please t' meet y', I guess," she sneered.

Arthur nodded. "Likewise. You wanna sit down, I gotta get another chair." Jacoby tilted slightly as if he were himself about to attend to this polite detail.

"Forget it, old man. I ain't no hothouse flower!"

Soames chuckled, leaned back in his chair and crossed his legs. "Sit down, Art. This won't take long. Bernie's got a job for y'." Soames nodded to Bernie, "Go ahead and give him your stuff."

Bernie lifted the Gladstone bag she had been carrying and placed it on Arthur's desk. Opening the bag and reaching inside, she extracted a cloth-bound ledger and dropped it directly on top of the accounting sheets Arthur had been working on before Soames arrived. "Here," she said. "I need you to check my numbers—make sure everythin's legit. Know what I mean?"

"I'm not a lawyer, Miss," Arthur observed. "I'm an accountant. I'll be happy to review your accounts and rectify any errors. But, if you need legal counsel, ..."

"Yeah—whatever!" Bernie snarled. "Just do it. I need it by 4:00 tomorrow afternoon." Having said this, she turned to go.

"Wait a minute," Arthur said fearfully. "How do I do I notify you?"

Bernie was already out in the hallway again. Without turning around, she said, "I'll call you. Just remember—4:00 o'clock tomorrow. At the latest!"

Arthur gazed in silent bewilderment at Soames as they heard Bernie and Perelli's footsteps clattering down the hallway toward the elevator. "What's this all about?" Arthur asked.

Soames chuckled again and lit a cigarette. "Don't worry about it, Art. It's just a small operation she's running—you know." Soames winked at Jacoby through a thick cloud of smoke.

"You mean bootlegging, I suppose," Arthur said bleakly.

"Like I said, Art," Soames replied, serious now, "it's just a small-time operation."

"Does her father know about this?"

Soames studied the lighted end of his cigarette for a moment. "Probably, though he'd never admit it. For Pete's sake, Art—you know the drill!"

"You I know. Her I don't. Larry says she's bad news."

Growing visibly annoyed now, Soames leaned forward and glared at Arthur. "Look at it this way, Art. You're doin' me a personal favor. Alright?"

"Very well. But I don't want any trouble."

Standing up, Soames was smiling again. "Don't worry. You'll be paid very well."

Arthur wanted to say getting paid was not what worried him, but he decided to keep silent—at least, in any further dialogue with Soames. He would discuss the matter in confidence with his partners.

"Oh, one other thing," Soames said as he stepped on the lighted cigarette he had dropped on Arthur's otherwise impeccably clean and shiny hardwood office floor. "You could be getting a call from a new guy I'm doin' some business with. Name's Emmett Spears."

"What's that about?"

Soames shook his head contemptuously. "You always gotta ask questions! Haven't you figured it out yet, Art? Askin' too many questions ain't healthy." Again Soames paused momentarily, studying the older man for some reaction.

Arthur was implacable. "It's business. You don't ask questions, you don't get answers."

Again, the secretive smile. "The guy just wants t' check me out—make sure I pay my bills. Alright?"

"I suppose," Arthur replied softly.

Stepping close to him, Soames patted him on the back. "Atta boy!" he said. Take it easy, Art."

As soon as Soames left the office, Arthur opened the ledger Bernie had dropped on his desk and began perusing its various entries. After only a few minutes, he picked up his candle phone receiver and called his senior partner. "I think we got a problem, Larry."

"What kind o' problem?" Larry asked irritably.

"A big one. It's about that Roach woman and some new client named Emmett Spears. I think we better talk about it in your office."

Larry sighed wearily. "Oh, alright. Come on over."

Arthur and Larry had known each other for more than twenty years, ever since they had first met while working for the Niles Canyon Railroad—a company that had long since gone out of business. Though their personalities and temperaments were radically different, they trusted each other implicitly.

Entering Larry's office, Arthur closed the door behind him and, without saying a word, handed Bernie's ledger to his partner. Then, he sat down and waited in silence while Larry skimmed several pages of Bernie's entries. Larry quickly came to an identical conclusion. Closing the ledger, he looked up angrily. "Woman's a complete idiot!"

"Yeah, but that ain't the only problem. Soames wants us t' meet with some guy named Emmet Spears."

Larry frowned and shook his head. "Not good. He's a high mucky-muck with the Knights Templar! You know what they are, don't y'?"

Arthur's face turned white with fear. "The Klan!"

Larry nodded and picked up his phone. "We gotta tell David."

* * *

167

Harry Lee's twenty-eight foot "junk" rigged sailboat was tied up at the same dock where Adam had tied his longboat when they went sturgeon fishing a week before. It was a wide, shallow-hulled boat with a high stern and rigging that consisted of two short masts rigged with numerous downhauls and sheets. Jack had never seen such a clumsy looking sailing vessel.

"Why do you want me to do this?" he had asked Adam.

"'Cause I gotta get my sugar 'cross the Strait. Don't you be askin' too many questions, boy. Less you knows 'bout this, the better." That was the extent of Adam's explanation, except for his statement that, for each trip across the Carquinez Strait, Jack would be paid twenty dollars.

Jack had known for some time that Adam supplemented his income from vehicle repairs with another type of business. He had not known exactly what that business involved, only that it was always conducted two times a week and late at night. He had heard rumors in Huey's barbershop that Adam was somehow involved with bootlegging. For forty dollars a week, Jack didn't care.

"You ready go, Jack?" Harry asked as he held out his hand to help Jack aboard.

"Sure." Ignoring Harry's offer of assistance, Jack nimbly jumped into the boat.

Swiftly moving to the stern, Harry grabbed the long wooden tiller and waved for Jack to untie the bowline from the dock. The strong current of the Napa River quickly drew the junk out into the main channel. Pointing his craft due East, Harry leaned forward and yanked on the downhaul of the forward sail. Quickly, the big square of batten-ribbed canvas rose and caught the gentle morning breeze. "You come sit here," Harry called out to Jack, pointing to a hatch directly behind the center mast.

They sailed in silence for several minutes, Jack wondering what he would be asked to do next. There had been no pre-embarkation instructions on how to operate this bulky craft. Apparently Harry believed in learn-as-you-sail training. As he surveyed the boat's many different lines, pulleys, and capstans, Jack realized Harry's method was probably best. Never before had Jack seen such complicated rigging.

They were approaching the mouth of the Napa River where it flows into San Pablo Bay when Harry gave his first command. "You take blue downhaul. Pull up sail and tie to capstan." Suddenly Jack noticed that every one of the downhaul and sheet lines had been painted a different color. The paint looked fresh, as if Harry had just recently marked them expressly for Jack's benefit.

As soon as he raised and secured the mizzen sail, the junk gained momentum. Glancing astern, Jack saw that Harry was grinning. "You learn fas'," he said. "Make much money!"

"What's the name of your boat?" Jack asked.

"*Dragon Queen*," Harry answered proudly. "Velly safe. Velly easy sail. You watch. You listen." As he spoke, Harry shifted his tiller hard to port. "Come about!" he shouted.

Jack ducked, knowing that both sail booms would instantly swing inboard.

"Tighten green and blue!" Harry ordered. Again, Jack swiftly executed this command and felt the *Dragon Queen*'s wide hull heel over—but only slightly—as she tacked closer to the wind. Clearly the *Dragon Queen* was much more stable than Del's *Sweet Harmony*.

They were moving swiftly now as Harry guided his boat out of the Napa River estuary. Once there were several hundred yards of open water between the *Dragon Queen* and both shores of San Pablo Bay, Harry signaled Jack to take the helm.

Harry sat beside Jack in the stern. "*Dragon Queen* got many line. You not worry 'bout tiller. Fix line firs'." He studied Jack's face intently for several seconds. Then, smiling, he said, "I go forward now. Wind change, you say port, starboard. Yes?"

Jack nodded, his eyes fixed on the two sails above. He felt Harry touch him lightly on the shoulder, and then he was gone. Jack was now in command of the *Dragon Queen*!

But Jack's lessons were just beginning. A twenty-eight foot junk responds much differently from a twelve-foot catboat. He felt the boat's weight and sluggishness even now as he nudged the *Dragon Queen* into a close reach for greater speed. Noting that the edge of the forward sail was beginning to luff, he leaned forward to loosen the blue sheet.

"No! No! Green sheet!" Harry shouted at him.

As soon as he restored the blue downhaul to its original tautness and released the green sheet, he felt the boat surge forward. *How will I ever get this?* Jack wondered.

Harry waved at him cheerfully from the bow. "You good sailorboy, Jack!"

Jack waved back. Though he didn't care for the *Dragon Queen*, he definitely liked Harry.

*   *   *

"Papa! We're going to the Claremont? Oh! That's wonderful!" Del exclaimed when her father told her the news. Though she had never been there, Del had often heard from her friends at school about how luxurious the Claremont spa resort was and she had seen photographs in several newspapers and magazines that showed the magnificent white ramparts of this castle-like edifice built high in the East Bay hills overlooking San Francisco Bay.

"I have reserved a suite of rooms for the weekend, and your Uncle Charles and Aunt Lucy will be staying with us so we can all celebrate your birthday."

"Ruby too?" Del asked.

"Ah …" The Judge hesitated. "I do not think so, Adelaide. I'm afraid they do not allow Negroes at the Claremont. But you may be sure you will have plenty of maids to attend to your needs—and your Aunt Lucy, of course."

"I think that's very unfair, Papa. I want Ruby to come too."

"Out of the question," the Judge said firmly. "However, I do want Ruby to go with you to the city tomorrow. You need shop for new attire that is suitable for a young lady. I have booked tickets for you on *The General* for 10:00 AM."

"We're going to San Francisco by train?" Del asked breathlessly. Only once before had she traveled to the celebrated City on the Bay, and that had been when she was only five-years-old. She remembered little of the experience now except the long and tedious journey on the ferry from Vallejo and back.

Her father nodded. "Missus Woolsey and her daughters will also be accompanying you. I want to be sure your choice of clothing is in the best of taste."

"You mean that snooty Colleen will be going with us? Oh, Papa! How could you!"

"Adelaide," her father somberly declared, "I will not allow you to say such things! Colleen Woolsey is a perfectly delightful young woman."

Del decided then and there that her father was a very poor judge of women. But she knew better than to voice that opinion. She would simply have to put up with Colleen Woolsey and her meddlesome mother as best as she could.

CHAPTER THIRTEEN

"The Sheik"

IT WAS RAINING HARD THE following morning as Del and her traveling companions waited on the covered platform at the Benicia Depot. Colleen was being her usual standoffish self, and Mrs. Woolsey prattled incessantly about the many discomforts of traveling by train that she had experienced on her own past trips to Oakland. *The Woolseys*, Del ruminated, *are so provincial!*

Del loved that word *provincial*. She had only recently discovered it while reading an article in *McClure's Magazine*, a publication her father subscribed to on the recommendation of Del's Aunt Lucy.

"You *do* have enough money to buy things, I hope," Dolores Woolsey asked doubtfully. Being the wife of a penurious banker, Dolores supposed that Judge Lanham, too, counted every penny.

"Papa has accounts at all the big stores," Del answered sweetly. "You don't need to worry."

Dolores nodded with tight-lipped approval. "We have several accounts ourselves, of course," she affirmed. She was certainly not going to allow a thirteen-year-old girl to think the Woolseys were any less prepared for this shopping expedition than the Lanhams. "George does not like to charge things. He prefers to pay cash for every purchase," she added righteously.

Suddenly all conversation was stopped by the hooting whistle of *The General* as it rounded the bend from Suisun Bay toward the Benicia Depot. At almost the same moment, another loud whistle from the opposite direction announced the approach of the giant *Solano* train ferry, which was maneuvering into position to dock at the First Street ferry terminal. Train yard workers in knee-top rubber boots and black "slickers" scurried back and forth across the tracks in preparation for the *General*'s arrival. Two switch engines stood hissing steam on side-tracks parallel to the main line.

Del and her friend Maggie clasped hands and squealed with delight at all this activity and excitement. "Have you ever taken the train before?" Maggie asked.

"I've taken the train to Sacramento with Papa several times, but never to San Francisco," Del answered. "We always took the ferry from Vallejo," she added, being careful not to say she herself had made that journey only once.

"The train doesn't go to San Francisco, silly!" Colleen said archly. "It only goes to Oakland. From there you have to take a ferry to San Francisco."

"I know that!" Del snapped back. "I only meant I never went to San Francisco by train before."

"Well then, why didn't you say to Oakland?" Maggie asked.

Del waved her arms in exasperation. "Oh, for Heaven's sake, Maggie!"

Again, the arriving train sounded its whistle—much closer this time. Looking down the track to the East, Del saw the giant steam locomotive emerge from behind the buildings of the Alta Manufacturing Company. It steadily made its way toward them, its big brass bell clanging repeatedly, puffs of white smoke shooting up from its boiler exhaust pipe. Dell shuddered as this steel-faced monster loomed larger in its relentless approach toward her, its single illuminated headlamp like the burning eye of a Cyclops.

Once it had passed, though, her fear turned into curiosity—first about what was inside the two long and windowless mail cars following the coal car, and then about the people in the passenger cars, several of whom were staring back at her. With a loud squeal, the train pulled to a stop. Almost immediately passengers began to get off. Those with umbrellas waited in the rain for their luggage to be unloaded; those without, rushed to find shelter inside the train depot.

"Come along now, girls!" Mrs. Wolsey declared impatiently. "We don't want to be the last ones on board." Opening her large black umbrella, she almost poked out the eye of another pedestrian standing beside her.

"Gee whiz, lady!" the man yelped. "Why don't y' wait 'til y're out in the rain b'fore you open that thing?"

In haughty response, Dolores simply raised her chin and looked away.

Ruby slipped her arm in Del's, gently coaxing her to let Dolores and her daughters go on ahead. "We got lots o' time yet. Dat train ain' goin' nowhere 'til them that's on gets off an' them that's goin' gets on."

Having watched the train ferry loading process with Jack many times in the past, Del knew Ruby was right. Besides, she was so irritated with Maggie she almost hoped she and Ruby would be separated from the Woolseys throughout the entire trip to Oakland.

But it was not to be, for Dolores and her daughters had already pushed and shoved their way onto the vestibule platform of one of the coach cars and Dolores was now frantically waving at Del to do likewise.

"Miss," said a Negro porter who suddenly appeared beside Del, "dat lady ast me t' he'p you aboard." Apparently in her zeal to keep everyone together, Dolores had tipped the porter and sent him on a mission to recover the rest of her party.

"Oh for Heaven's sake!" Del declared again. Then, turning to Ruby, she said, "Come on. I suppose we have to go."

The porter, who was carrying Dolores's umbrella, opened it as soon as they emerged from the covered waiting platform and held it over Del and Ruby while they made their way to the coach car.

"Thank you, sir," Del said to the porter as he helped Ruby and her up the steps.

Startled by this expression of gratitude from a white girl, the porter smiled broadly. "You is mos' welcome, Miss!"

Dolores showed no such gratitude, irritably snatching her umbrella when the porter handed it to her and seizing Del's wrist, she declared, "Hurry along now. Colleen and Maggie are saving our seats."

Colleen and Maggie had already laid claim to three rows of seats, two of which had been reconfigured to accommodate four passengers facing each other. Colleen sat guarding the foursome and Maggie sat guarding the third row for two.

"Maggie and Del, you come up here and sit with us," Dolores said as she sat down beside Colleen in the foursome. "Ruby, you can sit back there."

"I'll sit here, if you don't mind," Del announced as she slipped into the twosome seat. Then, turning to Ruby, she asked, "Do you mind if I sit next to the window, Ruby?"

"'Course not, honey. You go ahead an' sit wh'evah you wants," Ruby replied with a sly smile. It was clear to both of them Dolores wanted to distance her daughters and herself as far as possible from Del's Negro traveling companion.

Though she was angered by Dolores' racial prejudice, Del was not surprised. As her father had explained to her on numerous occasions, "Some people in California are still fighting the Civil War on the losing side."

Del focused all of her attention now on the activity in the train yard. Things looked so different from inside the train. How she wished Jack could be with her to experience the thrill of this new perspective!

First of all, there was the exhilarating feeling just of being a passenger rather than a spectator—a special person on the inside of this magnificent transportation machine, attended by scores of train yard workers and catered to by dozens of porters and conductors. *What a sense of prestige and power!* she almost said aloud. Then, there were all the purely physical sensations of movement beyond your own control—of the sudden jolt as one of the switch engines coupled with the cars behind you, of the surprise at seeing the elaborate steel superstructure of the *Solano* passing majestically overhead while your part of the train was pushed onto this vessel's enormous deck.

As Del had anticipated, it was another twenty minutes before all of the passenger cars had been loaded aboard the *Solano* and she felt the vibration of the ferry's powerful engines rumbling beneath her. She was somewhat disappointed to discover her section of the train had been loaded onto one of the two inside tracks, for that meant she would not be able to see anything as the *Solano* made its passage across the Carquinez Strait to Port Costa.

But the long scenic ride down the eastern coastlines of San Pablo and San Francisco Bays more than compensated for this initial disappointment. Del relished every moment of this part of their journey, soothed by the rhythmic rocking of the coach car as it rolled along the tracks, fascinated by the broad expanse of water that seemed to stretch forever under the overcast sky, and hungrily devouring every architectural detail of the communities through which they passed— each one larger and more populous the closer they drew to their final destination. How different this journey seemed from the ferry ride she had taken with her father eight years before!

Not once did Dolores or her daughters look out of the train windows, however. They were too preoccupied with their own chatter about the latest fashion displays in two mail-order catalogs they had brought with them. Seated beside Del, Ruby had quickly dozed off and was softly snoring.

Everyone stood up with excitement, though, when the train pulled into the Oakland terminal. Del had never before seen such a busy place. There were hundreds of people on the station platform, all rushing in different directions. "This way, girls!" Dolores commanded as they stepped off the train and turned to the left. Several yards ahead, Del saw a large green sign with white letters announcing, "To San Francisco Ferry." Eagerly, she ran toward this sign.

"Wait for us!" Dolores cried out sharply. "You might get lost"

Del ignored this warning, forcing the others to hurry after her.

* * *

By the time they arrived at the San Francisco Ferry Terminal just before noon, it had stopped raining. A pale sun was visible through the thick cloud cover over the city. "Maybe we can have a picnic in Union Square after all," Maggie said hopefully.

"Don't be silly!" Colleen scorned. "The benches will all be soaking wet."

"It doesn't matter," Dolores asserted. "We shall have lunch in the Galleria Tearoom."

Del was delighted by such an idea. For the Galleria Tearoom at the Emporium department store in San Francisco was one of the most elegant restaurants in the city. Del had often heard her father say so, though she had never been there herself. She worried, though, that Ruby might not be allowed to dine with them.

Dolores flagged a taxicab on the Embarcadero in front of the Ferry

Terminal. Climbing into the back of the cab, she and her daughters promptly claimed the large forward-facing passenger seat while Ruby and Del occupied the two small fold-down seats facing to the rear. "

As their cab moved slowly up Post Street toward Union Square, Dolores and her daughters continued to discuss what each of them hoped to purchase that day. Del and Ruby rode in silence, focusing their attention on the fascinating panoply of Post Street. Men in black bowler hats and matching three-piece suits rushed swiftly past elegantly attired ladies without so much as a single admiring glance. Burly workmen in overhauls wrestled huge wooden crates and barrels from the back of double-parked delivery trucks, and a policeman on every corner frantically gesticulated to keep the traffic moving.

At the entrance to the Emporium, a uniformed doorman sprang forward and, with much fanfare, ushered their party through the highly polished brass-framed glass entrance doors. The ground floor of this legendary department store was larger than several football fields, filled with clusters of glassed-in display cases and ornate maple wood counters, each cluster offering a different category of merchandise—everything from hats, handbags, and gloves to perfume and jewelry. White marble columns rose two stories on all four sides, forming a rectangular atrium that revealed five additional floors of open galleries. At the center above these galleries was a magnificent stain-glass dome—the San Francisco Emporium's signature icon. In the center of the main-floor lobby, on a platform stage directly beneath the glass dome, a string trio serenaded the shoppers with lively tunes from Victor Herbert operettas.

While they stood surveying this vast indoor marketplace, a beautiful young woman attired in a rhinestone tiara and long white evening gown greeted them with a radiant smile. "Welcome to the Emporium, ladies! I'm Winter," she introduced herself in a voice that was as warm and inviting as summer sunshine. Holding out a tray filled with small white sachet packets tied with sparkling silver ribbons, she warbled sweetly, "Please take one of our favors."

"Thank you, my dear," Dolores said to the young woman. Then to Del and her daughters she said, "Go ahead, girls, help yourselves."

Colleen and Maggie promptly did so. Del, noting that the lovely white Winter lady had looked askance at Ruby, took two of the favors and gave one to Ruby.

"We have a special waiting room for your servant, Madame," Winter explained coolly to Dolores. She gestured toward an area near the entrance that had been enclosed by ornate Japanese screens. "It's over there to the right behind those screens. When you've finished shopping, just let our concierge know and he will summon her for you."

"Why can't she come with us?" Del asked.

Winter fixed Del with a very unfriendly stare. "I'm, afraid it's against store policy, Miss."

Leaning close to Del, Ruby whispered in her ear, "It don't matter, honey," and humbly walked toward the servants' waiting area.

"This is ridiculous!" Del declared. But Winter had moved on with her tray of favors, and Dolores and her daughters were already walking toward the millinery department."

* * *

With the 1921 release of Rudolph Valentino's wildly popular silent film *The Sheik*, Arabic merchandise had become all the rage in women's fashion magazines like *Vogue* and *Harper's Bazaar*. Women's hats especially reflected the influence of Hollywood's romanticized Middle East. Prominently displayed in the millinery department were dazzlingly bejeweled tiaras and cloches designed to shroud the face in shadow and mystery. Also displayed, however, were many of the broad-brimmed hats and arm-length gloves of the pre-war era. The Emporium always catered to a wide range of tastes.

Still being very much a tomboy, Del had little interest in such niceties of women's fashion. So she watched with much amusement now as Colleen and her mother tried on several of the latest millinery designs. One of these was a pea-green pillbox hat topped with a decorative felt extension that looked suspiciously like a Coptic cross. As Colleen struggled in front of a face mirror to fit this item properly on her head, Del couldn't resist a comment. "I bet Father Cardoni would like that one!"

All of them giggled at this, including the female clerk behind the counter. Del suddenly realized how much fun the company of women could be—even snooty ones like Colleen. She only wished that her Aunt Lucy and Ruby could be with them as well.

Aware that these customers were not seriously interested in the latest hat fashions, the store clerk suggested an alternative. "Perhaps you ladies would like to visit our cosmetics department. We're offering free facials today."

"Oh yes!" Colleen exclaimed. "Let's do that!"

"Let's have lunch first," Maggie said. "I'm hungry, Momma."

"Well, yes. It *is* almost one o'clock. I'm a little hungry myself, and they do have such delicious salads here at the Galleria."

"All you think about is food!" Colleen protested to her younger sister.

"Come along, girls!" Dolores had made up her mind and was already leading the way to the bank of elevators at the back of the store.

* * *

The Galleria was on the second floor. Several other hungry shoppers were already queued up in front of the hostess' desk, and it looked as if most of the tables were occupied. The din of high-pitched women's voices everywhere, Del thought, was almost deafening.

"We'll never get a table!" Colleen protested. "Let's go back downstairs to the cosmetic counter and come up here later."

"I'm hungry!" Maggie insisted.

"I'll find out how long we'll have to wait," Dolores announced and marched to the head of the line at the reservations desk. Del watched, amused, as Delores cajoled with the tall and very attractive young woman who was restaurant hostess. At length, Dolores returned to say, "It will be just a few minutes wait."

Colleen made a face to signal her disappointment. Her silent protest did not last long, for the hostess kept her promise and soon seated them at a table close to the scrolled iron railing defining the outer perimeter of the mezzanine restaurant. "Thank you, Miss," Dolores smiled at the hostess. "This is perfect."

Indeed it was, Del thought as she looked out across the broad expanse of the open atrium filled now with the lilting strains of the theme song from *Student Prince* and the constant hum of shoppers milling in the lobby below. A dapper *maitre d'hotel* presented each of them with a folio sized menu ornately decorated with a gold-leaf border and filled with lists of salads, sandwiches, and hot entrees that made

Del's mouth water. "I know exactly what I want," she announced before the waiter appeared to take their order.

"And what is that, my dear?" Dolores asked solicitously.

"The chicken marsala."

"Oh yes!" Dolores agreed. "That does sound good. I believe I'll order that too."

"I want a tuna fish sandwich," Maggie announced.

Arching a disdainful eyebrow at her younger sister, Colleen declared that she would have the Crab Louis.

Their orders were promptly taken and served, and the deliciously prepared food quickly softened everyone's mood. The conversation became animated and friendly, focused especially on the most recent motion pictures. "Have you seen *Robin Hood* yet, Del?" Dolores asked.

"No," she replied. "Is it good?"

"Oh, it's wonderful!" Colleen exclaimed. "Momma took us to see it in Martinez last week. You simply *must* see it!. Douglas Fairbanks is so dashing!"

"I think it's dreadful what happened to William Taylor!" Dolores observed, swiftly changing the conversation to her own topic of special interest—the latest Hollywood scandal.

"Who's he?" Maggie asked.

"Only the most famous cinema director in Hollywood," Colleen said deprecatingly.

"Oh yes. I've read about him in *McClure's*. He made *Huckleberry Finn* and *Anne of Green Gables*, didn't he?" Del put in, eyeing Colleen to let her know she was every bit as clever as this pretentious young woman. But then, turning to Dolores, she asked, "What happened to Mister Taylor?"

"He was murdered in his own home. It happened just a month ago. It's been in all of the papers—even the *Benicia Herald New Era*. I'm surprised you and your father haven't read about it."

"My father doesn't read the gossip columns," Del replied defensively. "And he doesn't let me read them either."

"This isn't just gossip" Dolores scolded. "It's a very big case, and your father, being a judge, should certainly know about it."

"Maybe he does but he didn't want to tell me about it," Del said. "He's very protective, you know."

Dolores nodded approvingly. "Well, yes. I suppose that's understandable."

"Did they catch the murderer, Momma?" Maggie asked anxiously.

"Not yet. There are several suspects. There's Mister Taylor's houseman, Edward Sands, who claims he was not on duty the night of the murder. And then there's the actress Mable Norman who, some newspapers say, is having an affair with Sands. But I think it's Mister Taylor's valet, Henry Peavey. He *is* a Negro, after all!"

"What does that have to do with it?" Del demanded angrily. "You're blaming him just because he's a colored person?"

Dolores paused several seconds before she responded icily. "Well, what about that awful man Tucker who kidnapped Jack Westlake? Niggers all are alike, if you ask me!"

Del was so infuriated she almost jumped up from the table and ran to the elevator. "He didn't kidnap Jack!" she declared. "He rescued him when that truly evil man James Soames beat up Jack and forced him to run away from home."

"You don't know that," Dolores insisted.

"I most certainly do! Jack told me all about it himself last spring."

"You haven't seen him since then?" Colleen asked. "I thought you two were best friends," she added laconically.

"We *are* best friends!" Del retorted. "We will *always* be best friends! But, after Mister Tucker was forced to close his garage and Jack gave up his job at Huey's, nobody's seen either of them."

"What about his mother?" Dolores asked. "Surely she has seen her own son."

"I doubt it," Del said. "Jack was pretty mad at his mother, and so was Mister Tucker. Besides, I've heard that Jack's mother is still seeing Soames."

"How do you know that?" Colleen demanded.

Del bit her lip, aware that she was allowing herself to gossip—something both her father and the nuns at Saint Catherine had often told her is sinful. "I don't know really. It's just rumors."

"Disgusting!" Dolores declared, and hers was the last word on the subject.

After lunch, they took an elevator up to the women's clothing department on the fifth floor and found their way to an area filled with open racks of young women's blouses and dresses. Interspersed among these racks were numerous manikins draped in the latest fashions. One of these displaying a black velvet tunic with a white chiffon lining and matching *soutache* instantly caught Colleen's eye. "Momma!" she declared. "This is the one I want."

Dolores made a face. "Oh goodness no! You're much too zaftig for anything like that!"

"What's *zaftig*?" Maggie asked.

Dolores' face reddened. Brushing a hand across her own ample bosom, she explained, "Well, you know. Big at the top."

Both Maggie and Del giggled, only intensifying Dolores' embarrassment. Then, turning to Del, Dolores said, "Now you, my dear, could certainly wear something like this. You have the perfect figure for it.

"Flat-chested!" Colleen sneered.

Del had never heard a conversation like this before, so she was somewhat puzzled. Still, she had to admit the black tunic was very chic. "I think it's a little old for me," she suggested. Then, walking toward another manikin displaying a straight-lined burgundy dress with lace tulle, she touched the fabric and said, "I like this better."

"Flat-chested!" Colleen sneered again. " Flat bottoms and hips too. I hate these new Paris fashions!"

"It's all the rage these days," her mother insisted with a slight twinge of sympathy for her buxom daughter. Then, noticing that Maggie had wandered off out of earshot, Dolores added with a mischievous wink, "I wouldn't worry, Colleen dear. Men still prefer a full-figured woman."

"May I help you, ladies?" asked a slim sales clerk who had approached them with quiet diffidence.

"I'd like to try this on," Del said, pointing to the burgundy dress on the manikin.

"Of course, Miss," she answered. "I'm sure we have it in your size. Come with me, please, and I'll show you to a fitting room."

"Even their sales clerks are flat-chested!" Colleen declared, now thoroughly exasperated.

* * *

"What a lovely view!" Lucy Forrest exclaimed to her brother as she and Judge Lanham sat gazing out across the vast expanse of San Francisco Bay on the sunny April afternoon of Del's birthday. It was Lucy's first visit to the Claremont, and she luxuriated now in the casual elegance of the hotel veranda.

"I knew you would like it," Clyde Lanham replied with a smile. There was nothing he enjoyed more than pleasing his plump and pretty younger sister. "I hope Charles does as well," he added.

He knew his brother-in-law was an extremely fastidious man, not easily impressed by even the most luxurious accommodations. As Chairman of the Board of West Coast Financial, Charles Prescott Forrest had traveled to most of the world's capitols and built an empire based on his company's lucrative investments in the railroad and mercantile shipping industries.

"Oh, I know he'll love it!" Lucy affirmed. Then, leaning forward in her chair, she pointed down at the sun-filled glade directly below them where Del was playing badminton with three other girls her own age. "And just look at your daughter! What a wonderful time she's having! Has she ever played lawn tennis before?"

"I don't think so. There's not much lawn tennis in Benicia, I'm afraid."

"Well! She certainly learns fast! She's beating the pants off those other girls!"

"That's because she plays with boys all the time. She's very competitive. As a matter of fact," the Judge added, his tone suddenly solemn, "I've become rather alarmed about that lately. After all, this is her fourteenth birthday. It's time for her to acquire the graces of a young lady, and she's never going to do that if she continues to hobnob with those low-brow ruffians in Benicia."

Lucy fixed her brother with a reproving stare. "Oh Clyde! Don't be ridiculous. You know perfectly well that tomboys always blossom into the best of women."

"I know that is your hypothesis," he answered with a condescending smile. "But it is not one I share. I have already spoken to Sister Rosemary about this matter, and she fully agrees with me that it's time for Adelaide to make new acquaintances."

"Clyde—you didn't! What a dreadful thing to do! The nuns will surely think you're a pompous ass!"

"As a matter of fact," the Judge said archly, "Sister Rosemary has suggested I enroll Adelaide as a boarder at St. Catherine's Seminary. That way, she is sure to have much greater supervision in her daily activities."

"I thought that was *your* job," Lucy retorted briskly.

Clyde nodded respectfully, but not to concede his point. "Of course. But as you know, dear sister, I have a very busy schedule and cannot devote as much time to parental tasks as I would like."

"It seems to me Ruby has been an excellent surrogate."

"Ruby is a good woman with a loving heart," Clyde acknowledged. "She has a very limited capacity, however, when it comes to … ah … social refinements."

Lucy was silent. She knew her brother was right on this point, but she felt very uncomfortable about admitting it. She had great respect for Ruby's folk wisdom and childlike faith. At last she said, "I think we should discuss this some other time, Clyde. Right now I'm in a very good mood and I don't want to spoil it, if you don't mind!"

"Of course not. When do you expect Charles to arrive?" he asked in an effort to switch to a more neutral topic.

"Not until after seven, I'm afraid. He said he hopes to catch the five-twenty up from Monterrey. But you know how those banker meetings are. They go on forever!"

"How about a cup of tea?" Clyde suggested.

"Splendid idea!" Lucy jumped up. "Lead on, brother! But no more talk about sending Del to a nunnery!"

As they walked across the high-ceilinged lobby toward the *Fleur de Lys* tearoom, though, Lucy herself continued on the same topic. "You must give this matter much more thought, Clyde. I would suggest taking her into the city to the opera or to some concerts. If you like, I can come up once or twice a month and take her myself."

"That would be very kind of you," Clyde observed cautiously. He knew Lucy was a veritable pit-bull when it came to differences of opinion with her brother.

"She's much too young for a coming-out party," she admitted. "However, I'm sure there are some cotillions she might attend—perhaps right here at the Claremont. I'd be only too happy to chaperone. Would you like me to enquire for you?"

Shaking his head in good-humored resignation, Clyde said, "Of course, dear Lucy."

Lucy rose on her tiptoes and kissed his cheek. "Dear brother!" she quipped. "There may be hope for you after all!"

1924

The Lido

CHAPTER FOURTEEN

"I'll See You In My Dreams"

IT WAS 4:00 AM ON February 4, 1924. Sam Geddis was having a familiar nightmare. His mother was standing beside his bed, a butcher knife raised high over her head, her eyes glittering down at him with hellish fury. Behind and all around her, flames crackled. Though desperate to flee, Sam could not move.

Suddenly he was wide-awake and sitting bolt upright in his bed. His whole body was tense with alarm. He sniffed for the acrid stench of smoke, but there was only the stale air of his bedroom. In this the darkest hour before dawn, he could see nothing. Was someone else in his room? He listened intently, but all he could hear was his own shallow breathing.

Finally summoning the courage to get out of bed, he moved toward the bedroom door. He felt sure he had locked it before he went to bed, just as he had done every night since he and Tully moved back with their mother two weeks before. Dr. Merriweather had assured Sam that, after nearly three years of clinical treatment for what Merriweather called "a temporary mental disorder," his mother was fully recovered. Sam did not believe it.

He had begged his paternal aunt and uncle—Harry and Sarah Nielson—to keep him and Tully at their home in Oakland at least a few weeks more.

"I'm sorry, my dear," his aunt had said forlornly. "There's nothing we can do. The Court has ordered us to send you to live with your mother."

189

Immediately after her release from the Napa sanatorium, Florin had rented a small two-story house at the far west end of K Street in Benicia. Located on the shore of Southampton Bay, it was the only residential building in that part of town. Kevin Patterson had approved of this arrangement because he hoped it would discourage unwanted intruders.

When Sam and Tully moved into this two bedroom house, Sam immediately became suspicious because his mother again insisted that Tully sleep with her. At first, Tully was also surprised by this requirement. Now nine years old, he had grown accustomed to sharing a room with his brother at their aunt and uncle's house.

Tully did not resist, though. In fact, he quickly reverted to his earlier infantile attachment to his mother. Sam knew something was very wrong about this. He decided he should phone Merriweather. The young doctor's advice did not help.

"This is all quite normal," Merriweather explained. "Your mother is just trying to reassure Tully that she still loves him, despite their long separation. As the older brother, you must try to be more understanding, Sam."

"Oh, I understand alright!" Sam retorted angrily. "Momma is still crazy as a loon, and she's doing everything she can to make Tully as crazy as she is! She still gives him tub baths!"

There was a pause at the other end of the line as Merriweather pondered what this fourteen-year-old boy had just told him. "Again, Sam, you shouldn't worry. Like any mother, she's probably she just checking to be sure Tully bathes himself properly," he said, even though he too thought such behavior bizarre.

"Tully's been bathing himself properly for three years!" Sam declared, his voice cracking with frustration. "He doesn't need anybody's help! She's doing things to Tully—bad things! I know she is, and you've got to help us!"

Another pause, much longer this time. At last Merriweather said, "Tell you what, Sam. I have to drive over to Fairfield on business tomorrow morning. I'll drop by on my way back home. What time do you and Tully get out of school?"

"At 3:30, but we usually don't get home until almost 4:00 because we have to ride our bikes from way over on East 3rd Street."

"Alright then," Merriweather said. "I'll try to be at your house by 4:00 o'clock. Stay calm, Sam," he added soothingly. "I'm sure there's a reasonable explanation and we can work things out."

Merriweather kept his promise. When confronted with his former patient, though, he wavered in his resolve to ask the questions that, as a clinician, he knew he should. He had worked closely with Florin during the thirty-six months of her confinement, conducting weekly therapy sessions with her and studying every case history he could find about women who exhibited similar symptoms of what psychologists of the time called *hysteria*.

In 1924, the science of psychology was still in its infancy and based primarily on intuitive guesswork. Freudian analysis was the only tool available to clinical psychologists. In this case, the Freudian paradigm indicated a very troubling prognosis—one that Merriweather was reluctant to make.

Besides, Florin was a very canny patient—highly skilled at manipulating others to do her own bidding as well as at concealing her true thoughts and deepest feelings. Few women could match her guile, and fewer men could discern it—even highly educated and intelligent men like Scott Merriweather.

When he met with Florin and her sons that afternoon, Merriweather was quickly disarmed by Florin's solicitous vagaries. He decided the best course to follow was one of indirect observation in a non-threatening social environment. He therefore invited Florin and her sons to a Quaker Friends meeting in Berkeley. He felt sure the non-judgmental Quakers would induce Florin to share some of her deepest and perhaps even her darkest secrets.

*   *   *

When he first entered the one-story wood frame Quaker Meeting House in Berkeley the following Sunday afternoon, Sam was puzzled. Merriweather had told him they were going to a kind of church, but this was like no church Sam had ever seen.

There were no pews or oblong stained glass windows. There was no sanctuary with an altar and pulpit. Instead, the interior was a barren 25- by 50-foot room with open-beamed walls and ceiling, wood floor, and straight-backed chairs lined up against all four walls. In the center of this room stood an enormous table hewn from raw oak. The only lighting in the place came from four widely separated square windows in each of the long walls and two pull-chain light bulbs fixed to the ceiling rafters.

Although there were more than thirty other people already present, the room was completely silent. Some of the congregants sat with their hands folded in their laps, their heads bowed and their eyes closed. Others simply stared straight ahead as if they were in a trance. No one seemed to notice when Merriweather, Florin and her sons entered.

After they were seated, the silence in the room continued for another fifteen minutes until a heavy-set man in glasses stood up and announced in deep and somber tones: "This is a sad day for humanity. Early this morning, two Chinese and three Negro men were lynched and brutally murdered in Vallejo. We should remember them in our meditations."

"Remember them," several voices responded, almost in unison.

"Let us join together then, friends," said a handsome young woman who stood up and took several steps forward, her head bowed. Immediately, most of the others in the room stood and moved to gather around the table. Touching Florin's shoulder to follow his example, Merriweather now also stood and joined this mystical convocation. Those already in the group readily made room for the four newcomers, but there was no physical or eye contact.

Again, several minutes of silence passed until the handsome young woman began chanting in monotone words that Sam had never heard before—*om mani padme hum*. She repeated this mantra several times until most of the others joined in, including Merriweather. Mystified, Sam realized this must be some form of a chant, though he had no idea what it meant. He began to feel very uncomfortable.

Just when his discomfort started turning into impatience, someone in the circle said, "I'll fetch our refreshments." Instantly, the chanting stopped and everyone began milling about the room in friendly conversation.

"Scott, so glad you could come! I haven't seen you in months!" It was the young woman who had initiated the chanting. She embraced Merriweather now as if he were a long lost brother.

"Oh come on, Natalie!" he replied. "It hasn't been that long!" Then, turning to Florin, he said, "Florin Geddis, this is Natalie Brighton. Natalie is the founder of our Friends Meeting here in Berkeley."

"*Enchante!*" Florin lisped sweetly. "I am so happy to meet you, *Mamselle Brighton*! Doctor Merriweather has spoken very highly of you. These are my sons Tully and Sam."

"Thank you, Missus Geddis," Natalie murmured amiably as she clasped Florin's hand in both of her own and then, in turn, the hands of Tully and Sam. "Your boys are very handsome!" she added with a coy smile at Sam. "I understand you are interested in joining our Meeting. I certainly hope you do. We always welcome newcomers to our community. Come, let me introduce you to everybody."

Soon, the room was filled with animated conversation as several platters heaped with home-made rice cakes and sliced apples were brought out of an adjoining kitchen and placed on the table in the center of the room. While she guided Florin and her sons around the room, Natalie interspersed her introductions with a brief history of her organization, which she called the Berkeley Friends Meeting.

"We just opened this house a few weeks ago as an extension of our West Coast headquarters in San Jose," Natalie explained. "We did so at the request of several members of the University faculty here. As you can see, we have already attracted many new members. We call ourselves 'Beanite Quakers,' after Joel and Hannah Bean who first established our College Park Association in 1889. Unlike other more traditional Quakers, you see, Beanites do not evangelize. Nor do we have a pastor. We consider each member of our faith group to be his or her own pastor. We believe true faith comes only from within the individual, not from any hierarchical priesthood or ritualistic practices."

Both Florin and Merriweather nodded approvingly at this last distinction.

In his innocence, Sam understood nothing they said. It didn't matter. What interested him most now were the rice cakes. He had not eaten since breakfast, and it was already late afternoon.

"Go ahead, Sam," Natalie urged with an ingratiating smile. "Take as much as you like. You too, Tully."

While the boys munched on their apples and cakes, Merriweather introduced Florin to Roger Prendergast, the man who had reported the lynching in Vallejo. "How did you hear about this?" Merriweather asked anxiously.

"It was in the *Vallejo Times Herald* this morning," Roger replied.

"Do they know who's responsible?"

"All the evidence points to the Ku Klux Klan. They hanged the poor fellows by their wrists and then disemboweled them, leaving them to suffer a slow and agonizing death."

"Good Lord!" Merriweather declared. "I had no idea the Klan was active here in California."

"I'm afraid the Klan is active in many states," Prendergast observed grimly. "According to yesterday's *Examiner*, their membership nationwide has swelled to more than three million. It's rumored that, here in California, they're backed by the Republican Party."

"That's no surprise to me," said Natalie. "That dreadful Party boss Howard Roach is head of the Masons, after all."

"Griffith's *Birth of a Nation* hasn't helped matters," Prendegast averred.

"I have not seen it," Merriweather said. "But I can well imagine what an effect it has had on the masses."

"All the more reason for us Beanites to make ourselves visible in this crisis!" Natalie declared firmly. "We are planning a May Day vigil at the Capitol building in Sacramento." Turning to Florin, she said, "I hope you and your boys will join us."

Florin looked in silent bewilderment at Merriweather. She had no idea what Brighton or Prendergast were talking about.

This was precisely the reaction Merriweather had anticipated. "I'll explain this to you later, Florin," he assured her in a confidential whisper.

*   *   *

As they rode back to Benicia on the train that evening, Sam sat staring out of the window at the storm clouds hanging low over the mountains west of San Pablo Bay. He did not look forward to spending yet another night in his mother's house. For, though her relationship with Tully had not changed since her incarceration, her attitude toward Sam was radically different. Gone was her insipid obsequiousness. In its place were long periods of hostile silence, broken only by an occasional harsh rebuke.

Clearly, his mother resented Sam because of his testimony during the murder trial. He fully realized now that Florin's distracted courtroom demeanor had been a deliberate ruse, much like the grief she had shown after his father's suicide. Clearly too, there was no one who could help him. Merriweather had fallen completely under his mother's spell, and his Quaker friends were as gullible and insipid as kindergarten children.

The only person who might understand Sam's situation was Jack Westlake. After all, Jack too had been betrayed by his mother. But Jack had run away to live with Adam Tucker in Vallejo, and no one in Benicia seemed to know Tucker's home address. For, soon after Jack's departure, the Child Welfare Committee had boycotted Tucker's auto repair shop, forcing him to close down and seek employment elsewhere.

Sam would learn all this from Del a month later when he met her at Rankin's grocery store in Benicia. "I haven't seen Jack for months," Del reported. "I've heard plenty of rumors, but you know how people are in this town! So how are you and Tully doing?"

"Not so good," Sam said. "My Mom's still not right."

Startled, Del asked, "What do you mean?"

"I'm not sure," Sam lied. He had always liked Del because he knew she was open and honest. But she was still the daughter of Judge Lanham—the man who had been chiefly responsible for his mother's getting away with the attempted murder of her own children!

Besides, Del had changed since Sam had last seen her. At fourteen, she seemed self-conscious and aloof. The sharp angles of her tomboy frame had become rounded and supple. "Girls grow up much faster than boys," he remembered his mother often telling him.

As if she had read Sam's thoughts, Del stepped closer to him and touched his arm. "It's alright, Sam," she said softly. "I know it's been hard for you. But things will get better."

"I sure hope so!"

"Of course they will!" Del declared emphatically. Then, with the spontaneity of the tomboy Sam remembered, she asked, "Why don't you come sailing with us next Saturday? There's a bunch of us sailing on the Henshaks' yacht down to Alameda and back."

"But I don't know how to sail," Sam protested.

"You don't have to," Del assured him. "Just come along as a passenger. It'll be lots of fun."

For the first time in weeks, Sam felt happy. He accepted Del's invitation.

*   *   *

During the last week of March every year, the Solano County Fair was held at the fairgrounds in Vallejo. Farmers and vendors from miles around came to show off their prize livestock and peddle their latest wares. A feature attraction in 1924 was the farm equipment exhibit. Ever since 1886, when the first Holt Brothers Link Belt Combined Harvester was sold, mechanized farm equipment had become the focus of interest among California ranchers and grain growers.

At the entrance to the fairgrounds, a large pavilion had been erected to display the latest-model tractors, harvesters, and road grading equipment. Being a "natural born" mechanic, Adam had insisted this would be the first place he and his boys—Jack, Billy, and now Francis Flanagan—would visit on opening day. Francis had moved in with them two months before when he went to work as an apprentice at the Dodge Brothers Dealership in Vallejo where Adam was the chief mechanic. The four stood together now next to one of Henry Ford's latest small tractor models—the Fordson Model F.

"Now dat's de tractor you wants!" Adam declared as he leaned close to examine the Model F's compact and efficient engine.

"Price be right too," Billy observed as he fingered the tag hanging from the steel driver's seat."

"That's 'cause they's mass produce, jus' like the Model T. Ol' Henry, he's one smart fella!" Adam picked up one of the printed flyers lying on a table next to the display model. "Says here she delivers 20 horse."

"Ain't got as much power as the Massey-Harris 3," Francis said. "She delivers 15 horse on the drawbar. That's half again as much as the Fordson."

"Yeah an' cos' *three* times as much," Adam retorted, emphasizing his point by thrusting three fingers of his left hand close to Francis' face.

Jack had climbed up onto the Fordson and was moving the steering wheel back and forth, pretending to drive.

"Get down from there, boy!" ordered a heavy-set man in a three-piece suit who had suddenly stepped out of a curtained-off area near the display model. "We don't allow children on our tractors."

"He didn' mean no harm, mister," Adam said.

"All the same, he's gotta get down from there—right now!" The intruder's face instantly turned beet red. Clearly, he was furious that a Negro would dare to challenge him. "If he don't, I'm callin' the constable."

Jack was already back on the ground and moving away to a different vendor's display—a large wooden rack hung with various engine parts.

Shrugging his shoulders indifferently, Adam said, "Come on, boys. Le's go get us some kettlecorn,"

Together, they exited the farm equipment display and headed down a cinder path toward the concession area where scores of food stands had been erected. Stopping in front of a hand-printed sign announcing FRESH KETTLECORN—PENNY A BAG, Adam reached into his pocket and pulled out a dollar bill. Handing it to the man behind the counter, he said, "Gimme eight bags. You got any soda pop?"

The vendor took the dollar bill and gestured to his right. "Over there in that ice barrel. Nickel a piece. That'll be twenty-eight cents all together." Reaching into his pocket apron, the vendor quickly gave Adam his change.

"Thanks, Adam," Francis said as they walked on. "Real gen'rous of y'."

"Yeah. Thanks Adam," Billy and Jack echoed.

"Tha's my treat f' the day," Adam replied, grinning. "From here on, you pays y'r own way."

They were now approaching the center of the fairgrounds where a calliope filled the air with its thumping and jingling music and a Ferris wheel rose thirty feet above the fairground, its gondolas filled with screaming and laughing riders. There were hundreds of patrons in this area because, in addition to the calliope and a miniature ride-on train for children, there were numerous diversions for adults. These included skill-challenge games such as a ring toss, a BB-gun shooting gallery, and, most popular of all for male patrons, the strength test.

This concession was easy to find, for it was clearly marked by a large banner labeled BEAT THE GIANT. On a raised platform beneath this banner stood a huge, muscle-bound man in leopard-skin boxing shorts. Easily seven feet tall, this performer clasped a large wooden sledgehammer in his hands as if he were poised to wield it as a weapon against anyone who came too close.

To the left of the platform rose a fifteen-foot high pole with a metal gong attached to its top. At the foot of the pole was a kind of seesaw board. This was the strength-testing device. The object of this contest was to hit one end of the seesaw board hard enough to make a round metal disk at the other end fly all the way to the top of the pole and ring the gong.

Jack immediately recognized the man standing next to the platform. It was Belcher Keet, son of the Gypsy Queen whose family he and Del had met at Basilio Park. Belcher had the same trance-like gaze Jack remembered from their first encounter.

As Adam and the boys approached, Belcher took the sledgehammer from the giant's hands and raised it above his head. "Who's gonnah challenge the Giant?" Belcher demanded. "Nickle a try." Then, looking directly at Jack, he asked, "How 'bout you, boy?"

"Go ahead, Jack," Francis urged his friend. "That don't look so hard. Heck! I've swung a sledge like that plenty o' times."

"Then, why don't you do it?" Jack suggested.

Francis nodded with a confident grin. "Sure. Why not?" Stepping forward, Francis gave Belcher his nickel and, grabbing the sledgehammer, approached the strength-tester. Spreading his feet wide, Francis raised the heavy tool above his head and slammed it down on the strength tester. Instantly, the metal disk flew up the pole—but only halfway, when it fell back down again.

"Sorry, kid," Belcher said with a condescending smile. "Wanna try again?"

"That thing's rigged!" Francis snarled.

"That so?" Belcher replied, still smiling. Then, turning toward the stationary figure on the platform, he said, "So how 'bout it, Noah? Want t' show 'em how t' do it?"

The giant responded almost like a robot, slowly and stiffly stepping down off the platform and walking toward Belcher. Taking the sledgehammer in one hand, he raised it effortlessly and seemed only to let it drop of its own weight on the end of the seesaw board. This time, the metal disk flew all the way up the pole and slammed into the gong with a loud "clang." Having performed this feat, the Giant gave the sledge back to Belcher and returned to his place on the platform.

A dozen spectators emitted Ooo's and Ahh's in admiration. Francis, however, remained skeptical.

"It jus' lev'rage," Adam explained to the boys. "It ain't how hard y' hit it; it's where y' hit it." Then, facing Belcher, he said, "Gimme that thing."

"Gimme y'r nickel, first," Belcher demanded.

Adam paid Belcher and took hold of the sledgehammer with his left hand. Raising it above his head much as Noah had done, he let it fall and duplicated the Giant's achievement.

At the sound of the gong, all of the spectators applauded. Belcher glowered at Adam. He did not appreciate having his ruse exposed. "OK, nigger," he growled. "You go away now."

Adam stood his ground for several seconds, fixing Belcher with an expression Jack had never seen in Adam's face before. It was not a look of anger or resentment but of weary sadness. It was as if Adam were asking this man, *When will you people learn?*

At length, Adam turned to the boys and said, "Come on. Le's get outa here."

As if they were attached to Adam by an invisible chain, Billy, Francis, and Jack followed him in sullen silence back to the parking area. All of them had had their fill of the Solano County Fair.

They were met with much greater disappointment when they arrived back at Adam's shack. While they were gone, someone had broken in. The front door had been torn off its hinges and, in a pool of blood near the threshold, lay the shotgun blasted remains of Peewee.

"Damn!" Adam growled as he leaned over to examine the Peewee's shattered body. Francis and Jack stood behind him, dazed with terror and shock.

"They cleaned us out!" Billy groaned as he entered the building and saw the emptied shelves and shattered table and stools.

Following Billy inside, Francis exploded with rage. "Goddam dirty bastards! Who done this?"

Still stunned speechless, Jack remained outside. "Poor Peewee!" he murmured, tears streaming down his face.

"He done what he could," Billy observed as he extracted a shred of bloodied denim cloth from the dead animal's jaws. Holding this trophy up, he added, "Took a good chunk out o' somebody's ass!"

"What are we going to do now?" Jack asked. "Report it to the police?"

Adam chuckled. "Won't do no good. This ain't no robbery. I's a threat."

"What d' y' mean?" Francis asked.

"Rival gang," Adam replied. Then, turning to Billy he said, "Go get the shovel. We gotta dig up our stash an' get out o' here now."

Nodding, Billy did as he was told and followed Adam to the rear of the shed where Adam had stacked a pile of abandoned car parts and rubber tires. Moving several of these items aside, they exposed a barren patch of soil where Billy immediately began digging.

In a few minutes, he unearthed a large sea chest sealed with bands of copper. Together, Adam and Billy lifted this chest out of the ground and carried it out to the truck.

"Get in, boys," Adam said as he climbed into the cab and started the engine.

"Where are we going?" Jack asked when Adam turned onto Virginia Street and headed west toward the Napa River.

"Someplace else" Adam said.

CHAPTER FIFTEEN

"I Want To Be Happy"

EMMETT SPEARS HAD DRUNK FEAR and resentment with his mother's milk. His father Silas had been a Confederate foot soldier in Savannah, Georgia when General William Tecumseh Sherman's Army devastated that city in December of 1864. By the time Emmett was born eleven years later, Silas had been eaten up with bitter memories of that battle—memories that prompted him to binge on "white lightning" and beat his wife and children mercilessly.

Emmett's mother Cora did not fault her husband. Like most of their white sharecropper neighbors, Cora and Silas blamed Negroes and "carpetbaggers" for everything that had gone wrong in their lives. Emmett witnessed his first lynching at three years old. He would see many more before, at seventeen, he ran away from home to Savannah. There he enlisted in the United States Navy and, after six months of basic training, was assigned as second class seaman aboard the destroyer *USS Comstock*.

Because of his well-nurtured hatred of Negroes, Emmett quickly rose to the rank of petty officer in charge of the ship's coal stokers. For eighteen months, the *Comstock* patrolled the waters off the coast of Guatemala. Emmett's shipboard experience only intensified his deep-seated hatred of "niggers"—a term he applied indiscriminately to every person whose skin shade was darker than his own. "Lazy, filthy buggers!" he had often declared to his fellow officers. "They're all alike. Only thing they understand is the lash or the brig."

In the fall of 1913, the *Comstock* sailed through the Golden Gate to the Mare Island Naval Shipyard for refitting. While his ship was in dry-dock, Emmett applied for and was assigned to duty as a supply officer billeted in Vallejo. He remained in this post until he was decommissioned at the end of World War I.

Emmett quickly found civilian work as a yard boss at the Alta Manufacturing plant in near-by Benicia. When he interviewed for this job, Emmett made no bones about his racial prejudice.

"Sounds like somebody we need around here," plant manager Ed Johnson told him. "Ever since we started building dredges, we've had to hire a lot o' the local Chinks and Portagees 'cause they're the only cheap labor we can get. Damn Chinks don't speak no English and the Portagees comes to work drunk most days. You think you can handle that?"

"You won't have any more trouble, sir," Emmett said confidently.

Johnson wasn't sure. Emmett's small frame and facial features made him look like a starved rat, and his high-pitched voice was anything but commanding. "Well," he said cautiously, "I guess we'll give you a try. Report here Monday morning, 7:00 o'clock sharp."

* * *

In his first hour on the job, Emmett proved his mettle by challenging Leonardo Rocha—one of the biggest and toughest Portuguese workers at the plant.

Nursing a bad hangover, Rocha had come to work that morning in a foul humor. Instinctively, Emmett spotted him as a perfect mark. A foot taller than Emmett, with the arm and shoulder muscles of a bull, Rocha was pushing a cart filled with newly forged steel bars from the foundry building to the machining shop when Emmett stepped in his path and ordered him to increase the size of his load.

"What're y' talkin' about?" Rocha bristled. "Can't y' see ain't no more room in this here cart?"

"Then find a bigger cart," Emmett replied with calculated calm.

"Listen, you," Rocha snarled, "I been usin' this cart ever day since I been here. Ain't no scrawny newcomer like you tellin' me what to do!"

"That so?" Emmett said, still keeping his own fury in check. "We'll see about that." Emmett nodded curtly and walked out of the foundry building.

Crossing the alley into a supply shed, Emmett located a porcelain container labeled in red letters—*Bright Dipping: Handle with Care*. Opening this container, he carefully poured several ounces of its liquid contents into an empty milk bottle he retrieved from a trash barrel. Then, hiding the bottle behind his back, he walked back into the foundry building and again ordered Rocha to find a larger cart.

As Emmett expected, Rocha responded with his fist. When the bigger man reared back to fell his adversary, Emmett quickly dodged and, in the same instant, flung the acid contents of the bottle at his attacker. Instantly, Rocha bellowed in pain and covered his face with his hands.

The incident had occurred so suddenly that none of the other workers in the foundry knew what had happened until they heard Rocha's outcry. "What the hell's goin' on?" demanded a smelter named Steve Vascos as he rushed to Rocha's aid.

"Go get a bucket of water and douse him!" Emmett commanded and promptly walked out of the foundry building again—this time, going directly to the plant manager's office where he reported the incident.

Johnson whistled in amazement. "Jesus, Emmett! You don't fool around, do y'? Is Rocha hurt bad?"

"Nah, he'll be alright. It was just a low concentrate. The boys are fixin' him up. But, like I told y', them niggers won't cause you no more trouble."

Emmett was wrong about the extent of Rocha's injuries. The man's face had been so badly burned that he died of blood poisoning two days later. Emmett had been right about the effect of this incident on the other workers, however. From that day on, no one at the plant ever questioned Emmett's directives—not even Johnson.

As for the injustice of Emmett's assault, no one at the Alta plant or in the town of Benicia cared. In addition to being a notorious drunk and bully, Rocha was a childless bachelor. He had no ties to the community. He had gotten what he deserved.

Still, news of Emmett's ruthless attack spread quickly in the communities on both sides of the Carquinez Strait. It had been Spears, in fact, who had engineered the 1924 murder of the five Negro and Chinese men in Vallejo as well as the break-in at Tucker's shack. Word of Spears' atrocities had even caught the attention of Howard Roach, who promptly enlisted Emmett as a henchman for the inner circle of his Masonic Lodge in Martinez.

*   *   *

"Close the door and have a seat," Roach said when Emmett entered the County Supervisor's office in the late afternoon of August 12. "I got another job for y'. Seems Tucker still don't get the message."

"You mean that dumb nigger's makin' trouble again?" Emmett asked irritably.

"Afraid so, Emmett. An' this time we gotta do the job right"

"We'd o' done it right the las' time, only the Nigger went into hiding. Anybody know where he's at now?"

"The boys tell me he's living in some Chink house over on the east side of Vallejo. Shouldn't be too hard to find him. Chinks take bribes just like everybody else," Roach said with a knowing wink as he handed Emmett a leather pouch filled with one hundred dollars in small bills. "Here, spread it around. But don't waste it. You do it right this time, you get to keep whatever's left plus another hundred."

*   *   *

Emmett knew exactly what to do. Immediately after leaving Roach's office, he took the car ferry from Martinez to Benicia and drove to a bait shop in East Vallejo. Owned by a half-breed Korean named Cody Park, the bait shop was located at the entrance to a fishing pier that doubled as a footbridge to the Coast Guard Lighthouse just off Sandy Beach.

Like the buildings on either side and across the dirt-surfaced Sandy Beach Road, Park's shop was a one-story windowless structure made of weathered wooden planks and covered with flat sheets of corrugated steel—all scrap material that had been hauled there on barges from the Mare Island Shipyard at the end of the Great War. It was in an area most Vallejo residents referred to as "shanty town."

Most of Cody Park's customers were land-bound fisherman, too poor to own or rent a boat. Nevertheless, Park's humble enterprise was profitable. For, in addition to fresh bait, he also sold large quantities of laudanum in unmarked glass bottles he filled himself and stored behind the counter. These items he distributed only to customers he knew personally—most of them Asians. Sometimes, though, Park made an exception. Emmett Spears was one of these.

"Ah, Meesta Spear," Park said as soon as Emmett let the heavy oak entrance door slam shut behind him. "How many bottle you want?"

Looking around the dimly lit interior of Park's shop to be sure no one could eavesdrop on their conversation, Emmett waved his hand impatiently. "Don't need any dope today, Cody. Need a little favor instead." Extracting three one-dollar bills from his pocket, Emmett laid them on the counter top.

Park smiled knowingly. "Sure. You want nice young China girl—yes?"

"No China girl. I just need y' t' tell me where somebody lives. You ever heard of a nigger named Adam Tucker?"

"Sure. I know him. He come here buy bait plenty time. He live with Harry Lee over on Magazine Street."

"What's the house number?"

Park looked surprised. "House number? They got no house number. You drive long time. You see pigpen next to wood house."

"So how do I get to Magazine Street?"

"You go back Sonoma." Park pointed toward the northwest. "You come to Magazine, you turn left. Then you go maybe five mile. You see pigpen house on right."

Emmett was already heading out the door when Park held up the dollars and called out cheerfully, "Thank you, Meesta Spear."

* * *

Realizing he would need help to execute his plan, Emmett drove to the Brewery on West H Street in Benicia. Since it was late afternoon, he knew he would find his henchmen Tom Stark and Lou Bolger there, drinking beer and rolling dice at the bar. Emmett wasted no time with greetings. "Come on, boys," he said, "we got a job to do."

The two men exchanged quick glances and, without a word, followed Emmett outside to his 1923 Buick sedan, which was parked in the street directly in front of the Brewery.

"You got your pistols?" Emmett asked as Stark climbed into the front passenger seat and Bolger into the back.

"Sure," Stark replied, patting the front of his jacket where he kept his Colt revolver in a shoulder holster. "What's up?"

"We're gonna get us some niggers," Emmett said grimly as he turned left onto First Street and headed north toward Military Way. "Maybe a couple o' Chinks too."

"Yahoo!" Bolger cheered, extracting his own revolver from its shoulder holster and aiming it at several passing storefronts.

"Put that damn thing away!" Stark growled. "Somebody could see y'?"

"Scew 'em!" Bolger retorted.

"Save y'r anger, boys," Emmett said. "You'll get plenty o' chances to blast away soon."

"So who we gonna do?" Stark asked.

"Adam Tucker an' some o' his gang. Act'ly, all of his gang, if we're lucky."

"You found out where he's hidin'?" Stark asked eagerly.

Emmett did not answer. He felt no need to provide any more details. Concerned that he might need additional reinforcements, though, he made a right turn at Military and drove to Morgan's Roadhouse, a small tavern a few yards beyond the main entrance to the Benicia Arsenal. Leaving his engine running, he got out of the car and went inside. Within minutes he returned and made a U-turn, heading back toward Vallejo.

As Emmett's car ascended the highest hill on the road from Benicia to Vallejo, Stark noticed through the rear window that another black sedan was coming up fast behind them. "Who's that?" he asked.

"Jimmy Torrance and a couple o' his boys," Emmett replied. "They got a Tommy Gun—just in case."

"This is gonna be fun!" Bolger declared gleefully.

When they reached the outskirts of Vallejo, Spears turned his car onto Magazine Street, which looped back eastward again and quickly became a narrow dirt road that wound crazily up and down the range of hills defining the border between Vallejo and Benicia.

Darkness was approaching fast as the two vehicles moved slowly through the open countryside. So far, they had passed only three houses, none of which had a pigpen.

As they reached the crest of the next hill, Emmett suddenly pulled his car to the shoulder, turned off its engine, and stepped out. "From here on we walk," he announced. "Get the shotgun out o' the trunk," Emmett commanded, at the same time signaling the men in the vehicle behind to follow his lead.

Fifty yards below was the dark silhouette of a two-story building. Behind it, Emmett could see the wooden posts of a fence surrounding a rain-shelter. "This is it," he said.

"Don't see no lights," Torrance remarked.

Emmett ignored this observation. "From now on, nobody talks. Spread out an' stay behind me. When we get close to the entrance, Jimmy, you take your boys and go around back. Me and my boys 'll cover the front. Anybody comes out, shoot 'em."

Fifteen yards from the house, Emmett stopped again and pointed with both hands, directing Stark and Bolger to take positions on opposite sides of the front door. Then, with gun drawn, he walked to the entrance and knocked.

There was no response. Emmett waited for a minute and knocked again, this time more forcefully. Still there was no response, so he tried the door latch. It was not locked. He pushed the door open and immediately stepped back and to the side. For all he knew, armed men might be waiting for them inside.

"Guess nobody's home," Bolger declared.

"Go ahead in, then," Emmett ordered, still keeping to one side of the doorway. "I'll be right behind y'."

Stark and Bolger moved swiftly, their guns at ready. "Anybody here?" Bolger asked cheerfully, as if he expected someone to answer with a cordial greeting.

Emmett did not move from his position of safety until he heard Stark announce that he had found a lantern and was lighting it.

"What a bunch o' pigs!" Bolger declaared as he stood in the middle of what appeared to be a front parlor. The only furniture in this room was a large hand-hewn table strewn with soiled eating utensils and a few empty bottles. The naked floorboards were covered with scuffmarks and gritty with dirt and leftover scraps of food.

Emmett led the way into the kitchen at the back of the house and unlocked the rear-entrance door to admit Jimmy Torrance and his two cohorts. He then directed Stark and Bolger to search the second floor.

He and Torrance's men lit another lantern and began opening all of the built-in cabinets in the kitchen.

"Bingo!" Seth Warner, one of Torrance's men suddenly declared. Holding up a rolled up sheet of paper he had found in one of the cabinets, he spread it out on the kitchen counter-top revealing what appeared to be a navigation chart. "This is the Carquinez Strait," Warner, who was a seasoned local fisherman, explained. "And somebody's plotted a route from Crokett to Glen Cove. Look here," he said, pointing to a strait line that had been drawn on the chart with black ink.

Emmet leaned over the chart and pointed to one of several hand-written notes. "Looks like dates and times. They're runnin' their sugar across the Strait at night."

The sound of footsteps on the stairs signaled that Bolger and Stark had completed their search. "Ain't nothin' up there but some old Army cots," Stark reported. "You find anythin'?"

"We got what we need," Emmett said, as he rolled up the navigation chart and handed it to Warner. "Put this back where you found it."

"But how we gonna know where an' when to catch 'em?" Torrance asked.

Tapping his own forehead with an index finger, Emmett replied contemptuously, "Got it up here." Then, heading toward the front door, he commanded, "Douse them lamps an' let's go."

*　*　*

Standing on the long wharf built by the Contra Costa Beet Sugar Refining Company in Crokett, Jack watched as six Chinese dockworkers silently and efficiently wheeled handcarts laden with 100-pound bags of refined sugar onto *Dragon Queen*'s deck. Jack was apprehensive because a bright half moon illuminated the swift-running surface of the water and the steep slopes of the hills on both sides of Carquinez Strait. The *Dragon Queen*'s sails would be clearly visible to anyone standing on either shore.

But Tucker had insisted that this shipment had to go through, no matter what the risks. He was already a week behind schedule with the deliveries he had promised his customers in Yolo and Placer counties. Any delay now was out of the question.

According to the pocket watch Tucker had given Jack, it was now

2:45 A.M. High tide was at 3:44. Jack had to reach Glen Cove before then or the trucks waiting there for pick-up would depart without their cargo. Every link in Tucker's distribution chain was an independent entity. Continuity depended on everybody's strict adherence to a preset schedule.

Right now, Jack felt as if he were the most important link in that chain. He also felt as if he were not being paid enough for the related risks. After all, he was only fourteen. Most boys his age were still playing kick-the-can. At this ungodly hour, he mused bitterly, most of them were asleep in bed!

"You go now!" Eddie Zhao, the coolie boss, shouted up at him from the wharf next to the *Dragon Queen*.

Jack waved silent acknowledgement and quickly released the lines securing his boat to the dock. He had been doing this for more than a month now so that the rituals of casting off and pointing the *Dragon Queen* at the right angle to catch the maximum advantages of wind and current were almost instinctive. Still, he couldn't help feeling that this night was special—that something unexpected was going to happen.

Crossing the Carquinez Strait was no easy task, even under the best of weather conditions. With an eight- to ten-knot current that constantly shifted direction because of the uneven shoals on both sides of the Strait and a West wind that could be equally fickle in its strength and direction, maneuvering a twenty-eight foot junk was a challenge even to the most seasoned of sailors. Still, as he carefully tracked the effects of these changes on his cumbersome craft, Jack couldn't help feeling proud of his newly acquired skills.

Just when he reached the mid-point of his route and was feeling most confident, he heard the loud roar of an approaching powerboat. Glancing over his left shoulder, he saw the bow of this steel-hulled vessel high in the water bearing down on him at full throttle. Within seconds, the wooden deck under Jack's feet erupted and he felt himself being catapulted high into the air and then dumped precipitously into the icy waters of the Strait.

His body plummeted deep beneath the surface. Terrified that he might be caught in a whirlpool, Jack began flailing frantically to combat the powerful force of the current. Then he remembered what Harry Lee had told him about the best way to survive in such circumstances. "No fight current. Spread arms and legs. Warm body rise in cold water."

Sure enough, this strategy worked. Within seconds of following Harry's advice, Jack felt himself rising. When his head broke through the surface, he immediately gasped for air. But, in doing so, he also inhaled water, adding to his fear of drowning. Again he willed himself to relax, rolling over on his back so he would float face up. The current moved him forward swiftly, but in what direction he had no idea. He realized that, if he did not get out of the water soon, he would freeze to death. Already he felt the muscles in his arms and legs growing numb.

Suddenly something struck the back of his head. Twisting his upper torso, Jack saw what looked like a broken off segment of one of the junk's cedar masts. Immediately, he threw his arms around it and held on with all of his remaining strength. He could see clearly now that he and the mast fragment were moving directly upstream in the center of the main channel—a good three hundred yards from the nearest shoreline. He knew enough about the current here to realize there was no escaping its force. He would continue to be swept along in mid-channel, perhaps for miles upstream.

Desperately, Jack tried to pull himself up on top of the mast to escape from the icy water. But the cylindrical fragment rolled, dumping him back into the water and almost causing him to lose his grip. Exhausted, Jack's mind went blank. Even the terror of death deserted him. He felt his arms growing weaker by the second, the numbing cold seeping into his bones.

*   *   *

"Over there, Marco! See it?" Nicholas Skoulikas shouted to his younger brother as they deployed their nets.

"There's somebody hangin' onto that log," Marco said.

"Start the engine!" Nicholas commanded.

"What about the nets?"

"We'll have to drag 'em. Hurry up. He can't last much longer."

The small one-cylinder engine sputtered several times before Marco got it started. Slowly their fishing craft moved forward, just barely exceeding the speed of the current. "Jesus!" Marco exclaimed. "He just let go! He's gonna drown for sure!"

Nicholas moved swiftly, grabbing one of the spare cork floats they used for their nets and tying it to one end of a rope. The other end he lashed to the bow. They were now only a few yards away from the body floating face down in the water. Standing up in the bow, Nicholas stripped off his heavy jacket and , with the float tucked under one arm, jumped over the side and began swimming toward Jack.

Within minutes, the two men had Jack in their boat and Nicholas was vigorously pumping on his chest to revive him. Water gushed from Jack's mouth, and he began choking. His eyelids fluttered. "He's comin' aroun'!" Nicholas shouted exuberantly.

"He's one lucky kid!" Marco observed. Then, pointing at several large pieces of debris floating in the water, he shouted, "Look at that!"

"Wonder what happened? Must 've been a wreck." Looking down at Jack, Nicholas realized the boy was shivering so he quickly covered him with his own heavy jacket. "Don't worry, kid," he said. "You're gonna be OK."

*   *   *

Jack awoke seven hours later, the light of the noonday sun shining directly into his eyes through the open cabin hatch of a barge tied up at the First Street Pier in Benicia. When he sat up, he saw that he was in one of four wooden bunks, two built on each side of the barge cabin. He heard the voices of two men and a woman coming from the deck above. Tossing back the woolen blanket someone had covered him with, he realized he was naked. So he wrapped the blanket around himself, stood up, and climbed the wooden steps leading up through the hatch.

"There he is!" Nicholas announced cheerily. "How you doin', boy?"

"I'm alright, I guess," Jack answered blearily.

"You come with me, boy," a woman growled fiercely as she swept past him toward another cabin at the stern of the barge. "I'll rustle up some grub."

"Go ahead, boy," Nicholas said. "Dorcas is a good cook. She'll take care of y'."

"Thanks, Mister." Jack paused, suddenly remembering the manners his mother had taught him. Moving awkwardly in his blanket toward the two heavily bearded men, Jack reached out his hand in greeting. "I mean, thanks a lot. You fellows saved my life. My name's Jack Westlake. What's yours?"

"I'm Nick Skoulikas," said the older of the two men, startling Jack by giving him a big bear hug. Then, turning toward the other man, Nicolas said. "This here's my brother Marco."

Marco also hugged Jack, gruffly declaring, "Now we are brothers forever—yes?"

Jack was bewildered. He had never been hugged by a man before, nor did he have any idea what Marco had meant in saying they were 'brothers forever.' He assumed it must be some ethnic custom.

Jack had often heard about the Greeks who lived on the barges on the waterfront, but he had never met any in person. They tended to be a clannish lot—men who lived in the night more than the daytime. Their women were even less sociable—poor, superstitious, and irritable creatures who led hard lives and regarded all outsiders with suspicion. The sullen Dorcas was obviously one of these women.

"What happened to my clothes?" Jack asked, feeling somewhat more comfortable now—at least, with the two men.

Nicholas pointed up at a clothesline stretched between the two cabins on the barge. Jack immediately recognized his own Navy surplus pea jacket and Army surplus shirt and trousers hanging from this line. "Thanks," he said again.

"You go eat, boy," Marco said.

*　　*　　*

An hour later, after Jack had eaten and put on his dry clothes and shoes, Marco ushered him up First Street to Alessio's bus terminal. There he gave Jack a quarter for his fare back to Vallejo.

Much to Jack's surprise, neither of the men had asked him how he had wound up floating in the Carquinez Strait that morning. Apparently, they thought it was none of their business. As for the woman—Dorcas—though she had fed him well, she had remained surly and silent as he sat eating her generous serving of fish stew in the barge's galley. These were very strange people, Jack thought. At the same time, though, he had a new and profound respect for Benicia's Greek community. Never in the future would he allow anyone to say anything bad about them.

The Benicia-Vallejo Stage Line, as the Alessio brothers called their enterprise, consisted of a single 1914 Buick, with a maximum passenger capacity of fifteen. It had wooden bench seats and a canvas top with roll-up tarpaulins on either side that the driver would pull down whenever it rained. The bus made regularly scheduled runs between Benicia and Vallejo—twice daily during the week and six times each Saturday and Sunday.

Since it was Saturday, most of the seats on the bus were already occupied when Jack climbed aboard. Every other passenger was a woman because this was the bus that transported the local prostitutes for their weekly shopping spree in Vallejo. They were a gay and boisterous crowd and greeted Jack with lascivious leers and coquettish giggles.

"Move over, Maddie!" shouted Ramona Krebs to the woman beside her. "I want this one for myself!" This remark evoked guffaws of laughter from the other women, for Romona was the heaviest, oldest and ugliest of their company.

Jack blushed with embarrassment and desperately searched for an empty seat close to the driver so that, he hoped, he would be safe from the aggressive advances of these notorious sirens. But then he saw a familiar face framed in bright red hair. Sitting in the last row at the back of the bus was Becky Partridge, and she was eagerly waving to him. "Come on back here, Jack," she called out. "There's room next to me."

As Jack timidly maneuvered the narrow aisle between the bench seats, Ramona turned and glared at Becky. "Hmf!" she declared indignantly. "Guess he ain't so pure and innocent as he looks!" Again, there was an outburst of laughter.

Becky grabbed Jack's wrist and pulled him down beside her, immediately throwing her arms around him and kissing him vigorously on the cheek. This evoked loud cheers and whistles from the other women.

Jack swallowed hard and tried to look calm and collected, but his heart was racing. He couldn't repress the excitement he felt at seeing Becky again. In the past year, she had been at the core of all his most compelling adolescent fantasies. "Hi Becky," he said as nonchalantly as he could.

"Jack!" she purred. "Gosh! How you've grown up! So tall and

handsome!" Then, touching his cheek lightly with her fingertips, she added with sisterly scorn, "But you need a shave, mister!"

The bus started moving now, its old engine roaring loudly and its wood-frame chassis creaking under its heavy load. The other women ignored Jack and Becky, absorbed with their own conversations.

Feeling his chin, Jack realized he did indeed have a three-day beard. "Sorry," he said and immediately regretted having said it. After all, it was not as if Becky were a high-class lady to whom he owed gallantry and respect. Like all the other women on this bus, she was a common whore!

But then he remembered the Bible story Mrs. Moran once read in Sunday school about the woman Jesus saved from being stoned to death—and Jack immediately felt ashamed. He gazed at Becky—at her lovely blue eyes, somewhat sadder and more worldly wise than he remembered them from the last time they met but still filled with warmth and friendship for him. "How are you, Becky?" he asked. "It's good to see you."

Again, she kissed him—lightly this time, as if she were afraid to touch him. "Good as can be expected, I guess," she replied. Quickly she looked away, biting her lip. Recovering her composure quickly, she beamed happily at him. "What's this I hear about you almost drownin' in the Strait last night?"

Jack was astounded. "What do you mean? How'd you hear about that?"

"Oh, it's all over town! It'll prob'ly be in the *Benicia Herald* next week. I can just see the headline now: 'Brave boy survives perilous boat accident!'"

Jack shook his head in dismay. "First of all," he explained coldly, "it wasn't an accident. Somebody tried to kill me. And, second of all, I didn't do anything brave. It was the Greek fishermen who were brave. If it hadn't been for them, I'd be dead right now."

"Golly! What happened, Jack? What do you mean somebody tried to kill you!"

"It's a long story. I don't think want to hear it," he added, suddenly realizing Becky shouldn't hear it because such knowledge could be dangerous for her as well as for Adam, Billy, Francis and himself.

"Come on, Jack!" she insisted, tucking her hand under his arm. "I'm your friend. I want to know all about it."

"I really can't talk about it," Jack said with finality. "Sorry, Becky."

She withdrew her hand, clearly annoyed with him. They sat in silence for several minutes as the bus rumbled out along West Military toward Vallejo. When it began the long uphill ascent on Benicia Road, the roar of its engine operating in low gear was so loud that it obliterated all conversation. As they coasted into Vallejo, though, the only sound was that of the wind passing. The other passengers had resigned themselves to only occasional spurts of conversation.

"Jack," Becky said with iron determination. "I want you to tell me everything that happened. If you've been involved with something illegal, so what?" She glared sternly at him. "You think what I do is legal?"

Her question triggered a montage of images in Jack's brain—the image of his mother naked with Soames, images on the French postcards Francis Flanagan had once shown him, images of Becky with her customers. All now flashed before his eyes, reminding him of the nightmares that had troubled him in the past year. *What did this mean?* Jack wondered. *Did this happen to everyone? Were we all no different from dogs in the street?*

Jack didn't have an answer. *Maybe*, he thought, *nobody does.* He looked at Becky and saw the desperation in her eyes—the hopeless yearning for something better than the life she had. That much, perhaps because of his most recent near-death experience, Jack now understood.

"I work for Adam Tucker," he began. "You know him, right?"

Becky nodded

."I've been working for him and living with him for three years now," Jack explained. "He's been kind to me, but he's not just a mechanic. He's a bootlegger. Well, anyway, he's sort of a bootlegger. He delivers the sugar bootleggers use. It's still illegal." Jack stopped talking. He resolved to say no more.

"And that's why somebody tried to kill you last night," Becky promptly observed with the stark perceptiveness of her profession.

Jack nodded.

Again, she slipped her hand under his arm and, putting her lips close to his ear, murmured, "It's alright, Jack. I understand. Don't be afraid. I won't tell nobody. Just promise me somethin'."

He looked at her, puzzled. What could he possibly promise anyone—let alone a woman of Becky's reputation?

She held up her free hand, signaling him to wait before he spoke. The bus was pulling into the Vallejo terminal. The other passengers quickly got out and moved like a flock of noisy geese toward the central shopping area on Georgia Street.

Still grasping Jack's arm tightly, Becky guided him into the terminal waiting room—a small, foul-smelling place containing nothing but a few decrepit wooden benches, an unattended ticket counter, and a chalkboard listing bus fares and departure times to Napa and other North Bay destinations.

"Come see me at the Lido," she urged excitedly. "I want to give you a present." Then, opening her purse, she extracted a calling card with her name printed on it. Using the stub of a pencil, on the back of this card she wrote the name *Sadie* and pressed the card into Jack's hand. "Come next Tuesday afternoon at 4:00 and ask for Sadie. She'll help you find me." Then, fixing him with a devilish smile, she said, "It won't cost you nothin', honey!" Once more she kissed him—to his astonishment, this time on his mouth. Then she quickly exited the terminal.

CHAPTER SIXTEEN

"SomebodyLoves Me"

JACK HAD WALKED MOST OF the way back from the Vallejo bus terminal to the house on Magazine Street when he encountered Adam's truck coming in the opposite direction.

"What the hell happened to you?" Adam demanded angrily as he stopped to pick Jack up. "I been lookin' all over for y'! You los' me a lot o' money las' night, boy!"

When Jack related the events of the past eighteen hours, though, Adam's anger subsided. "You're a brave boy," he affirmed. "You didn't tell them Greeks nothin' about what we's doin', did y'?" he asked with a worried scowl.

"No sir," Jack said, nonetheless apprehensive about what he had told Becky. He decided the less said about that, the better.

"Guess somebody done found out where we's hidin'. Looks like we gonna have t' move again," Adam said.

"Where to?" Jack asked.

"Napa," Adam answered. "Got me some friends works for the 'lectric railroad up there. We has t' lay low for a while. Maybe go t' work for the railroad 'til the heat's off."

As soon as they returned to the house, Adam and Billy again dug up the old sea chest they had buried—this time, under the rain shelter in the fenced-in pig pen—while Jack and Francis collected their clothing, Adam's guns and mechanic's tools, the Army cots and blankets and loaded them into the back of the truck.

Driving back into Vallejo, Adam stopped briefly at the Monticello

Wharf on Georgia Street to phone his friends in Napa. "We's all set, boys," he assured them when he returned a few minutes later, climbed into the cab, and headed north.

*   *   *

For the next several days, Billy, Francis and Jack were at loose ends while Adam worked with his friends to find all of them some form of employment and a more permanent place to stay than the boarding house in Napa where they rented bunk beds for a dollar a night.

Adam paid Jack for his latest nocturnal run across the Strait, even though the attempt had failed and Adam now also had to reimburse Harry Lee for the loss of his boat. Over the past two years, Adam had accumulated a considerable hoard of cash from his sugar-distribution business. It never occurred to him simply to abandon his boys and let them fend for themselves.

Eager to see Becky again, early Tuesday morning Jack took a bus from Napa to Vallejo. There he transferred to the Benicia-Vallejo Stage Line. Since he had several hours to kill in Benicia, he decided to spend them near the First Street Pier where he could watch the train and car ferries coming and going. He never tired of this spectacle.

He also hoped to see his new Greek fisherman friends Nick and Marco—to thank them again and to repay them for his bus fare to Vallejo. But there was no sign of them on their barge. Apparently, they were asleep after a long night of fishing. There was no sign of Dorcas either. Jack was grateful for that. He did not like or trust the woman—a feeling he supposed was mutual.

By one o'clock, Jack grew hungry so he walked up First Street to Mary Lou Hewett's soda fountain. Huey was asleep in his own barber's chair when Jack entered the shop. On Tuesdays, business in town was always slow for Huey. Mary Lou, though, had several luncheon customers.

"Well, look who just blew in!" she declared as Jack mounted one of the few vacant stools at the soda fountain. "Jack Westlake, what you doin' in town?" Every customer at the counter immediately turned to look at Jack, and Mary Lou waddled over to him as fast as her swollen ankles would allow. "Ain't seen you in a dog's age, honey! Goodness—

how you done growed up! What's this I hear 'bout you almos' drownin' in the Strait las' Friday?"

Jack suddenly realized he had made a mistake seeking sustenance at Mary Lou's soda fountain. Now he would have to make up a whopping good story because Mary Lou was sure to press him for details. "What's the lunch special today, Mary Lou?" Jack asked, hoping to dodge her question with one of his own.

"Sausage an' fried beans—only two bits. You want that?" she asked.

"Yes. That sounds good."

Within minutes, Mary Lou served him a steaming plate of sausage and beans along with a thick slice of freshly baked bread. Leaning on the counter directly in front of him, she said, "Now, while you're eatin', s'pose you tell me all about what happened Friday."

Jack had quickly stuffed his mouth full and was chewing vigorously. He waved his hand, pleading for her to wait.

"You want some soda pop?" she asked, determined to get another nickel out of him.

"Just some cold water. Wow! Those sausages are hot!"

"Best linguica in Benicia," she proudly affirmed as she served Jack a glass of water. Again she leaned toward him, eager for an answer to her first question.

Jack was not good at making up stories. He wracked his brain for several seconds before he finally spoke. "Well, you see, it was like this. I was doing some night fishing in a skiff I borrowed from one of Adam's friends when all of a sudden I hooked into a big sturgeon. I mean, he had to be a real monster! He pulled me all the way around Dillon Point." Jack quickly scooped up another large mouthful of sausage and beans to give himself time to think of what he would say next.

With the trace of a skeptical smile on her face, Mary Lou remained stubbornly attentive.

"I guess I hit a rock or something," Jack continued, "because all of a sudden the skiff started filling up with water so I had to jump out and start swimming."

"How come you didn't cut the line?" Mary Lou asked with a smirk.

Now Jack knew he was really in trouble. "I didn't have a knife," he blurted.

"A fisherman in a boat without a knife? You gotta be kiddin' me, Jack!"

"No. Honest! I thought I had one but I must've left it back at the dock."

"Then y' shoulda let the Sturgeon take your rod," Mary Lou observed with ruthless pragmatism. "So what happened then?"

"Well, next thing you know I got caught in the current. It just took me right out into the main channel. And that's when Nick and Marco rescued me in their boat."

To Jack's enormous relief, another customer signaled Mary Lou for service. "You was real lucky," she said. But, as she moved away, to the man sitting several stools apart from Jack she commented loud enough for everyone to hear, "Ain't that somethin'—a fisherman in a boat without knife? I'll tell y' that beats any fish story I ever heard!"

Jack writhed under the sudden close scrutiny of Mary Lou's other patrons but breathed a sigh of relief. However incredulous Mary Lou might be, she had apparently heard enough for the time being. Taking a big gulp of water, Jack slipped a quarter under the edge of his plate and left the soda fountain to head back down First Street toward the waterfront again.

To minimize the chance of further encounters with old Benicia acquaintances, Jack decided to wait inside the depot until his appointment with Becky at 4:00 o'clock. On one of the benches in the waiting room, he found an abandoned copy of the *San Francisco Examiner*. He opened this paper and held it up in front of his face, pretending to read intently. This, he hoped, would discourage anyone from engaging him in conversation.

Jack actually became very absorbed in this paper when he came across a story about Matt Frabizio—the sixteen-year-old boy he and Del had first seen playing so skillfully at the Benicia Buccaneers' baseball game two years before. According to the *Examiner*, the San Francisco Seals had just recruited Frabizio. The report quoted Seals Manager Ernie Frobish as saying, "This kid's a natural. I'm betting he'll break all our home run records next season."

At 3:35, the passenger train from Sacramento was scheduled to arrive. Always fascinated by the elaborate train-yard activities associated with such arrivals, Jack left the depot and went outside to watch.

"That's the 4034. She's SP's newest engine," he overheard one of the yard workers say to another by-stander as they stood on the platform. The yardman pointed eastward toward the Alta Plant where the largest steam locomotive Jack had ever seen slowly moved toward the depot, emitting thick puffs of steam and heralding its approach with the repeated clanging of its bell and the ear-splitting hoot of its of its whistle.

This locomotive was not only remarkable for its size. It was also designed much differently from any Jack had ever seen. The cab was at the front of the locomotive rather than the rear. This made sense, Jack thought. In fact, he had often wondered why someone had not thought before of putting the cab in the front. After all, it would make it much easier for the engineers to see the road ahead.

Fascinated, Jack ran down the platform steps to get a closer look as this giant new powerhouse rolled past the depot and stopped almost directly in front of him. Greedily, he studied every detail of its newly manufactured parts—the huge white-rimmed wheels, the 22-inch high-pressure cylinders directly behind the cab, and the enormous boilers easily twice the length of other engine boilers.

Checking his pocket watch, Jack suddenly realized it was past 4:00. He would be late for his appointment with Becky. Fortunately, the Lido was only a stone's throw from the depot.

As Jack pushed open one of the double doors into the saloon on the ground floor, he was startled by the formal grandeur of the place. Damask scarlet fabric covered the interior walls. Brass door fixtures and decorative urns, polished to a high sheen, reflected the light from an ornate glass chandelier suspended from the ceiling. The thick pile of an Oriental rug covered most of the polished hardwood floor, and heavy midnight-blue drapes closed over the oak-framed windows, muffling all sound both outside and inside. Groups of luxuriously upholstered chairs and sofas were arranged around low mahogany tables where several couples sat chatting quietly.

Instead of the usual long wood-framed bar with shelves behind it crammed full of bottles, in the Lido there was only a small service bar. Beside it stood a gray-mustached man in a black three-piece suit, white shirt and black cravat. His face, though florid, was expressionless. His bright blue eyes glittered like glass. There was an ominous stillness about this personage. Standing stiffly with his hands clasped together in front of him, he looked more like a wax figure in a museum than a living human being.

"May I help you, young man?" said someone with a deliciously contralto voice.

Jack turned around to see a tall woman in a royal blue evening gown standing behind him. She was not attractive in any conventional sense. Her figure was thin and angular—almost manly. She had a long, narrow face, smooth olive complexion, and sharply defined facial features. Her raven-black hair was tied up in a bun at the back of her head, giving her the look of a stern schoolmarm. It was her piercing gaze, however, that told Jack everything he needed to know—this woman was in command!

Thoroughly intimidated, Jack blurted out his name and fumbled in his pocket for the calling card Becky had given him. The woman took the card and examined both sides of it. Then, nodding curtly, she disappeared through a curtained interior doorway.

Jack stood waiting nervously for several minutes until the curtain in the same doorway parted again to reveal a much more exotic denizen of the Lido. With a doll-like face and bleached blond hair, this woman was dressed in a bright pink kimono, the front of which she kept tightly closed with both arms across her very ample bosom. Moving toward Jack with simpering steps, she trilled invitingly, "You must be Jack! I'm Sadie. I'd shake your hand, honey, but …" she looked down with feigned modestly at the front of her kimono. "Well, I ain't 'xactly dressed for formal introductions—if y' know what I mean," she winked. Then, with a taunting giggle, she asked, "You ready, honey?"

Jack thought he knew what this woman meant—that she was about to take him to see Becky. But he wasn't at all sure. He was in very unfamiliar territory and his adolescent imagination was working now at a furious pace. "Y .. yes," he stuttered. "I g … guess so."

Nodding and laughing, Sadie pointed at Jack's feet. "First, you gotta take off them shoes."

"Why's that?" Jack asked, surprised.

"House rules, honey. All our gentlemen customers has to do it.

That's how we keep 'em from runnin' off without payin'. Soon as you're finished, you come back out here and see Al over there. Then, you'll get your shoes back."

Obediently, Jack removed his shoes and offered them to Sadie. Still clutching her kimona, Sadie shook her head. "No. You give 'em t' Al an' he'll give y' a ticket."

As Jack approached the wax figure in the black suit, Al moved like an automaton behind the service bar to retrieve a packet of numbered tickets. His eyes still expressionless, he took Jack's shoes, gave him a ticket, and dropped the shoes in a box behind the bar.

"Thanks," Jack said. But there was no response. The man simply resumed his wax-museum pose.

"You can tip 'im later," Sadie said.

When he turned to look again at Sadie, he saw that she had let the front of her kimono fall open to reveal her tight-fitting corset, garters and black silk stockings. Giggling at the shocked expression on Jack's face, she grabbed his hand and pulled him through the curtained doorway. "Come on, honey. Becky wants t' show y' a good time."

Sadie led him through a dimly lighted corridor toward an exterior door. As she opened this door, Jack found the courage to ask: "Who was that other woman I met back there?"

"That, young man, is Missus K. T. Parker. She's owns this joint." Obviously annoyed with Jack's ignorance, Sadie let go of his hand and marched ahead of him along a gravel path between two rows of detached wood-frame buildings. Each building was just slightly larger than a privy. All were solidly constructed and neatly painted, however, and the entrance door to each was marked with its own highly polished brass numeral and matching lockable door latch.

"Becky's here in number six," Sadie explained coolly. "Just knock and she'll let you in, you lucky boy!" Then, turning to go back to the main building, she added, "You got one hour, buster. I'll come fetch you, so you better be ready."

Jack looked around at the other buildings, wondering if each of these too were occupied by one of the women at the Lido. *This is like a damn factory!* he thought with disgust. But then he remembered Becky's beautiful blue eyes and glorious red hair, so he knocked on her door.

Immediately, he heard someone inside disengaging both chain and deadbolt locks. Barefoot and wearing a simple white cotton nightgown, Becky stood in the doorway looking like the picture of youthful innocence. Without any word of greeting, she took his hand and gently pulled him inside. Then, closing and double-locking the door again, she embraced him and kissed him on the lips—lightly at first but soon hungrily and passionately.

*   *   *

Half an hour later, they lay naked in each other's arms. Though exhausted from their lovemaking, Jack felt a sweet lassitude he had never before experienced. It was as if someone had released him completely from life's burdens of toil and doubt. All he wanted to do now was remain supine on Becky's bed, relishing the warmth of her body against his own, cherishing her gentleness.

Becky had indeed been gentle. Though she knew all the tawdry tricks of her trade, she had used none of them in her ministrations to Jack—encouraging him to do only what seemed to him natural and made him feel confident. She knew this was his first experience of sex. She did not want it to be terrifying and sordid as hers had been when, at twelve, she had been raped by a man three times her age. Sitting up in bed, she gazed down at him. "So how d' y' like Becky's crib, Jack?" she asked with a puckish grin.

Startled by this question, for the first time Jack took note of his surroundings. The eight-by-ten foot room was barely large enough to contain Becky's four-poster bed. There were only two other pieces of furniture—a wooden stool and a small vanity with an oval mirror. Since the building was windowless, the only light came from a single electric lamp on the vanity. The wall studs and ceiling beams beneath the sloping roof above were exposed, which meant the room was cold in winter and hot in summer. The only admirable feature of the place was its impeccable cleanliness. The bed sheets were obviously changed daily, the floor swept and mopped. Everything reeked of yellow soap and ammonia. Clearly, this was not a room in which anyone was encouraged to stay for long.

"Crib? What do you mean?" Jack asked. He had never heard this word used to describe a bedroom before.

Becky chuckled. "Oh Jack! You're so innocent!" Stroking his cheek affectionately, she said, "It's OK. It's good that you didn't know about cribs, actually. That's what they call these little houses we use."

"You mean for …?" He was unable to finish his question. His brain teeming with images of men and women copulating like dogs in the street, Jack suddenly felt sick to his stomach.

Becky nodded solemnly. "Yes, Jack. That's what I do for a living—remember?"

"I guess I'd rather forget," Jack answered, noting how sharply her hardened expression contrasted with the soft, smooth curves of her naked body. Then he said, "I'd like to see you again."

"Sure," she replied. "But you'll have to pay next time." She hesitated, afraid that what she was about to say next might be too harsh. With her eyes downcast, she added, "And every time after that too."

There was a long pause as Jack studied her face. "Why do you do this, Becky? You're so much better than this."

"Damn-it-all, Jack!" she declared angrily. "What the hell do you know about it? Do you think I do this because I want to? I do it because I have to. At least here they give me three meals a day and a roof over my head, and they pay for the doctor when I get sick. Ain't nobody else gonna take care of me like that." Now it was Becky's turn for a deliberate pause. The corners of her mouth turned down in bitterness. "Are *you* gonna take care of me, Jack?"

Jack could not answer her, though he desperately wanted to say yes.

Furious with his silence, she got out of bed, walked over to the vanity, and looked at herself in the mirror. "I thought so!" she mocked as she vigorously brushed her hair and rouged her lips to let him know she was preparing for her next customer.

Jack got out of bed too, walked over and stood behind her. Putting his arms around her, he pulled her close to him and kissed her neck. Immediately, she turned around and kissed him passionately on the mouth. "Oh Jack!" she cried. "I wish things was different! I wish I wasn't such a sinful woman!"

Unaccountably, the words came to him. They were from a hymn he had learned in Sunday school. "Those who love are born of God," he said.

He felt her shudder in his arms. "Let's go back to bed," she urged.

* * *

At exactly 4:00 P.M. one week later, Jack again entered the saloon at the Lido. This time, though, an armed bouncer immediately stopped him at the door. "What d' y' want, kid?" the man demanded.

"I ... er ... I came to see my friend Becky," Jack answered feebly.

"Sorry, kid," the bouncer said, his rigid manner softening slightly. "Becky don't work here no more. She's dead."

"Dead!" Jack cried out, reeling under the shock of this news. "But ... but how?"

"One of the Johns slit her throat."

"Slit her throat!" Jack roared, his shock and grief now turning to fury. "Who, for God's sake?"

The bouncer shrugged indifferently. "Who knows? It's a rough business, kid. Things like that happen." Then, seeing that Jack was about to move toward the curtained interior doorway, the bouncer grabbed his arm. "You better be on your way, kid. Ain't nothin' you can do."

"The hell you say!" Jack snarled, jerking himself free and smashing his fist into the man's face.

But the bouncer was bigger and stronger than Jack. He immediately wrestled Jack to the floor and knocked him unconscious with a rabbit punch.

The next thing Jack knew, he was lying on the boardwalk in front of the Lido surrounded by several men who were looking down at him and laughing derisively. As he massaged the back of his neck and struggled to his feet, one of them—older than the others—gave him a hand to help him up. "What happened, son?"

"They tossed me out because I took a punch at this guy in there. Some rotten bastard murdered my girlfriend!"

"You talkin' about Becky?" another man asked.

"Yeah," Jack said, eyeing this man suspiciously. "You know her?"

"Nope. But I heard about it. Just 'bout everybody in town's heard about it by now. You from out o' town, kid?"

"Vallejo, but I used to live here. When did it happen?"

"Last Saturday night—way after curfew. The police was here and everythin'. They didn't arrest nobody, though. The bastard who done it musta got away."

"Are they trying to catch him?" Jack asked.

"I doubt it," yet another man said. "She was nothin' but a two-buck tramp. Police aroun' here don't bother with whores much." Then, with a leer at his companions, he added, "Leastways, not dead ones."

All of the others laughed uproariously at this—all except the older man who had helped Jack to his feet. Shaking his head in disgust now, this spectator walked away. In stunned silence, Jack followed him up the street as far as the bus station. There, he walked into the public restroom, locked the door, and wept bitterly.

*   *   *

"Let it go, boy," Adam advised when Jack told him later that day about what had happened to Becky. They were sitting on the running board of a one-ton truck in Hooper's Garage in Napa, where Adam and Billy had recently found employment as auto mechanics.

"Let it go!" Jack raged. "How can anybody let it go? Becky was murdered, for God's sake! Somebody's got to pay, damn-it!"

Adam looked at him with sad eyes. "She was a whore, boy. Nobody cares about whores in this worl'. Leas' of all in Benicia where 'spect'ble white folks runs things. Look what they done t' me jus' 'cause I took you in when you run away from your Momma. 'Spect'ble white folks don't like niggers and whores. You bes' remember that," he warned, "'cause now, boy, you's a nigger too."

Jack knew what Adam meant. Still, he was shocked and infuriated by the presumptuousness of Adam's remark. He Jack Westlake, after all, was a white man; and Becky, a white woman. *There is a difference!* he heard an angry voice scream somewhere deep inside of himself. But he kept silent. For now Jack's grief overwhelmed all bitterness and resentment.

Adam too sat in silence, munching on the chicken sandwich Jack had brought him for his supper. Still chewing, he announced, "I found a job for y', boy—over at the Holland House."

"What kind o' job?" Jack asked indifferently.

"Bellhop and houseboy," Adam said, licking his fingers. "Act'ly, it's three jobs," he added with a sly smile. "Shoeshine boy too. They was real int'rested when I told 'em how good you is at shinin' shoes."

"There isn't much money in that," Jack said bitterly.

"You play it right," Adam replied evenly, "you can make good money. Lots o' rich folks stays at the Holland House—folks that tips real good. You walk on over there now an' see Tom Mullens. He works the front desk. You tell'im I sent y'."

Jack put his head in his hands. *What's the use?* he almost said aloud. *I don't want to do anything. I'd rather be dead like Becky!*

Adam punched Jack hard in the arm. "You git, boy!" he declared angrily. "You ain't free-loadin' off o' me no more!"

1925

Diamond Beach at low tide, showing decayed
hull of Black Diamond Mine coal barge

CHAPTER SEVENTEEN

"Yes Sir, That's My Baby"

WHEN JACK STARTED WORKING AT the Holland House in Napa, his first assignment was washing pots in the hotel kitchen. He worked side-by-side with two other men—a young Japanese named Jimmy Osawa and a much older Irishman named Micky Lafferty.

Jimmy, who loaded dirty dishes and silverware into the wire trays that ran on a canvas conveyer belt through the hotel's big steam washing machine, spoke no English. He communicated only with quick little nods or shakings of his head. Micky chattered like a magpie, a lighted cigarette between his lips dribbling ashes everywhere as he unloaded the clean dishes and silverware and sorted them into separate wooden bins.

"Where y' from, kid?" Micky demanded to know only minutes after Jack began his first day. "Looks to me like you ain't washed pots before," he sneered when Jack did not answer. "You better get yourself some rubber gloves."

"I'll manage," Jack said sullenly.

"Don't get smart with me, sonny!" Micky warned. "Y're low man on the totem pole around here, so you best respect your elders!"

Again, Jack did not respond or even make eye contact. He began extracting the greasy pots and pans from the deep side-by-side sinks he was supposed to use to clean them, placing each item on the adjoining counter top and then filling both sinks with hot water.

"Here, boy," Micky said, resting his hand lightly on Jack's shoulder and handing him a pair of thick black rubber gloves. Micky's face was so close to him that Jack could smell the man's stale, whiskey-reeking breath.

Jack flinched and stepped aside quickly to keep his distance. "Thanks," he said curtly.

As if he had read Jack's thoughts, Micky leered at him. "That's it, kid. You'll get it right—sooner or later!"

It was almost time for the hotel dining room to open, so the kitchen was noisy as cooks shouted commands to each other and waiters ran in and out carrying trays full of clean glass water goblets and place settings into the hotel dining room. Frying fish and potatoes; roasting pork, chicken and beef; and simmering soups and sauces created a dissonance of aromas. As Jack dipped the first cast-iron pot crusted with rancid beef gravy into his sink, he felt as if he would vomit.

"You need to use this, kid." It was Micky again, sidling up to Jack and pressing the long wooden handle of a wire scrubbing brush into his gloved hand.

Jack only grunted acknowledgment and began rubbing the wire brush vigorously against the inside of the cast-iron pot caked with a thick and long since hardened coating of animal fat.

"An' this is what y' need to cut the grease, sonny," Micky said as he poured a lye solution from a clear glass jug into the sink Jack was using. Touching Jack's shoulder again, he added, "Like I said, kid—you'll catch on."

Looking down at the hand on his shoulder, Jack snarled angrily. "Hey, hands off, old man!"

Micky jumped back in mock terror. "Oh sorry, kid! Y're real touchy, ain't y'? Too bad for you, buddy!" Micky returned to his assigned duties, but not without a coy wave and wink at Jack.

For the next two hours, everyone was busy. Waiters ran in, shouting customer orders at the cooks and wrangling with Micky to speed up the supply of clean plates and utensils. The head chef shouted a constant barrage of commands at his cooks while the cooks squabbled over access to the stovetops and ovens. There was no time for the calculated innuendo. Anyone who hesitated or balked was immediately bombarded with obscenities.

This didn't bother Jack. Working with Adam and his fellow bootleggers had inured him to such frenzied bullying and verbal abuse.

He knew there was nothing personal involved. It was all part of the momentum of labor under duress. It was later, when the pace of work in the kitchen began to slow, that Jack began to feel uneasy.

Again, Micky approached and touched Jack's shoulder. "So, kid, how'd it go? Think y'r gonna like this job?"

Grabbing Micky's wrist, Jack spun the much smaller man around like a doll and yanked his arm sharply up behind his back, making him cry out in pain. "What'd I tell you about the hands, you creep! Now leave me alone!"

"Sure, kid," Micky whined. "I was just tryin' t' be friendly. You don't have t' be mean about it."

Releasing Micky, Jack pushed him hard so that he stumbled and almost fell. "I don't need your friendly stuff—understand?"

Micky stood staring at Jack for several seconds, his weasel-black eyes flickering with wrath. Then, slowly he removed the stub of his cigarette from his lips and neatly spat on the floor between them. "Screw you, kid!"

*　　*　　*

When Jack returned to work the next day, Tom Mullens stopped him at the service entrance. Tom was a stocky man with thinning brown hair and a broad, pleasant face. His expression now was anything but warm and friendly. Being the assistant hotel manager, Tom was responsible for making sure quarrels between the help were kept at a minimum.

"Come with me, Jack," Tom said grimly as he led the way through the hotel lobby into his small office behind the front desk. Closing the office door, he gestured toward a straight-back chair. "Sit down. We gotta have a little chat."

Jack did as he was told. *Now I'm in for it!* he thought, without understanding why.

Tom leaned against a large oak desk covered with stacks of newly printed menus. Crossing his arms, he glared angrily at Jack. "Micky tells me you hurt him bad yesterday—almost broke his arm. What's this about?"

"Micky's a damn Ethel!" Jack declared. "He tried to mess with me, so I twisted his arm and told him to back off."

Tom's stern expression softened into a chuckle. "Listen, kid," he said. "You over-reacted. Sure, maybe Micky's kind o' weird. But he's harmless."

"I'm not so sure about that," Jack retorted. "Whatever he is, I don't want him messing with me."

Tom shifted a stack of menus on his desk chair to make room to sit down. "Don't worry. He won't mess with you again 'cause you scared the crap out of him. Just do your job right and things'll be fine. Fact is, you're not gonna be washin' pots for long. It's just a place we start newcomers to see what kind o' stomach they got. Adam told me you was tough, an' I can see that. Give it a week. Then, if you behave yourself, I'll move y' out to the bar where you can make some good tips. Deal?"

Jack was surprised by this sudden show of generosity. He had expected to be reprimanded for roughing up Micky—perhaps even fired. He smiled and nodded eagerly. "Sure. That'd be great. Thanks, Mister Mullen."

"Good. Now, go to work and keep your cool. 'Cause, if you do somethin' stupid again, I'll fire your ass! You got it?"

"Yes, sir." Jack stood up, wanting to shake hands. But, even though he was smiling, Tom's arms remained crossed in front of his chest. Tom Mullens would put up with no nonsense—a trait Jack definitely admired.

* * *

Tom was as good as his word—better, in fact. For, only two days later, he gave Jack a full-dress uniform, complete with crisp white jacket, and assigned him to tend bar in the hotel's luxurious saloon.

All four walls of the Cartwheel Lounge, as this popular cocktail lounge and dining room was called, were lined with dark mahogany panels. Plush maroon carpet covered the floor wall-to-wall; and, from the 12-foot high ceiling hung eight large cartwheels, the rims and spokes of which were mounted with small clear-glass electric light bulbs. This was the only illumination in the place, except for lighted candles in glass bowls on each of several dozen widely dispersed tables and a row of recessed electric ceiling lights above the bar. Stretching across the full length of the wall behind the bar was an enormous mural depicting a nude woman sprawled seductively on a crimson divan.

"This is where you put all the dirty glasses," Tom explained, pointing to a large removable wooden bin behind and below the surface of the bar. "When it's almost full, you just press this button and Jimmy will come pick it up." Then, pointing to a large drawer built into the wall beneath the mural, Tom said, "Clean glasses are in here." He pulled open the drawer, revealing that it contained a removable tray full of highball and stemmed cocktail glasses loaded from inside the kitchen. "Your friend Micky keeps this one supplied," he murmured, winking at Jack. "So be nice to him, OK?"

Jack nodded with a grimace.

"All the good stuff—imported wines, brandies, scotch, whiskey—is stored in those." Tom pointed to several pad-locked oak cabinets directly beneath the mural. "Strictly for our best customers. I'll give you a list. Everybody else gets the bathtub," he said, pointing to a row of spigots just below the bar top. Each spigot was marked with a printed label— *Scotch*, *Rye*, *Gin*, *Rum*, and *Brandy*.

Jack nodded. He knew all about "bathtub"—one source of wood alcohol for all. The color and flavor were added through each spigot to simulate the various types of liquor.

"Now for what's most important," Tom said, moving to a large cash register behind and at the far end of the bar. With its enormous keyboard and lacquered cabinet, this antique machine looked more like a one-armed bandit than a cash register.

Tom punched a key labeled *TOTAL* and a drawer popped out soundlessly. There were two sections in this drawer. One held various denominations of currency arranged in orderly slots and the other, though now empty, was labeled *CHARGE RECEIPTS*. Pointing to the receipt section, Tom explained, "This is where we put our most important customers' bar tabs. The bills and coins are to make change for cash-bar customers." Gripping the side panels of the drawer, he gently lifted it out its tracks to show how it could be removed. "At closing time, you bring the whole thing to me in my office. When it gets real busy, I'll stop by every so often to pick up the surplus cash and give you whatever small bills and change you need. You got all that?"

Jack nodded confidently.

Tom smiled at him and reached out to shake his hand. "Well alright, Jack. Go to work."

* * *

Friday evening, two weeks after Jack had been working the bar in the Cartwheel Lounge, Mullens called him aside to explain that two of the Leighton brothers from Benicia were about to arrive with several guests and that Jack should cater to their every whim. Mullens then gave the same instructions to the table waiters assigned to the Cartwheel Lounge, and they immediately pulled together several tables and set them with platters of canapé.

Jack knew about the Leighton brothers. They were, as *Benicia Herald New Era* editor Brad Pincus once reported, members of "the most interesting and flamboyant clan that ever resided in Benicia." Morton Leighton, the *pater familias*, had served briefly as United State's envoy to Panama in 1912. After contracting malaria a year later, he returned to Benicia where he recovered and served as Justice of the Peace until his death in 1921.

The Leighton family was well known for its generous hospitality to several upper echelon officers at the Benicia Arsenal. But it was Morton Leighton's eccentric sons, Alexander and Wyatt, who gave the family its reputation for flamboyance. Wyatt, the younger brother, was especially famous for the many pranks he had played on local townsfolk as a boy as well as for his widely celebrated reputation as a humorist and Hollywood screenwriter. Alexander, though more subdued in his personality, had already made *San Francisco Examiner* headlines with his achievements as a budding architect.

Before these distinguished guests even entered the Cartwheel Lounge that evening, Jack recognized the loud voice of Florence Henshak.

"I've always said, 'men are *such* pigs!'" Florence declared as she led the party of six through the entranceway. It was not Florence's characteristically crude remark that caught Jack's attention, however. Rather it was the strikingly beautiful young woman to whom she spoke—Susanna Fisk, the wife of Ford production-line supervisor Elmer Fisk and the daughter-in-law of Jack's self-appointed savior Charlotte Fisk.

Attired in a black cloche and a simple lavender frock cut in the straight-line fashion of the day, the angel-faced Susanna drew admiring glances from every one of the several dozen men seated at the bar. Though she basked in such admiration, Susanna was obviously accustomed to it.

"Name your poison, kiddoes," Oscar Henshak declared as he plopped himself into a chair before any of the others.

"Allow me, Susanna," said Wyatt, ostentatiously pulling back a chair from the table for Susanna. At six feet and three inches, Wyatt towered over every other man in the Cartwheel Lounge except Jack.

"Oh thank you, sir. You're so gallant!" Susanna warbled with an ingratiating smile.

"I'd 've thought *you'd* be doing that, Elmer," Florence said to Susanna's bland-faced husband.

"Looks like Wyatt beat me to it," Elmer remarked and then added with a sneer, "Typical! Wyatt always plays chief bull in the cow pasture."

"When you've got a hammer," Wyatt quipped with a wink at Susanna as he seated himself to her right, "the world is your nail."

"You behave yourself, young man, or I'll tell your Momma on you!" Florence warned.

"Wouldn't do any good," Alexander quipped. "His Momma thinks he's the chief bull in the cow pasture too."

"So what are we drinkin'?" Oscar repeated. Then, summoning a waiter his side, he said, "I'll have a Jack Daniels neat with a glass of water on the side."

"Susanna," Wyatt asked solicitously, "what's your pleasure, my dear?"

Glancing flirtatiously over her shoulder at Jack who was now busy taking care of other customers at the bar, she asked the waiter, "Does your bartender know how to make a Pink Lady?"

The waiter, surly and skeptical by nature, hesitated slightly. He did not like Jack, for he thought he was arrogant young upstart. He quickly covered himself, though. "Oh yes, madam. I'm sure we can fill your order."

"I'll have a Manhattan, straight up," Wyatt announced.

"The same for me," Alexander said.

"Florence? Speak up, woman!" Oscar barked.

"I think a glass of champagne would be nice."

"So where's your stock broker friend?" Oscar asked Wyatt who had begun to whisper an off-color joke in Susanna's ear.

Ceremoniously extracting a large gold watch from his vest, Wyatt glanced at it. "Should be here any minute now."

Just as he spoke, a short, barrel-chested man in a pin-stripe suit entered the lounge, accompanied by two garishly attired women—one on each arm. Though plump and shapely, both women were heavily rouged to disguise their age. One wore a tight-fitting lime-green satin sheath that accentuated every curve. The other was draped in a bright red evening gown covered with glittering sequins. Noticing them as they entered, Jack thought he recognized the woman in red as one of Mrs. K. T. Parker's "girls."

"Hey Mark!" Wyatt called over the rising volume of conversation in the lounge. "Over here!"

As Mark approached their table, his close-set eyes immediately focused on Susanna. "Hey, what are y' doin', Wyatt? Already movin' in on somebody else's tomato? Ramona here's s'posed t' be yer date." Turning to the woman in red, he said, "Can't say I didn't warn y' honey. This guy's a real lady killer!"

"Don't pay any attention to him, Miss!" Wyatt said to the woman in red. "He's got the manners of a racetrack stable boy."

"Speakin' o' manners," Mark retorted, "Ain't y' gonna innnerduce us?"

Without rising from his chair, Wyatt announced with mock civility, "Mister Mark Fassio, please meet my friends Mister and Missus Oscar Henshak and Mister and Missus Elmer Fisk." Then, waving contemptuously at his older brother, he said, "You already know this clown."

Fassio nodded with a smirk at Alexander, and to the others said perfunctorily, "Please t' meet ya's." Pushing the woman in red forward as he might a show horse, he announced, "This here's Ramona Krebs. Her friends call her Rummie," he added with a knowing wink at Wyatt. Then with his arm encircling the waist of the woman in lime green, he said, "And this beauty's Gloria Buck. Grab a seat, girls," Fassio commanded as he himself sat down, his gaze still fixed salaciously on Susanna.

Just then, the waiter returned with the drinks the others had already ordered. Mark caught his eye. "What y' got on tap, buddy?"

"Some very fine Canadian ale."

"Bring us three mugs o' that," Mark said without so much as a glance at either of his female companions.

"Wyatt tells me you're a stock broker," Oscar said, taking the first sip of his Jack Daniels. "That true?"

"Yeah, an' I got a real hot tip if anybody's int'rested."

"We're all ears," Alexander sneered.

"Buy American Bridge. It's really takin' off an' the sky's the limit," Fassio declared triumphantly.

"Isn't that the company that's building the new bridge across the Carquinez Strait?" Oscar asked.

Fassio's eyes glittered with the anticipation of a sale. "You got it!" he declared. "Believe me, you can make a real killing with this one. You know how many cars an' trucks are gonna be usin' that bridge? Thousands every day, and with tolls at 75-cents per car and 15-cents per passenger, that bridge'll make millions in no time! Besides, we're paintin' the tape."

"Painting the tape?" Susanna asked as the waiter served the three mugs of ale Fassio had ordered. "What does that mean?"

Gloating over his own superior knowledge, Fassio explained. "Everybody who buys stock watches the ticker tape, pretty lady. You know what that is, don't y'?"

Susanna looked at her husband, her lovely brown eyes pleading for help. Elmer dutifully intervened with calm assurance. "Of course, I have a machine in my study at home."

Visibly disappointed that he had not been able to play on Susanna's ignorance, Fassio pressed on with his explanation. "Anyway, here's how it works. My investment firm, Ostrander and Dunne, has branches all over the country—New York, Chicago, San Francisco ... you name it. The brokers in all our offices buy or sell shares at the same time. Of course, that makes the price of a stock go up or down all of a sudden, and that makes everybody else think there's a big run. So everybody jumps on the bandwagon—one way or the other. 'Course, when the price goes up, we sell and make a profit; and when the price drops, we buy in cheap and then drive it up again. Sweet an' easy as pickin' cherries!"

"Sounds to me like you fellas are breakin' the law with that scheme," Oscar remarked.

Fassio shook his head vigorously. "All perfectly legit. You interested?"

"I'll look into it," Oscar said, still skeptical. "You got a business card?"

"Sure." Fassio immediately produced two cards and gave one each to Oscar and Elmer.

Having heard her fill of this boring topic, Susanna held up her almost emptied cocktail glass. "Mmm! This drink's delicious!" Turning to her husband, she said, "I think I'll have another, dear."

"I'll try one of those too," Florence chimed in.

Wyatt signaled to the waiter. "Pink Ladies for *all* the ladies!" he ordered magnanimously. "In fact, let's all have another round. This one's on me!"

By the time the Leighton party finally finished dinner two hours later, everyone was feeling magnanimous—especially Susanna who walked up to the bar to give Jack a ten dollar tip and blow him a kiss.

When Jack returned to the boarding house that night, he was feeling very full of himself. Flaunting his ten-dollar tip, he told Adam about his encounter with the beautiful Susanna Fisk and declared his intention to become a rich man and marry a woman just like her.

"That's fool's gold, boy," Adam said. "You bes' stay away from married womens. They nothin' but trouble."

* * *

Del and Sam were standing together on Diamond Beach, gazing silently westward at the two high hills guarding the narrows into San Pablo Bay. The April sky was dark with rain-filled clouds and a brisk gale was kicking up whitecaps in the main channel of the Carquinez Strait.

"I love this!" Del murmured softly. She had released her hair from the confines of the braids Ruby had tied up for her that morning. It felt wonderful letting her long, auburn locks fly freely behind her.

Sam looked at her, unable to quell the thoughts that came to him as he watched the wind press Del's cotton frock against her body, clearly revealing the supple curves of her thighs, hips and small but shapely breasts. "Me too," he said. "I bet it'd be fun sailing out there now."

She glanced at him with a taunting smile. "How about flying up in those clouds?" she asked. "Do you think you could do that?"

"For Pete's sake!" Sam declared. "I've only had two lessons. How would I know? Besides, I don't think that old Jenny they take me up in could handle this kind of weather. It's nothing but wood, wires and canvas. Probably get blown all over the place."

Del studied him seriously for a moment, her hazel eyes full of confidence. "I'll bet you could—anyway, someday soon."

"Maybe so," Sam replied, warm affection for this lovely young woman flooding through him so powerfully now that he wanted to hug her. Yet, the very thought of such intimacy with anyone—even a trusted childhood friend like Del—sent a tremor of revulsion through him, for it reminded him of his mother's ongoing incestuous relationship with Tully.

They were brazen about it now. Tully slept in his mother's bed every night. They even bathed together. This ten-year-old boy was like a helpless whining infant who clung to his mother wherever they went.

"Sam, what's wrong?" Del asked, frightened by the expression of fury and repugnance in his face. When he did not answer her question, she seized his hand. "Sam, talk to me! What is it?"

He shook his head and pulled away from her. "I don't want to talk about it. Just forget it, OK?" Folding his arms across his chest, he stared out again at the dark clouds over the Strait.

They stood in silence for several seconds, Del desperate to probe his thoughts. "It's your mother, isn't it?"

He looked around at her fearfully. "What do you mean?" he demanded.

"She's still not right, is she?"

"No," he said bleakly.

"You need to talk to someone about it," Del urged.

Sam realized Del was right. He did need to talk to someone. But to whom? Merriweather and his Quaker friends had only made matters worse with all their chanting and convoluted counseling about his need for acceptance and understanding. They knew about his mother and

241

Tully's warped relationship. Yet, they had insisted Sam continue to put up with it in silent resignation. "I can't do this any more," he declared. "I've got to get away."

"Where will you go?" Del asked. When he did not answer this question, she said, "Maybe you should talk to our priest, Father Cardoni."

Sam glared at her. "A priest! Are you kidding? I've had enough of that damn religion stuff already with those goofy Quakers!"

"What do you mean?" Del asked, feeling both offended and embarrassed. She knew Protestants had little respect for the Catholic clergy. Still, Sam's vehemence seemed to her excessive. "Father's a good man. He's old but he's very wise."

"There's nothing anybody can say or do," Sam said dejectedly. "I'll just have to handle it myself … somehow." His voice drifted off to a whisper.

"Do you want me to talk to Papa about it?"

"No!" he roared at her. "Don't you dare! Your father's the one who let her off in the first place, for God's sake!"

"Don't swear like that, Sam!" Del retorted. "You have no right to blame Papa. He was the presiding judge. He had to follow the law. There wasn't enough evidence to prove your mother's guilt. You know that perfectly well yourself! Maybe if you talked to him now, though, he could give you some good advice."

"I don't want anybody's damn advice!" Sam snarled. Then, sulking, he turned away from Del and walked briskly toward the steps leading up the bluffs to West K Street.

Feeling helpless and overwhelmed with sorrow for her friend, Del let him go. She knew something was very wrong in Sam's life—something perhaps even evil. Precisely what it was, though, she did not know. Nor did she have any idea how she could help her friend. Instinctively, she murmured a *Hail Mary* and then turned to look out across the water again.

Suddenly she noticed a female Mallard moving slowly down the beach. Four small brown objects were following her—so small and round they looked like tiny rubber balls attached to her with invisible strings. At length, Del realized the tiny balls were baby Mallards and that their mother was leading them toward the water.

Del felt panic in her heart for the ducklings. The waves in the Strait were high and rolling in fast. *Surely they will drown!* Del thought. *How can a mother duck lead her babies to such a fate?*

That is precisely what the adult Mallard did, though, and Del watched fascinated and delighted as the little brown balls bobbled along over the waves, indifferent to everything but their mother's forward movement. Del wished Sam had been there to see this miracle of 'Mother Nature.'

CHAPTER EIGHTEEN

"Sleepy Time Gal"

SWIRLS OF DUST WERE FLYING across the improvised airstrip behind the Rivers' barn as Sam made his way toward the waiting Jenny. Standing beside this flimsy-looking two-passenger Army Air Corps training plane was the tall, big-boned figure of Sharon Rivers, Sam's flight instructor.

Today Sam was going to take his final solo flight test. If he passed it, Sharon would sign the certificate allowing him to become a licensed pilot in the State of California. He had been preparing for this test for almost a year now, and he felt confident he would pass it without a single hitch. Sharon had already started the Jenny's engine as Sam approached.

Pulling his goggles down over his eyes and snapping the strap of his leather helmet under his chin, Sam sprinted the remaining distance to the plane, climbed into the forward cockpit, and strapped himself in. Then, after double-checking the operation of his wing flaps, he gave Sharon a "thumbs-up." His whole body tensed when she yanked the wooden chocks from in front of the Jenny's wheels and jumped clear of its wing.

Sam eased the Jenny forward, adjusting the throttle to increase the 90 horsepower engine's output. Within seconds, the biplane was bumping along the airstrip at fifty miles per hour. Sam pulled back on the joy stick and felt the aircraft rise gracefully in a gradual ascent. Sam relaxed as he banked slightly to the right and saw the open hay fields falling far below.

Circling back over the Rivers' ranch, he tipped his wings at the tiny figure waving to him from the airstrip. Then, pulling back on the joystick again, he pointed the plane at a small cluster of white clouds to begin the series of maneuvers he had to perform while Sharon watched from below.

Todd and Sharon Rivers had been born and raised in the western part of Calaveras County. Both were the children of beef cattle ranchers who had settled in that region during the 1850s. Their marriage had brought together a legacy of land and livestock ownership valued at more than a million in 1925 dollars. Though they were childless, they had continued the family business. By using hired cowhands—mostly migrant workers from southern California and Mexico—they freed themselves up to pursue their preferred avocation of flying.

Sharon especially had a fascination with aircraft because her older brother, Rex Scanlon, had been an Ace fighter pilot during World War I. His heroic death in a dog-fight over the Western Front had seared in her heart a determination to keep his memory alive by turning the romance of flight into a profitable enterprise.

When, through family connections in Los Angeles, Sharon had met the youthful Amelia Earhart in 1922, soon after Amelia had set an unofficial women's flying altitude record of 14,000 feet, Sharon felt sure that aeronautics was a field of endeavor where women could excel.

By attending various air shows throughout northern California, Todd and Sharon got to meet and swap stories with such famous barnstormers as Clyde Pangborn. It was through Pangborn that they also met Floyd Nolta who told them of his plans to start a crop dusting service in Glenn County, south of Sacramento.

Inspired by Nolta's idea, Sharon took some of the cash she had inherited from her parents' estate and bought a fleet of six Army surplus Jennies. Then, in 1924 she and her husband converted one of the family hay barns into a hanger, cleared a 600 by 20-yard swathe of level open pasture for an air-strip, and ran an advertisement in the *San Francisco Examiner* offering flying lessons.

Considering the distance of their ranch from the Bay Area—over 100 miles across mostly backcountry dirt roads—Sharon and Todd were astounded by the response to their newspaper advertisement. Within weeks, they had enrolled more than forty-seven students. Six of these had been referred to them by the California Forestry Service, a government agency keenly interested in training pilots for aerial fire reconnaissance. It was for precisely that job that Sam was now preparing.

Half an hour after take-off, Sam set his plane smoothly down on the Rivers' landing strip again and taxied slowly to a stop. Sharon ran up and let out a victory whoop. When he jumped down out of the cockpit, she gave him a bear hug. "Sam!" she declared exuberantly. "You did it! Absolutely flawless!"

Startled and intimidated by this tall, horse-faced woman's effusive praise, Sam pulled away from her. But, then, seeing the hurt expression in her eyes, he said, "Thanks to you, Sharon. You're a great teacher!" Her warm smile prompted him to add, "You're also a very good woman." He was surprised by his own words. It was something he had never said before to anyone.

Sharon threw back her head and guffawed. "My Gawd!" she exclaimed. "You are a peach!" Then, throwing her arm around his shoulders, she marched him toward the Rivers' ranch house—a sprawling one-story residence in an oasis of evergreen and oak trees. "You come have a nice cold glass of lemonade while I do the paperwork. Believe me, kiddo, you're a shoe-in for that Forestry job!"

Sam had never been happier in his life. At last, he would be free of his mother and able to pursue the career of his dreams.

* * *

Seated at the soda fountain in Fielding's pharmacy and ice cream parlor on First Street, Gail and Snooky were savoring the chocolate sundaes the owner's daughter Pam had prepared for them.

"So have you heard about the Monkey Trial yet?" Gail asked devilishly. She had not seen Snooky in several months and was eager to engage her friend on a topic that was sure to get her up on a soapbox. She liked nothing better than hearing Snooky rant and rave about politics or religion, unless it was hearing her belt out one of her favorite Gospel hymns. It was not Snooky's logic but her energy that captivated Gail.

Ever since they had been in high school together, Gail had loved to tease Snooky about her "blind faith" in the teachings of the Catholic Church. Gail had no particular prejudice against Catholics in general, though she had always thought such practices as the wearing of habits and saying the Mass in Latin were absurd.

"What monkey trial?" Snooky frowned. "That don't make no sense at all. You mean they're puttin' monkeys on trial in the courts now?" Then, she grinned and said, "Well, come t' think of it, I guess that does make sense. I mean, most o' them courtroom judges is just monkeys anyways."

Both women laughed so loud at this that Pam looked up from the novel she was reading in astonishment.

"No, Snooky. I mean the trial down in Tennessee where this teacher was arrested last month for teaching Darwin's theory of evolution."

"What's *that*!" Snooky squawked, still cackling over her own joke.

Gail sighed, realizing that she would now have to go into a long explanation before she could get to the really interesting part of their discussion. "Well, back in the 1850s," she began, "a scientist named Charles Darwin wrote a book called *The Origin of Species*. It was about some geological research he'd done. You see, he'd dug up a lot of fossils—I think it was in South America—and he discovered that ..."

"What's *fossils*?" Snooky asked.

"Old bones."

"Old bones." Snooky shook her head in disgust. "Jesus, Mary and Joseph! Why'd anybody wanna do that?"

Gail took a deep breath. "Anyway, by studying these fossils," she continued, "Darwin figured out that fish, reptiles, and birds all have the same ancestry. He said they evolved their different bone structures through natural selection."

"Hold on there, girl!" Snooky declared. "You're way over my head! You sound like a damn college professor or something! Where'd you learn all this goofy stuff anyway?"

"I read about it in *The San Francisco Examiner*. It's really very interesting."

"Yeah. I bet—all about old bones and snakes and such!" Snooky studied Gail's face in silence for several seconds. Their eyes locked and then, slowly, both of them began to smile. "You're leadin' up to somethin', ain't y'? You're gonnah try to get me worked up over somethin' again, ain't y'?"

Gail began to laugh, nodding vigorously. "Well of course, Snooks!

You know how much I love to get your goat! And I haven't seen you in so long!"

"That ain't my fault! I'm *always* around town. But this sounds like a pretty serious and complicated topic. I can handle serious, but I'm not in the mood for complicated right now. How 'bout if we save complicated for some other time?"

Gail had just filled her mouth with ice cream, so she nodded her agreement.

"Okee-Dokee. Now I have a serious one for you," Snooky said. "Have you heard from Jack lately?"

Gail winced at this question. "No," she said softly, hoping her one-word answer would be sufficient. She knew her friend was relentless, however.

"Last I heard he was workin' at some hotel up in Napa. Guess he must be livin' up there someplace with Tucker. Anyways, that's the rumor. Want me to find out more? I could ask around," Snooky offered "I'm pretty good at diggin' things up, y' know," she added with a grin.

Gail carefully placed her spoon on the saucer under her ice cream bowl. Then, dabbing her lips with a paper napkin, she sat in silence. She knew more about Jack's situation than Snooky did—much more than she was willing to share with her well-intentioned but meddlesome friend.

"I don't think so, Snooky," she said at last. "What good would it do? He's been with Tucker so long now, I doubt he ever even thinks of me."

"What about you?" Snooky asked caustically. "You stopped thinkin' o' him?"

"Of course not!" Gail seethed. "He's my only son. I'll never stop thinking and worrying about him! But what can I do?"

"We already talked about that—a long time ago," Snooky replied coldly.

"Mama, can I have more?" Alfie suddenly called out from his wheelchair behind them.

Snooky promptly spun around and, picking up Alfie's empty bowl, placed it on the marble-top counter. "Put a couple more scoops in this for me, will y' Pam?" Then, turning to look at Gail again, she said grimly, "For me, kiddo, this stuff never ends."

"I know," Gail murmured. Then, hoping her next response would discourage Snooky from further probing, Gail said, "Maybe you're right. Maybe I should at least try to get in touch with him. But how? Tucker's gone into hiding, and Jack's probably gone with him."

"Where'd you hear that?" Snooky asked, surprised and then suddenly suspicious that Soames may have told Gail something she herself had not heard through the grapevine.

Though it was now common knowledge in town that Soames and Tucker were rivals in the bootlegging business, no one but Gail knew how fierce that rivalry had become in recent months.

Nodding toward Pam, who was busily cleaning glasses in a tub of hot water behind the counter, Gail said, "Maybe we should talk about this someplace else."

"Good idea. Hey Pam!" she said to the girl. "How much we owe y'?"

"Thirty cents," Pam answered.

"My treat," Gail said as she drew three dimes from her change purse and placed them on the counter.

Out on First Street, the two women walked toward the waterfront, pushing Alfie in his wheelchair. They walked in silence for several blocks until they passed the charred remains of the old McClaren Tannery.

"So how'd you hear about Tucker goin' into hiding?" Snooky asked.

"Jimmy told me," Gail replied, still hoping desperately that she would not need to elaborate.

"Thought so," Snooky said. "Soames put him out o' bus'ness, didn' he? Prob'ly tried to rub him out too, huh?"

"I don't know anything about that," Gail lied. For several months now, she had learned much more than she wanted to know about Soames' illicit activities as well as about his bitter hatred of Tucker. On several occasions, she had even been forced to socialize with Ted Peters, Howard Roach and his obnoxious daughter Bernie when they dined with Soames and Gail at the Fremont Hotel in San Francisco.

Snooky and Gail were approaching the train depot now, so they stopped in front of the steps leading up to the waiting platform.

"Alright," Snooky resumed, "so here's what I'm gonnah do. I know a guy works the bar at Frank's Place. Frank used t' buy all his hooch from Tucker, so he's bound t' know somethin'. Soon as I find out where Jack's workin', I'll let y' know. But y' gotta keep it a secret from Soames. You know that, don't y'?"

"Please don't do this, Snooky!" Gail pleaded desperately. "It could make trouble for Jack. Just let it be."

"Oh, so you're scared Soames'll squeeze it out o' you, eh? Damn-it, girl! I don't believe you!"

"Let it be," Gail repeated firmly.

Fuming, Snooky grasped the handles of Alfie's wheelchair and pushed it across First Street.

"Bye, Pail," Alfie called out to her as the boy and his mother moved swiftly back up the street toward Military.

Gail waved to him, her eyes filling with tears. It was her worst recurrent nightmare—she was losing people again.

*   *   *

Frank's Place on West J Street in Benicia was a favorite hangout of local-area sportsmen. Open twenty-four hours a day and seven days a week, it offered a wide variety of recreational activities and entertainments. Frank Alessio, the owner and proprietor, had bought the three-acre strip of waterfront property for a mere $100 soon after the Turner Shipyard closed down in 1903 and property values in Benicia suddenly hit rock bottom. Along with the land, Frank had also acquired an abandoned coal barge anchored fifty yards off shore.

Frank quickly realized the old barge was a potential gold mine. Because of its location where the eastern shoal of the Carquinez Strait drops precipitously into the deep-water channel, schools of salmon, shad, and bass swept past this barge year-round. It was a natural magnet for sports fisherman.

Frank therefore salvaged an abandoned skiff he found in the tules along Southampton Bay, equipped it with a single-cylinder gasoline engine, and used it to ferry customers to and from the barge. At the same time, he converted the wharf and boathouse on his property into a tavern where he prepared box lunches for his customers. When they returned from the barge at the end of each day, for an extra dollar each, they could also purchase a hearty hot meal of barbequed pork and beans as well as a mug of Frank's home-brewed small beer.

With the coming of Prohibition in 1919, Frank discovered that his barge and shore-side tavern offered even greater business opportunities. By expanding his menu of alcoholic beverages to include bootlegged wine and brandy and adding a bunkhouse at the rear of his tavern, he provided sleeping accommodations to customers who liked to linger hours after they returned from their day of fishing on his barge. Then, by engaging the services of several local prostitutes and the talents of various local entertainers like Snooky Wells, Frank soon turned his enterprise into one of the most popular speakeasies in the North Bay.

It was at Frank's Place that Jack and a dozen of his drinking buddies from Napa, Vallejo, and Benicia gathered after work every Wednesday and Friday night to gamble in a back room Frank had set up for private parties. Since Wednesdays and Fridays were paydays at Alta Manufacturing and the Benicia Arsenal, such parties rarely remained private for long because the flood of customers in the public bar quickly spilled over into the high-stakes poker games.

These invasions often resulted in barroom brawls. Though only seventeen, Jack stood head-and-shoulders above most of Frank's customers and, when fired up with Frank's bathtub gin, he fought with the ferocity of a bull. By the late autumn of 1925, he had established a reputation as the unofficial card room bouncer at Frank's Place.

Felicia Boreman—or "Fleck," as her friends and customers called her—had lots of surprises in her bag of tricks. Her thick torso and bawdy sense of humor made her a great favorite among the men who congregated weeknights at Frank's Place.

By seventeen, Fleck had already completed her apprenticeship at the Lido when "K. T." Parker fired her for freelancing on the side. Since then, Fleck had developed her own business by teaming up with five other women in Benicia who shared her belief that Parker had an unfair advantage in the local white slave trade.

When Fleck sidled up to stevedore Mort Kendrick as he sat at the bar that New Year's Eve, it was with the deliberate intent of pitting him against Jack Westlake in a spontaneous fistfight that would drive Jack and his gang of rowdies out of town once and for all. These young "punks" had been wrecking her business lately by drawing too much attention to their card games and emptying her customers' pockets before Fleck and her girls could get to them.

Mort was the perfect foil for her plan. Though he was not a tall man, his 230 pounds of body weight was all muscle. What mattered most, though, was Mort's short fuse and his insatiable appetite for women. "How's it hanging, Mort?" Fleck asked by way of a greeting.

The big man turned on his stool to face her, a lascivious grin spreading across his broad and florid face. "For you, baby, I'm always ready!" he declared as he grabbed her wrist and forced her hand against his groin.

With her free hand, Fleck slapped him playfully on the cheek. "Steady there, boy! I'll let y' know when I'm ready for some action. How 'bout buyin' me a drink first?"

"Sure, baby. Whatever y' want." Mort leaned far over the bar and bellowed. "Hey Gino! Get your skinny ass down here! My girl needs a drink!"

At twenty-two, Gino was the youngest of the five Alessio brothers. He was the only one who did not yet have a business of his own, which is why he was bartending for his oldest brother Frank. Always cheerful and easy-going, Gino had little ambition and much preferred swapping jokes with customers at Frank's Place than working in any of his other brothers' several business enterprises—which included the Benicia-Vallejo Stage Line, a laundry delivery service, and a grocery store. Rocking his head from side-to-side in mock defiance, Gino waved his hand at Mort as if to say, 'Keep your pants on.'

This was not the response Mort wanted. Immediately, he stepped off his bar stool and strode down to the end of the bar where Gino was still busy refilling other customers' beer mugs. Shoving his way between two of these customers, Mort pounded his huge fist on the bar top directly in front of Gino. "Hey! You gonnah get my girl a drink or do I have t' come back there and bust y' one?"

Gino shrugged. "Sure, sure, Mort. Be right with y'."

Pounding with his fist a second time, even harder, Mort shouted, "*Now*, asshole!"

Gino jumped and moved swiftly to serve Fleck, who had commandeered Mort's barstool and was watching this little donnybrook with great amusement. The two men Mort had pushed aside glared angrily at him. Mort responded in kind and stomped back to where Fleck was giving Gino her order—a double shot of Old Crow. "You got some nerve stealin' my seat, bitch!" Mort growled at her.

Ignoring this rebuke, Fleck held up her glass in a toast. "Here's mud in y'r eye, Mort!" Emptying her glass in one swig, she wiped her mouth with the back of her hand and said, "Thanks for the drink, muscle-man. How 'bout another one?"

"Give her another and make it a double!" Mort barked at Gino before he could move away again. "An' two doubles for me," he commanded as he added a two dollar bill to the pile of change he had left on the bar.

"Hey! You're a real big spender tonight, Mort! What'd y' do? Whip them kids in the back room?"

Mort blinked confusion. "What kids?"

"That kid Jack Westlake and his crowd." Fleck pointed with her prominent chin toward a closed door at the back of the barroom. "You know, the ones with the poker game."

"Poker game? I didn't know nothin' about no poker game. When'd that start?"

Fleck shook her head in contempt of the man's ignorance. "You gotta be kiddin' me," she declared. "It's been goin' on for months now!"

"Well, I don't play cards," Mort retorted. "Only thing I bet on is the horses an' maybe a cock fight once in a while. Better odds."

Immediately, Fleck saw her opportunity. "How do y' know the odds in poker if y' never played?"

Mort frowned. Then, stepping back from her as if to move toward the card room, he said, "OK. So let's try it right now."

"Atta boy, Mort!" Fleck smiled encouragingly. "I knew you was a sport. Go get 'em, stud!"

"You ain't comin' with me?"

"Hell no! They'd never let a woman in there."

Mort shrugged and headed toward the card room. Although its closed door was clearly marked with a *private* sign, Mort did not bother to knock. He simply pushed the door open and entered.

It was only a few seconds before everyone in the bar heard Mort's big voice bellowing in defiance. "What the hell y' talkin' about! You sayin' my money ain't good enough?"

This was quickly followed by the sounds of a scuffle as several of the players tried to usher Mort out of their card room. "Le' go o' me, you assholes, or I'll break y' in half!" Mort shouted.

Someone in that room was unimpressed by this declaration, though. For suddenly Mort's hulking body came flying through the door and he fell flat on his back, his face covered with blood.

Before Mort could get to his feet again, Jack appeared in the doorway. His youthful features twisted in rage as he kicked Mort in the ribs and then grabbed him by the shoulders and began pounding the back of Mort's head on the hardwood floor.

Mort was not to be so easily subdued. Slamming his knee into Jack's groin, he forced Jack to stumble back toward the wall. Then, rising to his feet, Mort lunged and slammed his head into Jack's stomach with the force of a battering ram.

Stunned by this attack, Jack let his guard down. This was a big mistake, for Mort followed through with a series of fierce punches to Jack's face, one of which hit him so hard in the jaw that he saw stars and felt himself sliding to the floor.

By now, every customer in Frank's Place was standing in a half circle around the two combatants, egging them on with jeers and cheers. Frank, however, was cranking the wall phone behind the bar to call Police Chief Colpepper.

Mort was on top of Jack now, pummeling him relentlessly with a clear intent to kill. Wrapping his long legs around Mort's waist in a scissors grip, Jack rolled the heavier man over. In the same motion, he jabbed him sharply just below the rib cage. This inflicted so much pain that Mort groaned and stopped swinging at Jack's face. Jack scrambled on top of Mort and locked both of his arms in a full Nelson.

Though exhausted, Mort was still not ready to give up. Summoning every bit of his remaining strength, he broke out of Jack's hold, struggled to his feet, and slammed Jack against the wall so hard that Jack again saw stars. Immediately, Mort launched another powerhouse punch to Jack's face. His aim was off, though, so his fist merely grazed Jack's temple and slammed into the wall.

In the split second that followed, Jack stooped and brought his own fist up under Mort's jaw with such force that it knocked him cold.

Frank's Place filled with deafening cheers and applause as Jack stood panting over Mort's prostrate form. Never one to sympathize with a loser, Fleck Boreman quickly departed.

* * *

Word of Jack's barroom victory spread quickly in Benicia, even stirring up admiration among the members of Sabina Keet's gypsy camp. Most interested of all was her son Belcher who saw an opportunity to capitalize on Jack's prowess. Not knowing where Jack lived, Belcher consulted with Frank Alessio who told him Jack worked at the Cartwheel.

Aware that the Cartwheel Lounge was not a place where gypsies would be welcome, Belcher waited for Jack outside the service entrance. Since it was after midnight, Jack was startled when a tall, stoop-shouldered figure in a floppy broad-brimmed hat suddenly stepped from the shadows and asked, "You Jack Westlake?"

"Yeah. Who are you?"

"My name's Belcher Keet. We met a long time ago. You prob'ly don't remember 'cause you was just a kid then."

"Oh, I remember alright," Jack replied suspiciously. He remembered too the time two years before when, at the Solano County Fairgrounds, Belcher had rebuked Adam Tucker, calling him a 'nigger' to his face. "What do you want?" Jack demanded irritably.

"I got a proposition for y'. It'll make y' rich."

Jack did not like this man and he remembered now the wicked-looking dagger he had seen him wearing that first time they met at the Benicia ballpark. "That so? Well, how come you're sneaking up on me in the middle of the night like this? Some kind of shady deal you got goin'?"

"Well, it ain't 'xactly legal, if that's what y' mean. Ain't much that is these days, is there? Take you, for instance. I hear you're sellin' hooch in that there place." Belcher gestured with his head toward the building behind Jack. "That ain't legal neither."

Jack had to admit the man had a point. Still, there were far worse crimes than breaking the federal prohibition law. "So what's this about?"

"About the fight game. Y' see, I set up prizefights. It's a real popular sport these days, y' know. Lots o' money in it. An' the way I look at it, you got the makin's of a real champ. You could make a thousand bucks just for one match. So what d' y' say? We got a deal?" Belcher had slowly moved closer to Jack as he spoke so that, in the light cast from a street lamp, Jack could now make out the features in Belcher's expressionless face, the most prominent of which were his colorless eyes—eyes that seemed to glow from some inner fire.

Jack did not respond. Instead, he studied the man's face in silence for several seconds, searching for some sign of weakness or duplicity. At last he said, "What makes you think I'd be a champ? Only experience I got is barroom brawls. I ain't exactly Gentleman Jim Corbett, y' know."

"Won't know if y' don't try," Belcher parried. "I can get y' a good trainer—the best there is—and at no cost to you. A thousand bucks is a lot o' money," Belcher reminded Jack. "Why don't y' come down to the gym next week and give it a try?"

"What gym?"

"The one over by the barracks on Mare Island, where all the Navy guys work out," Belcher explained. "I got a friend who's a trainer over there. He'll get y' a sparring partner and give y' a few lessons. How about it?" Belcher asked again.

Again, Jack paused before he responded. He wondered what Adam would think about Belcher's proposition. "I'll think about it," Jack said. "How do I get a hold of you?"

Belcher chuckled. "You know where I live—in the gypsy camp over by Mount Herman. See y', kid." Belcher waved and walked away, heading toward a battered Model T parked several yards down the block from the hotel.

* * *

The next morning over breakfast Jack told Adam about Belcher's proposition. Much to Jack's surprise, Adam was very much in favor of it.

"You don't wanna use his trainer, though," Adam warned. "Belcher's a fixer. Jus' 'bout ever'body aroun' here knows 'at. He been fixin' everythin' from cockfights to pony races ever since them gypsies moved to these parts before the war. He don't give a hoot about you. Fact he's prob'ly settin' you up. So you let *me* fin' you a manager and a trainer. I know some o' the bes' in the bus'ness."

"What about going to that gym over on Mare Island?" Jack asked.

"You go ahead. Tha's a good gym. But don't you do nothin' 'til I says so. That Belcher come aroun' botherin' you, you tell him come talk t' me. You got talent, boy. You don't wanna waste it on no two-bit chiseler like Belcher Keet. You hear?"

That had been the end of their discussion. A full week passed during which Adam said nothing more about Belcher's proposition.

Then, early one Thursday evening, shortly after Jack had opened the bar in the Cartwheel Lounge and the place had very few customers, a stout bald-headed man in a dark-brown suit sat down on one of the bar stools and ordered a glass of ice water. When Jack served him, the man asked, "You Jack Westlake?"

"Yes, sir."

Reaching across the bar to shake Jack's hand, the man said. "I'm Marty Sobel. Your friend Tucker tells me you're lookin' for a manager and a trainer. That right?"

When Jack nodded, Sobel extracted a business card from his vest pocket and placed it on the bar. Then, taking a sip of his water, he said, "You stop by my office tomorrow morning at 9:00 so we can talk business. See y' then, kid," Sobel said and left.

*   *   *

The big fight was scheduled for October 19. It was to take place aboard Frank's fishing barge—a fact that had at first surprised Jack because he had never imagined the Alessio brothers would be willing to associate themselves with such a conspicuously risky enterprise.

After all, boxing had been outlawed in California ever since James J. Corbett defeated "Battling Joe" Choynski on June 5, 1889. That fight too had been on a barge anchored in the Carquinez Strait. Though it was an event that had ever since been celebrated as one of the high points in Benicia's history, many of the spectators and gamblers who attended had been arrested and fined.

Preparations for this latest barge battle had been made months in advance, even before Belcher had first approached Jack with his proposition in January. Reports of the upcoming match had spread like wildfire throughout the North and East Bay. Though no one but Belcher yet knew who *both* contenders would be, rumor that such a legendary event was to be re-enacted in Benicia fired everyone's imagination. Some in Benicia believed "Gentleman Jim" Corbett himself might put in an appearance.

Even among the faithful at St. Dominic's Roman Catholic Church, there was much excitement about this upcoming event. In his homily on Sunday, October 16, Father Cardoni did his best to warn his flock against the evils of greed. "It is our ignorance of God's love that makes us hostage to greed," he said. "That is the lesson of the Roman soldiers who cast lots for Jesus' garments. They were pagans who knew nothing of the one true God. All that mattered to them was winning."

Such oblique Scripture references to a current event fell like seeds on rocky ground. Few who heard them that Sunday understood their relevance.

"Papa," Del asked her father after Mass, "is it true Jack is going to fight in a boxing match?"

The Judge's expression was somber. "I certainly hope not, Adelaide. It is only a rumor. We must ignore such nonsense."

"But Papa, I'm so afraid for him!"

"Jack has been a reckless and foolish young man," the Judge said sternly. "He must reap what he has sewn. Perhaps he will learn from it."

Del was not at all satisfied with this harsh judgment. She realized, though, that her father might be right. She had not seen Jack for many months now, and everything she had heard about him was discouraging. His reputation for carousing and drunkenness, though celebrated by some in Benicia as evidence of his manhood, filled her with dread for her friend. "I'll say a Novena for him," she affirmed.

"That would be a good thing to do, my dear," her father replied, hoping this would put an end to all further discussion of the matter. Judge Lanham did not like deliberately deceiving his own daughter.

The fact was, however, that only five days before Josh Wyman had filed a petition with the Solano County Court requesting a cease and desist order against Frank Alessio and every other known party to the upcoming boxing match. The Judge had had no alternative but to honor that request. The consequences for Jack would not be good.

*   *   *

As is normal for autumn mornings on the Carquinez Strait, a heavy fog hung low over the water, reducing visibility to less than a few feet. Foghorns sounded repeatedly from every direction as Billy Sparks rowed Jack and his trainer, Tim Garner, across the 75-yard stretch of water between Frank's Place and his barge. Though it was only was 6:00 AM, theirs was not the only boat moving toward the barge. Jack could hear the clatter and splash of oars all around him. No one was under power because everyone wanted to avoid detection by the local constabulary.

They need not have worried at this early stage of the event, however, for the mayors of Benicia, Vallejo, Martinez, Concord, and even the Solano County seat in Fairfield were now all heading to Frank's barge in their own rowboats. They knew arrangements had been made so that there would be no intervention by law enforcement until the match was over and they had time to escape arrest.

Through the fog, Jack could now discern the black hulk of Frank's converted coal barge, its giant hull rising nearly twenty feet above the waterline. He could also hear the voices of men on the barge's deck calling out orders to each other as they tossed tie-up lines to the approaching rowboats. Billy shipped his oars and stood up in the bow, to catch the tie-up line, and Jack and Tim Garner quickly climbed up the heavy fish netting that had been dropped over the side of the barge.

"Where's Sobel's quarters?" Garner asked the man who helped him onto the main deck.

The man pointed to an open hatch. "Down below there."

Garner grabbed Jack's arm and quickly guided him down a stairwell to the next deck below. At the foot of the stairs was a large room that had been partitioned off from the rest of the boat by a hastily constructed wall of wooden planks. The room contained several wooden benches and tables. Each table was stacked with the various supplies that would be needed during the fight— towels, bandage, and gallon bottles full of water or wood alcohol to be used for cleaning wounds.

Garner handed Jack the canvas bag containing his boxing attire and told him to dress for the fight. Once Jack had donned his trunks and shoes, Garner ordered him to sit on a bench so he could tape up his hands and wrists.

All this was done with very little conversation between Jack and his trainer. As Jack had learned during the past three weeks of his intensive training, Garner was a man of few words. His training methods almost exclusively involved demonstration, occasional tactile prods, and frequent corrections expressed in scatological epithets.

Garner's only verbal instructions to Jack that morning had consisted of repeated reminders that he do a "jigaboo" dance in this fight. "You know this guy's big," he added by way of explanation. "So y' got to keep movin'. Keep goin' in low an' close with fast jabs to the gut an' kidneys. An', whatever y' do, guard your head. The lummox hits y' in the head, it'll explode like a rotten melon."

At sixty-two, Tim Garner was a seasoned professional. His small, wiry frame was deceptive. He had been in the fight game since he first went to work as a twelve-year-old water-boy for John A. "Patsy" Hogan in 1876. Hogan was the only contender to knock down John L. Sullivan during the first year of that Hall of Famer's career.

In 1882, Garner moved from Boston to San Francisco where he took a job as a trainer at the Olympic Club. While there, Garner had frequent opportunities to watch "Gentleman Jim" Corbett work with his sparring partners. Since then, Garner had trained some of the best prizefighters on the West Coast. Jack didn't realize it, but he was in the hands of a master strategist.

After taping Jack's wrists and hands, Garner put him through a series of rigorous warm-up exercises, which included jumping rope, shadowboxing, and punching-bag workouts.

Though Jack was famished by fight-time at 7:30, Garner had not allowed him to eat anything since late afternoon of the previous day. "You can eat your heart out, once you win this one, kid," was the only encouragement Garner offered.

A boxing platform had been erected in the large open hold of Frank's coal barge. A few wooden benches had been set up along the sides of this platform for spectators who had paid premium prices for ringside seats. Most, however, had to watch the fight from the main deck above—a circumstance that resulted in numerous impromptu fisticuffs long before the real match began. No one kept any record of the number present that morning. When the bell rang summoning the two contenders, though, the roar of the crowd aboard was deafening.

Draping Jack in a bright green hooded robe, Garner beckoned him through a long, narrow corridor on the starboard side of the barge that led to the open hold. As soon as they emerged, Jack's attention focused on the towering figure approaching from the opposite end of this arena. He recognized this personage immediately as Belcher Keet's brother Noah—the freak show Giant that he, Adam, Francis, and Billy had seen at the Solano County Fairgrounds three years before. Adam was right. Belcher had "set him up"!

* * *

Huey's barbershop was a busy place the next morning as customers came in not only to get their bi-weekly shaves and haircuts but also to share stories about the surprising outcome of the previous day's match. Jack Westlake had knocked out his much larger opponent in less than three rounds. In fact, according to eyewitness reports, Jack had almost killed his adversary.

Those reports had been confirmed that morning by Lillian Blodget, Dr. Trent's nurse assistant, who told *Benicia Herald New Era* editor Brad Pincus that Noah was now being treated for life-threatening injuries at the Vallejo General Hospital.

"That don't surprise me none," said Joe Patmos, one of the eyewitnesses at the fight. "Jack pounded that big dopey guy's gut like a jack-hammer. I ain't never seen anybody's fists fly so hard and fast. You shoulda heard that crowd! Ever'body was screamin' over an' over, 'Jack the giant killer! Jack the giant killer! Get'im, Jack!'"

"What I don't get is how come Noah didn't defend himself," said Steve Venizelos who had not attended the boxing match but had heard many second- and third-hand accounts of the fight from members of his Red Men lodge. "I've seen that guy lifting 200-poind bar bells at the County Fair. He should have been able to floor Jack with a single blow."

"Defend himself!" Patmos exclaimed. "Hell! That guy didn't know the first thing about boxing. He fought like a big baby, hobblin' aroun' the ring an' swingin' his arms like he was fighting off a bunch of bumblebees. All Jack had to do was duck and come in low. I'll tell you, Jack must've had a damn good trainer!"

"Who *was* his trainer, anyway?" Huey asked as he scraped away at Ted Sena's six-day-old beard.

Patmos shook his head. "Nobody knows! He was an old geezer—real short and skinny. Must've been somebody from San Francisco. Right after the fight, he disappeared—just like all the high rollers sittin' ringside. The sun was out full force by then so the fog was gone. You could see the tugboats tied up along the deep-channel side o' the barge. Must've been them tugs that brought all the big shots up from San Francisco. Anyways, it was them tugs what got'em out o' there real fast."

"What was the big hurry?" Wally Sykes asked.

"You kiddin' me?" Patmos replied. "They all knew they'd be in big trouble when the Feds come. And, sure enough, wasn't more than a couple minutes after them tugs took off when a Coast Guard cutter come flying through the Strait right at us. That's when all hell broke loose and everybody got off that barge fast as they could. Some fellers even jumped overboard and swam ashore."

"I hear there was a lot of money riding on that match. If everybody ran off like that, how'd they collect their winnings?" Venizelos asked.

"Damned if I know!" Patmos declared angrily. "I bet $20 on Jack with hundred-to-one odds. Never did collect. Feller took my money said he was one of your Red Man brothers, Steve. Never did see him again!"

"That's ridiculous!" Venizelos retorted. "Red Men wouldn't get mixed up in anything like that! What was his name?"

"Said his name was Ted Peters. Real flashy dresser and a fast talker. He even showed me his Red Men membership card."

"You got took for a sucker. Nobody named Peters in our lodge," Venezelos insisted.

"Oh yeah? Well I hear your lodge sponsors boxing matches at your meetings right here in Benicia. Wouldn't surprise me none if the Red Men was the ones set up this whole phony fight."

"We'd never do anything like that!" Venizelos declared. "We're an honorable national organization, started way back in the Revolutionary days by the Sons of Liberty."

Everyone in Huey's shop got a good chuckle out of this—everyone, that is, except Venizelos.

"I hear they already arrested Jack and the Belcher brothers," Bob Jensen put in, joining the conversation for the first time. "They're bound to catch the rest o' them crooks sooner or later."

"Don't be so sure," Venizelos warned. "My guess is there's too many big-time politicians involved. When that happens, only suckers like Jack and losers like the Belchers get caught. They'll take the fall for everybody else. Just you wait and see."

"Sounds t' me like you know a lot more 'bout this than you're lettin' on, Steve," Patmos sneered.

"Whoever's responsible, it sure don't seem fair," Huey said in an effort to ward off an impending fistfight in his own shop.

As it turned out, Venizelos was right. Jack, Belcher and Noah were each given a sixty-day sentence in the Solano County Jail, and the legend of "Jack the Giant Killer" quickly faded from public memory.

1926

Carquinez Bridge under construction

CHAPTER NINETEEN

"Someone To Watch Over Me"

HAVING COMPLETED HIS SIXTY-DAY SENTENCE on January 3, Jack was released from the county jail in Fairfield. Adam was waiting for him in front of the courthouse. The man's tireless loyalty to Jack astounded him. Every Sunday during the eight weeks of Jack's incarceration, Adam had visited him, bringing fresh fruit and cigarettes as well as news of what was happening in the outside world.

No one else had shown Jack such loyalty and generosity. Not even his own mother had come to visit him. She had sent only one letter expressing her dismay at his situation and warning him not to trust any of the other prison inmates. "They are very dangerous men," she had written. "They are not like you. You are a good boy. As soon as this is over, I feel sure life will be better for you. Read your Bible every day and remember what you learned in Sunday school." This letter had only driven Jack deeper into his feelings of bitterness toward his mother.

As for his childhood friends, none of them had come to visit him either—not even Del, in spite of her repeated claims of undying loyalty. She had written him two long letters telling him about her attendance at tea dances in San Rafael and Oakland and her many museum and theater trips to San Francisco with her Aunt Lucy.

Apparently she thought such prattle would cheer him up. What it did instead was reveal to Jack her childish naiveté and the tyrannical hand of her father. With mixed feelings of anger and sadness, Jack realized that Del probably didn't even know her father had been the one responsible for his incarceration. Clearly, their worlds were drifting farther apart—as, no doubt, her father intended.

Jack wondered, though, about his old friend Sam. How was he dealing with having to live with his lunatic mother? Del had only alluded once to this in her letters, though she did mention that Sam was taking flying lessons. That was the only news that excited Jack. *Good for you, Sam!* he thought. *When I get out of here, maybe I'll take flying lessons too.*

But Adam had different plans for Jack. As they left Fairfield in Adam's old pick-up truck and headed south toward Vallejo, Adam explained. "You gonna have a tough time gettin' work now, boy, 'cause most folks around here don't hire jailbirds. Only thing you got goin' for you is how strong an' fearless you is. Bes' thing for you is bridge buildin'."

"What do you mean?" Jack asked, bewildered.

"Ain't you been readin' the papers I brung you, boy? They's buildin' a big new car bridge across the Strait, an' they's hirin' jus' about anybody they can get. It's shif' work an' risky 'cause you got to climb them big bridge towers they're puttin' up. But the pay's good. Three dollar a day to start. Francis, he already makin' four dollar a day runnin' one o' them big cranes they use."

"That must be some bridge!" Jack declared.

"Biggest in the world," Adam said. "Gonna make big changes aroun' these parts." Then, with a sly glance at Jack, he added, "Good for business."

"You mean your *old* business?"

Adam smiled and nodded. "It'll sure be a whole lot easier gettin' across the Strait."

"What about Soames? It'll be easier for him too, won't it?"

Adam pondered this observation for a few seconds. "Maybe. Maybe not. I hear him and Roach put money into this bridge. Bought stock, jus' like a lot of other folk. But them two grocers what started the company owns most of it. Way I see it, that makes things pretty much even. We jus' gotta be smarter than Soames."

"How are you going to do that?"

"When I figures it out, I'll let y' know … maybe."

Jack shook his head in wonderment. *Good old Adam—still the sly fox!*

"Tell y' what," Adam said. "How 'bout I take you over to Morrow Cove so's you can see what they's doin'. Maybe you can talk 'em into hirin' y' right now."

"Guess I don't have much choice, do I?" Jack replied, remembering what Adam had told him the last time he was unemployed.

"Guess you don't, boy!"

*   *   *

As soon as they drove through the entrance gate to the construction site, Jack jumped out and stood gazing in astonishment at what he saw. Rising more than a hundred feet above the water in Morrow Cove were six pairs of steel piers. At the base of each pier was a circular concrete foundation. Together these piers supported an enormous superstructure made of an elaborate maze of interconnecting steel girders. Mounted on a barge anchored close to this structure, a steam crane was hoisting more steel girders up to the riveters working at its highest point. When he looked across the Carquinez Strait toward Crockett, Jack saw that an identical tower was being erected on the opposite shore.

The noise from the big steam-driven crane engine was deafening as it strained to lift the steel girders from a second barge anchored next to the crane barge. Teams of men on this barge shouted to each other as they lashed each steel girder to a cable and then signaled the crane operator to hoist it to the workmen above. "There must be hundreds of men working out there," Jack said to Adam as the older man stepped out of his truck.

"An' they's gonna need plenty more," Adam said. "Bridge ain't even halfway done yet." Pointing to a long wood-frame building with a large sign identifying it as property of the American Bridge Company, Adam suggested, "Bosses is in that shed, so how 'bout you go ask for a job?"

As Adam spoke, the door of the makeshift office building opened and a man dressed incongruously in a three-piece suit with a steel helmet on his head descended the steps and came toward them. "You boys get out o' here," he growled. "This is private property."

Ignoring the man's hostility, Jack moved toward him. "I came to

269

see if you're doing any hiring, mister. Name's Jack Westlake," he added, reaching out to shake hands.

The man in the helmet ignored Jack's greeting gesture, instead glaring behind Jack at Adam who was leaning against the hood of his truck. "We don't hire spades!"

Jack resisted the impulse to respond with his fists. "He's not the one looking for work, mister. It's me," Jack said grimly.

Still suspicious, the man studied Jack for several seconds. "You ever worked on a bridge before?"

"No. But I'm strong and I learn fast."

"Where you from?"

Jack glanced hesitantly back at Adam, who simply nodded. "I live up in Napa," he answered.

"You afraid of heights?" the man in the helmet asked, gesturing up at the structure behind him. "If you are, this ain't the job for you, kid."

Jack squared his shoulders. "I'm not scared of anything, mister."

"Pretty cocky, ain't y'?"

Jack did not respond. He had made his pitch. The man could take it or leave it.

Baffled by Jack's youthful bravado, the official reached up and removed his helmet. Wiping sweat from his forehead with the back of his hand, he said, "Well, I guess we could find *somethin'* for you to do around here. Pay's two dollars a day."

"I hear it's three dollars to start," Jack said.

"Oh yeah? Where'd you hear that, kid?"

"Friend of mine already works here—Francis Flanagan."

"You know Flanagan?"

When Jack nodded, the man looked down at his own dust-covered dress shoes. "Flanagan's a good worker," he admitted reluctantly. "He's got a smart mouth, but he earns his pay." Looking up at Jack again, he said, "Tell y' what. You come by here tomorrow morning at 7:00, and we'll give you a try. Two dollars is all I can offer a greenhorn like you though."

"Two fifty," Jack said. "Not a penny less."

For the first time, the official smiled. "Alright then, Jack. Two fifty it is." Putting his helmet back on his head, the man reached out to shake

Jack's hand. "My name's Bert Lasky. I'm the foreman, so you report to me."

* * *

The next morning, Jack was put to work on the Morrow Cove barge serviced by the crane Francis operated. Because of his height, strength and agility, Jack quickly became adept at grappling the block and tackle and attaching it to each girder so it could be hoisted to the riveters above.

After three weeks on this job, he was promoted to apprentice at three dollars a day and assigned to work with three seasoned riveters on the North tower.

Jack's new teammates were tough Irishmen from Port Costa, older than he but hardy and jovial. The oldest, Sean Hanrahan, had only recently emigrated from his native city of Cork. His brogue was so thick that even his fellow Irishmen sometimes had difficulty understanding him.

This didn't matter much while they were on the job, for each man had a specific task he performed instinctively. Sean stoked the portable kiln they used to heat the rivets. Larry Finn, a short but sturdy man in his early thirties, wielded the tongs for tossing each rivet to his younger brother Patrick who caught each rivet in a bucket and, using another pair of tongs, set it in place. Jack's job was to ram each rivet home with a steel sledge. Though he felt somewhat uneasy during his first hour on the job, Jack forced himself to heed his co-workers' warning: "Don't look down!"

Working in ten-hour shifts, with only a twenty-minute lunch break, the four men kept up a furious pace. As soon as they secured one steel girder on the rapidly rising superstructure, Francis' crane presented them with another. By the end of each day, Jack and his teammates were exhausted. Not so exhausted, though, that they had no time for what Sean called "a wee bit o' whiskey" at a nearby tavern in Vallejo.

One evening after work Jack invited Francis to join them, thinking he would enjoy the company of fellow Irishmen. He was startled by Francis' response. "I don't want nothin' t' do with them dumb drunks! And you shouldn't either. You better watch yourself, Jack. One o' these days, they'll be the death of y'."

"We never drink on the job," Jack retorted. "Up there, we're all business. You know that!"

Francis glared at Jack and spat on the ground. "Yeah. Well, it ain't none o' my business. You go ahead an' be a damn fool if you want to." Having said this, Francis spun on his heels and walked away.

* * *

By late February, the north- and south-shore towers of the new bridge were almost completed and work had begun on the central tower being erected mid-stream in the narrowest part of the Carquinez Strait. Jack and his team of riveters were now working more than 200 feet above the surface of the water below.

"Damn wind's gonna blow us off o' here today!" Patrick shouted to his teammates as they climbed the wooden ladder to the top platform. "Better tie up."

"Hell with that!" Sean barked. As the oldest member of their team, Sean considered himself the wisest. He was not about to take advice from a twenty-year-old. Besides, he was nursing a raging hangover and in no mood to look out for anyone else's safety.

"Patty's right! It's got to be 30 knots up here!" Jack shouted. Quickly, he unwound the fifteen-foot long coil of rope hooked to his belt. It was company policy that each riveter must tether himself to one of his partners so that, if one man should stumble, the other could immediately drop down on all fours and act as a human anchor. But this policy was difficult to enforce. Because it hampered their freedom of movement, riveters usually ignored it.

"Sometime, when a man's a damn fool, ain't no point in arguin'," Adam had once told Jack. "You jus' gotta save him from his own foolishness." So that's what Jack did, asking Larry to swap jobs with him and tether himself to his brother Patrick.

As Jack changed places with Larry, Sean scowled at him with blood-shot eyes. "What are you doin' over here, boy?"

"Just needed a little change. Gets boring doing the same job every day," Jack lied. Then, giving a thumb's up sign to Francis in the crane below, he signaled for the first girder to be hoisted.

Their work pace was slower now—partly because of the strong wind that often surprised them with sudden gusts, partly because Larry was unaccustomed to using the sledge, but mostly because Sean was deliberately slow in heating the rivets.

After their lunch break, Jack had hoped Sean's resentment would subside, but it didn't. What's worse, Sean's hands began to shake and twice during the early afternoon Jack saw him reel with dizziness.

By 2:00 PM, the wind had died down. But now a hot sun made them sweat profusely. Jack stayed as close to Sean as he could. He had to step back several paces, though, when he tossed each rivet across the open space into Patrick's bucket. It was during one of those three-second intervals that he saw Sean suddenly look down.

Instinctively, Jack dropped his tongs and grabbed Sean's wrist. The tongs clanged loudly as they fell, bouncing off of several crossbeams in the structure below. Jack tried to pull Sean upright, but the older man had already lost his footing. The weight of Sean's falling body slammed Jack down on the narrow platform where they had been standing. With his free hand, Jack clasped the edge of the platform to keep himself from being dragged off the opposite edge.

"Hang on Jack!" Larry shouted as the Finn brothers dropped their tools and moved as swiftly as they could across the twenty-foot I-beam separating them from Jack.

Jack felt as if his arm were being torn from his body now as Sean desperately clasped it with both hands, his legs flailing wildly beneath him. Then he saw Patrick, the lighter of the two brothers, drop off the platform. His safety line snapped taught as he wrapped both arms around Sean's torso. "I got him!" he shouted. "Pull us up!"

Still Sean clung desperately to Jack's arm, keeping Jack from getting up to help Larry as he struggled to haul Sean and Patrick back up on the platform.

Francis, watching all this from the crane cab below, quickly took action by cranking the end of lift cable high enough so Patrick could reach out and grab it. As soon as Patrick secured his footing on the block and tackle, he called up to Larry, "Cut the tether so Francis can take us down!"

Larry looked around desperately at Jack who, now freed from Sean's grasp, was standing up. "I ain't got a knife!" Larry shouted down at his brother.

"Me neither!" Patrick shouted back, his face white with fear.

Reaching into his overalls, Jack brought out a pocketknife Adam had given him, opened it, and slashed through the tether rope. As soon as he saw the tether had been cut, Francis slowly lowered Patrick and Sean to safety.

By this time, other workmen on the ground below them had summoned Lasky and he was heading toward the central tower in the company launch.

Jack looked at Larry and Patrick. "Guess we better head down. There isn't much we can do up here."

As the three men stepped down the ladder to the next lower platform, they heard the engine of Francis' crane roar at full throttle again. Glancing over his shoulder, Jack saw the wire-mesh personnel cage rising slowly toward them. Inside was their foreman. When the cage reached the level of the lower platform, Lasky called out to them: "You fellows are through for the day. I'll take y' down from here."

"It's only two o'clock," Jack said.

"Never mind that!" Lasky barked. "I saw what just happened up here. You're all nervous as hell. I can't risk no more accidents. Go home and rest up. Don't worry. You'll get your full day's pay."

"Fine by me," Larry said as he led the way into the cage. Jack and Patrick quickly followed.

* * *

Though it was only March 20, it was going to be an exceptionally hot day in Benicia. Del decided her only escape from the oppressive heat was to take a ferry ride across the Strait to Martinez. So she picked up the extension phone in her bedroom to call her friend Maggie, hoping she could convince her to go with her. But her father was already on the line downstairs.

"She's going to have to board at Saint Catherine's, Lucy," Del heard her father say. "I'll be traveling during the week, and I have to be sure she's being closely watched while I'm away. Ruby's getting too old to supervise everything Adelaide does."

"Why don't you send her down here to live with us?" Del's aunt replied. "I'll look after her and she can attend day school at St. Vincent's. She'll be much happier with that arrangement, Clyde, I'm sure."

"Thank you, Lucy. But that would be much too great an imposition on you and Charles. After all, you like to travel with Charles when he goes abroad."

"Now Clyde, that's a ridiculous excuse and you know it. I'd love to have Del stay with us. Charlie won't mind a bit."

"I'm sorry, Lucy. I've made my decision. I've already made a deposit for the boarder's tuition at St. Catherine's. The matter is settled."

"Del's going to be very angry with you, Clyde, and so am I."

At this point, Del carefully replaced the earpiece on her candle phone. *What was this about!* she thought angrily. *Papa is going away and hasn't told me about it! How dare he do such an awful thing!* She resolved to confront her father immediately, but then realized doing so would reveal she had been eavesdropping on his private phone conversation— something she knew he would never tolerate. She would have to wait until he told her of his plans himself.

Del did not have long to suffer in silence. That evening over supper, her father revealed the full story. "I have some very good news, Adelaide" he began. "I have been appointed to the Ninth Circuit. Such an appointment is a great honor and comes with a very handsome stipend." The Judge was surprised when his daughter greeted this announcement with silence. "What's wrong, my dear? Are you not happy to hear such good news?"

"Good news for you!" she replied bitterly. "But what about me?"

The Judge reached for his glass of burgundy and slowly moved it to his lips, giving himself time to carefully deliberate what he was about to say. "I realize, of course, that this may be a bit hard on you, my dear. For, in my new position, I will be obliged to travel a good deal. The Ninth Circuit covers seven states, you see. It is likely that I will be away from home most weeknights and even, on some occasions, during weekends as well. I have made arrangements for that, however. When you return to Saint Catherine's in the fall, you will be enrolled as a boarder."

"A boarder!" Del declared in feigned astonishment but with no disguise of her dismay. "Why should I have to board when I live right here in town, only a few blocks away from school?"

"You will be able to come home on most weekends, Adelaide," the Judge observed, very much on his guard now. "I think it will be much better if you live at school during the week, however, so that you can better concentrate on your studies."

"Concentrate on my studies! Have I ever done anything else?" Del demanded. "I've been an A student every year since I was in first grade! Next year, I'll be in four honors classes! Sister Rosemary says I'll probably graduate *cum laude*! I've never had a problem concentrating on my studies! Papa, this is ridiculous!"

She had touched a nerve. The Judge glared at her. "I will not tolerate such insolence, young lady! I have made up my mind. You *will* board at Saint Catherine's. The matter is settled."

Furious, Del hurled her napkin to the floor and ran into the foyer and up the stairs to her room. Throwing herself on her bed, she wept bitterly. For the first time in her life, she felt hatred in her heart—worst of all, toward the one person she had always loved and trusted most.

* * *

All three towers of the new bridge had been completed by September, and preparations were being made for installation of the two thrust-through spans. Since these spans were being assembled at ground level at the American Bridge Company's plant in El Cerrito, all the riveter teams had been reassigned to that location.

Each morning a company launch picked the riveters up at the bridge site and transported them down the coast of San Pablo Bay to the assembly plant. At the end of each workday, the same launch transported them back to the Morro Cove location.

Work on the spans was much easier and less hazardous than it had been on the towers, for each span was only twenty-five feet high. Nevertheless, ever since the near-death incident on the north tower, Jack had declined his teammates' invitation to join them for drinks after work. Though they teased him about it, they honored his decision. In fact, because of his bravery and quick thinking, they had chosen Jack to be their team leader.

"You're the boss, Jack," Larry had said with a grin. "Guess you think y' gotta set us a good example."

"Lots o' luck, boyo!" Sean had sneered.

* * *

Adam was pleased when he heard that Jack's was now the riveting team leader. "I got big plans for you, boy," he said one Friday night as he, Billy, Francis and Jack sat eating shrimp and fried rice at Wong's Garden Restaurant in Napa. "We's goin' into a new line o' bus'ness soon, an' I needs somebody to run a fleet o' trucks between Oakland and Jamestown."

"Jamestown! That's a long haul! What's your new line of business?" Jack asked.

"Transportin' moonshine," Adam said. "They got a lot o' trees over in the Sierra foothills, an' some o' the local farmers is turnin' the sawdust from them trees into wood alcohol. All we need t' do is pump it into tank trucks and bring it down to Oakland."

"Where do we get the trucks?"

"Don't you be worryin' 'bout that, boy!" Adam snapped irritably. "I'll get the trucks. What you gotta do is round up some more drivers. You, Francis an' Billy cain't do it alone. Maybe some o' them Irish you works with could help."

"I don't know, Adam. Larry and Patrick might be alright, but Sean ..."

"Soon's he know how much money he gonna make, Sean won't be no problem."

"How much is that?"

"Could be a couple hundred a week or more."

Jack whistled in amazement. He had to agree. Even an old reprobate like Sean Hanrahan could be induced to stay sober for pay like that. Still, Jack was curious about the details of Adam's plan. "Why do you need so many drivers?" he asked.

"Takes at leas' two drivers for every trip—one to drive the truck and one to ride shotgun in a follow car. Once Soames gets wind o' what we's doin', his goons 'll be on us like flies on a dead dog."

"How are you going to get the mazuma to buy all these trucks and cars and pay all these drivers?" Jack asked.

Adam rolled his eyes. "Boy, you as' too many questions! You jus' find me them drivers—you hear?"

"Yes sir," Jack smiled and shook his head in embarrassment. Adam had always come through in the past. There was no reason to doubt his ability to do so now.

1927

Carquinez Bridge opening day

CHAPTER TWENTY

_____

"On the Sunny Side of the Street"

IT WAS RAINING HARD THAT January morning in 1927 when Sam reported for his initial orientation meeting with the Forestry Service. Located at the end of a long muddy road that wound through thirty acres of open land planted with evergreen seedlings, the one-story wood frame building that served as the agency's headquarters was anything but impressive.

Six years before, the State Legislature had allocated $20,000 for the establishment of California's first forestry nursery. Though it was a princely sum for any state government project at the time, there had been no broad public support for the legislation. After all, the only major forest fire on record in Northern California had occurred in 1923, when 40,000 acres from Lucas Valley to Bolinas had burned. The notion that the average citizen had any stewardship responsibility where the State's forestland was concerned belonged to a much later generation. In 1927, a bare bones solution was all that any elected official deemed necessary.

Fire Warden Ralph Gallagher was reading the sports pages of the _Sacramento Bee_ when Sam entered this agency manager's tiny office. Gallagher did not look up from his paper until Sam said, "Excuse me, sir. Are you Mister Gallagher?"

Gallagher lowered his paper only enough to glare at Sam. "Yeah. I'm Gallagher. Who are you?"

"Sam Geddis, your new aerial fire spotter."

"Are you now! You don't look old enough to fly a kite, let alone an airplane!" Gallagher quipped with a taunting smirk. Immediately, though, he stood up and reached out to shake Sam's hand. "That's OK, kid. I guess you got to be young and foolish to take a job like this, right?" A tall scarecrow of a man in his late fifties, Gallagher had wide-set pale blue eyes that twinkled with good humor. He nodded toward the straight-backed wooden chair in front of his desk. "Take off your slicker and have a seat, son."

Sam removed his dripping raincoat, carefully draped it over the back of the chair and sat down. While Gallagher folded up his newspaper and searched through a stack of folders on his desk, Sam looked around at the several official-looking certificates and photos that hung on the walls of Gallagher's office. One of these showed Gallagher shaking hands with then Governor Young, whom Sam recognized from several newspaper photos he had seen. The Governor had generated much press coverage in recent months as a result of his efforts to create a new Department of Natural Resources, including a Division of Forestry.

Having located Sam's personnel file, Gallagher leaned back in his chair and spent several minutes scanning its contents—something, Sam thought, this government official should have done before Sam arrived. But Sharon had warned him in advance what to expect. "You're going to be working for a bunch of bureaucrats!" she had observed contemptuously. "Most of them don't know the first thing about flying airplanes or fighting forest fires. They're just pencil pushers who got their jobs through political pull. So don't be scared of them. Just stick to the facts and keep your opinions to yourself. Once you're in the air, you can pretty much plot your own course."

Gallagher finally looked up from Sam's file, his eyebrows raised in an expression of surprise. "Wow! This gal Rivers really thinks you're the bee's knees. She got a thing for you?" he asked, fixing Sam with a suggestive leer. "You got to watch yourself with older women, kid."

Sam bit his lip, squelching the impulse to rebuke Gallagher. "She was my flight instructor. That's all."

Gallagher nodded—his tongue in his cheek, however. "So how come you want to be an aerial spotter? Your daddy a pilot?"

Determined to follow Sharon's advice, Sam said flatly, "My father's dead. He was in the oil business."

Gallagher looked up from the folder with an expression of surprise.

"Geddis! Of course! You're Talcott Geddis's boy! So how come you're not in the oil business like your daddy? Gotta be a lot more money in that for you than spottin' forest fires."

"My mother sold the business after my father died," Sam said coolly.

Gallagher studied Sam for several seconds, like a cat watching a mouse. Failing to elicit any further response, he shifted his gaze back to Sam's personnel folder. "Guess you realize this is only a part-time job—late summer months mostly. Pays forty bucks a week. You living home with your Momma?"

Sam had anticipated this question. "For now, but I plan to move out as soon as I can get some other work. Maybe do some crop dusting or fly for the mail service."

Again Gallagher nodded, his pale blue eyes still flickering with disdain. "Well, good luck to you, kid. Anyway, first thing you got to do between now and May is memorize some maps and weather charts. Your territory covers eight different counties all the way north to Redding, west to the coast, and east to the Nevada border." As Gallagher spoke, he opened a drawer in a large wooden filing cabinet behind his desk and extracted two thick packets of folded papers bound together with string. Handing the packets to Sam, he said, "Don't lose these, kid. Government property," he warned. "You lose 'em, you pay for 'em."

"Thanks." Sam placed the packets on his lap without looking at them. He was determined not to show any curiosity about their contents. To do so, he thought, would only signal a lack of self-confidence—no doubt triggering yet another wisecrack from this insolent bureaucrat.

"Any questions?" Gallagher asked, leaning back in his chair and locking his hands behind his head.

"What airport do I fly out of?"

"We got two Jennies in a hangar over at the old Army flight training facility in Fairfield. When you come back here in May, I'll take you over there and show you the ropes."

"Only two planes?" Sam asked, startled that a State agency could be so poorly outfitted.

"Only got one pilot," Gallagher winked. "So two's more than we need."

"You mean I'm your only spotter?"

"First and only, kid. We're on a tight budget." Gallagher smiled indulgently. "Look at it this way, kid—you're a real pioneer! Any other questions?"

"Not now, I guess."

Gallagher reached across his desk to shake Sam's hand again, at the same time giving him a business card. "Good. So I'll see you here May 1st—7:00 AM sharp. You got any questions in the meantime, give me a call at the number on that card."

Pulling on his raincoat again, Sam tucked the packets of paper under his coat and turned to go. "Thanks, Mister Gallagher."

"Oh—one more thing," Gallagher said as he came out from behind his desk and handed Sam an official-looking brown envelope. "A little advance payment, just to keep you interested!" Gallagher winked and slapped Sam on the back. "Welcome aboard, kid!"

*　*　*

"Your father means well, Adelaide. He just doesn't understand what families are all about," Del's Aunt Lucy explained as they sat together in the Tea Room at the Saint Francis Hotel. They had just come from a matinee performance of Mozart's *Die Fleidermouse* at the San Francisco Opera.

In spite of her delight with this outing, Del was now in a gloomy mood. She had expected her father to attend the performance with them. At the last moment, he had changed his mind, insisting that he had to work on an upcoming case in Nevada.

"But he's known about this for weeks. How can he be so insensitive?" Del complained.

"Your father is *not* insensitive!" Lucy affirmed. "He's just devoted to his profession. He's a very good and honorable man. You should be proud of his accomplishments."

"Of course, I'm proud of his accomplishments. But I'm also very disappointed in him as a father!" Del declared irritably.

Lucy frowned. "You expect too much, young lady. He's had to be both father and mother to you. If your mother had not died so young, things might have been different. But your father has done his best. Oh and by the way, he has just made reservations for you to have your coming out party at the Claremont next month. You should at least be grateful for that!"

"Has he really?" Del exclaimed with delight. "Oh, Aunt Lucy— that's wonderful! When?"

"Saturday, May 12."

"That's less than a month away! How will I ever be able to get ready for it? I have a guest list to make and invitations to send. And, of course, I'll have to shop for a new outfit! I can't possibly do all that in just a few weeks!"

Lucy smiled reassuringly. "Your father and I have already prepared your guest list and the invitations are at the printers. As for your clothes—well, that's part of my commission this afternoon. As soon as we leave here, you and I are going shopping at the Emporium."

"You mean I don't get to choose who's coming to my own party?" Del was angry again.

Lucy reached across the table and grasped Del's wrist. "We have invited many of your best friends. I've made sure of that," Lucy said firmly. "But your father is paying a great deal of money for all of this, my dear. He has the right to invite only those guests he considers suitable."

"What does that mean?" Del demanded.

Lucy looked around the room, fearful that Del was on the verge of making a scene. She understood her niece's anger. After all, Del was almost seventeen. She was bright and mature and had good reason to resent her father's arbitrariness. Looking back at Del, she said as softly and calmly as she could, "I know how you feel, my dear. But, as we both know, your father is very old-fashioned and set in his ways."

"I don't care!" Del exclaimed, raising her voice so that several people at the next table turned and stared. "Papa's treating me like a baby! I'm a woman! Doesn't he realize yet that women have the right to vote?"

"Only if they're twenty-one, dear," Lucy observed, feeling somewhat embarrassed at having to raise this caveat.

Del was not listening. "For heaven's sake! What's wrong with Papa? Has he been asleep all these years like Rip Van Winkle?"

"That's enough, Del!" Lucy declared, becoming angry herself now. "You'll simply have to accept things as they are!" She signaled for the waiter to bring their bill of fare.

* * *

The Peekaboo Club in El Cerrito was hidden in a grove of oak trees behind a gas station on Lincoln Highway, just a few miles south of where the new bridge was being built. During the 1920s, it was one of the most popular dancehalls in the East Bay, not only because it served alcohol but also because it attracted some of the best jazz bands in the country. No less than Joe "King" Oliver himself was rumored to have performed there in 1921.

It was here that Adam had brought Jack, Billy, Larry and Patrick to meet one of Adam's most important prospective customers—Peekaboo Club owner, "Big Jim" Jeffries. Since it was 10:30 on a Friday night, the place was packed with happy couples, most of them now swirling on the big hardwood dance floor as a six-man band worked its way through a lively rendition of Oliver's signature piece "Sugar Foot Stomp."

Adam lead the way to the only empty table he could find in a dark corner at the back of the dance hall. Even here, the *wa-wa* of the lead cornet and the vigorous counterpoint of the trombone and clarinet players made conversation impossible, so the five men simply sat down and listened.

Adam and Billy immediately responded to the band's rendition of "Sugar Foot Stomp," bobbing their heads in time with its lively tempo. Never having heard jazz before, Jack and the two Irish brothers simply gazed around in amazement at the jubilation of every other customer in the place.

"These people are nuts!" Patrick declared.

"Or drunk," Larry quipped.

"I don't know," Jack said. "Looks like they're having fun."

Billy grinned at Jack. "Sure they is! That be New Orleans jazz—the bes' music in America!"

"It's nigger music!" Patrick blurted contemptuously.

"That so, how come they's so many white folk out there dancin'?" Billy asked, still grinning at Jack.

Surveying the hundreds of people on the dance floor, Jack had to admit there had to be something magical about this new kind of music. People of every color and social class seemed to be mixing and mingling like infants at play. Even several well-dressed white women were out on the floor kicking up their heels with Negro male partners.

That's something new! Jack thought. Only one week before, he had read in the *Vallejo Times-Herald* about a Negro man in Cleveland, Ohio, who had been lynched and hung for whistling at a white woman. When the band quickly transitioned into its next number—"Struttin' with Some Barbeque"—Jack couldn't help being caught up himself in the joyful vitality of this New Orleans jazz.

A waiter approached their table and asked, "You boys drinkin' or jus' lis'nin'? We got a cover charge here, you know. Two dollar a head."

"Two dollars!" Patrick declared. "You gotta be kiddin' me, nigger!"

"Take it easy, Pat!" Jack cautioned. "Don't get your Irish dander up. Just tell the man what you want."

Shaking his head in disgust, Adam pulled a thick wad of paper money out of his pocket and extracted a ten-dollar bill. Handing it to the waiter, he said, "Give us five beers."

"Yassah," the waiter said, suddenly all smiles. "That be good for two rounds. I bring 'em right over."

"Big Jim here tonight?" Adam asked the waiter.

"Sho' is!" Obviously impressed that Adam knew his boss, the waiter now became even more deferential.

"Tell 'im Adam Tucker says hello, will y'?"

"Yas suh!"

"Thanks, Adam," Jack said as soon as the waiter left.

"Yeah, thanks—I guess." Patrick was still visibly irate.

"You'll feel better after a couple of beers," Larry told his brother.

As the audience applauded the concluding bars of "Struttin' with Some Barbeque," the lead trombonist held up both of his hands. "Ladies and gents," he announced, "we is honored tonight to bring you the fabulous Miss Veronique LaRoque who comes to us all the way from Montreal, Canada!"

Several dancers groaned in disappointment at this interruption of their fun when a slender Negro woman in black tasseled dress and narrow-brimmed hat tilted rakishly over her pretty face stepped up to the microphone. Her wide-set eyes rolled in anticipation while she waited for the trombonist to play the opening bars of the next number— "The Saint Louis Blues." Then, rocking slowly from side to side, she mournfully intoned, "I hate to see that evening sun go down."

Suddenly, the Peekaboo Club became as silent as a sepulcher. Couples who had been stomping and jumping wildly only moments before now stood like statues to listen with reverence as Veronique LaRoque poured out her soul.

Patrick, Larry and Jack too were captivated. When Veronique began her second verse with the words: "Feelin' tomorrow like I feels today, I'm gonna pack my grip and make my getaway," Patrick exchanged glances with Billy and admitted, "You're right. That *is* the best music in America."

Her performance concluded, Veronique bowed her head humbly at the explosion of applause and cheers. Several customers shouted, "Encore! Encore!"

"So what'll it be, Veronique?" the bandleader asked.

"How 'bout 'Beal Street Blues,' Sam?" she replied with a knowing smile. She knew this W. C. Handy classic was sure to appeal to the culturally savvy in her audience. And she was right. Again, her audience was spellbound.

When the applause that followed finally subsided, the bandleader turned to Veronique and asked, "So tell me, Miz LaRoque, how come a New Orleans-born gal like you wound up in Canada?"

Veronique smiled coquettishly. "Well now, Sam, tha's a long story. You see it goes all the way back to the days when they put my granddaddy on the Underground Railroad and sent him north. First stop was Philadelphia—the City o' Brotherly Love. Only, when he got there, they wasn't much love. Them white brothers run 'im out o' town on a rail."

The drummer hit a snare, and the room erupted with laughter.

"So then he got back on the train an' went to the Windy City, Chicago. An', wouldn' you know? They blows him out o' that burg too—all the way up to Montreal!"

On this punch line, the band promptly swung into a jaunty rendition of *The Marseilles* and the dancers recaptured the floor. Suddenly, a tall Negro with snow-white hair emerged from the crowd and clapped his enormous hands on Adam's shoulders. "How you doin', old man?" he asked in a deep voice that sounded like gravel pouring into a huge iron tub.

Adam jumped to his feet and spun around, playfully jabbing at the big man's stomach. "Don't you be grabbin' me like that, fool!" he exclaimed. "You be scarin' these poor boys here." Gesturing at Jack and the Irishmen, Adam introduced them to "Big Jim" Jeffries.

Jeffries dragged an empty chair from another table and sat down, his long arms resting on the back of the chair. "So what you got goin', Adam?"

"Startin' a new business," Adam replied, glancing around to see if anyone might be listening.

"You ain't fixin' cars no more?" Jeffries asked, his eyes twinkling with friendly sarcasm.

Adam nodded. "Yeah, Billy and me—we's still fixin' cars. But tha's our day job. I got somethin' else in min'." Reaching into his shirt pocket, Adam extracted a pack of Lucky Strikes and shook the open end toward Jeffries. "You want one?" he asked.

"Nah. I give up on them things," Jeffries said. "Makes me cough too much."

Lighting up a cigarette for himself, Adam tossed his spent match into the big glass ashtray in the center of the table. "Who y' buyin' your hooch from these days, Jim?" he asked.

Jeffries leaned back and fixed Adam with a disapproving glare. "Who buyin' hooch? What you means! We runs a 'spectable place here, my frien'! Don't serve nothin' but sars'parilla an' ice cream!"

As Jeffries spoke these words, the waiter returned with five large mugs of beer. "You want one, boss?" he asked.

"Nah. Gimme a double Canadian Club—neat," Jeffries replied with a wink at Adam.

"You ain't servin' Canadian Club to this crowd," Adam sneered. "So where you gettin' your hooch?"

Jeffries glanced suspiciously at Jack and the Irishmen. "Your boys alright with this?"

"What'd I say? They's my business partners."

Jeffries nodded politely, but he was clearly skeptical about the white men. Standing up, he said, "Tell y' what, Adam—how 'bout you an' me take a walk back to my office." Calling out to the waiter who was now taking drink orders from customers at the next table, he said, "Leroy, you take care o' these boys. Anything they wants is on the house. You hear?"

Yas suh!" the waiter replied in astonishment.

Patrick took a big swig from his mug of beer. As soon as Adam and Jeffries were out of earshot, he smacked his lips and belched. "Now that's what I call a real gentleman nigger!"

Jack and Larry ignored Patrick's tasteless quip. Billy had already disappeared into the crowd in search of a dancing partner.

The band was now well into a hard-driving rendition of "Muskrat Ramble" and the dance floor was so crowded with frantic dervishes that several couples had jumped up on the tables.

His head bobbing to the rhythm, Larry remarked, "I think I'm really startin' to get the hang o' this!"

"What we need now," Jack said, "is a couple of those flappers out there."

"Let's go see if we can cut in," Patrick suggested.

"Looks to me like there isn't much cutting in," Jack remarked, nodding toward two young women and a black man who were kicking up their heels on a table top. It isn't about cutting in. It's about *joining* in!"

* * *

Hours later, Jack and Adam stood shivering together on the Martinez ferry dock. The dense morning fog obscured even the pilings at the end of the dock. It would be another full hour before the first ferry was scheduled to depart for Benicia at 6:30 A.M. Billy, Larry and Patrick were sound asleep in the back seat of Adam's Model A, which Adam had parked at the ferry terminal entrance gate.

"Some night out!" Jack said, breaking the long silence between them.

"Yeah. The boys had a good time," Adam observed. "Firs' time I ever seen a fella do de Irish jig in 4/4 time!"

Jack laughed. He didn't know what Adam meant by 4/4 time, but it didn't matter. He too had enjoyed the drinking and dancing at the Peekaboo Club. Even Adam himself had finally gotten out on the dance floor when Jeffries personally introduced him to Veronique LaRoque and she insisted Adam dance with her. They had all drunk and laughed and danced until the bar closed and the band played its last number at 4:00 A.M.

"So what did you and Jeffries talk about in his office last night?" Jack asked, hoping Adam would be too tired to be angered by the question.

Adam shook out a Lucky and lit up before he answered. "He gonna take everythin' he can get at two dollar a gallon. Soon's the bridge open, we goin' be rich."

Jack smiled at the man's undying confidence. "What do you plan to do with all your money?"

Adam puffed greedily on his cigarette. "Gonna buy me a big garage someplace an' get out o' bootleggin'. I's gettin' too old f' this bus'ness."

Gazing out at the fog for a moment, Jack was not sure he should pose his next question. It was one he had wanted to ask for a long time. "Were you ever married, Adam?"

The older man turned toward Jack, his eyes suddenly filled with sadness. "Not church married," he said. "Married in the flesh, like it says in the Bible. Pretty white gal, but she took off an lef' when Billy was born. Didn' want no part o' real marriage."

"So Billy is your son?"

Adam nodded and turned away again, inhaling deeply on his cigarette.

Jack put his arm around Adam's shoulders. "You're a good man!"

Adam shrugged. "Ain't got many choices in this life, boy."

"Do you believe in God?" Jack asked, knowing he was now way beyond his own depth; but something inside made him ask.

Slowly exhaling a thin column of smoke, Adam chuckled softly. "Question is—do He believe in me? I ain't figured that one out yet, boy."

CHAPTER TWENTY-ONE

S'Wonderful

BY 1:30 THAT WARM MAY afternoon, the main lobby of the Claremont Hotel looked like a florist's hothouse full of young women in tea dance dresses representing every shade of the color spectrum. Despite this variety in color, there was striking uniformity in fashion design. Practically every debutante's dress adhered to the straight-lines and short-skirts that were *de rigueur* in 1927. Many had adorned themselves with beaded necklaces drooping to their waists, and most wore their hair bobbed short under tight-fitting hats that looked like aviator helmets. Much to the chagrin of their parents and chaperones, all but a very few were heavily rouged.

Milling among these colorful blossoms, young men in black tux and white jackets eagerly solicited the prettiest girls for the right to sign their dance cards, while the less favored but nonetheless aggressive young women vied for the attention of the handsomest gallants. The din of high-pitched giggles and strained baritone voices was deafening as it echoed off the high, gold-leaf ceiling and mirrored walls.

Del in her new white "coming out" tea dress with matching hat, gloves, stockings and shoes was completely surrounded now by half a dozen young men who were complete strangers to her. Despite the elaborate instructions in etiquette all had received beforehand from doting parents, introductions for these young people were perfunctory and often downright rude. "Let go of my arm!" Del demanded of the skinny, acne-faced boy squeezing her elbow.

"But you must let me have at least one dance!" he pleaded.

Another much taller boy with a large head and broad shoulders pushed him away. "Beat it, Tyler!" he barked. "She's way out o' your league!" Then smiling ingratiatingly at Del, he announced, "I'm Dirk Van Zandt. Surely you know the Van Zandt family name. We own the largest cruise line on the West Coast."

Still annoyed, Del was unable to quell her curiosity about this interloper. She had often heard her Aunt Lucy extol the luxurious accommodations on the Van Zandt cruise ships. Besides, in spite of his bullying manner, this young man was extremely attractive—his flaxen hair, soft and silky; his wide-set blue eyes, twinkling with mischief. So she introduced herself and allowed Dirk to sign his name on the last available line of her dance card.

At precisely that moment, the giant double doors of the ballroom opened and a tall man in black tux and top hat emerged, holding up a sign with the words *THIS WAY PLEASE* printed on it in large black letters. Few noticed this sign, but all responded with cheers and applause when they heard the jaunty opening bars of "Five Foot Two, Eyes of Blue" emanating from the ballroom.

For several minutes, there was pandemonium as the young people crowded through the ballroom entrance and fanned out among the large circular tables that had been arranged on three sides of the dance floor. Every table had been set for fifteen guests, each with his or her own name card. No one but the parents and chaperones knew ahead of time where they were sitting—an arrangement that was the source of many protests as some youthful celebrants discovered they were sitting next to people whose appearance had little appeal.

Del was more fortunate, for to her right at Table Number One was her father and to her left sat her old friend Greg Henshak. Though this arrangement was not very exciting, at least it afforded her the comfort of the familiar—something Del felt she desperately needed at that moment.

Though still quiet and diffident, Greg was no longer the frail little boy Del remembered from eight years before. Long days of hard labor in his father's vineyard had tanned Greg's face and thickened the muscles in his arms and shoulders. His voice was deep and resonant now, his gaze steady and confidant. "Well, well! You finally did it!" he teased. "This is your big day! Congratulations, Del!"

"Almost a year late," she replied with only the slightest hint of resentment in her tone. "But Papa has been very busy. Better late than never, I suppose."

"You look gorgeous!" Greg affirmed with a reassuring smile. "Just like one of those models in *Vogue!*"

Del touched her friend's sleeve. "Thanks, Greg. You're an angel!" Searching around the room for her newest male acquaintance Dirk Van Zandt, she noted that he was sitting next to a strikingly pretty young woman in a rose-colored dress and flirting with her shamelessly. "Do you know a boy named Dirk Van Zandt?" she asked, hoping that Greg would have some scandalous story to report.

Greg shook his head. "Never heard of him. Why do you ask?"

Del did not have time to answer, for a sharp fanfare of horns from the orchestra suddenly interrupted all conversation and cued Judge Lanham to rise ceremoniously from his chair, walk to the front of the ballroom, and mount the short flight of steps onto the raised orchestra platform. Stepping to the microphone, he addressed the full assembly. "Welcome, all you young ladies and gentlemen, parents and friends!"

Polite applause filled the room. Del blushed, partly in anticipation of the words she knew her father was about to say but mostly in embarrassment at the scores of eyes that now focused on her, conspicuously set apart in her all-white attire. How she hated Emily Post!

"I'm sure you are all aware this is a proud day for me as I introduce my lovely and only daughter to this august gathering." Again, there was a smattering of polite applause. Motioning for Del to join him at the microphone, the Judge commanded, "Come up here, young lady, and welcome your guests."

Del felt Greg squeeze her hand encouragingly when she stood up and did her best to smile. But her whole body trembled as she moved hesitantly toward the dais where her father stood waiting with a dour smile. Fortunately, he had enough sensitivity to meet her half way and, offering his arm, ushered her up the steps toward the microphone. "Ladies and gentlemen," he announced, "I am pleased to present Miss Adelaide Clarabel Lanham of Benicia, California!"

Instantly, everyone in the ballroom stood and applauded. This accolade lasted for several seconds—an agonizingly long time for Del who in her wildest imaginings had never anticipated such, she thought, an undeserved accolade.

When the applause subsided at last, her father again spoke into the microphone. "And now, dear friends, I'd like you to join me as I lead my daughter in her first formal dance." Turning to the orchestra leader behind him, the judge declared, "Maestro, let us begin!"

The orchestra promptly launched into a lilting rendition of "I'm Falling in Love with Someone"—a waltz tune from one of her father's favorite operettas, *Naughty Marietta*. Del almost collapsed with embarrassment on her father's arm as he gracefully and gently guided her down the steps and out onto the ballroom floor where, after only a few seconds of solo dancing, they were joined by scores of other couples.

*   *   *

When the orchestra members took a break an hour later, Del joined the large crowd of young people who had gathered on the outdoor terrace adjacent to the ballroom. Many of them were smoking cigarettes, some for the first time.

"You don't smoke!" Dirk Van Zandt said to Del in astonishment when she refused his offer of a Camel.

"No," she replied. "And I probably never will. I tried it once, but those things taste awful!"

Dirk merely smiled condescendingly. "Karin's been smoking since she was twelve, haven't you, Sis?" he said to the puckish platinum blonde standing next to him.

"Of course. It's very much the thing to do nowadays. But I always use a cigarette holder," Karin added. "It's much more sophisticated and lady like."

"Ha! Lady-like, my foot!" Dirk snorted. "All you want to do is be an *It* girl!"

"What's an *It* girl?" Del asked, suddenly feeling abysmally ignorant.

"Oh you can't be serious!" declared a tall string bean debutante with sloppily applied mascara. "You mean you haven't read Elinor Glyn's new novel yet? Doesn't *anybody* read in Benicia? Where exactly *is* Benicia anyway? I never heard of it."

Furious, Del wanted to slap this girl in the face. The nuns at St. Catherine's Seminary had taught her a better strategy for dealing with such boors, however. Extending her hand to the string bean, Del said coolly, "I don't think I've had the ... ah ... pleasure of meeting you yet. You do have a name, don't you?"

"Patsy Pringle," the string bean said, thrusting out her hand and grabbing Del's. "So where *is* Benicia?" she demanded again.

Flabbergasted by Patsy's insolence, Del relented. "It's in the North Bay, on the Carquinez Strait."

"Afraid I'm still lost," Patsy shrugged dismissively. "Where's the ... what did you call it—*car-keen-is-straight*?"

Determined not to be bested, Del asked, "Have you ever taken the train to Sacramento?"

"Sure. Lots o' times. My uncle's in the State Assembly," Patsy was careful to point out.

"Then you'll remember crossing the Carquinez Strait on one of the big train ferries."

Blowing a puff of smoke, Patsy impatiently waved it away from her own face. "'Fraid not. I don't pay much attention to the scenery when I'm riding in a train. Too busy reading. By the way, you still haven't answered my other question. Can't *anybody* read in Benicia?"

"*I* read all the time!" Del retorted angrily. "Why are you being rude?"

"Oh don't take her so seriously!" said a young man who had just joined the conversation. He was short and stout and his hair was parted in the middle of his head. He looked like one of Tenniel's caricature illustrations in *Alice in Wonderland*, Del thought. "Patsy's just teasing," he explained. "She always does that when she meets somebody new. We've lived next door to each other ever since we were little kids, so I know all about her." Grinning, he abruptly introduced himself. "I'm Craig McCutcheon."

Del thought of retorting caustically that Patsy probably didn't have many friends. But then she remembered Ruby's words of wisdom: *Some folks hurts so bad inside they has to go aroun' all de time hurtin' other folks outside.* She also realized that the name *McCutcheon* seemed very familiar. "Are you related to Mister Bertrand McCutcheon?" she asked.

Craig beamed at her gleefully. "He's my grandfather! Do you know him?"

"My father does. I think they go hunting together sometimes."

"Sure! The Grizzly Island Club. Grandpa gets a big kick out of that bunch. He couldn't hit the broad side of a barn door with a coal shovel, but he loves to brag about his fox hunting days when he was young back in 'merry old' Scotland."

Del suddenly decided she liked Craig McCutcheon. She was glad to see that Patsy had drifted off to join another group of smokers. "Do you go duck hunting?" she asked.

"Me?" Craig laughed. "'Fraid not. Hunting's not my game. I prefer sailing." Then he added with a wink, "As long as I have a good crew to do all the winching and pulling!"

"You're a sailor!" Del exclaimed with delight. "So am I! Do you race?"

Again Craig laughed. "Only if I can skipper," he said. "I have a 45-foot schooner. That's too much boat for me to handle on my own—even in light air. I guess you could say I'm strictly a seat-cushion sailor."

Del laughed. "Where do you keep your boat?"

"At the Corinthian in Tiburon. It's really my father's boat, but he lets me take it out every now and then. Mostly then," he chuckled. "You see, Father takes racing pretty seriously."

"So do I," Del said, without wishing to seem brusque. She simply wanted Craig to know that she took pride in her own sailing abilities. She felt confident this amiable young man would take no offense.

"Great!" he shrugged. "For me, it's just something to do for fun."

"So tell me," Del said. "What's this novel *It* all about?"

Again, Craig shrugged. "I don't know. Never read it myself. Patsy says it's about some older woman in Paris who seduces a younger man on a leopard-skin bedspread."

"What!" Del exclaimed, appalled that any young woman could be interested in such a plot.

Craig raised his eyebrows in bewilderment. "Yeah—sounds pretty stupid, doesn't it?"

"It's disgusting!"

Just then, the orchestra began playing again in the ballroom. "Guess it's too late for me to put my name on your dance card," Craig remarked as he followed Del back to her table. Offering her his personal calling card, he said, "Why don't you give me a call sometime? Maybe we can go sailing together."

"I'd like that very much," Del said, taking his card and quickly placing it inside her handbag.

*　*　*

Six days later—on May 21, 1927—the new Carquinez Bridge was dedicated. A long procession of automobiles filled with political dignitaries and businessmen from all over the State moved slowly across the giant thrust-through span between Vallejo and Crockett, followed by a parade comprising the Navy marching band from Mare Island, the Benicia Arsenal Drum and Bugle Corps, and groups of marchers representing such state-wide civic organizations as the Elks, the Moose, the Redmen, and the Boy Scouts of America. There were thousands of marchers and spectators at this history-making event.

Judge Lanham, Del and Ruby were part of this grand cavalcade, riding in the Judge's 1927 La Salle—the latest General Motors luxury car. Designed by Stanford University trained engineer Harley Earl, who had once custom designed a $26,000 automobile body for Hollywood film star "Fatty" Arbuckle, the La Salle was a sensation among America's rich and famous that year. Understandably, the Judge was extremely proud of his new acquisition.

At that moment, however, Del was more impressed by something else. "Isn't this a beautiful bridge!" she exclaimed. "Jack helped build it, you know," she added with pride.

"Did he indeed!" said the Judge. He was not pleased to learn that his daughter was still keeping herself informed about the activities of her ruffian childhood friend. "And just what did he do?" he asked disparagingly.

"He was a riveter," Del replied.

"And how did you come to know about that, young lady?"

"Sam Geddis told me," Del said, beginning to feel very uneasy.

"And when was that?" the Judge inquired, now becoming openly hostile.

"Oh, months ago when I ran into him at Rankin's. Why are you so irritable, Papa?" Del knew the answer to this question, but she was determined to defend her loyalty to old friends.

Her father did not answer.

"Papa!" Del insisted. "Why are you angry?"

"We shall discuss it at another time, Adelaide," he said at last. "This is an occasion for celebration. I suggest you simply enjoy it."

Del turned in her seat to look back at Ruby who had closed her eyes and was nodding, signaling to Del that she should silently comply with her father's suggestion. But Del preferred to sulk. Even later that afternoon when the Navy band played a rousing medley of Sousa marches during the ribbon-cutting ceremony, Del's mood did not improve.

Surveying the faces of the several bridge laborers who had been selected to stand with the American Bridge Company executive officers during this ceremony, she was disappointed to note that neither Francis nor Jack was present. The workers' impeccably clean overalls, polished boots, and high-sheen steel helmets suggested that none of these men had really been involved with the hard and dangerous effort that went into the new bridge's construction. All were probably managers and foremen dressed up to look like common laborers. *It's not fair!* Del mused bitterly.

* * *

"Jesus, Mary and Joseph! Where'd y' get these monsters?" Francis exclaimed when he saw the two white Pierce Arrow tanker trucks parked in front of Schuster's Garage.

"Bought 'em from Jim Busby over at the Dairy Maid plant," Tucker said proudly. "They jus' bought a whole fleet o' new Model T Red Crowns, so he sold the Pierce Arrows to me cheap."

"Still must've cost a lot o' money," Francis said doubtfully. "How'd y' pay for 'em?"

Tucker pursed his lips whimsically. "Bought 'em on the installment plan."

"*You* got a loan? First time I ever heard of a nigger gettin' a loan!" Patrick sneered.

"Oh, don't you be worryin', boy. I got my ways." Then, addressing Francis, Tucker asked, "Think you can service these trucks?"

Francis had already opened the front hood on one of the cabs and was fingering the multiple mechanical components of its giant engine. "I'll figure it out," he replied confidently. "Got lots o' power in this thing!"

"We gonna need lots o' power, an speed too," Tucker observed. "Gotta cover a lot o' miles."

"Who's driving these things?" Jack asked.

"During the day, it's you an' your Irish frien's. Nighttime it's me an some o' my boys. They's Negroes mos'ly. But it don't matter 'cause the bridge toll takers won't see 'em too good in the dark." Tucker chuckled.

"Are you going to keep those Dairy Maid signs painted on the sides?" Larry asked.

"Fo' sure I ain't paintin' *Tucker's Booze* on 'em!"

Everyone laughed. "Yeah. That's a pretty good disguise. But won't Busby complain?" Francis asked.

"He don't care. He got his money. 'Sides, it's free advertisin' for him."

"I've got to hand it to you, Adam!" Jack said. "You're one sharp businessman!"

"So when do we start?" Francis asked.

"First pick-up's tomorrow mornin'. Billy an' me's drivin'. Jack an' Francis, you be ridin' along with us so's you can learn the route an' how to handle these rigs. Larry, you an' your brother 'll drive in the follow car."

"What about Sean?" Patrick asked.

Tucker's expression suddenly became very serious. "He ain't goin' on this trip. I gotta be sure everbody's col' sober." Turning to Billy, he said, "Go get them roadmaps. They's in my rolltop in the shop."

Billy started to move toward the entrance to the garage.

"Hold on, boy You gonna need a key." Tucker reached into the pocket of his overalls and extracted a small key, which he handed to Billy. Then, he climbed up into the driver's seat of the truck Francis had been inspecting and started its engine. The others leaped back in astonishment at its loud roar, and Tucker grinned at them with satisfaction.

* * *

301

Sean Hanrahan was sitting alone at the bar in the Casa De Vallejo, a building that had formerly housed Vallejo's Industrial YMCA. Recently, an out-of-town brewery owner named Ronald Pilcher had purchased the ornate tile-rooved structure and was now renovating the place to become a luxury hotel. The first change Pilcher had made was to partition off part of the ground floor lobby as a taproom so that he could begin generating revenue before the rest of his hotel opened.

Since it was only 5:15 on a weekday afternoon, the taproom was empty except for Sean and the bartender, a heavy-set Dutchman named Niels Closson. "So what d' y' think o' this fella Lindbergh?" Sean asked in an effort to make small talk with the sullen-faced Closson.

"What about 'im?"

"Y'r not gonna tell me now y' never heard o' Charles Lindbergh!" Sean scowled.

"Yeah. I heard of him. So what?"

"He's one o' y'r people, ain't he? German guy?"

"I ain't German," Closson growled. "I'm Dutch. Big difference."

"Is there now!" Sean pushed his empty whiskey glass toward the inside edge of the bar. "So how about a refill, Dutch!"

Closson grabbed a brown unlabeled bottle from a shelf behind him and placed it on the bar next to Sean's glass. "Help y'rself, Irish!"

Sean immediately seized the bottle and filled his two-ounce glass, then tossed off the contents in one swig. Shuddering and shaking his head vigorously, he declared, "Jesus! That stuff could kill a horse!"

Closson did not comment. Instead, he opened a newspaper he had stashed under the bar and began reading. Restless, Sean reached into his shirt pocket and pulled out a pack of cigarettes. "Got any matches back there?" he asked.

Without looking up from his paper, Closson again reached under the bar for a small box of matches which he shoved down the smooth bar top toward Hanrahan.

Finally realizing that all attempts at friendly conversation with the bartender would be futile, Hanrahan lit his cigarette and refilled his glass. This time, he decided to sip its contents slowly. He was in no hurry to drink himself into oblivion. That would come later.

After several minutes of silence passed, Hanrahan asked, "I see you got a radio? How 'bout turnin' it on. See if you can get some music. This place is deader 'n a doornail!"

Reluctantly, Closson abandoned his open newspaper and walked toward the cash register at the far end of the bar. On a shelf beside it was a four-dial Freshman Radio. Closson switched it on and tuned it to a Sacramento station where a women's quartet was singing a jingle advertising Quaker Oats. When the jingle ended, a man's voice announced that the program was being broadcast from the ballroom of the Twain Harte Hotel in downtown Sacramento. "And now, ladies and gentlemen," the announcer said, "we are pleased to present Preston King's orchestra playing a medley of songs from that newest Broadway hit *Showboat*. To add to your listening pleasure, our own Sacramento song birds, Miss Lillian Spencer and Mister Vincent Capelli, will sing the lyrics."

A chorus of violins suddenly filled the taproom with the opening bars of "Why Do I Love You?" followed by the sweet soprano voice of Miss Spencer singing the first verse: "Why do I love you? Why do you love me? How can there be two, happy as we?"

Sean laughed. "Now there's a good question!"

"Nice song," Closson observed as he stood gazing at the radio with his arms folded and a blissful expression on his face.

It was a response that startled Sean. He had not expected sentimentalism from such an oafish barkeeper. Refilling his glass a second time, Sean raised it in a toast. "Sure and I'll drink to that, Dutchman!"

Closson turned and glowered at his customer. "It ain't a drinking song, Irish. You better go easy on that sauce or you'll be leaving here sooner than you think!" he warned.

Sean slapped a two dollar bill on the bar top. "How 'bout I just buy this bottle an' you shut up?"

Shaking his head in disgust, Closson walked back down the bar, picked up the bill, and returned to deposit it in the cash register. "Done!" he declared. "And so are you, once that bottle's empty!"

"Says you!" Sean was poised to retort, but he was interrupted by the arrival of two new customers, both wearing the gray overalls and heavy work boots of Mare Island shipyard workers.

The two men sat down at the bar, several stools away from Sean.

They did not even glance his way. "Give us a couple o' drafts," said the taller of the pair.

On the radio a deep baritone voice was now singing the lyrics of "Ol' Man River," the Italian-opera trained vocalist studiously correcting Jerome Kern's clipped consonants: "Old-a Man River, he don't-a plant-a taters. He don't-a plant-a cotton. And them that-a plants them is-a soon-a forgotten."

"What kind o' nigger shit is that?" one of the shipyard workers demanded.

Ignoring the racist hostility of this question, Closson placed two glass mugs of beer in front of the newcomers. "Two bits," he said.

"Sounds like jigaboo talk t' me," Sean said, confident that this would get the other men's attention.

The tall man looked suspiciously at him, sizing up the sincerity of this stranger's bigotry. He took a sip from his mug of beer and then, apparently satisfied, observed, "You got that right, mister. My name's Tom Stark. This here's Seth Warner. What's y'r name?"

Stumbling as he stepped off his bar stool, Sean eagerly moved to shake hands with Stark and Warner. "Sean Hanrahan and glad I am to meet two white gentlemen like yourselves."

Stark patted the empty stool next to his own. "Have a seat, Sean."

"Sure an' I'll be happy to do that," Sean replied. Gesturing toward the bottle he had just purchased, he asked, "Would y' care to have a wee spot o' me whisky, gents?"

Stark and Warner exchanged Cheshire Cat grins. "That's real kindly of you, Sean," Warner said.

Retrieving his bottle, Sean signaled to the bartender. "Give us a couple extra shot glasses, Dutch," he ordered.

*   *   *

Three hours later, the taproom was filled with smoking and drinking shipyard workers, store clerks, and businessmen from all over town. Closson's radio was now playing such popular tunes as "Bye Bye Blackbird" and "Fascinatin' Rhythm"—all of which were barely audible in the loud din of male voices.

Having long since emptied his bottle of whiskey and shared numerous rounds of beer with Stark and Warner, Sean was feeling no pain and his tongue was wagging freely about Adam's new bootlegging enterprise. Stark and Warner were all ears, for they knew their boss Emmett Spears would be very interested in such information.

"So where's the nigger gettin' his raw hooch?" Stark asked.

Sean scratched his head feebly. "Well now, tha's one I don' know," he reluctantly admitted. "Tucker's got a whole bunsh sh'pliers up in the Sh'erras. Lumber mills'd be my guesh. Damn nigger won' le' me ride along. Shaysh he don' wan' no drunks wreckin' hish trucksh. But I c'n fin' out easy 'nough."

Stark immediately pulled from his pocket the stub of a pencil and a small address book. Tearing out a blank page, he wrote a phone number on it and gave the paper to Sean

"Tell y' what, Sean. You find out, you give me a call at this number. Could be good money in it for y'," Stark added with an encouraging smile.

"Happy t' oblige, Tommy me boy! How 'bout another roun'?"

Warner pointed up at the big wall clock behind the bar. "We gotta get goin'. Wives'll be mad as wet hens we don't get home soon." This was a lie. Neither of these men was married. But it was an excuse they assumed any drunken Irishman would believe.

"Shorry t' hear tha', boysh." Sean gazed at his empty mug, dimly realizing that, now out of cash, his evening of fellowship was over. "'Shbeen nishe talkin' to y'."

Stark slapped Sean heartily on the back and stood up. "Likewise. Don't forget, Sean ol' buddy. You're gonna call me, right?"

Sean nodded despondently. He was still nodding after his companions had left and Closson growled at him, "Time for you to go home, Irish."

* * *

Adam and Billy were eating breakfast at Dewey's Roadhouse in Napa that morning when Jack entered, accompanied by his old friend Sam Geddis. Though Jack had often said good things about Sam to Adam, the two had never met. Nor had Adam shown any particular interest in doing so. Despite his loyalty to Jack and Francis, Adam had very little trust in white people generally. In Adam's eyes, the son of a wealthy white oil magnate was especially suspect.

"Good morning!" Jack greeted them cheerfully. "I see you're eating Dewey's greasy sausages again, Adam. Don't you know those things 'll kill you?"

Adam looked up from his plate, an annoyed expression on his face. "Don't you be sassin' me, boy! I eats what I wants when I wants it. Who's this?" he asked, pointing his fork at Sam.

"This," Jack announced with his hand on Sam's shoulder, "is the Charles Lindbergh of California—Sam Geddis!"

Billy rolled his eyes at the newcomer. Adam leaned back in his chair, chewing vigorously on the large forkful of sausage and egg he had just stuffed into his mouth. He motioned for Jack and Sam to sit down. As they did so, Adam continued chewing and scrutinizing Sam's face.

Sam returned Adam's suspicious gaze with a broad smile and reached across the table to shake his hand. "Glad to meet you, Mister Tucker," he said amiably.

Adam simply nodded, irritated that Sam had ignored his disability. "I don' shake hands, boy, 'cause I ain't got no right han'." To emphasize this point, Adam held up his hook. "You can shake hands with Billy, if you wants."

"Sorry, Mister Tucker!" Sam blushed and immediately turned toward Billy, who duly shook Sam's hand. Since Billy's mouth too was full at that moment, he only grunted his greeting.

Jack stood up. "I'm going to get a mug of coffee. You want one, Sam?"

"Sure. Thanks," Sam replied, his eyes still focused on Adam. "Jack tells me you're having a lot of success with your new business, Mister Tucker," he said. "Any chance you're hiring extra help?"

Adam was startled at the boldness of this question. His astonishment quickly turned to anger. "Jack got no bus'ness tellin' you nothin'!" Adam growled. "What kind o' bus'ness you think I'm in, boy?"

"I hear you're in the trucking business." From what Jack had told him, Sam knew enough about Adam to realize the older man had a special fondness for candor. "Don't ever beat around the bush with Adam," Jack had warned him. "You want to say something, get right to the point."

"You got some balls, boy!" Adam observed, but he couldn't repress a smile. "So how come you lookin' for a job?"

"I already have a job," Sam said. "I work for the Forestry Service. But it's only part-time and it doesn't really start until this fall. I need a full-time work right now."

"What kind o' work you do?" Adam asked.

Jack returned with the two mugs of coffee. "Sam's a licensed pilot," he said as he sat down. "He's a fire spotter—the only one in northern California."

"What's that got to do with me?" Adam asked.

"Maybe you need to keep an eye on the competition," Sam suggested. "No better way to do it than from an airplane. I already know all the roads from Oakland to the Sierra foothills." Sam glanced quickly at Jack, fearful that perhaps he had already gone too far with his candor.

Adam stabbed another chunk of sausage with his fork and popped it into his mouth. After chewing for several seconds, he swallowed and said, "Still don't see what it's got to do with me."

"Come on, Adam!" Jack declared. "You know Soames is already losing business to us. It's only a matter of time before he figures out our routes and tries to ambush us somewhere out in the Gold Country. In a plane, Sam can spot them miles ahead and give us a warning."

"You got your own plane, boy?" Adam asked Sam.

"Well, no." Sam hesitated. "But it would be easy enough to rent one."

"Rent one!" Adam exploded. "Where y' gonna rent an airplane? Ain't no airports around here."

"Actually there is," Sam said. "Right near here—just a few miles north on the Silverado Trail."

Having cleaned his plate, Adam pushed it away. Turning to Sam, he said, "Tell y' what. S'pose you an' Jack show us this airport. I'd like to see if you c'n really fly one o' them planes."

"We can do it right now, if you like," Sam replied.

"Then, les' do." Standing up and handing Jack a ten-dollar bill, Adam said, "You go pay for this. Come on, Billy. We's gonna see us an air show."

CHAPTER TWENTY-TWO

"Blue Skies"

JUNE 12 WAS DEL'S SEVENTEENTH birthday. Because she had completed her eleventh grade at Saint Catherine's Seminary with A's in every subject and had dutifully followed her father's advice to make friends with many of the young people he had invited to her debutant party at the Claremont, her father thought it was only proper he should reward her with a special birthday gift—a brand new Ford roadster she could use whenever she chose to attend tea dances or other chaperoned social gatherings at the homes of wealthy families in Oakland, Sausalito and Burlingame as well as in the better communities of the North Bay.

Del was ecstatic when she first saw her new canary yellow car with its black convertible top, wire wheels and balloon tires. "Papa! It's beautiful!" she declared, throwing her arms around her father's neck. "Thank you so much!"

Not one to be effusive in his expression of affection, the Judge kissed Del gently on the forehead, patted her back and quickly disentangled himself. "You are very welcome, my dear," he said beneficently. "I just hope you are careful while driving it. I have hired an instructor to give you lessons."

"Oh Papa! I'm sure I'll be fine. Can we take it for a spin right now?"

"Well, I suppose we can," the Judge allowed. "I will have to do the driving, however, until after you have completed your lessons."

Del eagerly climbed into the passenger seat, devouring with her eyes and touching with her fingertips every detail of the vehicle's plush interior—its polished wood-framed control panel with built-in speedometer, gas gauge and clock; its black leather upholstered seats; and its chrome-plated window cranks and door handles. "Maggie will simply die with envy!" she exclaimed.

"The envy of others, my dear, is not something to be desired," her father pontificated as he turned the key in the ignition and pressed the electric starter button. The roadster's efficient little engine immediately began purring smoothly. The judge released the hand brake, depressed the clutch, dropped the floor shift into first gear, and steered the car out of the driveway onto West Third Street. Within a few minutes, they were heading north along the paved highway toward Cordelia.

Del became very excited when she saw that the speedometer indicated they were traveling at forty-five miles per hour. "Papa," she asked, "can we put the top down?"

"I do wish you would learn the difference between *can* and *may*, Adelaide!" he answered irritably. Nevertheless, he brought the roadster to a slow stop on the shoulder of the road. "You must first release these to put the top down," he explained as he reached above the windshield and flipped open two metal latches. Then, he stepped out of the car and carefully pulled the canopy up and back into the well behind the seat. Next, he opened the rumble seat hatch and reached inside to extract the well cover—a narrow strip of canvas edged with snap-on grommets.

As he attached the well cover, Del gasped in surprised delight. "You mean there are extra seats in the back too!"

"Yes, my dear. This is what is called a rumble seat. It can accommodate two additional passengers."

"Oh Papa! That's wonderful! Now I shall be able to take all my friends for a ride as well!"

"Certainly not *all* at the same time, Adelaide!" the Judge corrected sternly. "This is not a touring car or a bus! And you must be very careful about passengers who ride in the rumble seat. It can be very dangerous, especially for small children."

"Of course, Papa. I shall always be very careful," she assured her father.

* * *

The Judge's warning was reinforced many times during the two weeks that followed when Del took her driving lessons from Roger Smythe, a volunteer safety officer for the Benicia Police Department. In his late sixties, he was a widower with two wayward daughters who had long since departed for parts unknown. Smythe was a patient and humble man who had lived in Benicia all of his life. Having worked most of it as a rural delivery postman, he knew every highway and country road in Solano County. It was all of these traits that had prompted the Judge to hire him as his daughter's driving instructor.

Del was a respectful and obedient pupil under Smythe's gentle tutelage. Once she had completed her driving lessons, however, she quickly discovered the excitement of driving her peppy little car fast on the country roads that wound through the hills of Sonoma, Napa and Solano counties. She also found many among her new acquaintances who were eager to introduce her to the world of late night house parties and even a few speakeasies.

With her father traveling out of state during the summer months, often weeks in succession, Del had many opportunities to pursue these interests unhindered. Even though Ruby rebuked Del several times for staying out late and coming home with liquor on her breath, Del dismissed these rebukes as prudish and old fashioned.

She never expressed this opinion to Ruby in so many words, for she had too much respect for Ruby's native intelligence. She also knew that Ruby would never betray her to her father—unless, of course, she did something really outrageous! This Del had absolutely no intentions of doing.

On the night of July 4th, however, things seemed to spin out of control. Del had been celebrating the holiday at the Henshak's hilltop mansion in Benicia with several of her new friends from the Corinthian and Vallejo yacht clubs. As it happened, Florence Henshak was away visiting with her now married daughter Rowena in Newport Beach and Oscar was on a weeklong golf outing with some of his cronies in Sacramento. That meant the only resident adult present in the Henshak household was their groundskeeper and general handyman, Wally Sykes.

Though now in his early fifties, Sykes was as fond of reckless partying as the young people who had gathered that night to watch the fireworks over Carquinez Strait. No less than five different displays were visible from the broad terrace and swimming pool at the back of the Henshak residence.

These began at 8:45 P.M., with the first and most distant display in Concord, overlapped a few minutes later by the much closer and louder display in Martinez. At 9:15, Benicia launched its display from a barge anchored just a few yards off the end of the First Street pier. This was accompanied by flashes and "pops" from virtually every back yard in town as well as by the wild hooting of switch-engine whistles on both sides of the Strait. Fifteen minutes later, the communities of Crockett and Vallejo began firing off their displays.

"Coney Island got nothin' on us!" Sykes declared to Craig and Del as the three stood together gazing at the shooting streaks and exploding blossoms of multicolored fire.

"Coney Island?" Del asked. "What's that?"

Wally stared aghast at her. "You mean you never heard o' Coney Island?"

"*I* have," Craig said quickly in an attempt to rescue Del from her own provincialism. "It's in New York, isn't it?"

"Brooklyn, actu'lly," Sykes corrected. "My home town. Coney Island's *only* the most fabulous amusement park in America! They got roller coasters there'd scare the pants off Attila the Hun. Why you can see the Coney Island fireworks from five miles out to sea! But this is a pretty darn close second," Sykes allowed, as he stretched his long skinny arms out toward the now climactic chatter of exploding rockets above Benicia's First Street pier.

"I've never been to New York," Del commented wistfully. "I hope I will someday."

Wally placed a consoling hand on Del's shoulder. "Sure you will, baby! Your papa's a big-time judge. One day soon he'll prob'ly hire a whole train t' take you an' your friends cross country on the Transcontinental Railroad—all the way to Coney Island!"

"He's not *that* rich!" Del protested. Sykes was notorious in Benicia for his tendency to exaggerate. She did not want her father's reputation marred by this foolish old loudmouth.

"Let's drink to the Transcontinental Railroad!" Craig said whimsically, raising his highball glass.

"To Brooklyn and Coney Island!" Sykes shouted.

"What's going on here?" Dirk Van Zandt demanded as he joined the threesome.

"Mister Sykes was just telling us about Coney Island," Del explained.

"What's with this Mister Sykes! Don't be so doggone formal, Del. All my friends call me Wally!"

Del gave the older man a look that said she regarded him not as a friend but as a busybody who had no business trying to fraternize with Greg's youthful guests.

"Well sure, Wally, old buddy!" Dirk declared, slamming Sykes on the back. "We're happy to call you Wally. Wild Man Wally—the party animal. Right?"

Sykes eyed Dirk fearfully. "I ain't wild," he protested. "I just like t' have fun. Nothin' wrong with that, is there?"

"Certainly not," said Patsy Pringle who, having walked from around the other side of the swimming pool, now entered the conversation. "I definitely prefer the company of older men," she added with a deprecating sneer at Dirk. "They're much more sophisticated than callow youths."

Dirk laughed and slammed Wally on the back again. "Yeah. Good old Wally here. He's real sophisticated, ain't y', Wally?"

In the bright flare of the first rocket from the Crocket display, Del noted that Wally's face was twisted with both fear and resentment. "I know a thing or two," he managed to say.

They all stood watching in silence as the Crockett fireworks illuminated the sky over the Carquinez Bridge where the headlights of vehicles moved slowly across the Strait like a living necklace of sparkling diamonds.

"I'll bet it would really be something to see this from the bridge?" Craig remarked.

"Yes," Patsy agreed. "So why didn't you arrange for us to be on the bridge during the fireworks instead of way up here on your patio, Greg?"

"Don't know," Greg shrugged. "Just didn't think about it, I guess."

"You can see much more from here," Del insisted. "Greg and I have watched these fireworks every year since we were little. Believe me, the higher you are the better."

Patsy responded to this challenge by waving to her friends Joanna Newman and Fred Saunders, who were watching the fireworks from the other side of the swimming pool. "Jo, come over here!" she commanded. "I want your opinion about something."

Joanna was twenty-one, already in her junior year at Mills College. She had traveled with her parents to Europe numerous times and had won four women's tennis tournaments in the Bay Area. Patsy therefore considered Joanna an authority on just about every topic.

Tall and athletic with thick ankles and a protruding Irish chin, Joanna seemed to Del the antithesis of everything feminine. "So what's up?" Joanna asked jauntily as she and Saunders approached.

Patsy pointed toward the lights on the bridge. "Don't you think our view of the fireworks would be much better from over there on the bridge than from way up here on Greg's patio?"

Joanna glanced quickly at the bridge. "Who knows? Yeah, maybe. But then what would we do for drinks? You know the bridge toll takers would never let us pass with a car full of booze!" she laughed and turned to Greg. "Speaking o' that, Greg, how 'bout somebody making me another Daiquiri?"

"Coming right up!" Sykes declared, quickly scurrying around the pool toward the wet bar.

Joanna elbowed her host. "Hey Greg, your man Wally's a real Ace of a butler. Great sense of humor. Where'd your parents dig him up?"

"He's been working for them ever since I can remember," Greg replied. "He's not really a butler, though. Just sort of a general handyman."

"He's handy alright!" Turning to Saunders, Joanna said, "Come on Fred. You need a refill too. Let's go back to the bar."

"Good idea, Jo," Patsy said. "This fireworks thing is getting boring. Let's all go get a refill."

Though Del was not happy about letting Patsy take over in a game of Follow-the- Leader, Craig grabbed her hand and firmly pulled her after the others. "Come on, Del. Don't be such a party-pooper!" he scolded.

As they gathered around the wet bar and Sykes busied himself filling their orders, Joanna recounted her last conquest at a women's tennis tournament in Santa Barbara. "It was a real love fest," she boasted. "My opponents got all the loves. Ha-ha! My coach tells me I'll be an Olympic champion someday."

"Except women don't compete in the Olympics," Dirk sneered.

Caught by this remark in the midst of taking the first gulp of her newly mixed Daiquiri, Joanna sprayed rum and lemon juice all over the front of Dirk's white shirt and trousers.

"Wow!" she declared. "Your Momma's really been neglecting your education, kiddo! Suzanne Lenglen took two gold medals and a bronze in the 1920 tennis Olympics! And how about Helen Wills? She won both singles and doubles gold in the Paris Olympics of 1924! And I guess you never heard of Gertrude Ederle. She took a gold and two bronzes for swimming in the 1924 Olympics."

Everyone laughed uproariously—everyone, that is, except Dirk whose face turned beet red.

"Guess she really clipped your wings, didn't she, sonny?" Sykes quipped.

Dirk glared murderously at Sykes, but said nothing.

"Oh that's perfect, Jo!" Patsy exclaimed. "Dirk, you're such a schlemiel!"

Though she was amused, Del couldn't help feeling sorry for Dirk. Patsy had gone too far. In an effort to soften the blow, Del changed the subject. She pointed toward the rapid flashes of color over the hills to the West. "Looks like Vallejo's finale."

"So what do we do now?" Joanna asked. "How about some jazz? Got any good records, Greg?"

"Sure," Greg said. "I'll go get some."

But Patsy stopped him in his tracks. "Bor-ing!" she spat out. "How about we go down there." She pointed toward First Street where the sound of music and exploding cherry bombs was now echoing up the hillside.

Greg shook his head. "Believe me. You don't want to go down there," he warned. "Things get pretty wild on nights like this. Street's full of whores and crazy drunks."

"No kidding!" Patsy exclaimed. "Let's go!"

"How about a nice moonlight sail over to Port Costa," Sykes

suggested. "They got live music over there in the Granary Barn. Some pretty good bands too."

"We could always drive over," Del said.

"No," Joanna retorted. "I like Wally's idea much better. Just look at that moon! You guys are all sailors, aren't you? You got a boat handy, Greg?"

"Yes," he answered. "But it's only a fourteen footer. It'd be kind of risky with seven people."

"Oh, come on Greg!" Patsy barked. "Where's your sense of adventure? Let's go!"

* * *

Ten minutes later, they were on the dock at Striker's Landing while Greg rigged his boat for sail. As part of his preparations, he handed out life vests.

"Who needs these filthy old things?" Patsy protested. "We're all good swimmers and the water's like glass out there."

"You ever sailed in the Strait?" Greg asked.

"Of course not! We only sail in Frisco Bay."

"Then I guess you don't know about the deep channel up here. We've got an eight-knot current out there, even in the calmest weather. So everybody wears a vest. Skipper's rules!" he affirmed.

"He's right," Del said. "We all wear vests on the Strait."

"Oh what the hell! Who cares? Let's just do it." Joanna put on her vest, and the others followed her lead.

"Not much inboard in this thing," Saunders observed as he gingerly stepped down onto the deck and helped Joanna aboard.

"Girls forward; guys aft," Greg commanded. "Except for you, Dirk. You're the biggest, so you get to straddle the mast."

Ignoring Greg, Dirk promptly seated himself in the stern. "You push off, Greg. I'll take the tiller."

"You don't know these waters," Greg told Dirk. "Besides, this is my boat. So you sit where I told you."

Del was delighted by Greg's calm self-assurance. "You'd better do as he says," Del warned.

"Yeah, dummy!" Patsy seconded. "Haven't you had enough humiliation for one night?"

"I've had enough from you, you stupid bitch!" Dirk growled, but he relinquished the tiller to Greg and squatted into position just forward of the mast.

Grasping the main sheet, Greg directed Craig to take the port jib sheet and Saunders to take the starboard. "You can push off now, Wally. Thanks."

Wally dropped the bowline into the boat and, with one foot, pushed it away from the dock.

"Aren't you coming too, Wally?" Joanna called out.

"Nah!" he waved. "Not enough room. You kids have fun."

Greg eased out his sheet, and a gentle breeze filled the mainsail. Because the heavily laden boat was low in the water, he knew it would be a very slow reach across the Strait.

Looking upstream, Craig saw the lights of a large tanker anchored at the Shell Refinery dock a mile to the east of where they were crossing. "How often do those tankers come through here?" he asked Greg.

"We get a dozen or so every day," Greg replied. "More at night, unless there's a really heavy fog."

"It's awful pretty out here," Patsy said with uncharacteristic awe. "Just look at that moon, will you!"

"How long will it take us to get across?" Craig asked.

"Shouldn't be more than a few minutes," Del answered. "The Strait's less than half a mile wide here."

"Is that where we're going?" Joanna asked, pointing directly across the Strait at a cluster of lighted buildings on the opposite shore.

"Yes," Greg answered.

"Then, why are you heading so far upstream?" Saunders inquired.

"Tide's going out and the current's too strong in the deep channel," Greg explained patiently. "So we have to enter it well above Port Costa and drift down. There's not enough air to carry us directly across."

Feeling left out of the conversation, Dirk reached into a back pocket and extracted his silver flask. "Anybody want a swig?"

"What's in it?" Joanna asked.

"Brandy."

Joanna made a face. "No thanks. That stuff doesn't mix too good with rum."

The others fell silent now as everyone scanned the dark hills that seemed to rise like waking giants ahead of them. In the distance, they heard the sound of a train whistle. Then, suddenly, the bright beam of a locomotive's headlamp flashed out across the water as it rounded the bend just beyond the Carquinez Bridge and headed due east toward Martinez. They were now about fifty yards from their destination and could feel the strong current of the deep channel slow the boat's progress.

"Coming about!" Greg warned as he turned the boat and its boom moved slowly from port to starboard. Craig and Fred managed to duck just in time.

Again, the locomotive sounded its whistle as it approached train ferry switching yard along the shore in front of Port Costa. The thunder of the big steam engine's wheels and the clatter of its following freight cars filled their ears. "Wow!" Craig declared. "This is a busy place! Tankers, ferries, trains!"

Greg was concentrating on steering his boat, its over laden hull difficult to control in the strong current. "Damn!" he swore when it suddenly struck something hard beneath the surface of the water. "Must 've hit a rock."

"Hope you didn't punch a hole in this thing," Patsy remarked. "It would be a long walk back across that bridge."

"It'll be alright," Greg said, trying to allay his passengers' anxiety. "This boat's built solid." But he was not as confident as he wanted to sound. He knew that the submerged rocks on the southern shoals of the Strait had sharp edges that could easily damage his boat's thin wooden hull.

Out of the strong current in the shipping channel now, they were drifting slowly. Greg released the main sheet and guided his boat carefully toward a narrow stretch of sandy embankment. Del stood up in the bow. As soon as she heard the crunch of wood on sand, she jumped over the side. Grabbing the bowline, she pulled them up on the beach.

Joanna clapped her hands. "Good job, Del!"

Everyone but Greg climbed out of the boat and walked up toward the railroad tracks where they waited while Greg secured his boat with the bowline and the boat's anchor. The first he tied to a wooden piling at the water's edge; the second he wedged between two rocks several feet above the beach. He had no way of knowing how long they were going to stay at the Granary. If it was late when they returned, the tide could rise and leave them stranded.

As they walked across the maze of railroad tracks toward the brightly lighted Granary building, they were greeted by the sound of loud music and laughter. "What fun! I'm gonna get plastered!" Patsy announced.

*　*　*

Patsy had fulfilled her ambition. When the six friends emerged from the Granary at 2:30 A.M., Patsy had to be carried between Fred and Dirk—neither of whom was very steady on his feet. Craig and Joanna too were staggering and leaning heavily on each other. But they were happy drunks and whooped with laughter every time they stumbled. Even Del, fighting the effects of both alcohol and fatigue, struggled to keep herself from stumbling. Only Greg seemed steady on his feet as he led them down to the boat, which had risen with the tide and was now half-filled with water.

"Wha'sh ma'er?" Craig asked when he saw the expression of dismay in Greg's face.

"We've got a leak," Greg replied grimly. "I'll have to go back and ask the bartender if he has a bucket or something we can use to bail this thing." The others watched in puzzlement as Greg headed back up the slope.

A few minutes later, Greg returned carrying an empty glass beer pitcher. "This is all I could get," he explained. "The bastard charged me ten dollars for it!" he added angrily. Immediately, he began scooping water out of the boat. But it was a long, slow process. It was almost half an hour before he managed to scoop out most of the water. The others, incapable of helping him, had simply flopped down at the edge of the railroad tracks above to watch.

Dragging the sodden life vests out from the cubby where he had stored them, Greg tossed them up toward his passengers who sat staring at them for several seconds. "Put them on," Greg ordered. "And make sure they're secure. If we don't make it across, you're gonna need them!"

Fumbling awkwardly with this safety gear, Greg's passengers slowly managed to don their vests. Del and Joanna struggled to wedge the totally unconscious Patsy into her vest but were unable to secure its straps, so Greg had to tie Patsy in with a length of rope he cut from the bowline.

Once everyone had climbed into the boat, Greg hoisted his mainsail and they were underway. Fortunately, the incoming tide and a brisk eastward breeze made it easier for them to make good headway in their reach back toward Benicia. The moon was low on the horizon, however, its former brightness obscured by dark clouds. The only artificial lights they could see were on the two buoys marking the channel and on the lampposts on the ferry terminal pier in Benicia.

Everyone was silent, the only sound that of the boat's bow pushing through the water. Greg was grateful for this. He was tired of his guests' rowdy garrulousness. Although he could feel water around his ankles and knew that there was a slow leak in the bottom of his boat, he felt sure they would be able to make the crossing safely.

Then suddenly he stiffened with fear, for a huge dark mass loomed off to his right. Not more than a hundred yards away, a tanker ship was bearing down on them. They were directly in its path. "Wake up! Wake up!" he shouted.

"Oh my God!" Del screamed and vigorously shook Joanna and Dirk into wakefulness.

"What do we do?" Craig demanded.

"Look!" Fred shouted. "There's a tug coming up on the port side. Maybe he'll see us!"

Greg leaned hard on his tiller to reverse course. It was his only choice. He had to get out of the path of the oncoming ship. He had no time to warn his passengers that he was going to jibe. With the sudden shift in direction, the sailboat's boom shot across the deck, nearly knocking both Craig and Fred into the water, while Dirk sat paralyzed in the center of the boat, clinging desperately to the mast.

Greg felt a momentary sense of relief as his craft moved starboard, avoiding a direct collision with the oncoming steel bow of the tanker— now less than twenty yards away. But the huge wake from ship's bow hit them broadside, capsizing the sailboat and dumping everyone into the ice-cold water of the Strait.

*　*　*

"What on earth were you thinking?" Del's father demanded, his normally expressionless face darkened with fury. "Or, perhaps I should ask, were you thinking at all last night?"

"No, Papa," she answered, dropping her eyes in shame. She was lying on the sofa in the front parlor, her head propped up with a pillow Ruby had retrieved from her own bed. "We were all very drunk, except Greg."

"Thank the Lord!" the Judge said. "If it hadn't been for him, you would probably have all drowned!"

That was not quite true. Although Greg had been sober enough to get them all into his boat and avoid their being run down by the tanker ship, it was not he who had rescued them. Rather, it was the crew aboard the tugboat. Although the laws of navigation prohibited such a rescue effort by any tug assigned to accompany an oceangoing vessel through inland waters, the skipper of this tug, Bart Dougherty, was a man whose heart was in the right place. Del felt sure that *Miss Trudy*'s being the escort tug for that particular freighter on that particular night was truly an act of God—a direct answer to the quick silent prayer she made as she struggled to the surface after Greg's sailboat had capsized.

"I am confiscating the keys to your car, young lady," the Judge announced. "I have also arranged for your Aunt Lucy to stay with us here in Benicia until you return to school this fall. For the rest of the summer, if you wish to visit with your friends out of town, you will have to ask your Aunt to drive you."

"Oh Papa!" Del pleaded feebly. "Please don't take my car away. I promise I shall *never* do anything like this again!"

"No, young lady," her father replied with grim finality. "You most certainly *will not*!"

1928

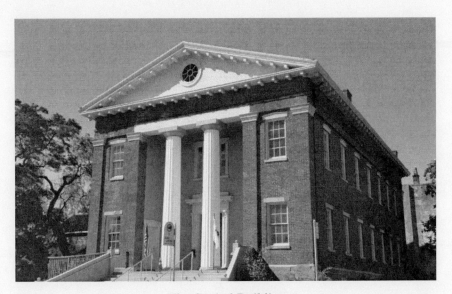

The Capitol Building

CHAPTER TWENTY-THREE

"You Took Advantage of Me"

BY FEBRUARY OF 1928, TUCKER'S new enterprise was thriving. Word had traveled fast among the hundreds of speakeasies and roadhouses along Lincoln Highway—all the way from Napa to Oakland. With the opening of the new Carquinez Bridge the year before, many new establishments had sprung up along the back roads winding eastward into the hills of Contra Costa County and westward to the shorelines of the Napa River and San Pablo Bay.

Tucker's two tanker trucks made the long round trip between Jamestown and Oakland twice each week, usually on Mondays and Thursdays. Apart from two alternate Lincoln Highway routes, one to the north and east through Sacramento and the other directly east through Stockton, most of the roads east of Sacramento and Stockton were unpaved and unmapped. Often little more than hay-wagon trails, those few roads marked by signs had names like Gopher Gulch and Blackbird Hollow. It was only by exploring these routes months ahead of time that Tucker had managed to plot the best routes.

Armed with pistols, Billy and Patrick drove one tanker at night, using the southern route. Adam and Eddie Zhao followed them in a separate car. Adam carried an Army-issue Colt automatic; Eddie, a double-barreled shotgun. Also armed with pistols, Jack and Francis drove the second tanker during daytime hours. They used the northern route through Sacramento to Placer and then headed southeast toward Jamestown. Larry followed them accompanied by a new member of

Tucker's gang, Ted Sena. Both men wore shoulder-holstered pistols. Sena also carried a Tommy gun.

Jack had known Sena from the days when he worked as a shoeshine boy in Huey's barbershop. "You can trust this man," he had assured Adam. "He's been in the business a long time, and he knows how to keep a secret."

Still, Adam was skeptical. "We's in a war here, boy," he cautioned. "We needs somebody can use a machine gun an' ain't scared t' die."

"Sena's your man," Jack said. "I've done some checking. He was a machine gunner for the French air corps during the Great War. Earned the *Croix de Guerre*. Just like you, Adam, he's a tough old geezer, and he isn't scared of anybody."

"Le' me talk to him," Adam said. When he did, Adam hired Sena immediately. That was late in June of 1927.

When, a month later, Sam demonstrated his well-developed aeronautical skills, Adam quickly saw the value of air reconnaissance and hired him. "Now you gotta get yourself a plane," he told Sam.

"That's easy," Sam said. "I'll talk to Sharon and Todd."

"How you know you can trust 'em?" Adam asked.

Sam smiled. "Because they're in the bootlegging business too. Not like you, exactly. They provide air courier service for a bunch of distilleries all the way from Fresno to Chico. They'll rent us a plane and a hangar, if the price is right."

"Whatever it takes," Adam nodded. "You set it up, boy."

The Rivers were eager to cooperate. They agreed not only to provide a hangar and use of their airstrip but also to lease to Adam an Army surplus De Haviland DH-4 bi-plane. This two-man aircraft was equipped with two .30-caliber Marlin machine guns in the nose and two .30-caliber Lewis machine guns in the rear. Its 421-horsepower engine delivered both the range and speed Adam would need to provide protection for his vehicles as they traversed the deserted back roads between Jamestown and Davis. The Rivers also offered room and board in the bunkhouse on their ranch so Adam's flight crew would have ready access to the De Havilland.

Since air reconnaissance would be effective only during daylight hours and Ted Sena was the only member of the gang familiar with aircraft machine guns, Adam switched him from daytime follow-car duty to gunner on the De Havilland.

"So who's taking Sena's place in the follow car?" Larry asked.

"How about Sean?" Patrick suggested.

Tucker frowned. He still did not trust the older Irishman, but he knew he needed a white man.

"Why don't you let Jack ride with Larry?" Francis said. "Sean can go with me in the truck. Don't worry. I'll keep him on the straight and narrow."

Adam studied Francis' face for several seconds. Though only nineteen, Francis had the hard eyes of a man twice his age. Better still, Adam knew Francis was a committed teetotaler. "You's gonna have t' watch 'im like a hawk, boy," Adam warned.

"Don't worry. I know all his dumb harp tricks. I'll fix it so he moves in with me. That way I can watch him day and night. He gets out o' line, I'll kick his Irish ass all the way back to Cork!"

Larry and Patrick both laughed. Jack said, "I'll vouch for that. I'll keep a close eye on him too."

Reluctantly, Adam nodded. "He don't get no gun. He jus' a extra set o' eyes, you hear?"

"Agreed," Francis said.

* * *

At first, Gail did not recognize the tall young man standing in her doorway. His face was in shadow cast by the bright mid-morning sunlight behind him. His voice, deep and resonant, was even less familiar. "Jack?" she asked hesitantly, feeling rather than perceiving his identity. "Is that really you?"

"Hello, Mother," Jack said softly. He was shocked and saddened by the changes in her. Though her figure was still slender and graceful, crow's feet were visible at the corners of her eyes. Her long brown hair, tied up in a tight bun at the back of her head, revealed strands of gray at the temples.

"Yes, Mother," he replied. "I know it's been a long time, but I'd like to talk to you about something. Can I come in?"

"Oh Jack, of course!" Gail exclaimed, throwing herself at him and clasping his face in her hands. "It's so good to see you! My God! How you've grown!" Her eyes filled with tears as she said, "Come in, dear. I'll fix you a nice breakfast."

"Thanks, but I've already eaten," Jack said as he followed her inside. He had forgotten how small her apartment was and suddenly felt remorse at not having visited her sooner. *How lonely and sad you must be!* he thought.

"Sit down, Jack," his mother urged. "I'll make a pot of tea." Quickly filling an iron pot with water and setting it on the stove to boil, Gail sat down in her armchair, its mohair fabric worn smooth as silk. "Are you still working for the bridge company?"

"No, Mother. They let everybody go as soon as the bridge was finished. I'm back working for Adam now."

She turned to face him, a worried look on her face. "Really! So what are you doing? Has he opened another garage or something?"

"No. He still works as a mechanic for an outfit over in Vallejo. But he's started another business on the side." Suddenly Jack stopped himself, realizing that any information he shared with his mother about Tucker's trucking enterprise she would probably share with Soames.

Gail was not to be put off. "What kind of business?"

"Trucking," Jack replied, hoping she would ask for no additional details. "I'm one of his drivers."

"Well! You certainly are a Jack of all trades, aren't you?"

They both laughed at her pun. Apparently satisfied with Jack's explanation, she moved on to another topic. "Have you seen anything of Del or Sam lately? I understand Sam earned his pilot's license and is working for the Forestry Service."

"Yes. I heard that too." Jack spoke hesitantly, worried that his mother's questioning was again leading him into dangerous territory. "I haven't seen Del for a long time. I did get a couple of letters from her while I was in jail. But she's moving in different circles nowadays. You know—high society and all that."

"There's no reason you can't still be friends," his mother observed, but there was a note of fatalism in her tone. Smiling sadly at her son, she said, "We all go our separate ways as we grow older, don't we, dear?"

Jack seized his mother's hand. "Mother, I want you to move out of here! Get yourself a nicer place—a house maybe. I'm earning good money now so I can help you."

Gently releasing herself from his grasp, she stood up and moved toward the stove. "Why would I want to move? I've been living here for almost twelve years now. It's close to my job, and I'm really quite comfortable. A single woman doesn't need much, you know."

"But this place is so small. You need more space, Mother—at least a place with hot and cold running water! And look at this," Jack said, pulling at some loose strands of stitching on the cushioned arm of her sofa. "You need new furniture. And you should have an electric iron and a washing machine. They have wonderful new kitchen appliances these days. I can buy them for you."

"Jack!" she said firmly. "I don't need it. Save your money. You may meet a nice girl someday and want to get married. That would make me much happier than any new furniture or appliances." She reached over the stove, opened a cabinet door, and extracted a round metal box. Removing its lid, she placed it on her kitchen table. "Have some sugar cookies. I baked them yesterday. It's a recipe from your Grandmother Tillie."

Tillie Westlake was Jack's paternal grandmother. She had died just before his father was killed in the Great War. Though the old woman had lived with them while Jack was very young, he remembered very little about her. Since Tillie's death, Gail had rarely mentioned her, except occasionally to praise her baking skills. Jack knew his mother was using the cookies now as a distraction.

He stood up and walked toward her. Taking both of her hands into his own, he implored, "Mother, you have to listen to me! I want you to free yourself of Soames. He's a very bad man—a thief and a murderer! You've got to break up with him before it's too late."

"No, Jack!" Gail retorted, pulling away. "You listen to me! My relationship with Soames has nothing to do with you! It's none of your business! Do you understand?"

"No, Mother. I don't understand. I guess I never will."

The pot of water was boiling now, so Gail filled her porcelain teapot and dropped in a tea caddy. "We'll have to let it steep for a few minutes," she said. Again, she motioned toward the cookie tin. "Go on, Jack. Have one. It will sweeten your disposition."

Defeated, Jack took one of the cookies and sat down again to nibble on it.

"Have you heard that Charles Lindbergh is coming to California?" Gail asked. "I'll bet Sam is very excited."

"Is he coming to the Bay Area?" Jack asked, aware now that all he could do was try to make small talk.

"I don't know. I think the paper said San Diego. But one never knows these days. They say soon there will be passenger air service all the way from Los Angeles to New York. I find that hard to believe." Gail tested the strength of her tea and filled a cup for each of them. "Do you still take cream and sugar, Jack?"

"A spoonful of sugar will be fine, thanks."

As she served the two cups and saucers and motioned him to sit down at the table, Jack felt like a little boy again. But the feeling dissipated quickly when Gail said, "So tell me more about this new job of yours. You said you are a truck driver. What kind of trucks and where do you drive them?"

"It's a delivery service," he answered, desperately searching for a way to remain ambiguous. "We cover a lot of different areas, all around the Bay."

Gail looked at him suspiciously over the edge of her teacup. "And what kinds of things do you deliver?"

"I really can't say." Jack decided it was the only right answer to offer. He was not going to lie to his mother—even now when he was so thoroughly disappointed in her.

Gail eyed him warily. "Is it something illegal? Jack, you're not involved with bootlegging again, are you?"

Jack pushed back his chair and stood up. Carrying his cup and saucer over to the kitchen counter and setting it down. Then, without turning to face her, he sighed. "I guess it's just as you say, Mother. What I do has nothing to do with you. It's none of your business! I'm leaving now!"

Gail remained seated and silent as Jack stepped outside and closed the door. Only then did she begin to weep.

* * *

Florin Geddis leaned on her kitchen sink and stared out at the row upon row of deteriorating wooden merchant ships anchored in Southampton Bay. Etched against the gray late October sky, the old ships were like gloomy ghosts silently reminding her she was now completely alone.

Three months before, Sam had moved out to share lodging with Ted Sena at the Rivers' ranch in western Calaveras County. Although Sam told his mother in January that he had accepted a job with the Forestry Service, he did not explain when that job would start. When he was away during the spring and early summer, she assumed he was working but did not know where or for whom. She had ceased to care. *C'est comme son pere!* she thought bitterly.

Now this latest blow! Two days ago, Merriweather had taken her Tee-Tee away and sent him to a private boarding school in Grass Valley, more than a hundred miles away. The foolish doctor had made some feeble excuse about Tully's needing a "good" Quaker education. "*Quelles betises!*" she declared aloud.

But there was no one to hear her—no one who felt any compassion for her lonely plight. Since Florin had been released from the sanitarium four years before, even her friend Gail had avoided her. Nor, despite all her protestations to the contrary, did that Quaker woman Natalie Brighton show any sympathy. Natalie's initial solicitousness had been purely political! *Quest-ce-que je faire?* Florin asked herself.

She knew the answer—the *only* answer. Entering her bedroom, Florin found the small bottle of laudanum she had hidden in a drawer beneath her undergarments. She brought it back into the kitchen and emptied its contents into a wine glass. Then, filling the glass with a Merlot she had recently purchased, she carried it into her living room and sat down in her favorite wingback chair.

She considered putting a record on her Victrola, but then dismissed this thought. She knew the laudanum would quickly take effect. In a matter of minutes, she would be completely free of her loneliness.

* * *

Sean regained consciousness and opened his eyes. He was sitting alone in complete darkness, his wrists and ankles bound tightly to a straight-back chair. The only sounds he heard were those of wood intermittently bumping against wood; the only sensation, that of bitter cold seeping into the very marrow of his bones.

Sean's first impulse was to call out, "Hey! Anybody here?" His instincts told him to keep silent, though. Wherever he was and whoever had put him there had done so with malice. He tried to control the terrifying thoughts that were racing around in his head.

After a few minutes, his eyes became accustomed to the dark and he was able to make out the dim outline of a large rectangular opening at one end of the building he was in. Through this opening, he could see two lights shining in the distance, several hundred yards away. Gradually, he became aware that separating him from these lights was a wide expanse of open water. The much closer sounds of wood clunking against wood told him he was in some kind of a boathouse.

His fingers were numb with cold. He thought of rocking his chair, hoping the weight of his body might cause it to break and loosen the ropes around his wrists and ankles. He quickly abandoned this idea, realizing he might be close to the edge of a dock and could tumble himself into the water. Sean closed his eyes again, the vaguely remembered words of an old Gaelic prayer drifting through his head. At length, he again slipped into unconsciousness.

"Ding-dong! Ding-dong!" mocked a reedy male voice.

Jolted into wakefulness, Sean saw a rat-like face, only inches away from his own. "Did you have a pleasant rest, Mister Hanrahan?"

Sean blinked, almost blinded by the bright light from a kerosene lantern the stranger was holding. The light revealed two other men standing on either side of his interrogator. They looked vaguely familiar to Sean, but he couldn't remember where he might have seen them before. "What's goin' on?" Sean demanded angrily. "Why you got me tied up like this?"

The rat-faced man stepped back, at the same time bringing the lighted lantern so close to Sean's left cheek that he could feel its heat. "We have a few questions to ask you, sir."

That reedy voice again—caressing but menacing! Sean stiffened with terror. "W .. what d' y' want?" he stuttered. "I d' … don't know from nothin'!"

"Aw, come on, old chum," one of the other men said with mock solicitousness. "Don't give us that line. After all what you told me and Seth the other night at the Casa de Vallejo? You know plenty!"

Desperately Sean tried to remember, but his brain was still foggy from whatever it was he had been drinking earlier. "Like what?" he asked fearfully.

"Like what routes your nigger boss uses for his deliveries," hissed the man with the reedy voice.

"Who the hell are you?" Sean demanded, trying to recover some of his own Irish bravado.

"Allow me to introduce myself. My name, sir, is Emmett Spears," the rat-faced man said, brushing the side of Sean's cheek with the white-hot globe of his lantern. When Sean yelped in pain, Spears added, "That's just a little taste of what's in store for you, muttonhead!

Terrified, Sean felt the warmth of his own urine—a response Spears was quick to detect.

"I see you're beginning to catch on."

The other men chuckled derisively.

"Come on!" Spears snarled. "We don't have all night. Spill it!"

"I only went with Tucker's boys once," Sean whimpered. "It was the night route they took from Livermore through Stockton and then straight across to Jamestown."

"What nights of the week?"

"Just Tuesdays, I think."

"Where do they keep their trucks?" Spears barked.

"Back of Schuster's Garage in Vallejo, where Tucker works."

Spears nodded to Stark. "Very good, Mister Hanrahan. But we also need to know the day route the nigger uses and which days of the week?"

Desperate, Sean tried to remember what Tucker had said months before. "Up Lincoln Highway through Sacramento and then to Placerville. From there, I think they take some road south toward Jamestown. I don' know for sure!"

"I know that road," Stark said. "It's the old Forty-Niners' route. Goes through Columbia."

"Which days?" Spears repeated, moving the hot lantern close to Sean's face again.

"Jesus!" Sean yelped in pain. "I don' know!"

"Not good enough, my friend," Spears snarled. Turning to Stark, he said, "We're done with this fool. Get him into the boat."

"What d' y' mean?" Sean cried out. "I tol' y' everythin' I know!"

"Take a look at your dogs, old buddy," Stark chuckled. "You got some new shoes."

Glancing down, Sean suddenly realized both of his feet and the legs of his chair were stuck in a box of hardened concrete. When Stark and Seth grabbed the corners of this box and lowered Sean into the stern of a run-about, Sean cried out, "What are y' gonnah do?"

"We're goin' fishin'," Stark explained, as he started the boat's engine. "And you're gonnah be the bait."

Speechless with terror, Sean began to scream. Instantly, Stark gunned the big inboard on his Chris Craft, completely drowning out Sean's screams as they sped out across the open water into San Pablo Bay.

*　　*　　*

Since it was Mischief Night, Adam was not surprised both of his tank trucks had been splattered with wet yellow paint. Parked in the open behind Schuster's Garage, they were easy targets for pranksters. "Wipe that stuff off before it dries," he told Patrick Finn and Eddie Zhau, handing them several rags he had retrieved from the back of his car. "An' hurry it up 'cause we's runnin' late."

While Billy warmed up the engine of the truck they were going to use that night, Patrick and Eddie quickly carried out Adam's orders. Ten minutes later they were on Lincoln Highway, heading south toward Livermore.

Using the southern route, it was more than a three-hour drive from Vallejo to Jamestown. Once they were past Stockton, though, the roads across the Central Valley were level and straight. At that time of night, their truck and follow car were the only vehicles in transit, so they made good time. As they entered the foothills of the Sierras, their progress was slowed by long hill climbs and sharp curves.

"What's that?" Patrick exclaimed as they came over a rise and the truck's headlights revealed an obstruction in the road ahead.

Billy shifted into low gear and the truck's engine whined in protest. "Looks like a tree fell across the road."

Seconds later, they saw figures moving behind the obstruction. Then, simultaneously, eight sets of automobile headlights flashed on— four on each side of the road.

"Jesus! It's an ambush!" Patrick shouted, quickly unholstering his pistol.

"Hang on!" Billy ordered, shifting into high gear and flooring his gas pedal. Their heavy rig quickly picked up speed on the downward slope. But as they roared through the gauntlet of bright headlights, dozens of men opened fire on them with pistols, rifles and Tommy Guns.

Without doors or windows, the truck cab gave Billy and Patrick no protection. Torn to pieces in a hailstorm of bullets, Billy lost control of the truck, which careened off the road into a ditch. The empty tank trailer rolled over on its side, toppling the cab and hurling Patrick out onto the rock-strewn embankment where he was knocked unconscious.

Following in their car more than a hundred yards behind, Adam and Eddie had not seen the roadblock until they crested the hill. The tank truck had already run off the road. Adam slammed on the brakes, stalling his engine. Eddie reached for his shotgun in the back seat. Instantly, several in the ambush party turned their fire on Adam and Eddie.

With bullets pinging off the hood and grill of his vehicle, Adam restarted his engine and backed up the car to turn it around. Eddie tried to fend off the attack by firing both barrels of his shotgun. But the rear wheels of Adam's car spun in the loose gravel at the side of the road for several seconds before he could gain traction. That's when two bullets smashed the front windshield and slammed into Eddie's right shoulder.

By now, the tank truck had caught fire. Just as two of the ambush party's vehicles began to move onto the road in pursuit of Adam, the truck's gas tank exploded. This gave Adam the time he needed to get a head start on his pursuers.

Thanks to Francis, the V8 engine of Adam's 1924 Buick sedan had been modified to provide maximum speed. Because of this and his superior knowledge of Calaveras County's back roads, Adam easily eluded and outran his pursuers. Eddie Zhao was bleeding profusely, though. Adam knew his partner would be unconscious, perhaps even dead, before they reached the Rivers' ranch.

* * *

"What the hell happened?" Todd Rivers asked as he helped Adam lift Eddie's limp body out of the car. Awakened by the sound of voices, Sam and Ted ran toward them from the bunkhouse, both shouting the same question.

"We was ambushed. Somebody leaked our route," Adam replied angrily.

Sharon held the front door open as they carried Eddie inside and gently laid him on the Rivers' living room sofa. His clothes were covered with blood and he seemed to have stopped breathing. Sharon leaned over Eddie and pressed her fingertips against his throat. "I'm afraid he's gone," she said.

Adam shook his head slowly. "They got Billy and Patrick too."

"We've got to go back and rescue them!" Sam declared. "We can take the plane."

"You'll have a tough time doing that in the dark, Sam," Sharon gently reminded her former pupil. "Biplanes don't have headlights."

Adam collapsed in a chair, his face twisted with anger and grief. "Ain't no use. The truck blew up. They's gotta be dead."

"I still say we should try!" Sam insisted.

Todd glanced at the clock on the mantle piece. "It'll be light in a couple of hours. I'll take our truck. Adam, you can come with me, and Sam and Ted will cover us from the air."

Adam closed his eyes and slumped forward.

"He's been hurt!" Sharon shouted, moving swiftly to catch Adam before he collapsed on the floor. Yanking open the front of his jacket, she exposed a bleeding gash just below his collarbone. "Looks like a glass cut. Todd, go get my kit!"

*   *   *

All Saints' was an important and solemn feast day in the Lanham household, as it was for many parishioners of Saint Dominic's Church in Benicia. Indeed, sometimes it seemed to Del that Catholics generally were obsessed with death. Despite the early hour, Saint Dominic's was filled to capacity—mostly gray-haired men and women, kneeling with their heads bowed in studied grief.

Every year since her mother's death, Del and her father had attended 6:30 Mass on All Saints Day to pray for Clarabel Lanham's immortal soul. Though she was only five years old when her mother died after a long bout with influenza, Del felt a special kinship with her now as Father Cardoni led the congregation in their recitation of the Canticle for the Dead.

"Salvation, glory, and power to our God," the priest began.

"Alleluia," all responded in unison.

"His judgments are honest and true."

"Alleluia."

"Sing praise to our God, all you his servants."

"Alleluia."

And so it went, on and on. The continuous pattern of utterance and response was supposed to ease the troubled spirit and soothe the grieving heart. But for some like Del, it was only numbing to a still sleepy brain.

Images of her dead mother came back to Del in fleeting fragments as she tried to concentrate on the meaning of the priest's incantations: "The wedding feast of the Lamb has begun … and his bride is prepared to welcome him." *What is the connection between these words and the living, breathing being that was your mother?* asked a voice somewhere deep inside of her. *Who was your mother? Why should she matter to you?*

Dell trembled in fear of these questions. Surely it was blasphemous to entertain them. How often had the nuns warned her that Satan is forever at work trying to poison our conscious thoughts, especially when we pray. "Always say the words aloud," Sister Rosemary had repeatedly urged during Catechism class. "The very act of uttering holy words will protect you from the Evil One."

But Dell's thoughts continued to meander. They were not thoughts, really, but the recalled images of women she had known: Those of her mother—pretty, slender and frail; of Ruby—most of the time jovial and always sturdy and steady; of Craig's mother Betsy—petite and perky as a Scotch Terrier; of Jack's mother—full of sorrow and stoic determination; of Sam's mother!

It was this last image that loomed large and frightening—Florin's dark and beautiful but empty eyes during the murder trial coupled with the recent newspaper report of her attempted suicide. Del shifted her gaze toward the bank of lighted candles to the left of her pew. Each burning candle represented some parishioner's prayer for a dead or a living soul. Del became aware that she was *really* praying now not for the soul of her own mother but for that of a mad woman!

"Hail Mary, full of Grace, pray for us sinners now and at the hour of our death," Del murmured. The words on her lips were not the same as those others spoke at that moment —neither the words of the priest, "Bring all who have died into the company of heaven with Mary, Joseph and all your saints" nor the response of the people, "and give us also a place in the unending fellowship of your kingdom."

Everyone stood up, Del included, and together recited the *pater noster* in Latin. Del felt a sudden flood of warmth overwhelming her—a feeling of love and forgiveness that could not be expressed in the words of any language.

CHAPTER TWENTY-FOUR

"How About Me?"

B ECAUSE SAM HAD BEEN LIVING at the Rivers' ranch, he was surprised when Patterson called him to report that his mother had tried to kill herself. "What happened?" Sam asked.

"Apparently your mother became very depressed after Tully left," Patterson explained. "So much so that she overdosed on laudanum. Luckily, her friend Gail Westlake found her unconscious and called the police."

"Where is mother now?" Sam asked.

"She's back in the sanitarium, under Dr. Merriweather's care. I'm afraid she'll have to remain there for quite some time. Needless to say, Tully is very upset, Sam, and he needs to come home."

"But how can he? There's nobody there to take care of him."

"I'm afraid that's going to be your responsibility," Patterson said.

"How am I supposed to do that?" Sam protested. "I have two jobs. I can't just up and quit both of them!"

"I'm sorry, Sam, but you may have to take some time off. Tully's very upset right now. He needs the support of a close family member."

"What about Aunt Sarah and Uncle Henry? They took care of both of us before. Why can't they take care of Tully now?"

"I'm sure the Nielsens would be willing enough, but the situation is quite different now that your mother is back at the sanitarium. According to your father's trust, you're the back-up trustee and your brother's sole surviving guardian, so you'll have to stay with him at your

339

mother's house in Benicia—at least until he's ready to board again at Stonehaven."

"How can I do that? I work way out on the other side of Galt! That's hours away from Benicia!"

"As I said, Sam, you'll have to take some time off."

Sam was silent. He wanted to tell Patterson that the lives of other men depended on him. His quitting now would put Adam's entire enterprise at risk because only Sam could fly reconnaissance over the daytime route.

The importance of this had been proven a month earlier when Soames had once more tried to ambush Jack, Francis and Larry as they drove their truck north on the return trip from Jamestown. Sam and Ted had attacked the ambushers from the air, strafing them with machine gun fire, killing several members of Soames' gang and driving the others off. No other ambush attempts had been made since.

It was Patterson who broke the silence. "Look, son, you don't *have* to work. There's plenty of money in the trust for you and your brother, as well as to pay for your mother's care. You can hire a live-in house keeper, even take some college courses, if you want."

"I'll have to think about it," Sam said. "I need to talk to my bosses first."

"Whatever you tell your bosses, Sam, you have to bring your brother home." When Sam did not respond, Paterson said, "Trust me, son. It'll be alright."

"That's easy for you to say!" Sam snarled and hung up the phone.

Almost immediately, Patterson called again. "I have some good news for you, Sam. Bert McCutcheon has just offered to buy your mother's property for $20,000!"

Although it encompassed fifty acres of prime real estate in the hills north of Benicia, the Geddis property had been abandoned ever since the fire in 1920. Despite Patterson's repeated urgings that Florin sell her property, she had ignored his advice.

Now that Sam was able to act in her behalf, Patterson encouraged him to accept McCutcheon's offer. "You can reinvest that money in stocks like Radio Corporation of America and Standard Oil. They pay excellent dividends, Sam."

Sam knew nothing about the stock market and had never taken

much interest in his father's estate. "How do I buy that stock?" he asked.

"I have a good friend who's a very reputable broker," Patterson assured him. "He'll be glad to help you. As soon as I set a closing date with McCutcheon, you'll need to come to my office to sign the papers. Would next Tuesday morning at 9:00 be a good time for you?"

"I suppose," Sam said reluctantly.

"I'll have to check with McCutcheon, but that should be alright. Oh, and there's one other thing," Patterson said. "I've made arrangements for us to meet with the headmaster at Stonehaven in the afternoon on the same day. Hope that's agreeable, Sam. I'll drive you up there in my car if you like," Patterson suggested, doing his best to sound off-handed.

Sam was immediately suspicious. "Why do *you* need to come?"

Patterson hesitated. "Let's just say it's part of my fiduciary responsibility, Sam. I am a back-up trustee for your father's estate, after all."

"Whatever you say," Sam allowed, feeling hopelessly trapped.

As soon as he hung up, Sam telephoned Adam Tucker and asked him to meet him on Diamond Beach at 6:00 the next morning. He wanted to be sure their meeting was secret. At that early hour, Sam knew Diamond Beach would be deserted, especially since the Strait would still be cloaked in heavy fog.

*   *   *

Jack and Adam were already waiting for him when Sam arrived at Diamond Beach. Jack had parked his black 1924 Ford sedan along the bluff above the beach. Climbing into the back seat of the car, Sam got right to the point. "I have some bad news," he announced. Adam and Jack listened patiently while Sam explained his predicament. When he was finished, neither of them said anything for several seconds.

"Don't you be worryin', boy," Adam said at last. "We work it out."

"Maybe Sharon could teach *me* to fly," Jack offered.

"Sorry, Jack," Sam warned. "Even if she did, it would take months. The De Havilland is a hard plane to maneuver."

"F'rget it. We don't need no plane," Adam said.

Jack and Sam both looked at Adam in astonishment. "What do you mean?" Sam asked. "Without air cover, you have no protection."

"We dump the moonshine an' sell somethin' else."

"Something else? What else? Peanut butter?" Jack retorted sarcastically.

"Hash," Adam replied. His face was expressionless as he stared through the car windshield across the Strait at the distant hills slowly becoming visible through the morning fog.

"Hash!" Jack was angry now. "What the hell is that?"

"I know what he's talking about," Sam put in. "He means hashish. It's a plant. The Chinese grow it and use it as a pain killer."

"Smart boy!" Adam smiled at Sam. "Ain't only Chinese uses it, an' it ain't jus' a pain killer. Niggers, spics, an' white folk uses it too—t' get high on. An' they pays good jack. Much as ten dollar a pound."

"Never heard of it," Jack confessed, feeling embarrassed at his own ignorance. "How do you know about it, Sam?"

Sam laughed and winked at Adam. "I read about it in London's *John Barleycorn*. They say London used it himself."

"So where do people get this stuff?" Jack asked.

"It grow in the ground—jus' like a weed," Adam explained patiently. "Fac', tha's what some folk calls it—*weed*."

"It's illegal," Sam pointed out, "in California, anyway."

"An' tha's why folks is willin' t' pay good scratch fo' it," Adam pointed out. "They don' wanna get caught growin' it theyselves, so they pays other folks t' grow it."

"Let's see if I have this right, Adam," Jack said. "You're going to grow this weed someplace yourself and try to sell it. Is that it?"

"No. I ain't growin' it, but I knows plenty o' folks that does an' I can get it from 'em cheap."

"And then sell it at a much higher price," Sam added to complete Adam's thought.

Adam nodded. "Like I say, you a smart boy. Bes' part is, hash is a lot easier t' move than booze. You don't need no big trucks 'cause you jus' packs it in one-pound sacks an' sells it by the ounce." Adam smiled at Jack. "You can get a whole lot o' them sacks in the back o' this here car, boy." Then, turning in his seat to face Sam, he said, "See? We don't need you an' your plane no mo'. So you jus' go on home an' take care o' that baby brother o' yours."

"Wait a minute!" Jack declared, perplexed. "What about all your other customers—the ones who buy your hooch? They're not going to like this. You already lost a lot of customers when you switched from using the tankers to using flatbeds and milk cans. Now, you'll lose *all* of them!"

Adam shook his head. "Not all, boy. Jus' them we don' need. We keep supplyin' our bes' cus'mers 'til we switch 'em to hash—real slow an' easy like. That'll make Soames' an' his boys think we's gettin' out o' the bus'ness." He chuckled softly. "You got to keep makin' changes in this line o' work, boy. What work one day don't always work the next. Now, s'pose we go get us somethin' t' eat!

"Not me," Sam said as he stepped out of the car. "I have to meet with Gallagher up in Davis." Sam stood with the car door open, gazing at Adam for several seconds. He wanted to tell this man how grateful he was and how much he admired him. But he knew Adam considered all such expressions of gratitude redundant, so he simply closed the car door and headed back along West K Street toward his mother's house.

Jack and Adam waved to him as they passed him on their way to Vallejo.

*   *   *

The meeting with McCutcheon had gone smoothly. By 10:30 Wednesday morning, all the necessary property transfer papers had been signed and McCutcheon's certified check for $20,000 deposited in the Geddis account at the Bank of Italy. As they left the bank, Patterson suggested he and Sam immediately head north in Patterson's car.

It was a three and a half hour drive from Benicia to Grass Valley, the small town in the Sierra foothills where Stonehaven School was located. *En route*, Patterson disclosed more details about Tully's situation. "I'm afraid your brother has developed a rather unhealthy relationship with one of the teachers at Stonehaven," he began. "Apparently it's affecting his studies and causing a great deal of gossip at the school."

Sam felt a sudden tightening in his abdomen. "What do you mean by an unhealthy relationship?"

"Well ... " Patterson paused, racking his brain for the right words. "Doctor Reuger calls it ... er ... an obsession. Sort of hero worship, I suppose," Patterson suggested, adding his own more palatable interpolation. "He told me he has not yet discussed the matter with either Tully or the teacher, but he believes he must do so sooner than later. He says it may be necessary for Tully to withdraw from school."

Sam exploded in frustration. "Dammit! I knew something like this would happen!"

Patterson was astonished. "How could you possibly know?"

Sam shook his head slowly. "It's just the way Tully's been for a long time now. I don't know. It's like he thinks he's a girl instead of a boy. Sometimes when I used to come home after school, I'd find him in mother's bedroom wearing her dresses and stuff."

"Did you tell Doctor Merriweather about this?"

"Sure—plenty of times. But Merriweather told me to ignore it. He said it was just a phase Tully was going through."

"Doctor Merriweather was probably right," Patterson said, trying to put the best face he could on what he himself considered bizarre behavior.

"No," Sam corrected. "Mother made him that way!"

"Your mother was not well, Sam."

Sam grimaced at Patterson's euphemism, but he remained silent until they turned in at the gated entrance to the school.

Stonehaven was situated in a wooded glen several miles east of Grass Valley. A cluster of mostly one-story wood-frame buildings erected in a helter-skelter pattern that made the place look more like a trailer camp than a school campus. Patterson parked his car in the gravel driveway behind an old school bus. Apart from this empty vehicle, the place seemed deserted. As Sam stepped out of Patterson's car, the only sounds he heard were the harsh cries of ravens and jaybirds in the redwoods that towered overhead like giant sentinels.

Patterson led the way along a footpath that wound between the buildings until they came to one fronted by a covered porch. "This is the administration building," Patterson said. "Anyway, that's what Reuger told me on the telephone."

Climbing the steps onto the porch, Patterson knocked on the entrance door and Sam peered through one of the windows. "Doesn't look like there's anybody here," Sam said.

"Perhaps we should check around the back," Patterson suggested.

"Let's try the door first. Maybe it's not locked." Sam turned the knob and the door opened, admitting them into a dark, narrow hallway leading to the back of the building. Although there were several interior doors on both sides of this corridor, none of them was open. "Hello," Patterson called out. "Anybody here?" When there was no immediate response, Patterson turned to Sam and shrugged.

Suddenly one of the interior doors opened, admitting light into the hallway. Framed in the open doorway was the silhouette of a short, plump woman. "Mister Patterson, is that you?" she called out.

"Yes, ma'm," Patterson answered diffidently.

"Please wait in my office. Doctor Reuger will see you presently." The woman promptly turned and went back inside, leaving the door open for them to follow. She was seated at her desk typing when they entered the small room she referred to as her office. Not much larger than a broom closet, it had only one narrow window. Apart from her desk and chair, the only other pieces of furniture in the room were two rickety ladder-backs lined up against the wall facing her desk.

"Good afternoon," Patterson said with an affable smile. "You must be Louise Kapowsky. I'm delighted to meet you. This is Samuel Geddis, Tully's older brother."

The woman did not look up from her typing. "Sit down, please," she answered with a brusque nod. Louise, it seemed, had no interest in small talk. Though diminutive in size and bland in appearance, she was obviously determined to focus on the more important task of typing a letter for her employer.

Accordingly, Patterson and Sam sat down and waited in silence. Through a closed door connecting Louise's office with her boss's, they could hear the sound of two male voices.

Several minutes passed, during which Sam became increasingly restless and impatient. "Maybe you should tell Doctor Reuger we're here," he said to the woman.

Still not looking up, Louise snapped, "He already knows. You'll have to wait. He's in a very important conference right now."

"We had a 3:30 appointment," Sam rejoined. "It's already 3:45."

Louise did not respond but continued typing.

At last, the inner office door opened and a very athletic looking man with shoulder-length blonde hair emerged. His pale blue eyes immediately focused on Sam, his small but sensuous mouth curling in a sly smile of recognition. He said nothing, however, and exited quickly through the door into the hallway.

"You may go in now," Louise said, still without looking up from her clacking typewriter.

Reuger's office was not much larger than Louise's and furnished almost as sparsely. Sitting at a roll-top desk against one windowless wall was an emaciated man in his sixties, attired in a dark-blue suit that looked as if it had not been pressed or cleaned in months. With his back to them, Reuger was leaning over his desk making notes in a cloth-bound ledger. When at last he turned to face them, his face was expressionless. "You're Patterson?" he inquired in a hollow voice and without so much as a glance at Sam.

"Yes, sir," Patterson replied with the icy caution he usually reserved for a hostile courtroom witness.

"Have a seat," Reuger said. Then, crossing one long, thin leg over the other and leaning back in his swivel chair, he got directly down to business. "That fellow I was just talking to is the teacher I told you about. His name's Ralph Pyncheon. He teaches history and coaches our cross-country and Lacrosse teams."

"You mean he's the man who has this … er … irregular relationship with Tully?" Patterson asked.

Reuger nodded. "Things have gotten more complicated since we spoke on the phone last week, Mister Patterson," he reported without the slightest sign of emotion. Suddenly shifting his attention to Sam, Reuger said, "You'll have to take your brother home with you today, young man."

Visibly shaken by this blunt announcement, Patterson said, "I think you should explain to Sam what has happened, Doctor Reuger."

"I assume you already did that," Reuger answered.

"I only told him what you told me," Patterson prevaricated. "This is a serious matter and very upsetting for Sam and his family."

Reuger's face remained expressionless, his voice flat and hollow. Addressing Sam directly, he said, "Pyncheon and your brother have become the object of some very ugly gossip. The other students are scandalized, and already we've received letters from several parents threatening to withdraw their children."

346

"So why don't you get rid of Pyncheon?" Sam demanded. "Why should Tully have to leave?"

"I agree, Doctor Reuger," Patterson said. "Tully is only fourteen years old. Surely he can't be blamed for this situation."

"This is a progressive school, Mister Patterson," Reuger said dismissively, "not a court of law. We do not seek to blame anyone but only to create a controlled environment in which children may learn to be content and cooperative members of adult society."

"But, in forcing Tully to leave, you are *ipso facto* blaming him, are you not?" Patterson asked.

Reuger blinked slowly, his lids more like those of a sleepy reptile than of a man. "Apparently you are not familiar with the terms *progressive school* and *controlled environment*, Mister Patterson. Allow me to explain. Our mission here at Stonehaven is to ensure that all of our students are comfortable with each other. We do so by establishing certain norms of behavior for the community at large and by shaping each student's behavior to conform with those norms through positive reinforcement."

"What do you mean by *positive reinforcement*?" Patterson asked, visibly annoyed by Reuger's pedagogical jargon.

"To the degree that each student adheres to our community norms, he is rewarded and progresses. To the degree that any student deviates, he is discouraged through negative peer pressure that impedes his progress. In severe cases, the individual's failure to conform may result in expulsion."

"So you're saying Tully is a threat to Stonehaven's controlled environment?" Patterson asked.

"Precisely," Reuger said, raising one eyebrow slightly as if he were surprised by Patterson's quick apprehension. "That is why it is necessary for Tully to withdraw from Stonehaven at once."

"But what if your community norms are unrealistic and unfair?" Patterson asked, again trying to set a logical trap for his adversary.

Reuger smiled for the first time. "In our experimental model, Mister Patterson, such terms are value laden and therefore meaningless. Where community norms prevail—as is the case here at Stonehaven— perception is 100 per cent of reality. In that context, what is ethical depends solely on each specific situation. There are no absolutes."

By now, Sam was completely flummoxed. Turning to Patterson, he asked, "What the hell is he talking about?"

Patterson did not answer Sam's question, though he shared his exasperation. Rising slowly to his feet, he addressed Reuger with the grim solemnity of a hanging judge. "There may be no absolutes in your controlled *school* environment, Doctor Reuger, but I assure you there are in the realm of jurisprudence. Your decision to expel Tully is completely arbitrary! If you persist in it, I will have no choice but to petition the court in Tully and Sam's behalf."

Reuger remained seated, his entire body as still as stone. Staring at Patterson out of dead eyes, he said, "You may do whatever you wish, sir, but you will have to remove Tully from the school premises today. I have arranged for his luggage to be packed. You will find it in the gymnasium where Tully is waiting for you." Turning his back to them again, Reuger called out to his assistant. "Louise, take Mister Patterson and Tully's brother over to the gymnasium."

Louise immediately appeared in the open door to her office. "Yes, Doctor Reuger. Follow me, please," she commanded without making eye contact with either Patterson or Sam.

"Come on, Sam," Patterson said softly. "Let's go and get Tully. There's obviously nothing we can do about this right now."

"I don't believe this!" Sam declared, still standing his ground. "You son-of-a-bitch!" he shouted at Reuger. "What about the tuition we paid? Aren't you even going to refund our money?"

Without turning around, Reuger observed matter-of-factly, "That's forfeit. You and your lawyer need to review the terms and conditions of our contract."

With his fists clenched, Sam moved toward Reuger. But Patterson grabbed his arm. "Come on, Sam. We have to go."

Still fuming, Sam turned and followed Patterson out of Reuger's office. Louise stood waiting for them in the hallway. "This way," she ordered and marched briskly toward the rear entrance of the building.

Outside, Louise led them along another path that wound between several single-story classroom buildings. Peering through the windows of these buildings, Sam noted that there were still no signs of students or faculty. Just beyond the class buildings, the path sloped up to a large red barn on the crest of a ridge. As they approached the entrance to this structure, they heard the sounds of children shouting as if they were engaged in some kind of game activity. The voices came not from inside the barn but from an open field behind it.

Sam remembered now the first time Merriweather, Tully and he had visited Stonehaven's campus two years before. Pyncheon had led them on an introductory tour, exuberantly pointing out the amenities and facilities of the school in his crisp Australian dialect. Sam had been suspicious of this man even then. His garrulous amicability seemed much too intense to be sincere. What troubled Sam most then was the way Pyncheon had continuously kept his arm draped around Tully's shoulders as they moved from one part of the campus to another.

Louise opened the entrance door to the barn. Following her inside, they saw Tully sitting beside a woman on one of the tiered wooden benches that had been set up on all four sides of this gymnasium. The woman was holding Tully in her arms, rocking him gently as he wept, his forehead pressed against her temple. Sam immediately recognized Natalie Brighton.

"Hello, Sam," Natalie said as they walked toward her across the open quadrangle of space between the benches—an area large enough for a basketball court.

Startled, Sam asked, "Miss Brighton! What are you doing here?"

"I teach here. Ever since I married two years ago. My last name's Pyncheon now," she explained with a forlorn smile.

"You're *married* to that Ethel?" Sam exclaimed.

Tully looked up quickly. "He's a nice man and he's my best friend!"

"Your best friend!"

"Take it easy, Sam!" Patterson cautioned.

At the same time, Natalie reached out toward him with a pleading gesture. "I know it's hard for you to understand, Sam," she said softly. "But you really must try. Tully's in a lot of pain right now."

"I don't understand *any* of this!" Sam declared angrily. "You people are just plain nuts! Come on, Tully! Where's your stuff? We're getting you out of here!"

"I don't want to go!" Tully cried, throwing his arms around Natalie's neck and sobbing.

Natalie kissed Tully's tear-streaked cheeks. "I'm sorry, dear," she warbled as she gently disentangled herself and stood up. "You really do have to go now."

Suddenly, Sam threw himself on the hardwood gymnasium floor, kicking his feet and flailing his arms. "No! No! I don't want to go!" he screamed, his newly baritone voice cracking into shrill soprano.

Sam was appalled. Tully had thrown temper tantrums when he was much younger and had no other way to retaliate against Sam's bullying, but seeing his brother—now nearly six feet tall—kicking and screaming on the floor like an infant was too much.

When Natalie bent over Tully and tried to calm him, he jumped to his feet. "No! No! I won't go! You can't make me!" he bellowed. Then, whirling around, he ran out of the gymnasium.

"Oh dear!" Natalie exclaimed

"What do we do now?" Sam asked Patterson.

Baffled, Patterson turned to Louise who was already moving toward the gymnasium exit. "I'll get Doctor Reuger," she said.

* * *

Reuger had responded quickly. With help from a burly Mexican groundskeeper, he used a syringe to sedate Tully. He then ordered the Mexican to carry Tully's unconscious body across campus to Patterson's car. Fifteen minutes later, Patterson and Sam were on the road back to Benicia with Tully stretched unconscious in the back seat.

For a long time, Sam stared out of the passenger-side window in silence as they drove through the rolling hills toward Sacramento. When he finally spoke, it was almost in a whisper. "Tully can't live with me. I can't take care of him."

"You don't really have a choice, Sam" Patterson grimly replied. "You're Tully's brother—his closest living relative. In two more years when you're twenty-one, you'll have full fiduciary responsibility. So right now you need to concentrate on what you're going to do with the money from the sale of your mother's property. Whatever happens where Tully's concerned, you'll both need a steady income."

The muscles in Sam's jaw hardened. "Damn it! When do I get a chance to live *my* life?"

"I think you already are," Patterson observed.

CHAPTER TWENTY-FIVE

"How Long Blues"

FOUNDED IN APRIL OF 1900, the Vallejo Yacht Club was one of the oldest organizations of its kind on the West Coast. During the 1920s, it was the only yacht club in the North Bay. Located on the Napa River where it flows into San Pablo Bay, the Vallejo Yacht Club is directly opposite the Mare Island Naval Shipyard. Not surprisingly, therefore, many of its officers and members were affiliated with that federal government facility. The club's first commodore, in fact, was William J. Wood, a master sail maker at Mare Island Shipyard. One of the club's most celebrated members was the American novelist Jack London, who berthed his ocean-going ketch *The Snark* there from 1910 until his death in 1916.

By 1928, the Vallejo Yacht Club had become the final destination for many of the major regattas in the Bay Area. As soon as they crossed the finish line that ran from the Carquinez Bridge to the mouth of the Napa River, boats from such other long-established clubs as the San Francisco Yacht Club in Belvedere Cove (1869), the Corinthian in Tiburon (1886), and the Encinal in Alameda (1890) tacked up-river to the Vallejo Yacht Club. There, skippers either commandeered empty slips or simply dropped anchor in the river and used their dinghies to get to the clubhouse dock.

Del's father had been a member of the Board of Directors at the Vallejo Yacht Club since 1914. Although he was not a sailor, his reputation as a jurist had earned him an honorary membership. The Judge rarely participated in any of the club's social activities, and he had agreed to serve on the Board only because he felt obligated to provide some form of service in exchange for his membership.

Ever since she first began competitive sailing in 1921, however, Del had been very much a part of the club's activities. In 1923, she was elected captain of its single-class boat racing team and, by her sixteenth birthday, had a shelf full of trophies hanging on the wall in the club's front vestibule as proof of her significant sailing skills. At eighteen, she was appointed Assistant Editor of the club's monthly newsletter as well as a member of the club's Activities Planning Committee. Everyone— young and old—at the Vallejo Yacht Club knew Adelaide Lanham.

But it would not be accurate to say everyone liked her. Many of the younger male members resented her, if for no better reason than simply because she was both a woman and an excellent sailor. Like most competitive sports in the early decades of the 20th Century, yacht racing was male dominated. Many of the adult members' wives and daughters also regarded Del's accomplishments with suspicion. Though Del strove to be gracious and congenial to everyone, her achievements were regarded, especially by the club's oldest generation of members, as unladylike.

Of this contingent, Florence Henshak was Del's severest critic. "I simply cannot understand why Commodore Spinks nominated Adelaide for the Planning Committee," Florence complained to Vice Commodore Reggie Hoyt as they stood together on the second floor veranda overlooking the Yacht Club marina. "The girl is a terrible Tomboy and has absolutely *no* social graces. She has been spoiled rotten by her father."

"Now-now, Florence," Reggie placated. "You shouldn't be so harsh. I'll have to agree, Adelaide does occasionally seem a bit pushy for someone so young. But that's the point, isn't it? She's young."

At seventy-three, Reggie was one of the oldest and most venerated members of the Vallejo Yacht Club. He had earned his reputation as a peacemaker many years before while he represented Solano County in the State Assembly—an elected office he held for nearly twenty years. He was also one of the founding members of the Vallejo Yacht Club. It was Reggie, in fact, who had intervened on behalf of Jack London when the Board had threatened to suspend the famous author for drunkenly disorder on the club's premises.

Florence glared at Reggie, his full head of white hair and matching white handlebar mustache reminding her that this ancient was a throwback to a much earlier age and that his gentle nature was probably more a sign of senility than of wisdom. "That's no excuse!" Florence declared. "Adelaide is the daughter of one our most distinguished members and should know her proper place in society!"

"Perhaps that is part of the problem," the gentle sage offered. "Having lost her mother at a tender age, the poor child has had no model of feminine modesty. Clyde, as you know, is very … ah … resolute. As they say, the apple does not fall far from the tree."

"Ach!" Florence expostulated. "You men are all alike! No wonder the suffragettes are taking over! Only last week I read in the papers that now even the British Parliament has succumbed to these brazen hussies!"

"Oh dear!" Reggie replied in feigned distress.

"Just look at what this has done to our young women today with their scandalous short skirts, their drinking and smoking! The Lord only knows what dreadful things they do in the back seats of automobiles! They call it *spooning*, but I call it something else!" Florence was in high dudgeon now.

"I share your concern, Florence my dear," Reggie offered soothingly. The old fellow was not without subtlety. He deftly parried Florence's aggressive thrusts by changing the subject. "Oscar tells me Adelaide is going to skipper the *Carte Blanche* in this year's Gate-to-Strait regatta. I must say that shows remarkable confidence in the young lady's yachting skills." The *Carte Blanche* was the Henshaks' 33-foot ketch and the Gate-to-Strait regatta was the most challenging and competitive event of the Bay Area's annual racing season—a thirty-seven mile run from the Golden Gate to the mouth of Carquinez Strait.

Florence stiffened. "Oscar is a fool! With all due respect, Reggie, I must remind you that Adelaide Lanham is most definitely *not* a lady!"

Reggie simply smiled and sipped at his mug of hot coffee.

* * *

Del had been preparing for the big race months in advance. As early as March 7th, while she was visiting with her friend Craig McCutcheon at his parents' home in Tiburon, she had asked him if she could do a trial run of the Gate-to-Strait course as skipper of his father's six-meter ketch, *Sassy Lass*.

"Of course!" Craig had immediately replied. "Fact, I've got just the lad for your first mate. He's a Brit—a really charming fellow named Colin Clarke. He's out here at Berkeley as an exchange student from Oxford. He also happens to be a crackerjack sailor. To be expected, I suppose, since his father's an Admiral in the British Navy."

Del bit her lip. "Sounds pretty intimidating."

"Not at all. Colin's one of the nicest guys I've ever met. I know you'll like him. Why don't I give him a call? We can meet him for lunch down at the club."

"Better call Greg too since it's his father's boat I'll be racing and Greg will be part of my crew," Del said.

Half an hour later, Del, Greg and Craig followed a tuxedo clad *maitre di* into the Corinthian Club's luxurious dining room. They were seated at a window table affording a view of the Tiburon marina, which was almost completely filled to capacity now with graceful sailing vessels and sleek wooden powerboats. The sky was overcast, and a brisk wind off the Bay was churning the water in Tiburon Cove. Watching the frantic back-and-forth motion of the scores of tall masts in Corinthian's marina, Del observed, "Not very good weather for your fellow members, I guess."

"Right," Craig replied. "Most of them are bankers and lawyers. Like me, strictly sunshine sailors."

"Mmm! Crab Bisque!" Del exclaimed as she perused the folio-sized Corinthian Club menu. "Perfect for a day like this!"

"Absolutely!" Greg agreed.

"Along with a bottle of sparkly, of course," Craig added as he signaled for the wine steward. Suddenly standing up, Craig declared, "Aha, here he comes!"

Del turned around and noticed that, walking toward them directly behind the approaching sommelier was a tall young man dressed in brown plus fours with matching socks and shoes, plaid crewneck sweater, and tweed jacket complete with leather collar, cuffs and elbow patches. His pale bespectacled face and head of thick unruly black hair, she thought, gave him the look of someone who had just emerged from a long night of scholarly endeavors.

"Craig, my good fellow!" the young man chirped as he stepped quickly around the steward and vigorously pumped Craig's outstretched hand.

"Colin Clark, these are my friends Adelaide Lanham and Greg Henshak."

Greg and Del promptly stood up to greet the newcomer. Smiling broadly at both of them, Clark eagerly shook hands with Greg and bowed to Del. "Delighted to meet you, Miss Lanham.

Disregarding Colin's Old World gallantry, Del reached out to shake his hand. "Please, Colin. Call me Del."

Unaccustomed to such an assertive greeting in women, Colin raised his eyebrows but quickly adjusted by gently taking her extended hand into his own as if he would kiss it. "Del it is then," he conceded. Promptly seizing the back of the chair in which she had been sitting, however, Colin affirmed his own indigenous protocol. "Please, Del, do make yourself comfortable."

"Your order, sir?" asked the steward, who had stood waiting patiently beside Craig during these introductions.

"A bottle of Dom Perignon, Roger, please," Craig said over his shoulder.

"Oh I say! Champagne!" Colin declared. "Jolly good idea! Nothing like hair from the dog, as you Yanks say!"

Del giggled. She liked this Brit immediately.

"Out celebrating again last night?" Craig asked as all four of them sat down.

"*Mais sure*! Big fund-raiser at the Top of the Mark for Mister Hoover. 'Chicken in every pot' and all that, you know. Met some smashing people! Clara Bow was there!"

"Oh come off it!" Craig reprimanded. Making a face at Del, he added, "Colin's a master of the hyperbole."

"Not in the least! She really *was* there, though I fear I couldn't get anywhere near her to introduce myself. She was completely surrounded by salacious railroad executives!"

Everyone laughed, though Craig shook his head disapprovingly. "I didn't invite you here to tell us about your exploits with the *It* girl, Colin," he scolded. "Del needs a good first mate for a sail in the Bay. Are you up for that?"

"Not too early in the morning, I hope," Colin shot back. "I rarely get my sea-legs much before high noon, I fear."

"An afternoon sail would be fine," Del assured him. "How does 2:00 o'clock suit you?"

Colin reached across the table toward her. "Let's shake on it then, shall we?" he asked with a taunting smirk.

*   *   *

Although the members of its Board of Directors did not know it, The Vallejo Yacht Club was one of Adam Tucker's regular customers. The club's steward, Fred Housel, had made a cash-only gentlemen's agreement with Adam to purchase his product on an as needed basis. Fred trusted Adam because they had worked together at the Benicia Arsenal years before.

Every week during the racing season, Jack and Francis would deliver six five-gallon milk cans full of wood alcohol to the service entrance at the club. On special occasions like the upcoming Gate-to-Strait regatta, they would deliver a dozen or more of these cans to accommodate the anticipated increased demand for mixed drinks.

"Hope this is enough," Housel said to Jack as the three men stored the cans in the icehouse behind the kitchen. "We got a lot o' people comin' here this weekend. Could be several hundred!"

"You run low, you give us a call. We can be down here with more in no time," Francis assured him. "How you fixed for hash?"

Housel looked surprised. "You guys sell that too?"

"It's one of our newest products," Jack replied. "You interested?"

"You better let me talk to Adam about that." Housel was suspicious. Perhaps these two young men were trying to do business on their own and cutting Adam out. *Typical of young saps!* he thought contemptuously.

"Suit yourself," Jack said. "Just give us a couple of days notice."

Housel decided he might be over-reacting. "I could use some extra help hookin' these cans up and tendin' bar next Saturday. Either o' you fellas int'rested?"

Housel was referring to the technique he used to connect the contents of each milk can with the mixing tanks he had set up under the bar. Fitted to the top of each can was a small hand-pump. This, in turn, was attached to a rubber hose that fed into a mixing tank behind the bar. It was an elaborate system and became very cumbersome to operate when the bar was busy.

"We'll do it for a dollar an hour each," Francis said, fully aware that his wage demand was unreasonably high.

"Son-of-bitch!" Housel barked. "You drive a hard bargain! But I guess I got no choice. Be here at seven o'clock sharp Saturday morning, and don't plan on leavin' before midnight!"

"We'll be here," Francis said.

Francis shook his head in amazement as he walked out to the truck with Jack. "Jesus! Poor goof must be really desperate. Never thought he'd settle for that one!"

* * *

On the morning of Saturday June 10, the sky over San Francisco Bay was almost cloudless and the water's surface as smooth as glass. These were not ideal conditions for any sailor. For regatta skippers, they were disastrous because it meant slow going for everyone throughout the entire thirty-seven mile run from the Golden Gate to the Carquinez Strait. With a fair wind of fifteen knots or more, the distance could be covered in two hours. But in quasi-still air, it could take twice that time—especially for the yawls and ketches whose larger hulls and deeper keels slowed their progress no matter how much sail they deployed.

Nevertheless, there was plenty of excitement at the starting line located just a few yards due East of the narrows where San Francisco Bay meets the Pacific. No matter what the weather conditions, the clash of currents at this point is always a challenge and the crews aboard every boat were constantly scurrying fore and aft adjusting sails and rushing from port to starboard to hike out and keep their boats from heeling over.

The larger boats, like the Henshaks' twelve-meter ketch *Carte Blanche*, were forced to hang back for almost half an hour after the warning gun sounded for the sloop class. Since there were twenty-three vessels in the combined ketch and yawl classes, these boats often came so close to each other in maneuvering for position that there were only inches between them and skippers and crewmembers exchanged a continuous barrage of epithets and threats.

During the past five years, Del had participated in scores of single-class races sponsored by the Vallejo Yacht Club. In many of these, tough U. S. Navy officers from the Mare Island Shipyard had made it clear to her that women skippers were a particular nuisance.

Del was frightened, though, when a deep male voice suddenly bellowed as she made her final tack toward the starting line, "Fall off, bitch, or we'll ram this boat up your ass!" Jerking her head to the left, she saw the bow of a fire-engine red yawl moving on a collision path toward the port side of her own boat. Stitched in ragged red letters on its white mainsail was the yawl's name, *The Red Baroness*, and crouching on its foredeck was an enormous ape of a man in white yachting shorts and a red-and-white striped shirt, his simian face twisted in murderous rage.

As the starboard boat, *Carte Blanche* had the right of way. Still, Del's instinct for safety prompted her to respond by adjusting her tiller. Just then, Colin roared back at the aggressor, "Starboard to you, mate! Touch us, and you're out of the race!"

The bully shook his fist at Colin, but *The Red Baroness*' skipper must have realized his bullying strategy wouldn't, for he turned his own boat away and, in doing so, trapped himself in irons.

Still trembling with fear and anger, Del waived to her first mate. "Thanks, Colin. You're a gem! Hope you brought your brass knuckles, though. That goon's sure to come after you!"

Colin flashed her a confident smile. "Rule Brittania!" he shouted.

The Committee boat fired its second gun, signaling the beginning of the yawl and ketch class race. Del eased up on her main sheet to catch as much of the light air as she could. *Carte Blanche* was in fourth place as Del guided her across the starting line. Still, the going was slow. None of the boats under way was making more than five knots as they moved eastward toward Alcatraz Island.

Del could only hope that, once they rounded the far end of this first natural course marker, a shifting current might work in her favor. She was only one boat length behind the third-place starter, a wide-beamed yawl named *Lucy Goose*. Del felt confident she could overtake this boat easily because *Carte Blanche* was much narrower abeam.

They were on a broad reach now, which meant that turning northward would force them to tack most of the way up San Francisco Bay toward San Rafael. Del checked her pocket watch. It was 8:45, and the sun was already beating down on them relentlessly, promising temperatures in the high 90s for the rest of the day. This could be a long and tedious run. At least, Del thought, she would not have to contend with *The Red Baroness*. That boat, she felt sure, was far behind them.

As the *Carte Blanche* approached the turning point at the north end of Alcatraz Island, Del tapped the tiller to steer her boat closer to shore. "What are you doing?" Greg shouted angrily. "Keep her to starboard! There are rocks over there! You'll run us aground!"

Suddenly Del remembered that the tide was going out. They would have to go above the *Lucy Goose*—something Del was very reluctant to do because she knew she would lose air. Nevertheless, she took Greg's advice. She smiled, remembering that she had been in almost the same predicament during her first regatta seven years before!

"Keep her on a close reach," Colin advised. "The current should be stronger farther out."

He was right. When they had sailed—or, more accurately, drifted—about twenty yards to starboard of the *Lucy Goose*, Del felt a sudden surge of movement.

Colin had been holding up his right arm with his palm open. He dropped it now. "Tack to port!" he barked.

As she yanked at her tiller and shouted "Coming about!" Del noticed that the *Lucy Goose* was reaching on a path parallel to the one she had followed earlier. Though the other boat was slightly ahead of her, it was moving slower than the *Carte Blanche*. Del was gaining momentum and would soon be able to force *Lucy Goose* to tack to port. Another competitor would be in irons!

So it went for almost a full hour—a fleet of sixty-eight boats constantly tacking and maneuvering as it made its ponderous way up to the point where San Francisco Bay narrows and then opens into San Pablo Bay. As they tacked toward China Camp, though, Del noticed that a bank of storm clouds had formed over the peak of Mount Tamapias to the West and she felt a light gust of cool air. She didn't need directions from Colin. "Coming about! Greg, release the jib!" she commanded.

Colin ducked down as the two booms swept across the deck. Instantly, *Carte Blanch* began moving swiftly. Within a few minutes they were almost abreast of the lead boat—a sleek-hulled yawl named

Bungy Buster. Colin gave her the thumbs up sign. "Atta-girl, Del!" he jubilantly declared.

* * *

Two hours later hundreds of spectators lined both banks of the Napa River, and cheers went up as the first boats approached the finish line. A sloop named *Gusty Girl* was in the lead, followed closely by two others of the same class named *Cormorant* and *Vamp*.

Reggie and Clyde Lanham were standing together on the Vallejo Yacht Club veranda, peering through their field glasses at the lead boats. "Looks like Encinal has the sloop class in the bag," Reggie observed, referring to the fact that both *Gusty Girl* and *Cormorant* were skippered by members of the Encinal Yacht Club in Alameda.

"*Cormorant* is Victor Hartz's boat, isn't she?" the Judge asked.

"Yes, I believe she is."

Lowering his field glasses, the Judge said, "Del told me Victor's daughter is skippering the *Cormorant* today."

"Better have a closer look, Clyde." Reggie was still studying the lead boats through his glasses. "That's definitely Victor at the helm. Not surprising. Victor is very much the take-charge type."

Clyde raised his field glasses again. "Hmmm. So it seems. You're right, of course. I've had to deal with Victor several times in my courtroom. A more arrogant jurist I have rarely encountered. How unfortunate for his wife and daughter!"

"Oh, I doubt they mind much, Clyde. Victor is a very wealthy man. Money talks, you know—especially where women are concerned." Suddenly, Reggie's masculine cynicism changed to amazement. "My God, Clyde! Look at that!" Reggie exclaimed. "It's the Henshak's ketch neck-and-neck with Van Zandt's *Red Baron*! They've caught up with the sloops!"

"Come on, Del!" the Judge cheered. "You can do it!"

It was fortunate neither of these gentle old men could hear the virulent exchanges between Colin and *The Red Baroness*' first mate at that moment. The battle between the two boats had been raging for nearly half an hour. Unfazed by the crewmen's invective, Del was concentrating on one thing—finishing first.

As the two boats sped forward, she jigged her mizzen sheet, thereby giving *Carte Blanche* the quarter of a boat-length advantage she needed. When the brass cannon on the Committee boat fired, she knew victory was hers!

* * *

The celebration that followed half an hour later was like nothing Del had ever seen. It was the first time any Vallejo Yacht Club member had won in the Gate-to-Strait race. Doc Blackburn's Montezuma Jazz band was playing a frantic rendition of the "Tiger Rag" and club members and guests were wildly hooting, prancing and kicking both inside and outside of the clubhouse. Booze in the clubhouse bar was flowing like water. Everyone clutched a mug or a cocktail glass filled with some concoction.

Desperate for help, Housel had put both Francis and Jack to work as bartenders. The three men were swamped with requests for drinks. Surrounded by dozens of fawning admirers, Del did not at first notice her two childhood friends. But, as she made her way toward the buffet at 5:30, she suddenly recognized Francis replenishing a large glass bowl with caviar. "Francis!" she exclaimed in delight. "What are you doing here? I haven't seen you in ages! How *are* you?"

"Well now, ain't you the cat's meow in your little sailor suit!" Francis replied, his eyes twinkling with mirth.

"Same old Francis! Still the smarty-pants!" Del declared, throwing her arms around his neck and kissing him on the cheek.

Francis grinned in delight. "If it gets me a hug like that, why should I change?"

"So why are you working here?" Del asked, her arms still around his neck. "I thought you were going to be a millionaire, like Henry Ford."

"Don't worry, Del" Francis said confidently. "I will, but things like that take time." He grabbed her wrists and pushed her away from him, but he did not let go of her. "Jeepers!" he exclaimed. "You're a knock-out! How about another kiss?"

"Don't be fresh!" she scolded coquettishly. She liked Francis and thought him very handsome. Just then, though, she was thinking of someone else. "Have you seen Jack lately?"

Francis pointed toward the bar where Jack was now in animated conversation with a tall, slender young woman whom Del immediately recognized as Victor Hartz's daughter, Deirdre. "There he is. Kind of busy, as you can see," he winked.

"Guess I'll have to do something about that!" Del kissed Francis lightly on the cheek again and disappeared into the crowd.

"Jack! How are you?" Del exclaimed as she rushed up to him.

"Jack's been telling me all about bridge building," Deirdre explained with an expression on her face that told Del this raven-haired beauty had already staked her claim.

"Really! Has he told you about how we used to go mud sledding yet?"

"Mud sledding?" Deirdre looked both surprised and dismayed. "What in Heaven's name is that?"

Jack silenced Del by taking her in his arms and kissing her on the lips. "Let's keep that a secret, baby!" he whispered in her ear.

Del quickly extricated herself. "Familiarity breeds contempt, mister!" she scolded. She shuddered with pleasure, though, at the unexpected spontaneity of Jack's embrace.

"You're such a doll! I couldn't help myself!"

"It's been a very long time," Del reproved, annoyance mixing with sadness in her voice. "I missed you, Jack. Why haven't you at least called me to tell me how you're doing?"

Jack looked away from her toward Housel who was signaling him from behind the bar. "Sorry, ladies," he said. "I have to get back to work."

"What a man!" Deirdre declared when Jack had gone. "I could really get goofy over him."

"Oh no you don't!" Del affirmed. "He's mine!"

*   *   *

Although it was almost midnight by the time she and her father left the victory party at the yacht club and both of them had immediately gone to bed, Del tossed and turned restlessly for hours. She heard almost every one of the twenty-two freight and passenger trains that rumbled along the tracks between Port Costa and Crocket that night—the clattering racket of their wheels and couplings echoing loudly across the Strait, the high-pitched screeching of their whistles crying out like frightened birds as they passed each other heading east and west on the parallel tracks. Never before had these noises disturbed Del's sleep. After eighteen years of hearing them nightly, she had come to regard them as a kind of lullaby.

This night was different, though. Del's thoughts were filled with images and sounds of her past and present—mostly they were images of Jack and the sounds of his voice when they played together as children and, earlier that evening, when he had stopped her in the Vallejo Yacht Club parking lot as she got into her father's car. "Del, can I see you tomorrow?" he had asked plaintively.

The Judge had been startled by this and at first seemed annoyed. When he saw the expression of yearning in his daughter's moonlit face, though, he smiled. "Hello, Jack. How are you, son? Why don't you come over to the house tomorrow and have lunch with us?"

"Oh yes, Papa! That would be wonderful!" Del was overwhelmed with surprise and delight at her father's sudden show of hospitality toward her old friend. Was it because her father had drunk too much champagne at the victory party? Was it because he was so pleased with her winning the regatta that he had momentarily let down his guard? She did not know. She did not care. All she cared about was seeing Jack again and learning all she could about what had happened to him during the last seven years.

So it was arranged. Jack would come to the Lanham manse at 1:00 P.M. the next day, right after Del and her father returned from Sunday Mass. Del's only regret was that she would not be able to spend time alone with him, that her father would be monitoring every moment of their visit together. But at least she would see him, and it was that prospect that had kept her awake. Somewhere, commingling with all the crazy images and sounds in her head, Del heard the words: *Love will find you!*

* * *

But their reunion was not to be. When Jack joined Adam, Ted and Francis for breakfast at Dewey's Roadhouse early the next morning and shared with them his plan to lunch at the Lanham home, Adam immediately bristled. "How many time I gotta tell you, boy, you got no truck with highbrow folk?"

"Del's my friend!" Jack retorted. "We'll *always* be friends. She told me so herself."

"Don't make no diff'rence," Adam said. His voice was flat; his face, expressionless. "You's a po' orphan boy an' tha's what you always be."

"Besides, we're outlaws!" Francis interjected irritably. "And you want to make whoopee with a judge's daughter? Don't get me wrong, Jack. Del's pretty and smart, but she'd be big trouble for us."

Busy chewing on his sausage, Ted Sena said nothing. But the world-weary expression on his face clearly indicated he too agreed with Adam.

Jack was furious. "That's all you care about, isn't it? Saving your own skins! What am I supposed to do? Just ignore their invitation? That would *really* be crude!"

"Crude is what we is, boy," Adam said as he reached across the table in front of Jack for a plate full of corn muffins. "You bes' get use' to it."

Jack sat in sullen silence. He realized the risks he would be taking if he were to renew his friendship with Del. His feelings for her now went far beyond friendship. Not since the afternoon he had spent with Becky at the Lido five years before had he experienced such a flood of emotion. There was no way of knowing what he might reveal to Del if he were to follow his heart. It could be dangerous for all of them, Del and her father included.

"Alright," he conceded. "I won't go and I won't call her." He got up from his chair and left the restaurant. He needed to get away from these men—these cruel captors of his fate!

* * *

"How could he do this to me!" Del protested as, two days later, she sat in the Lanhams' kitchen while Ruby prepared their supper. "No wonder he didn't come for lunch! He's a coward *and* a whoremonger!"

"Shush now, chil'!" Ruby scolded. "Don't you be talkin' like that! Where'd you get such a bad word? How you know he be like that?"

"Because Missus Hewitt told Istey and Istey told me—just this morning! She said he was with one of those women down at the Lido! Oh, Ruby! It's awful!" Del buried her face in her arms on the kitchen table and began to sob uncontrollably.

Ruby abandoned the pot of soup she was stirring and walked over to Del, leaning over her and gently massaging her back. "It jus' gossip, honey. Don't you take no stock in it."

Del lifted her tear-streaked face. "Why would Missus Hewitt gossip about something like that?" she protested.

Ruby shook her head sadly. "I don' know, chil'. Some people is awful cruel sometime. It the devil's work! When she say it happen?"

"Just after Jack almost drowned in the Strait. You remember. It was in all the local papers!"

"Land sakes, chil'! That be a *long* time ago! Mus' be five years or more. Jack was jus' a boy back then. Prob'ly didn' even know what he was doin'!"

"Oh, he *knew* what he was doing alright!" Del declared angrily. "Jack's smart. He's always been smart!"

Ruby sat down in the chair next to Del now and enclosed Del's hands in her own. "Listen to me, honey," she urged. "Men ain't never smart 'bout them things."

Del's lips quivered. "So it's true then!"

Ruby squeezed Del's hands with all of her strength. She wanted to tell this distraught and frightened young woman that Jack meant her no harm, that what he had done was normal for boys his age. But she knew there is a time to be silent and a time to speak. This, she recognized as a time to be silent. So she simply embraced Del and rocked her gently in her arms.

Overwhelmed by the warmth of this woman, Del felt suddenly at peace. Soon she would be going off to college in Philadelphia, thousands of miles from Benicia. Her life was about to change radically. Pressing her cheek against Ruby's, Del said. "I love you, Ruby!"

"I loves you too, chil'," Ruby crooned.

Chapter Twenty-six

"Let's Do It"

BECAUSE OF ITS PICTURESQUE LOCATION on City Beach in Benicia, during the 1920s the Anderson Hotel was one of the North Bay's most popular vacation resorts. Many of its guestrooms offered picturesque views of the Carquinez Strait, and its wine cellar was reputed to contain some of the finest domestic and imported vintages. Though local rumor had it that the Anderson was a trysting place for wealthy philanderers and their concubines, it was nonetheless considered several notches above the brothels of lower First Street.

During the summer months especially, fashionably dressed men and women from out of town would promenade along the boardwalk that ran from the waterfront end of West F Street all the way across the high bluffs to Gull Point. Moreover, there was an unwritten ordinance that only the most respectable families of Benicia could use the clean sandy beach in front of the hotel.

On the night of August 12, 1928, the small but elegant dining room in the Anderson Hotel had been reserved for a private party. Contra Costa County Superintendent Howard Roach had made the arrangements well in advance, issuing invitations only to those friends and acquaintances who could best support his campaign for a seat in the State Assembly.

Among his most valuable supporters were land speculator Bert McCutcheon, rancher Tom Horvath, amateur winegrower Oscar Henshak, Martinez Mayor Paul Frobish, Delta Dredging Company owner Zack Clements, Southern Pacific Railroad Vice President Russell

Bancroft, and Leo Caputi who was branch manager of the Bank of Italy in Martinez. Included too were Howard's daughter Bernie, his attorney David Stern, and his long-time allies James Soames and Ted Peters. The guest of honor on this occasion was Republican United States Senator Blake Hilliard.

As soon as everyone had been seated at the banquet table and their champagne glasses filled, Howard stood up and declared: "A toast, gentlemen! To Senator Blake Hilliard, our most distinguished representative in the nation's capitol. May you continue to serve the great State of California for many years to come, sir!"

"Here! Here!" McCutcheon declared as the men rose from their chairs and clinked glasses. Bernie remained seated. She viewed such masculine ceremonies with utter contempt.

A tall man with a thick head of silver hair and the ruddy complexion of a bourbon aficionado, Hilliard smiled beneficently at everyone present. "I thank you, Howard—lady and gentlemen all!" The man's booming base baritone filled the room as it had the floor of the United States Senate for almost twenty-eight years. "I welcome this opportunity to join with all of you this evening. And, if I may, I should like to make a toast of my own." Raising his glass, Hilliard intoned, "To the party of prosperity—Republicans!"

Cheers went up all around, and everyone sat down as two waiters in tux and tails brought out the appetizer, raw oysters on the half shell. Bernie quickly gulped down three oysters in rapid succession.

"No need to rush, lass," Bert McCutcheon brayed at her from the opposite side of the table. "I'm sure there's plenty more in the kitchen."

Bernie simply glared at him and continued feeding herself apace, despite the frown of disapproval her father bestowed on her. Her gluttony was just the sort of behavior he dreaded most. He had tried to dissuade Bernie from attending this meeting, knowing she would inevitably commit some horrendous *faux pas*.

Russell Bancroft, one of the first guests to arrive, had claimed a seat to the Senator's right. He leaned into the Senator now and mumbled, "Howard never could control that bitch!"

Hilliard simply responded with a politic nod and smile.

The gaunt-faced Clements, sitting to Hilliard's left, raised an entirely different subject. "So what's your take on the proposed amendment to curtail riparian rights, Senator?"

"It's an outrage!" Hilliard growled. "A socialist conspiracy, and it must be defeated!"

"Actually, I am somewhat ambivalent about it," Clements said. "The benefits that might accrue to our business are at least worthy of consideration."

Hilliard frowned. "How is that possible, sir?"

"If it should become law, our dredges will be in even greater demand than they are today," Clements replied matter-of-factly. "Water drawn off from the Sacramento River is bound to reduce levels throughout the Delta. If, as is rumored in Sacramento, the federal government builds a dam up in Redding as well, that could further exacerbate the problem."

"You need not trouble yourself about a federal dam, sir. I assure you, President Hoover has no interest in meddling with our State's affairs." Hilliard raised a long, bony index finger and shook it in Clements' face. "Take care, sir, that you remain faithful to The Party!"

*　　*　　*　　*

An hour later, the Anderson Hotel dining room was filled with cigar smoke. Every guest, including Bernie, had taken advantage of the management's after- dinner amenities, which included both Cuban cigars and a fine imported brandy. The six-course repast they had just consumed, as well as the several magnums of champagne they had imbibed, put everyone in a contented mood. Conversation was flowing freely and amicably.

Noting the lateness of the hour, Howard stood up and tapped the side of his water glass several times. "Gentlemen, it is almost 9:00 o'clock. I think it's time for us to get down to business. We have a full agenda, and I don't want any of you to risk a scolding from your wives." This attempt at humor elicited only a few polite chuckles. None of these men cared in the least what their spouses thought.

"The first item on our agenda is the upcoming election in November, especially as it involves the proposed amendment to limit riparian rights. We must kill this amendment, gentlemen! My attorney David Stern here has prepared a counter-proposal I'll submit to the State Assembly immediately after the election." Howard deliberately avoided pointing out that his ability to do so was contingent on his first being elected to the Assembly. That was another item on his agenda he would bring up only after he had secured everyone's approval of his counter-proposal. "David, would you please give everybody a copy?"

A stout man in his early fifties, Stern reached into the Gladstone bag he had kept close beside his chair throughout the evening and extracted a stack of unmarked envelopes. Taking one of these for himself, he passed the others around the table. "This document is highly confidential," he warned. "You may make notations on it if you like, but please return it to me in the envelope before you leave tonight."

"Yes—by all means!" Howard said. "But be sure you also add your signatures to the master copy I'll distribute after we have agreed on a final draft."

"Aye—that's the key," barked McCutcheon as he opened his envelope. "We must *all* agree!"

The men sat in silence for several minutes reviewing the contents of Howard's counter-proposal. Bernie, who was more interested in her cigar and brandy, left her envelope unopened and simply sat glowering at her father. She knew nothing about the law and had no interest in it. For Bernie Roach, all laws were made to be broken.

As Howard had expected, Tom Horvath was the first to respond. Dropping the four page document on the table in front of him, he looked up with a smile and said, "Looks good to me!"

Next to speak was Oscar Henshak. "Sure. I'll sign it."

Then, Mayor Frobish observed, "You know I've been with you on this for a long time, Howard. I'll sign it too—as is!"

"There are a few minor changes in wording I might make," Russell Bancroft observed. "But, generally speaking, I'd say it makes everything pretty clear."

"Very clear," Caputi echoed. "I'll sign it."

"Sure. Why not?" Soames said.

Peters nodded in agreement. "Looks alright t' me."

"It's done, then," declared the Senator. "Go ahead, Howard. Pass around your master copy and let's get on to the next item on your agenda."

McCutcheon and Clements, however, were still studying Howard's counter-proposal. When Clements finished perusing it, he looked up and said, "I'm not sure this is necessary. After all, the wording of the original amendment is pretty vague."

As he spoke, Clements drew a folded two-page document from the inside pocket of his dinner jacket, opened it, and began reading aloud: "... nothing herein contained shall be construed as depriving any riparian owner of the reasonable use of water of the stream to which his land is riparian under reasonable methods of diversion and use, or of depriving any appropriator of water to which he is lawfully entitled." Looking around at the others, Clements commented, "These words are from the amendment now before the State Assembly. Frankly, gentlemen, I see nothing in them that threatens the rights of private property owners."

There was dead silence for several seconds as the other men wrestled with the convoluted legalese Clements had just recited. In fact, no one else at the table had ever read the original text of the proposed State Constitutional Amendment. They had drawn their understanding of it from conversations with others of their own political persuasion who themselves had not read the Amendment.

The silence in the room was broken when Billings, his face now beet red with righteous rage, roared at Clements. "You, sir, do not understand the language of the law!" Then, drawing on the rhetorical flourishes that had made him famous during his long career on the floor of the United States Senate, Billings elaborated. "Such wording is designed not to edify and clarify but to obfuscate and deceive. I put it to you, sir, that it opens the floodgates to a disastrous taking not only of riparian rights but also of the most fundamental rights of liberty as they are defined in out nation's Constitution."

At this point, massaging his brow in perplexity, McCutcheon broke in and asked the question that was on the minds of most of those present. "What the hell is this all about, anyway?"

Horvath, the only one present who had a direct interest in and therefore a clearer understanding of the issue, was quick to explain. "Senator Billing's is absolutely right! What this is about is the rights of ranchers and growers like me. Ever since 1886, California law has protected our rights based on the Riparian Doctrine of English common law. The water in any lake, river or stream on or next to my property belongs *exclusively* to me. And, believe me, we ranchers and growers need every drop during the dry summer months. But a bunch of damn socialists in the Assembly want to change all that and force us to share our water with big cities like San Francisco and Los Angeles. That's gonna put us out of business!"

Bernie had heard enough. "What are you old geezers waiting for? Go ahead and sign the damn thing!"

Although Bernie's father winced, the Senator beamed at her with delight. "Dear lady! How right you are!" Then, to her father, he said, "Circulate your master copy, Howard. We shall *all* sign it!"

As the master copy was passed around and signed, Howard introduced the second item on his agenda. "You all know that, even to get this counter-proposal before the Assembly, you're going to need an advocate in Sacramento. That's why I'm throwing my hat in the ring this November and I'll need your help getting out the votes—the right kind of votes, that is!"

"We know what you mean alright, Howard," Russell Bancroft assured him. "You don't need to worry. SP already has the machinery you'll need to move things along."

"And, thanks to a little help from my friend Leo here," Frobish added with a knowing wink at the banker, "I've got the Contra Costa bosses in line. We're ready to go."

"That's swell," Howard said with an ingratiating smile, but there were lingering lines of apprehension on his brow. "We're gonna need more than just the Contra Costa votes, though. We have to get at least Alameda and Santa Clara in the South Bay and Sonoma and Napa in the North. We've got to take control in San Francisco too."

"Sonoma's already in the bag," Henshak reported confidently. "Napa should be easy. My brother-in-law, Luke Cavanaugh, is Chairman of the Board for the Napa interurban line. He's got friends on the town council in every burg from Napa to Calistoga."

"That's good news, Oscar. What about the big urban districts?"

Billings chuckled confidently. "I'll handle that for you, Howard. My constituents in Oakland and San Francisco have already joined forces with the rural counties up north to block any changes in the *status quo*. It's all part of the good old Federal Plan. We defeated the Los Angeles Plan in '26 and we'll do it again in '28."

"How you gonna do that?" asked the always-skeptical McCutcheon.

"I believe it's called gerrymandering, Bert," Soames replied with a sly smile.

Several of the others raised their eyebrows at the bald-faced candor of this observation, but no one contradicted it.

"Thank you, Senator," Howard said, deliberately ignoring McCutcheon and Soames' brief exchange. "That brings us to the next item on our agenda. We need a name for ourselves—something that sounds very official and respectable."

"How about The Fixers?" Bernie suggested sarcastically.

"That's not at all amusing, young lady!" Bancroft retorted.

"Why do we need a name?" McCutcheon asked. "I thought this was a private meeting and we were all supposed to be anonymous."

Howard fumbled nervously with the papers he had laid out on the table in front of himself. Glancing briefly at Soames and Peters, he said, "Well, of course, some of us may prefer to remain anonymous. But, if that's the case, I'll have to remove those signatures from my counter-proposal. We need to release this document to the press well in advance of the upcoming election to avoid the usual Democratic Party charges of collusion. Our document should be released under a letterhead with the names of its most distinguished supporters—such as Senator Billings and Mister Bancroft here. I think we need to identify ourselves as some kind of a statewide commission. Again, gentlemen, I'm open to any reasonable suggestion." As he said this, Howard deliberately avoided making eye contact with Bernie.

"Maybe we should table this item for a later meeting," Clements said. "Or perhaps each of us can give you our recommendation individually and let you make the final decision."

"Splendid idea, Zack!" the Senator declared. "Do we all agree?"

Everyone except Bernie nodded.

Visibly relieved, Howard began collecting his papers into a single pile. "Thank you, gentlemen. You have all been most cooperative. I think we can call it a night. Don't forget to return your envelopes to David."

* * *

Howard and Bernie Roach's engagements that night were not over. After the meeting at the Anderson Hotel, they joined Soames and Peters for drinks at the Pastime Card Room on First Street. Sitting in a booth at the rear of this dingy and dimly lighted working class establishment, they ordered a bottle of brandy and four glasses. Since it was almost 10:30 on a weekday night, there were very few other patrons in the place.

"That was easy," Peters observed, referring to the results of the meeting just ended.

"Not as easy as you think," Howard said. "We have to keep a sharp eye on that Clements fella. He's pretty shrewd and he don't give a damn about politics. All he cares about is his dredges." To Soames, he said, "You better tell your boys to keep close tabs on him."

"Don't worry, Howard," Soames said confidently. "I got six men working for him as dredge operators. They'll keep track of the scuttlebutt, and two of my girls are bookkeepers in his Antioch headquarters office."

"I'm talkin' about Clements himself. We need to know who his cronies are—what clubs he belongs to, that kind o' thing."

"Better find out who his whores are," Bernie opined.

"Clements is a strict Methodist. He doesn't do that kind o' thing!" her father corrected irritably.

Bernie laughed. "Yeah, sure!" she mocked.

"I'll put somebody on it," Soames said. "So what's the plan for rigging these districts? The Democrats and Progressives are makin' plenty o' trouble down in Los Angeles. Up here in San Francisco and Oakland too."

"Billings and Bancroft will have to deal with Los Angeles," Howard said. "Only thing we gotta do is make sure they get the hooch an' hash they need for bribin' the niggers and chinks down there."

"Taken care of," Soames assured him. "I got a deal goin' with Johnny Chase. He gets shipments down from Canada every week. Bancroft's on board too. SP 'll provide the freight cars for shipments south."

"Good!" Howard nodded. "You got Oakland and San Francisco covered too, right?"

Soames' eyes flashed with contempt. "You worry too much, Howie!"

"This is a whole lot more complicated than you think, Jimmy!" Howard snapped. "We got to get ready for *after* the election too, y' know."

"So what's the plan for *after*, Howie?" Peters asked with a snide smile.

"We got to buy us some retired California judges. Get 'em to serve on a panel that'll re-draw the districts in our favor. You heard what Billings said about the Federal Plan. Gettin' to the retired judges should be easy. It's the Ninth Circuit judges we got to worry about."

"You mean Honest Abes like Judge Lanham, I suppose," Soames casually observed, surprising Howard with his knowledge of the Ninth Circuit roster. "Hell! That pompous ass lives in Benicia, my old stomping grounds. You want him out o' the picture? No problem!"

"It's not just Lanham," Howard cautioned. "There's at least three others on the Ninth Circuit who'll need watching. Cubberly and Santoyo, for instance. They make no bones about their preference for the Los Angeles Plan,"

"What the hell is the Los Angeles Plan?" Bernie demanded.

"Yeah," Peters said. "I'm not too clear about that either."

Rolling his eyes, Howard explained. "Up 'til a couple o' years ago, it was easy for us Republicans t' control the State legislature just by re-drawin' district boundaries so we had more votes than the Democrats. But Los Angeles got so big that now it's harder to change district boundaries without somebody blowin' the whistle on us. Two years ago, the Democrats tried to push through a ballot for reapportionment based on population only. They called it the All Parties Plan. But the Republicans jinxed it by calling it the Los Angeles Plan. Whatever you call it, we don't want it. That's why we need the retired judges."

"Now I get it," Peters said. "You gotta line up your old ducks ahead of time. So what's that have to do with me and Jimmy?"

"Right now, nothing except be ready when I need help gettin' rid o' the bad apples."

"I got just the man for the job," Soames announced.

Howard looked worried again. "Not Spears, I hope. He's messed things up with small-timers like Tucker too many times already."

Chuckling, Soames shook his head. "Nah! This fella's a lot meaner and smarter than Spears. A real pro from Chicago named Lester Gillis. Maybe you know him by his alias—Baby Face Nelson."

"Baby-face Nelson!" Bernie exclaimed. "You mean he's comin' to California?"

"He's already here," Soames replied, clearly proud of his insider knowledge about this notorious bank robber and ruthless killer. "He and his wife are hiding out with Chase over in Sausalito because he's on the lam. The FBI's declared him Public Enemy Number One."

Suddenly aware that he might be dealing with more than he could handle, Howard turned to his daughter and said, "Come on, Bernie. I'm tired. Let's go home."

* * *

The Capitol Building at the northwest corner of First and G Streets has long been one of Benicia's greatest sources of pride. Even before California was admitted to the Union in 1850, no less than six municipalities—including Benicia, Columbia, Monterrey, Sacramento, San Jose, and Vallejo—competed to become the permanent site of the State Capitol. Erected in 1853 expressly for that purpose, Benicia's Greek revival structure remains today the preeminent symbol of the city's claim to historical fame.

It was here on November 6, 1928, that a group of local amateur performers staged "The Benicia Follies"—a musical review comprising song and dance routines from some of the then most popular Broadway shows. The featured performer in this review was the beautiful and talented soprano Susanna Fisk. This entertainment had been advertised weeks in advance through announcements in both the *Benicia Herald New Era* and the *Vallejo Times-Herald* as well as in printed flyers posted on the doorways and in the display windows of various shops and taverns throughout both Vallejo and Benicia.

The moment he saw Susanna Fisk's name printed in large black letters on one of these flyers at the entrance to the Pastime Card Room, Jack rushed to purchase a ticket. Jack did not tell Adam or Francis about this, for he knew they would ridicule his interest in such "high class" entertainment and that Adam, once again, would warn him about the hazards of chasing rich married women. Jack didn't care. With the woman he truly loved now gone from his life forever, he had sunk into deep depression and had reverted to his former habits of drinking and carousing

By the time Jack arrived at 7:00 on the night of the performance, the second floor of the Capitol Building was already filled to capacity. Every one of the bench seats set up for the audience was occupied and the standing room space at the back of the hall was crammed with bachelors, their breath reeking of whiskey and their loud voices defiling the place with obscenities.

Frank Pisciotta, now Benicia's Police Chief, had stationed six of his brawniest deputies at the entrance to the hall, armed with pistols and nightsticks and clearly eager to break the skull of anyone who threatened to disrupt the performance.

The speaker's rostrum at the front of the meeting hall had been converted to a temporary stage with a drawn curtain. The members of a small orchestra comprising a pianist, a flutist, a cornet player, two violinists and a tuba player sat in chairs to the right of the stage. In front on either side of the stage, Klieg lights on metal stands had been set up—each operated by a stagehand.

Just as Jack shouldered his way to the front of the standing spectators, the Klieg lights flashed on and the orchestra began playing a medley of sprightly show tunes. This overture had the wanted effect of calming everyone in the audience, even the raucous spectators at the back of the hall.

When the overture concluded, the curtain opened slowly on squeaking pulleys to reveal a canvas flat crudely painted to resemble a railroad depot and waiting passenger train. Standing center stage in front of this flat were four men in loose-fitting white trousers, dark blue blazers, and straw hats who promptly launched into a barbershop quartet rendition of *Toot, Toot, Tootsie, Goodbye*.

While the four singers took their bows and the curtain closed in front of them, Benicia Mayor Tom Borden stepped up on the stage. "Welcome, ladies and gentlemen, to the 1928 Benicia Follies!" he declared. "Pretty clever, opening the show with a goodbye song, wouldn't you say?" he asked. Except for several disparaging hoots from the back of the hall, Borden's attempt at humor evoked little audience response.

"Well, don't worry, ladies and gentlemen" Borden bravely continued.

"There's plenty more to come. Now I'd like to introduce our next sensation of the evening—Benicia's own mistress of the banjo, Snooky Wells, and that master of the mandolin, Silvio Iglesias This talented duo will perform for us a classical piece called ..." Squinting at his cue card, the Mayor hesitated.

On this cue, Snooky and Silvio stepped through the closed curtain to take center stage. "*L'Appuntamento*," Iglesias announced with a smile that revealed two rows of perfectly even white teeth beneath his drooping black mustache.

"It's Italian," Snooky explained to the Mayor. Then, with a wink at the audience, she added, "You don't want to know what it means, Your Honor." The many Italians and Portuguese in her audience roared with laughter as Snooky began strumming the opening bars of this fast-moving mazurka.

The applause that greeted Snooky and Silvio's virtuoso duet was deafening. Everyone stood up, calling for an *encore*. Snooky knew her audience and, signaling with a nod to Silvio, led the entire assembly in a sing-along version of *She'll be comin' 'round the mountain*.

Once more, Borden mounted the stage to introduce the next performer—a tall, gawky fourteen-year-old named Renata Vasquez whose mature contralto voice astonished everyone as she sang *Look for the silver lining*.

Next on the program was a local magician—Father Joseph Benedetto, a Dominican priest well known in town for his slight-of-hand tricks and his wry sense of humor. The climax of Father Joseph's performance occurred when he magically extracted coins from various parts of Mayor Borden's anatomy and suggested that, for a small monthly stipend, he would be willing to offer the Mayor some valuable tips on how to balance the town budget.

Smiling sheepishly, the Mayor waved the priest off stage and announced, "Now, ladies and gentlemen, we have a special treat as Benicia's lovely songbird, Missus Susanna Fisk, and Saint Paul's talented choirmaster, Clarence Holloway, sing for us a medley of tunes from *Showboat*."

This was the moment Jack had been waiting for. He was not disappointed. When the curtain opened to reveal another painted flat representing a stern-wheel riverboat tied up at a dock, standing center stage was the delicious Susanna attired in the hoopskirt and sunbonnet costume of Edna Ferber's heroine, Magnolia.

Susanna's eyes were downcast in modesty as she waited for the orchestra to play the introduction to Oscar Hammerstein and Jerome Kern's "Make Believe." When her eyes opened and her lips parted to sing, Jack felt as if she were directing every word solely at him:

> *Only make believe I love you,*
> *Only make believe that you love me.*
> *Others find peace of mind in pretending,*
> *Couldn't you?*
> *Couldn't I?*
> *Couldn't we?*

Instantly, Jack was smitten. Susanna's sweet soprano voice, her inviting smile, and the sure expressive movements of her hands affected him like an aphrodisiac! When she sang the words: "Make believe our lips were blending in a phantom kiss or two or three," Jack trembled with desire.

"She got nice bubs!" one of the rowdies behind him quipped. "I'd sure like to take a bite out o' that!"

Instantly Jack's left elbow shot up under this miscreant's chin, snapping his head back into the face of another male spectator. Within seconds, Jack was in a melee of flying fists. Within minutes after that, Pisciotta's men dragged Jack and two other rowdies out of the hall and locked them up for the night in the town jail.

*   *   *

Much to his surprise, Jack was released at noon the next day. "You're one lucky son of a gun!" Pisciotta said contemptuously as he handed Jack his wallet, pocket change and car keys. "Some lawyer from Martinez come over this morning and bailed you out."

"A lawyer? Whose lawyer?" Jack asked, dreading the prospect of yet another stint in the Solano County jail.

Pisciotta shook his head in bewilderment. "He didn't say. He just paid your bail and told me to give you this." Reaching into a drawer in his desk, Pisciotta extracted a business card and gave it to Jack, "For the life o' me, I can't figure why anybody'd give a tinker's damn about the likes o' you!"

Ignoring this insult, Jack looked at the unfamiliar name and phone number on the card—*Bernard Metzger, Attorney at Law.* Turning the card over, Jack saw that someone had scribbled two words on the back of it: "Call me."

As soon as he left the police station, Jack walked across First Street to Mary Lou Hewitt's ice-cream parlor where he asked to use her phone.

When the local operator put him through, a woman answered briskly, "Metzger and Colson."

"My name is Jack Westlake. Mister Metzger asked me to call him."

"One moment, please," the woman said.

It was several 'moments' before Metzger finally came on the line. "Mister Westlake," the man declared affably. "This is your lucky day!"

"What do you mean?"

"There's a pretty lady who wants to meet you Tuesday afternoon at the James Hotel in Martinez. You're supposed to meet her in the lobby there at one o'clock."

"What pretty lady?"

"I'm just a messenger, buddy. Can't tell y'. Just be there." Having said this, the lawyer hung up.

It's Susanna! Jack almost shouted his joy. Dumbfounded, he left the ice-cream parlor, got into his car and drove back to the boarding house in Napa. Francis and Adam were both away at work when Jack arrived. Since he was scheduled to drive to Jamestown for a pick-up that night and he had not slept well in jail the night before, Jack went to bed.

* * *

"Where was you las' night?" Adam asked as they climbed into the cab of the flatbed and Adam noted the ugly bruise on Jack's cheek. "You out drinkin' again? You bes' watch youself, boy!" he warned.

"Don't worry about it," Jack retorted. "I can take care of myself!"

Adam nodded, but his facial expression did not indicate agreement. Though troubled by Jack's reckless behavior, Adam made no further attempts to ask about Jack's nocturnal carousing until they returned to the boarding house at 3:00 the next morning. "This is the las' trip we makin' to Jamestown, boys," he announced. "Tomorrow, you and Sena finish up the deliveries and pay-offs down in Oakland. From now on, we's sellin' hash."

"Who are we selling it to?" Jack asked, surprised that Adam had made such an abrupt change in plans. He had known it would happen eventually, but not so suddenly.

"Francis and Sena got their pick-up and delivery lists. You'll get yours next Sunday night, 'less you wants t' stop workin' this gig." Adam eyed Jack suspiciously. "Like I told y', we's workin' solo on this. Is you in, boy, or ain't you?"

"Are you telling me *I'm* finished?" Jack asked, worried now that he had lost Adam's trust.

Adam's eyes glittered with menace. "It up to you, boy. I ain't foolin' with you no mo'. You gots to stay sober or you's out the game, you hear?"

"Yes, sir," Jack said, thoroughly humbled. "I'm with you, Adam. You *know* that!"

Again Adam nodded, but again Jack saw doubt in the old man's face.

* * *

A former boarding house for itinerant day laborers, the James Hotel in Martinez had recently undergone significant renovations by its new owners who hoped to attract a better class of clientele, especially management level employees and clients of the Shell Oil refinery that by 1928 had become the largest employer in the City of Martinez.

A new and luxurious front lobby had been added as well as an adjoining coffee shop where gentlemen could bring both their business associates and their families to dine in elegance and respectability. Being strict Methodists, the new hotel owners refused to serve alcoholic beverages of any kind and carefully screened every customer seeking overnight accommodations. Only single "gentlemen of business" or married couples were allowed to register for a room.

Susanna was waiting for Jack in the hotel lobby as he entered. She was dressed in the latest fashion of women's casual attire—which included a chocolate-brown cloche, gold necklace and bracelet, V-necked woolen sweater with alternating rust and beige stripes, a matching beige pleated skirt, flesh-colored silk stockings, and plain brown shoes with three-inch heels. Susanna's tight-fitting sweater conspicuously revealed her voluptuous upper torso and instantly caught Jack's hungry gaze.

His heart pounding furiously, Jack rushed toward her. She smiled at him invitingly but held up her hand, warning him to keep his distance. Then, glancing nervously toward the clerk behind the registration desk, she slipped her arm under his. "Let's go into the coffee shop," she murmured. "We can talk better there," she added with a flirtatious wink.

At Susanna's request, they were seated at a small table for two as far as possible from the large street-front window in the coffee shop. As soon as the headwater moved away, Jack leaned toward Susanna and reached under the table to touch her knees. "My God, Susanna!" he declared breathlessly. "You're so beautiful! I want make love to you right now!"

Raising the fingertips of her left hand to her lips, Susanna blew him a kiss. At the same time, with her right hand she pushed his hands off her knees. "I know, dear," she warbled sweetly. "But you'll have to be patient."

Jack was so excited by the wildly erotic images swirling inside his head at the moment that he could barely contain himself. "I *can't* wait!" he insisted. "Let's get a room here in the hotel and go upstairs right now!"

"Not here, dear. I have a better place for us. Do you have a car?" When he nodded, she said, "Good. You can follow me in mine. It's the red and black coupe parked out front."

At this point, the waiter returned and took their order. When he moved away, Jack reached under the table and again clutched one of Susanna's knees. She quickly encircled his hand with her own and her lips again shaped a kiss. "Please, dear!" she whispered, gently pushing his hand away. "We must be careful. The walls in this place have both eyes and ears."

"Then why did you ask me to meet you here?"

Shaking her head at Jack's naiveté, Susanna explained. "I'm a married woman, Jack, and you're a much younger and very handsome man. Look around. Do you see any other couples like us? This is strictly a hotel for businessmen and their families. That's why I chose it for our first meeting. My husband knows this hotel and would never guess I'm here to meet a lover."

"You're amazing!" Jack said. "I guess you've done this before." He regretted these words as soon as he spoke them.

Susanna was quick to respond. "If you want me, Jack, you're going to have to take me as I am. Life has not been easy for me with these Fisks. They're dreadful people, especially Elmer's mother. She's a nosey bitch!"

"So I've heard," Jack replied, recalling the many reports he had heard of Charlotte Fisk's meddlesomeness.

The waiter returned with their coffee. "Is there anything else I can get for you, madam?" he asked, eyeing Jack suspiciously.

"That will be all, thank you," Susanna answered. When the waiter moved away again, she said to Jack, "See what I mean?"

"Self-righteous bastard!" Jack growled.

"Drink your coffee," Susanna commanded. "I'll leave first and wait for you in my car. You pay the bill." She promptly stood up and left the hotel.

*   *   *

Fifteen minutes later, Jack was following Susanna's shiny new red and black coupe up a winding dirt road that climbed into the wooded hills west of Martinez. *Where is she going?* Jack wondered. *Why is she taking me way out here in the woods?* There were other questions Jack might have asked himself had he been thinking more clearly at that moment. But he was in love—blindly and helplessly so.

At length, Susanna pulled her car into a clearing in the woods. In the middle of this clearing was a small log cabin, its windows shuttered for the winter. She drove her car around to the rear of this building so it would not be visible from the roadway. Jack followed her lead. "What is this place?" he asked as both of them got of their cars.

"It's Elmer's hunting lodge," Susanna explained contemptuously. "He and his friends use it during the summer when they come out here to shoot rabbits and crows."

"Rabbits and crows!" Jack expostulated. "What kind of hunting is that? That's what little kids do!"

"Exactly!" Susanna smirked. "And that's the kind of hunter my husband is—a little kid!"

Jack moved swiftly, taking Susanna in his arms and kissing her. "You have a real man now, darling!"

Laughing, she grasped Jack's hand and pulled him after her as she ran around to the entrance of the cabin. Extracting a key from her handbag, she opened the padlocked door and, taking Jack's hand again, led him inside.

Jack could see very little in the darkness, but Susanna quickly found a kerosene lantern and, lighting it with a box match, placed it on a large oak table in the center of the sparsely furnished one-room cabin.

"Close the door, dear," she commanded as she slowly removed her hat, necklace and bracelet and carefully placed these items on the table. Then, turning to face him, she broke into song, her lilting soprano voice filling the room with lyrics from an operetta:

> *Come! Come! I love you only,*
> *My heart is true,*
> *Come! Come! my life is lonely*
> *I long for you.*

"Do you like that song, dear?" Susanna asked sweetly as she began to open the buttons on the back of her sweater. "It's called 'My Hero'," Susanna explained as she let her sweater fall to the floor, revealing her naked breasts. "It's from a beautiful operetta I sang the leading role in once called *The Chocolate Soldier*," she continued as calmly as if she were still fully clothed. Then, holding out her arms toward Jack, she warbled, "Now *you're* my hero! My sweet chocolate soldier! Come to me, darling!"

For the next two hours Jack had an experience he had never imagined possible. Susanna's love making was as calculatedly tantalizing as her stage performance. It was as if she had rehearsed her part in their encounter hundreds of times before, pacing and choreographing every word and gesture to match the musical score of an orchestra playing inside of Jack's head. By the time they left the cabin together later that afternoon, Jack was completely in Susanna's thrall.

* * *

Located on the southwestern shore of San Pablo Bay, China Camp was a community of ramshackle one-story buildings erected during the 1840s to house immigrants from Canton, China. The earliest of these immigrants had been lured to California during the gold rush years.

Because they had been fishermen by trade in their native country, they found the marshlands of eastern Marin County an ideal location for their settlement. It provided not only ready access to the abundant marine life in San Pablo Bay but also isolation from the then inhospitable Caucasian communities in other parts of the Bay Area. By 1880, the population of China Camp had grown to more than 500 residents, most of whom harvested grass shrimp and oysters.

By 1928, however, the population of China Camp had dwindled to less than 150 as the younger generations wandered off to find work, first as gandy dancers for the Central Pacific Railroad and then as poultry farmers in Napa, Solano, and Sonoma counties.

Both Harry Lee and Edie Zhao had been born and raised in China Camp. So it was not surprising Adam knew many of the people still living in that community. It was from them he had learned about the lucrative market for hashish and marijuana—both plants that flourished in the rich soil and temperate climate of the Marin foothills.

A dense fog lay over San Pablo Bay that morning in late November as Adam, Francis, Ted, and Jack stood at the end of the long dock in Rodeo. They were waiting for the longboat to arrive from China Camp with its cargo of cured hashish and marijuana. Impatiently checking his pocket watch, Francis said, "They're late. They should have been here an hour ago."

"Don't you be worryin', boy. They be here," Adam retorted. "Tha's thick fog out there an' the tide's out. They's got a heavy load, so they gotta move slow."

"How many pounds?" Ted asked.

"Four hundred," Adam said.

Francis whistled in astonishment. "That's a lot o' hash!"

"Lot o' cash too, boy," Adam observed with a sly smile.

In the distance, they heard the dying rattle of a small boat engine being turned off. This was quickly followed by the sound of oars splashing in the water. Gradually, the dark silhouette of a longboat with three men aboard became visible.

"Here they is," Adam said. "Get ready to catch the line."

Francis had already moved to the end of the dock and was calling out to the approaching boat, clearly visible now as it drifted closer. One of the men aboard stood up in the bow and tossed a line toward Francis. He caught it deftly and pulled the boat to the left side of the dock. There he secured it to a pier as the man in the bow climbed out and walked toward Adam.

"Nice day, huh?" the man said. "Nobody see."

"Good thing you got here now, Danny," Adam replied with an edge of annoyance in his voice. "Fog be gone soon. Hurry up! We gotta get them boxes loaded."

"Sure! Sure!" Danny held out his hand. "You pay first, yes?"

Grumbling, Adam reached into his pocket and pulled out a thick roll of bills. While he counted them out in Danny's open hands, the men in the boat began unloading wooden crates onto the dock.

Not to be rushed, Danny re-counted the money Adam had given him. Adam, in turn, ordered Jack and Francis to open several crates to check their contents.

When he had finished re-counting his money, Danny looked up and said, "Okee-dokee. You take boxes. We go now."

There were sixteen crates that had to be transported to the cars, each crate weighing approximately 30 pounds. "How about helping us load these crates into our cars?" Francis asked with a disapproving frown.

"Ah no," Danny said with a slight bow that was more deprecating than courteous. "We go now so nobody see." Danny promptly released the slipknot Francis had tied in the bowline, jumped back into his boat, and pushed off.

"Who are those guys?" Jack demanded angrily.

"Never mind that," Adam barked. "Let's get these crates to the cars."

Working swiftly, the men carried two crates at a time until four were loaded in the back seat of each vehicle. By the time they were finished, the fog had lifted so that they could see the buildings in the town of Rodeo.

Adam handed Jack a folded sheet of paper. "You got the drop-offs in Hayward," he said. Then, without any further explanation, he climbed into the front seat of his sedan and started its engine. "Le's go!"

As the other three vehicles turned onto Lincoln Highway, Jack pulled his car to the side of the road and looked at the list of addresses on the paper Adam had given him. He was astonished to see thirty-five different customer names on this list. It would take him several days to make his deliveries and collect payment for each. Most troubling of all, he knew none of the names on the list.

* * *

When Jack and Susanna met again at Elmer's hunting cabin a week later, he pleaded with her to leave her husband and live with him—though he had no clear idea of where that would be. He didn't care. His only goal was to possess this woman completely.

Touching his cheek with her hand, Susanna sighed. "Poor dear! You just don't understand, do you? My life is very complicated. I can't just run off and leave Elmer. He and his family are rich and powerful. They would ruin us both."

"But I can't go on living without you, Susanna!" Jack protested desperately. "There has to be a way!"

She studied his face for several seconds before she spoke. "There is," she said at last, "but I don't think you'll like it."

"Anything! Tell me!" Jack insisted.

"Elmer has a big life insurance policy on himself. If something happened to him, I would be a very wealthy woman." She paused again. Then kissed Jack on the lips, confident that this was all she needed to say and do.

"You want me to kill him? I'll gladly do it!" Jack declared.

"You'd have to make it look like an accident," she warned. "That wouldn't be easy. But, if you mean what you say and you can do it the right way, I promise I'll live with you."

* * *

Susanna's promise was all Jack needed. As soon as he returned to the boarding house in Napa that night, he decided to seek advice from Francis whose ruthless pragmatism Jack had long admired. "If you really hated somebody, how would you get rid of him?" he asked.

"Kill the bastard," Francis snapped.

"Yes, but how?"

"Depends on who he was. If he was just some bum, I'd trap him in an alley someplace and plug him right there. If it was somebody important, like a big-time politician, I'd have to track him for a while—find out where he goes every day, who his friends are—stuff like that. What're you askin' me these questions for, anyway?" Francis scowled.

"I have a friend who needs to get rid of somebody—somebody pretty important."

"So you want me to tell y' how t' do it?" Francis laughed derisively. "Forget it, Jack!"

"How about if I told you there's good money in it for you?"

"I don't do contracts. I don't need it, 'specially now we got this new hash bus'ness goin'. Tell your friend to go fly a kite!"

* * *

Jack realized he would have to get rid of Elmer Fisk on his own. So the next time he met with Susanna, he told her about Francis' strategy. She immediately agreed to give Jack all the information he needed to begin tracking his prey, including the routes Elmer followed to and from work at the Ford Plant in Richmond every day and the names of the restaurants and taverns where he met friends and business associates. Because Elmer was a creature of habit, it was easy for Jack to track him—an activity he pursued for several weeks.

But he had difficulty coming up with a specific strategy for making Elmer's death look accidental. Eventually it was Susanna who told him what to do. He would follow Elmer home from work in his car one afternoon as Elmer took his usual shortcut from Richmond to Martinez on a deserted back road that wound through the mountains east of Lincoln Highway. Since there were several sharp turns in this road with a precipitous drop on one side, Jack would force Elmer's car off the road at one of these turns, causing it to plummet down the side of the mountain. "You'll have to make sure he's dead, though, Jack!" she warned, her beautiful brown eyes dark with murderous hate.

Jack shuddered at the image that flashed in his head at that moment as he saw himself sliding down a steep mountain slope to check whether Elmer was really dead and then perhaps having to strangle him with his own bare hands. Nevertheless, he was determined to do whatever necessary to possess this woman.

He did not have the killer instinct, though. Each time Jack tried to carry out Susanna's plan, he found himself unable to do so. He began to feel sorry for Elmer and to question Susanna's motives. If she were capable of plotting the murder of her own husband, might she not also be capable of abandoning Jack once she got the money from her husband's insurance policy? The answer to these questions came soon after Jack's last attempt.

*   *   *

It had been raining hard for several hours that late Friday afternoon as Jack followed Elmer's big Buick sedan along the winding mountain road toward Martinez. The surface of this dirt road was slippery with mud, making it difficult for both drivers to keep control of their vehicles. Elmer's Buick was at least fifty yards ahead of Jack's new Dodge, moving much faster than usual. Perhaps Elmer had recognized Jack's car and realized he was being followed.

Whatever the reason, the Buick suddenly spun out of control as it approached a sharp curve. Jack slammed on his brakes and watched in horror as Elmer's big sedan seemed to leap off the road and plunged headlong down the side of the mountain.

Jumping out of his car, Jack ran to the edge of the road. Looking down, he saw that Elmer's vehicle had landed upside down more than a hundred feet below. Its wheels were still spinning. Black smoke was coming from its engine. Seconds later there was an explosion as the gas tank ignited and engulfed the Buick in flames. There was no doubt about it. Elmer Fisk was a dead man.

Slowly, Jack returned to his car and, turning it around, headed back toward El Cerrito. Guilt-ridden, he thought of reporting the incident to the local police. But he did not, deciding this would only raise suspicions about his culpability. Certainly he would have difficulty trying to explain why he was on that backcountry road at the time. He also decided not to phone Susanna to tell her what had happened. She would find out soon enough and would assume he had been responsible.

Though Jack had not directly caused Elmer's death, he realized he had been instrumental in it. Had he not followed Elmer that afternoon, the man might not have driven so fast and lost control of his car. From his past experience in court, Jack had learned what it meant to have means, motive and opportunity. He had all of these and all enough to convict him of murder. Certainly Judge Lanham would think so!

Jack's feelings of guilt plagued him for weeks after the incident, completely eclipsing his former desire for Susanna. He made no attempt to meet her again at their usual trysting place. Before long, Jack began to realize his feelings for Susanna had not been love but lust. *I have done a terrible thing!* he told himself.

Jack's remorse turned to fury when, two months later, he read a wedding announcement in the *Vallejo Times Herald*. Beneath a glamorous photograph of the smiling Susanna and Alexander Leighton was the following brief report: "Mr. and Mrs. Robert Copeland of Davis, California, announce the marriage of their daughter Susanna to Mr. Alexander Leighton of Benicia, California. Mr. Leighton, a well-known architect with the firm of Watson and Slone in San Francisco, will be honeymooning in Boca Raton, Florida, where Mr. Leighton is currently designing several new luxury homes." There was no mention at all of Susanna's former marriage to Elmer Fisk.

1929

The Alamo Rooms

CHAPTER TWENTY-SEVEN

"Happy Days Are Here Again"

NEW YEAR'S DAY WAS ALWAYS celebrated in Benicia, but 1929 broke all records for enthusiasm. With the 10:00 P.M. curfew suspended for the holiday, every bar and brothel in town did a land-office business. First Street swarmed with local citizens and out-of-towners forming impromptu parades. Crewmen and passengers danced together on the ferry decks. Cherry bombs exploding in back yards terrified hundreds of dogs, cows, pigs and chickens. As Benicia's church and firehouse bells rang in the New Year, Southern Pacific engineer Sergio Parente sounded the whistle of Locomotive 1486 in a one-note rendition of "Auld Lang Syne" that echoed in the hills on both sides of the Carquinez Strait.

Like many communities across the nation, Benicia had resonated with the economic boom of 1928. On May 16 of that year, nearly half a million shares sold on the New York Stock Exchange, setting an all-time high. On August 27, the United States joined fourteen other nations in signing the Kellog-Briand Peace Pact—an event hailed by the national press as "a universal renunciation of war." When, on November 6, *laissez faire* proponent Herbert Hoover defeated Roman Catholic populist Al Smith for the Presidency, many believed this Republican Party victory guaranteed another decade of explosive growth and prosperity.

In Benicia too, prosperity was evident. During the summer of 1928, two new auto service stations had been constructed at the intersection of First and J Streets. Then, in December, Alta's management announced plans to close its parent facility in Marysville and concentrate all its efforts on the production of dredges—what had become a high-demand product in the Sacramento Delta, whose channels and banks were constantly shifted by the floods of spring. At the same time, just across the Strait in Martinez, the Shell Oil Company expanded its business by building a new refinery. On New Years Eve day, a front-page report in the *Benicia Herald New Era* announced that 1929 promised a job for every able-bodied citizen on both sides of the Carquinez Strait.

The brothels of Benicia too had prospered. No less than fifteen different establishments now operated at the waterfront end of First Street. Thanks to her entrepreneurial spirit and generous under-the-table contributions to selected members of the Town Council, Terry Duckworth had her own house called the Alamo Rooms. Located directly across the street from the Lido, Terry's enterprise was in stiff competition with that of Mrs. K. T. Parker. In fact, it was rumored that Mayor Tom Brady had his own secret entrance to this newest establishment.

Home from college for the Christmas holidays, Del welcomed the New Year in the much more dignified environs of the Lanham manse on West G Street. There in her father's well-appointed dining room, she clinked champagne glasses and exchanged hugs with her father, her Aunt Lucy and her Uncle Charles.

Charles Forrest was a stockily built man in his early fifties with thinning black hair and a thick moustache that tickled Del's cheek when he awkwardly embraced her. Charles' preferred mode of communication was governed by the manly protocols of business. "Now then, my dear," he insisted as they sat down at the table Ruby had prepared for their midnight repast, "you must tell us all about your first semester at Mount Saint Joseph's."

"Shame on you, Charles," Lucy scolded. "If you read the many letters Del has sent us you would already know!"

"My dear Lucy," he replied condescendingly, "I acknowledge I have relied too much on you to apprise me of the content of Adelaide's letters." Then, turning to Del, he said, "Please forgive me, my child. Your uncle is a very busy man. Besides, I would much rather hear about it from your own pretty lips."

Del and Lucy exchanged knowing glances. "Thank you for asking, Uncle Charles," Del replied, deliberately ignoring her uncle's heavy-handed flattery. "It's a very beautiful campus and the instructors are all very bright. I'm especially enjoying my courses on literature and philosophy. We're studying the works of John Henry Newman and G. K. Chesterton. What clever men they are!"

"Indeed." Charles' comment was enigmatic. Though he had heard of these British authors, he had never read any of their books. He was much more interested in learning about Del's social contacts. "And what do you think of your Uncle Ward and your Aunt Chloe?" Ward Forrest was Charles' younger brother, a prominent Philadelphia attorney whose wife Chloe had taken it upon herself to be Del's surrogate parent while she was on the East Coast. Charles' own opinion of Chloe was that she was a frivolous eccentric—an opinion he hoped his niece would now corroborate.

"Oh! Aunt Chloe! I love her! She's such fun, and she's introduced me to all sorts of fascinating people!"

"I see." Charles grimaced. "And what sorts of people might *they* be?" This question evoked another stern look from his wife.

"Artists and musicians and writers. Many are *very* famous!" Del declared. "I even met the prima ballerina Anna Pavlova! They all come to her salon in Rittenhouse Square on Sunday afternoons."

"And what about your Uncle Ward? Has he introduced you to any of *his* friends and acquaintances? He too knows a great many influential people, you know."

"Really, Charles!" Lucy declared irritably. "Let the poor girl talk. You can't expect her to be interested in a bunch of stuffy old bankers and lawyers!"

"I would remind you, dear sister, that *I* am a lawyer and Charles is, in a sense, a banker!"

Lucy rolled her eyes. "Oh Clyde! Don't be ridiculous! You know perfectly well what I mean. Adelaide is a young lady. It's only natural she should be more interested in arts and letters."

"It is my intent," Clyde soberly announced, "that Adelaide should broaden her horizons as much as possible. That, after all, is the definition of a liberal education."

"Oh please don't argue!" Del protested. "Aunt Chloe and Uncle Ward have both been very kind! They've gone out of their way to make me feel at home with *all* of their friends. They've taken me to concerts at the Academy and all sorts of museums and wonderful restaurants in Philadelphia. I'm ever so grateful!"

"There, boys!" Lucy affirmed. "You have your answer! You haven't the least thing to worry about. Now, then, let's have some of Ruby's delicious herring."

* * *

"Things 're not going well," Roach said to Soames as the two men sat together in the lobby of the Fairmont Hotel that afternoon in February. "This fella Lanham's makin' a lot o' trouble. You seen the reports in the papers. We gotta stop that son-of-a-bitch!"

Soames exhaled a thin column of cigarette smoke from his lips. "So what do you want to do, Howard?"

Roach glared at Soames. "You know what we gotta do!"

"You're talking about assassination, Howard? That's pretty radical, isn't it?" Soames taunted.

"Of course not!" Roach snorted. "That would be stupid! It'd make Lanham a damn martyr for the Democrats. I'm thinkin' suicide. Or, anyway, somethin' that *looks* like suicide."

"The Judge is a Republican, Howard. But he's squeaky clean with the rank and file—both Democrats and Republicans. To make it look like suicide, you'll have to dig up some dirt on him first—something really nasty the newspapers 'll latch onto."

Sucking vigorously on his cigar, Roach smiled and, leaning forward, blew a thick cloud of smoke directly at Soames. "Now you're talkin' my kind o' language!" he declared exuberantly.

Soames coughed and waved smoke from his face. "Jesus, Howard! Blow your stogie someplace else!"

Howard chuckled. "Sure, Jimmy. Sorry about that," he added, though his apology was anything but sincere. Blowing cigar smoke in people's faces was one of Roach's favorite ways of getting their attention. "How 'bout women? Lanham's a bachelor. He's bound t' have nookie stashed away someplace."

Soames shook his head. "Like I said, Howie. He's a regular Boy Scout."

"How do you know?"

"I got somebody workin' on it. One of the best snoops in the bus'ness. He's been rootin' around for months. So far, he's come up completely empty-handed."

"Maybe the Judge likes boys," Roach suggested, inspired by his own ambivalent predilections.

"Nuh-uh. We gotta make somethin' up. Maybe bribe one of the clerks that works for him in San Francisco. Get her to plant some papers in his office files. Make it look like he's on the take."

"Good idea, Jimmy! So go do it, and do it quick!" Roach snarled. "We ain't got much time left. This judges' panel thing's comin' up for a vote in the Assembly next month! You know anybody at *The Examiner* who'll write it up for us?"

"Yeah. I know a fella. But he don't come cheap."

"Don't worry about that," Roach said, crushing the stub of his cigar in an ashtray beside his chair. "Just make sure he does it."

"How about the follow-up? You want me to handle that too, right?"

"What d' y' got in mind?" Roach asked cautiously.

"Soon as the news hits the papers, some o' my boys 'll pay the judge a visit one night while he's home alone. His daughter's away at college now and his housekeeper takes off most weekends," Soames explained. "Should be easy to make it look like a suicide."

"How do you know all that?" Roach was genuinely surprised by Soames' thoroughness.

"We been watchin' him. Ain't that what you wanted?"

"Well, yeah sure. But who you gonna get to do the job?"

"Baby Face 'll handle it."

"You sure?"

"Like I told y' before, Howie. That guy's a pro. Best in the business!"

Roach stood up. "Alright, then. Do it, but be sure you let me know ahead o' time. I don't like no surprises."

Their meeting over, the two men left the hotel.

* * *

By what presumption do we pathetic mortals boast there is a God who loves and cares for us? The universe is much bigger than that—millions of stars in billions of galaxies engulf and diminish us. Time, beyond our puny half-witted perceptions, does not exist. Immortality is but an illusion of the human ego, a fabrication our conscious minds use to disguise the all-consuming fear in our primitive brains— the only true source of our "higher" thoughts.

What, after all, is the origin of such "higher thoughts"? Is it not simply a product of natural selection? Through some freakish biological mutation, we humans developed a large skull that allowed the cortex of our brains to swell and thus provide us with a larger capacity for memory. It is our memory that enables us to recall the events of the past and thus hypothesize the idea of conscience. Other animals do not do this. Some freakish mutation has also caused our eyes to move forward and closer together in our skulls, thus giving us depth of perception—a capacity that prompted us to hypothesize the illusion of infinite time and space. But time does not exist. There is no heaven or earth; there is only now. All other species know this—or, rather. sense it. It is completely instinctive!

History is but the chronicle of rank and repetitive human stupidity. From time immemorial, we men have murdered each other over the charred and broken refuse of natural and man-made disasters. Desperately, generation after generation, we have fought the same war for survival. Generation after generation, we have learned nothing from it. Were there some divine order to any of this, our progeny would learn from us. But they never do. Instead, we all and always move swiftly and ineluctably to our own oblivion. We are but lemmings, and God is not.

As she read these words in the thick book she had found the day before in the ship's library, Del felt the dark depression of her father's death coming over her like a lava-flow of blood. Desperate to escape this feeling, she looked out at the bleak sky looming above the surface of the ocean. Its appalling emptiness stretched as far as the eye could see.

What horrors lurk beneath that surface? she asked herself. *Is there really no heaven—no mercy—in the universe after all?*

Del was completely alone in her recliner chair on the promenade deck. A blustery wind that morning had kept all the other passengers inside. She had wanted it that way. She had needed to be alone like this ever since the *Olympic* had left the New York harbor three days before. Her Aunt Lucy had desperately tried to keep Del busy with the many activities and diversions available aboard this enormous luxury liner—sending her to ballroom dancing classes, playing shuffleboard and paddle ball, attending lectures, listening to the quartet play waltzes and popular tunes from the latest Broadway musicals. But it was only solitude Del craved—to be alone with her darkest thoughts. Her Aunt and Uncle—poor dear and optimistic souls!—could never have understood the depth of her despair.

Suddenly Del felt a silent presence close at hand. Looking up, she saw a tall man with a thin mustache and goatee standing beside her chair. He said nothing. He simply stood there looking down at her. His gaze was full of sadness, as if he were reading her thoughts. When at last he spoke, it was in the gentlest of tones. "Are you enjoying your book?"

Del laughed nervously, feeling a sense of disappointment and even resentment at this question. Obviously the stranger had no idea what she had been thinking and feeling. Focusing her thoughts and not wishing to be impolite, she said, "It's not really that kind of book." She paused, struggling to find the words she needed to explain. "It's not a book anyone can enjoy, I mean."

"May I see the title?" the stranger asked, sitting down in the deck chair next to hers.

Suspicious now, Del simply raised her book up so that its title—*On Being Nothing*—would be visible to this stranger.

"Ah yes," the man said with a nod. "Sir Charles Sprague—a cynical and very depressing writer. Tell me, my dear," he said with a smile. "Why do you read such a book? You are young and beautiful. You are on a magnificent ship with many beautiful people. You should be happy." He spoke slowly and carefully, revealing that English was not his native tongue. His accent sounded distinctly European—probably Swiss or French.

Del thought carefully before she answered. She was not sure she wanted to continue this conversation. It was becoming much too quickly intimate and personal. "I found it in the ship's library," she said. "It's interesting—different from anything I've ever read before" she added, hoping this comment would discourage further questions. Couldn't this intruder see she wanted to be alone?

The man was not to be dissuaded, however. He lay back on his deck chair and, pulling his overcoat around himself, made it clear that he was settling in. For several minutes, he said nothing.

Satisfied that this was the best she could expect, Del continued reading. She had difficulty concentrating, however. Though wary of this interlocutor, she felt the need to identify him better—at least to get a name so that she could report this encounter to her Aunt Lucy. After all, her aunt had sternly cautioned her against speaking with strangers during this voyage. "May I ask your name, sir?"

"But of course," he said, rising from his chair and standing up to make a curt bow. "My name is Alain Courant. I hope you will forgive me for not introducing myself at the outset, my dear. But, you seemed so preoccupied with your thoughts that I did not wish to intrude."

"Oh, Monsiuer Courant!" Del exclaimed, leaping to her feet. "It's an honor to meet you, sir—such a famous author!" Del had never read any of Courant's books, but she had heard much about them. The teaching Sisters at Mount Saint Joseph's College had often praised him as a great contemporary Catholic writer.

"The honor, my dear, is all mine," he assured her with a warm smile. "And now—may ask you to tell me your name?"

Del blushed with embarrassment. "Of course! My name is Adelaide Lanham." She startled herself in using the old-fashioned name her father had given her. At the same time, though, for the first time in her life she felt proud of that name. She realized that, in its very utterance, she had bestowed dignity on herself—a dignity, she suddenly understood, that her father had always wanted her to have.

"That is a very beautiful name," Courant said, taking hold of Del's right hand and kissing it in a gesture of Old World gallantry that startled her. "Most suitable for such a beautiful young lady," he added. There was no flattery in this remark. It was made as a simple statement of fact.

Del was overwhelmed with gratitude and a sense of calm self-confidence she had not experienced in weeks—ever since she first learned of her father's ignominious death. "Thank you." Del sat down on her deck chair again. "You have no idea how much I needed that."

"Ah, but you see, I have a daughter of my own." Courant smiled. "Though she is younger than you, she has taught me much."

"Please sit down, sir." Del gestured at the chair next to her. Gazing out at the ocean again, another wave of sorrow swept over her.

For a long time Courant sat beside her in silence, his own gaze also fixed on the bleak seascape. "You are very sad," he said at last. "Would you like to talk about your sadness?"

"My father committed suicide three weeks ago," Del said without looking at him.

Courant remained silent. Both of them now were listening only to the sounds of the ocean waves and the constant hum of the giant ship's engines propelling them eastward across the Atlantic.

Del was grateful for his silence. How unlike the fawning and intrusive solicitousness of her aunt and uncle and of so many of her friends! They seemed determined not to let her grieve.

It was Del who spoke first. "Are you writing a book now?" she asked.

"I am," Courant replied. "Actually, I am working on two books. One is about a country priest whom I knew when I was a child. He was a very humble and holy man. Like you, he was also very sad."

"Why was he sad?"

"He was sad because he had grown tired of his life's work," Courant explained. His parishioners and their petty vanities bored him. He no longer saw any purpose to his vocation."

"Did he leave the priesthood?" Del asked somewhat fearfully.

"Ah no! He knew he was being tested, as all of us are tested all of our lives."

Startled by this observation, Del looked around at her new friend. "What do you mean? I don't understand."

Courant reached inside his overcoat and pulled out a small black book from which he extracted a paper bookmark. Handing this to Del, he said, "Perhaps this will help you to understand." Then, glancing at his pocket watch, he stood up. "I must go now, for I have promised to meet some friends in the gymnasium. I'm sure we shall see each other again."

"I hope so, sir." Del did not want him to leave. She took the bookmark and, looking at it closely, realized it was also a prayer card. "Thank you for this," she said.

"You are most welcome, my dear. Goodbye for now, then." Briskly, Courant walked away from her toward the stern of the boat and at last disappeared through a doorway.

Del watched him go and then read the words printed on the bookmark. They were from Psalm 34:

> *Magnify the Lord with me;*
> *Let us exalt his name together.*
> *I sought the Lord, who answered me,*
> *Delivered me from all my fears.*
> *Look to God that you may be radiant with joy*
> *And your faces may not blush with shame.*
> *In my misfortune I called,*
> *The Lord heard and saved me from all distress.*
> *The angel of the Lord, who encamps with them,*
> *delivers all who fear God.*
> *Learn to savor how good the Lord is;*
> *Happy are those who take refuge in him.*

After she had read these words once, Del read them again. Then, with her eyes closed, she listened again to the sounds of the ocean and the ship. Inexplicably, she felt comforted. She hoped one day she would be able to read Courant's book about the country priest.

* * *

With its dark oak-paneled walls and damask draped windows rising two decks to a white plaster ceiling from which were suspended a dozen crystal chandeliers, the first class dining room aboard the *Olympic* was as intimate and elegant as that of an 18th Century English castle. Thick carpeting muffled every sound the tuxedoed attendants made as they moved among the tables like devout votives in a chapel. Each white linen covered table was round and set with sterling silver utensils and clear crystal glasses to accommodate a maximum of only six guests. In the center of each table was a small bouquet of orchids surrounding a lighted candle floating in a glass bowl.

All of these details captured Del's attention for the first time as she entered the dining room with her aunt and uncle that evening. Though they had dined there together every one of the three nights since they first boarded the *Olympic* in New York, until now Del had been oblivious to her surroundings aboard ship. Her thoughts had been only of the dark horror of her father's sudden and inexplicable death.

"Good evening, Mister and Missus Forrest and Miss Lanham!" the *maitre di* murmured cordially as they approached the dais upon which he stood waiting for them. "I understand you will be dining with Monsieur Courant this evening, is that correct?"

"Yes," Charles replied unenthusiastically. Though both Del and her Aunt Lucy had been thrilled by the world-famous author's invitation to join him for dinner, Charles was suspicious of the man's motives. Artists and writers Charles Forrest had always regarded as cultural parasites.

The *maitre di* nodded deferentially. "Follow me, please." As he led this party across the dining room, a string quartet on the small balcony above the entrance began playing a Strauss waltz. Looking around the room, Del noted that none of the diners already seated seemed to notice this lovely melodic intrusion. They were much too preoccupied with their own conversations and gustatory raptures.

Del understood this preoccupation, but she was startled when she saw that Alain Courant was not alone at his table. A very attractive and fashionably dressed woman was seated beside him, her slim figure bent attentively toward him as they conversed. Del immediately wondered if this woman were his wife or only a traveling companion.

"Ah, Miss Lanham!" Alain declared, rising to his feet and smiling warmly at Del. Then, turning to her aunt and uncle, he said, "And I take it you are Mister and Missus Forrest?" In response to Charles' curt nod, Courant bowed courteously. "Delighted to meet you both! Allow me to introduce you to my editor, Madam Aimee Dupree."

Closer to this woman now, Del realized that Madam Dupree was elderly—the lines in her face and neck indicating that she was probably at least in her late fifties. Suddenly Del felt more at ease, for she assumed that surely this woman could not be Courant's mistress.

At nineteen, Del had already read *Anna Karenina* and *Madame Bovary*, so she was aware of the difference between American and European views on adultery. What she was not yet aware of, however, was how little age differences have to do with romance, at least for Europeans. It was a topic that neither the faculty at Mount Saint Joseph's College nor her very worldly-wise Aunt Chloe had been willing to discuss.

As soon as Del and her aunt and uncle were seated, Courant asked for their preferences in wine. When this question evoked no immediate response, he said, "May I suggest the Chateau Margaux. Nineteen twenty-nine has been an especially excellent year for this varietal."

"Of course, Monsieur Courant," Lucy promptly replied. "I'm sure you are much better judge of such matters than we Americans."

"You are too modest, madam," Courant replied. "I understand that some of your California wines are quite remarkable, though I've never sampled them."

"Most of our grapes are from Italy," Charles said disparagingly. "I'm afraid it's an infant industry in America. We still have much to learn from you Europeans."

At this point, the sommelier approached their table and solicited their order. Their assigned *chef du range* then distributed the folio-sized menus. Copies of the menu had already been delivered to Del and her aunt and uncle's cabins earlier that afternoon so that they could consider in advance what dishes they would choose for each course. Such advanced decision-making was preferable because many of the main course dishes were prepared tableside.

Soon after her first encounter with Alain Courant, Del had swum several laps in the ship's pool—an exercise that so refreshed her and whetted her appetite that she studied the dinner menu in her cabin with relish. She had decided on smoked chicken with Oriental salad for her appetizer, Risotto Primavera for her main course, and chocolate soufflé for dessert.

"Good heavens!" her Aunt Lucy scolded when Del gave her order to the *chef du range*. "How could you possibly pick Chinese chicken salad and Rissoto with all these other wonderful delicacies to choose from!"

"But Aunt Lucy, I love Chinese and Italian food—just like Papa." Her own words cut through Del like a knife. Lucy, realizing this, said nothing. Instead, she grasped Del's hand under the table and squeezed it in a desperate attempt to console her.

"And you, madam?" the *chef du range* asked Lucy. Before she answered, Lucy checked to be sure Del had not broken into tears. Though her face was pale and her lips trembling, Del managed to repress her grief. "As an appetizer, I'll have the Lobster Veloute and the Russian salad, please. The Sea Bass brushed with tapenade will be perfect as a main course. I think I shall wait to decide on dessert."

Nodding, the *chef du range* moved on to take the others' orders—a procedure that required several minutes, especially because Charles and Lucy became involved in an altercation when Charles ordered Steak Diane for the third night in succession. Lucy scolded him for having such tediously bourgeois taste. In the meantime, Del concentrated on the soothing effects of the Bach partite the orchestra was performing.

By the time the main course had been served, everyone was relaxed and engaged in animated conversation, mostly about the delicious food they were eating though this topic sometimes led into such other subjects as travel and international politics. It was Charles who first brought up the latter. "So what do you think of Young's plan to reduce German reparations payments, Mister Courant?"

"It is an outrage!" Madam Dupree declared, startling Charles with her unladylike intrusion. "The Germans need to make full restitution. Your Mister Young should stay out of it!"

Courant smiled benignly. "Ah my dear Aimee! She has very strong feelings on this matter. You must pardon her. Her husband was killed in the Great War, you see."

"Do not patronize me, Alain!" Dupree retorted. "The Huns have always been bellicose. If we reduce reparations, they will only rebuild their war machine and attack us again."

"You may be right," Charles cautiously agreed. "I have dealt with their bankers on many occasions and found them to be very shrewd business men."

"Treacherous, you mean!" Aimee affirmed, her hazel eyes flashing with anger.

"So tell us about your itinerary, Mister and Missus Forrest," Courant suggested in an effort to change the subject. "Will you be spending some time in France?"

"Oh yes," Lucy replied, grateful for Courant's intervention. "We will spend a week in Paris, of course, and then on to Lourdes and Chartres."

"I have a very good friend who is a priest at Notre Dame. If you like, I will give you his name. I know he would be delighted to give you a guided tour of the cathedral."

"That would be wonderful!" Lucy said.

"I hope he speaks English," Charles put in.

Courant smiled indulgently. "Ah yes. Father Paul is fluent in several languages, including English." Reaching inside his dinner jacket, Courant extracted a fountain pen and his calling card. "I shall write his name and address on the back of my card for you. Please give him my best regards when you see him."

* * *

Later that evening Del strolled with Alain Courant on the promenade deck, with Lucy and Charles following several paces behind them. Lucy was determined to chaperone Del but she did not want to seem intrusive in this endeavor. Unconcerned, Charles was satisfied simply to smoke his nightly cigar. Madam Dupree had declined to join them, announcing after dinner that she preferred to play cards in the ship's casino.

"Why is Madam Dupree so angry and vengeful?" Del asked Courant.

Courant nodded solemnly. "Yes. I understand why you would think that, my dear. But, like you, she is grieving. Anger is often a part of grief. Sadly, she has not yet gotten beyond that, even though more than ten years have passed since her husband's death. But I assure you, she is a good woman and a great help to me in my work—the very best of editors."

"I'm sorry, Monsieur Courant. I did not mean to be insensitive. I too am still very angry. I cannot believe my father would kill himself and I don't believe the terrible things the newspapers have said about him. They have charged him with taking bribes. I *know* my father would never do such a dreadful thing!"

Courant stopped walking suddenly and looked at Del in astonishment. "Your father was in politics?" he asked.

"No. He was a judge—a member of the Ninth District Court."

"Indeed!" Courant was impressed. "He must have been a very remarkable man."

"He was!" Del declared vehemently. "Everyone respected him—everyone but the newspapers!"

"Perhaps he had a few detractors," Courant said grimly. "Honorable men often do." They resumed walking. Both were silent for several minutes. At last, Courant said, "I am not very familiar with domestic American politics. Was there some political issue on which your father had strong opinions?"

Del did not answer his question immediately because she herself was not entirely clear about the political issues in California. "I was away at college when all of this happened," Del explained. "But I do remember, before I left for college last fall, there were several articles in the *San Francisco Examiner* about some new law the Republicans were trying to push through the California State Assembly. I think it had to do with the appointment of judges to redefine voting districts. Papa was very opposed to this. He said it would not be fair to the people who live in southern California, and he was quoted in the newspapers for expressing his opposition. Even though he's a Republican, Uncle Charles says Papa was right."

"Clearly your father was a man of considerable integrity and courage." After pondering his own words, Courant said. "You said your father is alleged to have committed suicide. I hope you don't mind my probing, Adelaide. But was your father home alone when this happened?"

"Yes," Del replied. "Our live-in housekeeper Missus Hicks was off for the weekend." For the first time, Del realized the significance of this fact.

What Courant said next brought it into focus. "I am afraid, my dear, there may have been foul play here. Has there been any kind of investigation following your father's death?"

"No," Del answered. "I don't think so anyway. Do you think there should be, Monsieur Courant?"

"Please, Adelaide! Call me Alain. You are not a child. You a very bright young woman and we are friends." Smiling confidently, he added, "Equals, I hope! As for my answer to your question—most certainly there *should* be an investigation. What do your Aunt and Uncle think?"

"Aunt Lucy hasn't talked about it. She's been terribly distressed by it and has been doing everything she can to hide her feelings on my account. But Uncle Charles is infuriated. He says all the politicians in California are corrupt. He doubts anything will be done."

Again, Courant paused momentarily before he spoke. "You must not become discouraged, my dear. These things often take time. Justice will prevail."

"Do you really think so?" Del asked, suddenly unable to control her tears.

Courant wanted to touch Del's shoulder to comfort her. Knowing her watchful aunt and uncle might misconstrue such a gesture, however, he resisted this impulse. Instead, he offered her the scented linen handkerchief tucked in the breast pocket of his dinner jacket and gently asked, "Did you read the prayer card I gave you this morning?"

"Thank you, sir," Del replied as she dabbed her cheeks with his handkerchief. "It really did help, but sometimes it's very hard to believe God is merciful."

"A bit less of Charles Sprague and a bit more of vigorous daily exercise might help, my dear," Courant advised with a smile. "Tomorrow morning at 7:00, why don't you join me here on the promenade deck for a good brisk walk?"

Del looked up into this tall man's bearded face, caught now in light from one of the large windows in the ship's casino. It was a calm and gentle face, like that of the image of Christ on the prayer card he had given her. She knew this was a man she could trust, and so it was agreed. Every morning at 7:00 for the remainder of the cruise, Del and Courant would meet to walk three full circuits of the promenade deck and afterwards eat a hardy breakfast together in the second-class dining room.

On one such occasion, Del posed a question to her new confidant. "I've been thinking about what I'll do when I return to California. Do you think I should stay there and not return to Mount Saint Joseph's next semester?"

"Why would you want to do that?"

"Because of Ruby, our housekeeper. She will be all by herself while I'm away. She's getting old and I'm worried about what might happen if she gets sick. My father's estate attorney says I should sell the house and move in with my aunt and uncle in Santa Barbara until I finish college.

But I don't feel right about that. Poor Ruby would have to move in with her relatives in Vallejo, and they are very poor."

"It is good of you to care for your old friend, Adelaide," Courant said. "But I hope you won't give up your studies. Is there a college or university near your home town in California?"

"Well, there's Mills College in Oakland and the University of California campus in Berkeley," Del said. "I could probably apply for admission to either of those."

"Are they Catholic institutions?" Courant asked. "Somehow, from what you have told me about your father, I suspect he would want you to complete your undergraduate studies at a Catholic college."

Instinctively, Del felt for the Sacred Heart medal she had worn around her neck since she was confirmed at Saint Dominic's Church ten years before. "You're probably right, Alain. There is Saint Mary's College in Moraga. Actually, that's a little closer to Benicia than Oakland or Berkeley. Perhaps I should apply there."

"Aha! You see?" Courant smiled. "You have answered your own question!"

Chapter Twenty-eight

"Singing in the Rain"

Since it was 3:30 on a Friday afternoon, the Bank of Italy had closed. While the tellers emptied the registers and tallied up the transactions processed that day, bank president George Woolsey conferred with his floor supervisor Chester Bollinger. A short, bald-headed man in his early thirties, Bollinger nodded repeatedly as George reviewed the names of customers who had made large deposits or withdrawals during the past week. One of the customers who had made an especially large withdrawal—nearly $5,000—was Mrs. "K. T." Parker, owner and proprietor of the Lido.

"Did Missus Parker give you any idea of what she was planning to do with all that cash, Chester?" Woolsey asked.

"No, sir, she did not," Bollinger replied, nodding and speaking as softly so none of the tellers might overhear his answer.

"What denomination were the bills?" Woolsey asked, not in the least bit concerned about being overheard.

"All one hundreds, sir. She asked that they be wrapped in separate packets of $1,000 each."

Woolsey looked worried. "Very unusual, don't you think?" he asked without really expecting Bollinger to reply.

"Yes, sir," Bollinger nodded. "Very unusual indeed."

"Perhaps we should inform the Mayor," Woolsey said.

"Yes, sir," Bollinger murmured compliantly, though he very much disagreed with his boss. He knew the man was an inveterate busybody with a downright prurient interest in Mrs. Parker's business dealings.

The low rumble of an automobile engine outside suddenly distracted Woolsey and he walked across the lobby toward one of the large glass windows facing First Street. As usual, the Venetian blinds in these windows had been drawn at precisely 3:00 P.M. Woolsey lifted one of the slats and peered into the street.

"Come over here and look at this, Chester" he called out.

Glancing around nervously, Bollinger noticed that several of the tellers were now watching them. Swiftly, he moved to Woolsey's side. "The tellers, sir!" he gasped.

"Never mind that!" Woolsey barked in a loud voice. "Now we know what that Parker woman's up to."

What the two men saw was a black limousine pulled up at the curb in front of the police station on the opposite side of the street. Standing on the driver's side of this vehicle was Police Chief Pisciotta in his uniform, featuring the wide-brimmed white cowboy hat made popular in the 1920s movie star Tom Mix. Pisciotta was leaning down talking with the woman driver, one cowboy booted foot propped on the running board. Because Pisciotta's hat blocked their view, Woolsey and Bollinger could not see her face.

"That's Parker!" Woolsey rasped. "And look at that! She's giving him a package!"

"You think it could be some of that money she withdrew this week?" Bollinger asked breathlessly.

"You're darn right!" Woolsey declared.

"Guess we better not tell the Mayor, then," Bollinger suggested.

"Guess not," Woolsey admitted, shaking his head in disgust and marching back to his office.

* * *

Adam had asked Jack and Francis to meet him at the Pastime on First Street that rainy April afternoon. Because it was Saturday, there were no parking spaces on First, H and I streets, so Jack had to park his car in front of St. Paul's rectory on East J and run several blocks through the heavy downpour. Annoyed with himself for forgetting to bring an umbrella, Jack was soaked by the time he reached the back entrance. As he opened the door and stepped into the dimly lighted and smoke-filled card room, he wondered why Adam had chosen this place for his meeting after he had so long avoided visits to Benicia.

Jack did not realize customer policies had changed radically since Joe Paterno owned the Pastime in the early 1920s. Now under new management, the popular bar and card room no longer refused service to Negroes and Orientals. Though he was a distant cousin of Paterno, the new owner Rick Lusardi welcomed everybody's business. Five years of uninterrupted prosperity had opened up Benicia's bars and brothels to just about anybody with loose change in his pocket.

It was not that the demographics of the town had changed. Benicia was still divided West and East between the rich and the poor and north and south between the righteous and the lawless. But racial and ethnic diversity had long been a characteristic of Benicia's transient population. The Chinese had first come in 1879 as "gandy dancers" when the Southern Pacific routed its main line through Benicia. Many of them had been fisherman in their country of origin, so they and their children continued to fish for and sell carp and striped bass to the Benicia canneries. In 1900, several started a Chinese lottery at the Washington Hotel on the corner of First and D Streets. Negro porters working on the many passenger trains that stopped daily in Benicia regularly patronized the Washington Hotel. They had always been welcome customers at Harry Gee's Public Café on First Street.

The only faces Jack recognized when he entered the Pastime now were those of Adam and Francis. Four other men sat with them at one of the round card tables—two Negroes and two Orientals. All were engaged in animated conversation, smoking cigarettes and drinking mugs of beer. The only other customers in the place were five Southern Pacific yard workers playing pinochle several tables away. Completely absorbed in their game, they ignored Adam's party.

Looking up, Adam shoved an empty chair away from the table with his foot. "Sit down, Jack," he said perfunctorily. The other men immediately stopped talking and stared at Jack. Even Francis' gaze seemed wary.

Turning first to a lean-faced Negro on his right, Adam said, "This here's Marvin Daniels." Marvin nodded curtly. "That fella in the suit an' tie is Hector Chan. Next to him's his brother-in-law Paul Lau. The big buck's Jimmy Whittaker. Boys, meet Jack Westlake. He keep the books. You get a new cus'mer, you tell Jack. You lose a cus'mer, you tell Jack. You get money from a cus'mer, you give it—*all* of it!—to Jack an' he give you back yo' cut. You got a problem, you tells *me*!"

Chan and Lau smiled slightly, but Daniels and Whittaker's faces hardened. Jack stared back at them, forcing himself to say, "Pleased to meet you."

A fat man wearing a soiled white apron entered the card room and approached Jack "What 're y' drinkin'?"

Jack gestured toward the others at the table. "Whatever they're having."

"Two bits," the fat man said, extending his open palm.

Jack handed him a dollar bill. "Here," he said. "Get me a couple of nickel cigars too."

The fat man nodded sullenly and returned to the bar.

"So what's this about?" Jack asked Adam. "Why are we meeting here instead of Vallejo?"

"We got new business here," Adam explained. "Four different places in town now—here, the Brewery, the Washington Hotel, and Frank's Place. I got my eye on Wink's an' Campy's too. Maybe even the Lido."

"You're going to solicit customers at the Lido?" Jack asked. "That's not a good idea, Adam. You know Parker's in cahoots with Pisciotta."

"Jack's got a point," Francis put in.

Adam was quick to respond. "This is a high stakes game, boys. We gotta take everythin' we can get. Fact, I'm thinkin' o' doin' some bus'ness over in Frisco too," he added defiantly. "They's big money in that town."

Francis exchanged quick glances with Jack. "That's Soames' home turf," Francis said. "Ain't we already got enough trouble with his thugs over here in the North Bay?"

"You gettin' cold feet?" Adam snarled at Francis. "Maybe you should go back to fixin' flats, boy."

Undeterred, Francis said, "We don't know nobody in Frisco, Adam. Besides, me and Jack ain't slick enough to deal over there."

"As a matter of fact, I know many people in the city," Hector put in. "So does Paul. We have many friends and relatives in Chinatown."

Adam glared at Francis and Jack. "There's your answer, boys! Hector here's a college man. He know what's what in Frisco. So don't you be worryin'."

"You went to college?" Jack asked Hector, registering surprise but already alerted by the man's neatly tailored suit and superior command of spoken English.

Hector smiled proudly. "Yes. I have a bachelor's degree in business from San Francisco State. I run my father's export/import operations as well as his several restaurants in the city."

Francis was not impressed. "How'd you get hooked up with us?" he asked.

"Through my cousin, Danny Wong. You're familiar with him, I presume?"

Francis looked at Adam. "The wise guy from China Camp?"

Adam nodded. "Chinks is all related to each other, one way or another."

Jack was troubled by this racist remark. It was unworthy of his old mentor. "What's that got to do with it?" he demanded.

Shaking his head in contempt, Adam lighted a cigarette. Then, leaning back in his chair, he studied Jack's face for several seconds while slowly releasing coils of smoke through his nostrils. "In this bus'ness, boy, you gotta have connections!"

"Maybe so, but Francis is right," Jack said. "We don't need to stir up any hornets' nests in San Francisco."

"You all makin' good money," Adam affirmed. "You do what I say, you make even more." Then, scowling at Francis and Jack, he asked, "So is you with us or is you ain't?"

"Depends on who's gonna run things in Frisco. Don't ask *me* to do it!" Francis declared emphatically.

"Not me either," said Jack.

"Hector's in charge of Frisco," Adam explained, visibly annoyed by their resistance. "Only thing you two gotta do is keep the record straight an' make sure the dope gets from China Camp to Frisco. Maybe help Hector get it to them fancy hotels where the white folks don' like niggers an' chinks."

Again, Francis and Jack exchanged glances. "What about Marvin and Jimmy?" Jack asked, focusing his eyes on the two Negro men. "What do they do?"

"Marvin and Jimmy's takin' over Vallejo and Oakland," Adam explained. "Guess you can figure out why," he added with a wink at Marvin.

The fat bartender returned with Jack's mug of beer and cigars. "Keep the change," Jack said off-handedly.

"Big spender, huh kid?" The bartender sniffed and walked away.

Jimmy Whittaker chuckled derisively. Jack shot him a warning look. A tall, muscular man in his forties, Jimmy had the bulging abdomen and sloping but powerful shoulders of a Samurai wrestler. His facial features, though, were small and childlike. It was as if Jimmy's body had grown and matured but his face had not. The man leered at Jack now, his small black eyes glittering defiance. *Go ahead, boy, make your move!* they seemed to say.

"You still ain't answered my question," Adam said grimly. "You boys with us or not?"

Jack knew he was taking a big risk in speaking so frankly, but he felt he had to. "You're moving too fast, Adam. Why not just stick with the customers we have? You said yourself we're already making good money. Why get greedy?"

"Everybody greedy," Marvin said. "You think white folks is the only ones got a right to be greedy?"

"Yeah. That what he think!" Jimmy insisted, ominously rolling his shoulders.

Adam raised his hook. "Hold on! Don't matter what Jack an' Francis think. I wanna know what they gonna *do*."

"I'm not sacrificing myself to a golden calf," Jack answered, surprising himself with his own biblical allusion. "But that's what you're asking us to do, Adam. Soames and his gang won't sit still for this. Neither will Parker."

"So you're scared," Adam said, stubbing out his cigarette in an already overflowing tin ashtray. "Tha's too bad, boy. Must've been that rich bitch you got mixed up with. I tol' you t' stay away from her."

"You were right about her," Jack admitted. "And I learned from the experience."

"What you learn, boy?" Adam taunted.

"I learned it's stupid to chase after things you can't have. All you wind up with in the end is big trouble."

"You got that right," Francis said, even though he could see Adam was now shaking with rage.

"May I make a suggestion?" Hector asked calmly.

Adam's anger shifted to Hector. "This got nothin' to do with you!"

"On the contrary, Adam, I believe it has everything to do with me—with all of us, in fact. You have worked with Francis and Jack for a long time. You have told me they are good men. Maybe we can work out some kind of compromise here."

Startled by Hector's intervention, Adam asked, "Wha' d' y' mean?"

"I already have many Caucasian business associates who can handle our deliveries to the hotels and men's clubs in San Francisco. Jack and Francis do not need to be involved with that end of the business. As for this local brothel owner—Parker I believe you said his name is?—we probably don't need his business. I'm sure the establishments in San Francisco have many more prosperous customers than he does."

"Parker's a woman," Jack corrected.

"All the more reason not to do business with her," Hector observed with a knowing smile. "Would you two gentlemen be willing simply to transport product from China Camp to our warehouse in San Francisco?"

Again, Francis and Jack exchanged glances. "Sure," Francis said, "long as we don't mess with the whores here in Benicia."

Adam smiled and winked at Jack. "There you go, boy—you're off the hook!"

Jack still didn't like Adam's plan to expand his business into San Francisco. He decided his best strategy, though, was to accept Hector's compromise—for the time being, at least. "You still want me to keep the books?" he asked Adam.

Adam glanced around at the others as he spoke. "That what you good at, boy, so that what you do. Now we got that set, s'pose you lay out the plan for Frisco, Hector."

"I'll be happy to," Hector said, stretching his neck and smiling around at everyone as if he were the keynote speaker at a political convention. "First, allow me to explain what may not be entirely clear to all of you. The commerce we envision between China Camp and San

Francisco is a two-way matter. In other words, the marijuana grown and cured in China Camp is to be sold to our customers in San Francisco as well, of course, as to your customers in the North and East Bay areas. At the same time, our cocaine-based products—mostly bottled and labeled in Hong Kong as cough medicines or cordials—are also to be sold to pharmacies and taverns throughout the Bay area."

"In other words, this is sort of a partnership between you and Adam. Is that it?" Jack asked.

"Not exactly," Hector gently corrected. "Each of our organizations remains a separate business entity, keeping total control of our respective production and pricing practices as well as our profit margins and the commissions we pay to our distributors."

"So, if you sell a pound o' weed to some fat cat in Frisco for $500 and we can only get $200 for the same pound in Oakland, we lose," Francis snarled.

"Ah no!" Hector assured Francis with an ingratiating smile. "Adam and I have worked out a very equitable plan for negotiating any profit disparities. Is that not so, Adam?"

Adam nodded. "Like I says, you got a problem, you tells me."

*   *   *

"I still don't like this," Jack said to Francis as the two of them left the Pastime half an hour later and headed toward their cars. The heavy rainfall earlier was now only a light drizzle.

"Me neither. This Hector fella's way too slick. He's pullin' one over on Adam for sure!"

"I can't believe Adam would let this happen. Do you think he's hiding something from us?"

"Who knows? Maybe he's got a deal goin' with those shades from Oakland too," Francis snarled. "One thing I *do* know, Jack. From now on, I'm packin'. You better do the same!"

"I have a better idea. I hear SP's planning to build a railroad bridge across the Strait from Bull's Head to Martinez. Maybe you and I could get a job working on that bridge."

"Where'd you hear that?" Francis asked.

"A friend of mine who works at the Port Costa switching yard.

He says SP's already got the plans drawn up and they're going to start driving pilings next month."

"Jesus! That's bad news for Benicia. But you're right. It could be good news for us. Your friend know who's doing the hiring at SP? It'd be nice to make an honest living for a change."

"I'll find out," Jack said.

CHAPTER TWENTY-NINE

"Mean to Me"

SOON AFTER JACK AND FRANCIS had joined the construction crew of the new railroad bridge in early May, Adam was hired as head mechanic at the Dodge Brothers dealership in Vallejo. Jimmy Whittaker and Marvin Daniels found work as ditch diggers for the Solano County Roads Department. Income from their day jobs, combined with the cash they earned selling hashish, made this core membership of Adam's gang wealthier than any of them had ever imagined possible.

Adam knew Jack and Francis were smart enough not to spend their money recklessly and draw unwanted attention to his gang. Jimmy and Marvin, though, he would have to watch. He decided the best way to keep everyone in line was for the five of them to live together. So on a clear Sunday afternoon in September of 1929, Adam assembled his four key henchmen and drove them out to an abandoned farmhouse in the hills northeast of Napa. As they stood in the gravel country road that dead-ended in front of the farmhouse, Adam explained the advantages of his plan.

"Ain't nobody lived here since the War and they ain't hardly anybody ever comes here now. Owner's an ol' timer name o' Randolph lives in Napa. Says he'll rent the place for fifty dollar a month. That be ten dollar a piece. You ain't gonna fin' nowhere cheaper 'n that."

Jimmy was the first to object. "What you wanna do this fo'? Place is a mess. Look at all them busted windows!" Glaring at Jack and Francis, he added angrily, "I ain't livin' with no damn white boys!"

"Me neither," Marvin echoed. "Sally won' like it neither." Sally was

Marvin's younger sister—a seventeen-year-old prostitute who shared lodgings with her brother and worked nights for her pimp on the streets of Vallejo.

"Don't matter what Sally like," Adam barked. "An' don' matter what *you* likes. You do what I says or I's cuttin' you out."

Realizing they had no part in this conversation, Jack and Francis wandered off to make a closer inspection of the old farmhouse and its outbuildings, which included a privy and a large hay barn. The wood siding of these dilapidated structures was warped and full of knotholes. The roof of the barn sagged in the middle, as did the roof over the porch in front of the house. A cylindrical pile of sandstone midway between the barn and the house indicated that the only source of water on the property was an open cistern.

"All the comforts of home!" Jack observed sardonically as he tried to turn the rusted crank used for lowering and raising the missing water bucket.

"Yeah. Ain't got electricity or telephone neither," Francis observed, suddenly remembering he had seen no utility poles along the road out of Napa. "Wonder if they got heat in this place."

"Let's go inside and find out," Jack suggested.

They climbed the rickety wooden steps up to the rear entrance of the house. When Jack lightly touched the outside latch, the door swung open, admitting them into a hallway that ended at the front entrance. Through the glass panes of the front door, they could see Adam on the porch fumbling with a set of keys to open a padlock. "Come around back," Francis shouted. "Door's open."

Minutes later the five men were standing in the kitchen, which was one of two large ground-floor rooms, the other being a parlor on the opposite side of the hallway. Against one wall of the kitchen stood an enormous iron wood stove, capped by a metal pipe connected to an opening in the brick facing of what once must have been a fireplace.

"Ain't got no chairs or tables or nothin'," Marvin declared in disgust. "How we s'pose' t' live in this dump?"

"Don't you be worryin'," Adam said confidently. "We make do. We's movin' in nex' week."

*   *   *

As usual, Adam had been right. Before the five men and Marvin's sister Sally moved into the farmhouse, he had managed to scrounge up used beds, chairs and tables at various rummage sales in Vallejo and Napa. For the next six months, they enjoyed complete anonymity in their remote country hideaway and the customer base for Adam's hashish distribution business grew rapidly throughout the North and East Bay areas.

By early December of 1929, Adam was completely out of the contraband booze business—a fact that he assumed had led Soames and his associates to think Adam's gang had disbanded.

Because of their different work schedules, the six co-habitants rarely saw each other except after work on weekdays when they all sat down at the kitchen table in the farmhouse to eat the meals Sally had agreed to prepare for them in exchange for her room and board and six ounce weekly allowance of hashish.

"You ain't cooked these chittlin's right!" Marvin complained as he sampled their evening fare one Friday night.

"I's in a hurry," Sally barked in a voice as shrill as a terrier's. "You wanna cook 'em more, do it yourself."

Like her brother, Sally had large, wide-set eyes that stared out at the world as if she were in a constant state of surprise. Her other facial features, though, were much more delicate than his. Her small mouth, drawn down at the corners in a perpetual pout, gave her a puckish look. Her coloring was almost Caucasian. She was, as her brother often proudly pointed out, a 'high yaller.' That and Sally's slender figure and long shapely legs made her a most desirable commodity on the streets of Vallejo.

In the short-skirted flapper dresses she regularly donned as the uniform of her trade, Jack thought Sally looked like one of the chorus girls in Busby Berkeley's *Whoopee!* Jack never expressed this opinion, however, for he knew it would prompt Marvin's wrath. Marvin had no problem with his sister's selling her charms to strangers as long as she was out of his sight. When she was in his company, though, he was her fiercest protector.

"Don't you be sassin' me, gal!" Marvin warned as he stood up from the table and carried his plate over to the stove where he scraped his undercooked chitterlings into the still hot frying pan.

Sally answered her brother with a sullen stare, then, flounced out of the kitchen to go upstairs and make final preparations for her night on the town.

"Guess she fix yo' wagon!" Jimmy sneered.

"I wants you all back here by midnight," Adam announced, abruptly changing the topic of discussion.

"Why's that?" Francis asked.

"Rumor's out Baby Face Nelson's in town. He's big trouble, so I wanna be ready case he decides t' pay us a visit. An' I wants you boys to work in pairs tonight."

"You mean me with Marvin, right?" Jimmy asked, eyeing Jack and Francis with open hostility.

Adam nodded, but he added, "We's all in this together. Nigger or not, Nelson 'll cut y' down. From now on, we's doin guard shifts here ever night."

Jack had read several recent newspaper reports about Baby Face Nelson. "I hear the FBI has issued an order for his capture dead or alive," Jack said.

"He's gonna be dead if I sees 'im," Jimmy boasted.

Adam glared at Jimmy. "You bes' hope you *don't* see him, fool!"

* * *

By August of 1929, construction of the new Southern Pacific railroad bridge connecting Bull's Head Point on the north side of the Carquinez Strait with Martinez on the south was well under way. All of the ten concrete supports for the bridge had been set in place. Giant crane-bearing barges had been anchored at the base of each support to begin work on the superstructure. Many Benicians were alarmed because the new bridge would re-rout all future train traffic from Cordelia to Martinez, completely bypassing Benicia. With both the Carquinez vehicular bridge and the newer railroad bridge in place, local business in Benicia would soon come to a standstill.

No longer would the depot at the waterfront end of First Street swarm with passengers forced to wait while their cars were moved on or off one of the ferries. No longer would Benicia be the principal shipping point for local farmers and fishermen. Only the Alta Manufacturing plant and the Benicia Arsenal on the east side of town were to be connected with Southern Pacific's main line by railroad spurs. Perhaps most worrisome to the town fathers was the inevitable loss of patrons at Benicia's many bars and brothels—enterprises that had been a major source of local government revenue for more than half a century.

One of the first businesses to be affected by news of this imminent change was the branch office of Ahern's Import/Export Company where Gail had been earning a modest but gradually increasing wage for the past ten years. Her boss Ira Jacobs had done everything in his power to induce her to remain on the job, even shaving his own salary increases to enhance Gail's. Though such a practice was not authorized and he had to "doctor" the monthly expense reports he sent to Ahern's central office in San Francisco, Ira had been willing to risk anything just to see Gail at her desk every weekday.

When Ira entered his office at 7:30 on the morning of October 4th—the first Monday of the month—he was startled to discover sitting at his desk a heavy-set man in a brown suit and matching bowler hat, smoking a cigar and casually leafing through a stack of cloth-bound ledgers Ira usually kept locked in a closet behind his desk. "Who are you?" Ira demanded angrily. "How'd you get in here?"

The man looked up and grinned, still clenching the cigar in his yellowed teeth. "You must be Ira Jacobs," he said. Then, glancing down at the opened ledger in front of him, he observed with undisguised sarcasm, "Interesting set o' books y' got here, mister."

Quickly surveying his office, Ira noticed that Gail's desk too had been violated, several of its drawers pulled open and the papers she had neatly stacked on top scattered haphazardly. Some had even been tossed on the floor. Outraged, Ira shouted at the intruder. "Who are you and what are you doing here?"

The stranger scowled and stood up, quickly removing the cigar from his mouth. "Take it easy, bud!" he warned. "You got some explainin' t' do 'bout these here books!"

"You still haven't answered *my* questions," Ira said resolutely. "Who are you and how'd you get into my office?"

Popping the cigar back in his mouth, the intruder sat down again. "Name's Blake Butterfield, private detective. Your boss give me the keys and told me to come check you out. So sit down, little man, an' listen up!"

"You mean Mister Livingston gave you the keys to this office? I don't believe you! I'm calling his office right now!" Ira reached for the candle phone on his desk.

Butterfield quickly grabbed it and pulled it away. "I said sit down, Jewboy!"

Not since he was a child had anyone made such a pejorative reference to Ira's Jewish heritage. He knew there was unspoken hostility in the reactions of some of his non-Jewish business associates, but overt anti-Semitism was rare in Benicia—a town whose long history of ethnic diversity made anti-semitism a non sequitur for most long-time residents. Trembling with rage and fear, Ira obeyed Butterfield's command and sat down on the bench he had placed in his office for visitors.

"Atta-boy!" Butterfield nodded. "Now, here's what you need to know. First off, looks to me like you been keepin' two sets o' books here." Butterfield gestured at a ledger and a check register that lay open on the desk in front of him. "Ledger shows you gettin' a weekly wage of forty dollars and your helper, this Westlake woman, gettin' eighteen. But your check register shows you're payin' her twenty-five an' payin' yourself only thirty-three. That ain't too smart, Ira. Your boss finds out, you could be in big trouble."

"What's the difference?" Ira asked, anger and resentment overcoming his fear. "Gail's a valuable employee. She's worth every penny. Besides, it's not costing the company anything 'cause her extra pay's coming out of my salary."

Butterfield shook his head in disgust. "You Hebes are all alike! But you're right, Ira. It don't matter much 'cause your boss is closin' this office down soon an' you an' your girlfriend'll be out o' work anyways."

"Why?" Ira demanded. "We have a thriving business here!"

"Guess you ain't been readin' the papers lately, have y', Jewboy? Ain't you heard about all the banks closin' around the country? And what do you think's gonna happen once they open that new railroad bridge over there?" Butterfield gestured toward the East.

Ira was silent. For several months, he had in fact been following the bad economic news in the papers and on the radio with much apprehension. But he had been fearful of alarming Gail and his mother by showing his anxiety.

Butterfield smiled indulgently and stood up again. "Tell y' what, Ira. I'm gonna do you a big favor. Gimme fifty bucks an' I'll keep my mouth shut about you're tryin' t' cook y'r books."

Outraged, Ira leaped to his feet. "You get out of my office now! I'm not giving you a nickel!"

Still smiling, Butterfield moved indolently toward the entrance door. "You'll be sorry, Jewboy. Once the word's out on you, you won't be able to get a job cleanin' latrines."

"Get out!"

Just as Butterfield opened the door, Gail appeared outside. Flashing a quick sardonic smile back at Ira, the man tipped his bowler at Gail and headed up the street.

"Who was that?" Gail asked as she entered the office. Then, seeing the desperate expression in Ira's face, she asked, "What's wrong?"

Ira had moved behind his desk and flopped down in his chair. Covering his face with his hands, he said, "They're closing the office."

Gail almost staggered from the shock of this announcement. "But why? What happened?"

Dropping his hands in his lap, Ira stared hopelessly at Gail. "I'm sorry, Gail! There's nothing I can do. Soon as SP opens their new bridge, Benicia's a ghost town. You and me—we're both gonna have to find new jobs."

"When are they closing the office? Who told you this?" Gail demanded, resorting to the controlled anger she always relied on to help her deal with crises.

"That goon in the brown suit. He's a private detective. Livingston hired him to check our books. He told me they're closing this office soon." Remembering Butterfield's parting threat, Ira added, "He didn't say exactly when, but it could be any day now."

"My God, Ira! That's dreadful! What will you do?"

Clasping his jaw in his right hand, Ira looked forlornly at Gail. "Right now, it's what *you'll* do that worries me most, Gail. At least mother and I own our house, and I can probably find some kind of work over at the Alta plant or at the refinery in Martinez. You know I'd invite you to move in with us, but mother would never allow that."

Gail removed her woolen shawl and draped it over the back of the chair at her desk, then busily began picking up the papers on the floor.

"Don't worry about me, Ira. I'll figure something out," she said, keeping her face averted so that Ira would not see her deep distress. Only two weeks before, she had broken off her relationship with Soames when she learned that he was conspiring with Baby Face Nelson to murder Tucker and every member of his gang, including her own son. Now completely on her own, she had no idea how she would manage to survive.

Ira got up from his desk and walked over to Gail where she stood leaning over her desk. He wanted to put his arms around her to reassure her, but he was terrified such familiarity would offend her. "I can lend you some money to tide you over for a while," he suggested. "A few hundred dollars if need be."

Gail turned to him and, taking his sad bullfrog face in her hands, brought it close to her own. Her eyes filled with tears as she kissed him gently on the cheek and murmured softly, "Ira, you're *such* a good man! I know you mean well. But I couldn't possibly accept that. You know, if your mother found out, she'd be terribly angry."

"I don't care!" Ira declared. "My mother is a cruel and wicked woman! I'm not afraid of her. I … I love you, Gail. I want to marry you!"

Still holding his face in her hands, Gail placed an index finger on his lips. "No Ira. That would never work. You are a dear, kind man. But I do not love you. I would never make you happy."

"Why not let me be the judge of that?" he pleaded.

"No," she repeated and stepped away from him. Pointing to the clutter on both of their desks, Gail smiled and said, "I think we should clean up this mess before a customer comes, don't you?"

"I meant what I said about the loan," Ira repeated firmly. "No strings attached either—no interest charge, no payment schedule, nothing!"

"Very well, Ira," Gail said. "I will consider your very generous offer, but only if it becomes absolutely necessary."

Realizing this was the best he could expect and feeling relieved that after so many years of hiding his true feelings for Gail he had at last summoned the courage to express them, Ira followed Gail's lead and began gathering up the books on his desk and storing them in the cabinets where they belonged.

* * *

Jack awoke suddenly in the middle of the night, his nostrils stinging with the odor of kerosene. In the bed next to him, Francis was snoring softly. Apart from this, the house was silent. Jack pushed back his covers and got out of bed. Fumbling for his trousers, he pulled them on and made his way to the bedroom window. He could hear a light rain falling but could see nothing in the pitch-black darkness outside. The smell of kerosene was even stronger now, seeping in through the open window.

Then he heard it—a soft rustling sound in the high grass that grew in the back yard of the farmhouse. Someone was out there, prowling around. Jack quickly returned to his bed and retrieved the revolver he always kept loaded under his pillow. Moving as quietly as he could toward the bedroom door, he carefully lifted the latch and stepped out into the second floor hallway. There he stood for several seconds listening. He could hear nothing but his own shallow breathing. He knew that, if he tried to walk downstairs, the warped wooden steps would creak under his weight and alert whoever might have entered the house.

As he approached the top landing, Jack could see the dim light of the lantern they kept illuminated every night in the kitchen for whoever had guard duty. Not sure what time it was, Jack did not know who was down there. Whoever it was, he must have fallen into a deep sleep. The smell of kerosene was now so strong that it would surely alarm anyone even partially awake.

Jack decided he had to risk being heard. He carefully moved down the stairs, placing his feet only on the outer edge of each step to minimize the creaking. When he reached the bottom step, he could see into the kitchen. Marvin was sprawled in a captain's chair at one end of the kitchen table, his eyes closed and his mouth wide open. On the table directly in front of him stood a half-filled bottle of whiskey.

"Wake up, Marvin!" Jack shouted as he swiftly moved to the front door. Sliding back the bolt, he yanked the door open and moved to one side, his gun at ready. Just then something heavy slammed against the side of the house, only a few feet from the door. Instantly, the entire front porch burst into flame. Jack leaped back, bumping into Marvin as he ran out into the hallway.

Jack fired several shots wildly into the wall of fire that now filled the open front doorway.

"What the hell!" Marvin shouted. "Wha' happen?"

His question was answered immediately by the sound of shattering wood and glass as someone outside raked the front of the house with machinegun fire.

"Get down!" Jack ordered, grabbing Marvin's arm and yanking him down onto the floor. "Follow me!" he shouted, as he scrambled toward the rear entrance of the house.

Already the entire first floor was filling with smoke as flames roared up the outside walls. Upstairs, the others were awake now. Sally was screaming hysterically as Francis and Adam scrambled for their guns and started firing wildly out of the second floor windows.

Their shots were answered with another stream of machinegun fire, this time aimed at the upper floor. Whoever was firing at them had moved around to the back of the house, evidently to block any attempt at escape.

Jack and Marvin were coughing violently. Jack realized both of them might soon be overcome with smoke. Rising to a crouch, he turned toward the front doorway again. If there were only one attacker, he might be able to get clear of the burning building, circle around it, and surprise the attacker from behind. If the machine gunner had accomplices, though, he would run into a hailstorm of bullets. It was a chance he would have to take.

Covering his face with his left hand, Jack lunged forward. Flames seared his bare feet and chest as he sprinted through the open door, across the burning floor of the porch, and dove into the steaming grass in the front yard.

When he jumped to his feet, a bullet whizzed past his shoulder. Looking up, Jack realized it had come from a window on the second floor. He dodged behind a tree trunk and waited for a few seconds to catch his breath. Then, he ran several yards farther into the darkness and began circling around toward the back of the house. As he did so, he saw someone leaning out of an upstairs window. It was Sally, screaming in terror. Someone was behind her, trying to push her through the window.

Another burst of machinegun fire raked the upper floor. Jack watched in horror as Sally's face exploded with blood and both she and the man behind her fell back into the smoke-filled bedroom. From another second floor window, someone was firing a pistol at random, his face obscured by thick smoke.

A flash of machinegun fire in the darkness about twenty yards behind the house revealed the location of their attacker. Jack swiftly moved in that direction, still hoping he could surprise the shooter. But whoever it was must have gone around to the front yard again. As Jack tried to follow, he heard a car door slam. An automobile's engine roared and its wheels spun in slippery mud and gravel as it sped away into the night.

"You hurt?" someone behind him asked in a hoarse voice.

Turning, Jack saw Francis and Adam standing directly behind him holding their guns, their naked bodies etched in black against the raging conflagration. Jack looked down, suddenly aware of the painful second-degree burns on the soles of his feet. "I'm OK," he said. "What about you?"

"We jumped out of our windows soon's we heard that car leave," Francis explained. Looking back at the house that was now totally engulfed in flames, he added, "Only problem is now we ain't got no clothes."

"Where's Marvin and Sally?" Adam asked.

"I'm afraid they're both dead," Jack answered, shaking his head. "I saw Sally get shot in the face and Marvin must've succumbed to the smoke. The last I saw of him was in the front hallway."

"What about Jimmy?" Francis asked.

"He was with Sally when she got shot. He probably caught it too."

Adam said nothing. Dropping his pistol on the ground, he covered his face with his hands. His shoulders were shaking, but there was no sound.

Francis and Jack looked at each other. This, they realized, was how Adam expressed his grief.

1930

The Bank of Italy

CHAPTER THIRTY

"Love for Sale"

O N JANUARY 5, 1930, IRA received formal notice that Ahern's branch office would close in two weeks. The notice had come as no surprise. After the devastating effects of the stock market crash three months before, he had expected it much sooner. That morning, he and Gail tried to keep busy filing papers and scouring customer account books for unpaid or overdue balances. For Ira, this search was mostly a way of trying to cover his distress.

When, by noon, neither the phone had wrung nor any customers entered the office, he stood up from his desk and walked across the office to stare out into the street. "I'm sick of this," he announced. "Let's close shop and go out for lunch. My treat. I have some business to do at the bank, as well, and I want you to come with me."

Gail was startled by both of these announcements. Never before had Ira offered to take Gail out for lunch, even after he had declared his love for her. As for Ira's inviting her to go to the bank with him—that was not just surprising to Gail. It was intimidating. Although she knew Ira trusted her to make accurate entries in the company ledgers and to keep all such records confidential, she had never been a witness to any of Ira's banking transactions. She couldn't help wondering whether Ira was about to do something rash such as embezzling company funds. If that were his intention, she wanted no part of it.

Realizing that Ira's invitation might simply be an expression of loneliness and despair, though, Gail accepted. "Thank you, Ira. I'd love to have lunch with you," she said amicably. "But are you sure you want to leave the office unattended? What if a customer comes? You know how people often *do* drop by during the lunch hour."

Still staring out into the street and irritably jingling the change in his pocket, Ira replied, "Don't see much traffic out there now, do you? Haven't all morning. We'll just hang a sign in the door telling them we'll be back at 1:00."

* * *

Ten minutes later, Gail and Ira were seated at one of the long tables in Marcelo Paz's "Working Man's Café." Paz, who had emmigrated from the Azores to Benicia in 1874 when he was twelve, had worked hard for years—first, as a janitor at the Washington House and, then, as a scraper at McClaren's Tannery. By the turn of the century, Paz had saved up enough money to purchase a storefront on First Street where he established his restaurant.

Having worked at the tannery himself, Paz understood the needs of the hundreds of single men who labored there for subsistence wages. By offering them "three squares for a dollar a day," Paz quickly won a faithful clientele. Though the tannery had long since ceased operations, the Working Man's Café remained a favorite of locals accustomed to cheap and hardy *sopas* served family style.

"How's bus'ness?" Ira asked Marcelo when the big-bellied man set their plates of sourdough bread, boiled onions and linguica in front of them.

"Is pretty good so far," Marcelo replied with a shrug. "When the train ferries stop, who knows? Maybe we go away." By *we* Marcelo meant himself and his wife and three children, all of whom lived in an apartment above his restaurant.

"Where will you go?" Ira asked.

Again Marcelo shrugged, his sad eyes and drooping black mustache accentuating the fatalism long since etched in the lines of his face. "Maybe we go to Petaluma. Raise chickens." Noting a fleeting glint in Marcelo's eyes, Gail realized his answer had not been serious. Never one to share personal matters with his customers, Marcelo was simply dodging Ira's question and giving himself an excuse to end the conversation.

"He's a cagey old bird," Ira observed as Marcelo headed back to his kitchen. "I've known him for almost thirty years, handled hundreds of shipping orders for the spices he uses. Not once in all that time has he given me a straight answer. Guess, like a lot of people in this town, he doesn't trust Jews."

"He's had a hard life. Perhaps he doesn't trust anyone," Gail suggested.

"That's too bad," Ira replied, though he thought Gail was wrong.

"Yes, it is." Gail heard the resentment in Ira's voice, but she was determined not to feed it with her own suspicions.

They ate their meal in silence, both finding ample entertainment in the constant bickering among the members of the large Portuguese family sitting at their table. When this noisy group suddenly leaped up from their benches and left the restaurant, Ira turned to Gail and said, "I guess you're wondering why I want you to come to the bank with me."

"It *is* a little unusual, Ira."

"I want to show you something so you'll feel better about borrowing money from me. I know you are a very proud woman, and I respect that. But don't you Christians believe people are supposed to help each other in times of need?"

"I'm afraid I'm not a very good Christian, Ira," Gail countered, annoyed that her boss should try to cloak his own ulterior motives in the garb of Christian charity.

Sensing her disapproval, Ira nodded and stood up to pay for their meal. This done, he gestured to her to follow him across the street to the Bank of Italy.

*   *   *

The eyes of every teller and customer were on them as they entered the bank lobby. The assistant bank manager, Chester Bollinger, immediately approached Ira with a solicitous greeting. "Ah, Mister Jacobs, how are you today? How may we help you, sir?"

"I need to get into my deposit box," Ira replied. His tone was abrupt, for he instinctively distrusted Bollinger.

"Certainly, sir. Right this way," Bollinger murmured, swiftly moving toward a partitioned area at the rear of the bank lobby where the vault was located. Signaling for one of the tellers to admit them to this inner sanctum, he stepped aside to allow Ira to enter first. When Ira motioned for Gail to follow, Bollinger looked startled. "Do you wish the lady to accompany you, sir?"

"Of course!" Ira barked. "This is Missus Westlake. She's my office assistant."

"Then, I'm afraid I shall have to ask her to sign your entry card as well, sir," Bollinger said, eyeing Gail suspiciously. "Bank policy, you know."

"Whatever!" Ira sniped as he signed and dated his card, then handed it to Gail for her signature.

Once he had completed all the necessary gatekeeper functions, Bollinger opened the thick steel door of the vault and guided them inside. "May I have your key please, Mister Jacobs?" he asked in a voice that was almost a whisper.

Gail watched all these apparently sacrosanct rituals with both astonishment and amusement. This was the first time in her life she had ever been inside the vault of a bank. The whole idea of anyone's having a bank safe deposit box was something she had only read about in novels and newspapers.

"Do you wish to use a private booth, sir?" Bollinger asked as he handed the long, narrow metal box to Ira. When Ira nodded, Bollinger re-opened the steel door and lead the way into a closet-like room furnished with a single table and chair. Pointing to a small button switch mounted on the wall, he murmured, "Please ring when you're ready to come out, sir."

"Yes, yes. I know!" Ira snapped irritably. As soon as Bollinger had left and closed the door behind him, Ira locked it from inside and, opening the metal box, began extracting packets of different-colored paper embossed with the names of such companies as Radio Corporation of America, Western Electric, American Telephone and Telegraph, and General Motors. Holding several of these documents up so Gail could examine them more closely, he proudly explained, "These are securities I've been accumulating for several years now—both stocks and bonds."

Though she was impressed by this hoard of paper, Gail couldn't help expressing skepticism about its value. "Aren't you a little worried about what's been happening on the stock market recently?"

Ira smiled indulgently. "I assure you, Gail, these particular stocks will hold their value. We're going through some hard times right now, of course. That's mostly because too many fools have been buying stock on the margin. But surely you don't think people will stop buying cars and radios forever. Someday, these stocks and bonds will be worth millions! So, you see, my dear," he beamed at her, "you shouldn't worry at all about borrowing a few hundred dollars from me."

Gail was dumbfounded. Until now, she had never given much thought to the new technological inventions that had wrought so many changes in American industry as well as in the lives of millions of average citizens. For the first time in her life, Gail saw the future as Ira saw it—with the eyes of a dreamer who had complete faith in the accelerating momentum of free enterprise and scientific progress. At the same time, she felt intimidated by Ira's zealotry.

What he said and did next intimidated her even more. Thrusting several stock certificates into her hands, he declared, "If you will have me as your husband, dear lady, this will *all* be yours!"

* * *

As soon as Gail left the office that afternoon, she went to see her friend Snooky Wells. Since 1922, Snooky and her son had lived in the first-floor garage space of a small cottage on East 7ᵗʰ Street—a cottage Alta Manufacturing had erected for its management personnel.

Alta Plant Manager Edward Johnson had agreed to let Snooky occupy this space in exchange for her services as a laundress and cleaning woman. After installing an old sink, toilet and gas stove and connecting these to the city utility lines, Johnson had made no further changes to the garage space, which had a dirt floor and neither windows nor electric lighting.

Ever resourceful, Snooky had gradually made the place livable by scavenging used furniture at various house and fire sales around town. To provide some modicum of privacy, she had separated her toilet from the rest of her living space by suspending old canvas sails from the open beams in the garage ceiling. For illumination, she used wax candles and two kerosene lanterns, also items she had scavanged from house and fire sales.

Though she was sorry for her friend's hardship, Gail always felt comfortable visiting her. After eating supper and playing several hands of Pinochle with Alfie until he went to bed at 10:00, the two women sat down at Snooky's kitchen table and sampled her bottle of bootleg brandy. "So what's this awful thing that happened?" Snooky asked.

"Aherns is closing their office in two weeks, so I'm going to be out of a job!"

"Uh-oh!" Snooky grunted. "That really *is* bad news!" Quickly taking a deep draft of her brandy, she asked, "So what 're y' gonna do?"

Gail stared at her friend in desperation. "I don't know, Snooky! I broke up with Soames last month, so I can't rely on him. I'll have to find some other kind of work. But what and where, I have no idea."

"You broke up with Soames!" Snooky threw up her arms like an excited cheerleader. "Hooray for you! So what made you finally get it?"

"I found out he's planning to murder everybody in Adam Tucker's gang, including Jack" she said grimly. "The man is pure evil!"

Snooky whistled in astonishment. "Wow! He really told you that?"

"I overhead him telling somebody else on the phone. He didn't know I was listening."

"Have you warned Jack about this?"

"I don't know where he is," Gail anguished. "I haven't heard from him in months. For all I know, he could be dead already!"

Snooky reached across the table and grabbed both of Gail's hands. "*I* know where he is," she said calmly. "He's working on the new railroad bridge."

Gail felt her heart skip a beat. "He is? Are you sure? How do you know?"

"Friend o' mine. Fella who works for SP. So stop worryin'. Jack's gonna be alright."

"Not if he still has anything to do with Adam. Believe me, Snooky, Jimmy's a very dangerous man and he's working with one of the most notorious killers in the country—Baby Face Nelson."

"Baby Face Nelson!" Snooky almost jumped out of her chair. "What's *he* doin' in California? I thought he was a Chicago mobster."

"Believe me, he's here. I met him in person two months ago at the Saint Francis Hotel in San Francisco. He's a little man, but one of the most frightening I've ever met. While we were dining at the hotel, he got into an argument over some silly thing with his wife. All of a sudden, he reached across the table and slapped her in the face. Hard too! Split her lip and made her bleed! The poor woman was terribly upset."

"How come the waiters didn't throw him out o' there?" Snooky asked. "I mean, the Saint Francis Hotel—that's a pretty classy joint, ain't it?"

"I think they were too frightened. I tried to get up and leave the table myself, but Jimmy grabbed my arm and forced me to sit down again. He didn't say anything. He just tilted his head toward Nelson. When I looked, I saw Nelson had opened the front of his dinner jacket to reveal his shoulder holster. I'm sure, if anybody tried to interfere, he'd have pulled out his gun and started shooting."

"Thank God you broke things off with Soames!" Snooky declared. "So now let's talk about your employment problem. You still playin' piano at The Majestic?"

"Yes, but that's only Friday and Saturday nights. The most I can make there is three dollars a week."

Snooky thought about this for several seconds and took another deep draft of brandy. "You probably won't like me telling you this, but I hear K. T. Parker's lookin' for a bookkeeper over at The Lido. That's your specialty, ain't it? Maybe you should apply for the job."

Gail blushed deep red and both of them simultaneously burst into laughter. When their laughter subsided, Gail announced with a mischievous grin, "I do have another alternative." She then told Snooky about her visit with Ira to the Bank of Italy that afternoon and about his bizarre marriage proposal.

"Jesus! Why didn't y' take it?" Snooky exclaimed. "I sure would! What's wrong with you, girl!"

"I don't love him, Snooky. Ira's a nice man, and I know he would be good to me. But I couldn't do such a thing!"

"Don't sound so nice to me. Little creep's just like any other ugly son-of-a-bitch. All he wants is t' get into your panties and he'll pay any price to do it. So what's the difference between that and going to work for K.T. at the Lido?"

Gail had no answer. This was not the time for false pride. "You're right, Snooky. There probably really isn't much difference. But at least, if I took the job at the Lido, I would only do so with the understanding that my duties there would be restricted to bookkeeping."

"Lots o' luck with that one, honey!" Snooky smirked. "A classy-lookin' gal like you? K. T.'s sure t' hook you up with some of her best customers. So what's wrong with makin' a little extra on the side?"

"I am not a whore!" Gail insisted angrily.

"That so? Don't kid yourself. You been Soames's whore for years now!"

Gail hung her head in shame. She knew her friend was right and now she would have to live with the consequences of her own folly.

* * *

The following Saturday morning, Gail took the day off, telling Ira she needed the time to attend to some personal business. She offered no further explanation and he did not ask. Applying only a modest amounts of mascara and rouge and attiring herself in an ankle-length skirt and loose-fitting blouse with a high neck, she walked down First Street to the Lido. Though the many other pedestrians in the street paid her little notice, Gail felt as if all eyes were following her every step of the way.

Never having entered the Lido before, Gail was surprised by the elegant décor of its front lobby. She was surprised too by the polite greeting she received from the very formally dressed gentleman standing behind the service bar. "Good morning, Madame. How may I help you?" he asked with a slight bow.

"I'm here to apply for the bookkeeping job," Gail said, trying to keep her voice from quavering.

"Please have a seat. I'll tell Missus Parker you're here." The man quickly disappeared through a door behind the service bar.

Within minutes, a tall, stern-faced woman emerged through the same doorway and moved gracefully toward Gail, her hand extended in greeting. "How do you do, Miss?" the woman said, her dark eyes disconcertingly probing but her voice deep and caressing. "I'm K. T. Parker. And you are?"

"*Missus* Westlake," Gail said, firmly emphasizing her married title but courteously rising from her chair and shaking the proprietress' hand. When Parker smiled slightly, Gail added, "My first name is Gail."

"Al tells me you're looking for work as a bookkeeper," Parker said, getting right down to business. "Come into my office and let's have a talk." She turned and led the way back through the same door behind the bar.

Much to Gail's amazement, Parker's office was very business-like. Well lighted by frosted glass windows in the two exterior walls and an array of stained glass lamps suspended from the twelve-foot ceiling, the room was furnished with a large oak desk and leather-upholstered armchair facing the single entrance door. Aligned against one wall were half a dozen matching oak file cabinets, and placed directly in front of Parker's desk was a single straight-back chair. Apparently, Mrs. "K. T." Parker rarely, if ever, met with more than one of her employees at a time.

"Please sit down, Missus Westlake," Parker said, gesturing toward the straight-back chair as she ensconced herself behind her desk. Then, folding her perfectly manicured hands on the immaculate green blotter of her otherwise empty desktop, Parker raised her chin and studied Gail in silence for several seconds. "Why don't you tell me a little about yourself?" she asked.

Gail was not at all prepared for such an open question. She had expected Parker to immediately ask about her specific qualifications as a bookkeeper. Calming herself with a deep breath, Gail said, "I … well, I'm now working as a bookkeeper at Ahern's Export/Import office here in Benicia. I have been for more than ten years now. But, you see, well … just recently I learned our office is to be closed soon. That's why it has become necessary for me to seek a new position."

"I'm sorry to hear about your misfortune, Gail," Parker commented. Then, leaning forward slightly, she inquired with the hint of a smile, "You don't mind if I call you Gail, I hope?"

"Oh, of course not," Gail answered, though in fact she very much resented this infamous woman's familiarity.

Parker nodded. "Good. You see, I was hoping you might tell me a little more about yourself, not so much your work experience. For instance, do you consider yourself an honest person?"

"Excuse me?" Gail asked, now shaking with anger.

"Come now, Gail," Parker reproved, still with the same hint of a smile. "I'm sure you how important it is for a bookkeeper to be honest.

It's especially important in our business because ... well, so many of our customers are inclined to be dishonest."

Gail couldn't help seeing the wry humor in this observation and her anger subsided. "I see what you mean, Missus Parker. I consider myself honest to a fault and I feel sure my current employer would agree."

"Your word alone will suffice, my dear," Parker observed reassuringly. "Now then, let me explain what I need you to do for me." Gesturing toward the oak file cabinets, she said, "Though it may be surprising to you, we must keep very detailed records on all of our workers and clients because the city has very strict reporting requirements. Every month, I must submit to the Mayor's office an accounting not only of our revenues but also of our health records. You see, every one of my girls must submit to weekly physical examinations by Doctor Trent. The results of these examinations must be recorded and included in our monthly reports. Keeping track of these records and preparing the monthly reports will be your primary responsibility. It's tedious and time-consuming work, but it must be done. Do you think you can handle it? If so, I will pay you forty dollars a week."

Surprised but pleased that Parker was being so forthcoming and generous, Gail nodded eagerly. "I'm very good with details," she said confidently.

"Excellent," Parker nodded curtly. "When can you start?"

Even more surprised by the suddenness of Parker's offer, Gail hesitated in her reply. "My manager says he expects our office to close in two weeks. But we're not completely sure," Gail added, not wishing to seem too eager.

Parker pushed back her chair and stood up. Opening a drawer in her desk, she extracted a business card and handed it to Gail. "As soon as you know exactly when you'll be available, please call me at the number on my card. That's my private phone number, so I'd appreciate it if you would keep it confidential."

Glancing at the card, Gail noticed that it revealed only Parker's name and phone number. "Of course," Gail replied as she too stood up, realizing the interview was concluded. "Is there anything else you need to know?" Gail asked, still astonished by the alacrity of Parker's decision.

"No," Parker answered flatly. "Is there anything else *you* need to know, Gail?"

Again Gail hesitated, her brain swirling with questions—none of which she dared to ask. "Thank you for your time, Missus Parker."

"You are very welcome. Good day."

*   *   *

Five miles northwest of Benicia is a mountain range rising more than 400 feet above sea level. This region is collectively referred to as Blue Rock Springs because of the jagged ridge of volcanic rock at its summit and the several natural springs that cascade down its grass-covered slopes. At the highest point of elevation, a solid mass of rock rises like a castle tower. For that reason, this promontory had come to be known locally as Castle Rock.

It was here in early March that Tucker had brought Jack, Francis, and Hector to show them his new hideout. Adam knew his gang would no longer be safe in any kind of rented lodgings, whether in a remote farmhouse or a in crowded city slum where they were now living as tenants of a rented apartment. They would have to find a place without any traceable address. Castle Rock seemed to offer the perfect solution. Apart from Lincoln Highway leading north out of Vallejo, there were no roads within a mile of Castle Rock.

After leaving Jack's Buick sedan parked on the shoulder of Lincoln Highway, Adam had led his party on foot across the mile-wide stretch of open fields northeast of Vallejo and up to the summit of Blue Rock mountain. When they finally arrived at the base of Castle Rock, all four of the men were breathless from the climb and sweating profusely.

"How you gonna get supplies up here?" Francis asked as he mopped his brow with the large red bandanna he always carried. "You'll need a damn mule train!"

Adam grinned. "Not mules, boy. Camels. I got a friend over at the Arsenal who'll lend us five of 'em for the job."

"You mean they still have camels over at the Arsenal?" Jack asked in astonishment. "I thought they got rid of those stinky things a long time ago."

"Nope. The old Commandant had a real soft spot for 'em, so he kep 'em and bred up some more." Adam explained. Then, chuckling softly, he added, "Guess he must 've figured the Army'd need 'em to fight the Mex'cans again."

Francis already knew about the retired Arsenal Commandant's fetish for camels and was not the least bit surprised by such bureaucratic foolishness. Just then, he was more concerned about practical matters. "How can we be sure nobody else comes up here?" he asked. "Ain't there some kind o' public park down there?" he asked, pointing down the slope toward the southeast.

Grinning again, Adam replied, "Park be way over other side the mountain. 'Sides, ain't nobody come up here 'cause of all the poison oak an' rattlers."

"You mean snakes?" Hector asked, anxiously looking around in the high grass at his feet. Having been raised in the city, he knew little about the hazards of the wild. "I wish you had told me about this before, Adam."

"Don't you be worryin', Hector," Adam chuckled. "Snakes is just as scared of us as we is o' them. 'Sides, they don't come out much in daylight. 'Course, you gotta watch where you steps in them rocks." Adam pointed to the base of Castle Rock where an aggregation of medium-sized rocks formed a kind of dry moat.

Looking both to the east and the west of where they were standing, Hector noted that the entire ridge was strewn with rocks and boulders. Remembering what he had read about the habitat of rattlesnakes in college, Hector protested, "This whole area has to be infested with snakes!"

Adam ignored this remark and waved the others to follow him as he climbed over the ridge to the northern side of the mountain where the grassy terrain rose in a gradual slope to the crest of Castle Rock.

"Jesus, Mary and Joseph! You can see for miles around up here!" Francis declared as they fanned out across the thirty-foot wide plateau of volcanic rock, long since smoothed flat by centuries of wind and rainfall. To the south, they could see the rooftops of Vallejo and Mare Island Shipyard as well as the broad expanse of San Pablo Bay beyond. To the north, they could see the full length and breadth of Hidden Valley—a region so named because it was completely enclosed by two parallel mountain ranges converging at both ends.

Gazing down at the rolling hills of this valley, Hector remarked, "This would make a perfect site for a golf course!"

"Is this where you plan to set up camp?" Jack asked, referring to the flat promontory on which they stood. "Must get pretty windy up here during the winter."

"No," Adam said. Gesturing down the northeastern side of Castle Rock toward a thick cluster of scrub oak, he explained, "They's a cave down there behind them trees. We can stow our hash inside an' set up camp under the trees."

"What about snakes?" Hector asked.

"When we moves in, they moves out," Adam answered abruptly.

"So when do we do this?" Jack asked.

"Thursday night," Adam replied. "We gotta move fas'. Soames ain' done with us yet. You can bet on that." Addressing Jack and Francis, he said, "You boys 'll come over to the Arsenal after work Tuesday to help load up the trucks. Hector, you tell your boys to get the stuff we lef' in the barn over by Napa. Everbody gotta be at the main gate by five o'clock sharp."

Hector nodded. "We can do that, but I hope you don't expect me to spend the night up here. You're going to have to get rid of those snakes first."

"You jus' send Paul and some o' his coolies," Adam retorted. "We gonna need help settin' up camp, but we don' need you."

"Fair enough," Hector said.

"Let's go!" Adam moved swiftly back down the mountain toward Jack's car. The others followed him in silent compliance.

* * *

When Adam and Francis arrived at the Arsenal entrance gate at 6:30 Thursday evening, eight dust-covered sedans were waiting for them. Inside each sedan were a driver and four passengers. Four cars were filled with Negroes; two, with Orientals. The only faces Jack and Francis recognized were those of Adam, Paul Lau, and "Big Jim" Jeffries, owner of the Peekaboo Club.

The front doors of the first sedan in line opened and Adam and Jeffries stepped out to greet them—Jeffries with a warm smile and firm handshakes, Adam with a scowl and a reprimand. "Y'r late!" he growled. "Thought you knocked off work at 5:30."

"That's *s'posed* to be when we get off," Francis said irritably. "But one o' the crane barges broke off its moorings just at quittin' time, so everybody had to pitch in to recover it."

"You boys need a union!" Jeffries quipped.

"Yeah, right!" Francis retorted bitterly. "Only SP don't hire union men."

"Come on! We got work to do! Follow us," Adam ordered as he climbed back into the driver's seat of his car and started its engine.

"Can't you see these boys needs a res'?" Jeffries mocked as he too got back into Adam's car.

Jack and Francis returned to Jack's Buick and followed the other vehicles as they turned into the main gate of the Arsenal and drove slowly along the winding uphill road that led to the Arsenal Camel Barns. As he parked his car side-by-side with the others, Jack noticed four Army lorries lined up beside one the sandstone buildings. In front of the other, a uniformed African American soldier was talking with Adam. After a brief exchange, the soldier nodded and turned to open a large oak double door. Adam signaled for his men to get out of their cars and follow him and the soldier inside.

This was the first time Jack had ever seen the inside of these Camel Barns, one of two Arsenal storehouses that, in 1864, had been converted to a stable for a contingent of camels. In 1855, then U. S. Secretary of War Jefferson Davis thought camels would be useful for transporting military supplies in the desert areas of the Southwest. His plan for these animals never materialized. After the Civil War, most of the original herd was auctioned off. A few of their offspring still survived on the premises of the Benicia Arsenal, however, and were occasionally on display during Benicia's parades and street fairs.

Though there were only five dromedaries stabled in this Camel Barn, a rancid smell made their presence conspicuous. "Pew! What a stench!" Francis declared as he and Jack entered the building. "Sure hope Adam didn't store our food in here."

Jack noticed that twelve oblong wooden crates had been stacked to the right, just inside the entrance. Each crate was marked in thick black letters with the label *U. S. Army.* "Those look like rifle boxes to me. I suppose there could be some canned fish in them, though."

All of Adam's men were now standing in a semi-circle listening to his instructions. "This here's Sergeant Hayes. He an' his men are gonna bring out the camels and load 'em in one o' them trucks over there." Adam gestured toward the stack of crates and a pile of khaki-colored canvas bags piled shoulder high against the wall opposite the entrance door. "This stuff, we loads into the other trucks. Le's get t' work. We gotta have all this up to Castle Rock by sundown."

*   *   *

Jack awoke just before sunrise the next morning, the prone bodies of other men scattered around him in every direction. A few had wrapped themselves in the Army issue blankets Adam had distributed the night before, but most had been so exhausted they simply dropped on the ground and fell asleep in the clothes they were wearing.

The move to Castle Rock had taken longer and required more effort than anyone had anticipated. Because of the long trek up the mountain slope, they had not managed to get all their supplies to the summit until almost midnight. Still, Jack noted with concern, the gun crates and supply bags remained fully exposed on the open ground in front of the cave. Looking up toward the top of Castle Rock where Adam had posted the only sentinel, Jack became even more alarmed when he saw that the man was slumped over his rifle, obviously asleep.

Every muscle in his body ached as Jack untangled himself from his blanket and slowly got to his feet. What he craved most at that moment—a hot cup of coffee—he could not have. Lighting a brush fire at any time on the mountaintop, Adam had warned everyone the night before, was forbidden because it might reveal their location. Trying to find a kerosene camp stove in one of the scores of canvas supply bags was also out of the question. Jack had no idea which one to search.

Reaching into his shirt pocket, Jack found his crushed pack of Camels. Carefully extracting one of the three remaining but flattened cigarettes, he lit it with a box match and sat down on the ground again to watch the bright red disk of the sun as it began to emerge above the horizon. It was going to be a hot day, and much work still had to be done.

Since he first announced his plan the previous Sunday, Adam had elaborated on it in great detail. He said they would need to dig a twenty-five yard long trench on the northern perimeter of the campsite because this was their most vulnerable flank in the event of an attack. He also insisted that at least two connecting trenches leading to the mouth of the cave would have to be dug. Adam showed them trenching charts he had obtained from former comrades in arms who still worked at the Benicia Arsenal.

"This how they done it on the Western Front," he explained, reminding his youthful civilian lieutenants of an earlier time. Though Jack had lost his father in France, he knew nothing about the details. His mother had never talked about it. Like most Californians, the parents of Hector and Francis had been little affected by the Great War because the vast majority of the Americans who fought in Europe had been recruited from states in the Midwest and on the East Coast.

Contemplating all these preparations and remembering their most recent disastrous encounter with Baby Face Nelson (or whoever it was had set fire to their farmhouse), Jack realized they might soon be engaged in the final battle with their old rival James Soames.

"Hey boy!" Adam called to him from the trees at the mouth of the cave. "Get on up here. We got mouths t' feed."

Jack jumped up and ran up the hill toward Adam who had already set up four kerosene cook stoves and was busily unpacking cans of baked beans and bags of potatoes. Adam's call for assistance had wakened several others who also eagerly joined in preparing the morning meal.

An hour later, twenty-three Negro and Chinese workers were hard at work digging the first trench while Adam, Francis, Jack, and Big Jim Jeffries set up machine gun emplacements—one surrounded by sand bags at the summit of Castle Rock, two directly at the mouth of the cave, and one each on the far left and right flanks of the encampment. When Jeffries, also a Great War veteran, suggested they put two of the machine guns in the perimeter trench, Adam disagreed. "Soames' boys takes 'at trench, they be usin' them guns on us," Adam warned.

Jeffries nodded, acknowledging that his service as a mess-cook aboard a Navy cruiser gave him little understanding of military strategy in land combat. He proposed one defense tactic that Adam liked, however—a tactic Jeffries had learned from his youthful days hunting blackbirds. "How 'bout we hang some tin cans in them trees over there," he suggested, pointing to a large cluster of oaks on the ridge about forty yards to the west of the cave. "Tie some trip wires t' them cans so's we can hear in case somebody sneak up there at night."

"How about them trees over there?" Francis added, nodding toward a patch of scrub oak clinging to an escarpment a dozen yards east of Castle Rock.

"Good," Adam said. "We's gonna post guards there too."

By twilight, all of the necessary defense preparations had been completed and Paul Lau and the laborers he recruited had returned to their homes in China Camp. Once the supplies had been stored and the defensive trenches dug, their job was over. A shooting war with James Soames and his gang was not part of the agreement Hector and Paul had made with Adam.

To celebrate their accomplishment, Adam opened a cask of corn whiskey. Everyone except the three men assigned to guard duty sat around the entrance of the cave to celebrate. No one became intoxicated, though. The men were much too tired from the day's labors. All but the watchmen were asleep in their tents by 9:00 P.M.

CHAPTER THIRTY-ONE

"Bidin' My Time"

"LOOKS LIKE YOU REALLY PUT the finish to Tucker's gang," Soames said to the short, pudgy-faced man sitting with him in Howard Roach's Martinez office. "Nobody's seen hide or hair of him or any of 'em for months."

"I didn't get everybody in that house," Nelson snarled. "Just a couple o' niggers. Don't know whether Tucker was one of 'em or not. The way I see it, I still got work t' do."

"That's right, Lester," Roach agreed. No one ever referred to Nelson as "Baby Face" in his presence, for to do so would be to risk being shot. "Baby Face" was a nickname others had given this vicious killer when, at ten years old, Lester M. Gillis first began his career as a petty thief in the slums of Chicago. "Adam's a shrewd old nigger," Roach said. "Wouldn't put it past him to be up to no good someplace. Maybe he's pushin' drugs. I hear there's good money in it. It's also a lot easier to distribute than booze. You better have some of your boys look into that, Jimmy."

Soames frowned, He had not thought of this angle. "That's Chink business," he said. "But I'll put Spears to work on it. If anybody can sniff Tucker out, it's Emmett Spears."

"When you find that damn nigger, be sure t' tell me," Nelson insisted. "I don't like unfinished business an' I hate niggers!"

* * *

Jack sat on the edge of his cot, smoking a cigarette. A gentle late

October rain was falling on the tent canvas above his head. Ordinarily, this sound was like a lullaby for Jack. But tonight he had been unable to sleep. He couldn't put his finger on the reason for his restlessness. It had been a long day, working ten hours slamming rivets on the Benicia Bridge and then making late night hashish deliveries to customers in Fairfield and Vacaville. Still, it was not physical exhaustion that was bothering him.

Then he heard it—the distinctive sound of rattling cans. Quickly, he pulled on his poncho and picked up his Winchester. Grabbing a handful of live rounds from a box next to his cot, he chambered a shell and stepped outside into the rain. It was not a heavy downpour but the steady ice-cold rainfall that is typical late autumn weather in the North Bay.

Jack stood still for a moment listening, but he heard nothing except the steady patter of raindrops. The only light in the camp came from a single kerosene lantern hung at the entrance to the cave where two sentinels were posted

Cautiously, Jack made his way up the slope toward the light. As he ducked under some low-hanging tree branches, he saw that the two men assigned to guard duty were playing cards. They seemed totally absorbed in their game. "Did you fellows hear those cans rattling just now?" he asked.

Startled by the sound of Jack's voice, the younger of the two men looked up, a ferret-faced eighteen-year-old named Benny White. "Ain't heard nothin'," he answered morosely.

"You're supposed to be on guard duty, not playing cards," Jack reprimanded. "Maybe that's why you didn't hear it."

"Maybe you jus' havin' bad dreams, boy," the other and much older sentinel said without looking up from his hand of cards. Only his profile was visible to Jack—a thin, stoop-shouldered man with a lighted cigarette dangling from his lips.

Jack's impulse was to grab both of these men and knock their heads together. "Pick up your rifle and come with me, Benny," Jack commanded.

"Who put you in charge, boy?" wheezed the older guard, still not looking up from his cards. Jack had never spoken to this man before.

He knew only that his name was Homer Johnson and that he was a recent recruit from Richmond.

Ignoring Johnson's rebuff, Jack started to move toward the cluster of trees on the ridge west of the cave. He wasn't sure this was where the rattling sound had originated, but he was determined to investigate. Behind him, he heard Johnson say, "You stay here, boy. I'll go check it out."

The two men walked in silence across the fifty yards of open space between the cave and the dark cluster of trees on the ridge, Johnson following several yards behind. As they drew closer to their target, Johnson moved up the slope above Jack. Though he was still fuming with resentment toward this man, Jack was glad Johnson had taken the initiative. He was obviously more experienced with stealth reconnaissance than Benny White.

Their eyes had adjusted to the darkness now so they could see the outlines of the trees against the glistening surface of the rain-slicked rocks on the ridge. Johnson stumbled, dislodging several small stones that cascaded down into the cluster of trees. Again, they heard the clatter of the tin cans, immediately followed by the sound of running feet. Jack raised his rifle and fired blindly in the direction of the fleeing intruder. Johnson did the same. Then, both men ran around to the other side of the trees and fired a second time.

"What's goin' on?" Adam called out from the mouth of the cave below them.

"We got a prowler!" Johnson yelled back.

Rousting several of his other men, Adam led them up the slope to join Homer and Jack. "You see him?" Adam asked, holding a lighted lantern up to Jack's face.

"No. Just scared him away."

Adam shook his head. "Ain't good! Now they knows where we is." Turning to the other men, he said, "You boys spread out. Search the whole area." Reaching inside his poncho, Adam extracted a pocket watch. "It be dawn soon. Jack, you an' Homer stay here. Me an' some o' the boys'll check out the trees over on other side o' the ridge."

* * *

When Adam and his search party returned to the cave almost an hour later, they had found nothing. Nevertheless, Adam had left two of his men on the western face of the ridge to supplement the sentinels already stationed on Castle Rock. Everyone in the encampment was now on high alert.

"I'm goin' into town today," he told Jack and Big Jim Jeffries. "Gotta make a couple o' phone calls."

"Who y' gonna call?" Jeffries asked with a sarcastic sneer. "Fed'ral agents?"

"Gonna call your fly-boy friend," Adam replied, looking directly at Jack. "We needs air support."

"Sam's working for the Forestry Service now," Jack said. "He may not be able to help us."

"He damn well better!" Adam retorted.

*　*　*

Todd and Sharon Rivers had not seen or heard from Sam since they let him use their De Havilland fighter plane to foil Soames' attempted ambush almost two years before. They were startled, therefore, when he landed his brand new Vega 5 on their private airstrip that Sunday morning in early December and taxied it to within twenty yards of their front patio where they were drinking coffee and reading the *San Francisco Examiner.*

"Who the hell's that?" Todd exclaimed, jumping up and running inside to get his shotgun.

Sharon put down her paper. "Don't know. But that sure is one gorgeous flying machine!" Shading her eyes against the bright morning sun, she watched as the pilot killed his engine and stepped out of the cockpit. Weighing just over two tons, with a body length of nearly 28 feet and a wingspan of 41 feet, the Vega 5 was Lockheed's newest and fastest passenger plane. Sharon had read about this sleek and powerful new aircraft, but she had never seen one.

Because Sam was still wearing his flight helmet and goggles when he killed the Vega's engine and stepped out of the cockpit, Sharon did not recognize him. Even so, she waved a friendly greeting as he approached the patio. Her ever-suspicious husband was much less hospitable. Slipping two shells into his double-barreled Remington, he cocked it and pointed it directly at their visitor.

"Woah, Scott! Don't shoot! It's me—Sam Geddis!"

Squealing with delight, Sharon ran down the patio steps to greet him with a big hug. "Sam, it's so good to see you! What a delightful surprise! What are you doing out in our neck of the woods?"

Removing his helmet and goggles, Sam pointed toward his plane. "I thought you guys might like to take a ride in my new chariot. What do you think? Isn't she a beauty?"

"Boy-o-boy!" Todd enthused as he trotted toward the plane and immediately began stroking the smooth steel skin of its bright blue fuselage. "She sure is! What's the horsepower?"

"Four fifty," Sam proudly announced. "Carries four passengers and has a cruising speed of 155 miles per hour."

Scott whistled in amazement. "Mind if I check out the instrument panel?" he asked.

"Help yourself."

"So how'd a small-time crook like you rate such high-class transportation?" Sharon asked with a sarcastic grin.

"Well, she doesn't belong to me, of course," Sam admitted. "Property of the U. S. government, on loan to the Forestry Service. My boss is thinking of buying a couple of these for our spotter fleet. This model has a range of almost a thousand miles—just what we need to cover the big territory we have. Besides, the payload capacity will be great for transporting fire crew personnel."

"You still haven't answered my question, Sam," Sharon said. "How do you rate such a privilege?"

Sam blushed. "I'm the fleet captain now. Got the promotion just last month. They told me to take her out on a test flight today."

"So you decided to show off to your old flight instructor, huh?" Sharon threw her arm around Sam's shoulders, giving him another hug. "Good for you, Sam. I'm real proud of y'. Come on up and have a cup of coffee."

The sudden roar of the Vega's engine made both of them jump, their heads snapping around to see Todd waving gleefully at them from the pilot's seat. Sharon immediately ran toward the plane and started banging on the cockpit door with her fists. "Todd, what the hell do you think you're doing?" she exclaimed. "Shut it off, you lunatic!"

Todd opened the cockpit door and leaned out. "Come on, climb aboard, you two, and let's take her up!" he shouted.

Walking slowly toward the plane, Sam shook his head and made a thumbs-down sign. Todd promptly turned the engine off and exited the cockpit. "Sorry, Sam," he said sheepishly. "Just couldn't resist."

"Don't worry," Sam said with a smile. "I'll take you guys up. But I'm afraid I'll have to be the pilot. Government regulations, you know."

"Of course!" Sharon concurred. "Todd, I don't believe you! Didn't your Momma teach you any manners?"

The three friends laughed and headed back toward the patio where Sharon quickly served fresh coffee and home made donuts.

* * *

After they pumped Sam with more questions about his fast-track career with the Forestry Service for several minutes, Sharon asked, "Have you heard from Adam lately?"

Sam was startled by the question. There was even a note of embarrassment in his reply. "Not for quite a while," he said. "I've been pretty busy what with my job and having to take care of Tully, you know."

"How's he doing?" Sharon asked.

Again, Sam sounded embarrassed. "I'm afraid he ran away. Just a couple of weeks ago, in fact."

Sharon frowned. "What happened? Where'd he go?"

"Well, it's sort of a long story," Sam replied, his gaze shifting in an effort to avoid eye contact with either Todd or Sharon. "After they sent mother back to the sanitarium again …" he paused. "Maybe you didn't know about that."

Sharon and Todd shook their heads simultaneously, and Sharon grasped Sam's hand in sympathy.

"They had to do it because, after I went to work for the Forestry Service full time and Tully went off to boarding school up in Grass Valley, mother started drinking and taking drugs. It got so bad she overdosed and almost died. That's why they sent her away again. Then, when the headmaster at Tully's boarding school found out, he expelled Tully—the bastard! Mother's lawyer told me I had to move back to Benicia and take care of Tully. I hired a live-in housekeeper so there'd be somebody in the house when Tully got home after school every day. But he hated that housekeeper and he missed Mother. He also missed this weird teacher he had up at Stonehaven—that's the private boarding school where he was. He hated the public high school in Benicia too. He was like a wild man."

"How old is Tully now?" Sharon asked, her voice filled with compassion.

"He turned fifteen just last month, and that's when he ran away."

"Where'd he go?" Todd asked.

Sam hung his head. "I don't know. I think he may have gone to San Francisco. That's where he told me his teacher friend lives."

"Did you try to find him?" Sharon asked.

"I called the police in San Francisco and my lawyer has made some enquiries. But so far, nobody's had any luck."

"That's awful!" Sharon gasped. "So who is this teacher you mentioned?"

Sam looked to his left, out at his plane. "Name's Pyncheon. He's a damn Ethel an' I think he seduced Tully."

"Good God!" Todd growled in disgust. "You've got to find him, Sam. That creep'll wreck your brother's life."

"So what the hell am I supposed to do?" Sam demanded angrily. "I've already done the best I can!"

"It may be too late for you to do anything," Sharon said softly.

"What are you talking about, Sharon!" Todd demanded. "Tully's his kid brother, for God's sake!"

"The boy's fifteen. He's probably already made up his mind," Sharon tried to explain, knowing her husband would still probably not understand. "He's may have been homosexual for a long time. I've known people like that."

"It was mother's fault," Sam mumbled.

Sharon looked startled. "Your mother? What do you mean, Sam?"

Sam shook his head and sat in silence for several seconds. "I'd rather not talk about it, if you don't mind."

Sharon grabbed Sam's hand and squeezed it. "Of course. We understand, Sam."

Again there were several seconds of silence as the three friends tried to collect their thoughts.

Todd was the first to speak. "I think I better tell you, Sam. Adam's in a lot of trouble, and he needs your help. He called us the other day and asked how he could get in touch with you."

"What kind of trouble? He have a brush with the law?"

"It would probably be better if he had," Todd said. "It's a lot worse than that, I'm afraid. Soames has hired a hit man from Chicago named Baby Face Nelson to go after Adam and probably just about everybody who's ever had anything to do with him. That's why you saw me go for my shotgun when you flew in here. Two weeks ago, Nelson set fire to Adam's house and killed three others who were living there with him. Adam, Jack and Francis barely managed to escape. You ever heard of Baby Face Nelson?"

"Of course," Sam said. "His name's been in all the papers. He's on Hoover's Most Wanted list. But I didn't know he was in California."

"He's in Vallejo!" Sharon announced grimly.

"Jesus! So how can I help?"

"Adam and his gang have gone into hiding," Todd said. "They need you to do some air reconnaissance for them in case Soames and his gang try to go after them again."

"Where are they hiding?"

"We don't know," Sharon said. "I think you'd better talk to Adam about that yourself. I have a telephone number where you can reach him."

Sam gestured toward the Vega. "I can't do reconnaissance for Adam with that thing. It's strictly government property."

"We still have the old De Havilland," Todd assured him. "You can use that if you need to. You still in touch with Ted Sena?"

Sam shook his head. "Sena's dead. Somebody shot him in a barroom brawl back in February. Anyway, that's what the papers said. But I think it must have been one of Soames' thugs got him. Sena wasn't the kind to get into barroom brawls. He was too old and too smart for that."

"Then I guess you'll have to teach Jack or Francis how to use that machine gun on the De Havilland," Todd advised as he stood up. "Let's go take a ride in that new rocket ship of yours," he suggested with a smile.

"Good idea!" Sam declared. "I need to clear my head from all this."

*   *   *

Gail had been working at the Lido for almost two months and was feeling very comfortable in her new job. Parker had set up a desk and chair for Gail in her own office and carefully reviewed with her all of the accounts already established, including those assigned to some very wealthy and prestigious clients. These included several railroad and banking executives as well as two members of the California State Assembly. Gail was amazed by the complete confidence her new boss seemed to place in her.

Because Gail worked only weekdays between 8:30 A.M. and 4:30 P.M. and spent all of her time on the job inside Parker's office, she rarely encountered any of the male customers who frequented the Lido. In fact, Parker seemed determined to protect Gail from such exposure. The only other employee Gail saw regularly each day was Al Russo—the taciturn manikin in black who served as bartender and watchdog in the Lido's front lobby.

It was early December, and First Street was decorated for the coming Christmas holiday as usual, with a holly wreathe hung at the top of every lamp post and the customary crèche or Santa Clause display in every store window. This year, however, there were far fewer stores open than there had been the year before. Although the new railroad bridge was still under construction, several merchants had already closed shop in anticipation of the economic hardship soon to be visited upon the town of Benicia.

Among the shops that had closed were Wilson's Dry Goods, Dalton's Music Store, Ewing's Haberdashery, and Graf's Bakery. Most of the bars and brothels at the waterfront end of First Street were still open for business, however. As long as the passenger and freight trains continued to stop at the Benicia depot to be loaded on and off the *Solano* and *Contra Costa* ferries, there continued to be a plentiful supply of transient patrons for these enterprises.

Most of Benicia's working class residents were already suffering, however, not only from the closing of local businesses but also from the general economic panic that was spreading nationwide and that some newspaper pundits were already beginning to call "The Great Depression."

Ever since September, there had been a hiring freeze at the two largest commercial employers in Benicia—the Alta Manufacturing plant and Dougherty's Cannery. An increasing number of unskilled laborers were being laid off daily at these facilities because of a slow-down in demand for their products. Although the Arsenal continued to operate under federal government funding, many of the troops stationed there had been reassigned to deal with protest riots and wildcat strikes in other parts of the nation. The civilian Benicians who had been food service and maintenance workers at the Arsenal suddenly found they were no longer needed.

Most severely affected by all of this were the Portuguese and Italian families who lived in the boarding houses and small cottages on the East side of town. By far the largest proportion of Benicia's permanent population, most of these residents were renters. For generations, they had eked out a subsistence existence as day laborers at the tanneries and canneries. When household breadwinners lost their jobs in 1930, their entire families suffered.

Probably no one was more aware of this growing problem than the proprietors and workers at Benicia's brothels. These, after all, were the women who for years had been the principal providers of emotional solace to the tired and discouraged male wage earners of Benicia—men whose wives, exhausted from child-bearing and living in constant fear of spousal abuse, had turned away from their husbands and sought consolation in Holy Mother Church.

At first, it was a source of amusement to Gail when she learned from Snooky that several of the women who worked at the Lido, including K. T. Parker herself, attended daily Mass at Saint Dominic's Church. Such behavior offended Gail's Protestant sensibilities, for it seemed to her the height of hypocrisy. Early one Friday afternoon, however, she had a conversation with Parker that opened her eyes to a new way of perceiving this paradox.

"Gail, I want you to set up a separate ledger for a charitable account." Parker announced. "Many families in town are suffering terribly from recent lay-offs. Some are on the brink of starvation. I believe we must do something about that. So I'm asking each of our girls to make a weekly contribution from their earnings to purchase groceries for the poorest families. I'm putting you in charge of managing this project. I expect you to keep the account record and to oversee the purchase and distribution of the groceries."

Gail was stunned. How was it possible this hardened purveyor of carnal sin could even conceive of such an idea? She sat in silence, staring open-mouthed at her boss.

"You seem surprised," Parker said, arching one of her perfectly shaped eyebrows. "Do you think that, because I operate a brothel, I am without compassion?"

Gail shook her head vigorously. "Oh no! Of course not, Missus Parker!" Gail blurted, suddenly realizing the hypocrisy of her own preconceptions. "I think that's a wonderful idea! I'll be happy to help."

"Good," Parker responded curtly. Then, stepping to the wall safe behind her desk, she opened it and extracted a canvas bag. Handing the bag to Gail, she said, "Here's the first week's collection. Please tally the amount. Then you and I will sit down this afternoon and make a list of the groceries to be purchased. I have already identified six families who are in greatest need. As soon as we have made up the list for each family, you will go to Rankin's and have the orders filled and delivered anonymously to each family tomorrow morning."

"Anonymously. You mean you don't want the families to know who donated the groceries?" Gail asked, further astonished that this tough businesswoman was not only generous but also humble.

"Anonymously," Parker repeated emphatically. "We don't need any publicity about this. For us, even good publicity is bad. You know the old saying: 'No good deed goes unpunished.'"

Gail couldn't help smiling. "I see your point, but keeping things secret won't be easy."

"Well, do the best you can," Parker said and left the office to attend to other matters.

Gail had been right. Within less than two weeks after the first grocery distribution, everyone in Benicia knew the truth. News of Parker's generosity had been leaked through a variety of sources, one of the first being Bobby Sessions, the fourteen-year-old delivery boy at Rankin's grocery store.

Bobby told his girlfriend Isty Hewitt; Isty told her mother Mary Lou; and Mary Lou told her husband Huey the barber. Once Huey knew, the news of Parker's charitable donations circulated around town like wildfire. By Christmas Day of 1930, the ladies of the Lido were widely hailed as "angels of mercy."

1931

The Vallejo General Hospital

CHAPTER THIRTY-TWO

"Wrap Your Troubles in Dreams"

MUCH TO EVERYONE'S SURPRISE, EIGHT full months had passed without any further signs of danger. The warm nights during the summer and early fall of 1930 had made sleeping in their tents uncomfortable, so most of Adam's men slept on the open ground in front of the cave. They were awakened at dawn each morning by the sound of a biplane circling low overhead. Jack derived much comfort from this, knowing that it was Sam doing his daily flight reconnaissance.

The months of uninterrupted tranquility at Castle Rock made most of Adam's men complacent, as did the growing success of his hashish distribution business. Several of the men began to argue that they should re-locate to more comfortable quarters in Vallejo or Napa. Everyone was making good money and few saw any reason why they should continue to deny themselves the amenities of a comfortable bed and bath. Adam, however, was firm. "This war ain't over," he insisted. "Soames an' his boys are still out there an' sooner or later they gonna find us."

Then, on the morning of New Years Day Sam's plane did not appear. This was particularly troubling to Jack because winter was the slow season for aerial fire spotting in California. Besides, Sam was not one to carouse on New Years Eve. Like Francis, he was a teetotaler. He would have little reason to interrupt his normal reconnaissance flight over Castle Rock.

As usual, Jack was up at sunrise. Emerging from his tent, he lit a cigarette and scanned the horizon for Sam's plane. Glancing up at the summit of Castle Rock, he noted that, again, the sentinel on duty was slumped over his machine gun, obviously fast asleep. Jack decided he should climb up and replace this careless watchman.

Just as he started up the slope, though, something slammed into the ground a few inches to his right. This was immediately followed by the crack of a rifle resonating from the valley below. Instantly, Jack dropped flat on the ground and rolled to his left. Two more shots rang out, both striking the startled sentinel who tumbled and rolled down the hill.

By now, most of the sleeping men had been rousted out of their tents. Several were running toward the cover of the oak trees at the mouth of the cave. Others were crawling on their stomachs, some firing their pistols down the hill at targets they could not see. From the cover of the trees in front of the cave, Adam was shouting, "Keep down! Keep down, y' damn fools!"

Jack rose to a crouch and ran as fast as he could toward the trees. Glancing quickly behind him, he saw a dozen or more men firing rifles and pistols as they advanced rapidly up the hill, dodging in and out behind boulders to avoid being hit by return fire. Just as he reached the cover of the oak trees, Jack heard machine gun fire. It came from several directions. He spun around and fired downhill at the attackers. But his pistol lacked the range for accuracy.

"Over here, Jack!" Someone roared at him from behind. It was Big Jim Jeffries. He was trying to attach an ammunition belt to the machine gun he had carried and mounted in the perimeter trench. Jack, unlike Jeffries, had practiced setting up and firing several of Adam's machine guns so he knew exactly what to do.

"Perfect!" Jeffries declared with a triumphant grin as he aimed the now armed machine gun at the far left man in the line of attackers and swept it in an arc of rapid fire. Jack watched in awe and terror as men toppled over in front of him like pins in a bowling alley. The message was quickly apprehended. The attackers scattered and retreated back down the mountainside.

Cheers went up all around and Adam began ordering his men to set up two more machine guns at strategic points in the perimeter trench. He also ordered two men to climb to the top of Castle Rock to operate the abandoned machine gun at that location. An eerie silence settled over the mountainside as they waited for the next attack. Jack scanned the terrain below with a pair of field glasses. There was no sign of movement.

"Look down there," Jeffries suddenly said, pointing toward a large vehicle moving slowly into the valley from the direction of Lincoln Highway.

Through the field glasses, Jack saw a long flatbed truck carrying a Howitzer field cannon. Lowering the glasses, Jack stared at Jeffries. "They've got a long-range cannon!" he announced bleakly. "We're sitting ducks!"

Jeffries gripped the handles of his machine gun tighter and stared fiercely down the slope, but he said nothing. For the next twenty minutes, the defenders watched in helpless dread as the cannon was unloaded from the trailer and prepared for firing.

Then they heard it—the distant sound of an airplane engine. Looking up, they saw the craft moving in a wide circle high above them. *Was it Sam?* Jack thought in desperation. *Oh please, God —let it be Sam!*

But, as the unspoken prayer formed in Jack's brain, another sound struck terror into his heart—the piercing whistle of an incoming Howitzer shell followed by an enormous explosion that blew a hole in the side of the mountain just a few yards from the mouth of the cave. Dirt and shattered rock thrown up from the blast cascaded down on them like hail. The first explosion was followed almost immediately by another, and then another. Jack heard the screams of men as the third round found its mark.

They were trapped, Jack thought. If this cannonade continued much longer, most of Adam's men would be dead or wounded. Again peering through his field glasses, Jack noted that several columns of armed attackers were again advancing up the face of the mountain.

"Get ready, boy!" Jeffries snarled, snapping a bayonet to the barrel of his Army-issue carbine. "We's in for it now!"

The bombardment continued, more rounds finding their targets and more of Adam's men screaming in pain. Then suddenly it stopped, and the approaching attackers, within range now, began opening fire again. Three of the four machinegun emplacements Adam had set up returned fire, as did several of his riflemen. But they had already taken so many casualties during the bombardment that Jack knew their fate was sealed.

Just at that moment, though, he heard the roar of an airplane engine accompanied by the rapid fire of two airborne machine guns. It was Sam's De Havilland. The plane swept in fast and low, its blazing guns cutting a wide swathe in the advanced column of attackers. The cannon began firing again, this time aimed higher to hit Sam's plane. But the De Havilland was moving too fast for the stationary cannon.

After the first pass, Sam banked his plane and made a second run across Soames' scattering band of foot soldiers, decimating their ranks. Banking his plane a third time, he made a run at the men firing the cannon. Through his field glasses, Jack saw someone in the rear cockpit of the De Havilland lean out as the plane swept low over the Howitzer. He heard several small explosions followed by a single big explosion. When the smoke cleared, he saw that both the cannon and its crew lay in scattered pieces. Again the defenders cheered.

Jack felt a firm hand on his shoulder. Looking around, he saw Adam standing behind him along with six other men armed with bayoneted rifles. "Come on, boy," he said calmly. "Time for a counter-attack." Addressing all of his men, Adam raised his hook straight above his head and waved it. "Don't nobody shoot 'til you see this."

Jack grabbed his Winchester and followed as Adam led the way slowly but steadily down the slope. Gesturing with his left hand, Adam signaled for them to spread out as they descended. Gunfire from below immediately resumed, but the attackers were much fewer in number now and quickly distracted by yet another assault from the air. When the De Havilland came in low with its guns blazing, most turned their rifle and Tommy Gun fire on the plane.

Jack and the others were moving fast now, spreading out in an ever-widening arc as they reached the bottom of the slope. All eyes were on Adam, watching for his raised hook. Out of the corner of his eye, Jack suddenly noticed that smoke was pouring from the tail of Sam's plane. Still focusing his attention on Adam, Jack heard the plane's engine begin to sputter. Within seconds, its nose dropped and the plane crashed, tumbling in forward somersaults until it burst into flame. At almost the same instant, Jack saw Adam raise his hook.

They were so close now they could see the faces of the enemy.

Dropping to one knee, every one of Adam's men took careful aim at a face and fired. This lethal volley so terrified Soames's men that many of them scattered in desperate flight. Three of them armed with Tommy Guns regrouped behind the long-bed truck, however, and opened up on Adam's squad with withering fire.

Five of Adam's men were killed instantly, and Jack was knocked to the ground with bullet wounds in both his left leg and his right shoulder. As he lay in helpless agony, Jack saw Adam turn around to look at him. In that instant, someone jumped up on the truck bed and yelled. "Die, you damn nigger!" A score of rounds tore into Adam's back, hurling him to the ground, face down.

It's over! Jack thought just as he lost consciousness.

* * *

Ezra Coghill was just opening his service station on Lincoln Highway that morning when he heard the cannon fire and multiple explosions. Coghill's was the last stop for travelers heading north out of Vallejo. "Didn't know they was a quarry over that way," he said to his first customer, a cattle farmer named Larry Stokes.

"They ain't," Stokes said, stepping out of his Model A and shading his eyes against the bright morning sunlight to study the two columns of black smoke now rising above Castle Rock. "Those ain't just sticks o' dynamite goin' off neither. You bes' call the sheriff, Ezra."

At that moment, however, Solano County Sheriff Karl Hedrick was otherwise occupied. He was still sound asleep in one of the rooms at the Casa de Vallejo where, the night before, he had engaged the personal services of one Lucile Barnes.

Tim Larson, Hedrick's deputy in the Fairfield office, did not know this, of course, and he was very irritated by the note of urgency in Coghill's phone call. "What are y' talkin' about?" Larson demanded. "That's Hidden Valley. Ain't nothin' over there but the old Richardson homestead and that burned down eight years ago."

"I'm tellin' y', y' gotta send some men over there right now," Coghill insisted. "They's a full-scale war goin' up in them hills!"

* * *

It was almost noon before two Solano County police cars and an ambulance from the Vallejo General Hospital finally turned off of Lincoln Highway onto the dirt road that wound eastward through the hills into Hidden Valley. Sheriff Hedrick was driving the lead vehicle. Astonished by what he saw when he rounded the last bend in the road and the valley came into full view, Hedrick slammed on his brakes.

The entire valley below and the slopes rising on either side were covered with a carpet of green. Directly in the center of this carpet was a large black gash, its jagged edges defined by smoldering field grass. A mile ahead and below them, half a dozen vehicles were parked helter-skelter.

"Gimme them field glasses," Hedrick barked at Raymond Scofield, the officer sitting next to him. "Jesus H. Christ!" the Sheriff exclaimed as he peered through the lenses. "They's bodies all over the place down there! What the hell happened here?"

"Mind if I take a look, Sheriff?" Scofield asked calmly. Taking his time, the older and more experienced officer scanned both the vehicles below and the northern slope of Blue Rock mountain. "Looks like there's bodies all the way up to Castle Rock. Must 've been a major gang war." Turning to the young recruit in the back seat, he said, "Hal, you're gonna have t' go int' Vallejo an' call for more help. Better call Fire Chief Tillman and the hospital too. Tell Toby t' send out every ambulance he's got."

As Scofield stepped out of the police cruiser, Hedrick remained in the driver's seat. "I'll drive back to town with Hal," he explained to Scofield. "It'll take somebody with authority to get Toby movin' on this. He gets real uppity with city officials when they lean on 'im."

Scofield knew the real reason Hedrick wanted to go with Hal. The Sheriff couldn't stand the sight of blood. *Good riddance!* Scofield thought as he walked to the police cruiser behind them. Climbing into the back seat, he said aloud, "Let's go, boys. Sheriff's going back to get some more help."

The officer driving the second car greeted this announcement with a disgusted shake of his head, released his hand brake, and drove on. About twenty yards before they got to the parked vehicles, Scofield ordered the driver to stop. "Draw your guns," he cautioned. "There may still be a few trigger-happy goons in this bunch."

The driver killed the engine, and the three policemen moved out in different directions to search for survivors, Scofield first walking back to the ambulance to warn the two hospital orderlies they should stay in their vehicle until he summoned them.

The other policemen moved cautiously among the scattered bodies, calling out each time one of them found a possible survivor. Suspicious that some of the combatants might be hiding in the parked vehicles, Scofield inspected each of these first.

As he approached the long-bed truck that had carried the Howitzer to the battle site, he heard the sound of movement. Crouching low, he peered underneath the trailer carriage. "Anybody there?" he asked. "Don't move! We're police officers and we're armed."

"Help me," Soames answered feebly.

Moving closer, Scofield glimpsed Soames' shadowy form as he tried to raise himself from the ground. A bullet lodged in his pelvis made the effort too painful, though. Groaning, he collapsed on his face.

"Lie still, mister" Scofield said gently. "Help is on the way." Scofield stood up and called out to the other officers. "Got one here. How many live ones you got so far?"

One officer held up two fingers; the other, three.

"OK. I'll bring in the meat wagon. You boys go on up the hill and see what you can find."

What they found were the dead bodies of eight Negroes, including that of "Big Jim" Jeffries who had been the first of Adam's counter-attack squad to die. They did not even bother to inspect the smoldering pile of twisted metal and charred wood that had once been the De Havilland. The bodies of Sam and Francis had been torn to bits when the plane exploded.

* * *

The battle at Castle Rock was headlined in all the Bay Area newspapers the following morning, complete with grisly photographs of dead bodies. The scores of reporters who swarmed over the site less than an hour after the police first arrived came away with conflicting stories about what had happened and who was involved. None of the dead had been identified, and most of the wounded taken to Vallejo General Hospital were in shock. Of the wounded, only the identities of

Jack and two of Soames' henchman, Tom Stark and Seth Warner, had been reported accurately.

As soon as Del got the news, she telephoned the Lido. She knew Jack's mother would be frantic. Mrs. K. T. Parker answered the phone and told her Gail had already been driven to the hospital in Vallejo. Del then called Greg Henshak and, together, they drove to the hospital in Del's roadster. They had to park three blocks away from the hospital's main entrance at the intersection of Tennessee and Sutter streets because of all the other vehicles already parked in that area.

Two policemen stopped them at the outside entrance, allowing them into the building only after Greg assured them he was Jack Westlake's brother-in-law and that Del was his first cousin.

"That was quick thinking, Greg," Del said admiringly as they approached the duty nurse at the front desk. "I just hope you don't have any outstanding traffic tickets," she added with a puckish grin.

"Don't worry," he assured her. "The Vallejo police are not known for their efficiency."

The duty nurse brusquely directed them to a ward on the second floor—a large rectangular room that reeked of disinfectant and was lined on each of its long walls with hospital beds, half a dozen of which were occupied by wounded Negro men. At the far end of the ward they found Jack, sitting up in a hospital bed with his arm in a sling and his leg in a full-length cast. Gail was sitting beside his bed, her face pale with anguish. Jack looked up and smiled wanly as they approached.

"How are you, Jack?" Del asked anxiously.

"He's very lucky," Gail answered for him.

"What happened?" Greg asked. "The reports in the papers are very confusing. How'd you get involved with this, anyway?"

Jack shook his head. "You don't want know," he said grimly.

"Of course we do!" Del insisted. Then, noting the annoyed look on Jack's face, she tempered her declaration. "Well, maybe not right now. The important thing is you're alive. Where's Francis? The papers said he was involved with this too."

"He was in the De Havilland with Sam. They were both killed when it crashed," Jack said, his eyes dark with despair and grief.

"Oh my God!" Del gasped. "Jack, that's terrible! What about Adam?"

The muscles in Jack's face tightened. "Adam's dead too That bastard Nelson got him—shot him in the back with a Tommy Gun!"

"You mean *Baby Face* Nelson, the gangster from Chicago?" Greg asked in astonishment. "His name wasn't even mentioned in the newspaper reports."

"That's because somebody paid off the police," Jack said bitterly. "The son of a bitch's being treated right here in this hospital—in a private room, for God's sake!"

"How do you know that?" Greg asked.

"One of the nurses told me. She said Nelson's in cahoots with the hospital manager, some guy named Tobe Williams."

"Jack! That's awful!" Del exclaimed. "Somebody should report it to the FBI."

"Nobody's got the guts," Jack spat out.

"Well, *I* do!" Del declared.

"You don't want to get mixed up in this," Jack warned. "Nelson's here under an alias. He's probably got policemen guarding his room right now."

Torn between her feelings of rage and grief, Del began to weep uncontrollably. "I don't believe this!" she cried.

Greg put his arm around her shoulders. "Take it easy, Del. There's nothing anyone can do about it right now."

"That's true, Adelaide," Gail put in, startling Del with the use of her formal name. Del hadn't seen Gail Westlake in more than ten years. Though at thirty-nine Gail was still an attractive woman, her once lush chestnut brown hair, cut short and bobbed now, showed signs of gray, and wrinkles marred her once smooth brow and wide-set eyes. "Life isn't fair, my dear."

This forced Del to recover her composure. "Is there anything we can bring you?" she asked Jack.

Jack shook his head. He too was visibly discouraged.

"Well, at least there's one thing you don't have to worry about," Greg announced. "You'll have a job waiting for you as soon as you get out of here, Jack."

"What do you mean? He won't be able to work again for months!" Del protested.

"I'm not talking about manual labor," Greg explained. "I'm talking about his managing our vineyard. When father died last winter, I had to take over the business and I just don't have the talent for it. I need help with all the paperwork. So, what do you say, Jack? You willing to take that on?"

"Of course he is!" Gail answered for her son, her face suddenly lighting up with hope. Then, smiling at Jack, she declared, "That would be wonderful for you, dear!"

Jack frowned. "It's nice of you to offer, Greg, but I don't know squat about grape growing."

"Maybe not, Jack, but you can learn. So think about it, will you? You don't have to make a decision now. Just know the job is yours if and when you want it."

*　*　*

Late the next afternoon, Del again visited Jack in the hospital. This time she was accompanied by one of her instructors from Saint Mary's College—a Dominican friar named Michael Flynn. In addition to being a Professor of Canon Law, Flynn had been Del's academic advisor and close friend ever since she transferred to Saint Mary's College in the fall of 1929. When they saw Flynn's clerical collar, the police guards at the entrance to the hospital had waved them through without question.

Jack was surprised when Del appeared. He had not expected her to return so soon—or even to return at all. Fatalistically, he supposed his involvement in the slaughter at Castle Rock was enough to drive Del away from him forever.

He had not been completely mistaken. After returning home from the hospital the day before, Del had fallen into deep depression. Try as she would, she could not reconcile her feelings of affection for Jack with her long-held belief that he had deliberately abandoned and betrayed her in pursuing his life of crime.

Her first impulse had been to confide in Ruby. But Ruby, now in her late fifties, had grown feeble during the past year, handicapped by crippling arthritis and the early onset of dementia. That is why, late the night before, Del had telephoned Flynn.

Though he was thirty-seven and a studious scholar, Flynn was almost childlike in his ebullient playfulness. Tall and portly, with bright red hair and sparkling green eyes, he never seemed to take anything seriously—whether it was some ponderous papal encyclical or the latest ravings of popular evangelists like Father Charles E. Coughlin. Flynn made light of even the most extreme pronouncements of contemporary atheists like Aldous Huxley and Clarence Darrow. It was Flynn's sense of humor that Del had always admired most.

"Jack," Del said as she took his hand affectionately, "there's somebody I'd like you to meet." Turning to the friar, she introduced him simply as "my friend Michael Flynn."

Jack, his mistrust immediately aroused by Flynn's clerical collar, nodded coolly at the newcomer. "I don't need a priest yet, Del," Jack said bitterly.

Flynn emitted a big belly laugh, his rich baritone voice echoing throughout the entire hospital ward. "Humble servant of the Lord, it's for sure I am, sir!" he declared. "But priest I am not—at least, not yet. I love my cakes and ale far too much!" This was followed by another infectious belly laugh that forced both Del and Jack to smile.

"That's a big relief!" Jack said as he reached out with his good arm to shake hands with Flynn. "So tell me, Mike, why are you here?"

Flynn was quick to respond. "I've always been fascinated by gangsters. When I read about your exploits in the newspapers and Del told me she knew you, I insisted she introduce me," Flynn prevaricated with a wink at Del. "You see, I've never had the privilege of meeting a real gangster before!"

Taken off guard, Jack did not know what to say. He had never thought of himself as a gangster—an outlaw, yes, but he was an outlaw with principles. Still, given his current situation, he couldn't blame Flynn for seeing him as a gangster. "Sorry to disappoint you, Mike," Jack said at last, hoping his answer would be taken as an expression of humility. "I'm not John Dillinger. Just a poor fool who got mixed up with the wrong crowd."

"Ah, we are all poor fools, my friend!" Flynn laughed. Then, raising an open hand as if he were holding something in it, he addressed the invisible object, "Alas! Poor Yorick!'" he declaimed. "I knew him well, Horatio; a fellow of infinite jest, of most excellent fancy."

"Sounds like Shakespeare," Jack said with a whince.

Nodding his approval to Del, Flynn said, "A true man of learning!

You have excellent taste in your choice of male companions, my dear!"

Del blushed but couldn't constrain an admiring glance at Jack. In spite of everything, she felt very proud of him at that moment. "Thank you, Michael. I know Jack's a good man at heart."

"A good man at heart," Flynn echoed, his tone changing like quicksilver from mirth to sternness. "Do I detect a slight note of condescension?" Shaking a pudgy finger at her, he scolded, "Not becoming in a young woman of your sophistication, I fear. And certainly not a quality that will advance your career in the legal profession."

"You're going to be a lawyer?" Jack asked, suddenly intimidated, though not particularly surprised, by this news.

"One of the best," Flynn said. "Provided, of course, she follows my advice to the letter!" he added with another wink at Del.

"I've applied to Stanford Law School," Del announced proudly. "Michael, who is my academic advisor at Saint Mary's, seems to think I have a good chance of being admitted."

"Good for you," Jack said grudgingly. "I just hope you pass the bar soon enough to defend me in criminal court. I'm bound to be indicted for this."

"Now there's a depressing thought!" Flynn said. "Are you depressed, my friend?"

"No," Jack sneered. "I'm a realist. I know how the law works. Once you get your name in the papers, you're guilty until proven innocent."

"I think we need to educate your friend in Constitutional law," Flynn said to Del.

"You mustn't worry, Jack," Del assured him, despite her own anxiety. "We'll do everything we can to help you." With a sudden flood of feeling, Del threw herself at Jack, clasping him in her arms and weeping uncontrollably. "Oh Jack! This is terrible!"

Flynn stood watching their grief in silence for several seconds, his own face full of sorrow. Then, closing his eyes, he began to pray silently.

* * *

A week later, Del was in Flynn's small office on the campus of Saint Mary's College for her regularly scheduled Wednesday afternoon conference. "I saw Jack again last Friday," she said. "We were alone and he told me all about what's happened to him in the last five years." She hesitated, nervously averting Flynn's steady gaze. "It was awful!"

"How awful?" Flynn asked without expression.

"He's been selling narcotics and probably had all sorts of affairs with disgusting women." Burying her face in her hands, she wailed, "Oh my God!"

Flynn remained motionless, waiting until at last her sobs subsided and she sat staring hopelessly at the crucifix on the wall behind Flynn's desk. At length, Flynn suggested softly, "We need to pray for him, Del."

"Pray for him!" she exploded in rage. "I've been praying for him for years! What good has it done?"

"You're very angry right now," Flynn remarked, still keeping his voice low and his eyes steadily fixed on Del's. Again, he waited several seconds before speaking. At length, he asked, "Do you think Jack is sorry for what he has done?"

Del stood up and began pacing back and forth. "Oh God! How should I know? He *said* he was. But what does that mean? He's a bootlegger and a murderer!"

"You do remember how our Lord treated the woman caught in adultery, don't you?" Flynn asked, still keeping his voice low. "And what about Dismus—the confessed murderer who died beside him on a cross?"

Del stiffened, clenching her fists and rolling her eyes at the ceiling. "I'm not Jesus!" she cried desperately.

"Yes you are, my dear," Flynn corrected. "Whether we like it or not sometimes, we are all part of the Body of Christ." When Del did not respond to this, he asked, "How long has it been since you received Communion, by the way?"

Del turned on him, her face twisted in fury. "How *dare* you ask me that! You're not my confessor!"

"No," Flynn admitted, "but I am your friend. Please sit down, Del. We need to talk like friends."

Suddenly exhausted, Del slumped into her chair again. "I don't know what to do, Michael! Please help me!" she whispered, her lips trembling and her eyes again flooding with tears.

Flynn's impulse was to stand up and walk around his desk to embrace her. He remained seated, however. He knew it was not sympathy Del needed at that moment. "Take some deep breaths, Del," he commanded. "Do it along with me. Ready? Breathe in … breathe out … breathe in … breathe out." He repeated these commands several times, each time following them himself until at last Del too was breathing deeply and in time with him. "Feel better now?" he asked.

Del smiled and nodded. "Yes, Michael. Thank you."

"Don't thank me, my dear," he said. "It is the work of the Holy Spirit. Are we ready to talk rationally about this?"

"Rationally?" Del asked, lapsing momentarily into her earlier feelings of confusion and resentment.

"You are an extremely intelligent young woman, Del. Intelligent people are always rational when they're faced with a perplexing problem," Flynn lectured.

"You're talking like a man!" she retorted, but there was a smile on her face.

"Ah, good!" Flynn chuckled. "You're back to yourself! Let's begin by exploring some alternative possibilities."

Del tilted her head quizzically. "What do you mean by alternative possibilities? I hope you're not going to start spouting a bunch of scholastic solipsisms!"

"You know me better than that, Del!" Flynn gently scolded. "Consider, for one, the possibility that Jack may not have told you the whole story. Perhaps he is leaving out some important details that may lessen his culpability."

"Like what, for instance?"

"Well, did he recount in detail what has happened to him in the past several years? Not to be cliché, but the devil really is in the details, you know!"

Del looked surprised. "No," she said. "He didn't. He probably knew I didn't want to hear about it."

"Precisely!" Flynn stood up and, walking to the single window in his small office, gazed out at the mountains east of the college campus. Their golden slopes were turning russet now, reflecting the fiery red of a hot summer sunset. "Which indicates, to me at least, that Jack has strong feelings for you. Would I be wrong in saying that perhaps he even loves you—I mean, as a man loves a woman?"

Furtively, Del pulled a handkerchief from her purse and dabbed her tear-streaked cheeks. Her voice was hoarse when she answered. "Perhaps. I don't know any more. It's been so long since I saw him last and so much has happened."

"Do *you* love Jack?" Flynn asked, fully aware that he might be driving his point into a broken heart.

"I did once," she answered bleakly. "Not any more, though. We're two different people now, Michael. We live in completely different worlds."

Flynn turned to face her. "There's only one world, Del," he said and then added wearily, "It doesn't change much. What changes is how we perceive it—'now through a glass darkly, then face-to-face.'" He was deliberately alluding to a biblical passage with which he knew Del would be familiar.

"I'm not there yet, Michael," Del answered grimly.

"We are all in a different place, my dear," he observed, moving closer to her. "But I hope you won't object if I conduct my own investigation into the devilish details of this matter."

Startled, Del looked up at the big man now standing directly in front of her. "No," she said. "It's something you have to do, I suppose."

Flynn nodded. "It's time for Vespers, so we'll have to end this now." Leaning over her, he made the sign of the cross on her forehead. "Go in peace, Del."

* * *

Jack was still using crutches when, in early August, he moved into the small car-barn apartment Greg had prepared for him on his parents' property in the hills above Benicia. At first, Jack had felt very uncomfortable with this arrangement. For he was now not only a crippled convict on parole but also an untried manager responsible for overseeing a vineyard that employed two dozen farm workers and encompassed more than 200 acres.

Every morning at 6:00, Jack would awkwardly dress himself and hobble across the Henshaks' once neatly manicured but now neglected and weed-choked lawn toward the main house—a sprawling two-story ranch house, surrounded on three sides with a large porch. With Greg's father deceased and his mother transplanted to her daughter's home in southern California, the Henshak manse was an unkempt bachelors' quarters. The elegant furniture and family portraits that once filled the house had been placed in off-site storage and most of its bedrooms locked to discourage vandalizing guests and servants. Florence Henshak did not trust either her son or her faithful caretaker Wally Sykes to look after the belongings she had left behind.

When Jack entered the house on this particular morning, Wally was in the kitchen cooking sausage while Greg sat at the barren oak table in the dining room reading the *San Francisco Examiner* and drinking coffee from a large porcelain mug.

"Good morning," Greg said without looking up from his paper.

"How's the leg this morning?" Wally asked as Jack entered the kitchen and poured a cup of coffee for himself.

"Still pretty stiff," Jack answered. "The hospital doctor said that's the way it'll be for another couple of weeks at least." Returning to the dining room, he very carefully eased himself into a chair.

Greg folded his paper and reached for one of the oranges Wally had placed in a cracked ceramic bowl on the table. "Think you're up to a tour of the vineyard this morning, Jack?" he asked.

"Sure. Guess that's the only way I'm going to learn about all the different varietals you have. Afraid the line drawings in those books you gave me don't help much."

Greg nodded as he popped the first wedge of an orange into his mouth. "Mmm! These are pretty tasty! You ought to try one."

"Do you harvest citrus?" Jack asked.

"We used to. But there's too many other growers in the south to make it worthwhile. We do make lemon cello sometimes. The Christian Brothers over in Martinez are a lot better at it than we are, though."

"Lemon cello was one of Adam's favorites," Jack remarked, his voice suddenly filled with sadness.

"Sorry I mentioned it," Greg said. "I didn't know."

"You boys want griddle cakes with these sausages?" Wally called out from the kitchen.

"No thanks, Wally," Greg answered. "It's going to be too hot out there in the vineyards this morning for those lead balloons you cook up. Unless *you* want some, Jack" Greg added.

"Sausage and scrambled eggs 'll be fine for me. Nice of you to offer, though, Wally."

"My pleasure, my boy!" Wally chirped as he scraped the cooked sausages onto a platter and began cracking eggs into a bowl. "Scrambled eggs comin' up!"

"There was a phone call for you last night, after you went to bed," Greg said to Jack. "Some fellow named Michael Flynn."

Jack grimaced. "What did *he* want?"

"He didn't say. He just left his name and a phone number. He wants you to call him back. You know him?"

"He's one of Del's teachers over at Saint Mary's. She brought him with her to the hospital while I was there. A real joker! I thought he was a priest at first, but he claims he isn't. Del says he's a friar, whatever that is!"

"Maybe he wants to convert you," Greg observed with a taunting smile.

"Hope not," Jack laughed. "Last thing I need right now is some goofy evangelist breathing down my neck."

Sipping from his coffee mug, Greg smiled slyly. "Remember Missus Moran, our Sunday School teacher?"

"Of course," Jack said, eyeing his friend warily. "You're not going to tell me *she* called here last night too!"

"No," Greg said, no longer smiling. "Poor old girl died three years ago. Some kind of cancer. She was a terrible busybody, but I always liked her. Remember that song she taught us? How'd it go now? 'Jesus loves me, this I know …' "

"'Cause the Bible tells me so," Jack intoned, completing the verse. Then, shaking his head vigorously as if he had suddenly tasted something bitter, he declared, "How can anybody believe that crap!"

Greg looked at his friend in sadness. "You're pretty bitter, I guess."

"I don't believe in fairy tales, if that's what you mean," Jack said.

"Maybe that's because you've been living in your own fairy tale and it turned out to be a nightmare."

"Easy for a rich kid to say!" Jack retorted. "I did what I had to do to survive. Nobody was paying my way."

"Still, from what I hear, you and Adam made quite a bundle over the past few years."

"How do you know that?" Jack snapped back. "You don't know *anything* about what it's been like for Adam and me!"

"OK, boys. Time t' quit your squabblin' and down some o' this good grub I fixed for y'," Wally insisted as he dropped a steaming platter full of sausages and eggs on the table and, handing each of them a plate and knife and fork, sat down to eat his own breakfast. "You want more coffee, you'll have t' wait 'cause I had t' make a fresh pot."

"Thanks, Wally," Greg said, grateful both for his cooking and his intervention.

"Yeah, thanks," Jack echoed, still bristling with resentment.

They ate in silence for several minutes until they heard a truck pull up in the driveway at the back of the house. "That 'll be Garcia and his boys," Wally said. "You better hurry up an' get out there, Greg, or them Mex'cans 'll be comin' in here 'xpectin' me to feed them too."

Greg stood up. "You ready, Jack?"

When Jack nodded and also got up from the table, Greg handed him a wide-brimmed straw hat like the one he was already wearing himself. "You better put this on, buddy. Pretty hot out there."

"Thanks," Jack said, smiling his gratitude as he followed Greg out onto the porch.

CHAPTER THIRTY-THREE

"Dancing in the Dark"

IT WAS A COLD SATURDAY morning in November. A stiff wind off the Strait pounded at the windows in the front of the Lanham manse, making them rattle in their frames. Del sat in the kitchen drinking her first cup of coffee and reading the mail she had picked up at the Post Office the night before. She relished the warmth emanating from the big cast-iron stove.

Ruby was still asleep upstairs. She slept late often now because of the heavy sedation Dr. Silas Wentworth, the new and youthful general practitioner in town, had prescribed for Ruby's arthritis. Long gone were the days when this faithful servant rose early to prepare breakfast for Del. Now it was Del who waited on Ruby—who swept and dusted, did the food shopping and cooked the meals, washed the dishes and took out the trash.

In spite of worsening economic conditions nationwide in the fall of 1931, Del could have hired someone to perform all these household chores. Her father had invested wisely over the years in railroad and oil company bonds that continued to generate a steady though modest income for his daughter. But Del did not like the idea of a stranger taking care of the one person in the world whom Del loved most.

Among the letters she read that morning was a long missive from Father Michael Flynn. He had recently taken his final vows and was now a full-fledged priest about to embark on his first assignment as the assistant pastor of a mission parish in Chiapas, Mexico. Del eagerly read his beautifully hand-written words:

Dearest Adelaide,

I know you don't like your friends to address you with that name, but it's high time you became accustomed to it since you will soon be entering a profession that is dominated by stuffy old men. I pity you!

I too must now become accustomed to being treated by others as if I were some kind of freak from another dimension. You cannot begin to imagine how awkward it feels to be addressed as "Father" rather than "Brother." My superiors tell me that, among the peasants in Mexico, it is customary to grovel before a priest and that I must honor that custom by commanding it wherever I go and whatever I do. I can only pray that Our Lord will give me the grace to bear such a heavy cross.

But enough about me! I have very good news to report about Jack. I met with him several times before I left for Mexico . I suspect that's so primarily because Jack regards me as a useful resource in his management of the Henshak vineyards. As you probably realize, I have many acquaintances—brothers!—who are affiliated with the Christian Brothers Winery in Martinez. That winery has recently become one of Jack's biggest customers, and the Brothers have quickly spread the word that Henshak grapes are among the finest available. In spite of the bad times we are in right now, I feel sure Jack's efforts will be richly rewarded.

I realize it must all seem very Machiavellian to you that I have used Jack's appetite for financial success as a means to capture his immortal soul! But Holy Mother Church has been doing this sort of thing for centuries, so it should come as no great surprise to you. In any case, I have managed to engage Jack in quite a few very interesting discussions on topics that touch his spirit. I just hope no one reveals to

Jack that I am now a priest, for that would undoubtedly terrify the poor fellow.

Nor, I hope, do you expect me to share the detailed findings of my investigation with you. It's not that I have become Jack's confessor and must therefore keep everything he shares with me in confidence. Jack doesn't even know what a confessional looks like. I doubt that he has ever even seen the inside a Catholic church! Nevertheless, I feel obliged to keep what he has told me in strict confidence.

I assure you, however, that Jack is indeed "a good man at heart." Despite all the secular laws he and his fellow bootleggers may have broken, they appear to have done so only out of dire necessity. As I'm sure you're aware, Negroes are still at the bottom of the social order here in America. Jack has told me that rival Caucasian gangs have repeatedly threatened and even murdered Negro members of Adam's gang. This forces me to believe the real evil here is racial bigotry—a subject you and I have often discussed. Remember what happened to the Scottsboro boys last March?

If anything, Adam Tucker is living proof of the injustice of such bigotry. He has guided and protected Jack ever since Jack was forced to run away from home ten years ago. It's no surprise that Jack has come to regard Adam as his adopted father. Isn't it interesting that now both of you are grieving orphans? All the more reason for you to be compassionate and forgiving toward each other!

As I think you already know, Del, Jack is by nature a simple man. His naiveté about faith and morals has made him especially vulnerable to temptation. I'm afraid the Baptist Sunday School education he had as a child did not prepare him for the evil he has had to face as a man. The horrors he most recently experienced at Castle Rock have left him bitter and cynical.

Jack is still a young man, however. Our heavenly Father will undoubtedly give him many future opportunities to grow in his faith. In working for his friend Greg, Jack is already on the path to redemption!

I would like to be able to continue encouraging Jack on this path. But, now that I'm so far away, I cannot—except, of course, through my daily prayers for both of you.

I know you will be very busy with your studies in the months to come, but I hope you will write to me whenever you can. I also urge you to continue your friendship with Jack and Greg. Both of these men are worthy of that.

Yours in Christ,
Michael

Del was not happy with Michael's letter. Michael seemed to gloss over Jack's selfish recklessness and make excuses for it by blaming his lack of adequate religious education. She knew Jack better than this pompous scripture-spouting priest! Worst of all, yet again a man whom she had trusted was abandoning her!

Trembling with anger and resentment, Del tried to calm herself by getting up from the kitchen table and walking into the front parlor where she stood for several minutes gazing out at the dark clouds lowering over the hills to the southwest. A heavy downpour was imminent.

Suddenly Del remembered she had planned a shopping trip to San Francisco with her friend Joanna Newman that afternoon. Her plans would have to be changed because of the inclement weather. She went to the wall phone in the foyer and picked up the receiver to call Joanna. "Jo," she said when her friend answered, "Would you mind awfully if we don't go into the city today? I just don't feel up to chasing taxis and trolleys in the rain."

"Great minds think alike!" Joanna declared. "I was just about to call you and make the same suggestion. I found out only yesterday that I have to write a lab report for my Chemistry class and it's due Monday. Do you believe the nerve of some of these college profs? We can go next Saturday if you like. Brad will be in town on business next week, so we can have lunch with him at the Saint Francis or someplace. I can hardly wait for you two to meet!"

Del had often heard Joanna praise her cousin Bradford Conklin. A graduate of Notre Dame, he had been a star quarterback while he was there and, at twenty-five, had already made a name for himself as a successful precious metals trader on the Chicago Commodities Exchange. "Still the matchmaker, eh?" Del said with a soft chuckle.

"Why not? You're a ripe plum, ready for picking. And, believe me, Brad's a swanky guy!"

"Alright, Jo. I'll take your word for it. Now go write your lab report."

"Okey-doke! See y' next Saturday, kiddo."

When Del next called the Henshaks' home number, Wally Sykes answered. "Del Lanham!" he exclaimed jubilantly. "How *are* you! I haven't seen you since that night you silly kids tried to cross the Strait in a teacup! I hear you're in college now and planning to become a lawyer. Just like y'r ol' man, huh?"

Del was not happy with Wally's flippant reference to her father, but she realized there was no malice in Wally's off-handed manner. "Is Jack there?" she asked, ignoring his questions, most of which she considered mere rhetorical babble.

"Greg and him's up in Calistoga peddlin' grapes this weekend. Prob'ly won't be back 'til Sunday night. You want Jack to call you?"

"No," she replied. "It's not important. I'll try again next week." Del did not want to give Wally the impression she was pursuing Jack——an impression she supposed Wally would probably convey to Jack anyway. "Thank you, Wally," she said and promptly hung up.

Del was relieved that she had not spoken to Jack after all. Calmer now than she had been a few moments before, she decided she needed to read Michael's letter again and think more carefully about what he had written.

Was Michael implying that she too should undertake the "investigation" he had begun? She wasn't sure. More importantly, she didn't know whether she wanted to. Her own life was already complicated enough, what with fall semester examinations coming up soon as well as the Christmas holidays. Her Aunt Lucy and her Uncle

Charles were coming for a weeklong visit. She would have to shop for gifts and make plans for meals and outings.

Then too there was this "swanky guy" Joanna said she wanted Del to meet. Brad Conklin sounded very interesting. It had been months since Del had dated anyone. Maybe it was time to stop dwelling on Jack's past offenses and meet someone new.

* * *

Jack made no attempt to return Del's phone call until late the following Wednesday night. "Sorry I didn't get back to you sooner," he said. "Greg and I have been pretty busy lately reeling in new customers for this year's Cabernet harvest. Business is really picking up!" he proudly announced.

So Michael had been right. Jack's new job managing the Henshak vineyards was restoring his spirit. "I'm glad to hear that, Jack," Del replied coolly. "I just hope it continues. The economic news isn't very good these days. Banks are closing all over the country." Unable to resist the temptation to remind Jack of his own shadowy past, she added, "Even Al Capone has been put out of business."

Jack sighed in exasperation. He knew little about Al Capone or banks closing in other parts of the country, for he seldom read anything in the newspapers except the sports columns. "I've been through hard times before, Del. This won't last forever," he assured her.

"Have you talked to your mother lately?" Del asked.

"You know what? I haven't," Jack admitted, but without the degree of remorse Del had been looking for. "You're right. I *should* call her. As a matter of fact, why don't you and I take her out for dinner? I hear there's a great new place that just opened up in Benicia. I think it's called Sparky's Fish Grotto."

"Your mother would probably like that," Del said, her tone of voice still edged with resentment. "When do you want to do this?"

"How about this coming Saturday night?"

"Sorry, Jack. I've already promised some friends I'd meet them in the city."

Jack's voice signaled disappointment, but he was in no mood to back down. "How about this coming Friday, then?"

Del hesitated. She did not like being pushed. "Alright," she said at last. "We'll go in my car. I'll pick you up at Greg's, say around 6:00. You'd better check with your mother first, though, to see if she'll be able to make it. Call me and let me know. Do we need to make a reservation at this restaurant?"

Jack laughed derisively. "Make a reservation at a fish joint in Benicia! Are you kidding me?"

Del was not amused. "Call me," she retorted and hung up. But then, glimpsing her own angry face reflected in the hallway mirror, she stuck out her tongue at herself.

* * *

Friday was fish night for most residents of Benicia during the 1930s, not only because so many were Roman Catholics but also because fish was the most plentiful and therefore cheapest supply of food in the Carquinez Strait. Those who could afford to dine out flocked to Sparky's Fish Grotto by the hundreds. A long line of hungry and noisy diners had formed at the roped-off entrance gangplank when Del, Jack and Gail arrived at 6:15. Many of those waiting to be admitted were large family parties, which meant that smaller groups of two or three would probably either have to wait longer or be forced to share a table with strangers.

Del had hoped for a more intimate and leisurely dining experience, but Jack and Gail seemed delighted with the prospect of eating "family style." As they waited in line, Jack and Gail greeted and bantered with several local residents they recognized. Having spent most of the past three years socializing with college friends and acquaintances in Moraga, Del felt distinctly out of place.

By the time they were finally shown to a table on the ferry's upper deck at 7:00, Del was fuming. Sensing her irritation but ignoring it, Jack insisted on ordering Martinis for all of them. "Come on, Del, cheer up," he urged, "this is a time to celebrate! We three haven't been together like this for years!"

Del exchanged a quick glance with Gail, who was also very much aware of Del's displeasure. "What's the house specialty?" Gail asked Jack as she studied the grease-stained cardboard menu the headwaiter had given her. "Besides Martinis, that is," she added with a wink at Del.

"Well, it's November," Jack replied, impervious to his mother's innuendo. "So that means striped bass or maybe, if we're lucky, sturgeon."

Still favoring his healing leg, Jack carefully turned in his chair to look around for a waiter.

The influx of patrons had now greatly diminished because most Benicians with families preferred to eat early. Still there was no sign of a waiter for their table. The irritable expression on Jack's face prompted his mother to say, "Be patient, dear. Someone will be here soon. We're in no hurry, are we?"

"Of course not," Del said as she gazed through the row of westward-facing windows in the restaurant. Over the hilltops to the west, long strands of dark cloud spread like the strokes of a painter's brush on the still pink canvas of the evening sky. "What a lovely view!" she declared, suddenly feeling comfortable in her surroundings.

Jack looked at her in pleased surprise. "Glad you like it, Del. I figured you might." Then, looking out of the windows himself, he said, "Looks just like it did when we were kids. Some things never change, thank God!"

"It's good to see you two together again," Gail said.

Almost immediately, Del bristled. "Together? We're not together, Gail. Not the way we were when we were children and certainly not in the way you're implying."

"And what way is that?" Gail challenged.

Del was silent. She looked at Jack, searching his face for some reaction. But Jack too was silent. He stared at Del now as if she were a complete stranger.

"Never mind," Gail said, embarrassed. "I'm sorry, Del. I should mind my own business."

"No," Del gently corrected, touching Gail's gloved hand where it lay on the table. "I'm the one who should be sorry. I'm not being fair. I know you mean well, Gail. But Jack and I are ..." She paused, groping for the right words. "Well, we're still friends, of course, but our lives are different."

"I understand," Gail murmured sadly.

Jack shook his head. "I wish *I* did," he scowled. "Where *is* that waiter?" he demanded, looking around the room again.

Just as he did so, a man in a short white jacket approached their table. "You folks ready to order?" he asked.

"It's about time!" Jack grumbled.

The waiter's eyes flashed defiance. "Sorry, mister! We're real busy tonight. Ladies, what can I get for y'?"

"I'll have the bass almandine, please," Gail promptly replied.

"The same for me, please," Del said.

"We're going to order drinks first," Jack asserted. Sweeping his hand in a circle, he said, "Martinis all around."

"Right!" the waiter snapped and quickly disappeared.

"That was very rude of you, Jack," Gail reprimanded.

Del wanted to say she agreed, but the glance she exchanged with Gail at that moment rendered any explicit statement unnecessary.

Aware that he had stepped out of bounds, Jack kept silent while the two women talked.

"Jack tells me you're going to law school," Gail said. "That's wonderful, Del! Very brave of you! I dare say there aren't many women lawyers."

"You've got *that* right! It's only this year that a woman has finally been appointed to the California bench," Del announced.

"God help us!" Jack protested. "Who is she?"

"Georgia Bullock," Del archly replied. "She also happens to be a colored person, Jack. I would think you'd at least be glad about that!"

Jack was saved from saying something else he would regret by the arrival of the waiter with their cocktails. Forcing himself to smile, he held up his glass to make a toast. "To Georgia Bullock—may she free us all from the pompous old men in California's courtrooms!"

"She'll do that and more!" Del affirmed, glowering at Jack and clinking her glass only with Gail.

The waiter, who still stood beside their table, asked if they wanted to complete their main coarse orders. Jack struggled to control his anger. "Give us a few minutes, pal, will y'?"

"Yes, please. That would be nice," Gail agreed sweetly. The waiter walked away. Turning to Del, she said, "Tell me more about your career plans, dear. I suppose you'll be going to law school right after you graduate from college next spring. Where would you like to go?"

"My first choice is Stanford, of course," Del replied. "They have the best curriculum for women lawyers. But I'll probably go to Hastings in San Francisco, instead, because it will be much easier for me to commute between there and Benicia. I can take the ferry every day from Vallejo instead of having to travel all the way to Palo Alto."

"Why don't you rent a room or an apartment in Palo Alto?" Jack asked.

Del gave Jack a look that confirmed his worst fear—Del considered his question boorish. "I can't do that because I have to take care of Ruby. She's not well."

"Sorry to hear that," Jack said. "I didn't know. What's wrong with her?"

"She's getting old, Jack. She has terrible arthritis and she's losing her memory."

"Perhaps you could hire someone to take care of her while you're away during the week," Gail suggested.

"I couldn't do that. Ruby has been like a mother to me."

Gail looked down at her cocktail glass, keenly aware that her son was watching for her reaction to Del's reference to motherhood. "You are a very good daughter, Del," she said. "I have often wished I had a daughter like you."

"You have a son who wants to take care of you," Jack put in. "I still do, mother. And I will, if you'll just let me. I'm making very good money now. Greg's vineyard is doing well and I'll soon be able to buy a house of my own. I wish you'd quit that job at the Lido and move in with me."

"I'm happy for you, Jack, and I'm grateful for your offer. But I'm doing fine." Nervously sipping at her drink, Gail reminded him, "We both need our separate spaces, son."

What Gail really meant she had not said. A year before, she had met a man at the Lido with whom she became romantically involved. His name was Vincent Farina. The owner of several gambling casinos in Nevada, Farina was one of Mrs. Parker's wealthiest business associates, though, so far as Gail knew, he had never been one of her customers at the Lido. He was also one of the handsomest and cleverest men Gail had ever met. A true "Dapper Dan," Vincent Farina was always dressed in the latest style of men's clothing and groomed impeccably. Best of all, he had a sense of humor. Gail had never before met a man who could make her laugh so easily and so often.

Immediately attracted to Gail, Farina began wining and dining her every weekend, taking her to soirees at luxurious resort hotels she had only read about and bestowing on her gifts of jewelry and clothing which he encouraged her to select at some of the most expensive boutiques in San Francisco. Wherever they went together, Farina treated her like "a perfect lady," proudly introducing her to prominent businessmen, famous entertainers, and government dignitaries.

Nor did Farina ever seem to have an interest in other women, though he was constantly surrounded with beautiful and flirtatious female admirers. Gail was his proudest prize. He had placed her on a pedestal above everyone else. It was this, at last, that had induced Gail to succumb to his charms.

Gail realized now how completely she had been deceived. Their whirlwind romance ended suddenly a month before when Gail discovered she had syphilis—a disease she could have contracted only from Vincent Farina. When she confronted him with this ugly truth, he had laughed at her. "Well, my dear," he had mocked, "what else could you have possibly expected? After all, did we not meet in a brothel!"

Again Del placed her hand on Gail's. "I wish you would consider Jack's offer," she urged. "Even if it's only for a little while." Glancing sidelong at Jack, she added, "You don't look well, Gail. Both of us are worried about you."

Though startled by Del's candor, Jack nodded his agreement. His mother looked pale and tired, especially at that moment. He suddenly realized that, as a woman, perhaps Del understood his mother better than he did.

Gail's voice hardened. "I think both of you should mind your own business," she replied. "I've already told you, I'm fine. I don't need anyone's help!"

"We all need each other," Del insisted. "Look at this place. It's full of happy families and friends. Isn't that the way it's supposed to be?" she asked, her voice trembling with emotion.

"I think I want to leave now," Gail said, rising from the table.

Jack also stood up. "Mother, please sit down," he pleaded. "We don't want to force you to do anything. We just want you to be happy."

"Happy?" Gail retorted angrily. "Do you know what happiness is, Jack? Are you happy now that your best friends are all dead? And you,

Del, are you happy now that you have to compromise your career to take care of a sick old Negro woman?"

Del stood up and put her arm around Gail's shoulders, gently guiding her back to her chair. "Please, Gail. Don't be angry with us!"

"Is something wrong, ladies?" the waiter asked.

Embarrassed now, Gail sat down.

"No," Jack said to the waiter. "I think we're ready to order. Ladies?" he asked.

"Is the abolone fresh?" Gail inquired of the waiter.

"Yes, Ma'm. Came in just this morning."

"Good. That's what I'll have."

"The same for me," Del said.

"And me," Jack echoed. "Oh, and bring us a bottle of *Chateau d'Yquem* if you have it."

"Yes sir," the waiter said with an approving smile and swiftly moved away.

"I'm sure we'll all feel better once we've had something to eat," Gail observed, calmer now.

"Oh yes!" Del agreed. "I'm starved!" Then to Jack she said, "*Chateau d'Yquem*? Jack, aren't you being a little extravagant?"

"Nothing but the best for my favorite ladies!" he replied with a gallant smile.

Nodding her approval, Gail smiled. "Now that, Mister Westlake, is what I call the right attitude."

"Let's all drink to right attitudes!" Del raised her cocktail glass, this time clinking it with both Gail's and Jack's.

"Is that you, Gail Fenton?" a woman suddenly called out from two tables away.

When Gail turned to look at who was addressing her by her maiden name, she immediately recognized Beth and Wendy Wentworth, twin spinster sisters who had been her teachers at the West End Grammar School more than twenty years before. Beth had taught arithmetic and Wendy music. Wendy had also given Gail private piano lessons. Now in their late sixties, both women were still the plump and jolly mentors she had always adored as a girl. They immediately got up from their table and rushed to embrace Gail.

Overwhelmed with joy, Gail burst into tears. "Oh Wendy! Oh Beth! How wonderful to see you again!" she exclaimed.

"And is this little Jackie?" Beth said, gazing up in awe at Jack as he stood, grinning down at the pixie-like twins.

"My! How you've grown!" Wendy gasped. "And such a ..."

"... handsome young man!" Beth declared, completing her sister's sentence.

Del laughed, unable to control her amusement at this duet. Her laughter evoked immediate and simultaneous smiles of friendly curiosity from the twins.

"And you, I suppose, are ..." Beth began.

"... Jackie's lady friend," Wendy continued.

"Well ..." Del hesitated. "Yes, we're friends," she allowed. "My name's Adelaide Lanham." Del had given them her full first name because she realized it was probably what these two elderly ladies would expect.

"The Honorable Judge Lanham's daughter!" Wendy exclaimed.

"Of course!" Beth continued. "We should have known. You have your father's beautiful eyes ..."

"... and strong chin," Wendy added. "You're much prettier than he, of course!" she quickly added with an admiring smile.

"Please, ladies," Jack said, still resonating pleasurably with his mother's toast. "Won't you join us?"

"Oh dear no!" Beth replied.

"Thank you, but we've already eaten," Wendy explained. "And we have to get home ..."

"To walk our little Toby," Beth cut in.

"Toby's our cocker spaniel," Wendy further explained. "He's old and crotchety."

"Not at all like us, of course!" Beth giggled.

"He keeps us on a very tight schedule. If we don't feed him and take him for his walks at the appointed times, ..." Wendy explained.

"... he becomes very cross. So, you see, we really must go now." Beth nodded to Wendy and then to Gail said, "But you must come have tea with us sometime soon, my dear."

Reaching into her handbag, Wendy took out a calling card and gave it to Gail. "We live close by here ..."

"… on West K Street," Beth specified. "We're at home most afternoons."

"But give us a call ahead of time to be sure," Wendy advised. "Our phone number is on our card, And, by all means, Jack …"

"… you and Adelaide must come too," Beth insisted.

As if on a prearranged signal, the sisters exchanged warm hugs with Gail, Jack and Del. "Bye-bye now!" they declared in chorus and promptly headed for the stairway down to the main deck.

"Goodness!" Del exclaimed, laughing out loud. "What a sketch they are!"

"Like something right out of a vaudeville show!" Jack quipped.

"Or *Alice in Wonderland*!" Del declared.

Gail's face was streaked with tears of happiness as she said, "They are the sweetest, dearest people I know!"

* * *

An hour later, Gail, Jack and Del were walking barefoot together in the sand along Diamond Beach, enjoying the cool but gentle breeze blowing across the Carquinez Strait. A full moon was rising over Mount Diablo to the east. Its bright light glittered on the surface of the water and turned the beach into a ribbon of white. None of them spoke, but they walked hand-in-hand like contented children after a sumptuous meal.

Suddenly, Gail began singing words from the latest popular radio tune—Kate Smith's "When the Moon Comes Over the Mountain." Del quickly joined in, the two women laughing as together they sang the last verse, "When the moon comes over the mountain, I'll be alone with my memories of you."

Jack vigorously applauded, so Del began singing her latest favorite, "Lady of Spain, I adore you." Now both Jack and Gail joined in.

Then, linking arms, the three of them sang and danced together along the luminous beach, their hearts brought together at last by the irresistible rhythm and bittersweet lyrics of Bing Crosby's "Dancing in the Dark."

1932

The Washington Hotel

CHAPTER THIRTY-FOUR

"I Guess I'll Have to Change My Plan"

DEIRDRE HARTZ WAS THE APPLE of her father's eye. As she spun the wheel of his thirty-three foot sloop *Cormorant* and eased the vessel into a smooth reach only a few yards off the rocky eastern end of Alcatraz Island, Victor Hartz turned to his wife Margaret and declared, "Now that's what I call precision!"

"And grace!" Margaret declared, glancing admiringly at her husband. "Just good genes, I suppose—from *both* of us!"

"I'll toast to that," Victor replied, raising his sailing mug filled with equal quantities of tomato juice and gin.

Victor and Margaret Hartz were a paragon couple. Though in their late fifties, they had the lean and muscular bodies of thirty-year-olds and the fair hair and perfectly sculpted facial features of Teutonic warriors. They were the envy of every other member of Alameda's Encenal Yacht Club. It was not only their good looks that awed everyone, though. It was also their very significant financial wealth and social prominence.

As a senior partner of Sherman, Hartz and Colby, one of San Francisco's most successful law firms, Victor had accumulated a hoard that allowed him to own fifteen percent of the Southern Pacific Railroad and ten percent of the Shell Oil Company, as well as elegant waterfront homes in San Francisco and Newport Beach. As the niece and principal heiress of one of California's wealthiest bankers, James T. McCracken, Margaret had brought to their marriage a degree of prestige and power unmatched by any other couple in the Bay Area. Having, in her now distant past, held star roles in such Broadway hits as *Student Prince* and

Naughty Marietta, Margaret still enjoyed some measure of theatrical celebrity on both coasts. She leaned back on the boat cushion in the *Comorant's* large cockpit now, stretching out her long, shapely legs to bask in the bright early September sun.

Closing her eyes, Margaret reminisced about the days when she bowed repeatedly before the roaring applause of theater audiences in New York, Boston, and Chicago. She luxuriated too in the belief that her husband's eyes were now greedily focused on her full and still firm breasts. She was Cleopatra on her barge drifting down the Nile; she was Queen Bess waving to her cheering subjects as she sailed passed them on the River Thames. It was not her twenty-two-year-old daughter's accomplishments that were foremost in her mind but her own. "I think we should send Deirdre to Europe in the fall," she announced, her eyes still closed.

"Why's that?" Victor had shifted his attention from the lean and supple figure of his daughter to the prow of his boat as it pointed due North toward Point Richmond.

"I'm concerned about this hot romance she seems to be having with that Westlake boy."

"Westlake?" Victor asked. "Who's that? Never heard of him."

"Yes you have!" Margaret countered, opening her eyes and squinting disapproval at her husband. "You met him at the club barbeque only last week. Big, strapping fellow. He works for the Henshak Vineyards in Benicia. He's very handsome, I must admit, but he's definitely not our kind."

Removing his sailing cap, Victor wiped perspiration from his brow and neck with one of the clean towels he always stowed in the cockpit cubby for that purpose. "Deirdre's smart enough to take care of herself," he said confidently. "I wouldn't worry about it."

Alarmed, Margaret sat upright. "But I *do* worry! And so should you!" she insisted. "Girls today are very reckless. You've no idea how many horrible stories I've heard about the disgusting things they do, and I'm not just talking about heavy petting in the back seat of a car! Do you know what I found in Deirdre's dresser drawer yesterday?"

Uninterested, Victor continued to gaze straight ahead.

"A box of condoms!"

"Only confirms what I said," Victor smirked. "Deirdre's smart. She knows how to protect herself."

"You're impossible!" Margaret declared.

"I have other more pressing matters to think about, Meg," Victor replied, still not looking at her.

"Like what?" Margaret demanded to know.

""Well, for one thing, do you realize that in less than two years, New York Central's stock has dropped from 168 to 34? Our SP shares aren't doing much better. I think Deirdre will have to be satisfied with sailing in the Bay rather than across the Atlantic this fall," Victor observed grimly. "She's finished college so it's time for her to find some kind of employment—if she can, that is."

"Are you saying we're going broke?" Margaret asked in panic.

"Not yet, but many people are. Some of my best client accounts, in fact, are delinquent by several months."

"I don't believe you! Surely you're exaggerating, Victor!"

"Perhaps you should read something more than the fashion pages in *Vogue*, my dear," Victor observed with undisguised contempt. "Unfortunately, no one in Washington seems to know how to fix this mess and that fast-talking governor of New York is making noises that sound increasingly socialistic. I wouldn't be at all surprised if he threw his hat in the ring for the next presidential election. God only knows what will happen if the Democrats take over!"

Margaret was not the least bit fazed by her husband's sarcasm and tough talk about business and politics. She had her own agenda and was determined to make him address it. "If Deirdre needs a job, then you need to find one for her. I'm sure there must be some sort of girl Friday thing she can do at your office."

"Sorry, Meg," Victor replied. "My budget's stretched to the limit. Actually, we're laying support staff off at the office right now."

"What about that Lanham girl you just hired? She's the same age as Deirdre."

"Del has a law degree, or will in a few months. We need to beef up our criminal defense team. That's the one area where there's growing demand right now. Besides, Del's coming on board as an intern at thirty dollars a week."

"That's disgusting!" Meg declared. "Practically slave labor. You should be ashamed of yourself, Victor!"

"It's what keeps you in diamonds and furs, my dear," Victor said, taking another swig from his sailing mug.

* * *

Jack was surprised by the large number of people who had shown up at his mother's funeral service in Saint Dominic's parish hall that October 10 afternoon. After all, Gail was not a Catholic, which is why the service was being held in the parish hall instead of in the church proper. It was only the very considerable influence Mrs. K. T. Parker had on the pastor (she was one of Saint Dominic's most generous donors) that had persuaded him to allow obsequies for a Protestant on church property.

The parish priests had not participated in the funeral rites, since doing so would be in violation of cannon law. Instead, the service was conducted by one of the church ushers, a wizened sage named Norman Agulha. Norman was the eighty-five-year-old patriarch of a large Portuguese family that had lived in Benicia for four generations. Norman and all of his brothers and their sons and grandsons had, at one time or another, been both altar boys at Saint Dominc's Church and patrons of the Lido. Norman was so old and feeble that he could barely walk and his voice, so weak no one could hear the mixture of Latin and Portuguese words he mumbled over Gail's closed coffin during the opening invocation.

It had not mattered. Many others were present to volunteer their lengthy epitaphs about a woman most of them knew only by her reputation as one of Mrs. K. T. Parker's "angels of mercy." Death was a subject the poor of Benicia were well acquainted with, however, and the number of Roman Catholic poor in town had tripled during the past nine months. Any occasion that allowed these hapless victims of circumstance to express their anger and despair was welcome.

One of the most vehement of those victims was Ted Sena's widow, Olivia. A tall, sturdy woman in her middle fifties, Olivia stood before the large assembly of mourners and proclaimed her anger with the eloquence of Hector.

"I did not know Gail Westlake, but I knew her son Jack," she began, nodding to Jack where he sat in a chair beside his mother's coffin. "Many in this town blame Jack's mother for his life of crime. They say she abandoned him. But what do they know? Her life, like ours, was hard. First, she lost her husband in the Great War. Then, left a penniless widow, she had to go to work for a Jew!"

Here Olivia paused to glower at Ira Jacobs who, trying his best to be inconspicuous, had taken a seat in the last row of chairs at the back of the parish hall. As scores of his fellow mourners turned to imitate Olivia's scornful stare, he hunched over and lowered his tear-filled eyes. *What have I done to these people?* he asked himself. *How have I deserved this?*

Not satisfied with the obvious pain she had inflicted, Olivia pressed on with her attack. "A Jew!" she declared vehemently. "Was it not the Jews who crucified Our Lord? Is it any wonder this poor woman turned to a life of sin? Is it any wonder her own son was corrupted by a nigger and condemned to a life of crime?" To these questions, many in Olivia's audience nodded their agreement.

Jack jumped up from his chair. "Enough, woman!" he shouted. "Shut your mouth and sit down!"

Startled but undeterred, Olivia turned her fury on Jack. "How dare you talk to me like that!"

"Shut up and sit down, Olivia!" a man called out from her otherwise spellbound audience. The man who spoke was Steve Venizelos, recently laid off from his job in the patterning shop at the Alta Plant. Jack was startled to see how time and hardship had aged Venizelos. Dressed in a tattered work shirt and soiled corduroy trousers, this man, once so particular about his personal appearance, now had long gray hair down to his shoulders and a matching shaggy beard. Thin and stoop-shouldered, he stood up and moved slowly to the front of the hall. "Go on, woman, sit down!" he commanded.

Olivia stood her ground. "I will not!" she shouted, her face turning red with rage.

"Fine!" Venizelos growled. "Then just stand there and listen. You're dead wrong about Ira. He's a good man. I know 'cause I done a lot o' bus'ness with him back in the days when I worked at the tannery. And you're wrong about Gail and Jack and Adam Tucker too," he said with a sympathetic glance at Jack. "You said yourself you didn't know Gail

Westlake. Well, I did and I can tell all of y' Gail was an honest and hard-working woman. She did her best to raise Jack to be honest and hard working too. You got no right to judge her, Olivia!"

Venizelos' declaration was greeted with loud applause, to which Olivia responded by marching to the back of the room and leaving the hall—a final act of defiance that prompted many in that assembly to clap louder and even to cheer at her departure.

Satisfied that he had said what he needed to, Venizelos returned to his seat. As he did so, a tall, slender woman in funereal black rose from her chair and walked to the front of the hall. There she turned to confront the other mourners, her face completely hidden beneath a large black hat and veil. The woman waited until the room was completely silent. Then, lifting her veil to reveal her face, she surveyed her audience and said, "You all know who I am."

Several women gasped and several men guffawed, for everyone did indeed recognize the stern features of Mrs. K. T. Parker. Ignoring these vocal expressions of self-righteous shock and scorn, she opened the small black prayer book she was carrying and read aloud from its text: " 'Come to me, all you who labor and are burdened, and I will give you rest. Take my yoke upon you, for I am meek and humble of heart; and you will find rest for yourselves. For my yoke is easy and my burden light.'

"All of you also know these words Our Lord spoke to his followers," Parker said, looking up to survey her audience with a steady gaze. "We are *all* His followers, and we are all here for the same reason—to honor the memory of a woman who labored and was burdened and to pray that she will at last find rest in the arms of Christ." Closing her prayer book, Parker stepped quietly to the bier, kissed the top of Gail's coffin, lowered her veil, and returned to her seat where she bowed her head in silent prayer.

Whether it was shock or fear that prompted their response, all now bowed their heads. Silence reigned in the parish hall for several minutes until Snooky Wells stood up and pushed her son Alfie in his wheel chair to the front of the hall. There, she turned his chair so that he faced the assembly and, shouldering her banjo strap, began strumming and singing a slow and mournful rendition of *Nearer My God to Thee*.

Snooky's dirge quickly inspired others to join in. These included

Jasper Papadopolis on his flute, Jorge Saraiva on his mandolin, and Kevin Caley on his fiddle. Next, Snooky began strumming the first few bars of *When the Saints Go Marching In*, slowly at first but gradually increasing her tempo until everyone began clapping and singing along with her.

The jubilant spirit this Gospel song aroused inside the parish hall soon spilled over into an impromptu parade down First Street to the old Washington House hotel, where Mrs. Parker had reserved the second-floor dance hall for Gail's wake. By the time the parade of mourners reached the hotel, its size had more than doubled. For nothing attracted a crowd in Benicia like the prospect of free food and alcoholic beverages. Parker had paid in advance for a plentiful supply of both. Always thinking ahead, she had known such a public ceremony would be as good for her business as it would for Gail's immortal soul.

Along one wall of the second floor dance hall, a row of long tables had been set up, covered with brown paper and laden with platters of freshly baked bread and large pots of *sopas*—the favorite fare of Benicia's Portuguese community. Tending and constantly replenishing the food on these tables were a dozen men and women in the colorful attire of Saint Dominic's Holy Ghost Society.

Unaware of the generosity of these people or of Mrs. Parker's part in purchasing the food and several kegs of beer for the occasion, Jack was nonetheless pleased to see such an outpouring of community support. He recognized many faces of the men who attended from the days when he worked as a shoeshine boy at Huey's barber shop and from the card games he had played at Frank's Place. He was disappointed, though, because Steve Venizelos was not among them. He had hoped to thank Steve personally for what he had said at his mother's funeral.

"So what do you think, Jack?" Snooky asked as she greeted him at the entrance to the hall. "Ain't this somethin'? Bet y' never thought your Momma was so popular, huh?"

"No. I guess not," Jack answered with a skeptical smile. He did not delude himself that everyone in this rowdy crowd was there simply to honor his mother's memory. "It's good to see you," he said, giving both Snooky and her son warm hugs. "How are you?"

"We're good, Jack. How you holdin' up?"

Jack motioned toward Greg who was standing directly behind him.

"Thanks to this guy, I'm doing pretty well. He gave me a job after I got out of the hospital. You two know each other? This is my friend Greg Henshak."

"Oh I know Greg awright! He prob'ly don't know me, though," Snooky chortled.

"Everybody in town knows you, Snooky," Greg said, shaking her hand. "You're such a fine musician. It's a pleasure to meet you in person."

"Likewise. Ain't every day old Snooky gets to shake hands with a millionaire," Snooky remarked with thinly disguised sarcasm. Turning to Jack, she asked, "You talked to K.T. yet?"

Jack winced. "No. I'm not so sure I want to, even though I appreciate what she said at the funeral."

"Nobody's all bad, Jack," Snooky said. "When they's hard times, we all gotta help each other."

"I suppose you're right, Snooky," Jack concurred reluctantly. He still felt deep resentment toward Parker, not only because she had induced his mother to work at the Lido but also because of what had happened to Becky Partridge eight years before. He had always blamed Parker for Becky's death. He suspected Parker was complicit in his mother's death as well.

Seeing the resentment in Jack's face, Snooky shrugged her shoulders. "Well, me an' Alfie gotta go do some sing-alongs." Touching Jack's cheek affectionately, she said, "You take care o' yourself, Jack."

Greg and Jack watched Snooky as she pushed Alfie in his wheelchair toward the raised platform at one end of the dance hall where the mustachioed Jorge Saraiva was already entertaining the crowd with a medley of fast-moving mazurkas on his mandolin.

* * *

A few minutes later Jack and Greg stood at the downstairs bar of the Washington House, hiding from the noisy throng above. Jack kept his eye on the main entrance. Of all the people attending his mother's funeral, Del was the one he had most wanted to see. "I wonder why she didn't show up," he said to Greg.

Greg shrugged. "I don't know, Jack, unless maybe she's too busy. She has a new job, you know, with Victor Hartz's firm over in San

Francisco. She tells me they're going to assign her to a case as soon as she passes the State bar."

Somewhat amused that he was now dating the daughter of the man who had hired Del, Jack was nonetheless annoyed that Greg was more informed about Del's activities than he. Frowning, he asked, "How'd you know about that?"

"Ran into her down at the depot a couple of weeks ago. She was on her way to Sacramento and I was waiting for Mother to come in on the train from Oakland."

"What about Ruby?" Jack asked. "Del told me Ruby's sick. If Del's working in San Francisco, who's taking care of her?"

"I don't know, Jack. She didn't say anything about that."

The two friends stood in silence for several minutes, listening to the thumping of dancing feet coming through the ceiling above them. Gail's funeral reception was rapidly turning into a drunken spree. A shiney-faced bartender pointed at Jack's empty beer glass. Jack nodded and the man promptly refilled it from a tap.

Greg emptied his own glass and held it out to the bartender. "I'll have another too, please," he said.

"Yah, yah," the man answered, speaking for the first time since Jack and Greg had entered the bar.

"You're new in town," Jack observed as the bartender filled Greg's glass. "What's your name?"

"Yah," the bartender answered. "My name iss Hans Schmidt. I come mid my brudder Otto long way in ship from Germany." Shaking his head, he added, "Not good in Germany now."

"Why's that?" Jack asked with casual interest. "What's wrong?"

"Bad things happen. No vork. Many riots."

"There isn't much work here either, Hans," Greg said.

Holding Greg's filled beer glass in one hand, the German placed his other on the bar top and fixed Greg with a desperate stare. "Still better here. No Nazis. No Hitler. Very bad man!"

Greg remembered reading something about a man named Hitler in the back pages of the *San Francisco Examiner* several weeks before. But he knew little about this man or his National Socialist Party except that it had something to do with German politics. He had never before heard the term *Nazi*. As for Jack, he knew nothing about any of this.

"Why do you say this fellow Hitler is bad?" Greg asked.

Hans relinquished the beer glass to Greg. "He vant to make super race und rule whole world," the bartender said, stressing the magnitude of Hitler's ambitions by stretching his arms out and making grabbing gestures with his hands. "So ve come to America. Find vork und live free mans."

"Good luck, buddy," Greg said as the bartender moved away to wait on another customer.

Someone touched Jack's left forearm. Looking down, he saw a woman's gloved hand and then smelled Del's familiar lavender-scented perfume. "Jack," she said timidly. "I'm sorry I'm late. But, most of all, I'm *so* sorry about your mother!"

Del was smiling up at him, but her face was full of sadness. Jack immediately embraced her. "Thank God you're here!" he declared. "I was beginning to think you …"

Del put her velvet gloved fingers on his lips and shook her head. "Don't say it, Jack. I know what you're thinking, but it isn't so. I *do* care!"

"Then why haven't you answered my phone calls?" he asked irritably.

Del shook her head and bit her lip. "I don't know, Jack. It's just that so many things have been happening lately. I mean, my course load at Hastings has been huge, and then there's Ruby's poor health, and now this …" she broke off, averting her eyes. She realized she probably should have been honest with Jack and told him she was spending what little free time she had with Brad Conklin, whose commodities firm had recently transferred him from Chicago to San Francisco. She didn't want to hurt Jack's feelings, though—especially not now while he was grieving over his mother's death.

"Alright, so you've been busy," Jack conceded. "But maybe I could have helped somehow. Why didn't you call me? Aren't we friends anymore?"

Touching his forearm, she said softly, "Of course, Jack. But …"

"But what?" Jack insisted.

Stepping back from Jack, Del gazed up at him with an expression of despair in her eyes he had never seen before. "Oh Jack—you have no idea! It's not only your mother's death that's so terrible. I just found out my firm is defending the man who murdered my father!"

"Murdered!" Jack exclaimed. "But I thought he … it was suicide."

"That's what the newspapers *claimed*," Del replied bitterly. "But the truth is somebody murdered Papa with his own shotgun and made his death look like a suicide. The police arrested a suspect in Vallejo just last month, and now Victor's firm is going to defend him in court! Oh God, Jack! I just don't know what I'll do!"

"All the more reason you should have called me!" Jack declared.

"Maybe you should back off, Jack," Greg warned.

Jack gave him an angry look. But he said nothing, realizing that perhaps he had come on too strong.

"Thanks, Greg," Del said. "I appreciate that."

"I really like your new look," Greg commented in an effort to lighten their conversation. "Especially your hair and your dress," he added with an admiring smile.

Pleased with Greg's flattery, Del touched the soft curls at the back of her head and moved her hips slightly to draw their attention to the ruffles on her black dress. "I have my new bosses' wife to thank for this," she explained. "She took me to her hair dresser and a very expensive women's boutique in San Francisco. She said I needed a new wardrobe if I was going to work in the city, and insisted on paying for everything herself."

"Wow!" Greg declared. "Sounds like you have a very generous mentor. Congratulations!"

"How'd you wind up working for Victor Hartz?" Jack asked, now feeling completely left out of the conversation.

"Well, you know how much I love to sail. Even after Papa died, I kept my membership in the Vallejo Yacht Club and crewed on other members' boats whenever I could. I guess Victor Hartz must have somehow found out I was going to law school, so one day last summer he came up to me at the Club and asked if I'd be interested in working for him as an intern. I suppose he felt sorry for me. I don't know. Anyway, I decided it was an offer I couldn't refuse. After all," she said with a peevish glance at Jack, "it's very hard for a woman to get started in the legal profession."

"So you've told me," Jack allowed with a sardonic smile.

"I'm sure you'll be very successful," Greg said.

Jack looked around the bar restlessly. Eager to talk with Del alone, he touched her shoulder and said, "Let's get out of here. It's getting too noisy."

"You coming with us, Greg?" Del asked when Greg made no effort to follow them.

"No. You two go on. I know you want to talk. Besides, I have to get to the house. Mother is having guests for dinner and expects me to be there when they arrive."

* * *

After saying goodbye to Greg, Del and Jack drove in her car to Diamond Beach. They stood close together now on the bluffs above, gazing in silence across the wind-swept water toward the Carquinez Bridge. Gulls wheeled noisily across the surface of the water while, higher up, the long-necked geese called stridently to each other in their eastward flight.

Suddenly unable to control his own pent-up feelings, Jack began to weep soundlessly. Del put her arms around his neck and kissed him lightly on the cheek. "Jack," she murmured softly, "I'm *so* sorry!"

Gently pushing her away, Jack dried his eyes with the back of his hand. "Thanks, Del. I needed that." Studying her upturned face, he suddenly realized that Del's kiss, though a sincere expression of her sympathy, meant nothing more. "I guess we've both finally grown up, haven't we, Del?"

"Yes," she answered, taking his hand and guiding him toward the steps down to the beach. "Anyway, we both have grown-up jobs to do. That's for sure."

At the bottom of the steps, they kicked off their shoes and walked together along the beach. "So now that you have this new job, who's going to take care of Ruby while you're working in the city?" Jack asked.

"That is a big problem," Del acknowledged, "because Ruby's health has gotten much worse in the past year. She's not only losing her memory, Jack. She's incontinent."

"What do you mean?" Jack asked, never before having heard the word *incontinent*.

"She can't control her bowels, and that makes taking care of her really difficult. It's hard enough for me to do, let alone asking some stranger to do it."

Jack made a face. "Yeah, I bet it is! So what will you do?"

"I went to see Father Joseph at Saint Dominic's about it. He suggested I ask Snooky if she'd be willing to help."

"Snooky!" Jack declared in astonishment. "For crying out loud! She's got problems enough of her own taking care of Alfie, doesn't she? How could she help you?"

"That's what I thought, but Father said he would ask her himself and she said yes if I'd agree to let her and Alfie move in with us."

"That woman has some nerve!"

"Actually, it's working out pretty well. For one thing, Snooky doesn't mind Ruby's incontinence because Alfie's had the same problem ever since he was born. I guess, after twenty-three years, she's just gotten used to it."

Jack shook his head in amazement. "How does anybody get used to something like that?"

"I don't know," Del replied. "But, so far, the three of them are getting along wonderfully together. They sing old Gospel songs, play card games, and listen to *Amos 'n' Andy* and *One Man's Family* on the radio. I haven't seen Ruby laugh so much in years."

"I'm glad it works out for them, Del. But how about you?" Jack asked. "What if Snooky gets sick. Then you'll have *three* people to take care of. You sure you can handle that?"

Resisting the impulse to say he was being too 'pushy' and pessimistic, Del looked in the distance toward the Carquinez Bridge and said, "I guess I'll have to cross that bridge when I come to it, Jack."

"I'd like to help if I can," Jack offered. Although he realized Del probably no longer had any romantic feelings for him, he still clung to the possibility that she might change her mind.

"Thanks, Jack, but we'll be fine," Del affirmed, hoping this response would discourage him from intruding any further.

Jack was not to be dissuaded, however. "What about this thing you have to do for your law firm? Didn't you say they're defending your father's murderer? If I were you, I'd quit that job."

"And do what?" Del asked, her eyes flashing with defiance. "I want to be a lawyer, Jack. The man who's been charged in this case still has to be tried in a court of law. I don't like the idea of being part of his defense team, but that's what lawyers have to do sometimes whether they like it or not."

"How can you defend someone if you think he's guilty?"

Del stopped walking and looked at Jack with pity. "It doesn't matter what I think, Jack. What matters is what we can prove. I guess it's hard for you to understand that. It is for most people, I suppose. But that's what justice is all about. Do you remember how you felt when you were sent to jail for fighting in that boxing match and all the people who made money betting on you got off scot-free? That didn't seem fair, did it?"

"No, and it was *your father* who sent me to jail!" he reminded her angrily.

"He sent you to jail because you got caught and the others didn't," Del corrected. "Maybe, if you'd had a good defense lawyer, you'd have gotten a lesser sentence. I'm sorry that happened to you, Jack, but the fact is you were proven guilty as charged. That may not seem fair, but it *is* just."

Again, Jack shook his head, utterly bewildered. "I guess you'll make a pretty good lawyer, Del, 'cause you sure seem to know all the answers."

Del reached out and took Jack's hand again. "Not yet," she said with a confident smile. "But I'm learning."

CHAPTER THIRTY-FIVE

"Night and Day"

IT WAS ALMOST MIDNIGHT ON a rainy night in early November. Del was reading a law brief in her father's study. A Cole Porter tune played softly on the radio, its haunting minor key and yearning lyrics distracting her attention:

> *In the roaring traffic's boom,*
> *In the silence of my lonely room,*
> *I think of you*
> *Day and night, night and day.*

Del looked up at the glowing face of the radio dial on the bookcase shelf in front of her. *Why?* she asked herself. *Why am I thinking about Jack, and why does it hurt so much?* Determined to quash such feelings, Del got up from her chair and went into the kitchen to brew a pot of tea. To her surprise, a kettle was already steaming on the stove and Snooky was sitting at the kitchen table playing solitaire. "What are you doing up so late?" Del asked.

Snooky's face was pale and her eyelids dark with fatigue. "Can't say for sure, kiddo," she mumbled, trying hard to seem off-handed. "Jus' one o' those things y' get when y're old, I guess. Tea'll be ready in a minute. You want some?"

"That's why I came out here," Del said, sitting down opposite Snooky and looking earnestly at her. "Come on, Snooky! You're not old, but you *do* look tired. Maybe all this care taking is getting to be too much for you. Why don't you take a couple of days off? Go see some of your friends at the Brewery. Maybe you need a new boyfriend," Del winked suggestively.

Scooping up her playing cards, Snooky briskly reshuffled the deck. "You kiddin' me? I need a new boyfriend like a hole in the head!" she spat out contemptuously. "Speakin' o' boyfriends, what's goin' on between you an' this Conklin fella?"

Del was instantly taken aback. She had invited Brad for dinner a month before and he had dined with them at the house several times since then. "What do you mean?"

"I mean—you two gettin' serious?" Snooky asked as she began laying her cards face down again.

Del's impulse was to tell Snooky to mind her own business, but the sound of the teakettle whistle distracted her. She got up to fill the teapot. "Brad is just a friend," she said coolly.

"He sure spends a lot o' time aroun' here for somebody who's just a friend," Snooky retorted, still concentrating on her card game.

"I take it you don't like Brad very much," Del said warily as she dropped four teabags into the pot and remained standing beside the stove, her arms crossed in front of her.

"Ain't for me t' say whether I like him or not," Snooky said. "But I *will* say I don't trust 'im."

"You don't know him," Del said, now becoming very annoyed. "Besides, it's really none of your business."

Snooky paused for several seconds, studying her upturned cards. "Honey, I know men a lot better 'n you, an' whether you like it or not I'm tellin' you Conklin ain't the right man for you. He may be rich an' handsome an' all that, but ..."

Del slammed the palm of her hand on the kitchen counter top. "I don't believe this! What right do you have to criticize my friends?"

Snooky did not respond. She continued to turn over her cards and match the reds with the blacks, the momentum of her play accelerating with the growing intensity of her own anger. When she finished turning over and matching every card, she turned in her chair to face Del. "I guess you're feeling pretty sure of yourself these days, ain't you, kiddo? Believe me, I know you better than you think. I watched you and Jack grow up so I know how close you two have always been. Maybe now

516

ain't the time. But, when the right time comes, Jack is the man for you."

Trembling with anger, Del tried to control herself by filling two teacups. "Dammit!" she cursed as the tea spilled over into the saucers.

Snooky stood up and moved to help her. "Sit down, Del," she commanded. Then, picking up the two cups and saucers, she rinsed them in the sink and, refilling them, set them on the table. "I know you're mad as hell at me right now, and maybe I deserve it," she said as she sat down and motioned Del to do the same. "But I spent too many years watchin' Jack's Momma throw herself away on bad men. I did some o' that myself in my day. But I'll be damned if I'm gonna sit by silent an' watch you do the same thing! You're too pretty and smart for that. If you don't like it, well … I guess that's the price I'll have t' pay!"

Stunned by this assault, Del walked back to her chair and sat down. Clasping her forehead with both hands, she stared down at the teacup and saucer on the table in front of her. She didn't know whether she wanted to roar or to weep.

"Listen to me, baby," Snooky urged, "'cause jus' maybe I see some things you don't. Believe me, this Conklin fella's got a mean streak."

Del dropped her arms on the table in exasperation and turned to stare at Snooky. "How do you know that?"

"Call it instinct, honey," Snooky said with a sly smile. "I got a nose for trouble, and Conklin's big trouble."

"What about Jack?" Del countered. "With all the awful things he's done, are you going to tell me he's not trouble?"

"Jack's done a lot o' stupid things. I'll give you that. But they ain't a mean bone in his body. You know how many times he's tried to rescue his Momma from that son-of-bitch Soames?"

"I know he tried," Del admitted. "But it never did any good."

"That's right 'cause his Momma was blind and stubborn. Don't get me wrong. I ain't sayin' she wasn't smart. She read a lot o' books and had a lot o' big ideas. But, you know what? Sometimes smart people are dumb. 'Wise dumbbells,' my Pappy use' t' call 'em." Snooky was pacing back and forth now, wringing her hands, groping for the right words. "They're so smart they talk themselves into doing stupid."

For several seconds there was silence between them as Del pondered

Snooky's last statement. "I know what you mean," Del said at last. "I've done that myself."

Reaching into her gunny sack, which she had hung on the back of one of the kitchen chairs, Snooky pulled out a pack of Lucky Strike cigarettes and lighted one for herself. "We all do that one way or another, baby," she said as she exhaled thin streams of smoke through her nostrils and sat down again. "We fool ourselves into thinkin' we can solve all our own problems. Some fools even think they can solve the whole world's problems, like that nutty politician Huey Long. But you know what? It ain't so. Jesus got it right. Anybody who wants t' save his own life 'll lose it, an' anybody willin' t' lose his life for Jesus 'll save it. You was raised a Catholic, honey, so you oughta know that."

"You sound like Father Flynn," Del answered, her tone of voice still despondent.

"Who's that?"

Del looked directly at Snooky, searching her haggard face for some assurance that this aging and uneducated woman was more sophisticated than she sounded. "He was my faculty advisor at Saint Mary's. He was just a Dominican Brother then, but now he's an assistant pastor at a mission parish in Chiapas, Mexico."

"Sounds like a pretty smart fella," Snooky observed, taking another drag on her cigarette. "Must have a lot o' guts too. Mexico ain't too safe a place for gringos these days."

Del nodded somberly. "He's written me several letters about that. He says the poor people there are terribly oppressed and that several of the mission priests have been threatened with their lives for preaching against the government."

"Priests ought t' stay out o' politics!" Snooky declared irritably.

Rubbing her eyes, Del stood up from the table. "I'm tired. I'm going to bed now."

"Not yet you ain't," Snooky said harshly as she dropped her cigarette into her empty teacup. "We ain't finished what we was talkin' about. You said I remind you of your priest friend. What 'd you mean by that?"

Del was openly defiant now. "Father Flynn says we're all part of the Body of Christ, so that means we have to be as perfect as he was. That's what you said too, isn't it when you talked about losing our life for Jesus? I can't do that, Snooky! Nobody can, except maybe saints! And I'm no saint!"

"Jesus never said we have to be perfect," Snooky replied calmly. "He just said we gotta tend his sheep. And you're already doin' that. Just look at what you're doin' for Ruby an' Alfie an' me, givin' us a home and three squares." She stood up and embraced Del. When she felt Del's body relax, Snooky said, "You can go to bed now, honey."

* * *

To develop its passenger service, in 1911 the Southern Pacific Railroad began running a special winter season train between Oakland and Reno, Nevada. During the 1920s, this "snow train" became very popular with Bay Area residents who enjoyed skiing and tobogganing in the Sierras and/or liked to gamble at the various casinos in Reno.

As the Thanksgiving holiday approached in 1932, Victor Hartz and his partners decided their office staff needed something to lift their spirits in the face of the continuing bad economic news. Accordingly, they reserved the club car on Southern Pacific's snow train and hired a caterer and a small orchestra to make sure the six-hour journey through the snow-covered Sierras to Reno would give everyone a chance to relax in each other's company and forget, at least for a few days, about stresses at work.

Del had invited Brad Conklin to be her escort on this weekend-long outing, and Deirdre Hartz had invited Jack. Jack's appearance came as a big shock to Del, for neither Jack nor Deirdre, who was now working as a filing clerk in her father's office, had said anything to Del about their relationship. Nor had Deirdre's mother, and this was what Del found most vexing. After all, Margaret had gone out of her way to build Del's self-confidence. Not telling Del ahead of time about Jack and Deirdre seemed like a betrayal.

"Jack! What a surprise to see you!" Del declared in feigned delight as she approached him soon after she and Conklin had boarded the train in Martinez.

"Hello, Del," Jack smirked sheepishly. Then, gesturing toward Deirdre, he said, "You remember Didi Hartz, don't you—from the Vallejo Yacht Club?"

Del deliberately slipped her arm under Brad's as she replied, "Actually,

Deirdre and I both work at her father's office in San Francisco, Jack."
Del was careful to use Deirdre's full first name to let Jack know how
much she disapproved of his using an affectionate nickname. Looking
up adoringly at Conklin, Del warbled, "Brad, this is Jack Westlake. We
grew up together in Benicia."

"'S'at so?" Brad said with a triumphant smirk as he exchanged a firm
handshake with Jack. "Swell meeting you, Jack."

Somewhat put off balance by the energetic conviviality of this tall,
muscular Adonis, Jack nodded and asked, "Have you met Deirdre
Hartz?"

"Oh yeah, sure," Conklin replied casually. "We know each other
real well. Hey, Didi! This is really a great idea your Daddy had bringin'
everybody up here to Reno. Do you guys ski?" Brad's question was
addressed to both Jack and Deirdre.

"Of course! Every chance we get!" Deirdre declared. "Jack's taking
lessons, and I'm sure he's going to be a very good skier. He's a natural
athlete," she added with an admiring glance at Jack.

"I'm still a beginner on the slopes," Jack admitted, "but I'm pretty
good at poker. Maybe you and I should play a few hands, Brad," he
challenged.

Brad shook his head. "Not a gambling man myself—not with cards,
anyway. I'd rather play the commodities market. The odds are a lot
better."

"You gotta be kidding!" Jack retorted. "You seen what's happened
to stocks these days?"

"Commodities aren't stocks, buddy," Brad retorted. He quickly
concluded that this smalltown rube knew nothing about investments
and that trying to educate him would be a waste of time.

"Come on, fellas! Cut the gab about business!" Deirdre insisted,
tugging on Jack's sleeve. "Let's go get some drinks. We're here to have
fun!"

At just that moment the club car jolted as the train started to move.
All four of them were almost knocked off balance. "Looks like the
engineer's already had a few too many," Brad quipped.

"I certainly hope not!" Del declared. "We have a long way to go!"

*　*　*

520

Three hours later, the two couples had joined a dozen other passengers on the observation platform at the end of the train. Everyone was bundled up in fur coats, hats and scarves as they stood ogling the passing winter landscape of high snow-covered mountains on one side and precipitous slopes on the other. The train was moving slowly now in its long ascent to the border between California and Nevada.

"Look! There's Donner Lake!" Deidre exclaimed, pointing down through a screen of evergreens toward a vast open space several hundred yards below. "That's where all those poor people froze to death!"

"Is it really?" Del asked, suddenly remembering what she had read about the ill-fated Donner emigrant party when it attempted to cross the Sierras in the late fall of 1846. Of the original eighty-seven emigrants, nearly half of them had died of starvation. "Is it true some of the survivors actually resorted to cannibalism?" Del asked, addressing her question to no one in particular.

"Oh yes," said a gray-haired man with a pockmarked face who suddenly joined in their conversation. "They had no choice. There was nothing else for them to eat in the dead of winter. The frozen bodies of their fellow travelers provided the only reasonable alternative."

"Reasonable!" Brad declared in disgust. "What's reasonable about that? With all this forest land, there had to be plenty of wildlife to hunt."

"Not in the dead of winter, my friend," the older man said. "I can see you're not familiar with the severity of the winters in these parts."

"Listen, mister," Brad replied with open resentment, "I'm a seasoned hunter. I've killed elk in the some of the most desolate parts of northern Michigan where the winters are every bit as severe as this."

The man with the pockmarked face smiled sagaciously. "My name's Fred Koontz," he said, reaching out to shake hands with Brad. "It's always a pleasure to meet a fellow sportsman. But you're wrong about this, buddy. You realize we're more than 6,000 feet above sea level here?"

Brad did not like being contradicted on any topic. Most of all, he resented this stranger's calling him "buddy." Looking down contemptuously at Koontz's extended hand, he asked, "What makes you such an expert?"

Del grabbed Brad's upper arm and squeezed it as hard as she could.

"Brad, don't be rude!" she scolded. "I'm sorry, Mister Koontz," Del apologized to her colleague. "This is my friend Brad Conklin. He's very smart, but sometimes he gets carried away with his own opinions." She gave Brad a harsh look.

Brad firmly removed her hand from his arm. "Sometimes, Del, you get carried away with your own opinions. This is man talk, so you better stay out of it."

"Take it easy, pal," Jack warned, stepping ominously close to Brad. "Maybe Mister Koontz is right. He's older than you and he's a native Californian."

Realizing he was outnumbered, Brad steadied himself, but not without a quick glance of defiance at Jack. Turning to Koontz, he sneered, "My mother always told me I should respect my elders."

"That's good enough for me," Koontz replied. Quickly changing the subject, he said to Del, "The boss tell you we'll be working together on the Spears case?"

"No. Not yet. As a matter of fact, I wasn't even sure I would be working on it. When did Victor make that decision?"

"He told me just a few minutes ago. Said you're gonna be assistant defense attorney and Bob Blanden will be the lead."

"But I only just passed the bar exam two weeks ago!" Del protested. "I've never been in a courtroom, except as an observer."

"Don't worry, Del. Blanden's an Ace. He's had years of courtroom experience. You'll learn a lot."

"When does all this begin?" Del asked, her anxiety not at all relieved by Koontz's assurances.

"Monday. We're having a strategy meeting with the senior partners in the morning and you and Bob are scheduled for a jailhouse interview with Spears in the afternoon. It's an interesting case. I'm looking forward to it."

"What's your role in this?" Del asked. She knew Koontz had joined the firm only a few months before and that his prior job had been with the Solano County Prosecutor's office. She remembered that Koontz had worked with Joshua Wyman during the Geddis murder trial, but she knew nothing about what he had done on that case.

"I'm doing the precedents work. Your primary job will be to help with that. Of course, you're also back-up for Blanden so you may get a shot at some real courtroom combat, young lady."

God! I hope not! Del almost said aloud. But she kept silent, realizing how timorous such an outburst would sound. Though her stomach was churning, Del was determined not to let anyone know she was afraid—least of all the three men she was talking to at that moment.

"Wow!" Deirdre exclaimed. "That's terrific, Del! Congratulations! Calls for a toast. Let's go back inside and get some champagne. Besides, I'm freezing!"

* * *

By the time the train arrived at the station in downtown Reno, everyone in Victor Hartz's party was tipsy. Brad and Deirdre were so intoxicated they had to be carried off the train and placed on luggage carts for the three-block walk to the Mother Load House, the casino hotel where Victor had reserved rooms for the weekend.

Jack had been amused by Deirdre's reckless drinking, but Del was furious with Brad who had become so obnoxious on the train that he almost got into a fist-fight with one of the Negro porters. It was only Jack's intervention that had prevented the two men from coming to blows. Jack had grabbed Brad's right arm and, twisting it behind him, forced him out into the vestibule between the train cars where the cold air promptly made Brad vomit and pass out.

After making sure their unconscious dates were safely secured in their separate rooms, Jack and Del returned to the hotel lobby. Occupying an entire city block, this enormous ground-floor space was decorated like a Medici palace and filled with scores of gaming tables and row upon row of one-armed bandits. Six bars and two coffee shops were open around the clock with scores of waiters and "cigarette girls" circulating constantly among the hundreds of guests and gamblers who patronized this luxurious adult playground. In the lobby's high ceiling, enormous fans circulated but did not dispel a thick haze of tobacco smoke. On the second floor mezzanine, three different orchestras took turns playing popular dance tunes from noon to midnight.

Del and Jack spent several minutes wandering around, watching over the shoulders of participants in the various casino games—which included Blackjack, Keno, Poker, Craps and Roulette. Never having been inside a casino before, Del was amazed at the lavish surroundings and mystified by the serious intensity of the players. "They don't look as if they're having much fun," she commented to Jack.

"A lot of these folks are high rollers," Jack explained. "They'll bet the family farm for a chance to win big, and the house odds are always against them. You're right. Most of the time, it's no fun."

"Then why do they do it?" Del asked.

Jack shrugged. "I don't know. Some people just like to take risks, I guess. It's not so much about winning or losing. It's about being in the game."

"Do you gamble?" It was a rhetorical question. Del had long known that virtually every adult male in Benicia gambled, whether it was at billiards in a bar or cockfights in a barn.

"I used to play a lot of Poker, but not much any more. Greg doesn't like card games and Wally's too much of a scatterbrain. Every once in a while I play a pick up craps game with some of our Mexican farm workers. It's just for fun, though."

"I hope you don't try to cheat those poor men," Del said disapprovingly.

"And risk getting a knife in my back?" Jack laughed. "Not me! Look over there, Del." Jack pointed to a stout old woman simultaneously playing two side-by-side nickel slot machines. Her heavily lined face was expressionless as she methodically pumped and pulled, working each machine as if she were in a trance. "Now there's somebody who's having fun!"

"You're kidding me!" Del declared.

"No. I'm serious. I'll bet she's eighty or more and, if she hits a jackpot tonight, you'll see her whooping and hopping around like a puppy with a bone. When you're as old and ugly as she is, hitting the jackpot's better than sex," Jack chuckled.

Del blushed. "Jack! You're disgusting!"

"Look over there," Jack pointed at several more senior players. "And there's another one. I'm telling you these old geezers love the bandits. They play 'em for hours at a time!"

As they passed several rows of slot machines, virtually every one operated by an elderly man or woman, Del had to agree. The slots were an obsession for these people. Suddenly she felt very sad. *Was this all they had in their old age? Didn't they have families or friends who cared about them? Didin't they care about anybody themselves?* "Let's get out of here, Jack," she said.

"Whatever you want. But we better go get our coats first," Jack suggested. "It's pretty cold outside."

*   *   *

"Your boyfriend's gone," Jack announced when Del met him at the concierge's desk twenty minutes later.

"What? How is that possible? He was totally unconscious!"

Jack shrugged. "I don't know. But the desk clerk just told me Brad turned in his room key and headed for the railroad station just a few minutes ago."

Del looked at her wristwatch. "It's almost 11:00. I don't think there are any passenger trains after ten o'clock."

"The desk clerk says there's a midnight freight to Sacramento that includes a couple of passenger cars. Maybe he's taking that."

"That selfish bastard! How can he do this to me?" Del started to move toward the hotel entrance. "I'm going to stop him!"

Jack grabbed her wrist. "Let it go, Del," he said gently. "Brad's not going to listen to you. You know that. Anyway, it doesn't really matter now, does it?"

Flush with anger, Del stared defiantly at Jack. The sadness in his eyes dissipated her resentment. She had expected Jack to be as angry as she. After all, he was Brad's rival for her affection. Suddenly she realized that it was she who was being petulant and selfish. She didn't really care that Brad had walked out on her. By far, Jack was the better man. "Thank you, Jack," she murmured.

Taking Del's hand, Jack nodded toward the street exit. "Let's take our walk."

They left the hotel and started walking down the main thoroughfare of downtown Reno. Most of the pawnshops and small cafes that filled the gaps between the all-night casinos and hotels had closed and both vehicular and pedestrian traffic was sparse. A light snow was falling on the already frozen slush left by the blizzard that hit the city three days before. They had to walk slowly and carefully to avoid slipping. Del clung tightly with both hands to Jack's arm and leaned close to draw warmth from his body.

Jack wanted desperately to put his arm around Del, but he resisted this impulse, sensing that she might think he was again trying to be overly protective. Since their last encounter on Diamond Beach, he had forced himself to accept the idea that Del's plans for the future did not include him. He wanted at least to preserve their friendship. "Do you think you'd like to learn how to ski?" he asked in an effort to break the silence between them.

Del smiled up at him. "I doubt I'll have time for skiing now that I'm involved with this defense case. It's thoughtful of you to ask, though, Jack. Besides, that's sort of a thing between you and Deirdre, isn't it?"

"Do I detect a hint of jealousy in that question?" Jack asked hopefully. Then, shaking his head, he said, "You women! You're all alike—warm one minute and cold the next."

Del gave his arm an extra squeeze. "Right now I'm cold and I need you to keep me warm."

"I'll be happy to do that any time," Jack affirmed. He wanted to say he'd like nothing better than to keep her warm for the rest of her life.

Almost as if she had read his thoughts, Del said. "It's a sweet dream, isn't it, Jack?"

"What?" he asked, feeling as if his heart had just missed several beats.

"You and I together, keeping each other warm," she said softly.

Jack stopped walking, took Del in his arms, and kissed her on the lips. "It doesn't have to be a dream, darling," he said.

Suddenly Del felt free. Pressing her lips to his ear, she whispered, "Jack, I love you!"

CHAPTER THIRTY-SIX

"The Song Is You"

THE OFFICES OF SHERMAN, HARTZ and Colby occupied three full floors of the Yerba Buena Building on Montgomery Street in downtown San Francisco. The senior partners' office suites were located on the uppermost floor, each comprising a large corner office and several adjoining rooms occupied by the partners' executive secretaries and clerical staff. A large conference room off a central hallway was furnished with an enormous oak table and twenty-four matching armchairs upholstered in luxurious red leather. Ornate floor-to-ceiling windows in two adjoining walls of this room provided natural lighting during the day and four crystal chandeliers illuminated it whenever the partners needed to confer with their corporate clients after normal business hours.

At 8:30 that Monday morning, all three senior partners were already seated at the head of the oblong table when Del followed Fred Koontz and Bob Blanden into the conference room. None of these executives stood to welcome them. Only Victor Hartz greeted them verbally. "'Morning, Bob. 'Morning, Fred." Then, with a condescending nod at Del, he added, "Adelaide."

Ordinarily, Del would have resented such ungentlemanly behavior. This morning, though, she didn't care. The past two nights and days she had spent with Jack filled her with joy and confidence. Jack had made love to her with a tenderness and patience that surprised her. He had also been sensitive to Deirdre's feelings, insisting that he and Del spend the daytime hours socializing with her while they were in Reno. It was only after Deirdre had retired to her room Saturday night that Jack and Del again openly expressed their love for each other.

Smiling graciously at the three senior partners now, Del sat demurely in a chair beside Fred Koontz. Del had met Victor Hartz's partners, Maxmillian Sherman and Claude Colby, only once during her very brief interview with them when she was first hired as an intern. Sherman was a tall, emaciated-looking man in his late sixties whose three-piece silk suit, though tailor made, hung on him like rags on a scarecrow. His long, narrow face, deep-sunken eyes, and balled head made him look positively sepulchral, Del thought. In sharp contrast, Colby was heavy-set with a conspicuously protruding abdomen and the thick pursed lips and glittering leer of a Sybarite. As she lowered her eyes and placed her notebook and fountain pen on the table in front of her, Del felt as if Colby were slowly and salaciously undressing her with his eyes.

"Alright then," Victor began, "let's get right down to business. We've prepared a dossier on this fellow Spears. It includes the police report filed at the time of his arrest and the Grand Jury's findings as well as a profile prepared by our private investigator, Clint Halsey. Halsey was supposed to be here this morning, but he couldn't make it because he has to testify in court." Pressing the switch on a tabletop intercom, Victor called to his secretary. "Kirsten, bring us the Spears casebook."

"Do we have a witness list from the County Prosecutor yet?" Blanden asked. A soft-spoken man in his late forties, Blanden was clean-shaven but otherwise inattentive to his personal grooming and attire. Though she had met him for the first time that morning, Del liked Blanden. He had an earnest open face with regular features, except for a pair of thick bushy eyebrows that grew in a straight line low over his brown eyes. They made Blanden look as if he were constantly peering at the world from under a hedge. When he immediately confided to her that he and his wife Sharon had four children, two of whom were adopted, Del concluded such a man could certainly be trusted.

"We're in the very early stages of this case, Bob," Sherman pointed out archly. "Everything we know at this point is in the casebook."

The conference room door opened and Kirsten Rayner entered carrying a briefcase and a stack of five loose-leaf binders. Kirsten had been Victor's secretary ever since he first joined the firm twenty-three years before. A tall redheaded Dane in her early fifties, Kirsten had the erect bearing and self-assurance of someone who knew how to handle her boss as well as her distant ancestors had known how to navigate the North Atlantic. With a confident nod to the three partners, she quickly distributed copies of the casebook and a pad and pencil to everyone seated at the table. "Will there be anything else you need, Mister Hartz?" she asked.

"I think you better stay and take shorthand minutes of this meeting, Kirsten. That way we'll all have an accurate record of everything we discuss today." Looking around the table, he asked, "Everyone agree?"

When the others nodded, Kirsten sat down in the empty chair at Victor's left and extracted a pen and stenographer's pad from her briefcase.

"Let's begin with the police report because the Grand Jury findings are based primarily on that document," Sherman directed. As the founding partner of the firm, Sherman had immediately assumed the role of discussion leader. "You'll find it on page sixty-eight." He paused for several minutes while the others perused the seven-page report prepared by the Solano County Sheriff's office. "As you can see, the evidence against Mister Spears is purely circumstantial. While Spears was living and working in Benicia at the time of Judge Lanham's death, there is not one scintilla of evidence that he either knew or ever had anything to do with the Judge. Spears was a low-level shop supervisor at the Alta Plant while Lanham was a respected Judge of the Ninth Circuit. The two men moved in completely different circles."

"Benicia is a very small town, Mister Sherman," Del observed evenly. "My father knew many people there and I'm sure even this man Spears had at least heard of my father. After all, as the police report states, Spears had been employed at the Alta Plant since 1924."

Sherman frowned, obviously annoyed by Del's youthful audacity. "With all due respect to your father's memory, Miss Lanham, I caution you not presume upon your heritage. When the senior partners have finished our analysis of this report, we will open this matter for general discussion."

"Adelaide *does* have a point, Max," Colby said, surprising Del by coming to her defense. "Benicia's a pretty small town. I've been there a few times myself. Hell, they just paved the streets in that burg a couple o' years ago! Spears probably *did* know about Judge Lanham. Being a working class type, he may even have envied the old gentleman."

"That's immaterial," Sherman retorted. "The Prosecution will have to show that there was some direct connection between Spears and his alleged victim. There is no indication of such a connection in this report."

"But didn't you just say we're still in the very early stages of this case?" Blanden asked. "How can we be sure Spears wasn't working for somebody else? Say somebody who knew the Judge and had some kind of a grudge against him?"

"We cannot base our defense on mere supposition," Sherman barked.

"You're right about that, Max," Victor said. "Obviously, what we need to do is dig deeper into this case. That's partly Halsey's job, but it's yours too, Fred. You're familiar with the archived case files in the Solano County Courthouse so you'll have to do some digging there. Adelaide, as the only native Benician here, you can help by interviewing local residents. Our purpose here today is to come up with some ideas about what to look for."

"Did your father have any particular enemies?" Colby asked Del.

"Father almost never talked about his work," she replied. "He was critical of State Assemblyman Howard Roach, though. He told me several times that he thought Roach was a corrupt politician."

"What do we know about Roach's background?" Victor asked. "That's certainly an avenue to explore."

Both Fred and Del were now taking notes.

Addressing Del, Blanden asked, "Did your father ever tell you why he thought Roach was corrupt?"

"Not that I recall," Del answered. "But I was in boarding school when father was appointed to the Ninth Circuit, and then he sent me off to college in Philadelphia." She paused, reluctant to admit what she said next. "I'm afraid I wasn't paying much attention then."

"I dare say," Sherman remarked disparagingly. "Be that as it may, I hope you are paying attention now."

"Come on, Max!" Colby scoffed.

"Seems to me I do remember a case involving this fella Roach's attempt to bribe some retired judges back in '28. Maybe there's some connection," Fred offered.

"By all means, look into that," Victor said, penciling a note of his own on the front page of the casebook.

"Did your father have any particular vices, Miss Lanham?" Sherman asked, determined to continue humiliating Del.

Appalled by this question, Del exchanged glances with Fred who shook his head slightly to caution her against a hostile response. "My father smoked cigars," she said with a coy smile at Blanden.

"That's hardly a vice, young lady!" Colby chuckled. "If it is, then I am surely damned!"

"This is not an occasion for levity, Claude," Sherman warned. Then, relentless in his interrogation of Del, he asked, "Did your father consume alcoholic beverages?"

Again Colby intervened, this time with a burst of laughter. "For heaven's sake, Max, everybody drinks booze in Benicia! It's an Army base. They got more bars and bordellos per capita than just about any other town in the Bay Area!"

"That's not fair!" Del protested. "There are many good and decent people in Benicia. As for my father, he rarely drank except for an occasional glass of wine with dinner. Are you being deliberately rude, Mister Sherman?"

"Enough!" Victor declared as if he were a parent reprimanding a room full of unruly children. "Max merely asked the question to explore the possibility that your father may have had enemies of some kind. The Grand Jury was clearly convinced there was foul play in this case, so we have to address that issue."

"It wasn't addressed at the time of father's death," Del said. "Why now?"

Victor looked sidelong at his partners, the hint of a mischievous smile on his face. "I guess you could say there's been a change in the political climate since then, Adelaide. Apparently evidence was suppressed in the first investigation."

"I take it you're referring to the discovery that the spent shotgun shells found at the murder scene did not match the ones the Judge used when he was duck hunting," Blanden said.

"Exactly," Victor affirmed.

"Who suppressed that evidence?" Del asked, startled to learn this for the first time.

"That's one of many things we don't know yet," Sherman answered. "All of which you people need to find out."

"Or as much as you can in the time we have to do it," Colby put in.

"Has a trial date been set?" Blanden asked.

"No," said Victor. "But the presiding judge Richard Gorman has a reputation for being a man of action, so we're going to have to get moving on this right away." Extracting the gold watch he carried in his vest pocket, he snapped it open. "It's 9:15. Unless any of you has something more to add, I suggest we adjourn now. Kirsten will transcribe her notes and distribute copies to everybody later today." Turning to Kirsten, he added, "Won't you?"

"Yes, sir," she confidently replied. "The typed transcripts should be ready by noon."

"Let's go!" Colby declared, pushing back his chair and struggling to his feet.

* * *

Although she had visited the Solano County Courthouse in Fairfield several times with her father, Del had never seen the inside of the County Jail—a five-story annex located at the rear of the Courthouse. It was not a place her father would have wanted her to see. With its gray sandstone exterior and high barred windows, this Victorian fortress had been designed for the express purpose of striking terror and despair in the heart of anyone who entered it. Blanden and Del had to pass through two separate steel-caged areas on the ground floor, in each of which their personal identification papers and brief cases were carefully inspected by armed guards, before they were finally admitted to a small windowless room where they were told they could speak with their client Emmett Spears.

This "interview room," as the prison guards called it, was furnished with a steel table and four steel straight-back chairs, all bolted to the concrete floor. The only illumination came from a single light bulb in the ceiling. Even this fixture was enclosed in thick steel wire mesh. They had to wait for several minutes before the heavy steel door through which they had been admitted opened and two guards ushered Spears inside, both his wrists and his ankles shackled together with chains.

Del was startled by Spears' calm indifference as the guards forced him to sit down in one of the chairs, further securing his shackled wrists and ankles to the frame of his chair. Clearly, they considered Spears a dangerous inmate. Del wondered why, for Spears was small in stature with narrow shoulders and thin arms and legs. Apart from his wrinkled face and gray hair, he looked as frail and harmless as boy of twelve or thirteen.

"Would you please remove the shackles from Mister Spears' wrists?" Blanden asked. "We may need him to sign some papers."

The burliest of the two guards scowled and shook his head. "Sorry, sir. Against jailhouse rules. You need him to sign somethin', knock on the door an' we'll come back." Both guards then left the room, locking the steel door behind them.

"Sorry," Blanden shrugged at his client.

Spears said nothing. His face was expressionless, though Del detected a glimmer of mockery in his small, close-set eyes.

"My name is Bob Blanden and this is my associate Miss Adelaide Lanham. We're here to ask you a few questions about the Grand Jury's indictment against you," Blanden explained.

"That's bullshit!" Spears snarled. His eyes flashed murderous resentment at Del. "You're related to that judge, ain't y'? What the hell *you* doin' here?" he angrily demanded.

"I already told you," Blanden said, fighting to keep his own anger under control. "Miss Lanham is my associate. She is a fully licensed attorney and has been assigned to help with your defense. Her relationship to Judge Lanham has no bearing on this case."

"That's bullshit too!" Spears declared.

Blanden paused several seconds before he responded. "You really don't have much choice here, Mister Spears. We've been appointed by the court to represent you in this case. Unless you have the resources to hire another defense attorney, you're stuck with us."

"So I'm a charity case. Is that it?" Spears spat out. "Fuck you and your charity!"

"Have it your way," Blanden said abruptly as he stood up and moved toward the door to call the guards.

Del shuddered, for Spears continued to glare hatefully at her. "Hold on," he said, rolling his eyes. "Awright! Awright! You got me, so set down an' le's talk."

Blanden returned to his chair. "No more obscenities!" he warned. "You keep talking like that and we're gone. Do you understand?"

"Yeah, sure," Spears hissed. "You got the hammer!"

Blanden opened his brief case and took out a thick legal-sized document. Placing it on the table, he pushed it toward Spears. "This is a copy of the Grand Jury's indictment. Have you read it?"

Spears nodded sullenly.

"Good. Then, you know there are a number of witnesses the prosecuting attorney has lined up to testify against you. We don't know yet exactly who they are or what they are likely to say. But clearly you've made some enemies. We need to know their names."

Spears smiled for the first time, but his voice was full of sarcasm. "I'm fifty-six years old an' I been all over the country. I got lots o' enemies," he said cagily. "Where do y' want me t' start?"

"Start with the first day you came to Benicia," Blanden said coldly.

"Well, let's see now. I guess that'd be when I went to work at the Alta plant back in '24. I had a run-in with one o' the Portagees that worked in the foundry. Big fella named Lenny Rocha, but he's dead. So he wouldn't be much of a witness now, would he?"

Jotting Rocha's name in his notebook, Blanden ignored Spears' taunt. "What was the nature of your quarrel with this man?"

"He wasn't doin' his job right."

"And what did you do?" Blanden asked.

"I was shop supervisor, so I reported him to my boss."

"Who was your boss?"

"Ed Johnson, the plant manager."

Blanden's patience was beginning to wear thin. "What did *he* do?"

"Nothin'," Spears replied with a smirk.

"Did any of the other workers at the plant see you quarrel with this man Rocha?" Del inquired cautiously.

Spears shifted his gaze to Del. He was watching her now like a bird of prey. "Yeah, prob'ly."

"What were *their* names?" Blanden asked.

"Hell! That was a long time ago. I don't remember!"

"Never mind," Blanden said, exasperated. "We'll find out. How long did you work at the Alta plant?"

"Couple o' years, I guess. Don't remember 'xactly. Like I said, it was a while back."

Blanden ignored the open hostility of this response and consulted the notes he had taken during the strategy meeting that morning. "Did you ever meet a man named Howard Roach?" he asked.

Del noted a flicker of recognition in Spears' eyes, but he shook his head. "Never had the pleasure. He somebody important?"

"Mister Spears," Blanden said ominously, "I suggest you take some time to refresh your memory. We're not going to sit here for hours and pick your brain. We'll get back to you in a few days. Hopefully by then you'll have something useful to tell us." Packing up his briefcase, Blanden snapped it closed, walked to the door, and pounded on it with his fist. "Let's go, Del."

Spears said nothing. He continued to stare at Del, though, when she stood up from the table and the prison guards entered to take Spears back to his cell.

"He's one of the most frightening men I've ever met," Del said as she and Blanden exited the County Jail.

"He's devious, that's for sure," Blanden affirmed. "I'm afraid we're not going to get much out of him. Looks like I'll have to rely on you to find out what you can about Spears and his job at the Alta plant."

Suddenly Del felt panicky. She knew very little about the Alta plant or anyone who had ever worked there. It was on the east side of Benicia in a part of town she had seen only on her way to and from Saint Dominic's Church on Sundays and Holy Days. Whom could she talk to? What references could she consult to learn more about this sprawling industrial complex?

* * *

By the time she returned home at 6:30 that evening, Del was exhausted. Snooky greeted her at the door with a glass of chilled Chardonnay. "You look beat, kiddo. Tough day at the office, I guess, huh?"

"You have no idea!" Del said, eagerly sipping her wine before she had even set down her briefcase. "Thanks for this. It's just what I needed."

Snooky followed Del into the dining room where Alfie and Ruby were deeply engrossed in a game of Hearts. "Why don't y' come into the kitchen and tell me what happened today?" she suggested

Giving Ruby and Alfie quick hugs, Del followed Snooky and sat down opposite her at the kitchen table. "OK. So tell me all about it, kiddo," Snooky said.

"We interviewed a new client at the County Jail this afternoon. I've never been so scared of anyone in my life!"

"Who was it?" Snooky asked.

"A man named Spears. He's the one who's been charged with murdering my father."

"You mean *Emmett* Spears!" Snooky exclaimed. "No wonder you was scared! He's the guy threw acid on Lenny Rocha!"

"Threw acid on him!" Del gasped. "Snooky, are you sure?"

"Sure I'm sure. It was all over town when it happened back in '24, though I s'pose you was too young to know about it."

"Did you know Rocha?" Del asked, suddenly realizing Snooky, with all of her many acquaintances in Benicia, might be a valuable source of information.

"Me? Not a chance! Rocha was big trouble. Got into bar fights all the time."

"Do you know what finally happened to him?" Del sipped again at her glass of wine, trying with little success to conceal the intensity of her interest.

"He died only a few days later. Acid ate right through to his brain."

Del almost choked on her wine. "That's awful! What about Spears? Was he arrested?"

"Nope. Like I said, Rocha was a bum. Nobody cared."

"Who told you Spears was responsible?" Del asked grimly.

"Steve Vascos. He worked in the same shop with Rocha, and he said he seen Spears do it."

"Did he report what he'd seen to the plant manager?"

"You kiddin? Steve's a Portagee. Johnson never woulda believed him. He's a bigoted bastard. I oughta know. He used t' be my landlord!"

"So Spears got away with it," Del concluded grimly.

"Yup."

"Does Mister Vascos still work at the Alta plant?" Del asked.

"Nah. He works over at the Arsenal now. He quit his job at the plant soon as he could after he seen what Spears done."

"I need to talk to Mister Vascos," Del said. "Do you think you could arrange that?"

"Yeah, prob'ly," Snooky replied, lighting a cigarette. "What do y' wanna talk t' him for?"

"I think he may be able to help us with this case."

Snooky slowly exhaled a thin stream of tobacco smoke before she answered. "OK. I'll see what I can do."

"Thanks, Snooky. I appreciate it, but please don't tell anyone else about this."

"You can count on me. I don't know about Steve, though. He's a real blabbermouth. You know how people are in this town. Word gets around fast."

"You don't have to tell Steve why I want to talk to him. Let me handle that."

"I see you're back on your old control kick again," Snooky retorted irritably as she emptied her whiskey glass and refilled it from a bottle on the kitchen counter. "People are gonna talk, kiddo, an' there ain't nothin' you can do about it!"

"You're probably right," Del admitted. "I'm sorry if I sounded bossy, Snooky. I didn't mean to. But I need your help with this."

"You want me to be your spy?"

Del shook her head. "No. But you know many more working class people in town than I do."

Snooky sucked fiercely on her cigarette. "You mean the drunks and bums."

"I didn't say that!"

Snooky shrugged. "It don't matter, kiddo. I know why you wanna keep everythin' hush-hush. It's a tough job bein' a snoop. You ain't had much practice yet. But you'll catch on. If y' wanna wheedle stuff out o' people, y' gotta take y'r time an' be sneaky like me!"

"We don't have much time, I'm afraid," Del said. "This case could go to trial soon, and we have to gather all the evidence we can before that happens."

"So ask me some more questions, counselor. Maybe I can give you some good answers."

Del was startled to hear Snooky use the word *counselor*. Apparently this woman knew more about courtroom protocol than Del had imagined. "Alright then. Did you ever hear of a man named Howard Roach?"

Snooky flicked the ashes of her cigarette into her already emptied whiskey glass. "Yeah. Gail told me about him. She said he was one of Jimmy Soames' cronies."

"Do you mean the same man who forced Jack to run away from home?"

"That's the one. A real prince!"

"Jack told me Soames was part of the gang that attacked Adam Tucker and his men at Castle Rock last summer."

"Yeah. Gail said Soames was makin' plans for somethin' like that. That's why she broke off with him—*finally*!"

"Was there anyone else Gail told you about?" Del had opened her briefcase now and was searching through it to find her notebook.

She said Soames introduced her to that mobster from Chicago, Baby Face Nelson. She said he's real mean. Carries a gun all the time an' beats up on women."

Very excited now, Del was furiously taking notes. "Where did Gail meet this man?"

"She said it was at the Saint Francis Hotel in the City."

"Did she tell you when this meeting took place?"

"Not 'xactly," Snooky frowned, trying to remember a specific date. "Must 've been at least three years ago, though, because it happened before Gail went to work at the Lido."

Del looked up from her notebook, her eyes sparkling with excitement. "Did she mention the names of any of the other people at that meeting?"

"Not to me. Anyways, nobody I remember, an' I us'ly got a pretty good memory."

"Yes you *do*!" Del declared. "You've been a big help, Snooky. Thank you so much!"

"If you're finished with the questions, maybe we should play some cards with Alfie and Ruby," Snooky suggested.

"That's a wonderful idea! Just let me freshen up a bit first." Del quickly carried her notebook and briefcase into her father's study and then went upstairs to the bathroom.

Del returned five minutes later, Snooky was still sitting in the kitchen waiting for her. "Say, I almost forgot. Jack called tonight, just a little while before you come home. He sounded real happy and he wanted to talk to you. So what's goin' on, Del? You too finally gettin' together?"

Del blushed and smiled. "Yes, Snooky. We are. It happened last weekend while we were up in Reno, and you'll be happy to know he proposed to me."

Snooky looked sternly at her. "Well? Did you accept?"

"Yes."

Snooky leaped to her feet. "Hallelujah! There is a resurrection after all!" she declared as she rushed around the table to embrace Del. "When's the happy day?"

Del hesitated. "We ... we haven't set a date yet. I told Jack we'd better wait until after this case is settled. There's just too much going on right now."

Snooky put her hands on her hips and frowned. "Don't you go gettin' cold feet now!" she warned.

"Don't worry. We *are* getting married!" Del affirmed. Then, picking up her empty wine glass, she said. "How about a refill so we can pledge a toast to it?"

"You got it, kiddo!"

Chapter Thirty-seven

"It Don't Mean a Thing If You Ain't Got That Swing"

As soon as Del arrived at work the next morning, she went directly to Blanden's office and told him everything she had learned from Snooky. "This is terrific, Del! Good job! I'll call Clint and Fred and put them to work on these leads right away." Then, with a frown of consternation, he said, "If you get that meeting set up with Vascos, I think you'd better take Clint with you."

"I'm glad you suggested that, Bob. As my friend Snooky says, I'm not very good at interrogating strangers."

"Don't worry. You'll get plenty of practice in this line of work. But, until the Prosecution sends us their witness list, we'll have to hold off on interrogating anybody but Vascos."

"Do you have any idea when that will happen?"

"Not really, but we can still do some background research on Roach. He's a State Assemblyman, so there ought to be plenty of news stories about him. I have a good friend who's a reporter at the *Examiner*. She'll get you a pass to the paper's archives. You free to go over there today?"

Del smiled. "I haven't checked the in-box on my desk yet, but I can't imagine there could be anything more important than this."

"I'll give you a call as soon as I've set up a time for you to go over to the *Examiner*."

* * *

Upon returning from lunch that afternoon, Del found Blanden's hand-written note on her desk. "Sorry I can't go with you today," it said.

"I have to meet with a client on a different case. The Hearst Building is at Third and Market, opposite the Call Building. The reporter you want to talk to is Esther Kaufman. Her office is in the City Room—on the 7th floor, I think. Happy hunting!"

Del had never been inside the Hearst Building, an enormous twelve-story structure covering an entire city block and containing the executive and editorial offices as well as the huge presses that daily produced *The Examiner*, one of the two morning newspapers that served San Franciscans during the 1930s. She was especially awed by the entrance to the Hearst Building, whose Corinthian columns and ornate lintel made it look more like the entrance to a pagan temple than to a newspaper office.

The marble walls and high frescoed ceiling of the ground-floor lobby also evidenced the grandiose if somewhat eclectic taste of the building's owner—William Randolph Hearst. On a raised dias in the center of this lobby stood the concierge, his royal purple uniform stitched in gold. When Del asked this haughty official to direct her to the City Room, he frowned disapprovingly and pointed toward a bank of elevators. "Seventh floor," he barked.

Exiting the elevator on the seventh floor, Del found herself in an enormous and deafeningly noisy room filled with desks, most occupied by men in shirt-sleeves busily talking on phones or pounding on typewriters. Copy boys were scurrying back and forth between these desks and a fenced-off area at the back of the room where a contingent of editors diligently marked up stories and either sent them back for revisions or tossed them in "out" baskets from which they were dispatched to the type-setting room on another floor.

Bewildered, Del stood surveying this frantic activity for several minutes before she finally noticed a woman working at one of the reporters' desks. In 1932, women reporters were a rarity—especially at large dailies like the *San Francisco Examiner*. Realizing she would be ignored unless she took the initiative, Del made her way through the maze of desks until she stood directly in front of the woman reporter, who did not look up from her typewriter. "Are you Esther Kaufman?" she asked.

The woman's head jerked up, her dark eyes flashing fiercely at

Del. "Yeah. Who wants t' know?" she asked with a distinct New York accent.

"I'm Adelaide Lanham. Bob Blanden said I should speak to you about a case we're working on. We need access to your paper's archives and he said you'd be willing to help."

"Oh yeah. Sure. Hold on a minute while I finish this," Kaufman said and immediately resumed typing.

Del stood watching in amusement. Esther Kaufman was a petite woman with a sallow complexion and coal-black hair, cut short with little attention to style. Del guessed she was probably in her early thirties, though it was difficult to be sure. Kaufman had a hard, almost mannish face with a large nose and thin rougeless lips. This was understandable, Del thought. After all, Esther Kaufman worked in a man's world. To be successful at what she did, she would have to be mannish.

Finished with her typing, Kaufman unreeled the sheet of paper from her typewriter and dropped it in the "out" box on her desk. Then, standing up and grabbing her handbag, she nodded perfunctorily at Del. "Come on. Let's get out o' here," she said. "It's too damned noisy!"

Del followed Kaufman as she led the way across the City Room and entered an elevator. "So where y' from?" Kaufman asked briskly while the elevator descended to the ground floor.

"I live in Benicia," Del replied hesitantly, unnerved by the abruptness of the question.

"Where's that?"

"It's in the North Bay, on the Carquinez Strait."

Kaufman gave her a vacant stare. "Sorry. Don't know where that is either. I'm a New Yorker myself. Moved out here five years ago, but I still can't find my way around—even in this puny burg you people call a city. Never was very good with directions, I'm afraid." She waved her hand dismissively. "Don't worry about it. Doesn't matter anyway. So, you a real lawyer or just one of Bob's little helpers?" There was sharp bitterness in this question.

"I'm a real lawyer," Del said matter-of-factly as they stepped out of the elevator. Already, she was beginning to feel uncomfortable with this tough-talking woman reporter. At the same time, she couldn't help liking Esther Kaufman. There was something about her blunt but obviously intelligent candor that Del found refreshing. "Where are we going?" Del asked.

"Lunch," Kaufman said as she led the way out of the lobby and onto Market Street. "There's a great little Jewish deli right down the street here. They actu'ly make kosher pastrami san'wiches—almost as good as New York. You eat yet?"

Del glanced at her wristwatch, which indicated that it was almost 2:00 P.M. "Oh yes. More than an hour ago."

"So you can have a cup o' coffee an' watch."

Del almost laughed aloud at the way Kaufman pronounced the word *coffee*, stretching out the first vowel as if it were two distinct sounds.

* * *

A few minutes later they were sitting face-to-face at a tiny table against the wall in a crowded delicatessen scarcely wide enough to accommodate their table and a single customer passing from one end of the place to the other. Behind a high glassed-in counter near the entrance, several counter clerks in crisp white aprons shouted at each other as customers also shouted out their orders.

"So what are y' lookin' for in our back-issues? How far back you gotta go?" Kaufman asked, chewing vigorously on the huge bite she had taken out of her three-inch thick pastrami and rye bread sandwich.

"I'm searching for articles about several California politicians," Del replied, trying to keep her response nebulous. "I'll probably need to go back three or four years at least."

Licking mustard from her fingers, Kaufman probed further. "What's the case you're workin' on?"

Don't you know how to use a napkin? Del felt tempted to ask. Instead, she said, "It's a murder trial and it's still pending. I can't tell you any more right now."

"Aw, come on! You can tell me. I'm a profess'nal—just like you. I ain't gonna break no rules!"

Del wanted to point out that Kaufman was working for a newspaper publisher who was notorious for breaking rules. But she decided there was nothing to be gained by being critical. "Sorry," she answered simply.

Kaufman nodded vigorously. "No problem. I'll take y' up an' show you the ropes soon as I'm finished here." Shifting to another topic, Kaufman asked, "Where'd y' go t' law school?"

"Hastings," Del answered, now very wary of this busy body. "The campus is right here in San Francisco."

Again, Kaufman waved dismissively. "Never heard of it. I figured someplace like Stanford or Berkeley. Doesn't matter. I'll take your word for it. Important thing is y' got it. How long y' been with Sherman's hack shop?"

"Just a little more than a year. By the way, Miss Kaufman, we're not a hack shop. Sherman, Hartz and Colby is one of the most respected law firms in California."

Kaufman nodded vigorously as she devoured the last of her sandwich and stood up. "Sure, kid. Anything you say. But let's dispense with the hoity-toity attitude, OK? My friends call me Esther. Come on. Let's go."

* * *

In spite of her tough demeanor, Kaufman was very helpful. She spent the rest of that afternoon showing Del how to use the newspaper's arcane cataloguing system and guiding her through the labyrinth of steel stacks that filled the entire tenth floor of the Hearst Building. She introduced her to several of the archive attendants, directing them to give Del access any time she needed it. She also set her up in a carrel with a lockable cabinet for storing her papers. When all of these tasks were completed at 5:30, Kaufman shook hands with Del. "OK. You're all set. You need anything else, you know where to find me. Gotta get back to work now. See y'."

For the next three weeks, Del diligently scanned through back issues of the *San Francisco Examiner*, hunting for any news story or editorial that made reference to Senator Hilliard, Howard Roach and Baby Face Nelson. Del found only one recent newspaper report about Nelson. A front-page story in February reported that Nelson had escaped from an Illinois State prison and apparently disappeared. Back issues of *The Examiner* contained numerous reports about Roach, however, especially in the years since he had been elected to the State Assembly.

There were even several news photos of Roach shaking hands with businessmen and other politicians at various public appearances—such as the dedication of a new primary school in Santa Rosa and the groundbreaking for a new hospital in Oakland. The man seemed to have traveled to every county in the State. Most recently, an August 1 front-page news photo showed him standing with U. S. Senator Blake Hilliard behind Babe Diedrickson as she received a gold medal for track during the Los Angeles Olympic games.

Del had often conducted library research for the papers she wrote in college, but she had never before spent so much time on newspaper archives. She was amazed at how much important national and international news she had missed. She had not known, for example, that in July some 20,000 veterans of World War I had marched on Washington demanding the veterans' bonuses Congress had promised them in 1924 and that they had been dispersed at gunpoint by soldiers and tanks under the command of General Douglas MacArthur.

Like most Americans in 1932, Del knew about the kidnapping of Lindbergh's infant son in March. But she had not known that, less than a year before, Japan had invaded Manchuria. Also, like most Americans in 1932, Del was indifferent to the ominous rise of totalitarian regimes in Europe and Asia.

Nevertheless, the more she scoured the newspaper archives the more difficulty Del had concentrating on her mission—to link Howard Roach with her father's murder. On the first Monday in September, she met with Blandon to express her frustration.

"I know what you mean, Del," he empathized. "With everything else that's going on these days, it seems as if the whole world is going to Hell in a handcart. But, believe me, *we're* making progress on this case. Thanks to the names you've dug up, we've been able to identify five witnesses whose testimonies could cast doubt on Spears' involvement with the murder. Best of all," he added with a triumphant smile, "yesterday we finally got the Prosecution's witness list."

"Really! May I see it?"

Blanden handed her two typed sheets of paper, each stamped at the top in all-cap letters—CONFIDENTIAL.

Del eagerly perused the first sheet with the names of the defense team witnesses:

- Clements, Zachary

- Bolger, Lewis
- Krebs, Madeline
- McCutcheon, Bertrand
- Peters, Theodore

The only name she recognized was that of Bert McCutcheon. She was surprised to see his name on this list. Bert, after all was her friend Craig's father—a man whose reputation as a staunch Presbyterian was known to everyone in Benicia. "I know Mister McCutcheon, she said. "He's rich and eccentric, but I can't imagine he'd be involved in anything like this."

"There are wheels within wheels in this case, Del," Blanden replied with an enigmatic smile. "Believe me. Take a look at the Prosecution's list."

Perusing this list, Del instantly understood what Blanden meant, for the list included the names of two powerful Republican politicians and Jack's worst enemy—his mother's old lover. Somehow, apparently this scoundrel had survived the battle at Castle Rock!

- Frobish, Paul
- Hilliard, Blake
- Roach, Howard
- Soames, James
- Stark, Thomas

Again, Snooky had been right. Soames was the link with Baby Face Nelson. "Looks like there's been some kind of a conspiracy," Del observed tentatively.

"Exactly! And Spears was their fall guy. Anyway, that's what we're going to try to prove in Court. We're having another strategy meeting with the senior partners tomorrow morning to rake through what we've found so far. So get ready, Del, because tomorrow we're going to have to convince our bosses."

* * *

That meeting had come in the nick of time, for on the same morning they received notice that the trial hearings were to begin on December 1. Blanden and his team had less than two weeks to prepare their case.

"Who are these people Bolger and Krebs?" Max Sherman demanded querulously as he reviewed the defense team's witness list.

"They're low lifes," Clint Halsey replied. A short, stocky man in his late fifties, Halsey had been a detective sergeant with the San Francisco Police Department before he retired to become a private investigator for Hartz, Sherman and Colby. His round innocent-looking face and jovial manner concealed the instincts of a ruthless and relentless sleuth. "Spears told me Bolger worked for him a while back when Spears was a hit man for Soames. Maddie Krebs is one of the old whores at the Lido in Benicia. Spears said she used to service some of his boys, including both Bolger and Tom Stark."

"So why do Bolger and Krebs matter?" Colby asked.

"Bolger matters because he's the one witness we have who can corroborate Spears' claim that he wasn't anywhere near Benicia when the Judge was murdered," Blandon said. "Explain it to them, Clint."

"Spears told me he and Bolger were on a fishing trip up in Klamath at the time, and Bolger confirmed it. As for Krebs, well, she says she got Stark roaring drunk one night and he told her all about Soames' plan to hire Baby Face Nelson."

"You know Stark will deny that," Sherman sneered. "Who's going to believe a whore?"

"Stark has a record a mile long—felony assault against a police officer, breaking and entering, hit and run manslaughter. You name it, Stark's done it," Koontz replied coolly.

"Are you planning to put Spears on the stand?" Victor asked.

"Probably, but not until we've worked through the other testimonies first," Blanden answered. "Initially, our purpose will simply be to cast doubt on the credibility of the Prosecution's witnesses. That's where Clements and McCutcheon come in. They were all present at a Republican Party meeting in Benicia where Howard Roach said Judge Lanham was somebody he wanted out of the way after the elections in 1928."

"Out of the way? Why should Roach want Lanham out of the way? What does that mean anyway?" Sherman asked.

"That's where Peters comes in," Blanden explained. "He was at another meeting in Benicia on the same night and he overheard Soames tell Roach he would use Nelson to murder the Judge."

"This is all hearsay, of course," Victor sighed. "No self-respecting trial court judge will allow it."

"This entire case involves hearsay!" Blanden declared. "The Grand Jury's findings are based on the hearsay of political heavies like Hilliard and Roach and Martinez Mayor Frobish, who's nothing but a big fish in a little pond. Soames is a bootlegger and Stark is one of Spears' former henchmen. Their credibility as witnesses is zero."

"Then Gorman will dismiss the case," Victor said.

"Maybe not," Colby countered. "Gorman's a Republican appointee. He's likely to side with Billings and Roach. Don't forget. This is an election year, and the stakes are high for the Republicans."

The partners were now in a state of utter bewilderment.

"We have two very big aces in the hole," Blanden announced proudly. "First there's the evidence that was suppressed during the first investigation of the Judge's alleged suicide. Fred has obtained a copy of the original investigative report filed in that instance and it clearly reveals the shotgun shells used to kill Judge Lanham were not the same as the ones he regularly used for duck hunting. Second, Del has come up with a courtroom strategy that could blow the current case wide open. Go ahead, Del. Tell them about your plan."

"It's really very simple," she began modestly. "I've developed some questions I plan to ask Spears if and when we put him on the stand. These questions are about the specific layout of the interior of our house in Benicia. If Spears can't answer these questions correctly, we'll know he has never been there."

"An interesting idea, Del," Victor said, raising his eyebrows in surprise and admiration. "But why not file a request for a closed hearing with Judge Gorman. If Spears answers prove his innocence, the Judge will probably dismiss the case before it goes to trial."

Blanden leaned back in his chair, his face hardened with determination. "That would be a Pyrrhic victory for us. Billings and Roach have cooked up this whole case to hide their political chicanery. We have a chance to expose them in a public trial. It's our civic duty to do so."

"So you want to use the courtroom to promote your own political agenda, Bob. Is that it?" Sherman asked with a crooked smile.

"Bob wants justice! So do I!" Del affirmed, startling even herself with the forcefulness of her declaration.

Yet again, Colby intervened. "I agree. If we expose Billings and

Roach, they'll be indicted not only for conspiring to assassinate a Ninth Circuit judge but probably also for a whole host of other crimes against the State. At the very least, winning this case in a public trial would be a big plus for the firm. I say we should go for the jugular."

"Too risky!" Sherman countered. "The whole thing could backfire on us."

"Let's vote on it," Victor said.

By a show of hands, with only Sherman opposed, the decision was made. They would proceed with a public trial.

1933

The "Manse" on West G Street

Chapter Thirty-eight

"I've Got the World on a String"

THE DEFENSE TEAM HAD WON, thanks in large measure to Del's closing argument, which Bob Blanden had insisted she deliver in court. It was Del, he argued, who had uncovered the most damning evidence against the prosecution's case because of her exhaustive search through the archived files of *The San Francisco Examiner* and it was Del whose relentless cross-examination of Spears had proven conclusively the man had never seen the inside of the Lanham house.

Their victory had made the front page of every major newspaper on the West Coast, and radio newscasts had carried the story all the way to Washington, D. C. The Deputy Director of the FBI himself had wired Del his personal congratulations, for not only had she pinned yet another murder rap on "Public Enemy Number One"—Baby Face Nelson—but also she had broken open one of the most insidious political conspiracies in the history of California.

State Assemblyman Howard Roach and United States Senator Blake Hilliard would each face ten-year prison terms and their co-conspirator Paul Frobish, five years. Other participants in Roach's conspiracy to bribe retired judges, including Russell Bancroft and Leo Caputi, also received prison sentences of two years each. Though issued summonses to appear in court, James Soames and Thomas Stark had fled the State. Their names had been added to the FBI's "most wanted" list. Because they had provided critical testimony on behalf of the defense, however, Bert McCutcheon and Zack Clements received only fines of $5,000 each.

All of this had happened only two weeks before Christmas of 1932—the day on which Del and Jack had planned to make a formal announcement of their engagement to be married. Del's sudden celebrity disrupted this plan, however. Swamped with solicitations from radio newscasters to tell her story on the airwaves and with invitations to speak at women's clubs and colleges all over the Bay Area, Del told Jack she had no time to plan for a wedding and that they should postpone their engagement announcement indefinitely.

Snooky was furious. "How can you do this to Jack?" she demanded late one Sunday night in early January when she confronted Del in her father's study.

"What have I done wrong?" Del fired back. "Do you have any idea how busy I am right now? I'm besieged with press conferences practically every day and my bosses are pushing me to make public appearances all over the State, even on weekends! I'm their poster girl, and new clients are banging down the doors of our office just to do business with Sherman, Hartz and Colby. What do you expect me to do, Snooky? Just toss all this to the wind?"

"All this fame and glory, huh? It means more to you than Jack or anybody else, don't it?"

This comment gave Del pause. Snooky had touched a raw nerve. Del knew the postponement of their engagement had crushed Jack's spirit. He had not called her since December 12 when she had first suggested they postpone their engagement announcement. *How typical of him to skulk off in silence!* she thought. *How typical of men in general!*

But these last words were not Del's. Rather they were the words of her new friend Esther Kaufman who, when Del told her after the trial that she was planning to marry Jack, had urged her to reconsider. "What d' y' need a man for?" Esther asked as they sat together eating lunch in Esther's favorite delicatessen.

"Jack and I love each other," Del answered firmly. "We always have and we always will."

"Phooey!" Esther expostulated. "Nothin' lasts forever! Least of all the hots y' get for some guy. It's all about hormones, kiddo—the same hormones monkeys have!"

Del knew nothing about hormones. It was a subject none of her teachers—even her college science instructors—had ever mentioned. "I guess you've never been in love, Esther," Del said. "I feel sorry for you," she added, though in fact she did not.

After nearly a month of seeing Esther almost every weekday, Del had gotten to know her well. Though often amused by her earthy sense of humor and grateful for her help in using the archives of *The San Francisco Examiner*, Del did not like Esther's frequent outbursts of bitterness—especially toward men.

"Oh yeah?" Esther retorted. "Well, I feel sorrier for you 'cause it's obvious you been readin' too many o' those sappy romances they publish in magazine like *Woman's Home Companion*!"

"I don't read magazines," Del retorted coolly. "I don't have time."

You ain't gonna have time when you're married either, kiddo. Believe me. Once your boy Jack ropes you in, you'll be hog-tied and branded. Ten-to-one he's already knocked you up. If not, it's for sure he'll do it soon as you two tie the knot."

Del reached for her handbag and stood up to leave. "You've gone too far! I thought you were my friend, Esther, but obviously you're not!"

Lowering her head and flailing her arms, Esther feigned contrition. "You're right! I *am* a bitch sometimes. Sorry! I got carried away. So don't go off in a huff, Del. Sit down an' let's talk."

Cautiously, Del resumed her seat. "Only if you can talk respectfully," she warned.

Esther stared at Del out of desperately hungry eyes. "Believe me, Del, I *do* respect you. Truth is I *adore* you, baby! That's why I hate to see you throwin' yourself away on some small-town jerk. You're better than he is—*way* better! You got it in you to be a real leader. Who knows? Maybe even the first woman President of the United States!"

"Don't be ridiculous!"

"So now you're sayin' the idea of a woman President's ridiculous?" Esther challenged. "You've definitely been readin' the wrong books, honey!"

"I've been reading law books mostly these days," Del pointed out with a tinge of sarcasm in her voice.

"Yeah, an' men write the law books—*all* of 'em! That's why women have been chattels all these centuries. You need to read some books by women writers."

"Such as?" Del asked, arching an eyebrow. She was prepared to retort that she had read many books by women writers and that Esther was insulting her intelligence.

"Such as Margaret Sanger, Emma Goldman, Alice B. Toklas, and Gertrude Atherton. There's a whole bunch of 'em. I'll make a list for y'." Esther was very excited now. She felt sure she had captured Del's attention.

"I've heard of Margaret Sanger, of course. She's a well-known advocate of women's rights, isn't she?"

"Damn right she is—'specially women's right to abortion. Fact, she just came out with a new book on that topic. It's called *My Fight for Birth Control*. If you're thinkin' about gettin' married, you better read that book first."

"I'm a Catholic, Esther. We Catholics don't believe in birth control."

"Yeah, an' that's why there's so many poor starving Catholic children! You people are just plain nuts!"

"I thought you were going to talk respectfully," Del cautioned.

"Right. Well, *you* I respect. But stupid people I don't. Anyway, you're a smart girl, so you should read Sanger."

Suddenly recalling the tall, stern-faced figure of Victoria Callahan shaking her axe at the women of the Lido fourteen years before, Del shuddered. "I'm not so sure. As for those other women authors you mentioned. I'm afraid I've never heard of them."

Esther's jaw dropped. "Y' gotta be kiddin' me! Hell! One time or another, they all lived and wrote right here in San Francisco. Matter of fact, Atherton went t' some private school in your hometown when she was fifteen. She didn't stay there long though 'cause they tossed her out for foolin' around with some o' the local boys."

"You must be talking about Saint Mary's Hall. That school closed a long time ago." Remembering Esther's earlier observation that she knew very little about the Bay Area, she said, "I thought you never heard of Benicia."

"After you told me about it, I did some digging and found out Atherton's mother sent her to boarding school there after she divorced her first husband. Guess her mom did Gertrude a big favor because that's where she first got interested in writing. She wrote a whole slew of novels. The best one was *Black Oxen*. That's definitely another book you should read. It's been around for quite a while. Came out back in '23, I think."

"What's it about?"

Esther responded with a coy smile. "Why don't y' read it yourself an' find out?"

"Perhaps I will when I get the time." Del glanced at her wristwatch and stood up. "I have to go back to the office now. Goodbye, Esther."

"Bye-bye, honey," Esther replied with a flirtatious wink as she popped the last fragment of a kosher dill pickle into her mouth.

* * *

It was a rainy Thursday morning in early February. Del was standing in line at the Martinez train depot, waiting to purchase her ticket to Sacramento where she was scheduled to speak before the State Assembly on behalf of a new bill giving the widows of public employees the right to claim their dead husbands' pensions. Suddenly she saw Jack standing under his open umbrella just outside the entrance to the depot. As soon as she purchased her ticket, she went outside to confront him. "Jack!" she demanded angrily. "Why haven't you called me?"

Startled, at first Jack didn't recognize her in her ankle-length mackintosh and wide-brimmed rain hat. "That you, Del" he asked sheepishly.

"You're damn right it is! So why haven't you called?" Del flinched, suddenly embarrassed by her own aggressive language.

Jack too was embarrassed. "What do you expect, Del?" he asked. "You made it pretty clear you're not interested in marrying me. You're too busy, you said."

"I did *not*!" Del almost screamed at him. "I *never* said that!"

Several other travelers standing nearby began staring at them. Jack took hold of Del's arm and firmly guided her to the far end of the waiting platform. "Maybe not in so many words," Jack admitted, keeping his voice low. "But that's the message I got. After all, you haven't called me either, have you?"

Del answered this question by breaking into tears. "That's not fair, Jack!" she blubbered. "I would have called, but I thought you were angry with me. After all, you *are* hot-headed!"

"So this was only a lovers' quarrel?" Jack asked, melting in submission to her tearful rebuke. "I'm sorry, darling. I just thought ..."

Del glared at him. "You thought wrong! You jumped to conclusions, just as you *always* do!"

There were tears in Jack's eyes now as he gazed down at her. He desperately wanted to take Del in his arms, but he still wasn't sure how she would respond. For weeks now, Greg and Wally had both urged him to phone Del and patch things up. "You can't let that beautiful lady get away, Jack," Wally had insisted. "She's the best thing ever happened to you!"

Seeing the tears in Jack's eyes, Del threw her arms around his neck and kissed him. "Oh Jack!" she cried. "I missed you so!"

Just at that moment, they heard the voice of a conductor calling out the "All aboard" for Del's train to Sacramento. Del looked around frantically. "I've got to go, Jack," she gasped, grabbing her suitcase and moving swiftly toward the steps down from the waiting platform. "I'll call you as soon as I get back. I promise!"

Jack's impulse was to run after her and try to help her with her luggage as she climbed aboard the train. But she was too fast for him. He shook his head and smiled sadly. *This is the way it's always going to be, I suppose*, he thought to himself.

* * *

Four days later Del did telephone Jack, humbly apologizing for not having called him sooner. "My presentation in Sacramento Thursday turned into a three-day junket of speaking engagements," she explained, unable to conceal the pride she felt in this achievement. "I didn't get home until late last night."

"Well, congratulations!" Jack said. "Sounds like you're in line for a political appointment. What's it going to be—Attorney General?" There was an unmistakable note of sarcasm in Jack's question.

Del decided she should ignore it. "No, Jack," she chortled. "I have no political aspirations—or prospects, for that matter. The speeches I gave were not about me but about this new widow's pension bill that's before the State Assembly right now. Many Californians are in favor of it."

"And you're its chief advocate," Jack observed, devilishly baiting her to elaborate.

Del did not take the bait. "Alright, Jack—enough of that! I'm calling to ask you to join some friends and me for a Saint Valentine's Day party in the city next Saturday night. We're going to this crazy new restaurant called The Red Rooster. It'll be lots of fun. I'd love it if Greg would come too."

"Sure. I'll be glad to go with you. I don't know about Greg. But he's right here with me now, so why don't you ask him yourself?" Jack handed the phone to Greg.

"I see you made the front page of the *Examiner* again this morning. Wow! You're becoming quite the celebrity!"

"Don't you start on me now too, Greg!" Del scolded. "Jack has already done enough balloon popping!"

"He's just jealous. So what's up?"

"I want you and Jack to have dinner with me and some friends in the city next Saturday night. Do you think you can make it?"

"Certainly! I'd be delighted!" Greg answered eagerly. "What time and where do we meet you?"

"I'm taking the 3:00 o'clock ferry from Vallejo. We can meet at the terminal there if you like. Let's say around 2:30?"

"It's a date. So where are we having dinner? Is this a tux and tails affair?"

"Hardly!" Del laughed. "We're going to this crazy new dinner club called The Red Rooster. It's in the Castro."

"In the Castro?" Greg's tone suddenly became guarded. He had heard rumors that the Castro was heavily populated by lesbians and gays. He did not feel at all comfortable about being seen in such company.

"Oh don't worry. Greg. You'll be perfectly safe!" Del reassured him. "It's just a goofy place where men dress up as female waitresses and put on a silly floorshow. Most of the customers are just normal people like us."

"Hmm," Greg replied. "Ah well, I suppose it could be fun."

"Good. Let me talk to Jack again, would you please?"

Back on the line, Jack asked, "How about if just you and I have dinner together Friday night, Del?"

"Oh Jack, you know I'd love to. But I promised Snooky and Ruby

I'd stay home and have dinner with them Friday. I've been away a lot during the past several weeks, and they've been pestering me to spend some time with them. Why don't you come over and have dinner with us?"

"That's not quite what I had in mind, Del."

"I know what you had in mind, dear," Del replied, feeling the blood rush to her face. "Maybe later in the evening, after everybody else has gone to bed."

"That sounds good to me," Jack said. "What time do you plan to have dinner?"

"I should be home from the city by six. But come earlier if you can. I know Snooky and Ruby would love to see you."

"I'll do my best," Jack promised, and the two lovers hung up, wishing each other sweet dreams.

*   *   *

When Del, Jack and Greg entered the San Francisco ferry terminal the following Saturday afternoon, they were greeted by a very chatty group of twelve people, most of whom worked with Del at her law office. Jack immediately recognized the Hartzes as well as Fred Koontz and Bob Blanden. He had met Blanden when he had gone to the Solano Court House to watch Del during her cross-examination of Spears. Greg knew the Hartzes, Craig McCutcheon and Joanna Newman, but there were seven others he did not know.

Del quickly and deftly introduced Jack and Greg to everyone, which included Claude Colby and his wife Ida, Bob Blanden's wife Christine, Kirsten Raynor, and Esther Kaufman. Since there were fifteen in their party, they broke up into three groups of five each and took separate cabs across town to the Castro district.

The Red Rooster dinner club occupied the basement and first floor of an old five-story warehouse. The entrance was down a flight of steps from street level through a single oak door with a sliding peephole indicating the place had once been a speak-easy. But now no one challenged them as they passed through this door into a large, high-ceilinged room filled with tables, each illuminated by a flickering candle in a crimson heart-shaped glass. The walls of the place were festooned with lace-embroidered white banners repeatedly declaring in glittering red letters "Happy Valentines Day."

Since it was 5:30 when they arrived, there were still several unoccupied tables. A tall woman dressed in a black tuxedo greeted them stiffly and summoned two garishly rouged men attired in red and white babushkas and matching dresses to move several tables together.

Victor Hartz, assuming his usual leadership role, commandeered a chair at the head of the long table and insisted everyone else sit in a "girl-boy" pattern. "We don't want anyone to feel left out!" he announced with a sardonic leer at Esther Kaufman.

"Don't worry about it, Vic," she sneered back as she disobediently seated herself next to Del. "Nobody ever leaves *me* out!"

So the tone was set for the rest of the evening. Every one of these fifteen people was gifted and intelligent in one way or another. None would be able to lord it over the other. They had gathered at the Red Rooster, after all, to see a freak show and would not allow any petty rivalries or jealousies to distract them from the rollicking fun of watching others make fools of themselves.

Nor would they be disappointed. Three transvestite waitresses quickly took orders for the first round of drinks. Almost simultaneously, a six-piece band burst into a lively accompaniment for the entrance of the Red Rooster chorus line. Kleig lights flashed on revealing a truly bizarre spectacle. Six men wearing red wigs and dressed in red and white *folies bergere* costumes pranced onto the small stage. Then, squealing with falsetto delight, they hoisted their skirts and kicked their heels high in perfect unison.

Almost every member of the audience applauded—except Jack, Greg and a few other newcomers to this experience who could only gape in amazement. Claude Colby whooped with delight and Esther Kaufman, clapping wildly, rose to her feet to encourage a standing ovation. Though several other audience members followed Esther's lead, no one else at her table felt compelled to do so. The general consensus seemed to be that The Red Rooster was not San Francisco's symphony hall.

As the chorus line pranced gleefully off the stage, a dwarf in top hat and tails hopped up on the stage and seized the microphone. Tipping his hat and bowing, he greeted his audience with a puckish smile. "Welcome to The Red Rooster, ladies and gentlemen. My name is Tristram Sills and I'm your host for the evening. Sounds like you enjoyed our Red Rooster Rockettes. Aren't they delightful? Let's all give them another hand," he suggested as he turned toward the six dancers still standing in the wings and led the audience in more applause.

"And now, dear friends, we have another treat—something that'll really warm your cockles." Tristam quickly covered his mouth with a white-gloved hand. "Ooops!" he said in mock embarrassment. "One does have to be careful about how one uses one's words, doesn't one?"

To this aside several audience members responded with snickers, though Del and most of the other women at her table thought Tristram's jest was tasteless. Unfazed by their response, Tristram blew a kiss at his audience and cleared the stage for the next performers.

Two men wearing house dresses and blonde wigs in pin curlers spent the next five minutes screaming and throwing pies at each other in a pantomime of squabbling housewives. Their antics climaxed when they tore off each other's clothes until both male actors were stripped to their boxer shorts.

This farcical interlude evoked gales of laughter as the actors picked up their clothes and scurried off stage, cuing Tristram to resume his Master of Ceremonies role. "Wasn't that fun?" he asked salaciously. "Well, believe me, folks! You ain't seen nothin' yet! But it's suppertime. So now, while our lovely waitresses attend to your gustatory cravings, our talented musicians will serenade you with a medley of songs from that fabulous new Hollywood musical *42nd Street*." Hopping down from the stage, Tristram bowed to the band and shouted, "Take it away, Maestro!"

As she sat listening to the music and sipping her wine, Del suddenly gestured toward one of the cross-dressers attending the table next to theirs. "I know that man!" she gasped. Turning to Jack, she declared, "It's Tully Geddis!"

"What?" Jack asked. "You can't be serious!"

"She's right, Jack," Greg admitted. "He does look like Tully—or anyway like his mother!"

This observation startled both Del and Jack. "That's sick!" Jack spat out in disgust.

"Sam *did* tell me once that Tully liked to dress up in his mother's clothes," Del said, her eyes filling with tears. "Oh Jack! This is so sad!"

"But why?" The question was posed by Kirsten Raynor who was seated directly across the table from Del. "The man you're talking about seems to me quite content with himself."

"Right!" Esther agreed. "There are lots o' guys like him! 'Specially here in the Castro. So what's your problem, Del?"

Exchanging quick glances with Jack and Greg, Del bit her lip. "Perhaps you don't understand," she said as calmly as she could to Kirsten who was studying Del now with smoldering disapproval. "Tully is a childhood friend of ours. His brother was killed in a terrible accident several years ago and his mother is in an insane asylum. She has been for years."

"What I understand," Kirsten observed coldly, "is that you Americans are purists. You expect everyone to be like you. We Danes do not think that way."

"Kirsten!" Bob Blanden suddenly put in. "You surprise me. I never realized you had such strong opinions, though of course you are certainly entitled to them."

"I'm glad you see it that way, Robert," Kirsten replied coolly. "Perhaps you and some of your colleagues have misconstrued my professional reticence. I assure you, outside of the office, I am very much my own person."

"Good for you, Kirsten!" Esther chimed in. "Me—I'm the same wherever I am!"

"That too appears to be part of the American character," Kirsten said with a pitying smile at Esther.

"Now hold on, there, Kirsten!" Claude Colby, who was sitting to Kirsten's right, had been listening to this conversation with increasing irritation. "If you Europeans are so darn superior, how come you're lettin' that maniac Hitler take over in Germany? Don't you realize he's nothing but a thug and a bully? Just look what he's doing to his own people—especially the Jews!"

"My German acquaintances tell me they admire Hitler because he makes the trains run on time," Kirsten replied dismissively.

"He has done much more than that," Ida Colby remarked, speaking for the first time. Ida, a stern-faced woman in her late forties with the high cheekbones and deep-set eyes of an Eastern European, spoke with a distinctly German accent. Her tone of voice was somber as she elaborated. "*Der Fuehrer*, as they call him now, has ordered boycotts of Jewish businesses throughout Germany, and he has banned all Jews from civil service jobs. One of his henchmen, a police official named Heinrich Himmler, is now establishing a concentration camp for political prisoners at Dachau. I assure you, Miss Raynor, most of those prisoners are Jewish intellectuals."

"How do you know all this, Missus Colby?" Bob asked. Though he had met Claude's wife before at several social gatherings with the senior partners, she had always seemed to him withdrawn and unapproachable.

"I have family in Germany, Mister Blanden. As a matter of fact, because of the boycott, my brother was forced to close his haberdashery shop in Munich only last month."

"That's horrible!" Joanna Newman declared. "Why haven't we heard more about this here in America?"

"Probably because we Americans already have problems of our own to solve," Craig McCutcheon opined. "I read just yesterday that the unemployment rate here is now at sixty-five percent!"

"You'd never know it in our line of business," Greg observed. "We can't produce grapes fast enough to meet our customers' demands."

"Then you're very lucky," Blandon's wife Christine said. "At the public school our children attend, most parents are on the dole. One of the fathers, who was a very successful investment banker four years ago, just committed suicide!"

"Yeah, and how do you think us doops in the newspaper business feel?" Esther demanded. "You know what my monthly salary is? Eighty bucks! How can anybody live on that? An' I work for the richest man in California, f' God's sake—William Randolph Hearst!"

"So do you think this fella Roosevelt will save us?" Fred Koontz asked, addressing his question to no one in particular.

"You people are all a bunch of cry babies!" Victor Hartz declared from his place at the head of the table. Holding up his cocktail glass, he proclaimed, "I say God bless America! The land of free enterprise! Even that radical Roosevelt has it right. 'We have nothing to fear but fear itself!'"

"So how come 'God Bless America' isn't our national anthem?" Esther demanded. "Can you believe some boob in D.C. picked a song that begins with 'Oh say can you see by the dawn's early light'?"

"Considering all the drunks Prohibition's made, that's actually a pretty good line," Jack quipped.

Claude Colby burst into laughter. "By golly, Jack! That's a real corker!"

"Jack ought to know!" Greg couldn't resist saying.

Del quickly came to Jack's defense. "That's not fair, Greg! After all, look at the business *you're* in. It's still illegal!"

"Prohibition's days are numbered," Victor affirmed. "There's an amendment to end it on the floor of Congress right now."

Already six sheets to the wind, Deirdre Hartz held up her empty glass. "I shay good riddansh! Lesh have 'nother roun'!"

With this suggestion, all agreed. While the table attendants were refreshing everyone's drinks, the band began playing the opening bars of "Too Many Tears." Everyone's attention was drawn to the stage where a tall and strikingly stunning female figure stood silently in an ankle-length black evening gown, its sequined fabric sparkling in the spotlight.

The performer's poignant interpretation of this Guy Lombardo favorite captivated every man and woman in the audience. Even Jack became convinced this sultry entertainer was a real woman, especially when he heard the concluding words of the song:

> *I'll never learn*
> *To smile again and sing,*
> *I gave you everything;*
> *And in return*
> *What did you leave me for souvenirs?*
> *Too many tears.*

It was only after they had awarded the talented chanteuse with several minutes of vigorous applause that the audience was shocked back to reality. At that point, Tristram hopped up on the stage and, grinning broadly, commanded, "OK, Larry, show 'em your stuff!"

The beautiful vocalist promptly obliged by removing his shoulder-length black wig and opening the front of his costume to expose his hairy chest and male genitals. Once more, the room was filled with deafening applause and laughter.

Jack was not amused. "This is getting boring!" he protested. "Don't these clowns have any other gags?"

"Hey Jack!" Joanna reminded him. "This is a gay nightclub. What do you expect?"

"Yes, but Jack's got a point," Craig said. "A little more subtlety and variety might help."

"Gays are an oppressed minority!" Esther retorted. Then, challenging Ida Colby, she mocked, "Just like the Jews in Germany."

"You know nothing about it, young woman," Ida rejoined. "I assure you, what is happening in Germany is no laughing matter!"

Though most of the others at the table now eagerly anticipated a heated argument between Esther and Ida, Del's focus of interest was elsewhere. She was still closely following the movements of the transvestite waitress she had identified as Tully Geddis. Rising from her chair, she whispered to Jack, "I'm going to talk to him."

Jack grabbed her wrist. "No, Del!" he implored. "Let it go. He won't understand."

"But I know he recognizes us!" she insisted loudly. "He's been looking our way repeatedly. We can't just ignore him!"

Greg stood up beside her. "If you really must do this, Del, I'll go with you. But I agree with Jack. I think Tully'd much rather avoid us. He looks pretty scared."

"Your childhood friend obviously made a decision about who he wants to be a long time ago, Del," Kirsten observed. "If he wanted to speak with you, I'm sure he would do so. Perhaps it would be wiser and more compassionate to honor his need for anonymity in this situation."

But Del stood her ground. "I disagree. What's compassionate about deliberately ignoring someone you've known all your life?"

"You may be entering the heart of darkness," Kirsten warned, alluding to Joseph Conrad's novel about a 19th Century European white man who wandered into the jungles of the Congo and adopted the cannibalism of the African natives.

"We're all entering the heart of darkness," Ida said grimly.

These remarks meant nothing to the other members of their party, however. None of them had ever read *The Heart of Darkness* or studied the dying days of European colonialism when Belgium, France, and Germany carved up the African continent to exploit its resources and oppress its inhabitants.

At that moment, Del had only one thought—she had to speak with Tully, to somehow reassure him she was still his friend no matter what may have happened. As she moved away from their table, both Jack and Greg tried to accompany her.

Holding up both hands to stop them, she said, "No. Please! Let me speak to him alone. Tully's afraid, and probably most of all of you two men!"

Shaking their heads, Jack and Greg sat down again. "She certainly has a mind of her own!" Greg declared as Del walked away.

"She cares about people," Jack said. "It's her greatest strength."

"And her greatest vulnerability," Kirsten added.

* * *

Tully was engaged in animated conversation with another costumed waiter when Del approached him. They seemed to be having some kind of an argument. Del waited for several seconds until the other waiter angrily walked away. "Hello, Tully," she said hesitantly.

Immediately, he turned and stared at her—the irises of his wide-set eyes were dark and fearful, like those of a faun staring at a predator. Recovering his composure, he asked, "Del, is that you?"

"Yes, Tully. It's me," she said softly and moved closer to him. "How are you?"

Tully linked his arm under Del's and guided her toward a door with an illuminated sign above it marked *EXIT.* He pushed the door open and led her into a dimly lighted exterior alley. As the heavy door slammed shut behind them, Tully released Del's arm and stepped away from her. "What do you want?" he demanded angrily.

"I ... I just wanted to say hello," Del replied, her chest suddenly tightening with dread.

"Why couldn't you just leave me alone?" Tully's deep voice was suddenly very masculine and aggressive. "The past is dead! We have nothing to say to each other."

"I don't believe that, Tully," Del retorted, becoming angry herself now. "You can't just cut yourself off from the people who were your childhood friends!"

Tully smiled cynically. "Childhood friends? Don't you remember how you and your friends, including my own brother, treated me when we were growing up? That wasn't friendship! It was pure bullying! Sorry, Del. I'm afraid I don't have very good memories of those days."

"I didn't bully you!" Del protested. "Neither did Jack and Greg!"

"No. You ignored me! If Greg and Jack are such good friends of mine, why didn't they come with you to say hello?"

"They offered to come with me. But I told them you seemed frightened."

"Frightened of them?" Tully asked. "More likely, they were frightened of me, Del. Surely you're smart enough to realize how people like me intimidate men like Jack and Greg."

"I think you may be exaggerating the effect you have on others, Tully. The truth is …" Del stopped herself in mid-sentence, realizing that what she was about to say would only make Tully more angry and defensive.

Tully stepped close to her now, his eyes flashing defiance. "The truth is what, Del? That they really don't care? That they consider me a freak? You know that's the real truth, don't you, Del? And that's what you really think too, isn't it?"

Del looked down at the cobble-stoned pavement, glistening with the moisture of the fog drifting in over San Francisco at this late night hour. Then, looking up, she gazed steadily at Tully. What she said next came from deep inside of her. They were words she did not recognize as her own but they came freely and exultantly. "None of us knows the truth in other people's hearts, Tully. But I know my own truth. I am your friend. I will *always* be your friend."

Tully smiled cynically. "I wish I could believe that, Del. But I don't. Our lives are very different."

Del reached out to touch Tully's satin-sleeved forearm. "I understand, Tully," she murmured compassionately. "You've had a lot of sadness in your life."

Tully covered his face with his hands and moaned. "You don't know the half of it! Mama finally did it!"

"What is it, Tully? What happened?" Del asked desperately.

"Momma hanged herself last week! Tied her bed sheet to the bars in the window of her room!"

"Oh my God, Tully! I'm so sorry! I didn't know!"

Dropping his hands, Tully exposed his tear-streaked face but his eyes were red with rage. "No. You didn't know! And you didn't care! Nobody ever cared! That damned psychologist Merriweather just locked her away in that hell-hole of a sanitarium and let her rot!"

"Did Sam know about this?" Del asked, desperately searching now for some common ground of feeling.

"Of course, he did! But he hated mother! He blamed her for everything!"

"I don't believe that!" Del said.

"You can believe whatever you damn please!" Tully roared. "Just leave me alone!" Then, yanking open the door, he re-entered the nightclub.

Del stood alone in the alleyway for several seconds, trembling—suddenly aware of the dampness and darkness that enveloped her, suddenly understanding what Kirsten Raynor had meant when she warned, "You may be entering the heart of darkness."

She did not have long to ponder this thought, for the fire door burst open and Jack rushed into the alley. "Del, what happened? Are you alright?"

She nodded mechanically. "I am, but Tully's not." She threw herself into Jack's arms. "Oh Jack! It's terrible! Tully's mother killed herself!"

Jack held her tightly for several seconds until her trembling subsided. Then, opening the fire door, he gently urged, "Come inside, Del."

CHAPTER THIRTY-NINE

"Stormy Weather"

ONLY A FEW DAYS AFTER the Saint Valentine's Day party in San Francisco, Ruby fell on the back porch steps of Del's house and broke her hip. As a result, she was now confined to a wheelchair. Then, two days later, Snooky was diagnosed with emphysema. Her physician warned her that she might be dead within a matter of months if she did not stop smoking.

Despite this ominous warning, Snooky refused to follow the doctor's orders. She continued to smoke two or more packs of Lucky Strikes every day. Consequently, her body was constantly racked with wheezing and coughing that diminished her appetite and disrupted her sleep.

At first, Del had pleaded with Snooky to stop, using every argument she could think of. When, after one particularly severe coughing attack, Del scolded Snooky for 'stinking up the house with her filthy habit,' Snooky became belligerent. "So you want me and Alfie to move out?" Snooky demanded. "Alright, we'll move out!"

Terrified, Del grabbed Snooky's wrists. "No! Of course not!" she cried. "I'd *never* let you do such a thing!"

"Well then, dammit, girl! Leave me alone! I'm fifty-one years old. I been doin' this since I was knee-high to a grasshopper, an' I sure ain't stoppin' now!"

Almost in tears, Del protested. "But you're killing yourself, Snooky! I don't want you to die!"

Snooky fixed Del with cynical stare. "Everybody dies sooner or later, kiddo."

At that moment, Del understood there was nothing she could do. She would simply have to accept the fact of Snooky's rapidly deteriorating health and probably imminent and painful death. Embracing Snooky, Del said, "I love you, Snooky." She felt the older woman's frail body shudder in her arms.

Chuckling with a rasping wheeze, Snooky declared, "Like Mae West says, honey, 'I ain't no angel!'"

*   *   *

Del knew she had to break the news of Snooky's worsening condition to Jack and again insist they postpone their marriage. On a rainy Saturday afternoon in early March, she arranged for Snooky and Alfie to see a motion picture at the Majestic Theater while she and Jack lunched alone together at the Union Hotel.

Del waited until they were drinking their coffee after lunch before she brought up the subject of Ruby's fall and Snooky's illness. After explaining their conditions to Jack in graphic detail, she said, "We can't get married now, Jack. It wouldn't be fair to any of us—least of all to you!"

"You sound like mother—pushing me away just when you need me the most!" Jack retorted. "What's wrong with you women?"

Del looked at him sadly for several seconds before she answered. "Call it our nesting instinct, Jack. We women know it's dangerous to overpopulate the nest. When you have too many chicks, one or more of them always falls out."

"Or gets pushed!" Jack snarled.

"It's very difficult for me right now, Jack," she replied, struggling to remain calm. "I'm afraid we'll just have to wait until things settle down a bit."

"That could be a long time!" Jack protested bitterly. "Do you really think it's going to get any easier? What happens if Snooky becomes bedridden? Then you'll have three invalids to look after! How will you do that and keep your big-time lawyer's job?"

"I suppose I'll have to hire someone to come in while I'm at work," Del answered wearily.

"Won't that be adding another chick to your nest? No matter how you look at it, Del, you're going to need help. Two paychecks are better than one, and you know I'll always be willing to help with Ruby and Snooky."

Del was silent. She had already thought long and hard about the point Jack was making. She knew the fame she had recently won as a trial lawyer was fool's gold in the face of the rapidly deteriorating national economy. Only two days before, her firm had lost yet another major client to bankruptcy, and the senior partners were talking about additional cuts in staff. What would she do if she lost her job?

Worse still, most of the stocks and bonds in her father's trust fund had declined in value during the past year, significantly reducing her monthly dividend and interest income. After the court decision had invalidated her father's alleged suicide, she had expected to receive a death benefit from his life insurance policy. That did not happen, however, because the company that issued the Judge's policy had gone into receivership.

What if she were to become pregnant soon after they were married, as Esther Kaufman had assured her she would? Even with two incomes, how could she and Jack afford children? Any form of birth control but abstinence was out of the question for Del. Since Jack was not Roman Catholic, she could hardly expect him to tolerate that.

Del reached across the table and grasped Jack's hand. "Please, dear! Please try to understand and be patient with me. I just need more time to work things out!"

As Del anticipated, though, Jack had lost all patience. He did not express this in words, but his drooping shoulders and bowed head spoke volumes. Reaching inside his jacket, he pulled out his wallet, extracted a five-dollar bill and dropped it on the table to pay for their lunch. Then, he stood up and left the hotel without a word of goodbye.

Torn between her anger at this rudeness and her fear that this might really be the end of their relationship, Del followed him into the street. By the time she got there, though, he was already driving away. She stood in the open doorway of the hotel, watching forlornly as his car moved slowly through the rain up First Street.

*   *   *

Early the next morning Jack stood alone, staring over the rock wall that divided the Henshaks' terrace and pool from the steep grassy slope that fell several hundred yards below toward West Military. A dense fog hung over the Carquinez Strait, obscuring everything more than a few yards beyond the wall. All Jack could hear was the mournful sound of the foghorn on Dillon Point. In his still groggy brain, Jack imagined that, if he were to climb over the wall at that moment, he would fall into an abyss and disappear forever. He lit a cigarette and inhaled deeply, hoping this mild narcotic would dispel such lunatic thoughts.

"So what are you going to do?" sounded a familiar voice behind him. It was Greg. The two friends had sat up late the night before trying to drown Jack's sorrow and disappointment with a bottle of Christian Brothers' brandy. It had not worked.

"Nothing," Jack answered bleakly. "There's nothing I can do."

Greg leaned with his back against the wall, trying to make eye contact with Jack. "Maybe you need to get away for awhile," Greg suggested. "Take a trip. It would give both of you some breathing space. Matter of fact, I've been thinking of sending you on a business trip to Europe anyway. The Brothers tell me sweet white wine is becoming all the rage these days but none of the other California growers have the right kind of grapes. They say, if we plant Reislings, we'll have a corner on the market. I hear the best Rieslings are grown in Germany."

"You want *me* to go to Germany?" Jack looked at his friend in amazement, suddenly remembering what Ida Colby had said about Hitler's brutal new government. "No thanks. I've had enough of gangsters to last me a lifetime!"

Greg nodded somberly. "I understand. But that's precisely why now is a good time to buy Riesling cuttings over there. The National Socialists are confiscating all the best vineyards. It's part of Hitler's plan to build up his economy and drive out the Jews."

"What do Jews have to do with winemaking?" Jack asked.

"Are you kidding? Haven't you ever heard of Baron Rothschild?"

"Yeah. He drives fancy racecars," Jack said contemptuously. "So what?"

Amused by his friend's lack of sophistication, Greg smiled indulgently. "Where do think the Baron got the money to buy those fancy racecars, Jack? His family's been in the winemaking business for two generations. Today, the Mouton-Rothschild vintages are among the best in the world. The Rothschilds are Jews, so naturally many of their fellow Jews bought vineyards in France and Germany back in the Twenties, figuring they'd have an inside track in the business. They're smart, those Jews. They stick together. Unfortunately, though, many of the ones who bought vinyards in the Rhine Valley are now being forced to sell their cuttings at a loss. That's where you come in. I need you to go over there and take advantage of the fire sale."

Jack glared angrily at Greg. "You're a damn vulture!"

"It's business, Jack. There's nothing personal about it. I feel just as sorry as you do about the poor Jews. In a way, by buying their cuttings, we're giving them a chance to raise enough money to get out of Germany before things get worse. And, believe me, things are getting worse for the Jews over there every day!"

"Why do you want to send me? Why don't you go yourself?"

"I will, if you really don't want to go. But I thought you might enjoy the chance to travel. You've never been to Europe. Del has, though. If you go, maybe you two will have some interesting experiences to share. Travel broadens everybody," Greg suggested feebly. "It makes you … well … more flexible and tolerant."

Jack ignored what he considered a thinly disguised insult. "Never been to Europe? Hell! I've never been outside of California! I'd get lost just trying to find the place. Besides, except for a few Chicano curse words, I don't know any foreign languages."

"Don't worry about it. Many Europeans speak English these days. It's become the international language of business."

"Is that so?" Jack answered skeptically. "But what do I do when I get there? I don't know anybody in Europe!"

"Not a problem," Greg said. "I've already made contact with one of the biggest growers in Germany—a man named Arthur Mehlman. He's Ida Colby's uncle. She told me about him while we were at the Valentine's Party. Mehlman says he's ready to make a very attractive deal. He's even offered to pay for packing and shipping the cuttings we buy if our order's big enough."

"What's big enough mean?"

"We could buy several thousand if the price is right. That's something we'll have to negotiate. We'll also have to make sure every cutting is from a new shoot before they're shipped. That could take some time. What do you say, Jack? You willing to do this?"

"You paying my expenses?" Jack asked, though he already knew the answer.

"Of course. So does that mean 'yes'?"

"What the hell! Why not?" Dropping his cigarette butt on the flagstone, Jack crushed it angrily under his foot and started walking back across the patio toward the entrance to the ranch house.

"Where are you going?" Greg asked apprehensively.

"I need some Java."

"Maybe you should talk about this with Del," Greg suggested.

Jack froze in his tracks. "Why? She doesn't care."

"You're wrong, Jack!" Greg said sternly. "She loves you. If you leave without at least telling her, she'll think *you* don't care. You don't want that, Jack. I *know* you don't!"

"I'll think about it," Jack said bitterly and entered the house.

* * *

"Don't you be fussin' now, chil'!" Ruby scolded as Del knelt down to examine Ruby's swollen feet.

"But Ruby, they must be very painful!" Del anguished. "Let me get some ice water and see if we can't reduce the swelling."

"It the end o' the day, honey. My feets always swells like that night times. It don't hurt much." But Ruby winced when Del tried to remove her slippers and raise her feet up with a pillow.

Del shook her head vigorously and stood up. "You wait. I'll get some ice." She left the front parlor she had converted into a downstairs bedroom for Ruby and Alfie to share and went into the kitchen.

"What's up?" Snooky asked as she sat at the kitchen table smoking and reading a newspaper.

"Ruby's feet are terribly swollen. I'm going to soak them in ice water. Do we have a large pan somewhere?" Del felt embarrassed asking this question. After all, this was her own kitchen! She should know where everything was stored. Having been very busy with her job as a lawyer and itinerant lecturer, though, Del had left many of the housework and meal preparation chores up to Snooky. As a result, her kitchen was no longer familiar ground.

Snooky grinned and got up from her chair. "Sure, kiddo. I moved the big pans out to the pantry so I wouldn't make so much noise bangin' aroun' out here every mornin' an' wake up Alfie an' Ruby."

"That's very thoughtful of you Snooky," Del smiled. "Thanks."

"Us Christians gotta help each other out," Snooky winked as she retrieved a large roasting pan from the pantry and placed it in the sink so that Del could fill it with water. "Speakin' o' that, what's new with Jack these days? I ain't seen him around lately. You two fightin' again?"

Del grimaced. "Not really. Anyway, *I'm* not fighting with *him*. But he's pretty angry at me because I told him I have to postpone our marriage plans again."

"Why'd you do that?" Snooky demanded irritably. "Your Aunt Lucy's been callin' here practically every day askin' me whether you've set a date yet. She says she wants to come up and help you with your *trousseaux* and all that kind o' stuff."

Reluctant to answer, Del concentrated on chipping pieces of ice into a bowl. "It's complicated, Snooky. I have a lot on my mind right now. I'm worried about you and Alfie and Ruby."

Snooky crossed her arms and leaned against the kitchen counter. "What's that got to do with you an' Jack? Come on, Del, you're not going to blame us for you gettin' cold feet!"

"I'm not blaming you and I'm not getting cold feet!" Lifting the pan full of water and ice out of the sink, Del started to carry it into the parlor. "Let's talk about this some other time," she said firmly.

With her arms still crossed, Snooky followed Del. "That priest friend of yours called here today," she announced ominously.

Del almost dropped the pan. "What priest? You mean Father Flynn?" she asked, suddenly filled with conflicting emotions of jubilation and dread.

"That's the one. He says he's back in Benicia on a little vacation from whatever it is he does down there in Mexico and he wants to see you and Jack."

"I'll call him at the rectory tomorrow" Del said and quickly dropped the subject by focusing her attention on Ruby. "Here, Ruby. Let me help you get your feet into this."

Ruby smiled compliantly as Del lifted her feet from the pillow into the ice water. Though she shivered from the sudden immersion, Ruby showed no other sign of discomfort.

Snooky moved closer to Ruby. Bending over and putting her arm around Ruby's neck, she asked, "How's that feel? A little better?"

Ruby rolled her eyes at Snooky. "Oh yes. That feel good! God bless you both!"

* * *

When Del phoned Jack two days later to invite him for dinner at her house the following Saturday evening, Jack's initial response was coldly indifferent. He was still convinced she had spurned him once and for all. When she also told him they would be dining with Father Flynn, he became angry. "What's he butting into this for?" he growled.

"He's not butting in, Jack! Why do you always think people are against you? For Heaven's sake, Jack! Just come! Dinner's at 6:30. I'll see you then!" Without giving him a chance to respond, Del hung up the phone.

* * *

Del and Snooky had conspired three days in advance to prepare a gourmet repast. The first two courses comprised French onion soup and a salad of winter lettuce with grapes, walnuts, feta cheese, and Ruby's special vinaigrette dressing. The main course consisted of broiled salmon with an *au gratin* potato casserole and *haricots verts* cooked with bacon. This was followed by a rich chocolate mousse Del had ordered from Margaret Hartz's favorite bakery in San Francisco.

As Jack left for dinner that evening, Greg gave him two bottles of the Henshaks' best vintage Chardonnay and an imported bottle of Benedictine brandy. This too had resulted from a conspiratorial phone conversation between Greg and Del two days before.

By 10:30 P.M., everyone was feeling mellow. Pleasurably fatigued from the dinner conversation, Alfie and Ruby asked to be wheeled into their bedroom. Soon after Snooky helped them into their beds, she also retired, coughing violently as she climbed the stairs to her bedroom.

Del listened anxiously and would have excused herself to help Snooky, but she knew there was little she could do and that Snooky would have insisted she go back downstairs to keep company with her guests.

Leaning back in his chair, Flynn patted his stomach contentedly. "Ahhh! Now that was what I call a feast. Didn't realize you were such a marvelous cook, Del!"

"I can't take credit for most of it, I'm afraid. Snooky prepared the main course and Ruby planned the appetizers. The wine and brandy were gifts from Greg. But thanks for the compliment anyway, Michael. It's the least I could do to celebrate your return to Benicia."

"And to celebrate your forthcoming nuptials!" Michael said, raising his brandy glass to toast Jack and Del.

"That may not happen," Jack said bitterly. "Del's too busy to get married."

"It *will* happen!" Del insisted irritably. "Just not right now. And it's *not* because I'm too busy. It's because I have too many responsibilities." Glaring at Jack, she added, "I *do* wish you'd try to be reasonable, Jack!"

"Now, now, children!" Michael said with a paternal chuckle. "No quarreling! You'll give me indigestion!"

"Sorry, Mike, but Del's the one who's being unreasonable!" Jack retorted. "She says she loves me but she won't let me help her."

"So now Jack's running off to Europe! Some help that's going to be!"

"Hold on a minute!" Michael leaned forward toward Jack, his normally bland and happy face marred by a frown. "You're going to Europe? Why's that?"

"It's a business trip," Jack explained, feeling somewhat dishonest about his answer. "Greg's sending me to negotiate a deal with some Jewish growers in Germany who are selling their Riesling cuttings at a big discount."

Michael's expression was even more troubled now. "Jewish growers, you say? Why are they selling at a discount?"

"Because the Nazis are confiscating their vineyards and forcing them out of business."

"Jack, you didn't tell me that!" Del exclaimed in astonishment.

"I thought Greg did," he curtly replied.

"So you are on a mission of mercy," Michael smiled. "Good for you, my boy!"

"Yeah," Jack sneered. "That's what Greg says, but I don't see it that way. Greg's just taking advantage of other people's misery to cut a good deal."

"It sounds like a fair enough exchange to me," Michael observed. "Often the things we do for selfish reasons benefit others. It's one of life's little paradoxes."

Del reached across the table and took Jack's hand. "Jack, I'm so sorry," she murmured affectionately. "I didn't know. You're very brave to do this!"

"Yes indeed!" Michael concurred. "Doing business with Jews in Germany right now is *extremely* dangerous. God be with you, my son!" Turning to Del, he said, "So it seems, Del, that Jack is being quite reasonable after all."

"It's only because Del refuses to marry me!" Jack insisted, annoyed that Michael had tried to sugar coat Jack's feelings of resentment.

"Jack!" Del shouted. "Stop saying that! I haven't refused to marry you! I just need more time!"

"Ah yes, time is always the culprit in the affairs of men," Michael observed. "It reminds me of the words of the Psalmist: 'Wait for the Lord, take courage; be stouthearted, wait for the Lord!'"

"What's that supposed to mean?" Jack snarled.

"Look at it this way, Jack" Michael suggested, leaning forward toward Jack. "You are both impatient to consecrate your love for each other, but the cares of this world are getting in your way. Isn't that so?"

Jack and Del nodded. In spite of himself, Jack was eager to hear the words of this savant.

"You'll pardon me, Jack, but in our profession we priests rely heavily on scripture." Michael reached inside of his suit jacket and extracted a small black prayerbook. Leafing through it, he quickly found the passage he wanted to read aloud. "Here it is—Paul's letter to the Philippians:

> So then, my beloved, obedient as you have always been, not only when I am present but all the more now when I am absent, work out your salvation with fear and trembling.

For God is the one who, for his good purpose, works in you both to desire and to work. Do everything without grumbling or questioning, that you may be blameless and innocent, children of God without blemish in the midst of a crooked and perverse generation, among whom you shine like lights in the world.

Closing his book, Michael slipped it back into his pocket and sat silent for several seconds, studying the expressions on Del and Jack's faces. "You *too* are the lights of the world—all the more when, apart from each other, you do everything without grumbling or questioning. It's sound advice, even for skeptics!"

"I still don't get it," Jack said, bewildered by Saint Paul's convoluted syntax.

"Let me try to put it in plain English. Paul was writing his letter to a group of newly converted Christians who lived at a time in history and in a part of the world where Christians were being persecuted as brutally as the Jews in Germany are today. They were frightened about what might happen in the future and were doing a lot of grumbling and questioning about God's mercy. It's a very old question: If God loves us, why does he let so many bad things happen? These early Christians were also worried because Paul had gone far away to strengthen other fledgling Christian communities. They felt deserted and betrayed by their spiritual leader. In a nutshell, what Paul was saying is 'Stop complaining and get to work. God will take care of you.' Or, to put it another way, distance makes the pure of heart grow fonder and, whatever you do while you're in Rome, don't do as the Romans do!" Michael chortled at his own final twist on scripture. "Does that help, Jack?"

"I guess," Jack allowed. "But it's probably easier for you and Del to understand than me. I'm not Catholic."

"Not yet." Michael smiled. "But don't worry, Jack. We're working on it. Aren't we, Del?"

Tears of joy were streaming down her face as Del answered, "Yes, of course!"

"Good. Now let's join hands and pray together for each other and for all those who are suffering in this crooked and perverse generation."

* * *

Jack had been scheduled to board the 10:00 A.M. train to Chicago at the Martinez depot on Tuesday, April 5. Because it was a weekday and Del had already left for work in San Francisco, only Greg accompanied him on the car ferry between Benicia and Martinez that morning. As they stood together on the upper deck gazing toward the receding shoreline of Benicia, Greg went over the details of Jack's long journey for the last time. He wanted to be sure Jack understood his itinerary and the importance of always carrying his passport and letters of credit in the money belt he had given him to wear under his clothing. "If you lose your papers, my friend, your goose is cooked!"

Jack nodded solemnly, but he was only half listening. Just then, his thoughts were elsewhere as images of his past seemed to rise up like ghosts, embodied now in the frantic flight and screeching of the gulls that swirled above the ferry boat's wake. Beneath his feet Jack could feel the rhythmic throbbing of its diesel engine, relentlessly reminding him that he was leaving everything and everyone he knew and loved behind—everyone he might never see again. "Promise me something," he said.

"What's that?" Greg asked.

"That, whatever happens to me, you'll look after Del. Make sure she's safe and happy."

Greg placed a hand on Jack's shoulder. "You know I'll do everything I can to make sure she's safe. As for making her happy, that's going to be your job, my friend."

"I hope so," Jack said grimly. "But we never really know, do we?"

CHAPTER FORTY

_____

"It's Only a Paper Moon"

IT WAS ALMOST TWO WEEKS before Del and Greg received their first postcards from Jack. The brief messages he printed on them were almost identical: "Got to Chicago at midnight. Really tired from the trip. Hard to sleep on a train—especially a chair car! Never realized how big this country is!" There was no greeting or sign-off, except for Jack's first name.

"Same old Jack!" Greg commented to Del when they compared these picture-less postcards. "All fact and no feeling!"

"He's frightened, Greg," Del remarked. "That's always the way he talks when he's frightened."

"You know what, Del? You're right! I never thought about it before, but that's what he *does* do when he's scared. He clams up!"

"At least he sent us cards," Del said. "That's better than nothing!"

They did not have long to wait before more postcards arrived. Four days later, Del received six postcards and Greg three, all postmarked with the same date. This time, they were picture postcards. Each depicted a different station stop on Jack's Transcontinental Railroad journey. Again, Jack's printed messages were short and factual. Of the Mohave, he wrote, "Miles and miles of desert. Like being in the middle of the ocean, without the water." Of Denver, he wrote: "Long lay-over here. Went to the Brown Hotel for a couple of drinks. Real fancy joint." Of Saint Lewis, he wrote: "Never saw so many hoboes! Only two passenger cars on this train now. Most of the others are boxcars full of bums. Really gives you a feel for how bad things are all over."

Three weeks passed before Jack sent another batch of picture postcards, all from England. Of Liverpool, Jack wrote, "First stop after a rough seven-day ride on the Atlantic. They ought to call this town *Cesspool*. I used to think Benicia was stinky and dirty!" Of London, he wrote: "You should see the buses here—two-deckers! Believe it or not, the cops here (they call them Bobbies) don't even carry guns. Believe me, they need them. All kinds of crazies in this burg, most of them Irish! Reminds me of the nuts I used to work with on the Carquinez Bridge."

The next piece of correspondence Del received from Jack was much different. On May 15, a thick envelope arrived post-marked Zurich, Switzerland. Opening it eagerly, Del read these words:

> *My Darling,*
>
> *I had to take the train to Zurich to send you this letter because the Nazis open every piece of mail sent in or out of Germany.*
>
> *Things are really bad in Germany. Hitler's goons are everywhere. They call themselves the "SS" and prowl around at all hours of the night in the cities and towns here, painting Nazi slogans on walls and smashing store windows—especially Jewish stores.*
>
> *Then there's the Hitler Youth. I guess they're supposed to be like the Boy Scouts. But they're really nothing but a bunch of young thugs. Yesterday, I went to Koblenz with Arthur on some business. Koblenz is the closest city to where I'm staying with the Mehlmans. We saw a bunch of Hitler Youth beat up an old Jewish man in the street. Nobody said or did anything, even though it happened in broad daylight and there were hundreds of people all around us. Arthur said nobody does anything because everybody's afraid.*
>
> *In spite of this, the Mehlmans have gone out of their way to make me feel welcome and safe in their home. They gave me the best room in their house with my own private*

bathroom! They have a very big house—almost as big as Greg's. They need it too because they have a big family. Besides Arthur and his wife and two kids, his father and two of his brothers and their families also live here. That's because they've already lost their homes and jobs—thanks to the Nazis!

The Mehlmans pray a lot. I guess you can see why! Every night before supper, they go through a big ritual. Arthur's wife Naomi lights candles on something she calls a menorah and Arthur's father Eli chants special prayers in Hebrew. Arthur says his father is a Rabbi. I guess that's sort of a priest among the Jews. I don't understand this stuff. But, whatever it means, it seems to work pretty well for the Mehlmans. They're all very kind and brave—and smart! Arthur's youngest daughter Hannah (she's only sixteen!) plays piano and violin just as good as anybody I've ever heard on the radio. Arthur says she wants to be a concert pianist. I just hope she lives long enough to do that!

The Nazis are watching us like hawks. Every few days, an open car full of armed SS men in black uniforms and boots comes by and demands to search Arthur's house and barns. They say they're looking for communists. But Arthur says they're really looking for Jewish fugitives they can haul off to one of their prison camps. That's why Arthur's relatives always take off during the daytime. I'm not sure where they go, but it's pretty obvious they're hiding from the Nazis.

After dark, everybody comes back and helps Arthur and me collect cuttings from his vineyards. Even with all this help, it's slow going because, unless there's moonlight, we can't see what we're doing. Working with lighted lanterns is VERBOTEN, as they say here, because somebody might see us and report us to the SS.

It's also slow going because we have to pack the cuttings in wooden barrels and hide the barrels in a cave until they're *shipped by horse-drawn cart to the Rhine River. It takes almost a full day to get these barrels to a river barge, and then it's another three days down river to Rotterdam. Yes, I said down river! I know that sounds crazy because, if you look at a map of Germany, you'll see the Rhine flows from South to North! But then I guess everything in this country is topsy-turvy!*

It'll probably take weeks for us to pack and ship the 10,000 cuttings I've purchased at a dollar per dozen. Mehlman wants to sell us a lot more and has even offered to lower his price on every extra thousand we order. I think we should at least double our order, even if we never plant all the cuttings. These poor people are terrified and I want to help them as much as I can. But it's up to Greg.

Please let Greg read this letter, and tell him to send his answer to the Zurich P.O. address on the envelope.

I'm not sure how soon I'll get back here to pick up my mail. The German border guards are very suspicious of everybody entering or leaving Germany. Anyway, I'll try to do it early next month.

He had signed this letter with the words *Love, Jack* and with a postscript *I miss you very much!* But it was not only these sincere expressions of his feelings that surprised and delighted Del. The sheer length of his letter astonished her. Never before had he been so voluble and articulate, even in his speech. "Something must have happened to make him write such a long letter," Del said to Greg when she shared it with him.

"He's learning" was all Greg could say by way of explanation when he had finished perusing Jack's letter.

"Learning what?" Del asked.

"Learning what it means to be truly courageous. Jack's had a rough life full of fighting and treachery. That taught him to be tough, but it didn't teach him to be courageous."

"I'm sorry, Greg, but I don't understand," Del said.

"True courage requires compassion. You know that, Del! That's why you insisted on talking to Tully alone when we were at The Red Rooster. When he comes back, Jack will be worthy of your love."

"He's already worthy of my love, Greg. I just hope he comes back!" Del paused for several seconds before she said, "I have something to tell you."

"What?"

"I'm pregnant."

Greg' mouth dropped open in astonishment. "Are you sure? I mean ..." Greg did not finish his next question. He had started to ask if Jack was the father, but he realized how crude and unfair such a question would be.

Del knew what he was thinking. "Yes, Greg," she said with a smile. "Jack is the father. There's never been anybody else. So, you see, he *has* to come back!"

Unable to control the sudden surge of pity he felt for Del, he embraced her. "Of course he does, and you *know* he will—come hell or high water!"

* * *

It was Saturday, June 6—almost a month later—before a second thick envelope arrived from Zurich. Though Del was eager to open this envelope, she decided to wait until the next day when she could share the contents of Jack's letter with Greg, Snooky, and Father Michael. Terrified by the frightening experiences Jack had recounted in his last letter and now entering the third month of her pregnancy, Del felt more vulnerable than ever before in her life. She wanted to be sure she would have emotional support if anything catastrophic had happened to Jack.

After noon Mass that Sunday, the four friends sat in wicker chairs on Del's back porch, sipping lemonade and trying to keep themselves cool with hand-fans. The early afternoon heat was oppressive, discouraging even quiet conversation. As Del opened Jack's letter, several picture postcards fell out into her lap. Instantly, she retrieved these and passed them around. Each postcard depicted a scenic region in Germany where Jack had been during the past month. There were color photographs showing the mountains and terraced vineyards on either side of the

Rhine River as it wound its way toward the North Sea. There were pictures of ancient castles perched high in the mountains, their ramparts rising above evergreen treetops.

"Looks very beautiful and peaceful," Michael observed as he passed each picture along to Snooky and Greg.

"Yes, and look at this," Del handed him a black-and-white photograph someone had recently taken of Jack standing with his arms around the shoulders of two men, one of whom was wearing a broad-brimmed black hat and had a long white beard. Several other men, women and children were also in this photograph. Del surmised that all were probably members of Arthur Mehlman's family. "They look happy, don't they?" she asked.

"Maybe they really are," Snooky answered, sensitive to the uncertainty in Del's question. "So why don't y' read the letter and find out?"

"Alright," Del said and began reading Jack's letter aloud.

> *My Darling,*
>
> *I'm sending you some pictures so you can see how beautiful it is here. The Rhine Valley reminds me of home, though the mountains are much higher and the Rhine is wider than the Sacramento. They don't have as many ferries as we do, but they sure have plenty of grain and coal barges.*
>
> *Tell Greg I got the telegram he sent to me in Zurich. It's good to know our first shipments got through. I guess the Nazis are too busy chasing Jews here to worry about vine cuttings.*
>
> *You're not going to believe this, but three weeks ago, an SS officer came by with flowers for Hannah. He said he was so impressed by her piano playing the last time he visited that he told his mother and she wants Hannah to give a recital at her "salon" in Munich. I figure the real reason this SS guy likes Hannah is because she's so pretty. She has blond hair and blue eyes. She doesn't look at all Jewish because*

*her grandmother was "pure" German and I guess Hannah
got her grandma's genes.*

*Naturally, Hannah got pretty excited about performing
for a bunch of high-class Germans. Arthur and Naomi
were scared, though. They don't trust the SS officer and
said they have to get Hannah out of the country before he
tries to abduct her. They asked me to take Hannah with
me to America where she can live with her Aunt Ida. They
said there's only one way I can do that safely. To get across
the border into Switzerland, I'll have to sign fake papers
that say Hannah is my wife. Arthur has a lawyer friend in
Koblenz who's drawing up the papers now.*

*Next Tuesday, if we can get across the border, Hannah and
I will take a train from Zurich to Paris, then fly to London.
From there, we'll take another train to Southampton where
I've booked passage for us on the Britanis when she sails
on June 28. With luck, we should be back in California
by mid-July.*

*Better get ready, Del, because as soon as I get back you and
I are getting married. No more stalling!*

Having finished the body of Jack's letter, Del stopped reading aloud.
She was reluctant to speak the words with which Jack had concluded his
letter—*I love you.* She wasn't even sure she believed them. "I just hope
he means it," she said, her voice trembling with dread.

"How can you possibly have any doubts?" Greg asked.

"But what will he say when he finds out I'm pregnant?" Del protested.
"And what if they can't get out of Germany? He's taking a terrible risk
bringing that Jewish girl with him."

"Are you afraid she will steal Jack's love from you?" Michael asked,
cutting to the heart of Del's protests.

Del was silent, appalled by her own selfish thoughts.

Michael took her hand. "Don't be afraid, Del," he urged. "Jack loves
you. His bringing Hannah to America is proof of his commitment to
what all of us believe to be good and true. He understands how Saint

Joseph must have felt when he learned Herod was about to slaughter the innocents. The angel did not tell Joseph everything he probably wanted to know. He just told him the next step to take."

"Yeah!" Snooky barked. "Like I already told y', Del, I ain't no angel, but I got an answer for that one! Call your Aunt Lucy and tell her you're ready to pick out your *trousseaux*!"

About the Author

A graduate of Cornell University with advanced degrees from the University of Pennsylvania and Columbia University, Bruce Robinson taught American literature and history until 1986, when he changed careers to become a technical marketing writer in the data communications industry, working for such major corporations as Lockheed, British Telecom, and Lucent Technologies. Throughout his career, Robinson. has been both an editor and a by-lined author of articles published in professional and general interest periodicals.

When he moved to Benicia, California in 1999, Robinson quickly developed an interest in the history of his new home town. This led him to write a series of oral history articles for the *Solano Historian*, based on in-person interviews with senior citizens who grew up in Benicia during the 1920s and 1930s. It is these interviews that have inspired him to write *Legends of the Strait*.